NOBLEWOMAN, OFFICER... AND DECOY

"Ma'am, this is a job for *Marines!*" Gutierrez said sharply.

"Sergeant," Midshipwoman Hearns shot back just as sharply, "it was *my* idea, *I'm* in command of the party, and I say that makes it *my* job."

"You're not trained for it!" he protested.

"No, I'm not," she agreed. "But let's be honest here, Sergeant. Just how important is training going to be, under the circumstances?"

"But—"

"And another thing," she said, deliberately dropping her voice so that only Gutierrez could hear her. "If— *when*—those pirates finally catch up with the decoys," she said unflinchingly, "they're going to realize they've been fooled if all they find are Marines. That was a Navy pinnace. Do you think they're not going to be suspicious if they don't find *any* naval personnel dirtside?" Gutierrez stared at her, his expression unreadable, as he realized what the young officer—and Grayson noblewoman—meant. That despite anything else she might have said, she *knew* the decoys were going to die ... and that she was deliberately planning to use her own corpse in an effort to protect the other personnel under her command.

"We don't have time to debate this, Sergeant. We need every minute we've got. I'll let you choose the rest of the party, but I'm coming. Is that clearly understood?"

Gutierrez stared at her for perhaps another three heartbeats. And then, slowly, obviously against his will, he nodded. . . .

—from "The Service of the Sword" by David Weber

BAEN BOOKS by DAVID WEBER

Honor Harrington:
On Basilisk Station
The Honor of the Queen
The Short Victorious War
Field of Dishonor
Flag in Exile
Honor Among Enemies
In Enemy Hands
Echoes of Honor
Ashes of Victory
War of Honor
At All Costs
The Shadow of Saganami
Crown of Slaves (with Eric Flint)

Edited by David Weber
More Than Honor
Worlds of Honor
Changer of Worlds
The Service of the Sword

Mutineers' Moon
The Armageddon Inheritance
Heirs of Empire
Empire from the Ashes (omnibus)

Path of the Fury
In Fury Born
The Apocalypse Troll
The Excalibur Alternative

Oath of Swords
The War God's Own
Wind Rider's Oath

With Steve White
Insurrection
Crusade
In Death Ground
The Shiva Option
The Stars at War I
The Stars at War II

With John Ringo
March Upcountry
March to the Sea
March to the Stars
We Few

WORLDS OF HONOR #4

THE SERVICE OF THE SWORD

DAVID WEBER

THE SERVICE OF THE SWORD: WORLDS OF HONOR #4

A Baen Books Original

Baen Publishing Enterprises
P.O. Box 1403
Riverdale, NY 10471
www.baen.com

ISBN: 0-7434-8836-9
ISBN 13: 978-0-7434-8836-5

Cover art by David Mattingly

First paperback printing, July 2004
Second paperback printing, June, 2006

Library of Congress Cataloging-in-Publication Number
2002043997

Distributed by Simon & Schuster
1230 Avenue of the Americas
New York, NY 10020

Production by Windhaven Press, Auburn, NH
Printed in the United States of America.

Contents

Promised Land

by Jane Lindskold

Judith had been very young when the raiders took the ship, young, but not too young to remember. There had been explosions, the shrill scream of tearing metal, the insidious tugging of air leaking from a ruptured compartment before someone slapped on a patch.

The battle had been muffled, somehow less than real, made distant by the swaddling vac suit two sizes too big, but the best they'd had intact. It had been muffled, less than real, but that didn't save the child.

Reality came through later, came through with a vengeance.

* * *

Despite everything he'd been through, all the time and energy he'd put into his training, into getting marks that wouldn't shame his family, when it came time for his middy cruise, someone had gotten cold feet. Michael Winton first heard the rumor that they were

1

going to put him on a system defense ship near
Gryphon from his roommate, Todd Liatt.

Todd was one of those people who always heard
things before anyone else. Michael had teased Todd,
that he, not Michael, was the one who should be
specializing in communications.

"You wouldn't even need a com set, Toad-breath.
Information seeps directly into your nervous system.
Think of the savings in time and resources that would
be."

Todd had laughed, even played along with the joke,
but there'd really never been a question where he
would concentrate. Tactics was the best specialization
for those who hoped for a ship of their own someday,
and Todd wanted command.

"Hey," Todd said, mock serious, "I've got four older
sisters and three older brothers. I've taken other
people's orders all my life. It's time I get a turn, right?"

But they'd both known Todd's desire was motivated
by an overwhelming sense of responsibility, a desire
to make things right. Michael was certain that the white
beret would fit Todd as naturally as his skin.

And himself? Michael didn't want command. He
hadn't even wanted a career in the Navy, not at first,
but now he was as devoted to the service as Todd was.
He just knew he didn't want to command a vessel.
Michael would never say so to Todd, but he knew too
much about the cost of command to long for it.

Communications appealed to Michael: the rapid flow
of information, the need to weigh and measure, to sort
and balance, were all as familiar to him as breathing.
He'd been playing some version of that game all his
life.

He was good at it too. His memory was excellent.
Pressure didn't fluster him. It seemed to focus him,
to make things clearer, contrast more acute. He felt

sure that no one who'd gone through a training sim with him had any doubt that he'd earned his standing on graduation.

Michael was proud of that class standing. It's very hard to be judged on your own merits when you're so highly born that people are automatically going to figure you were being carried. That's what made Todd's news almost more than he could take.

"You heard what?" Michael said to Todd, his voice taut with anger.

"I heard," Todd replied stiffly, unintimidated, "that you are going to be assigned to the *Saint Elmo* for her Gryphon deployment. Apparently, your singular ability to process information came to the attention of BuWeapons. They're working on some top secret sensor technology and they want the best people they can get for the trial runs."

Michael's response was long, eloquent, and suggested that he'd hung around with Marines at some time in his life. That was true. His sister was married to a former Marine, but Justin Zyrr had never used language like that in Michael's hearing.

Todd listened, his expression mingling shock and grudging admiration.

"Two years," he said. "Two years I share a room with you, and never do I learn that you can swear like that."

Michael didn't answer. He was too busy grabbing various items of clothing, obviously preparatory to storming out of the room.

"Hey, Michael, where're you going?"

"To talk to someone about my posting."

"You can't! It isn't official yet."

"If I wait until it's official," Michael said, his voice tight, "then it's going to be too late. Insubordination at least. Now I might be able to do something."

Todd was too smart to fight a losing engagement.

"Who're you going to talk to? Commander Shrake?"

"No. I'm going to screen Beth. If this is her idea, I need to know why. If it isn't her idea, I need to know so someone can't try to convince me that it is. When I know that, then I'll try Shrake."

"Forewarned is forearmed," Todd agreed.

Michael nodded. One thing his com training had taught him. Find a secure line if you want to discuss a sensitive matter.

He guessed it was pretty sensitive when you were going to place a person to person call to the Queen.

✳   ✳   ✳

The ship that had captured theirs had been from Masada. Judith had been too young to understand the difference between pirates and privateers. When she was old enough to know, she was also old enough to know that when it came to Masadans preying on Graysons the distinctions were so much fertilizer.

Her father had been killed helping to defend the ship. Her mother had died trying to defend her child. Judith only wished she could have died with them.

At twelve standards Judith was married to a man over four times her age. Ephraim Templeton had captained the Masadan privateer that had taken the Grayson vessel, and he claimed the girl child as part of his prize. If this was somewhat irregular, there was no one left alive to protest when Judith was not repatriated to her own people.

Even disregarding the difference in their ages—Ephraim had seen five and half decades by standard reckoning—Judith and Ephraim were not at all alike. Where Ephraim was heavily built, Judith possessed a light, gazelle's build. Her hair was dark brown, sun-kissed with reddish gold highlights. His was fair, silver mixed in increasing proportion to the blond. The eyes Judith learned to carry downcast lest Ephraim beat her for impudence were hazel, brown ringing vibrant green. Ephraim's eyes were pale blue and as cold as ice.

At thirteen Judith had her first miscarriage. When she had her second miscarriage six months later, the doctor suggested that her husband stop trying to impregnate her for a few years lest her reproductive equipment suffer permanent damage. Ephraim did as the doctor suggested, though that didn't mean he stopped exercising his conjugal privileges.

At sixteen Judith was pregnant again. When tests showed that the unborn child was a girl, her husband ordered an abortion, saying he didn't want to waste the useless bitch he'd been feeding all these years to no purpose, and what was more purposeless than breeding a girl child?

If before Judith had hated and feared Ephraim, now that emotion transformed into loathing so deep she thought it a wonder that her gaze did not sear Ephraim to ash where he stood. Her sweat should have been acid on his skin, her breath poison. That was how deeply she hated him.

Some women would have committed suicide. Some might have resorted to murder—which in Masadan society was the same as suicide, though a bit more satisfactory in that the murderer achieved something in return for her death. But Judith did neither.

She had a secret, a secret she held onto even as she bit her lip to keep from crying out when her husband used her again and yet again. She held onto it even when she saw the grudging pity in the eyes of her co-wives. She held onto it as she had from the moment she watched her mother bleed her life out onto the deck plates, remembering that brave woman's final warning.

"Never let them know that you can read."

✹   ✹   ✹

It hadn't been Elizabeth's idea to have him posted to a lumbering superdreadnought that would never even leave the Star Kingdom's home binary system. Michael's relief when he learned this was boundless. Even before their father's death, Beth had encouraged Michael to find his own place, to push his limits. Distracted as she had been by the heavy responsibilities she assumed after their father's tragic death, Beth still had made time for Michael, listening to the problems he couldn't seem to discuss with their mother, the dowager Queen Angelique.

To have found that Beth had suddenly changed would have been a new orphaning, worse in many ways, for on some level Michael expected it—indeed, knew he should strive for it, since it was his place to support his Queen, not hers to support him.

Now that he knew that he would not be undermining his Queen's policy, Michael made an appointment to see the Fourth Form dean. That he could almost certainly have demanded an appointment with the commandant of the Academy and been granted it occurred to him, but the option was as quickly rejected. The Navy could be—and was—officially unyielding where matters of birth and privilege were concerned. That didn't mean strings weren't quietly pulled in the background, but anyone who too blatantly abused his position could expect to pay a price throughout the entire course of his career. Besides, it would have been self-defeating. The appointment would have been granted to the Crown Prince, not to Midshipman Michael Winton, and being seen as Crown Prince Michael rather than Midshipman Winton was precisely what Michael was trying to avoid.

However, if his appointment with the dean came rather more promptly than even a fourth form midshipman who stood in the top quarter of his class could usually hope for, Michael wasn't fool enough to refuse it. He arrived promptly, sharp in his undress uniform, every button, and bit of trim in as perfect order as he and Todd could make them.

Michael saluted crisply when admitted to his superior officer's presence. Indeed, though there had been those who had expected the Crown Prince to indicate in fashions subtle or less so that in the past these same officers had bent knee before him, Michael had never given them reason. He knew, as those who were not close to the Crown never could, how human monarchs were, how an accident could make an eighteen-year-old queen . . . could make a thirteen-year-old crown prince.

Michael wondered how many of those officers who expected him to slight them realized how greatly in awe of them he stood. They had earned their ranks, earned their awards and honors. The long list of titles Michael heard recited on formal occasions had nothing to do with him, everything to do with his father.

He thought that Commander Brenda Shrake, Lady Weatherfell, might actually realize how he felt, for there was a warmth in her pale green eyes that spoke of understanding that in no way could be confused with indulgence or laxity. The dean's title identified her to Michael as the holder of a prosperous grant on Sphinx, but long ago Lady Weatherfell had decided that her calling was in the Navy.

Even the battle that had left traces of scarring on rather stark features, that had bent and twisted two fingers of her right hand, had not made her renounce her decision. Instead Commander Shrake had moved with all the wisdom of her long years shipboard to the academy, where, in addition to her administrative duties, she taught some of the toughest courses in fusion engineering.

Commander Shrake was a leader within an academy responsible for turning out competent naval officers on what anyone with any sense must realize was the eve of war. There was no room for indulgence in her job, but there was room for compassion.

"You wished to see me, Mr. Winton?"

Michael nodded stiffly.

"Yes, Ma'am. It's about a rumor."

"A rumor?"

Suddenly Michael felt the speeches he had been rehearsing since Todd's revelation the day before dry up and flake away. After a panicked moment, he forced himself to begin afresh and was pleased to find words came smoothly.

"Yes, Ma'am. A rumor about Fourth Form postings."

Commander Shrake smiled. "Yes, those rumors would be starting about now. They always do, no matter how carefully we keep the information to ourselves."

She didn't ask how Michael had heard and for that Michael was grateful. Getting Todd into trouble was not on his agenda, but neither was lying to the Fourth Form dean.

"And whose posting is it you wish to speak about?" Commander Shrake continued.

"My own, Ma'am."

"Yes?"

"Commander Shrake, I have heard that I am to be posted to the SD *Saint Elmo*."

The dean didn't even make a show of consulting her computer. Michael respected her for it. Doubtless the matter had been discussed, maybe even debated. Someone at Mount Royal Palace might even have leaked back news of Michael's call to Beth last night.

"That matches my own information," Commander Shrake replied. "Is that what you wished to know?"

"Yes, Ma'am, and no, Ma'am. I did wish to have the

rumor confirmed, Ma'am, but I," Michael took a deep breath and let the rest of his words hurry out on its eddy, "also wished to request another posting, Ma'am. One that isn't so close to home."

"You have a desire to see more of the universe, Mr. Winton?" asked the dean with a dangerous twinkle in her eyes.

"Yes, Ma'am," Michael replied, "but that isn't my reason for requesting a change of posting."

"And that reason is?"

"I want . . ."

Michael hesitated. He'd been over this so many times he'd lost count, and he still couldn't find a way to state his case without sounding pompous.

"Ma'am, I want to be a naval officer, and I can't do that if people start protecting me."

Twin silver arches of raised eyebrows made Michael flush.

"It is not the Navy's habit to protect her officers, Mr. Winton," Commander Shrake said coolly, and the scarred hand she rested on the desk in front of her was mute testimony to her words. "Rather it is those officers' job to protect the rest of the kingdom."

"Yes, Ma'am," Michael said, pressing on through he felt he'd doomed his case. "That's why keeping me back here isn't right. The Queen's brother . . ."

The damned words fell from his lips like bricks.

"The Queen's brother might have right to protection, but when I entered the academy I gave that up. It shouldn't start again now that I'm about to leave."

Commander Shrake steepled her fingers thoughtfully.

"And that's what you think this posting is, Mr. Winton?"

"Yes, Ma'am."

"And if I told you that Admiral Hemphill herself had heard of your qualifications and requested you?"

"I would be pleased, Ma'am, but that wouldn't stop others from thinking that I was being protected."

"And it matters to you what others think?"

"I'd like to say that it didn't, Ma'am," Michael said earnestly, "but I'd be lying. I could live with it if it was only me. I've done that before, but I don't like what it might make others think about the Navy."

"Oh?"

"Yes, Ma'am. If the Queen's brother is given a posting where he's not subjected to as great a risk of combat, then how long will it be before some other nobles start thinking that's their right, too?"

Michael paused, not knowing if he'd overstepped himself, but the dean nodded for him to continue.

"The Navy needs recruits, Ma'am," Michael continued, "from all elements of our society. I don't like to think what will happen if the word gets around that certain people are too valuable for dangerous postings—and that by implication other people are considered more disposable."

"Mr. Winton, surely you realize that this has always been the case. Frankly, certain people *are* more valuable."

"Yes, Ma'am, but they are valuable because of what they know, because of what they have learned, because of what they can contribute to the conduct of naval operations. They are not," Michael concluded, unable to keep a trace of bitterness from his voice, "considered more valuable due to an accident of birth."

"I see," Commander Shrake said after an uncomfortably long pause. "I see, and I believe I understand. What, then, are you requesting, Mr. Winton?"

"A more usual midshipman's posting, Ma'am," Michael said. "If the Navy truly believes I can be of greatest service in an SD orbiting Gryphon then I will give that posting everything I have."

"But you would prefer, say, a battlecruiser heading out to deal with Silesian pirates."

"I believe that is more usual, Ma'am," Michael said.

"I see," the dean repeated. "Very well. You have made your case. I will consider it and perhaps present the matter to the Commandant. Is there anything else, Mr. Winton?"

"No, Ma'am. Thank you for hearing me out, Commander."

"Listening is part of being a good commander," Shrake said, sounding rather like she had returned to the lecture hall. "Then if you are finished, you are dismissed."

*　　　*　　　*

Grayson and Masada shared certain attitudes towards women, a factor that was not at all surprising since the Masadans had originally been part of the Grayson colony. Both societies refused women the vote and the right to own property. Both considered women inferior to men, seeing as their main role supporting and upholding their homes and husbands. Both societies, to be blunt, considered women property.

But property can be valued and valuable. The Graysons came to see their women as treasures. Grayson men might refuse their women numerous rights and privileges, but in return they were enjoined to love and protect them. The protection might be smothering and binding, but usually it was not damaging.

The Masadans, after their separation from Grayson, grew to see women in a different light. Since the Masadan attempt to gain control of Grayson society had been thwarted by a woman—even as God's plan for Man had been thwarted by Eve—so women were perceived as the visible, living embodiments of sin and suffering. Few actions were considered out of line when inflicted on such creatures. Indeed, a woman might work her way toward redemption by accepting whatever was done to her.

On Grayson a man did not mistreat a woman, because she was precious. On Masada, theoretically, a man might treat any woman as harshly as he wished. Most were wise enough not to exercise this right because to do so would be to invite similar treatment of their own property. Individual owners might abuse their women as much as they deemed right to preserve the sanctity and order of their households. Most did.

One did not bother to educate property on Masada. On Grayson, higher education and formal degrees might be denied to women, but basic literacy and math were routinely taught. They had to be, if only because the daily maintenance of household technology in such a hostile environment required it.

Masada's less lethal planetary environment obviated that need, and no good Masadan patriarch was about to waste education on a mere female. Judith's parents, scions of a merchant family with ties outside the Grayson system, had begun her education earlier than most. They'd decided to have her educated beyond even the normal Grayson standards for a variety of reasons. One of these was that they did not wish to seem backward in the eyes of those with whom they sought to do business. Another was that they were good, God-fearing people who did not see how the ability to contemplate God's wonders and mysteries intellectually, as well as with the blind obedience of faith, could hurt anyone. Especially not in a faith which enshrined the doctrine of the Test.

Finally, there was an element of practicality. Even though propriety meant that a girl would not be exposed to the prying eyes of strangers, that didn't mean she had to be useless. A girl who could read,

write, and work sums could help with the business.
When her parents discovered that Judith had an almost
preternatural quickness with mathematics and logic patterns, they delighted in giving her puzzles and games
meant to enhance this ability.

But Judith's mother understood, as her father might
not have done, the danger that knowledge placed the
girl in when the Masadan raiders took their ship.
Despite her tender years, Judith understood her
mother's warning. Even within Grayson society she had
been encouraged to conceal just how much she knew.
Indeed, as she grew older she had concealed from her
parents just how much she had learned, fearing they
might view her education as complete.

That habit of secrecy and the knowledge it concealed
was why Judith didn't kill herself, why she didn't kill
the man who called himself her husband, lord, and
master. She had something else in mind. Something
that would hurt Ephraim Templeton a great deal more.

Judith began training for her revenge during the
first years of her captivity, continued after her
marriage, focused more intensely once Ephraim
began to try to father children upon her. She hoped
to put her plan into action before he could tie her
to Masada through their children. What she had
never realized was that she would care about those
little lives, even those never born.

On the day she learned that the child she carried
was a girl—a girl Ephraim did not plan to let live—
Judith knew she had no choice but to put her plan into
action.

Even so, she knew it was unlikely that she could save
this baby. Her hope was that she could save the next.

* * *

"I simply don't see how we can pretend to forget
that his sister is the Queen," said Lieutenant Carlotta

Dunsinane, assistant tactical officer of Her Majesty's light cruiser, *Intransigent*.

"Carlie, a slew of instructors and classmates at Saganami Island have been pretending it for the last three and a half years," replied Abelard Boniece, *Intransigent*'s captain. "Now it's our turn."

"But still . . ."

Lieutenant Dunsinane let her voice trail off. In her inflection was a wealth of unspoken knowledge, the awareness that the young man whose dossier glowed on the screen between them was next in line for the crown of the Star Kingdom of Manticore. True, Michael's sister, Queen Elizabeth the Third, was married and her first-born child would undoubtedly replace him as Heir in due time. But Michael Winton had been the Crown Prince for the last nine years. His social and political rank were not easy things to disregard.

Then there was the uncomfortable resemblance between Midshipman Michael Winton and his father, the much-loved King Roger III. The latter had died long before his time, victim of a freak jet-ski accident that had left the Star Kingdom grieving, and thrust Elizabeth and her brother into the public eye.

For Elizabeth, just a few years short of her majority, this scrutiny was something for which she had some training. For thirteen year-old Michael, still at an age when traditional forbearance shielded him from the greedy eye of the newsies, there had been little preparation.

The resemblance between father and son came across despite Prince Michael's apparent youth, extending beyond the Winton's clean-cut features and strikingly dark skin. It had something to do with the set of the youth's jaw, the manner in which he carried his head straight and square on his shoulders, even in the way he seemed unaware of the myriad gazes that

flickered in his direction and then politely away again—
an unawareness that was never rude or rejecting, simply
unaware.

To be fair to Prince Michael—*Midshipman
Winton*—Carlie reminded herself with the fierce
determination of one who is certain it is only a matter of time before she screws up, part of Carlie's own
uncertainty had nothing to do with Michael Winton
himself. The midshipman's dossier had given no indication that Michael Winton expected privileges or had
been given them, but Lieutenant Carlotta Dunsinane
couldn't quite believe this was so, and deep inside she
was steeled for trouble.

To make matters worse, as part of the RMN's
ongoing naval expansion, *Intransigent's* middy berth was
filled to bursting—and suddenly, cynically, Carlie
realized the reason why there had been a couple of
changes in those assigned to her care. Doubtless there
were those in a position to learn of Mr. Winton's new
assignment in advance, those who saw an advantage to
having their son or daughter serve on the Crown
Prince's middy cruise, an advantage that nothing as
trivial as a sudden change in posting could make
impossible.

As supervisor of *Intransigent's* middy berth, Lieutenant Dunsinane was under conflicting pressures. She
had to simultaneously guard and direct her young
charges, yet try to break them if there was anything
in them that needed breaking. This was never an easy
task, but it was going to be made more difficult with
a middy berth overloaded with scions of rank and
privilege.

Then there was the ATO's acute awareness that the
RMN desperately needed good officers—with the
emphasis on "good"—but there were those who thought
that any officer was a good officer with the fleet spread

so thin. So Carlie knew that there would be those in the command structure who would fault her for breaking *any* of those who had survived the gruelling three and a half T-years they'd spent at the Academy—not to mention fault her for wasting the money invested in that training.

And fault her even more if one of those whose training didn't pan out was the carefully watched, highly observed Prince Michael Winton. Yet she'd also be faulted if Midshipman Winton passed his cruise without proving himself.

Carlie swallowed an impulse to offer her resignation here and now.

"Mr. Winton will be reporting to you in just a few days, so you have time to prepare yourself," Captain Boniece continued. "May I offer you a word of advice?"

"I would accept your advice gladly, Sir."

"Give the young man a chance to prove himself before you condemn him."

"I'll do my best, Sir."

Carlie Dunsinane meant every word. She also knew how difficult keeping those words was going to be.

As she was leaving, she saw Tab Tilson, the head communications' officer, coming in with the latest dispatches. Before the door slid closed, she heard him say:

"More changes, Sir, I'm afraid."

The door slid shut before Carlie could hear what those changes were, but she sincerely hoped they had nothing to do with her already overcomplicated middy berth.

✳   ✳   ✳

Ephraim Templeton ruled his household with an iron rod—or more literally a very flexible whip and a willingness to use it. However, much of how he regulated his household was based on certain assumptions.

None of Ephraim's wives could read. Therefore, no effort was made to secure the library against them. None of his wives could use the computer beyond activating the simple pictorial icons used for routine household chores. Certainly, none of them could manage anything as complicated as programming.

Judith, however, could read. She was familiar with the more complicated computers used by the Graysons, and her parents had taught her elementary programming. This last, combined with ready access to Ephraim's household databanks, made it possible for Judith to continue her education.

Her mother's dying warning had also provided a hint as to along which path lay Judith's freedom. If the Masadans did not want her to know anything, then she would seek to know everything—and to keep her acquisition of that knowledge from them.

Judith's programmed safeguards would not have stopped a careful security check, but where there can be no mice, no one sets mousetraps. She had another advantage as well. She was not her husband's favorite wife. Indeed, in many ways she was his least favorite, but Ephraim did not dispose of her because she was a prize.

To his fellows, who hated the Graysons with singleminded fanaticism, Judith was presented as a soul redeemed from sin, a vessel who would carry within her womb those who would prove the undoing of their own forbearers. For this reason, Ephraim often took Judith with him when his duties took him away from home. She was a trophy: living, breathing proof that the Masadan struggle to conquer Grayson would not be in vain.

Initially, Judith, then only twelve, had hated these voyages. They forced her into increased intimacy with her husband, for Ephraim didn't bring any other of his wives. However, once Judith realized that during her voyages on *Aaron's Rod* she was free from observation—for jealous Ephraim kept her locked in the captain's quarters lest she incite unholy lust among his crew—she took advantage of her isolation.

Hacking into the ship's computer was Judith's first challenge, but one for which her education on Grayson's more sophisticated systems had given her the tools. Once she had access to *Aaron's Rod*'s computer, and safeguard programs in place, Judith immersed herself in the joys of forbidden knowledge.

While she was supposed to be praying or memorizing scripture, Judith familiarized herself with the ship's systems, starting with the basics of life support, engineering, and communications, moving from these into the more arcane specializations of weaponry and astrogation. Later, when she was fourteen, she began studying elementary tactics.

Had Ephraim but known, his youngest wife at fifteen was as well-educated—at least in theory—as any member of his crew. Instead he thought her something of an idiot, for her inability to memorize the scripture passages he set for her—even with the incentive of a beating for her failure—was nearly beyond belief.

But Ephraim didn't have energy to waste worrying about the deficiencies of a woman who, after all, hardly needed a mind to serve her purpose. As he had been when *Aaron's Rod* took the merchant vessel that had carried Judith and her parents, Ephraim continued to serve as a Masadan privateer.

Ephraim was very careful which ships he hunted. Most of the time he was content to masquerade as an armed merchantman, even to the extent of carrying regular cargos. The missile tubes and laser batteries that were part of his vessel could be turned to other purposes than self-defense, however, and when the situation was deemed propitious, unarmed ships fell before *Aaron's Rod*'s might.

Judith, of course, did not take part in these battles. When *Aaron's Rod* went into battle, she remained locked in the captain's quarters. Ephraim valued her sufficiently to provide a vac suit lest she die from a breach in the hull, but that suit was an uncertain refuge. Ephraim had no wish to have Judith become some other man's prize, so tied into her vac suit was a version of the dead man's switch, rigged so that if Ephraim died, or even if he viewed their situation as hopeless, Judith would also die.

What Ephraim didn't realize was that Judith knew all about the switch, and had disabled it while leaving the circuit sufficiently intact to hide her tampering from routine equipment checks. She re-checked the suit every time she put it on, reassured in the knowledge that the suit was only issued to her when the situation was critical, and her captors too distracted to do more than scan the telltales.

Thus Judith came to revel in her shipboard time.

As her confidence grew, Judith didn't restrict her education in ship systems to when she was aboard *Aaron's Rod*. Ephraim had purchased training simulation software for the use of his sons. Both the software and the VR rigs used for the most realistic training were expensive beyond Ephraim's usual prudent parsimony. However, he dreamed of one day commanding a privateer fleet with his sons as captains. The actions of this fleet would make the name Templeton famous throughout Masada, earning the clan a posting at the forefront of the action when the day came to make a decisive strike against the heretics on Grayson.

Fourteen year-old Judith discovered the best times to extract a VR rig from the lockers. Unlike her stepsons, who gloried in battle scenarios, she concentrated on the boring programs: Piloting a ship. Preparing for a hyper translation and adjusting to post-translation nausea. Checking and understanding astrogation coordinates. Scanning for communications.

In careful secrecy, Judith forced herself to learn how to get the most out of each of the preprogrammed routines that ran the essential ship stations, knowing that when her time came she would likely have to do without much in the way of a crew.

Judith was working her way through a particularly complicated scenario dealing with the aftereffects of a power surge following a return to N-space, when the VR rig was jerked off her face.

"What do you think you are doing?" Ephraim's senior wife hissed.

       ❋   ❋   ❋

Like every other member of his graduating class, Michael Winton was given an opportunity to visit his family before reporting to his new assignment. It was good to be home, though Michael's suite at Mount Royal Palace seemed unnecessarily large and rather empty without Todd's explosively effusive companionship.

Empty, that was, unless Beth's son, Roger, came exploding into the room. Roger was three T-years old, with all the energy and curiosity that could be wished for in that delightful age when a baby is becoming distinctly a little boy.

When Roger reached his sixth Manticoran birthday—which would make him just over ten, by standard reckoning—he would be subjected to a comprehensive battery of physical and mental tests meant to guarantee that he was suited to be the next king. Until then, Michael would continue to hold the title Crown Prince and be next in the succession. Remembering his own encounter with a similar battery of tests, Michael had no doubt that Roger would pass with well over the minimum requirements.

Seven more years to go, Michael thought without the least trace of wistfulness. *Then I can be just plain Prince Michael again—and if Beth has another kid or two, I'll drop so far down the succession I'll be like Aunt Caitrin, just another superfluous noble.*

He grinned at the thought, swinging a delightedly shrieking Roger around and around in circles. He thought there was probably no one less superfluous than Duchess Winton-Henke, his late father's younger sister, but he knew she'd enjoy the joke as much as he did.

All in all, Michael didn't mind having someone else make his bed, having the luxury to sleep late, the opportunity to wear something other than his uniform. The business of the Star Kingdom did not precisely stop because the Crown Prince was home from school, but Beth found excuses to avoid several formal engagements in favor of quiet evenings with her brother.

Even when Beth couldn't get free, Queen Mother Angelique might be available, and Roger always wanted a chance to play. For a few days, Michael could almost forget that his was a family any different from any other.

One evening after Justin had gone to put Roger to bed, brother and sister sat playing chess. Their only audience was Beth's treecat, Ariel, who sprawled drowsily across his human's lap. To Michael's complete surprise, Beth extended one long finger and tipped over her king, conceding the game to him.

"I haven't checkmated you yet!" Michael protested.

"You would have in two moves," Beth said, "and I have something I need to discuss with you."

Michael heard an odd twang in his sister's voice, a barely suppressed tension that warned him that the Queen was going to confide in him information that at least some of her advisors would rather she didn't—and that she was worried that their judgement, rather than her own, might be right.

Michael kept his observation of Beth's mood to himself, reaching instead for the chess pieces and beginning to methodically fit them into their velvet-lined niches in the polished hardwood box.

After a few moments, Beth continued, "I know where *Intransigent* is being sent."

Michael cocked an eyebrow at her. He'd been told that his new posting, the light cruiser *Intransigent*, was being sent to Silesia. He didn't know which sector, but he expected they'd be taking over one of the standard anti-pirate patrols. If that was the case, though, why did Beth look so thoughtful?

"Don't be a pig," Michael prompted when her silence stretched on. "Give."

Beth smiled at the bantering note in his voice.

"*Intransigent* isn't going to Silesia," she said, "at least not right away. She's being diverted to deliver new orders and relief personnel to a diplomatic contingent we have negotiating with the government of the Endicott System."

"Endicott?" Michael asked, not certain he had heard right.

Beth nodded. Stealing a few chess pieces from their velvet niches, she worked up a makeshift map on the board that still rested between them.

"This queen," she said, setting the carved ebony figure at one extreme, "is the Star Kingdom. This," she said, setting the white king at the other extreme, "is the People's Republic of Haven."

"They wouldn't appreciate your using a king,"

Michael teased. "They're a republic, not a decadent, top-heavy monarchy like us."

Beth grinned, but she didn't exchange the piece. Instead she drew imaginary, curving lines marking the sphere of influence ruled by each piece. The area ruled by the black queen was markedly smaller than the one ruled by the white king.

"Between our two less than harmonious governments," Beth went on, "is a certain amount of stellar real estate not claimed by either us or the Peeps. Unlike the People's Republic, the Star Kingdom of Manticore does not advocate a policy of forced annexation."

The Queen spoke lightly, but there was steel beneath her words, steel that had been forged and tempered through numerous battles in the political arena against those of Beth's subjects who felt that Elizabeth the Third, like her father before her, was a bit too fond of acquiring new extra-system responsibilities for the Star Kingdom. The conflict had come to a head with the acquisition of the Basilisk System in the very year Elizabeth had been born. Despite the passage of twenty-some years and the increasingly obvious predation of the PRH, the arguments against keeping the Basilisk System had not quieted in the least.

For Michael, his term at the Academy had only made him more certain, not less, that the policy followed by the Crown was the only sensible one. The words "Star Kingdom" might sound sweepingly grand, but when it came down to facts, before the acquisition of the Basilisk System, the Star Kingdom had only been one tidy little binary solar system.

True, the Manticore System had been blessed with three habitable planets. True, it commanded a wormhole terminus that was the envy of its neighbors and the heart of a profitable trade empire. But the fact remained that one home system, now supplemented by a second much poorer system, was a very small empire in the face of all the habitable worlds within the vast region commanded by the People's Republic of Haven.

Beth now placed two bishops—one white, one black, Michael noticed in amusement—on the board so that they occupied a space between the two spheres of influence.

"Between us and the Peeps," she continued, "are a variety of neutral entities. Right now Manticoran diplomatic focus is on two of them—the only inhabited worlds in a volume twenty light years across and rather conveniently placed between us and the Peeps. One of these," she touched the black bishop, "occupies the Yeltsin's Star System. The other occupies the Endicott System."

"The Graysons," Michael said, showing off just a little, "and the Masadans."

Elizabeth cocked an eyebrow at him, clearly impressed.

"Pretty good. I guess you did learn something at the Academy."

"Luck," Michael said modestly. "I just happened to do a paper on that region for a history class. Did you know that both those systems were settled long before Manticore?"

Elizabeth nodded, a sly grin spreading across her face.

"'Just happened to do a paper,'" she mused aloud. "Gee, anyone with a sneaky turn of mind would think you were anticipating what the Star Kingdom might need to do if the Peeps kept pressing our borders. Dad would be impressed."

Michael was pleased despite himself—as well as glad, not for the first time, that his dark skin hid his blush. Lest Beth realize his embarrassment, he kept talking.

"I even know," he said, "why you chose bishops to mark these systems on your tac board. Both Masada and Grayson are ruled by theocracies, one almost as crazy as the other."

"Almost?"

Michael shrugged.

"The Faithful of Masada are a splinter group off the original Grayson colony. If I had to pick between them, I'd pick the original Graysons. They're remarkably backward in some of their social customs, but they're marginally more tolerant than the Masadans. They have a higher tech base than the Masadans, too."

Elizabeth nodded.

"I agree with you. However, not all of my advisors are so certain that an alliance with Grayson is preferable to one with Masada. They point out that Masada is a far more habitable planet than Grayson. They also see the Masadans' technological weaknesses as our potential strengths. Not only wouldn't we need to worry about our ally getting uppity, but the Masadans should jump through hoops to have a shot at the technological jump-start we can offer."

Michael shook his head.

"I wish I believed that," he said, "but from what I recall from my research, the Masadans were willing to destroy the Graysons when they couldn't conquer them. Even after the Masadans were exiled from the Yeltsin System, they kept coming back and trying to take Grayson. Those don't sound like people who would be willing to jump through anyone's hoop."

Beth nodded.

"Again, I agree with you. However, not all my advisors are so reasonable and, despite what many of my subjects think, my whim is not what governs the Star

Kingdom. To complicate matters, we're probably years away from having to pick one group over the other. Hell, not everyone is even convinced that war against the People's Republic is inevitable. So for now, we're collecting information, learning everything we can about the Masadans and Graysons while they in turn learn about us—and while they learn about the Peeps."

"And if part of that learning experience," Michael said, understanding, "is a Manticoran light cruiser sweeping through as diplomatic limousine service, then all the better."

"You've got it," Beth said. "Before you start wondering, it's not pure coincidence that *Intransigent* has been chosen for escort duty. Apparently, the Masadans and Graysons are both misogynists. One of the sticking points in our negotiations with both societies has been that not only do we permit women to serve in our armed forces, but also that our 'kingdom' is actually a 'queendom.'"

If Michael hadn't already encountered some information on this social peculiarity he would have thought Beth was joking, but he already knew how blinkered both the Masadans and the Graysons were by elements of their religious heritage.

"The Graysons are showing some signs of thawing on that point," Beth went on, "but the Masadans are not. Some of my advisors thought that the Masadans might be distracted by, well, by . . ."

She stopped and Michael, uncertain when was the last time he had seen his sister so at a loss for words, waited in mild astonishment.

"They thought if you went out there," Beth continued in a rush, "that the Masadans might draw the conclusion that I was just a figurehead—a broody hen laying eggs to hatch the next generation of Winton monarchs. Certainly, Roger's existence would confirm their willingness to think that way. When a culture deliberately isolates itself as the Masadans have, it tends to interpret data solely through its own distorted viewpoint."

"And," Michael said, taking up the thread to spare Beth further irritation, "the Faithful of Masada might even be honored, if they think that someone holding real power came all that way to see them."

He considered the plan, then shook his head decisively.

"It's stupid, Beth. There's lots of information available that would counter any attempt to make you look like a 'broody hen' possessed of the right pedigree. Anyhow, I'll just be a midshipman. That's hardly a rank guaranteed to impress."

"Actually," Beth said, ignoring Michael's first point to concentrate on the second. "The Masadans may well be impressed. They're a hard society, one that seems to believe equally that God preordains their success and that success is proof that God favors someone. They're also warlike, and their leaders often lead in battle as well as in the political arena."

"So a prince who's 'warrior' enough to come up through the Academy and serve in a midshipman's berth would impress them?" Michael said dubiously.

"Let's just say it couldn't hurt," Beth assured him.

Michael decided to leave this for further consideration and turned to what seemed to be what he really needed to know. He suspected that Elizabeth's advisors had wanted this part of his briefing to come from the diplomatic corps, not from the Queen—just in case her sense of priorities was different than their own.

"How much do you want me to do when I'm there? As far as that goes, is the Navy being told that I'm wearing an extra hat?"

Beth's answer was equally direct.

"I want you to cooperate with the diplomatic service as much as seems reasonable. I do not want you to make any promises to anyone in my name or your own."

Michael's dark brown eyes widened in shock.

"As if I would!"

"I know you wouldn't," Beth said softly, "but you'd be astonished how many people don't believe that."

Michael snapped a few pawns into their velvet niches to cover his reaction. He'd supported Beth and her policies since the day she was crowned. It deeply angered him that anyone would believe he would usurp her authority.

"As for the Navy," Beth continued, pretending not to notice how upset he was, "*Intransigent*'s captain will be requested to release you for certain social and diplomatic receptions once the ship is within the Endicott System. Captain Boniece will be assured, however, that your 'second hat' is not to be allowed to distract you from your duties as a Queen's officer. Any briefings the diplomatic representatives feel you need in preparation for arrival at Masada are to be fit into your spare time."

After three and a half T-years at the Academy, Michael had a fair idea of how little spare time a midshipman had. He suppressed a groan.

"I live to serve my Queen," he said, keeping his tone light.

Beth reached over and patted his hand.

"Thanks, Michael. In a few years, the Star Kingdom is going to need all the friends we can get. Who knows? Maybe with your help we can find a way to win over both Endicott and Yeltsin."

"Right," Michael said, looking at the black queen standing all alone on her side of the board. "Maybe we can."

* * *

Dinah, Ephraim's senior wife, was a few years younger than her husband. They had married when she was fifteen and he seventeen. Their first son, Gideon, had already fathered an extensive brood of his own, and some of his sons were reaching an age where they could help crew their father's ship, even as Gideon had Ephraim's.

Now the senior wife stared at her rebellious junior, her anger evident.

"What do you think you are doing?" Dinah repeated.

Judith returned Dinah's gaze as levelly as she could, but meeting those steel gray eyes wasn't easy. Judith had been ten when Ephraim had first brought her into his home. For the two years before he had taken Judith as his youngest bride, Dinah had been a surrogate mother to the orphaned girl. The senior wife had been strict, but not cruel, coaching Judith on matters of etiquette, listening to her recitations, and standing between her and the resentment of Ephraim's other wives—all of whom knew perfectly well that he hadn't brought the Grayson girl home out of high-mindedness.

When a few years later, Judith had suffered her miscarriages, Dinah had sided with the doctor who had advised giving the girl a few more years to physically mature. She had held her ground even in the face of cutting remarks from Ephraim, who accused Dinah of envying the younger woman's youth and potential fecundity.

Now, hair as gray as those piercing eyes, her figure spread from the children, living and dead, she had carried in the thirty-eight years of her marriage, Dinah stood as accusing judge of her co-wife. What Judith didn't understand was why Dinah didn't immediately com for Ephraim or one of her sons.

"I wanted to see what it was like," Judith answered lamely. "I saw Zachariah using it and it looked like fun."

As Dinah set the headset in its rack, Judith could swear that the older woman looked at the program list and understood what was written there. But that was impossible, wasn't it?

For the first time in the four years she had lived beneath Ephraim's roof, Judith doubted that she understood how things worked.

"Come away, Judith," Dinah ordered, her fingers tapping the tabs for the shut-down sequence.

These were standard, the same as for every appliance in the house, so Judith shouldn't have been surprised, but something stirred within her, an inkling of an emotion so alien that she had all but forgotten what it felt like.

Hope.

Afraid to feed that strange emotion, Judith bent her head and dutifully trailed Dinah to the private chamber that, as senior wife, Dinah claimed as her right. The other wives slept in dormitories, an arrangement meant to prevent something vaguely referred to as Vice.

Judith had an idea that Vice might involve sex, but nothing in her experiences with Ephraim gave her any idea why this might be something to pursue. She'd filed this away as a piece of useless information, devoting her energy instead into devising ruses for leaving the dormitory unquestioned. During the two years she had resided with the other wives, she had come up with a large number of these and was careful never to use any one too often.

Dinah motioned Judith to a chair, then closed the door.

"Power surge following transit into N-space," Dinah said. "How useful is that?"

Judith actually started to answer, so matter-of-factly was the question put to her. Then she realized what this meant.

"You can read!"

"My father was very elderly when I was born," Dinah said levelly, "and his eyesight was failing. He never cared for the restrictions of recordings, and had me taught to read so that I could read scripture to him. Later, when my meekness and piety caught Ephraim's eye, my father commanded me to forget what I had learned, for it was well-known that the Templetons saw no use for women's education. I, of course, obeyed, never disabusing my lord and master of his assumptions regarding me."

Judith knew that Dinah's family had been poor and not well-placed within the Masadan hierarchy. An alliance with the ambitious Templetons, especially one that also disposed of a useless daughter, would have been worth a little lie.

"Did you know that I . . ." Judith asked, feeling every bit the child, all the confidence of her fourteen years fleeing.

"Could read?" Dinah set an audio recording of chanted scripture playing on her room's system. "I guessed. You were very careful, even when there were no men present. I commend you for that. Even so, there were times your gaze would rest over-long on some printed label or other bit of text. I was certain the day you saved little Uriel from harming himself.

Judith remembered the day quite clearly. Uriel had been a toddler when first she came to Ephraim's house. His mother, Raphaela, was great with child once more and chasing after the boy had been one of the many tasks bestowed on the Grayson captive.

Not able to transfer her hatred of Ephraim to any of his children, Judith's secret and her honor had warred against each other on the day that Uriel had reached for a brightly colored plug that superficially looked like any number of toys scattered about the nursery.

What it was, however, was a partially installed electrical system that a careless technician had not finished sealing.

For a moment that seemed far longer than it had been, Judith had stared at the chubby hand and the plug. Only the writing on the wiring revealed it for the danger it was. If she stopped Uriel, she might give away her secret.

The little hand had barely moved toward the apparent toy when Judith scooped Uriel away. Once she had soothed the screaming child, distracting him with an even more fascinating toy, Judith had returned to put the wires out of reach. Now that she thought back, Dinah had been present, but as the senior wife had made no comment, Judith had thought her too distracted by her own duties.

"That long," Judith said, and her inflection was a question.

"You were very careful," Dinah replied, "and Ephraim never noticed anything odd about you—except, perhaps, for wondering whether your apparent stupidity was a form of rebellion. I assured him that I thought not."

"You protected me," Judith said, almost accusingly. "Then and today. Why?"

"Then, today, and a dozen times since," Dinah answered. "Why? Because you were careful, because you were kind to those you had reason to hate, and because I pitied you. And for one reason more."

Dinah paused for so long that Judith thought she might not finish her thought.

"Yes?" the younger woman prompted.

"And," said Dinah, a strange light shining in her grey eyes, "because I thought you might somehow be the One prophesied, the Moses sent to lead us from this place and into a better life."

*   *   *

That Midshipman Winton was polite and dutiful to a fault, no matter how much work or how many practice sessions the ATO scheduled for him, didn't moderate Carlie's sense of unease regarding her royal charge.

Unless actually on duty, the young man was rarely without a cadre of hangers-on. Two of these—Astrid Heywood and Osgood Russo—had been transferred to *Intransigent* immediately after Michael's own assignment. The other three had already been assigned to the ship, but that didn't stop them from taking advantage of their proximity to the Crown Prince.

The presence of this cadre had split the middy berth into two groups, for the remaining six members seemed to go out of their way to avoid Midshipman Winton. To make matters worse, even ten days after the last member of the middy berth had reported for duty, Carlie was uncertain whether Michael did or did not encourage his followers. What she was certain of was that he did nothing to *discourage* them, and in her eyes that was just as bad.

Then there was the problem of Michael Winton's extra duties, duties that required him to spend a great deal of time consulting with the diplomatic contingent that was *Intransigent*'s reason for heading to the Endicott System. Carlie didn't doubt that once the diplomats had Prince Michael behind closed doors they bowed and scraped to him in the most abject manner. Certainly, Michael seemed even more distant and self-contained whenever he returned from one of these meetings.

That Michael couldn't take his toadies with him to these diplomatic sessions was one of the few good things about them, Carlie thought, but they served even more than his little cadre to emphasize that Michael Winton was someone apart from the rest of the middy berth. Hell, from the rest of *Intransigent*'s crew.

How different Michael Winton was had been reinforced at Captain Boniece's latest dinner. As was the practice of some of the Navy's better captains, Boniece periodically invited various of his officers to dine with him. On this particular night, both Carlie and Michael had been included, and Carlie kept a sharp—though she hoped not too obvious—eye on her charge.

The evening went smoothly, Midshipman Winton not speaking unless spoken to, but offering intelligent answers to those questions put to him. Carlie had even begun to think that maybe Michael wasn't as stuck-up as she had believed.

Then came the conclusion of the meal, and wine was poured for the traditional toast to the Queen. As the junior officer present, the duty fell on Midshipman Winton.

He needed no prompting. Nor did Carlie expect him to need such. Carlie had shared stories with many officers of her acquaintance, and all agreed that this stepping forth into the limelight in the presence of those who were for the first time your peers rather than those august others known as Officers was a landmark occasion in a career.

Raising his glass to just the right level, Michael Winton said in a clear, carrying voice: "Ladies and gentlemen, the Queen!"

"The Queen!" came the affirmation.

Carlie had sipped from her glass, using the action to cover a glance at her charge. Michael Winton had settled back into his seat, but he wasn't drinking the captain's excellent wine. Instead he was—Carlie was certain of it—he was smirking.

Lieutenant Carlotta Dunsinane, loyal officer of the Navy and therefore to the Queen it served, was shocked to the core. Her shock must have shown in her expression because the *Intransigent*'s communications officer, Tab Tilson, leaned toward her.

"Are you feeling all right, Carlie?"

"Fine," she managed. "Just got a little wine down the wrong pipe."

Tab nodded, reassured, and turned to answer a question put to him by Captain Boniece. When Carlie again turned her gaze to Mr. Winton, the prince was politely talking to his near neighbor, his expression as correct as it had been all evening.

But Carlie knew what she had seen, and again doubted to the depths of her heart whether this prince could ever humble himself from his position of power and privilege to embrace the life of service that was at the heart and soul of what it meant to be a true naval officer.

*   *   *

Michael didn't know if he was going to survive this middy cruise. It wasn't just the workload, though he had done a quiet survey of his own as compared to his fellows and knew that it wasn't just his imagination that Lieutenant Dunsinane heaped more on him than on any of the other eleven middies.

It wasn't that about half of his ostensible free time was taken up by the diplomatic corps briefings, briefings that—to him—seemed unnecessary, since his job was to be seen but, as Lawler stated over and over again, definitely not heard.

It was the isolation that was killing him.

Michael had lived for fifteen days now crowded into

a berth furnished with six double bunks, each bunk furnished with its tenant, and he had yet to have a decent conversation with anyone—not even with several people who, on Saganami Island, he would have called friends.

Michael wasn't a fool. He'd even expected something like this. It took time for people to get used to the idea that they were rooming with someone who, if he talked about his sister, was talking about the Queen. Michael and his first roommate at Saganami Island had been stiff and formal strangers for a few weeks, but eventually Sam had become comfortable enough with the idea of rooming with royalty that Michael hadn't felt like he was letting the Crown down by walking around in his underwear.

He and Sam had never become buddies, but they had become solid acquaintances. Maybe helped by a bit of distance, Michael had made his best friends among those who didn't have to share living quarters with him. Foremost among these had been Todd Liatt, who had bridged that final gap to become Michael's roommate later on.

What wouldn't Michael give to have Toad-breath here now! That psychic radar of Todd's would pin down why it was that Lieutenant Dunsinane never looked at Michael without her expression turning stiff as an armorplast bulkhead. But Todd wasn't here and Michael didn't want to think what Lieutenant Dunsinane would think of him if she caught him looking at her public record. It was pretty clear she didn't think much of him already.

Michael could have kicked himself up one side of the hull and around the other when he saw the ATO's expression there at Captain Boniece's dinner party. He'd been feeling so good about getting through that toast that he'd slipped, remembering how Beth had teased him regarding that very earth-shattering event while he was on his last leave.

"And don't forget you'll have to toast the Queen," she had said primly one morning over a very informal breakfast. "You're *my* officer now, you know."

Michael had seen an irresistible opportunity.

"Let me practice, Your Majesty," he'd said, and rising to his feet he'd picked up the entire plate of freshly toasted bread slices and up-ended them over her head.

Beth had shrieked like they were both kids again, and started throwing toast at him, her treecat Ariel joining the game with pinpoint enthusiasm. The sound had pulled Justin out of his drowsy perusal of the morning newsfax, and brought Queen Mother Angelique into the room at an undignified run.

The memory of Beth's reaction had brought a smile to Michael's lips, a smile he had instantly tried to suppress lest he be seen as irreverent at this most solemn occasion. Unhappily, he'd caught his own expression in a polished serving dish and knew the squelched smile looked worse than any open grin would have done.

He'd longed to talk to Lieutenant Dunsinane, to explain what had happened, but he couldn't seem to find an opening. Talking to the ATO was much harder than talking to the dean. Commander Shrake at least seemed to think Michael was a person. Lieutenant Dunsinane couldn't seem to see past the prince and everything Michael did only made her more formal and severe.

Michael knew he couldn't ask someone else to talk to her, though he was tempted to ask Lieutenant Tilson, the communications' chief. Whenever they met, the com officer seemed quite businesslike, as if he believed Michael was more interested in learning his duties than in reminding people he was the Queen's little brother.

But though Michael's nascent specialization in communications placed him frequently in Lieutenant Tilson's sphere, Michael couldn't talk to Tilson about his problems with Lieutenant Dunsinane. It wouldn't be right. Michael possessed a Winton's fierce loyalty and he wouldn't undermine the officer responsible for supervising the middy berth, even if Lieutenant Dunsinane had misjudged him.

Lieutenant Dunsinane wasn't the worst of Michael's problems. He hoped that if he worked hard enough, he might win her over. What really troubled him were the five middies who, despite everything Michael did to gently dissuade them, hung around him like a self-appointed honor guard.

Soon after the middy berth was fully assembled, Michael learned that the leaders of this corps were also newly reassigned to *Intransigent*. It didn't take Michael's lifelong immersion in politics to realize that the pair had gotten posted to *Intransigent* precisely for the proximity that would give them to the Crown Prince.

Astrid Heywood was a scion of one of Manticore's more powerful noble houses, the Honorable Astrid in civilian life. She was a pretty young woman, honey-blond, with enormous long-lashed blue eyes. Her slightly too regular features suggested that her attractiveness had been helped along with various cosmetic enhancements, but Michael doubted that most men his age would look beyond the melting glances Astrid kept casting in his direction to notice.

Astrid's mother, Baroness White Springs, sat in Lords where she was an increasingly vocal speaker for the Independents. Unlike the Crown Loyalists, each Independent supported Crown policy more flexibly. Michael didn't know how Baroness White Springs would react if her daughter was openly rebuked by the Queen's

brother, but he didn't think it would be good. The
Heywood family had to have put out a good amount
in favors or bribes to get Astrid moved onto *Intransigent* at such short notice, and Michael suspected the
baroness expected a solid return on her investment.

That calculating use by mother of daughter might
have made Michael pity Astrid, except for something
that had become all too apparent during the days Astrid
had been trailing him. Despite her intelligence and
willingness to work hard—traits proven by her completing Saganami Island—Astrid was one of those
impossible members of the Manticoran nobility who
really did believe that an accident of birth made her
better than anyone else. Astrid didn't see Michael's
attempts to avoid her as anything other than a fellow
dodging the awkward attentions of a pretty girl, simply because it didn't occur to her that anyone would
want to avoid her. Moreover, despite the logical twisting
involved in such thinking, Astrid's already good opinion of herself was enhanced by the fact that she now
shared a berth with the Crown Prince.

Osgood "Ozzie" Russo was a more subtle character, though one would never guess it on initially meeting this bright-eyed, laughing imp. His family was
connected to the incredibly rich Hauptman cartel, and
Michael was certain that Ozzie's transfer had been
bought outright. Whether the purchase price had been
in bribes or in concessions for supplies needed by the
rapidly expanding Navy, Michael had no idea, nor did
he really care—except to hope that the Navy proper
rather than some corrupt individual over in
BuPersonnel had benefitted.

Not surprisingly, given his family interests, Ozzie was
specializing in Supply. Logistically, he was brilliant, able
to glance at a complicated schematic and reduce it to
its component parts before Michael had finished

reading the headers. Although Supply was outside the line of command, and thus often discounted by ambitious sorts, Michael was enough of a history buff to realize that many battles had been won or lost even before they were joined due to logistical considerations.

The problem with Ozzie was that he apparently saw Michael as another resource to be cultivated for the future benefit of himself and his family—and he figured Michael should see him in the same light. Michael didn't like this one bit, but although Ozzie was not ostensibly connected to anyone in politics, money could be used as easily as aristocratic connections to obstruct the Queen and her policies, so Michael made certain not to alienate Ozzie, while quietly fuming beneath the other's fawning attention.

What united Astrid and Ozzie was a sense of superiority over their fellows, though ironically Michael was fairly certain that each privately thought little of the other. Like a lodestone attracting iron filings, these two had drawn the more amorally ambitious middies toward them. In doing so they had pushed away what Michael, at least, saw as the better elements of the middy berth, those who wanted to earn their rank on their own merit, not because of whom they knew.

Not wishing to be seen in the same light as Astrid and Ozzie—neither by Michael nor by the rest of the ship's officers—six of the middies hardly spoke to Michael. That two of these, Sally Pike and Kareem Jones, had been among Michael's circle of friendly acquaintances at Saganami Island, made this ostracization confusing as well as painful.

But there was nothing Michael could say to them that wouldn't make the situation worse, so he hauled his way through his day, wondering if what he was feeling was anything like what he'd heard about the isolation of command.

❋   ❋   ❋

At fourteen, after several very intensive sessions with
Dinah—sessions that were represented to a pleased
Ephraim as preparing Judith to resume her childbear-
ing duties—Judith had been initiated into the very
small, highly secret, and slightly mystical Sisterhood of
Barbara.

The Sisterhood took its inspiration from Barbara
Bancroft, the woman who had foiled the Masadan plot
to destroy all life on Grayson following the failure of
their attempt to seize control of it. Even before she
was captured by Ephraim, Judith had heard of Barbara, for on Grayson she was revered as the planet's
savior. The Barbara of whom Judith heard from the
Faithful was a completely different person: evil, conniving, traitorous, faithless, and blasphemous.

Indeed, the Faithful's version of Barbara Bancroft
was so horrendous that initially Judith wondered that
the Sisterhood had taken "this Harlot of Satan" as their
patron. After a few secret meetings with Dinah and
her cell, Judith understood that it was precisely because
Barbara was so vilified that these brave Masadan
women named themselves for her. However else Barbara Bancroft was represented by the Masadans, the
one thing the Faithful could not say of her was that
she was cowardly. Moreover, Barbara had won in her
battle against Masadan tyranny. She had paid a terrifying price for that victory, but she had won.

The Sisterhood had two goals. The first was to
educate and, when possible, to protect other women.
That protection was granted to any woman, but the
educational benefits were only extended to those
women who had been tried and found perfectly trustworthy. Maintaining secrecy was made easier in that
any woman who so much as learned to read a few
simple lines or do more complex mathematics than

could be worked out by counting on fingers was considered suspect by the Elders of the Faithful.

Tales of the punishments doled out to those who had transgressed were told in the nursery, repeated in sermons, and reinforced in a hundred little ways. There was even a sub-set of the Faithful who viewed these simple arts as the first step down the slippery slope to technological corruption. These, known as the Pure in Faith, refused to have even their men learn to read or write. As a result, the Pure lived in isolated enclaves and had little to do with the rest of the Faithful—other than providing some of the most ferocious and unquestioning soldiers.

Such indoctrination made it highly unlikely that any Masadan woman who took the daring step of joining the Sisterhood would betray her Sisters later. Indeed, that irrevocable loss of intellectual virginity drew the women closer to each other, bound by their awareness of the penalties all would share—even one who might later regret her learning and report the rest.

Judith rapidly discovered that the Sisterhood did more than teach forbidden arts and knowledge. The Sisters were also trained in dissembling so that the accidental revelation of their knowledge—even by something as casual as being seen to read a printed label—could not betray them.

But these were all elements of the first of the Sisterhood's missions. The second of the Sisterhood's goals was far more daring, perhaps impossible, for the Sisterhood hoped to someday lead an Exodus that would set the Sisters free from domination by their masters.

No matter how hard the Faithful tried to keep knowledge of the outer universe from their women, the truth had filtered in—often hinted at in the very restrictions and rulings the men enforced upon their women.

The Sisters knew that somewhere beyond the reach of Masada's sun were worlds where women were not regarded as property. There were worlds where women were permitted to read, write, and think; worlds where, so the most daring among them whispered, women were even permitted to live without male protectors.

From the day Ephraim had dragged the shocked and traumatized Grayson ten-year-old into the nursery, Dinah had dreamed that Judith might be the promised Moses who would lead the Sisterhood to freedom. Nor had the girl disappointed the older woman's hopes. From the start Judith had demonstrated both education and self-control—and the intelligence to hide both. Her innocent anecdotes about the life she had left, mostly told before she realized how dangerous they were, had confirmed the Sisterhood's most sacred hopes and dreams.

Thus Judith, while believing herself alone, had been cocooned within the watchful web of the senior Sisters. They had not dared draw her into their secret, not until they saw if Judith would, like so many women, perversely fasten onto her tormentor, envisioning him as a hero who had the right to treat her as a mere thing. Four years of brutal testing, two of those after Judith was married to a man who had set his seal on ostensibly stronger souls, were allowed to pass before Dinah confronted Judith and drew her into the Sisterhood.

Now, two years after Judith's initiation, faced with Ephraim's plans to abort her unborn daughter, confronting a future marked by similar abuse, Judith accepted the mantle the Sisterhood had set upon her shoulders. She would be their Moses, and, though hearing no divine voice to guide her actions, she decreed that the time for the Sisterhood's Exodus had come.

* * *

Although he understood the reasons, Michael still found the wholly male diplomatic corps bound for Endicott rather odd. Every political meeting he had attended since his father's death had been dominated by Beth. Even when Beth had been a minor, her regent had been their aunt Caitrin, the Grand Duchess Winton-Henke. This all male group was positively weird.

Then again, maybe the fact that gender and availability, rather than pure ability, had been key elements in selecting this group was why it was so peculiar. There was also the fact that much of the Manticoran diplomatic corps felt that its first task was preserving peace rather than preparing for war. Many of the best and the brightest among them were employing their energies trying to figure out how to work with the Peeps. Doubtless the Masadan mission was not an assignment those would seek.

Perhaps, too, the reality that Masada was not the Queen's first choice for an ally in this region of space had something to do with those who had volunteered. Those diplomats, like Sir Anthony Langtry, more of Her Majesty's way of thinking and ready to embrace the possibility that war could not be prevented would be striving to win over the Graysons.

The men who had volunteered for the Masadan mission were eager for any chance to prove themselves—as they most surely would if they could win the misogynistic and egocentric Faithful over to an alliance.

Forbes Lawler, a first-generation prolong recipient and former member of the House of Commons, was the head of the group. Handsome, with iron grey hair, and a lean, athletic build, Lawler spoke in a straight-at-them, square-jawed fashion that reminded Michael

of his first gym teacher. Although Lawler never said
so directly, he clearly hoped that in addition to bringing
new instructions he would soon be replacing the current ambassador.

Quentin Cayen served as Lawler's personal assistant.
Young enough to be a second-generation prolong recipient, Cayen tinted his hair silver at the temples and
affected reading glasses in an attempt to bring gravity to his otherwise boyishly plump features. Michael
thought Cayen looked rather silly, but since Cayen was
otherwise competent, and eager to please without being
offensive, the midshipman tried to overlook the other
man's cosmetic enhancements.

The last member of the delegation, John Hill, was
ostensibly a computer specialist. He was very knowl-
edgeable about the Masadans, including being familiar
with the Faithful's religious rituals and dietary restrictions. Hill was pretty clearly a spy, but Michael
thought he might well be the most competent member of the trio.

On the day *Intransigent* entered the Endicott System, Michael was working in the almost empty middy
berth when a memo requesting his attendance at a final
planning session came from Lawler. Since Michael had
a mess of homework—it might be called other things,
but it still felt like homework—he wasn't terribly
pleased. However, he knew his duty and reluctantly put
aside the fusion repair sim he'd been assigned by the
chief engineer herself.

"Where are you going, Michael?" Astrid asked,
setting her own reader aside, apparently prepared to
accompany him.

"Mr. Lawler wants me," Michael replied.

"Oh," Astrid said, disappointed, and turned back to
her work.

Michael, who had the vague feeling that Astrid had

been trying to get him alone for several days now, saw Sally Pike smirking, and thought he might be right. Relieved, he grabbed a few things, waved a vague farewell, and got out of there before Ozzie or one of the other hangers-on could decide to walk him to the diplomats' suite.

When Michael arrived, Lawler was pacing back and forth, barely containing his excitement.

"A notice just came from the bridge," he said, thrusting hard copy into Michael's hand. "There is at least one Peep ship in system."

"Doesn't the People's Republic have an embassy here, just like we do?" Michael asked.

"They do," Lawler agreed. "However, an embassy is no reason for the Peeps to station a heavy cruiser here, is it?"

Michael felt his eyebrows shoot toward his hairline. *Intransigent* was a light cruiser, and Beth had considered sending her on a diplomatic mission a rather heavy-handed move. Apparently, the Peeps were less subtle.

"It's the *Moscow*, Prince Michael," John Hill added. "Not one of their newest models, but not one of the oldest either."

"Has she been here long?" Michael asked, feeling odd, as he always did after existing within the Navy's rigid command structure, to be back among those who subtly deferred to him.

"Not long enough to state that *Moscow* is stationed here," Hill replied, with the vaguely exasperated note in his voice that Michael had learned was reserved for correcting Lawler's more extreme statements. "Nor would I say that *Moscow* was sent in anticipation of our own arrival, though that isn't impossible. Mr. Lawler's coming with new instructions has not precisely been kept a secret."

There was no real reason Lawler's arrival should have been, Michael knew, but he had a feeling that Hill was the type of man who kept secrets by reflex. Hill probably thought it would be a breach of basic security if he knew the color of his own socks.

"Ambassador Faldo is most impatient for our arrival," Lawler interjected happily, "but Captain Boniece tells me we cannot be shuttled planetside until tomorrow morning. That leaves us ample time to review."

For the next several hours, Michael tried not to think wistfully of the engineering sim he hadn't completed, nor about the trauma team drill Surgeon Commander Rink had promised to run for the middies. When the twittering of the com broke into Lawler's nearly uninterrupted lecture, Michael realized he'd been all but dozing.

"Ambassador Faldo wishes to speak with you and your shore party," the duty communications officer announced. "If you are free."

Lawler smothered a look of mild annoyance, then nodded.

"Please patch the Ambassador through."

"Just a moment, Mr. Lawler."

Cayen had leapt to his feet the moment the com chimed and, by the time the call came through, he had modified the desk unit so that the ambassador's face was projected on one of the cabin's bulkheads, sparing them the need to crowd around a terminal.

Ambassador Faldo, like Mr. Lawler, was a first-generation prolong recipient. Unlike Lawler, who managed to project incredible vigor, Faldo looked tired. His hair had apparently once been blond, but had now faded to a muddy gray with just enough of the original color left to make him appear molting. His eyes, sunk beneath puffy lids, were a washed-out brown, but their gaze remained direct and penetrating.

"The reaction," the ambassador began after minimal polite greetings had been exchanged, "to the presence of Prince Michael aboard *Intransigent* has been—to speak mildly—beyond my greatest expectations. Not only has the Chief Elder expressed a desire to meet Mr. Winton, but the Senior Elders are to be included in the reception. In fact, as far as I can tell, everyone who is anyone as well as everyone who wants to be thought anyone is attending some enormous conclave of Elders that the Faithful have 'coincidentally' announced will be happening at this time."

"That's wonderful, Sir," Lawler said.

"I suppose so," Faldo agreed. "However, it means I want to move up the time for our meeting tomorrow. We're to join the Chief Elder at precisely noon, and I want time to prepare for such an important event. The Chief Elder has honored us by putting at our disposal a meeting room at the Hall of the Just."

Doesn't want us talking where he can't try to overhear us, Michael wondered with inbred cynicism. *Probably. He knows that'll mean Faldo won't be able to give me too detailed a list of do's and don'ts. Maybe figures he'll be able to trip me up somehow.*

Michael listened attentively as plans for the next day's meeting were made, but nothing more significant was said, doubtless because of fear that either the Peeps or the Masadans would hear something they shouldn't. Tight-beam communications were good, but as a communications officer Michael knew all too many ways their security measures could be circumvented.

After the connection had been cut, Lawler resumed pacing, rubbing his hands together with vigorous enthusiasm.

"Well, that's very interesting, very interesting . . ." he was beginning, but Hill interrupted.

"It is indeed," he said. "There have been some

rumblings of discontent regarding how Chief Elder Simonds has been making policy. I wonder if this is his way of demonstrating to his own people how integral he is, and of convincing them that they do not want another leader."

"Mountain coming to Mohammed, and like that," Lawler said. "Yes. Well, we can let him play his games."

"In all deference, Sir," Hill replied, not sounding deferential at all, "I wouldn't use that particular analogy. The Faithful have rejected even the New Testament of the Christian bible. They view the Islamic faith— if they recall it at all—as a heresy."

Lawler looked momentarily nonplussed. Then he resumed his hand-rubbing.

"Right! That's why these briefings are so important. We don't want to make any mistakes."

Michael raised one hand, feeling more than ever that he was in school.

"Mr. Lawler, I really should report this change in schedule to Lieutenant Dunsinane."

Lawler waved his hand in a wide, breezy gesture.

"Do so, Mr. Winton. I shall write her myself requesting that you be freed from your more routine shipboard duties during this crucial moment in Manticoran diplomacy."

As Michael moved to com the ATO, he found himself wondering precisely what tomorrow would bring and hoping against hope that it would not include a very pissed-off Lieutenant Dunsinane.

*   *   *

Carlie looked at the memo from Mr. Lawler first with disbelief, then with anger. She continued staring at it for so long that at last the two emotions blended into a generalized confusion.

" . . . requests that Mister Midshipman Winton be relieved from a portion of his shipboard duties in order to be better able to serve the needs of Her Royal Majesty at this crucial diplomatic juncture."

There was more of the same, all soothing, all vaguely pompous, and all boiling down to what had already been clearly said in that first line. Midshipman Winton was being given a holiday from his responsibilities as a member of *Intransigent*'s crew so that he could go play prince.

She'd known that Michael would be going down to the planet with Mr. Lawler's contingent, but she hadn't considered that Mr. Lawler would be so bold as to think that a midshipman's shipboard responsibilities could be superseded by anything else. She'd figured that Midshipman Winton would fit his trips planetside into his free time. He'd managed his numerous meetings with Lawler and company then, hadn't he?

Her first reaction was to refuse. Then she thought again about that phrase "crucial diplomatic juncture." It was no secret that there had been a Peep presence in system. The Havenites weren't being either coy or subtle. The fact that the Peeps—like the Manticorans—were demonstrating an armed presence indicated their own awareness of how touchy the situation was.

Could the presence of Crown Prince Michael make a difference in how the Masadans felt about the Manticorans? Would she be doing something foolish if she stuck to regulations? Reluctantly, for she very much wanted to go by The Book, Carlie commed Captain Boniece and was granted his first available appointment.

Tab Tilson gave her a lazy wave as he exited the captain's briefing room, and Carlie had a moment to wonder if the communications officer was also present on Michael Winton's business. Then she was summoned into the captain's presence.

"Yes, Lieutenant?" Abelard Boniece looked amused

as he motioned her to a seat. "Your call said you needed to consult me regarding Mr. Winton. I have read the memo you copied to me. You may proceed from that point."

Carlie could have far more easily handled the captain's looking stern or even angry than she could the twinkle in his eye, but she straightened herself in her chair and tried to report as if in the middle of a battle.

"Yes, Sir. Frankly, I don't know what to do. This is Mr. Winton's midshipman's cruise. I feel that the distraction of playing diplomat has not been good for him."

Captain Boniece merely raised an eyebrow and Carlie hastened to explain.

"I knew from the start, Sir, that Mr. Winton was going to have these distractions. However, to this point they have been secondary to his shipboard responsibilities. Mr. Lawler is, effectively, requesting that we give them precedence."

"That is exactly what he's doing," Captain Boniece agreed. "Moreover, his request is not precisely out of line with what we were told to expect from the moment *Intransigent* was diverted to Masada."

"I suppose not, Sir," Carlie admitted grudgingly.

Captain Boniece met her gaze squarely, any hint of amusement gone from his expression.

"Have you been dissatisfied with how Mr. Winton is conducting himself, Lieutenant?"

"Not really, Skipper. He does his duties, but he doesn't seem much like the other middies."

"Perhaps," Boniece replied, "because Mr. Winton is not like any other snotty—not on *Intransigent*, nor on any other ship in Her Majesty's navy."

Carlie's eyes widened. The term was openly, sometimes even affectionately, applied to middies, but as far as she could recall, it was the first time she had heard it applied to *Intransigent's* berth.

Captain Boniece seemed to think he had made a point of some sort, for his smile momentarily returned before he continued his train of thought.

"Even as you have been observing Mr. Winton," he said, "I have been observing you, Lieutenant. It seems to me that you're trying to make Michael Winton into just one of everyone else. What you must understand is that even if he serves in the Navy for a hundred years, Michael Winton will never be just like anyone else. Even if Queen Elizabeth has twenty children, Michael will always be her only brother. I want you to accept this and work with it. That's an order."

"Yes, Captain."

The snap in his tone was such that Carlie started to rise and salute, believing herself dismissed, but Captain Boniece motioned for her to remain.

"I want you to think about something else, Carlie," he said. "Not only is Mr. Winton unlike everyone else with whom he serves—so is every member of this crew different from every other."

Carlie blinked at him, too startled to manage even a routine "Yes, Sir."

"Have you ever wondered, Lieutenant Dunsinane," Boniece continued, "why the assistant tactical officer is put in charge of the middy berth? After all, what do a dozen or so snotties have to do with planning an attack or defense, deciding whether to roll the ship or fire from all ports?"

"Yes, Skipper," Carlie said, too confused now to be indirect. "Honestly, I have."

"Tactics," Boniece went on, "is the most direct track to command, and a commander needs to learn to work with the most important asset the ship possesses—the crew. Unlike energy batteries or missile tubes, crews don't come with neat specs listing limitations and advantages. Crews are unpredictable, annoying, surprising, and astonishing."

Carlie, beginning to understand now, was feeling like a complete idiot. Boniece, however, wasn't done with drumming his lesson home.

"If you win your white beret, you're going to need to deal with every variation of human temperament. You're going to need to learn the way to get the best out of each one. Sometimes that's going to mean preferring someone who seems too junior to merit preferment. Sometimes that's going to mean passing up someone who, by The Book, has every advantage going for him. Once the ship leaves base, there's no supply room with spare crew members. You need to train your crew for diversity and flexibility—and contrariwise, you need to train them for perfect expertise in their departments."

Carlie nodded.

"I think that I haven't been treating my snotties," she grinned as she said the formerly tabooed word, "as they deserve. I'll remember that, Sir. And now that you mention it, Mr. Winton has been drawing rather more than the usual workload. I believe he can miss a few hours here and there. I would, however, like him to report back to the ship to sleep."

Captain Boniece cocked an eyebrow at her.

"I don't think Mr. Winton will forget where his duty lies," Carlie explained. "However, I suspect that Mr. Lawler might. I'd like to make certain that Mr. Winton has at least a good night's sleep."

"I support you on that, Lieutenant," the Captain said. "Now, tell Mr. Winton to get ready to go planetside, and remind him that we expect him to do the Navy proud."

❋   ❋   ❋

Judith had reasons other than her own crisis to set the Sisterhood's Exodus in motion.

From tapping into Ephraim's private communications channels, she had learned that envoys from other star nations regularly visited Masada. She had also learned that some of those envoys—specifically those from an enchantingly named place called the People's Republic of Haven—sought to win Ephraim's support in the Counsel of Elders with more than mere words.

Two of the vessels in Ephraim's privateer fleet, *Psalms* and *Proverbs*, had been offered technological modifications. Much of what the Havenite engineers did to the two ships merely improved their eyes and ears, but at Ephraim's insistence, their teeth had been sharpened as well. Since the Havenites were eager to show how useful they could be as allies they had agreed with few hesitations.

The modifications to both *Psalms* and *Proverbs* were carefully installed, so that the alterations were not evident in a routine external scan. Ephraim said this was because neither the Council of Elders nor the Havenites wanted anyone to detect the work and think ill of the acceptance of advanced technology. However, such care had been taken to conceal the modifications that Judith fleetingly wondered if the Havenites might suspect the dual use to which Ephraim turned his vessels.

In time *Aaron's Rod* would also be modified. It said something about Ephraim's essentially conservative nature that he had chosen to have ships other than his little fleet's flag undergo the modifications first. As with many other captains and their ships, *Aaron's Rod* was an extension of Ephraim's self and ego, and he did not wish that other self to be tampered with until he saw the results on others.

Judith feared that such extensive changes to *Aaron's*

Rod's systems could mean delaying the Sisterhood's escape until she could learn how to use these new devices and then train her Sisters. All of the women were without question brave, but—as could only be expected given their Masadan upbringing—all but a few tended to follow Judith's instructions by rote rather than with any intellectual comprehension of the tasks she set them.

There were exceptions. In the early years of their marriage, Ephraim had taken Dinah on his voyages, and she, like Judith, had striven to learn something about the various departments. Dinah's actual skills were woefully outdated, but at least she understood the concept of three-dimensional astrogation and tactics. Many of the Sisters persisted, no matter how carefully Judith explained, in visualizing their ship as sailing over a flat surface.

Dinah thus became gunnery officer and XO to Judith's captain. Dinah's eldest daughter, Mahalia, a widow who had been returned to her father's house after the death of her husband, was put in charge of Engineering. Ephraim's third wife, Rena, mother of many children, was head of Damage Control.

Naomi, the second wife of Gideon, was put in charge of the passengers—for Judith and Dinah were determined to take as many of the Sisters with them as they could manage. Indeed, removing the Sisters from Masada was the entire reason for this venture. The leaders were all too aware that there would be no second chance, and that those Sisters who were left behind would be intensively and painfully interrogated if their connection to the rebels was in the least suspected.

Judith knew nothing of the specific escape plans for the majority of the Sisters. That stage of the process was in Dinah's hands. Judith did know that there were multiple plans for each Sister, and that in most households only one or two women at most needed to slip away. Ephraim's household was extraordinary in its concentrated membership in the Sisterhood, but that was hardly surprising given that it was Dinah's household and Dinah was the Sisterhood's head.

Escape for Judith herself was comparatively close at hand. Along with Mahalia and Rena, she was to take the cargo shuttle, *Flower*. If they failed, the rest of the program would not even be put into motion, for without *Flower* they could not reach *Aaron's Rod*.

Judith was woefully aware how few trained people she had to crew *Aaron's Rod*—assuming the Sisters would even manage to get aboard the ship, subdue its caretaker crew, and get it out of orbit. However, the ship's computer contained numerous preprogrammed routines, and each of Judith's department heads had several assistants. Those assistants at least understood how to get the most out of what the computer could offer.

Judith was mulling over her options for alternate crew assignments—all her information memorized, for the first rule of the Sisterhood was to leave as few written records as possible—when Dinah signaled for her to join her among the noisy children in the nursery.

The older woman's eyes were shining with barely suppressed excitement.

"I believe God is parting the Red Sea for us," she said softly. Then she spoke in more usual tones. "I have just come from Ephraim. He summoned me to give orders for what is to be done during his forthcoming absence."

Despite Dinah's initial words, Judith's heart sank. Was Ephraim preparing to take *Aaron's Rod* out on another voyage?

"Absence?" she managed.

"Yes," Dinah said. "A delegation has arrived from one of the star nations—the one ruled by a queen."

Now Judith understood that light in the older woman's eyes. Judith had always favored the People's Republic of Haven as their potential sanctuary, both for its name and for the marvelous way it had declared itself the protector of the weak and the oppressed. Dinah, however, preferred the Star Kingdom of Manticore.

Dinah's preference wasn't only because the Star Kingdom was ruled by a queen—though that did make a difference to her. Dinah reasoned, rather cynically to Judith's way of thinking, that any nation that spent as much time talking about how it defended the oppressed as the People's Republic did probably had something to hide.

"Honestly, child," Dinah had said a trace impatiently one day. "Look at our own men and how they go on about loving God and doing his Will and battling the Apostate. We know that few of them love God as much as they love their own honor and position.

"Ephraim may say he wants to build and train his fleet so that he can be in the forefront when the battle against the Apostate comes, but he certainly doesn't mind the benefits he has garnered in the meantime. You wouldn't recall the day he was elected into the Council of Elders, but Satan in all His peacock majesty never was prouder. Was that honor enough? No, now Ephraim's trying to be promoted to Senior Elder—and him not even three score years."

Judith had agreed that Dinah had a point, but she found the monstrous creatures that adorned the Manticoran heraldry frightening and disturbing. She also didn't much like the idea of a ruling nobility. It sounded far too much like the hierarchy on Masada.

Dinah had another, more telling point, to offer.

"And why, if this People's Republic of Haven is so willing to respect other people's rights, why are they improving Ephraim's ships for him—even to their fighting capacities? I might believe they were motivated by simple altruism, but for how easily he swayed them to his way of thinking when it came to weapons."

Judith had to admit Dinah's argument had weight, but she also knew how persuasive Ephraim could be. In any case, it didn't matter whether she or Dinah were right. The Sisterhood had agreed to let God guide the path of their escape, and the arrival of the Manticoran vessel at the very time the Sisterhood was setting Exodus into motion did seem like an omen of His intent.

"Why would the coming of a Manticoran vessel mean Ephraim must leave home?" Judith asked.

"The Manticorans have sent someone very important to meet the Council," Dinah said, and though her voice was respectful, her eyes gleamed with mischief. "It seems that all these years we have been foolish in believing that such a powerful kingdom could be ruled by a weak woman. It seems that there is a prince who actually holds the reins, though he was but a child when his father died and so the Queen was crowned in his stead. Now a grown man, this prince has come here himself to meet with our Elders."

"And none of the Elders will miss such an important occasion," Judith said, her heart pounding with excitement.

"None," Dinah agreed. "Ephraim has ordered Gideon and his other sons to accompany him."

"Many other households will do the same," Judith said, "for is it not true that a man's strength is in his sons?"

"There's even more," Dinah said. "A well-informed source tells me that the Navy is pulling out for maneuvers."

"They aren't worried about a Manticoran attack?"

"Not in the least. Manticore wants allies, not another system to administer. The Navy, however, does not want the Manticorans to get too close a look at what we have."

Judith, thinking of the modifications that had been worked on *Psalms* and *Proverbs,* wondered if some similar tinkering might have been done to a few of the fleet vessels—just enough to whet the Admiralty's taste for what the People's Republic could offer, perhaps. She could see why they wouldn't want to show their hand without reason.

"God truly is with us," Judith breathed. "Surely we can escape from a few patrol boats."

They smiled at each other. It did seem that God had parted the Red Sea for them, for in none of their plans had they dared anticipate such a removal of the Masadan men from their households.

Yet this would not make the success of Exodus certain. Many households would be secured more tightly in the absence of their masters. Many women would be forced to accompany their husbands, and so be prevented from escape. Then there was each step of the escape itself: the taking of the shuttle, the subduing of the caretaker crew, getting the ship from orbit and to hyper limit. Judith's head swam. However, she had to admit that the omens were still too good to ignore.

The Sisters were committed to making the attempt, no matter the risks. Death was preferable to the life they would be leaving behind them. At last resort, Judith thought grimly, *Aaron's Rod* would make a spectacular funeral pyre. Perhaps some new Moses would be guided by the bright burning of that beacon and finally set her Sisters free.

* * *

Michael thought he was ready for anything. However, when Lieutenant Dunsinane told him that not only was he being relieved of some of his shipboard assignments so that he could accompany Mr. Lawler to the surface, but even smiled as she did so, he was so startled he nearly forgot to thank her.

"I've reviewed your work," Dunsinane went on when Michael finished stammering, a trace of her former severity returning, "and I see that you've kept up on your assignments. And don't thank me too fast. There's one limitation to your shore leave, Mr. Winton."

"Yes, Lieutenant?"

"Unless you are prevented by some serious impediment from doing so, you are required to return onboard each night in order to report."

"I will, Lieutenant," Michael promised. "According to Mr. Hill's briefings, the Faithful are very unlikely to schedule any meetings after the dinner hour. It violates one of their social customs. All I'd miss is Mr. Lawler's recap of events."

Dunsinane didn't quite grin, but Michael thought that the twitch at one side of her mouth might mean that she had detected the inadvertent note of relief that had entered his voice at the thought of avoiding a few of Mr. Lawler's exhaustive—and largely pointless—analysis sessions.

"I'm certain that Mr. Cayen would be happy to make a transcript for you," Lieutenant Dunsinane said so confidently that Michael had a sneaking suspicion that she had already arranged for this.

In fact, for the first time Michael had the feeling the ATO was working with him rather than against him, and he was determined not to be a disappointment.

*   *   *

One of *Intransigent*'s pinnaces took them down to a major Masadan spaceport first thing in the morning. *Intransigent* was not being permitted a close parking orbit. Indeed, she was being kept so far from the planet proper that Michael wondered if the Masadans were nervous about the possibility of attack.

I guess, he thought, *that a planet that's made a career out of attacking its closest neighbor would be nervous about getting similar treatment from its tougher neighbors. Maybe not, though. The Faithful really do seem to believe that God is on their side and nothing else makes much of a difference. Maybe they just figure they're keeping us out of sensor range.*

He smiled a bit at this last thought. If that were indeed the case, then the Faithful must not realize how sophisticated *Intransigent*'s sensors were. They were more than capable enough to insure that everything going on in the immediate area was available to her crew. Only a sufficiently large mass—like the planet itself—would keep something hidden.

The pinnace came down at what Michael knew was the largest and most modern facility of its type on Masada. Numerous elements in its design and construction showed the concentration the Faithful had dedicated toward building their fleet. He knew from his briefings that their navy swallowed a staggeringly large amount of their gross planetary product. Despite all of this, to Manticoran eyes, the facility was rather primitive.

Nothing he saw at the spaceport prepared him for the City of God itself. The number of people on foot was staggering. Men and women alike were bundled against the harsh weather, walking with bent heads and resigned postures against a biting wind.

Vehicle traffic was minimal and seemed restricted

to transport trucks. Indeed, their guide did not take them to a private vehicle, but instead directed them toward a stair leading to a dimly lit, rather forbidding tunnel.

"The Faithful," John Hill said in a neutral tour guide's tone, "do their best to prosper without undue technological interference. This means that even their most important men do not keep private vehicles in a city. Everyone uses mass transport."

"Right," said Lawler. "Forgot that for a moment."

When they had descended into the mass transit tunnels, Michael quickly realized that although all the Faithful might travel on the same rails, the accommodations were not equal. Women, clad from head to foot in all-enveloping robes, their faces veiled so that only their modestly downcast eyes were visible at all, were further sequestered in private carriages. These, Michael saw, had very few seats. He supposed it was some sort of mortification for the flesh.

Women traveling with children were permitted seats so that they might hold their children safely strapped on their laps. Carriages for men were always equipped with seats. This, apparently, was to make it possible for them to read or work, for Michael spotted few heads that were not bent attentively over some text or other.

An idle mind is the devil's playground, he thought, swallowing a wry grin lest their humorless guide think he was mocking the train system. *Isn't there a saying like that?*

He noticed that not all the carriages were equipped with equal degrees of luxury. The majority seemed to be furnished with simple benches of shaped plastic crowded tightly together, an aisle left down the middle. Some carriages, however, had padded seating, spaced further apart and aligned front to back. The carriage into which their guide waved them not only had padded seats, but curtained windows, and better lighting.

But then, Michael thought, *the Faithful believe that temporal success is a reflection of God's favor. Therefore, if someone has earned the right to travel in style, that's not an indulgence, because God favors him and so would want him to travel better than his more sinful fellows.*

As he settled into his own comfortable seat, the padding subtly conforming to his body to absorb the worst of the shocks and jolts, Michael couldn't help but think of the women he'd seen crammed into the standing carriages. It had been hard to tell, what with the heavy robes and winter cloaks they all wore, but some of those women had walked as if they were pregnant. Surely that alone was sufficient mortification of the flesh!

The curtains were drawn as soon as they were aboard the carriage, but Michael managed to peek out and get some feeling for the various stations as they flashed by. There were no advertisements, at least not in the sense there were on aggressively capitalist Manticore. Here the posters and streamers exhorted the Faithful to remember their responsibilities to God, and to those whom God had appointed to lead them on the path of righteousness. Printed in red or green against black backgrounds, the texts shouted at the eye.

Serve the Lord with fear and rejoice with trembling. Psalms 1:4.

Blessed are all they that put their trust in Him. Psalms 2:12.

The memory of the just is blessed: but the name of the wicked shall rot. Proverbs 9:7.

The way of transgressors is hard. Proverbs 13:15.

Nor were these sayings repeated only once or twice. Michael counted the piece about transgressors at least twenty different times. He thought there had been more, but apparently their train had switched onto an express track. They gained speed, slowing less and less frequently until, with a great squealing of brakes and a bone-jarring jolt, they came to a halt in a brightly lit, cleanly tiled station.

"The Palace of the Just," their guide announced, a thrill of pride entering his voice. "Follow me."

Michael did so, finding himself sandwiched neatly between Lawler and Cayen, Hill bringing up the rear. The steps they climbed were carpeted, the handrails gilded. Soft droning chants, like the voices of depressed angels came from hidden speakers.

Their guide stopped before an enormous door barred in gold.

"Your ambassador will meet you within. You will be given some time to pray and prepare for your meeting with the Elders."

Without a further word, he turned away, and Michael couldn't help but feel he was eager to be away from the contamination of their very presence.

* * *

At the appointed time, Judith began her deception. The usual attire for a Masadan woman was a long robe that covered the wearer from head to foot. In public, a veil was also worn, though in the shelter of the women's quarters this was not deemed necessary in any but the strictest households.

The advantage of this was that disguise as other than a woman was very easy. No one glimpsing someone in trousers and tunic saw anything but a male. To make matters even easier, Masada's planetary climate in general was cold. Ephraim's holdings were in one of the northerly reaches. A bulky coat and boots, both of which added to the concealment of a female form and manner of moving, were routine.

Needless to say, this disguise would not work for every woman. Judith, naturally neat and small-figured, could pass for a young man even without the coat. Although she had borne two children, the widow Mahalia had nearly died from the same illness that had killed her husband. Her emaciated form and the doubt that she would ever bear healthy children again was why she had been returned to her father's house after her husband's death. Even after she had recovered from her illness, Mahalia remained gaunt, hardly feminine any longer.

Rena's figure was distinctly maternal, or would have been had she not been also quite fat. As it was, her size was such that—at least when in coat and trousers—she made a large and convincing man.

The first stage of their deception was cutting their hair to the shorter style favored by spacefaring men, and never worn by women. The danger involved in this simple act was tremendous, for the three of them would be marked out for notice, even if Exodus was called off. Dinah had come up with several excuses to explain the oddity, but Judith still felt a thrill of fear when she felt cool air against her bare neck.

Men's clothing wasn't a problem. Ephraim Templeton was well-off, but he firmly believed that idle hands were the devil's playground. Laundry, mending, cooking, as well as child-tending and other "feminine" tasks were handled in the women's quarters. Dinah had long been such a superlative manager that Ephraim hardly ever listened to the reports she recorded for him. Making several sets of men's clothing in appropriate sizes and styles had been easy for the resourceful head wife.

Judith and her allies had also practiced adopting a man's gait and mannerisms. It had been hard at first to step out in the fashion trousers demanded, but oddly enough, boots made it easier. Even more difficult had been learning to look up and to make casual eye contact, for such directness was considered slatternly, even by a veiled woman, and was avoided even in the women's quarters except among close friends.

However, Judith didn't really feel like a woman once she'd donned her man's clothing. Only her eyes, still striking with their green rimmed in darker hazel, looked familiar. Once she had donned the very special contact lenses Dinah had insisted each woman wear, not even the eyes that gazed outward from the mirror were her own.

Mahalia and Rena were equally transformed, and Judith felt a thrill of satisfaction. If the rest of Dinah's planning was as thorough, Exodus might indeed succeed.

Although the Sisters had been tempted to carry out their deception under the friendly cover of night, Dinah had vetoed that. The Faithful did not approve of frivolous entertainment. Unless there was a major religious festival, streets and businesses grew quiet at the conclusion of the business day. This meant that the Sisters would find it more difficult to leave their homes. Moreover, morals proctors were more likely to make random vehicle checks after nightfall.

Therefore, Judith, Mahalia, and Rena crossed the chilly grounds toward the Templeton business property beneath a sun that shone with harsh brightness while granting no comforting warmth.

Flower was berthed in a voluminous hangar that protected the vessel from snow and ice. The hangar was large enough to permit cargo to be loaded and unloaded under cover. An attached hangar held *Blossom*, a smaller vessel, better equipped to carry people and used for ship-to-shore trading missions.

Blossom would have been the Sister's first choice, for the personnel shuttle was smaller and easier to maneuver. However, even with its cargo bay open, they could not squeeze in all the members of the Sisterhood. Even with the capacity of the heavy-lift cargo shuttle, it would be a tight fit. In fact, Judith was half afraid that if all of the Sisters succeeded in reaching the shuttle, she would be unable to get them all aboard.

Not, she reminded herself grimly, that all the Sisters would reach them safely.

No one challenged them as they entered the hangar. Ephraim, jealous of keeping his wealth in the family, employed his sons as free labor and crew. His desire to bring an impressive entourage to the conclave meant that all but those sons least in favor were with him. This meant that in turn the nonfamily employees were being kept very busy handling unaccustomed duties—and Dinah had promised that various small catastrophes would keep these unfortunate souls quite distracted indeed.

"First," Judith said, keeping her voice very soft, "*Flower*."

Mahalia and Rena nodded. Judith thought Mahalia looked a bit pale, nor was she certain that the fanatic light that brightened Rena's eyes was any better. Then she caught her own reflection in a highly polished side panel. She looked scared stiff.

She grinned at that frightened young face, and her own fears vanished. This, after all, was the easy part.

The pass-code to open *Flower*'s hatch was changed every sabbath, but Judith had found it easy to learn what the new one was. When Ephraim routinely copied the pass-code to those of his crew who might need to go aboard, unbeknownst to himself, he copied it to Judith as well.

There was no other security precaution in use here where Ephraim was secure. As soon as Judith pressed in "God hath made man upright; but they have sought many inventions," the hatch slid open, admitting them into a wide area lit only by stand-by lights.

Without further discussion, they went in three different directions: Mahalia to the small engine room; Rena to the cargo bay, and Judith to the cockpit.

She was running a standard systems check, trying to calm herself by imagining this was just another sim, when Mahalia signaled her on one of the small tight-beam communication units Dinah had somehow acquired for all of Exodus's most essential personnel.

"Isaac here. I have the engines warming," Mahalia reported, her voice very tight.

"Good. Meet me at the hatch in five," Judith said. "Routine check here will take me that long. I'll com Abraham to have cargo prepare for loading."

Dinah had insisted that they use code names, just in case some imp of Satan caused their communications to be overheard. Judith was Moses. Dinah was Abraham. Mahalia was Isaac, and so on. As a further precaution, the communication units transformed their voices into voices other than their own—and all selections were male.

Since Judith knew that Ephraim had several programs on *Aaron's Rod* that permitted him to display false images when contacting other vessels, she suspected that these communications units had been acquired to facilitate some similar ruse. It was all one to her. If they could turn Ephraim's pirate tools to the Sisterhood's good, it was a further sign that God approved of their cause.

Once Judith was certain *Flower* was in good running order and the systems warm-up was proceeding according to plan, she left the cockpit and joined Rena and Mahalia.

"Abraham says his sons are rising up to go into the Promised Land," she said, trying to sound confident. "We'd better deal with *Blossom*."

Judith had protested that she could disable the second shuttle herself, but Dinah had insisted that she take the others.

"They will have nothing to do but wait, as I understand it. In any case, you may need help."

A different code, "The dogs shall eat Jezebel," opened *Blossom*'s hatch, and instantly Judith was grateful Dinah had insisted she bring help. Before them, lounging in the very comfortable seat that was reserved for Ephraim himself, sat a large fair man of arrogant mien.

His name was Joseph, though he was more commonly called Joe. Joe believed himself Ephraim's bastard, and took liberties on this presumed kinship that a wiser man would not. Twice he had patted Judith on her rump, stopping only when she had threatened to tell Ephraim. She knew he also stole from ships stores and did a little trading in prohibited items.

Doubtless Joe resented the fact that Ephraim had not summoned him to attend the conclave along with the rest of his sons and this hiding from his proper duties was his little rebellion. If so, it was very brief.

Rena jerked something from the pocket of her baggy coat. There was a sharp barking sound, and Joseph lay still, blood spreading from his chest.

"Is he dead?" Judith asked, in a hushed, hoarse whisper.

Rena touched the man, then nodded.

Judith tried to think of something to say. She hadn't

even known Rena was armed. Then she decided it didn't matter. Rena had done what was needed, and what Joe would have done to them if he had gotten the upper hand did not bear thinking about. Turning them over to Ephraim would have been the least of it.

"Right," she said, her voice strong again, "I'll lock down the cockpit. You two know what to do."

Mahalia was already moving toward the engineering station.

Rena gave Judith a small smile before moving to her own assigned task.

"Trust in the Lord, Moses, and he will provide."

She patted her pocket and trotted aft to the cargo bay.

Judith shivered, and hurried forward.

❋ ❋ ❋

The first of the Sisters arrived soon after. These were well known to Judith, for they were from Ephraim's own household and the households of his sons. First among them was Naomi, a slight, pretty woman with hair as light as spider silk and nearly as fair. Gideon had never looked beyond her beauty to see the wisdom in her dark gray eyes, and she, in turn, had never raised her voice for him to hear.

Hated by Gideon's first wife—a stolid, extremely traditional woman whose resentment of her husband's second marriage was her only rebellion from the role Masadan society had cast for her—Naomi had turned to Dinah. In her father-in-law's first wife she had found more than comfort and understanding. She had found dreams that had made her bear Gideon and all that came with him in patience.

Under Naomi's direction, the Sisters set about reconfiguring the cavernous cargo hold of the freight shuttle so that all those who would take part in the

Exodus could travel safely. Much planning had been done in advance, and now Judith found herself reminded of some elaborate church ritual, everyone moving in calm but intensely emotionally charged order.

There were not enough vac suits for everyone—nor would there be on *Aaron's Rod*. This lack was a weakness in their plan, but one they couldn't avoid. Straps and padding could be scavenged from existing supplies and even ordered without raising comment, but there was no way that several hundred vac suits tailored for female plumbing could be acquired without raising comment. She wondered if that many suits even existed on all of Masada.

There were, however, a number of very nice military surplus hardened vac suits in the lockers, used, as Judith knew all too well, for boarding parties. These were issued to a handful of women code-named Samson's Bane, women who had proven their willingness to offer violence to men if needed.

Fleetingly, Judith wondered just how they had proved this willingness, but that hadn't been her department, nor did she doubt Dinah's judgement. Look at what Rena had done. . . .

Judith had her own suit, and Dinah had insisted she wear it.

"It's noble of you to want to take the same risks as so many of our Sisters must, but the reality is that without you we have no chance at all."

Judith accepted this, a touch reassured by the fact that the groundside warehouses had contained sufficient suits for the rest of the command crew and a few other key personnel. *Aaron's Rod* did have rescue capsules, and the plan was to move the most vulnerable into them in case of emergency. But hopefully, that would not be necessary. Hopefully they would simply launch, get to the hyper limit, and make the translation into hyper before anyone on Masada could catch up with them.

Judith's duty station for this stage of Exodus was in the cockpit. After donning her suit, she headed there and began working out the details for *Flower*'s rendezvous with *Aaron's Rod*. Happily such maneuvers were routine. Once she'd entered in the merchant vessel's parking orbit and a handful of other parameters, the computer could do the calculations.

Judith had deliberately left the cockpit door open, and was aware of a gradual rise in the noise level behind her as she worked. Crying of small children mingled with the soft voices of women soothing them and stronger voices giving orders. Subconsciously, then, she was prepared when Dinah's voice sounded over her com link.

"Abraham to Moses. We have everyone we're going to get. A few Sisters did not make the contact points, but God is with us. We have a full hold."

Judith felt her heart beating incredibly fast, but her voice was calm as she responded:

"Moses to Abraham. Close hatches. Report to cockpit. Moses to Exodus. Disconnect personal communication devices. Use shuttle intercom in case of emergency."

A handful of women had been filing forward as she gave her orders. Judith glanced over at the woman sitting at the sensors and communications station.

"Odelia, Naomi knows that we're in God's hands now, but even so, you may get calls regarding our passengers. I don't want to hear any of them—even if someone goes into labor. The only things I'm to hear are if something goes wrong with ship systems. Dinah will be primary on sensors, so only pass something on to me if she's missed it."

Odelia, a plain but strong woman from the household of a Senior Elder—and therefore someone with whom Judith had had only limited contact—nodded curtly.

"I'm on it, Moses."

Without giving any further instructions, Judith hit the release that opened the shuttle hangar doors. They slid easily and almost before she could wonder, Dinah reported:

"Scanning. No indication of any alarm sounding."

Judith brought up the shuttle's contragravity and fed power to its air-breathing turbines and watched the hangar walls beginning to move as it glided easily forward. She could tell from how Odelia's hand rose to her ear-set that the anticipated flurry of calls had begun. Odelia muttered into her throat mike, then Judith's own ear-set went live.

"Jacob in Engineering," came Rena's voice. "Everything looks good."

Judith resisted an urge to snap at her. Procedure was to report only problems. Then she forced herself to relax. After all, she was glad to know.

"Moses here. We'll be shifting to full flight mode. Ready?"

"Ready," came Rena's confident response.

Dinah commented almost casually, "We've been noticed. There are men running out onto the tarmac."

"Odelia, warn them back," Judith ordered. "I'm shifting for take-off."

Odelia touched her throat mike, and Judith knew that possibly for the first time since the Faithful had come to Masada the amplified voice of a woman giving orders—even if masked—was sounding.

She didn't have time to think about this, though, but concentrated on remembering the take-off and orbital boost sequences. The computer could have done it, but she wanted to prove to herself that she was more than back-up for the automated systems.

Her delight when the ship obeyed and launched gracefully from ground to sky, then began climbing, was so enormous that she cheered aloud. The surprise on the other women's faces was such that Judith momentarily felt embarrassed, but she forced herself not to apologize.

"We have angel's wings," she said instead, letting them share her joy. "According to the computer, we'll rendezvous with *Aaron's Rod* right on schedule."

There was a palpable reduction in tension, and Odelia relayed the information back to the passenger cabin and cargo hold. They weren't home free yet, but although Masada did have intercept vehicles, the rights of Elders were so firmly established that any domestic air traffic enforcement would waste valuable time before interfering with a vessel belonging to Ephraim Templeton.

Odelia had a file of appropriate responses to use if they were queried and an appropriate male dummy to fill her screen. Oddly, nothing came from the surface but an automated confirmation of their course and reassurance that there were no impediments.

"Could it be," Odelia asked, breaking the listening silence in the cockpit, "that everyone is so busy watching the Manticorans that they have slacked off on domestic traffic control?"

"I suppose so," Judith agreed, but she didn't feel at all confident.

The next strange thing happened when they approached *Aaron's Rod*. Judith was about to command the shuttle bay doors to open, when they slid apart on their own.

"Sisters," she said, checking and double-checking the angle and cutting back on the shuttle's speed. "Something isn't right."

✳   ✳   ✳

Chief Elder Simonds of the Faithful of the Church of Humanity Unchained was without a doubt the oldest looking man Michael had ever seen. His face was deeply lined. The skin sagged on his neck, but had drawn tight around the swollen knuckles of his hands. Eyelids drooped, but did not conceal a penetrating gaze.

Despite his appearance, Simonds was not the oldest man Michael had ever met—not by far, since the Faithful had decided that the use of prolong was an abomination against God—and so Simonds was quite likely younger than many of Michael's instructors at Saganami Island. Unlike them, however, Simonds had aged without even the slowing of that process that those first-generation prolong recipients could expect.

For the first time in his life, Michael realized that there was a strange power that came with the physical trappings of age. In Simonds' wizened face numerous deeply graven lines proclaimed not only his years, but made one imagine some wisdom must have been gained in his long life. It was an interesting lesson, and Michael suddenly understood why Quentin Cayen had tinted his hair to create the appearance that he was graying. Cayen knew the Masadans would respect the signs of age and had sought to acquire them.

For a fleeting moment, Michael wondered if he should have tried something similar. Then he rejected the idea out of hand. He was a prince of Manticore. Nothing would change that, and no cosmetic alteration would make him any more himself.

Greetings were framed in praise of God and His wisdom, but Michael had not grown to maturity in Mount Royal Palace without learning to hear the notes of self-congratulation in a man's voice—nor were they especially hard to detect here. Chief Elder Simonds was a man very pleased with himself.

With what Michael hoped would be taken for the modesty of youth before age, he set himself to listening silence while Ambassador Faldo and Mr. Lawler said the appropriate, flattering things to the Chief Elder, his attendant Senior Elders, and the very few mere Elders who had been permitted to attend this first private conclave.

He was doing very well until the doors slid open to admit a small contingent who were most definitely not Masadan. Like Ambassador Faldo's diplomats, they wore civilian clothes, but the styles were not Masada's flowing robes. Instead they were in the neat, trim-lined tailoring currently in fashion in the People's Republic of Haven.

As Ambassador Faldo handled introductions, Michael remembered that the Peeps also were wooing the Masadans. Chief Elder Simonds was too canny a politician to ignore this opportunity to show his other suitor the presumed mark of favor Michael's presence was assumed to be. Michael remembered the *Moscow* and forced his lips to keep from twisting into a cynical grin.

We see your heavy cruiser and raise it by one Crown Prince, he thought, but he let nothing of his amusement touch his manner as he replied to introductions.

Indeed, that was easy enough to do. Michael was one of a bare handful of people who knew that King Roger III's death had not been an accident, but an assassination—an assassination planned by and paid for by the People's Republic of Haven. Beth had been convinced against her own inclinations to keep the matter secret, and so Michael must do the same, but his tone was cool as he accepted Ambassador Acuminata's congratulations on his completing Saganami Island.

"I understand you are specializing in Communications," Acuminata continued. "That's an interesting choice. I would have thought Tactics, or perhaps Engineering would be more the Winton way."

Michael pressed his fingernails into his palm, well-aware that he was being accused of cowardice and lack of ambition. Acuminata was only echoing what some of the more obnoxious newsies had been saying for years.

He forced a smile.

"Communications are very valuable. You wouldn't believe what you can learn if you only listen and watch, then draw the obvious conclusions."

Acuminata blinked, but what he might have said in reply was lost when Chief Elder Simonds, aware he was no longer the central focus of the gathering, coughed.

"Shall we adjourn?" he said, and without waiting for a response swept out of the room.

The conclave was being held in an enormous hall where, to Michael's relief, the Havenite contingent was seated some distance away. To keep himself from glowering at them, Michael sought to distract himself by studying those individual Masadans who stood out from their fellows. The Faithful largely wore their hair and beards long, after the model of Old Testament prophets. Their formal wear continued the motif, consisting of flowing robes enhanced with heavily embroidered arm-bands and belts that almost surely marked achievements in individual careers.

Here and there, however, were men who wore their hair shorter, shaved their beards, and seemed less at ease in the long robes. Michael knew from Lawler and Hill's exhaustive briefings that Masada had a large navy, enhanced by a civilian merchant fleet. Doubtless these men had sacrificed their hair out of the practical considerations of space travel.

Michael's dark Winton complexion had drawn more than a few stares ever since they left the shuttle. Here he understood why. It was one thing to read that the bulk of the original members of the Church of Humanity Unchained had come from a limited segment of Earth's population. It was another to see it so openly demonstrated. Not only had the Masadans come from one stock, unlike the Manticorans, they clearly had not encouraged any immigration.

He noted a family resemblance among many of those seated together, and a seating order that seemed to indicate that age was given precedence. That made sense, given that their equivalent of a king was a chief elder.

Maybe we can work with that, he mused. *We respect family, so do they. Titles and such are passed down in order of birth in the Star Kingdom. I'd bet anything that there's a preference for age and experience here over youthful ambition.*

Michael's self-imposed task was made easier in that most of those gathered in the Conclave Hall were studying him in turn, their gazes holding curiosity, unease, or, most often, open hostility.

They have never learned, he thought, amused, *that being part of a crowd gives very little protection from being seen if one cares to look. These men may be bulls in their own herds, but they are cattle beneath the rule of these Elders who claim to speak for God.*

He felt very glad, then, to belong to the Star Kingdom of Manticore where, no matter that there was a House of Lords and House of Commons, a talented individual could rise on merit alone, and, where, best of all, no one claimed to have an exclusive idea what was the Will of God.

It rapidly became apparent, to Michael's relief, Lawler's frustration, and Faldo's resigned acceptance, that Chief Elder Simonds intended today's gathering of the Conclave of Elders to be his opportunity to show off his new prizes. Although questions were directed to the Manticoran guests, the answers were often given by Simonds or one of his toadies. It was long and wearying, rather like listening to a shout and its echo, so Michael let his attention drift.

It was for this reason he noticed when a messenger made his unobtrusive way to one of the family groups, one of those that Michael had noticed before because of the predominance of short-haired individuals.

Messengers were not uncommon. Any form of electronic communication was forbidden in this gathering of ostensible technophobes. However, there was something about the swift and purposeful way this messenger advanced that caught Michael's eye. He grinned to himself, wondering if some of Todd's preternatural awareness for human interaction had rubbed off on him.

The messenger did not speak with the head of the clan, but to someone who had to be an older son. Michael noted with mild curiosity that the son did not pass the message on to his father, nor did the father inquire after it.

Chain of command? he thought. *I'd bet anything they've served together and the father has learned to trust his son's judgement.*

Michael felt a familiar flicker of grief. His father had died when he was thirteen T-years old. He'd never know if Roger III would have approved of him and his choices. Given that there were times Michael himself doubted the wisdom of his entering the Navy, he supposed he should be relieved.

Chief Elder Simonds was declaiming something forceful and poetic about how God would guide his

Chosen to the path of greatest wisdom—a speech that was basically a put-down of someone who had had the temerity to actually suggest some sort of cost-benefit analysis of the advantages of an alliance with the Star Kingdom of Manticore—when Michael noticed another messenger heading for the spacefaring clan.

In the interim he'd checked the seating chart they'd been given and learned that these were the Templetons, headed by one Ephraim Templeton who apparently headed a prosperous merchant trading fleet. According to John Hill's briefing (when Michael consulted the notes he had stored on a discreetly concealed pocket computer) the Templetons were in the awkward position of having too much to do with hated technology to be trusted in high government, but of having too much wealth to be ignored.

This time Gideon Templeton, identified by Hill's amazingly comprehensive brief as the eldest son of Ephraim and captain in his own right of the trading ship *Psalms*, passed the communiqué to his father. Ephraim read it and Michael saw him scowl. He scribbled something for the waiting messenger and then returned his attention to what the Senior Elder was saying.

Michael would have bet anything that neither Ephraim nor Gideon were listening very closely any longer. There was a tension in their seated forms that spoke volumes. Nor was he surprised when he saw a message being passed to one of the highest ranking Senior Elders. The man's bushy eyebrows shot up to his hairline and he wrote a terse reply.

Moments later, the messenger had returned to the Templetons. Ephraim glanced at the note handed to him, nodded crisply, and motioned for his sons to follow him. Without interrupting Chief Elder Simonds' harangue, the entire group filed from the hall.

Even before this, the exchange of messages had caught the attention of many of the gathered Elders. Simonds apparently realized that he was losing their attention and said rather sharply:

"I have been informed by Elder Huggins that Brother Ephraim Templeton and his sons have been called from us in order to deal with a technological problem."

The sneer in his voice when he mentioned the hated technology, along with the fact that he denied Ephraim Templeton his title while granting it to Huggins were signals to everyone present that the Chief Elder would be quite offended if the gathering paid any more attention to this diversion. Michael saw heads snap front and center, like recruits at a dress parade.

Simonds was returning to his speech when Michael felt a tap on his shoulder. John Hill leaned forward and whispered very softly.

"Come with me."

Michael raised an eyebrow, but Hill shook his head, refusing further discussion. Trusting that the spy would have already consulted Faldo and that Faldo would cover his departure, Michael obeyed.

Out in the corridor, Hill said, "We're getting you off planet. Something hinky is up, and you'd better not be in reach of these fanatics. If it turns out to be nothing, we can make apologies then."

Michael blinked.

"Hinky?"

John Hill led the way briskly down an astonishingly empty corridor.

"I'm still gathering information. Will you trust me?"

For a moment Michael thought about how much Hill seemed to have collected about the Masadans, about his overly comprehensive knowledge of even the minutia of their culture. Then he gave a mental shrug.

This wasn't the time to get paranoid, not with what he'd seen out there on the conclave floor, not with the sudden departure of the Templetons, not with Simond's evident annoyance.

He nodded, then followed Hill as the other man moved briskly toward a stairway leading to the roof.

❋   ❋   ❋

Despite the doors to *Aaron's Rod*'s shuttlebay opening as of their own accord, Judith could see no good reason not to accept the invitation and several reasons why they should. Most importantly, the shuttle was far more vulnerable out in open space than it would be neatly parked within the hull.

She had no illusions that Ephraim would not be notified of the shuttle's unauthorized departure, only the hope that such notification would be delayed until he could not effectively pursue.

Judith was so busy concentrating on why *Aaron's Rod*'s bay doors had opened of their own accord that she didn't notice that she had managed a textbook perfect landing until she saw Dinah's smile.

"No contact from *Aaron's Rod*," Odelia reported crisply, "but sensors report several strange things, including a higher power load on the reactor and a higher readiness level from Engineering."

Judith frowned, but signalled to begin powering down the shuttle.

"Forward your report to *Samson's Bane*, and tell them to be ready. . . ."

Odelia gave a slight start, and held up her hand in mute interruption. Then she switched what was coming over her ear-set so the rest of the cock-pit could hear.

"Hey, Joe," a laconic male voice she recognized as Sam, one of the caretaker crew, said over an audio-only channel. "Looking good. We'll be bringing out the carry flats when pressure and atmosphere are re-established. Why didn't you take *Blossom*? We were a little surprised."

Judith made a quick motion for Odelia to put her on.

"Hey, Sam," she replied, trusting that the computer simulated male voice wouldn't sound too unlike Joe. "Before he left the big man ordered *Blossom* given a thorough scrub."

"Sounds like him," Sam replied. "Pompous prick. Big problem when his private limo has blood stains on the fabric. Pressure's almost up. See ya . . ."

He signed off, and Judith blinked. She knew she had to say something calming or many of the Sisters would panic. Dealing with a caretaker crew aboard *Aaron's Rod* had been in their plans, but it sounded like Joe, Sam, and who knew what others were doing more than minding the ship.

"I guess we weren't the only ones taking advantage of Ephraim being away," Judith said, making her tone matter-of-fact. "We all know Joe's been smuggling for years. Makes sense he and his pals would use a ship in orbit as a rendezvous point."

"Explains why we weren't challenged before this," Dinah agreed, rising to leave the cockpit, doubtless to spread her own form of calm. "Joe must have filed a flight plan. God works in mysterious ways. Sometimes even sinners can be His hands and feet. Let's not disappoint Him by refusing a miracle when He offers it."

Odelia had connected Zaneta, head of Samson's Bane, into the loop and now her voice came back, crisp and assured.

"We're going out before the men come in. There's no hope they wouldn't be suspicious if we left the shuttle armored up after they got here. This way they may overlook us. Pray for us."

Judith heard a soft murmur through the open cockpit door as those Sisters who must stand by and wait did precisely that. She lacked their faith, but found the soft, rhythmic sound oddly comforting.

"Odelia," she said to the com officer, "remind those who have suits to seal up. We don't know what other surprises there might be. Seal the inner locks of the shuttle as well, but leave the outer ones ajar, as if we're waiting for them to come aboard."

Odelia paled slightly, but she gave the order, even as she closed her own seals.

There was nothing they could do but wait, and they did so in silence, the only sounds Zaneta's terse report.

"We're off the shuttle, forming up on either side of the door."

"Lights show hatch into ship opening."

The next words were not meant for the waiting Sisters, but for Samson's Bane.

"Steady. Let them through . . . Miriam, you make sure that door stays open. We don't want to be sealed in the bay."

Odelia suddenly remembered that *Flower* had external cameras and turned them on. The image was distorted, for Odelia didn't take time to center, but the command crew watched as one, two, three men strolled through the door, heading toward the shuttle.

None wore even a vac suit, much less carried weapons. That was what made what followed so very ugly.

The fourth man coming through the hatch glanced casually to one side and caught sight of the suited figures flanking the portal. He started to cry out and Zaneta fired. Her shot caught him squarely in the throat and he went down, gouting blood.

The other members of Zaneta's corps were no less ready. The three who had already passed went down, then Samson's Bane were out of camera range as they moved into the body of the ship.

Zaneta's terse words came clear and unruffled.

"Two more in here, already down. Miriam! Take that man alive. We need to know if there are more. The caretaker crew should only have been two men."

Miriam apparently obeyed. A moment later her voice, dulcet, famous in her immediate circle for its graceful music, reported.

"He says there are three Silesians in the aft cargo bay."

"Hold him," Zaneta snapped. "Moses, which way do we go?"

Judith gave directions, reciting corridor turns from deck plans she had memorized, until her fingers made the computer bring up the schematics.

Ten men were dead, one captive before the boarding action was ended. The captive bleated that there were no others, alternately pleading for his life and—once he realized that his opponents were women—threatening them rather unconvincingly with God's wrath.

Shaken to the core, for the bloody bodies sprawled in the shuttle bay brought back long-buried memories, Judith kept one channel tuned to Zaneta's report as she moved toward *Aaron's Rod*'s bridge. Only by concentrating on her immediate responsibilities could she keep herself from sinking back into the terrified ten-year-old who had watched her parents reduced to similar bloody stillness.

"Prisoner says that he and his fellows came aboard with contraband earlier. Sam had brought his cronies when Ephraim ordered a change of watch so he could have all his sons with him at the conclave. Joe was to meet them with *Blossom* so they could take the goods off, Ephraim none the wiser."

"Did the Silesians have a shuttle of their own?" Judith asked, fitting herself into the captain's chair and snapping on read-outs. Reassuring activity from Engineering told her that Mahalia and her crew were in place.

"A small one, parked in the aft hold. Apparently, Joe managed an override there. Didn't want to risk the shuttle bay itself."

"Smart. Lock the man in one of the cabins. Check his shuttle. There might be things we can use."

"Right."

"And find out if anyone expects the prisoner."

"Right."

"Mahalia in Engineering," came a new voice. "Captain, we're in luck. The smugglers did some of the powering up so they could operate bay doors and the like. We're ahead of schedule there, though of course they didn't need to bring up the impellers."

"Good."

"Naomi here," came a voice that sounded rough, as if the owner might have been shouting. "We have a bit of a situation with the passengers. Some are panicking, claiming that the presence of the smugglers is a bad omen. Children reacted badly to going by the dead bodies."

Judith felt a trace of impatience. That wasn't her department! She was just supposed to fly the ship out of here. She schooled herself to sound calm.

"If you must, use sedatives. Did Wanda make it?"

"Yes."

"Have her lead prayers. Something from Psalms should be perfect. Maybe number thirty-seven?"

"Right. Sedatives will make evacuating in case of emergency harder."

"Put the worst cases in the life pods and seal them in."

And leave me alone! Judith thought. All she did was turn to Odelia and say, "Limit Naomi's bridge link or connect her to Rena in Damage Control. I need sensor readings to plot our course out of here."

"On it, Moses," Odelia said. "Sensors are coming up. Dinah has put Sherlyn on them."

"Smart," Judith said, and was pleased to see Odelia smile.

As she turned her attention to the astrogation plot, she noticed that Dinah wasn't yet at her own station, but stilled her annoyance. It wasn't as if she needed a gunner quite yet, and as XO Dinah was doubtless sparing Judith problems the captain wouldn't hear about until after this was all over and the Sisters were safe. Hadn't Dinah done her duty and made certain there was someone minding the sensors?

Judith immersed herself in her calculations, hardly aware when Dinah arrived and took over fielding those queries Odelia couldn't divert elsewhere. Data flowed over her boards, organized and perfect. A ship here, a ship there, planetary mass there, farther out a larger vessel that had to be the Manticoran ship. *Intransigent*, its beacon announced.

That should be our name, Judith thought. *If there has ever been anyone forced to hold their ground, it's us.*

Mahalia reported that *Aaron's Rod*'s impeller nodes were hot and ready just as Odelia, her voice so tight Judith hardly recognized it, said, "Captain, we have a communication from the surface. They're ordering us to hold our orbit and await the authorities. Do you have an answer?"

Judith touched the keys that snapped *Aaron's Rod*'s impeller wedge into existence and sent the privateer sweeping up and out of her parking orbit.

"That," she said, "is our answer."

*   *   *

What was supposed to be a sleepy watch was turning distinctly interesting. Carlie, at the Tac station on *Intransigent*'s bridge, listened to the reports coming in while she took her turn plotting intrasystem traffic.

Captain Boniece was not the type of commander to have his crew idle away an opportunity to gather information. Endicott might one day be an ally, in which case the information could be used to defend it. If it chose to side with the Peeps, well, the information would still be useful.

Intransigent did nothing overtly rude, but her sensors were so much better than the Masadans' that they took in a great deal that doubtless the Masadans assumed was out of range. Carlie knew, too, that Tab Tilson had requested the use of any middies who could be spared for what he promised would be an interesting training exercise.

Carlie remembered her own days as a middie and suspected that Tab was having them monitor all in-system and planetary communications. The sorting of order out of the myriad unshielded transmissions would be excellent training for the mad wash of information that flowed through the Combat Information Center in the midst of a battle.

And if they picked up some information on the Faithful's Navy, or on the presence of the Peeps in system, well, that wouldn't be a bad thing either. As the hours passed, the most interesting thing they found was how little evidence there was of either, almost as if both had decided to make themselves scarce.

Almost! Carlie snorted to herself. *Get real, woman. This is no coincidence.*

She noted with interest that a personnel shuttle, sleek and easily maneuverable, had detached from a

Silesian trading vessel and had entered a ship in parking orbit around the planet.

"Interesting," Boniece murmured when she passed this information on. "Beacon says the ship is *Aaron's Rod*, an armed merchie."

"If she's armed, the armament is well hidden," Carlie reported in response. "I wonder if there's a reason for them to hide their weapons?"

Armed merchantmen were often suspect since it didn't take much for one to turn pirate. This liaison with the Silesians—many of whom were themselves pirates—made this one even more suspect than usual

"Get a listing on *Aaron's Rod*," Boniece suggested.

Sally Pike, one of Carlie's middies doing a nervous turn on the bridge, reported, "She's registered to a Templeton Incorporated, Sir. She's also registered with the Masadan government as a privateer."

"Interesting," Boniece said again. "Does Templeton Incorporated have any other armed merchantmen?"

"Yes, Sir," Midshipwoman Pike replied with a promptness that made Carlie ridiculously proud, "*Proverbs* and *Psalms*. Both registered as privateers."

"It seems we should raise our estimate on the number of armed vessels available to the Faithful in time of war," Boniece commented.

"Privateers are hardly a problem, are they, Skipper?" commented an engineer with the lazy confidence of one who knows that his ship is in all ways superior.

"Guns," Boniece said, turning to Carlie, "what would you say?"

"I'd say, Sir," Carlie replied promptly, peripherally aware of Midshipwoman Pike listening with some astonishment to the ATO getting quizzed, "that anything that has guns and sidewalls can't be rated 'hardly a problem.' For that matter, even an unarmed vessel could ram."

"Paranoid," Boniece agreed, "but reasonable, and we cannot forget the psychology of the Faithful. In their own view, they are God's Chosen, and people who believe God is on their side are hard to predict."

The discussion went on and if Midshipwoman Pike was conscious of the fact that many of the questions tossed her way were something of a quiz she kept her concentration admirably.

Near the end of the watch, Carlie reported, "Skipper, there's a cargo shuttle rendezvousing with *Aaron's Rod*, one from groundside. ID Beacon says it's the *Flower*, currently adjunct to *Aaron's Rod*."

"Have the Silesians left?"

"No, Sir."

"I'd say then, we have a meeting. Interesting."

Later, just as the watch was changing, Carlie reported, "Captain, *Aaron's Rod* is powering up her impellers."

"Silesians still on board?"

"Yes, Sir."

"Tell your relief to keep the officer of the watch appraised."

"Yes, Sir."

✳   ✳   ✳

Carlie was back in her quarters, taking a breather before going to check on her middies, when a call was relayed to her.

"Restricted channel from the surface," the com officer, Midshipman Kareem Jones reported crisply.

"Very good. I'll take it here."

A face Carlie remembered forgetting after one of Captain Boniece's dinners formed on the screen.

"Lieutenant Dunsinane, John Hill," the face said. "I'm with the embassy here. I'd like you to request the return of Mr. Midshipman Winton to *Intransigent*."

All Carlie's old doubts about Michael Winton came flooding back.

"Has he done something wrong?"

"He has done nothing, but I suspect that a situation is developing where it may not be best for Mr. Winton's continued welfare that he remain planetside."

Carlie had seen tabletops with more expression than Hill was showing, but there was an intensity in his gaze that made a lie of all the stiff neutrality.

"Situation?"

"I don't dare say more," Hill replied. "I only request that as the officer directly responsible for *Intransigent*'s midshipmen you be prepared to say that he is returning on your order."

A crackle of static wavered across the connection, and Carlie knew she didn't have time to ask more questions.

"I'll send the order," she agreed. "He is due on board fourth watch anyhow."

"Th . . ."

John Hill's thanks, if thanks they were, were cut off. A moment later Midshipman Jones' voice came on, apologetic.

"I'm sorry, Lieutenant. The call was interrupted at the surface. Would you like us to try and reestablish it from here?"

"No, Mr. Jones, that won't be necessary. Send a message to Captain Boniece asking him to call me at his first convenience."

"Yes, Ma'am."

Boniece returned her call almost before Carlie could finish mentally framing her report.

"Yes, Lieutenant?"

Carlie explained about John Hill's mysterious call, finishing by saying, "So I agreed, Sir. I hope that was the right thing to do."

"Sounds to me like Mr. Hill wanted an excuse to get Mr. Winton—or perhaps it would be wiser to say Crown Prince Michael in this case—off the surface without creating a diplomatic incident. He didn't say anything about removing the rest of the diplomatic contingent, did he?"

"No, Sir. We were cut off, but I had no indication he was about to ask anything of the sort. His concern seemed solely for Mr. Winton."

"Interesting."

The captain bit into his lower lip for a moment.

"Sounds like Mr. Hill was apprehensive about a situation wherein either Prince Michael or Mr. Midshipman Winton would be facing a risk that the rest of the diplomatic contingent would not. Very strange."

"Do you think it's just a matter of his relationship to the Queen?" Carlie asked hesitantly.

"It could be, or it could be that Mr. Hill senses a situation developing where an officer in the Queen's service might be more vulnerable than a civilian diplomat."

"My apologies, Sir, but you're talking in riddles."

"Riddles are all Mr. Hill has left us with. Keep yourself available, Lieutenant. You may be needed."

"Yes, Sir."

The captain closed the connection almost as abruptly as had Mr. Hill. No longer in the least bit tired, Carlie straightened her tunic and went to review her other middies, vaguely seeking reassurance that they, at least, were out of danger.

✳   ✳   ✳

On *Aaron's Rod* Judith felt the sudden clarity that comes with having made an irrevocable decision. She should have felt it when she cut her hair or when she donned men's clothing or when she took *Flower* from the planet's surface, but it wasn't until she sat here, nothing but the star-filled emptiness of space in front of her, that she felt the last of the chains that had held her on Masada snap and leave her free.

"I'm plotting us the most direct course to hyper limit," she said crisply. "Odelia, let me know if anything new comes from the surface. Sherlyn, keep an eye out for anything moving on an intercept course."

An odd thought occurred to her.

"Connect me to Rena."

"Damage Control here."

"Rena. Has anyone taken a good look at the shuttle on which the smugglers came aboard?"

"I did, actually. My team seemed best equipped to inspect it."

"Where did it originate?"

"It's registered to a Silesian ship, the *Firebird*."

Sherlyn volunteered, "*Firebird* is here in system, Judith."

Judith nodded her thanks and continued, "How's it set in the hold?"

"Facing out toward the doors. I guess they turned it around somehow."

"Good. How confident do you feel about checking its piloting programs?"

"Pretty good. But, Moses, it's unarmed and unarmored. I don't think it will do as an escape vehicle."

"Good to know. Get acquainted with its piloting program. I may have something for you to put into it."

"Yes, Moses."

At least Masadan women are good at taking orders, Judith thought with a faint trace of humor.

Dinah had glanced over at her, but the older woman said nothing and when Judith volunteered nothing of her thoughts, returned to checking the weaponry boards.

Odelia broke the quiet that had settled over the bridge.

"Moses, surface is now insisting we return to orbit."

Judith nodded.

"Odelia, I don't think we can fool them for long, but let's mess up the works. Tell them you're Sam . . . Tell them we're taking the ship out on Ephraim's orders. That should at least slow them down long enough to talk with him."

Odelia nodded, the skin around her eyes tight with worry. Judith heard her query the computer for Sam's identification codes and instruct it to configure her voice mask to match his range.

Good. Thinking for herself. I suspect we're going to need a lot of that if we're going to get out of here alive.

That diversion bought them enough time that the planet had visibly receded, but at last the call came as Judith had known it would.

"They say they've spoken with Elder Templeton and that he has no idea what they're talking about. They sound really angry."

"Let them be angry," Judith said. "The more angry they are, the less energy they'll have for clear thought. Any sign of pursuit?"

"Several drives have gone active," Sherlyn reported, "including the *Firebird*'s. The only thing moving toward us are a couple of light attack craft."

"We're better armed than any of those," Dinah reported.

Judith knew that the Faithful's dedication to building a navy had not extended to extensive in-system defense. Simply put, the Graysons didn't want war, dedicating their energies to protecting their own system. The Faithful, on the other hand, had specifically designed their navy to take Yeltsin's Star back, and each LAC cut into offensive tonnage. They'd built just enough

LACs to keep their system from being a sitting duck while the rest of the fleet was away, and those ships were widely spread out. Nor were they likely to fire on a ship belonging to a prominent citizen.

"Good, Dinah," she said. "We may need to remind them of that. How do we look for offensive capacity?"

"Full-up," Dinah reported crisply. "Jessica reports that the magazines are well-stocked and that her crews have the tubes ready for loading. The energy mounts are powered up and ready. Point defense is standing by."

"As I recall specs for the LACs," Judith mused. "They're pretty much limited to one salvo each from their box launchers and a single spinal laser, right?"

"Right," Dinah confirmed.

"Well, we won't throw away missiles unless absolutely necessary, and we have the range on them."

"We're also armored in Ephraim's reputation," Dinah reminded her. "They're going to be reluctant to fire on the vessel of such a successful privateer."

But what Ephraim gives, Judith thought, *he can as surely take away.*

The hyper limit seemed very far away indeed. It seemed even farther when Odelia reported a few moments later:

"We have a call from Ephraim Templeton."

"Let us all hear it," Judith said, unwilling to let the man become a phantom to her companions.

Ephraim sounded very angry, what Rena called "beating angry." By the time Odelia put his transmission up, he was already in mid-flurry.

" . . . and I promise that only God's wrath will be greater than mine when we catch you. Turn around immediately!"

Judith grinned, forcing herself to seem more amused than she felt.

"Now there's real incentive."

"If you do not," the transmission continued, "I shall come after you myself, and my vengeance will be terrible!"

"Send back the following," Judith said. " 'Vengeance is mine, saith the Lord.' Then refuse further transmissions. I don't think we can talk him out of his course."

"Do you think he'll really come after us?" Odelia asked.

"Oh, yes," Judith said. "I'd guess he's already on his way. The question is whether or not he can get to either *Psalms* or *Proverbs* before we can get clear."

She glanced at the plot, which showed the planet not as far away as she had imagined, and suspected that Ephraim could catch up. Although her handling of *Aaron's Rod* had been competent, she was keeping the ship at a comparatively low rate of acceleration.

Part of that was because of her awareness of her delicate human cargo, which wasn't ready for space travel, but another part—and she had to be honest with herself—was because she was afraid to try and attempt anything too elaborate. Nor was she prepared, with her trained-by-rote Engineering crew, to risk reducing the safety margin on the privateers' inertial compensator the way a more experienced crew might have. Worst of all, the Havenite modifications to Ephraim's other ships had included upgrades for their compensators. Even with the same safety margin, they could pull a substantially higher acceleration than *Aaron's Rod*. With fully trained crews to get the highest possible speed out of them, their acceleration advantage would be even greater.

Still, there might be time for the Sisters to get away. Ephraim had been half the planet away from his estate when he was notified. She and her allies had disabled the *Blossom*, the only other ship to orbit vehicle available in his hangars. There might be time.

And if there wasn't?

Judith frowned, and, oblivious to her nervous crew, buried her face in her hands and tried to think.

"Would you mind telling me," Michael said as he chugged up the stairs after John Hill, "what is going on?"

"You saw those men exit the Conclave Hall?"

"Yes. Templeton. Shipping."

Michael kept his replies short. The program of exercise he'd been following shipboard, he was discovering, didn't prepare one to run up stairs.

"Someone has stolen a Templeton ship."

"So?"

"Right now Templeton has no idea who's stolen it."

"You do?"

John Hill tapped his ear, and Michael realized he was indicating something buried beneath the skin.

"I get better news than he does. There have been some interesting disappearances, some of which I may be the only one to have heard about."

"How?"

"Trust me."

"All right. But what makes it significant to us?"

"Let me just say that if anyone puts these disappearances together, they're going to remember you and wonder if your being here had anything to do with it."

"I don't understand."

"Templeton doesn't know this yet, but a woman was caught trying to leave her home. She was captured and under interrogation . . ."

Hill's inflection made clear that he meant something rather more severe than simple questioning.

"Before she died she admitted to the existence of an organization called the Sisterhood of Barbara and of something called Exodus. I'd like to believe otherwise, but I think the two events may be connected."

"Why . . . What does this have to do with us?"

"Nothing, but I don't think for a moment the Faithful will believe it."

They'd arrived on the roof by now, and to Michael's surprise a small air car was waiting for them. Hill ushered him aboard and spilled into the driver's seat and brought up the counter grav.

"Templeton took a similar vehicle out of here not long ago on his way to the nearest spaceport. You don't think the ban on technology applies to emergencies? This one is picking up some of his sons."

Michael shook his head in admiring disbelief.

"You were explaining why the Faithful wouldn't believe that we have nothing to do with this."

"Believe that their women, so good, so devout, so well-trained, would rebel without outside stimulus?" Hill snorted and banked the air car at a stomach-wrenching angle. "Easier to believe that such was instigated from without. They'll see you as the servant of your Queen."

"Which I am . . ."

"Except that to the Faithful, Elizabeth shares the dubious honor of being called the Harlot of Satan."

"Shares?"

"With Barbara Bancroft, the woman they blame for foiling their coup to overthrow Grayson."

"What about the rest of the diplomatic corps? What will happen to them?"

Hill shrugged. "I think they'll be all right. The Masadans are going to be very careful about respecting diplomatic immunity until they've made up their mind who they want to get into bed with. The thing is, it could be argued that you're not covered. You're a Navy midshipman, making a courtesy call, you see. . . ."

"Shit."

"In a bucket. So you've been recalled to duty. Lieutenant Dunsinane is such a stickler. . . ."

"That she is," Michael agreed. "Now that I think of it, my orders included having to report back shipboard every evening."

Michael could see they had now arrived at the spaceport. He was unsurprised to find *Intransigent*'s pinnace rising to meet them. Nor did John Hill disappoint him. The vehicle to vehicle transfer was managed as smoothly as if Hill had handled similar procedures numerous times before.

As he took the hand the flight engineer held out to him, Michael called back.

"Thanks!"

"I'll try to keep you posted," Hill shouted over the wind's roar. Then he banked the air car and sped away.

"What's going on, Sir?" the pilot asked once they were buttoned up and streaking for the edge of atmosphere.

"I'm not sure," Michael admitted. "I guess we just follow orders."

"And those are to get back to *Intransigent*," the pilot agreed.

Michael took advantage of the pinnace's undermanned state to drop into the tac officer's cubby and bring its tactical plot on-line. He easily located what had to be the hijacked Templeton ship crawling tortoiselike out-system. He thought about what John Hill had told him, about this improbable Sisterhood and their desperate Exodus, and felt a surge of sympathy for them.

If they're really trying to get away, why don't they run? he thought. *Why the hell don't they* run?

✳   ✳   ✳

Carlie couldn't keep her mind off her absent middy and John Hill's peculiar call, so it was almost a relief when *Intransigent* was moved to a higher level of alert and she found herself on the bridge, officer of the watch, while Captain Boniece met with his department heads.

"Our pinnace has left the surface," Midshipman Jones reported. "En route to rendezvous with *Intransigent.*"

Carlie acknowledged.

"How's *Aaron's Rod*?"

Ozzie Russo, another one of Carlie's middies, answered promptly.

"Still heading out-system. Looks like she's on a direct line for hyper limit, Ma'am."

"Hm."

"Lieutenant Dunsinane?"

"Yes, Mister Russo?"

"Why is she moving so slowly? There's not much traffic there."

"I couldn't say, Mister Russo. You sound like you have a theory."

Carlie saw the normally confident, even cocky, Ozzie color.

"Well, Ma'am, it reminds me of the first time my father let me take the helm of our yacht. It had looked so easy on the sims, but once I had all that to handle, I found out the sims hadn't really prepared me. Our pilot made me watch the tapes over and over again, just to get it through my head that I didn't know everything."

The midshipman finished in an embarrassed rush, his color even higher. Carlie, accustomed to Ozzie's more usual rich boy attitude of self-importance, was amused and pleased.

"You may well have a point, Mister Russo. I'll make a note of it."

"Yes, Lieutenant. Thank you, Ma'am."

Later still, the routine business was interrupted from Tactical.

"Lieutenant Dunsinane, a pinnace just launched from the surface. It's going great guns. A second just followed it, also going fast."

"Vector?"

"First one is heading for an armed merchantman, *Psalms*. The second is heading for armed merchantman *Proverbs*."

"Those are the other Templeton ships," Carlie said. "Inform Captain Boniece. Then tight-beam our pinnace and suggest she increase her accel. I want those people back on board."

"Yes, Ma'ams," eddied around the bridge.

Next interruption came from the com station.

"Call coming in from planetary surface, Lieutenant Dunsinane. Originating at their Palace of the Just. Caller identifies himself as one Ronald Sands."

"Get Captain Boniece on the line," Carlie said. "Let him know what's up."

"Captain Boniece is on, Ma'am," came the reply hardly a breath later. "He says for you to take it. He'll ghost."

"Right. Pipe it to the bridge."

Ronald Sands proved to be a man of middle years whose light eyes seemed focused on some visionary distance. He wore his light brown hair well past his shoulders and his full beard neatly trimmed. When he moved, though, there was carefully controlled energy that reminded Carlie that the Faithful eschewed prolong. Sands was probably no more than thirty, possibly younger than that.

"You are Lieutenant Dunsinane?" Sands began, his

tone almost concealing his disbelief and disgust. Carlie remembered hearing that the Faithful kept their women in isolation. This being the case, Sands was keeping his poise admirably.

"That is correct. Lieutenant Carlotta Dunsinane, officer of the watch, *HMS Intransigent*. How may I be of service?"

Sands' lips twitched in a very slight smile, one that was surely a concession to courtesy rather than an indication of any friendliness or warmth.

"I speak with the words of Chief Elder Simonds," he said.

Looking down at what was apparently a prepared script he read: "These are the words of Chief Elder Simonds: 'The people of the Star Kingdom have come to Masada speaking of mutual respect and the possibility of alliance. God in His infinite wisdom and greatness of heart has offered opportunity for the Star Kingdom to show the depth of its commitment to these words.

"'A vessel belonging to one of our most honored and respected citizens has been stolen by those who have no respect for the Faithful. Its course will take it near to you. We do not ask you to take the vessel, nor to fire upon it, only that you slow it in its progress so that it may be reclaimed.

As God has said: 'He that diggeth a pit shall fall into it; and whoso breakth an hedge, a serpent shall bite him.' 'Thus they go from strength to strength. They are a stubborn and rebellious generation. However, God has shown that mercy and truth are met together; righteousness and peace have kissed each other.'"

Carlie felt momentarily overwhelmed by this last spate of scripture, but she managed a courteous nod.

"Your request has been heard, however, I must consult my Captain."

"There is a time to keep silence, and a time to speak," Ronald Sands agreed. "We ask only that the time for speech not be delayed overlong so that these thieves may slip away unimpeded."

"You will have the Captain's response promptly," Carlie agreed. "*Intransigent* out."

When the transmission was broken, Carlie took a deep breath.

"Captain Boniece, your orders, Sir?"

Boniece spoke slowly. "It isn't our place to interfere in a domestic situation, but we were charged with assisting our diplomats. See if you can get a secure line to them. I'd like their advice."

"And if Ronald Sands coms again?"

"Stall him. I'm tempted to have someone do a search for appropriate Bible texts, but the Faithful would probably not be flattered."

"Right, Sir."

Remembering the quickly concealed look of distaste that had flickered across Ronald Sands' face when he had realized he was speaking to a woman, Carlie thought he wouldn't be flattered at all—but that they might not know it until it was too late.

*   *   *

Already shocked when the pinnaces were seen heading for *Psalms* and *Proverbs* well ahead of her imagined schedule, Judith listened to Ronald Sands' "request" with a sense of mounting horror. She had anticipated having to out-run *Psalms* and *Proverbs*, even tangle with a LAC or two, but never in her wildest dreams had she thought that the Manticoran cruiser might be turned against them.

She shivered. Then, horribly, matters grew worse.

Odelia, her face as white as milk, spoke into the stillness.

"Judith, Ronald Sands is comming the other outsider

ship, the Havenite *Moscow*. He's making the same
request of them. Their bridge officer has also asked
for time to consult his captain."

It's over. The traitorous voice that had whispered
through Judith's thoughts as she had struggled to adapt
their plans now repeated itself in mournfully triumphant song. *Give up. It's over.*

"No!" she said aloud, and the heads of her already
shocked bridge crew turned to look at her, clearly
wondering if their young commander had lost her
mind.

"It isn't over," Judith said aloud. "Didn't we swear
to die rather than surrender ourselves to slavery? Hasn't
God given us many miracles to prove He is with us?"

She saw Dinah nod, but everyone else remained stiff
and tense.

"We are not going to be taken by a few words,"
Judith said stubbornly.

A thought that had been dwelling in the corners of
her mind now came into sharp focus.

"The Faithful are not the only ones who could
request help from the Manticorans and the Havenites,"
she said. "What if we requested sanctuary from
Ephraim, what if we told these outsiders that we face
being returned to torture and death?"

Dinah responded so quickly that Judith wondered
how long she had been holding back a similar suggestion.

"What do we have to lose?" the older woman asked
reasonably. "We will need to ask someone's aid sooner
or later. Why not now?"

"We can't ask both of them," Odalia said reasonably.
"From what I've heard, they're adversaries, if not
outright enemies. We must choose one or the other."

Dinah looked at Judith.

"Captain?"

Judith licked her lips. She could think of many good reasons for favoring the Havenites. Their ship was larger and more powerful. They preached freedom and justice for all peoples. She remembered Dinah's words, though, remembering how the Havenites had modified Ephraim's ships. She remembered something else, too.

"Odelia, did you say 'he' when you spoke of the Havenite officer?"

"Yes, Judith." Odelia looked puzzled. "It was a male voice."

"But a woman spoke from *Intransigent*," Judith said. "Surely a woman would feel more sympathy for our cause."

Dinah, devil's advocate against what Judith knew would be her own choice, spoke, "But this Lieutenant Dunsinane may be commanded by a man."

"Still, he is a man who trusts his bridge to a woman," Judith said firmly. "He may listen to us."

There was no argument, so Judith took a moment to frame her request, then turned to Odelia.

"Put in a call to *Intransigent*. If possible, make it a tight link. We don't want Ephraim overhearing what we intend."

Odelia took a moment to consult the computer, then nodded.

"*Intransigent* is answering."

"Make sure you don't have the fake images up," Judith said. "It is time we were known as who we are."

Their eavesdropping on Ronald Sands's call had been audio only, so this was the first time Judith had seen Lieutenant Dunsinane. Her ears had not deceived her. The person facing her was a woman—a very young one, though older than Judith herself.

Then Judith recalled that the Manticorans had some medicine that permitted them to remain physically youthful, in violation, so the Faithful said, of God's will, for did not God say "There is a time to be born, and a time to die"? This was not the time to wonder about such things. If she didn't handle this right, the death time of the Sisterhood would be very close indeed.

"I am Judith," she said, deliberately leaving off the "wife of Ephraim" that was all the surname the Masadans granted their women. "I now command *Aaron's Rod* for the Sisterhood of Barbara. We have fled slavery on Masada."

"I am Lieutenant Carlotta Dunsinane," the woman responded courteously. "What may I do for you?"

"We request," Judith said, her heart beating far too rapidly, "that you assist us. Either grant us sanctuary from our enemies or at least prevent them from halting us in our flight. We have heard your monarch is a queen, and beg in the name of our shared womanhood that you assist us."

She didn't like how the word "beg" had slipped out, but it was too late for her to change it.

Dunsinane nodded her understanding.

"Judith, I am only officer of this watch and cannot answer for my Captain. I will contact him with your request and reply as soon as possible."

"We can only wait," she replied.

Dunsinane broke the connection, but they hardly had time to speculate on what her captain might think when Odelia indicated that *Intransigent* was signaling.

"Their captain wishes to speak with you," she said.

"Put him on," Judith said.

Captain Boniece was at least a man of some years, his commanding bearing reminding Judith of Gideon at his best. Nor did it hurt that he was darker than most Masadans. Judith knew it shouldn't matter, but she couldn't help trusting him more for not looking like her enemies.

"Captain Judith," Boniece said politely. "My watch officer has relayed your request. I am inclined to assist those who appeal to my Queen, however, I have one difficulty."

"Yes?"

"Some hours before *Aaron's Rod* departed orbit, a personnel shuttle and a cargo shuttle entered the ship. The personnel shuttle originated with the Silesian freetrader, *Firebird*, the shuttle from the surface."

He paused and Judith replied, "The cargo shuttle bore my Sisters and myself from slavery."

"And the personnel shuttle?"

"Belonged to smugglers transferring illegal goods which were to be picked up by allies in my husband's house."

She saw Captain Boniece's eyebrows raise.

"Can you confirm this?"

"We have the contraband," she replied, "and we have one of the Silesians."

"The rest?"

"Are dead. We could not risk their stopping us. Our course is most desperate." Judith managed a very small smile. "In any case, their lives were forfeit if the Faithful had caught them. Their cargo included liquor, drugs, and what I believe is pornographic material— any of which would have brought a death sentence from the Faithful. Indeed, we were probably kinder than the Faithful would have been."

"I note that you do not include yourself in the Faithful," Captain Boniece said. "Yet a moment ago you spoke of 'your husband.'"

Judith felt as if he was trying to trap her, and chose her words carefully.

"If we speak of faith in God," she said, "then we are all faithful, for we have trusted Him to guide us forth. However, if we speak of the Faithful of the

Church of Humanity Unchained, then we are not of that number. Those Faithful rate their women as property. We defy that right."

She shook with the wrath that rose within her.

"By their law I am the youngest wife of Ephraim Templeton. He wed me when I was twelve years of age, after murdering my parents two years earlier and stealing me away. I am Grayson born."

"Grayson?"

"That is unimportant," Judith said. "For my Sisters are all born of Masada but have seen their way to freedom. They are my people, and I will do anything to keep them from those who treat them as slaves. I tell you this. We are sworn to die rather than be taken."

Pity, wonder, and calculation crossed Captain Boniece's features. Then he turned as if listening to something outside of the range of the pick-up.

"Forgive me, Captain Judith. Two questions. One, can you confirm your Grayson birth? We are not looking to abandon your Sisters, but the matter is of some interest."

"I know my parents' names and where I was born," she replied. "I know the name of the ship we were on, the ship Ephraim took and later converted into one of those that even now pursue us. If the Graysons have records, these things may help."

"Indeed." Boniece's gaze met hers squarely. "I am inclined to assist you, at least to the extent of letting you make your own escape. However, I cannot do this without confirming that you are who you say you are. Are you familiar with those programs that enable one person to look like another over communication lines?"

"Very well indeed," Judith said.

"Then you understand our dilemma. Unless we are certain you are who you are, then we might be accused of assisting someone—say those from *Firebird*—to hijack *Aaron's Rod*. If members of my crew could board you, confirm that you are who you say you are . . ."

Judith frowned.

"Might you not seek to take us in turn?"

Captain Boniece shrugged. "There must be some trust. However, I will make it easier for you. Did you note the pinnace from this ship that left Masada shortly after your own departure?"

"Yes."

"She has aboard a crew of only four: pilot, co-pilot, flight engineer, and one passenger. The passenger is Midshipman Michael Winton, brother of the very Queen whose protection you invoked. Let them come aboard and confirm your account. After they do so, they will leave."

Judith frowned, sensing the unhappiness of her bridge crew.

"I must consult my Sisters," she said. "I will reply as soon as possible."

"Very good, Captain Judith. I will inform the pinnace as to her possible course change."

Judith thanked him and broke the connection, then turned to deal with Babel unleashed.

What had seemed like aeons ago, Sherlyn had reported the launching of the Manticoran pinnace, and that it appeared to be returning to *Intransigent*. Judith had filed the information away as unimportant. Now, however, the sleek vessel seemed to glow brighter on her plots.

"Men!" spat Odelia. "They'll get their men aboard and betray us. We might have had a chance if *Intransigent*'s captain was a woman, but a man . . ."

"You forget," Dinah said, "that the Star Kingdom knew they were sending *Intransigent* to Masada. They would have chosen a ship with a male captain from routine diplomacy if nothing more. Stop thinking with your womb, Odelia. These are men who serve with women, men sworn to the service of a queen. They have no hatred of women."

"I still don't like the idea of letting four men aboard," Odelia sulked. "They may behave differently away from their female associates. Men do revert to animality when denied the gentler voice of women."

"The responsibility is mine," Judith said, finding her voice at last. "I am captain by your own election. We have said much about how God is testing us. Let us not forget that Satan has his due. Remember how the Chosen People were led astray to worship a Golden Calf in the desert."

"This is no Golden Calf," Odelia said, confused.

"It is a temptation to turn away from what God offers us," Judith said, amazed at her own confident tone, though she thought she had no trust in any god. "All this Captain Boniece asks for is confirmation that we are who we say we are. He does not ask us to come to him. Instead he sends to us."

Sherlyn spoke, "Like Shadrach, Meshach, and Abednego they go into the fiery furnace, trusting we will not burn them."

"And do not forget," Dinah added, "they also send their Queen's own brother. They would not send him lightly."

Judith nodded.

"Odelia, connect me to *Intransigent*."

When Captain Boniece's features shaped on the screen, Judith said with what grace she could manage, "Captain, we would welcome your inspection team. My Sisters, however, are very fearful. We would be grateful if your men would leave their weapons aboard their vessel."

"That can be arranged," Captain Boniece said. "They will rendezvous with you as promptly as possible."

"And I will have an escort waiting to meet them," she replied. "Judith, out."

When the connection was cut, Judith said, "Send Samson's Bane to the aft cargo bay. Tell them to carry their weapons, but not to offer threat."

Odelia relaxed marginally as she relayed the instructions. Judith, watching the various pursuing dots on her plot, relaxed not at all.

※　　　※　　　※

Michael listened as Captain Boniece concluded his briefing.

"We'll send transcripts of our conversations with Captain Judith," Boniece said, "and of Ronald Sands' request on behalf of Chief Elder Simonds."

"May I ask, Sir," Michael said, "how you plan to respond to him?"

"That will depend on your report, Midshipman Winton. However, if you confirm that there is reason to believe Captain Judith's version of events, I intend to support her."

"Sir, that's going to pretty much destroy chances of an alliance with the Endicott System," Michael said, realizing even as he spoke that he was thinking more like a prince than a midshipman.

"I am aware of this, Mr. Winton."

Michael didn't think he was imagining the stress the captain placed on his surname.

"I have also consulted with Ambassador Faldo, and he has his own reasons for encouraging us. I have also heard Mr. Hill's report on the 'missing' people on Masada, and that seems to provide some external substantiation for Captain Judith's account of events."

"Yes, Sir. May I ask one more question?"

"Go ahead."

"Will the Ambassador and his contingent be in danger?"

Captain Boniece smiled. "John Hill thought you might ask. He said to tell you that arrangements for their safety had been made. You may make your report on the situation aboard *Aaron's Rod* without concern for them."

"Thank you, Sir."

"A reminder, Mr. Winton. The Sisterhood of Barbara is desperate. Captain Judith has openly admitted that they killed the smugglers they found aboard *Aaron's Rod* lest the Sisters be stopped in achieving their Exodus. John Hill reports that at least one dead man was found at the Templeton estate. Do not underestimate them. They may be lower tech than we are, but you can die from a knife wound as easily as from a pulser."

"Or from a punch in the kidney. Yes, Sir. I won't forget, and I won't let my crew forget."

"You are the senior officer, Mr. Winton. Don't forget that."

Michael hadn't, not for a moment. However, he wasn't about to act like some tin-plate godlet and forget that pinnace crew had all seen more action than he had.

"All right," he said, signing off and turning to his crew. "Captain Boniece has sent us transcripts. Let's review them while we approach. Then I'll give you a crash course in Masadan etiquette."

By the time the pinnace was easing into *Aaron's Rod*'s aft cargo bay, Michael had had numerous opportunities to be grateful for Lawler's rambling discourses on Masadan culture, and even more for John Hill's unobtrusive competence.

"These women," he concluded, "are going to expect us to lord over them. We won't do that, but let's not err in the direction of self-abasement. That would just confuse them."

"We'll follow your lead, Sir," Chief Petty Officer Keane Lorne, the pilot, said without looking up from his controls. He was busy gentling the pinnace into the gaping cargo hatch without the assistance of the boat bay tractors that would normally have handled a final approach. "Will they even want us all to leave the pinnace?"

"I don't know," Michael admitted. "Let's let them issue the invitations."

The pinnace came to an easy halt alongside *Firebird*'s shuttle.

When external readouts confirmed atmosphere and pressure had been reestablished, Michael walked to the hatch. He wore his vac suit, but carried his helmet in the crook of his left elbow, wanting to show both his face and a level of trust.

"I'll go first," he said, repeating earlier orders. "Follow on my command."

"Right, Mr. Winton," Chief Lorne replied for them all. "Luck."

Michael stepped out and trotted down the steps to stand on the deck. As he did so, the hatch into the cargo bay opened, admitting several figures, all, like him, wearing vac suits. Several of these women were quite obviously armed, but they kept their weapons at rest. Their leader, a broad-figured, grey-haired woman, carried no weapons and stepped ahead of them to greet him.

"I am Dinah," she said. "I believe I am the equivalent of executive officer. I am also one of those who established the Sisterhood of Barbara. What do you need to see to confirm our account of our actions?"

Michael was already convinced, but he had his orders from Captain Boniece. After all, unlike the Masadans, the Silesians did not sequester their women. It was possible that the hijackers were female Silesians masquerading as Masadan escapees. That seemed like a dreadful lot of trouble to go to just to take one armed, low-tech merchie, but Captain Boniece was putting his neck on the line in being willing to help Captain Judith and her crew. He had to be able to prove before a board of inquiry that he'd confirmed their need. Getting that confirmation was Michael's job.

"I need to see your passengers. Captain Judith spoke as if a large group is partaking in your Exodus."

He knew from the update from John Hill that both women and children were now being reported missing on Masada, but he didn't want to show his hand.

"This can be done," Dinah replied.

"I would like to speak with the surviving Silesian smuggler."

"This also can be arranged."

"I would also like to speak with Captain Judith."

"This, also, can be permitted."

"My crew," Michael said. "Would you like them to come with me or to remain here?"

Dinah's lips twitched in a tight smile.

"I care little, but some of my Sisters would feel safer if they remained here. Perhaps they can inspect the Silesian craft?"

"That will work," Michael agreed. "Let me introduce you."

He did so, and was pleased that the crewmen handled themselves well. They had left their weapons aboard, but each carried a com unit so compact it was unlikely the Sisters would even recognize it. He would know if anything happened to them.

"Commander Dinah," Michael said, "where would you have us start?"

"The Silesian smuggler is near here," she said. "Then we will go where you may observe the Sisters."

The Silesian smuggler was only too glad to confirm

what had happened. In fact, he'd been locked up, in terror for his life, for long enough that Michael didn't even have to tell him that *Firebird* had abandoned him to get him to tell everything—right up to and including admitting that they had been smuggling into the Endicott System for several years.

Michael promised that he would do what he could to get the Silesian repatriated, then followed Dinah toward a lift. Several of the armed women paced them, but as Michael offered nothing but courtesy, they had marginally relaxed.

"All the Sisters are not gathered in one place," Dinah explained. "About a third of our number are assigned to various stations."

Michael did a quick estimate.

"You're rather under-strength," he said.

"We are," Dinah retorted, "remarkable for what we have done. Do you realize that most Masadan women cannot read or do mathematics more complex than what can be counted off on fingers? That we managed this many Sisters who can at least ask the computer for assistance and understand what it tells them strikes me as remarkable."

"I apologize," Michael said, appalled at what he was learning. "How did you manage this much?"

"Judith was a great help," Dinah said. "She has actually been into space repeatedly."

"The rest of you haven't?"

"Only a few," came the placid reply. "I myself have not been for twenty years. Some of our Sisters were . . . unable to join us." Her face tightened briefly, but then she drew a deep breath and continued. "Fortunately, none of them were among our department heads."

"Right."

They progressed to what Michael guessed were

Aaron's Rod's common areas: dormitories, cafeteria, lounge. He was introduced to someone named Naomi who in turn introduced him to some of the women and children packed into these spaces.

"The ones experiencing the worst panic are in sickbay," Naomi said with a levelness that did not disguise her deep concern. "Happily, Elder Templeton did not stint on tranquilizers."

"Life support?" Michael asked Dinah when they had returned to the lift.

"In good shape," Dinah said. "I always made certain Ephraim took good care of such things. He was careful, too. A privateer cannot always go to the nearest port."

"What about facilities for all those people if the ship has to fight?" he asked as levelly as he could, hating the image of what a direct hit on one of those crowded cabins would do.

"We brought materials aboard," Dinah said, "but it is a weakness."

"I see." Michael looked around for several more seconds, then turned back to Dinah. "And Engineering?" he asked.

He had kept his tone as inflectionless as possible, but Dinah smiled grimly.

"Our engineers' training is limited to what we could achieve from stolen simulations," she told him. "I believe that is the reason Captain Judith has been holding us to a slower acceleration rate than our impatience to be away might otherwise dictate. She fears to cut our compensator's safety margin as a more experienced crew might."

Michael marveled at Dinah's calm.

"What were you before," he asked, "a teacher?"

"I was," she said. "Although not as you mean it. Remember, women are forbidden to learn. Officially,

I was nothing more than Ephraim Templeton's elder wife, and mother of his children—many of whom," she finished, "are doubtless crewing the two ships that now pursue us."

They had arrived at the bridge, and Michael, shaken to the core by everything he had learned, was unprepared for his first meeting with Captain Judith.

Seeing her image on a transmission tape had not prepared him for the intensity of her brown-rimmed green eyes, nor for her youth. His introduction to so many of the Sisters during his whirlwind tour had brought home to him that not only was this a pre-prolong civilization, this was also a civilization that used its women hard.

Judith, then, was hardly more than a child. He remembered hearing her declare that Ephraim Templeton had wed her when she was twelve years of age. He realized that she'd meant twelve T-years. She couldn't be more than eighteen now.

How old are you? he thought, then realized to his horror he'd spoken aloud.

She must have found his shock funny rather than offensive.

"I am sixteen T-years," she said. "And you? You look the beardless boy."

"I am twenty-one," he replied, matching her humor, "and neither of those figures matter in the least. Captain Judith, could your communications officer contact *Intransigent* for me? I want to make my report."

"There is a briefing room," Captain Judith offered politely, gesturing to a door at one side of the bridge.

"If you don't mind," Michael replied, "I'll speak to Captain Boniece from right here. It will save repetition."

Captain Judith appeared pleased by this indication

of trust, and if her mouth tightened as Michael reported the limitations of her crew's abilities Michael didn't blame her. After all, Dinah was right. What the Sisterhood of Barbara had done in achieving this much of their Exodus was remarkable. It couldn't be easy to hear of their abilities spoken of in such a fashion.

Captain Boniece listened with very little interruption, then spoke directly to Captain Judith.

"*Intransigent* will cover your departure, Captain," he said. "I suggest that you raise your accel to the maximum you feel your crew can safely sustain. We have no desire to get into a fire fight with Ephraim Templeton or any Masadans."

"We will do what we can," Judith replied. "I fear, however, Ephraim will feel differently. And there is something I must tell you, something about *Psalms* and *Proverbs*."

*   *   *

Captain Boniece had sent *Intransigent* to battle stations, so Carlie was at the ATO's station on the bridge when Ephraim Templeton learned that the Manticorans had chosen to support Captain Judith rather than himself.

That Templeton was furious was evident from the moment his thick-set figure appeared on the screen. However, though his blue eyes blazed with cold fury, he attempted to be polite.

"I understand that you were not receptive to Chief Elder Simonds' request that you assist me in regaining my property."

Boniece replied levelly, "I was not."

"That is your right, of course," Templeton couldn't quite conceal a sneer, "but what is this Sands tells me, that not only have you refused to assist, you have informed him that you will actively impede any effort to regain *Aaron's Rod*?"

"It is distinctly possible," Boniece replied, "that *Aaron's Rod* will be returned to you. However, it is currently in use."

"Currently in use?"

"The question of the ship is a delicate one, I admit," Captain Boniece said, his conversational tone at odds with the fist he clenched out of sight of the pick-up. "However, without it the people on board would have difficulty removing themselves."

"People?" Templeton looked appalled. "You don't mean those insane bitches do you?"

"Pardon?"

"I have been informed that *Aaron's Rod* was stolen by Silesian pirates who somehow lured away a large number of Masadan women and children. It is those women to whom I refer."

Boniece shook his head. Carlie, watching her board, realized that *Aaron's Rod* was increasing speed. Boniece was obviously talking to buy her time. Carlie watched, waiting to see *Intransigent*'s pinnace depart and bring her wandering midshipman to the relative safety of the light cruiser.

"First," Boniece said slowly, "I must disabuse you of the notion that the Silesians had anything to do with the taking of *Aaron's Rod*. Apparently, they were smugglers whose run happened to coincide with the arrival on *Aaron's Rod* of her new crew."

"New crew? Do you mean the women?"

"The Captain Judith to whom I spoke claims birth in the Yeltsin System," Boniece said. "She says her companions wish to emigrate from the Endicott System."

"Judith?" Templeton was so angry that he became momentarily incoherent. "That green-eyed whore . . . Is she behind this?"

"I suggest you speak with her yourself."

"Speak with a woman? Are you as crazy as they are?"

"I speak with women on a regular basis, Mr. Templeton. Umeko Palmer, my XO, is a woman. For that matter, I serve a woman—my Queen."

Templeton's sputter faded into something far uglier, an icy fury that made Carlie shiver.

"Captain Boniece, I advise you to cease interference in something that does not involve you or the Star Kingdom of Manticore. I will reclaim my ship and my property, with or without your assistance. Indeed, there may be others quite eager to assist me."

"Perhaps," Boniece replied, his tone equally cold. "However, I will not. *Intransigent* out."

He uncurled his fist and spoke in something more like his usual tones. Then he turned to Maurice Townsend, the tac officer.

"Guns, stand by. Com, get me Mr. Winton aboard *Aaron's Rod*, I want to know what's keeping him. Then place a call to *Moscow*. I want her captain to know that we'll view it quite unkindly if they interfere with Judith of Grayson's efforts to return home."

"Do you think they'll listen?" Townsend asked.

"I think so," Boniece said, grimly. "If they don't, then *Intransigent* is going to be responsible for starting a shooting war with the Peeps."

※　　※　　※

Judith had never even imagined someone with skin as dark as Michael Winton's. It reminded her of the night sky without stars. She corrected herself when he smiled at her as she concluded her report to Captain Boniece regarding the upgrades to *Psalms* and *Proverbs*. That smile and the brightness of his eyes put stars in the sky.

Perhaps it was because Michael Winton was so unlike any other man she'd seen—more a youth hardly out of boyhood in appearance than a man, his gaze the warm brown of a friendly animal's—but she found him easy to speak to. When he offered to delay his departure from *Aaron's Rod* long enough to make sure they were getting everything they could out of her inertial compensator, she accepted with ease.

It was at that moment that *Intransigent* signaled.

"We've had contact from Ephraim Templeton," Captain Boniece said bluntly. "I'm squirting a copy for your information. In brief, he's extremely angry."

"We never thought otherwise," Judith replied. "He will kill us all if he captures us, down to the least unborn babe."

Inadvertently, she cupped her hand over her abdomen as she spoke.

"He wants *Aaron's Rod* back," Boniece continued. "That may offer some protection."

"I doubt it," Judith replied. "He is like God—terrible in His wrath."

"Is Mr. Winton available?"

"I'm here, Sir," Michael cut in. "Captain Judith and I have just been discussing how to increase this ship's acceleration. Their engineers . . . aren't very experienced, Sir."

Captain Boniece blinked.

"I should have thought of that myself." He shook his head and gave Judith a quick, measuring glance. "In fact, it's remarkable that they have managed as much as they have, under the circumstances they must have faced. My compliments, Captain."

"I fear that Mr. Winton speaks only too accurately of our limitations," Judith admitted. "My Sisters studied hard, but the sims could teach any of us only so much, and—"

Sherlyn cut in, just as Judith became aware of staccato voices in the background of Captain Boniece's transmission.

"*Proverbs* and *Psalms* have raised their speed. They are splitting to go around *Intransigent* and come after us!"

Boniece returned his attention to her.

"Captain Judith, have you . . ."

"Yes. Ephraim is angry. He is coming for us."

"I am going to attempt to intervene, but it's going to be tough with them splitting that way. I don't want to be the first to fire."

"I understand."

Michael Winton leaned into the pick-up.

"Captain, I request permission to stay aboard *Aaron's Rod* and assist. Chief Lorne says PO O'Donnel knows his compensators backward and forward. I think we can increase her acceleration substantially if Captain Judith is willing to let him manage her safety margin."

"Mr. Winton . . ."

Captain Boniece seemed to be about to refuse. Judith never knew why he didn't. Was he thinking of the vulnerability of a pinnace out there against Ephraim's enhanced privateers? Was he thinking of how coordinating a rendezvous would restrict *Intransigent's* own maneuvers? Was he thinking how desperately *Aaron's Rod* needed every trained hand?

For whatever reason, Captain Boniece gave a crisp nod.

"Permission granted. You are to place yourself and your pinnace crew at Captain Judith's disposal."

"Yes, Sir!"

"Run for the hyper limit, Captain Judith. Good luck. *Intransigent* out."

*   *   *

Carlie tried not to voice her protest when Captain Boniece permitted Michael Winton to stay aboard *Aaron's Rod*, but something must have squeaked out. Boniece gave her a thin, hard-lipped grin.

"Well, ATO, I don't think anyone will think we've gone soft on our middies."

She managed an answering grin.

"No, Sir."

"Tactical, we're fighting defensive," the captain continued. "I do not, I repeat *not* want to fire on either *Psalms* or *Proverbs*. However, feel free to intercept their fire."

"You think they'll fire on us?" Maurice Townsend, the senior tac officer said in disbelief.

"Not on us, Guns," Boniece gestured vaguely toward where *Aaron's Rod* was picking up speed. "On her."

"They're splitting, Captain," Carlie reported, firing off coordinates.

"Above and below us," Boniece said. "Not bad. They know we can only keep our wedge between *Aaron's Rod* and one opponent. Ephraim Templeton's on *Proverbs* and he sounded angry enough to blow his wives and daughters into the heavens. We'll keep between *Proverbs* and *Aaron's Rod*.

"As for *Psalms*, I want point defense's perimeter extended to cover any fire from her. Send out a few decoys, too. They won't know for a while what they can ignore and what they can't. They can't be sure they didn't insult us beyond prudence.

"Remember, they've been modified. Their power plants and compensators are better, maneuverability increased. For all we know they've been up-gunned, as well. Don't make the mistake of thinking of these as just a couple of merchies."

Despite Boniece's warning, Carlie did find it hard not to underestimate *Psalms* and *Proverbs*. Not only were they merchies, they were from cultures several steps down the tech ladder from Manticore. It didn't take long—a couple of narrow misses on missiles—for her to realize that *Proverbs* and *Psalms* had an asset that nearly compensated for their disadvantages: killer crews.

Their warheads were pathetic by Manticoran standards, and their ECM was even worse. But even an old-fashioned nuke could kill if it got through, and their rate of fire was high. Their fire control must have profited from enhancement as well, for their targeting was excellent and their tac officers adjusted for *Intransigent's* dummies with thoughtful insight.

"I wonder," Tab Tilson commented after a particularly nasty brush, "just how many merchant vessels were 'lost' to this pair?"

"Too many," Boniece commented. "We may owe the Silesian pirates an apology."

There was a harsh laugh at that, but then *Psalms* put on a burst of acceleration, obviously trying to edge around *Intransigent* and get at Judith's ship. Ignoring the light cruiser, *Psalms* bore down on *Aaron's Rod*, seeking an angle where the other ship's wedge wouldn't protect her from attack.

Boniece was issuing orders with the measured calm that came over him when he was at his most intense, and Carlie felt her fingers flying to comply. One, two, three . . . She thought she had intercepted all the missiles heading toward *Aaron's Rod*, then another battery went off.

Four, five . . .

Aaron's Rod fired lasers, intercepting the incoming missiles neatly, but a fresh broadside followed on their heels.

"Captain," Carlie heard her own voice like a stranger's, "*Proverbs* is speeding up and edging around us to port. If we're not careful . . ."

"Keep us between *Proverbs* and her target," Boniece

commanded. "So far *Aaron's Rod* is doing some tidy defensive fire."

Carlie glanced at her board, but the hyper limit was still impossibly far away. She didn't know how much longer they could keep this on a purely defensive footing. The consequences if they did not, especially since to this point neither *Psalms* nor *Proverbs* had fired on *Intransigent* . . .

She couldn't let herself think about it. Then she saw it, a missile from *Psalms* slipped through the joint defenses.

"*Aaron's Rod* has been hit!"

*　　*　　*

Michael Winton had gotten off the bridge almost immediately. His peculiar rapport with Captain Judith didn't extend to the rest of her bridge crew—Dinah possibly excepted—and he knew he was interfering with her ability to command.

He convinced Zaneta, the head of his armed escort, to take him back to his pinnace.

"O'Donnel, they need you in Engineering," he said crisply, and waved at one of Zaneta's Samson's Bane. "She'll take you there. How far you reduce the safety margin is up to Captain Judith, but I think we're going to have to get as close to maximum military power as you can take us."

"Aye, aye, Sir."

The petty officer sounded calm, but Michael saw the truth in his eyes. Maximum military power would mean running the compensator with no safety margin at all. That would enormously increase the possibility that it might fail and kill them all . . . but it would also give Judith at least half again the acceleration she'd been able to maintain so far.

"Good," Michael approved as warmly as he could. "On your way, then."

O'Donnel nodded and went jogging away behind his guide while Michael turned back to the other two crewmen.

"As for us, I think we'll serve best as damage control," he went on, both to them and the listening Zaneta. "Can you introduce us to the Chief, Ma'am?"

Zaneta did so. Rena proved to be Ephraim's third wife. Michael couldn't help but wonder both how many women Ephraim had married, and what kind of man he was that they were willing to risk so much to get away from him.

He didn't ask. Rena made him rather nervous.

A battle from below decks, rather than the bridge, proved to be a strange and elusive thing, a little like a very bad nightmare where everything shifts at the least prompting.

Michael's first assignment was to repair a set of overheating relays for one of the impeller nodes. O'Donnel was obviously doing his job with the compensator, Michael reflected. *Aaron's Rod* was no longer crawling by anyone's estimate. In fact, he doubted that even when she turned privateer she'd ever needed to pour on the heat this way.

Chief Lorne was diverted to sickbay when Michael learned that he'd done time as a sick berth assistant before becoming a coxswain. So far, the Sisters had been unreasonably lucky, and Michael knew it. The most frightened might have required sedation, but no one had been seriously injured during the escape. Yet. But, then, *Aaron's Rod* hadn't taken any hits yet, either.

With Lorne in sickbay and O'Donnel nursing the ship's compensator, PO Parello, Lorne's copilot, ended up in gunnery checking a hinky laser mount. That left them spread out over the entire ship, but their personal coms kept all four of them in close contact.

The absence of titles and the first names that were all the women gave for identification created a sense of intimacy almost immediately. If it hadn't been that Zaneta followed him everywhere, Michael might even have felt accepted. Even she soon tucked her weapon in its holster, and held leads and lines without comment.

Then a missile impact rocked *Aaron's Rod*. Michael froze, waiting for Rena's report.

"Aft cargo hold breached," she snapped. "Seals holding. Mr. Winton, anything on that pinnace of yours?"

They'd already handed out the med kits, vac suits, and anything else from the pinnace's stores that Michael thought could help even the odds.

"No problem," he said.

Another shudder went through and this time Rena paled.

"Sheared off one of the lasers. We've lost two Sisters in gunnery control. Teresa is taking Dara to sickbay."

Michael waited to be sent, but Rena just gave him a sad smile.

"Nothing we can do for a part that's missing. Teresa sealed the compartment and we're not losing much."

More reports came in. Michael found himself down in Engineering, flat on his belly reprogramming software to divert around a damaged circuit. His universe resolved into small problems, each intensely important while it lasted, each superseded by yet another problem as overtaxed systems collapsed under the strain of compensating for their fellows.

He wondered why *Intransigent* wasn't doing more to protect them, and discovered to his shock that she was soaking up most of the damage. He'd forgotten how vulnerable these older model ships were. Forgotten if he'd ever known . . .

And the nightmare kept going on.

❋   ❋   ❋

When she could spare a glance from her own duties, Judith felt nothing but awe for what *Intransigent* was doing. The light cruiser was keeping *Proverbs* at bay with nothing more—at least so it seemed—than her presence. *Psalms* had slipped around, but very few of the missiles Gideon Templeton lobbed relentlessly at the ship carrying his mother, step-mothers, and even a few of his children, got through.

Judith remembered her lessons and did her best to keep the cruiser's wedge between *Aaron's Rod* and incoming fire. She was fully aware that she wasn't managing it as well as a properly trained helmswoman might have, just as she knew that her inexperience kept her from rolling *Aaron's Rod* with the sort of confidence that would have used the privateer's own wedge with proper efficiency. But she was doing the best she could. She knew that . . . and so did any God who might actually be listening.

Besides, she had other things to worry about, as well. Along with Dinah, she was also responsible for point defense, fighting to intercept the incoming fire that got past *Intransigent*. They did well, but she was aware of how the older woman was slowing, her breathing becoming labored.

"Dinah, you need to rest," Judith said.

"I will have time enough to rest," Dinah said. "How far to the hyper limit?"

"Fifteen minutes."

"I can last fifteen minutes," Dinah insisted.

Judith couldn't press. She needed to do so much. Odelia had received coordinates for their translation into hyper-space from Captain Boniece, but Judith still had to put them in. She had to adapt her tactics, such as they were, to systems that kept failing. Sherlyn's sensors were only giving partial information as missile strikes wiped away external feed.

Yet minute by minute, the hyper limit approached. Something had happened, for *Psalms* was no longer following so closely. Maybe *Intransigent* had gotten frustrated and fired on it. Maybe even the Havenite modifications to the Masadan engineering couldn't take the strain.

Five.

"Odelia, tell Naomi to have the passengers prepare for translation into hyper."

Four.

"Judith! *Proverbs* is dropping back. Sensors show . . . I'm not sure what they show. I think a drive is out."

Three.

"We're leaking atmosphere from aft. Life support isn't happy about it."

Two.

"Judith . . ."

Dinah's face was very gray. When Judith grabbed her, she saw the read-outs on the older woman's vac suit were flickering from green to amber.

"My heart . . . I can't breathe . . ."

One.

"Hyper limit fifty-nine seconds," the computer intoned.

Judith thrust Dinah into the captain's chair, praying to a God she desperately wanted to believe in for one more miracle. She took a moment to fasten the straps on the frighteningly limp figure.

"Odelia, we need a medic on the bridge. Now! I think Dinah's having a heart attack."

"Thirty seconds."

Judith could hear Odelia calling for a medic, giving the warnings, signaling *Intransigent* that they'd resume contact after they'd translated into hyper. She leaned to the astrogation panel, pressed the buttons as she had done so many times in sims.

There was a strange feeling and the universe seemed to hiccup abruptly. She had the impression of distant cheering coming over open com links. The bridge was strangely quiet.

Judith rose and cradled Dinah's head against her. She saw gray lips move, bent her head to listen.

"We're safe?" Dinah whispered.

"Safe," Judith managed a stiff smile.

"I think," Dinah coughed. "I will never see the Promised Land, but my daughters . . ."

"Will!" Judith completed fiercely when the other woman could not draw breath. "As will you."

"Moses . . ."

"You call me that," Judith said, "but you are truly Moses, I was only your handmaid."

Dinah's lips twisted in what might have been a wry smile, might only have been pain.

"Moses never saw . . ."

"The Promised Land?" Judith finished. "Moses doubted God, but you never did. God will send one more miracle."

But Dinah was very still now, and slowly, one by one, the telltales on her suit shifted to red, then black.

Judith, who had not lost control for one moment during those interminable hours of flight and battle, bent her head and wept.

✳   ✳   ✳

Carlie kept her gaze locked on the sensor boards, but there was no sign that either *Psalms* or *Proverbs* had followed them into hyper. Certainly *Proverbs* had shown signs of a drive malfunction, but *Psalms* might have had enough. She supposed they'd know someday, but right now it was enough to give her report.

"No sign of pursuit, Captain."

"Very good, Lieutenant. Com, contact Captain Judith."

Tab Tilson's voice held such concern when he spoke, that Carlie jerked her head around to look.

"Captain, Odelia—that's their com officer—says Captain Judith isn't available right now and would you talk to her?"

Captain Boniece blinked, but adjusted to the odd request.

"Put her on screen."

The screen took shape of image of a plain woman with round features and long hair drawn into a knot at the back of her head. Her eyes were red from weeping, but her expression tightened with determination as she looked at Captain Boniece.

"How may I help you?"

She sounded like she was offering to serve drinks, not in apparent command of a fighting ship's bridge.

"I had hoped to speak with Captain Judith," Boniece replied. "We registered no hits on the bridge. Is she . . ."

Odelia interrupted before Boniece could finish his rather awkward query.

"She lives, but Dinah . . ." She paused and gulped, tears welling back in her eyes. "Dinah is dying. Her heart."

Carlie doubted that Captain Boniece could make any more of this than she could, but he adapted smoothly.

"Medical emergency. It may be we can help. I'll send coordinates for taking *Aaron's Rod* out of the grav wave. Then our ships can rendezvous, and I'll extend every assistance my ship can offer. Is Mr. Winton available?"

"He is also with Dinah," Odelia said. "But I can link you to any or all of your other men."

Carlie saw Boniece relax marginally, and realized

that he had been dreading that his men—like the Silesian smugglers—might have been killed by these fanatics.

"Give me PO O'Donnel," he said.

*   *   *

Michael Winton came aboard *Intransigent* shortly after the two ships left the grav wave. He looked tired and thinner, but Carlie Dunsinane thought that impossibly he might well have grown several inches. Maybe it was that he now walked straighter, his head held like a prince—or like the Navy officer he'd proven himself worthy to be.

They'd already had his report, transmitted as soon as the immediate crisis was over. Reading between the lines of his neat prose it had been a tough couple of hours.

Simply put, *Aaron's Rod* was a good ship for her type, but she'd never been intended for the punishment she'd taken during that Exodus. For days to come there would be repairs to make, systems to bring back on-line. Though Michael never said so, Captain Boniece had been wise to leave the four *Intransigent* crewmen on board. Without their skills, *Aaron's Rod* could never have won that deadly race.

Even so there were the wounded and dead. Few enough if this had been a military action, but in this close-knit community of rebels, each loss had been felt as if it had been of, well, a sister.

Worst, perhaps, had been the heart attack suffered by Dinah, senior wife of Ephraim Templeton, and, Carlie now realized, the true leader of the Exodus. Judith had been ship's captain, but Dinah had been admiral. Her collapse, just when the Sisterhood should have been able to feel joy at their release, had nearly broken them.

Carlie watched as Michael turned to take one end

of the stretcher being extended out of the pinnace's side hatch. The other end was held by a green-eyed girl who Carlie realized with a shock was Captain Judith.

She covered her own reaction by stepping forward with the grav-assisted stretcher she'd brought from sickbay, no one questioning that an ATO would do the job of a medical attendant. The attendants were there, though, as was Surgeon Commander Kiah Rink, who immediately took charge.

"You'll save Dinah?" Judith asked, reaching out to Rink. "Tell us you will."

"I'll do what I can," Rink said, bending over the stretcher and taking readings, "and I'll do it better if you'll let me get her and my other patients to sickbay."

She softened.

"The oxygen was a good idea. So were the rest of the measures you took. You've done all you can. Let it go."

"Michael did it," Judith said, looking at him with pride. "Came to the bridge when we called for a medic. He had one of the kits from your pinnace. Your medicine is far better than Masadan medicine—and he had been trained that a woman needs different care than does a man."

Michael was too dark to show a blush, but Carlie had the distinct impression he was coloring.

"Why don't both of you escort the wounded to sickbay," she suggested. "Mr. Winton, when the wounded are settled, please escort Captain Judith to Captain Boniece, then report to me."

"I must return to my ship!" Judith protested.

"If you'll permit, Captain, we'll send over a relief crew," Carlie said. "I have one standing by, all women, under Commander Umeko Palmer, our own XO."

Judith smiled.

"Thank you for your consideration. I will accept your relief crew, but it does not need to be all women. The Sisterhood does not mind men—not if they are Manticorans."

With One Stone

by Timothy Zahn

It was Silesian space.

It was escort duty for convoys of Her Majesty's merchant marine.

It was going to be boring as hell.

Lieutenant (Senior Grade) Rafael Cardones stifled a sigh as the *Star Knight*-class heavy cruiser HMS *Fearless* slid smoothly into its slot in Sphinx orbit. It wasn't fair, and everyone aboard knew it. After all they'd gone through at Basilisk Station a few months back, and especially now with a shiny, brand-new-out-of-the-box warship wrapped around them, surely the Admiralty could have given them *something* more challenging than to run endlessly back and forth between Basilisk and the roiling cesspool of political chaos laughingly called the Silesian Confederacy.

"Nodes to standby," the ship's commander ordered in that smooth soprano of hers, and Cardones threw a surreptitious look at her. If Captain Honor Harrington was dismayed by the thought of escort duty, it certainly didn't show in her face. Her expression was almost serene, in fact, as if she didn't have a care in the world.

Of course, Cardones recalled, her expression had been nearly that serene as she ordered their former ship, the late lamented light cruiser *Fearless*, to charge off across the Basilisk system in pursuit of an eight-million-ton Q-ship owned and operated by the People's Republic of Haven. A Q-ship, moreover, that might as well have been a full-fledged battlecruiser for the weight of armament it carried.

While their light cruiser might as well have been a glorified LAC after all the gutting Admiral Sonja Hemphill had done to it in order to make room for her precious experimental grav lance. The fact that Captain Harrington had managed to keep the *Fearless* together long enough to find a way to use that self-same grav lance against the Peep Q-ship was irrelevant, as far as Cardones was concerned. To him, it had been borderline criminal stupidity on Hemphill's part, and the rumor mill had it that Captain Harrington had said so directly to her face at the Weapons Development Board hearing afterward. Not in so many words, of course.

He took another look at the captain's face. On second thought, he decided, that expression wasn't serene at all. Captain Harrington was looking forward to the chance to hunt down some pirates and kick their collective butt.

Maybe this tour wasn't going to be quite as boring as he'd first thought.

Across the bridge, Lieutenant Joyce Metzinger straightened suddenly in her chair. "Captain, I'm getting a signal from HMS *Basilisk*," she announced.

Cardones glanced back at the captain, saw a slight frown of surprise. She'd done a stint aboard *Basilisk*, he knew, before being given her first hyper-capable command. Tac officer, if he remembered correctly, the same post he himself currently held aboard *Fearless*. Was Admiral Trent simply calling to say hello?

He was half right. "Admiral Trent sends his greetings," Metzinger continued. "He also requests your presence aboard at your earliest convenience."

The com officer glanced at Cardones. "He also requests that you bring Lieutenant Cardones with you."

Cardones blinked. And he had *never* served aboard *Basilisk*. What in the world . . . ?

"Acknowledge the admiral's message, Joyce," Captain Harrington told Metzinger. She stood and half turned, holding out her arms to the treecat wrapped lazily across the back of her command chair. He leaped gracefully into her arms, then scampered up into his usual traveling position along her shoulders. "And have my pinnace prepared. Rafe?"

"Right away, Ma'am," Cardones said, already on his feet. An admiral's *earliest convenience* was any regular mortal's *five minutes ago*, and it would not do to keep Trent waiting.

The *Basilisk* was a superdreadnought, three and a half kilometers long and eight and a quarter million tons of fighting fury. Cardones eyed it as their pinnace approached, his thoughts balanced midway between future anticipation and future regret. To serve aboard a prestigious ship of the wall had been his dream ever since he'd put on the uniform of the Royal Manticoran Navy. But on the other hand, with a ship that size the sheer number of people aboard tended to make even senior officers mere cogs in a machine far larger than they were. Even if he someday made it aboard such a ship, he suspected he would look wistfully back at his days aboard smaller ships like the *Fearless*, where each person made more of a difference.

Especially since even cruisers could sometimes make their presence felt on the galactic stage if they were in the right place at the right time, as Captain Harrington had proved at Basilisk Station. All in all, it might not be such a bad thing to serve a while aboard the RMN's smaller ships.

The *Basilisk*'s boat bay was the usual scene of controlled chaos as Cardones followed Captain Harrington through the boarding tube to the sound of the side party's bosun's pipes. The boat bay officer of the deck and quartermaster were off to one side, conferring over a memo pad, while at the other side a work party was tearing into one of the fueling stations. He glanced once in that direction as he landed on the deck behind his captain, hoping they'd remembered to seal off the hydrogen tanks and clear the hoses before they fired up their cutting torches. He'd heard once of a party that had forgotten, and it hadn't been pretty.

Given the unusualness of Trent's invitation, Cardones would have expected the admiral to add to the novelty by coming himself to greet his visitors. But except for the side party there were only two people waiting for them: a tall man wearing the four gold sleeve rings and collar planets of a captain of the list, and an almost equally tall woman with the same four sleeve rings but the collar pips of a captain junior grade.

"Captain Harrington," the man said, stepping forward to meet them. "I'm Captain Olbrecht, Admiral Trent's chief of staff. Welcome aboard the *Basilisk*."

He smiled as he stretched out his hand. "Or rather," he added, "welcome *back* aboard."

"Thank you, Captain," Captain Harrington said, taking the proffered hand and shaking it. "This is Lieutenant Rafael Cardones, my tac officer."

"Yes," Olbrecht said, nodding as he extended his hand to Cardones. His eyes flicked across his face and down his torso with the sort of evaluating glance senior officers always seemed to give their juniors. "Welcome aboard, Lieutenant."

"Thank you, Sir," Cardones said. Olbrecht's grip was firm and precise, exactly the sort of handshake senior officers always seemed to offer their juniors.

"This is Captain Elayne Sandler," Olbrecht went on, releasing Cardones's hand and gesturing to the woman still standing a respectful pace behind him. "You'll be going with her, Lieutenant."

Cardones felt his spine stiffen slightly. On the trip over he'd come to the conclusion that there was fresh data on the Silesian situation that Trent wanted to discuss with the *Fearless*'s skipper and tac officer. But if he was now going to be split off from her . . .

"Yes, Sir," he managed, turning his head to nod to the woman.

She nodded back, her cool eyes giving him the same once-over Olbrecht had just performed. Apparently it was a technique senior officers were issued with their collar insignia. "This way, Lieutenant," she said, turning and heading off toward one of the lifts.

"Yes, Ma'am," Cardones murmured, looking at Captain Harrington. "Ma'am?"

"Go ahead, Rafe," she said, her voice calm and completely unconcerned. "I'll see you later."

"Yes, Ma'am," he said. Her voice might have been calm, but Cardones had caught the puzzlement briefly creasing her forehead. So this wasn't something she'd been expecting, either. He headed off after Captain Sandler, trying to decide whether that was a good sign or a bad one.

He caught up with Sandler at the lift. "Sorry to make such a cloak and dagger out of this," Sandler commented as she palmed the call button. "But you'll understand in a minute."

"Yes, Ma'am," Cardones said, settling for a neutral response as he watched Olbrecht and Captain Harrington disappear into one of the other lifts. Heading somewhere entirely different, apparently, than he and Sandler were bound.

The lift doors in front of them slid open, and they stepped inside. A minute later the car deposited them outside one of the *Basilisk*'s ready rooms. Sandler touched the release and stepped inside; forcing the tension out of his shoulders, Cardones followed.

There were six people seated around the long briefing table, all of them looking back at the newcomers. Cardones glanced down the double row, automatically taking in faces and rank insignia.

His eyes reached the woman at the head of the table. An admiral, he noted with mild surprise. He lifted his eyes from her collar to her face—

And with a surge of rushing blood in his ears the tension came roaring back like a hyper-space grav wave slapping him in the face.

It wasn't just an admiral. It was Admiral Sonja Hemphill.

"Lieutenant Cardones," she said, gesturing a slender hand toward the empty chair two places down from her left, between a pair of men wearing lieutenant commander's and ensign's insignia, respectively. "Please; sit down."

Her voice was even, almost calm. But Cardones wasn't fooled for a minute. This was the woman whose "innovations" had nearly gotten him and the entire crew of the *Fearless* killed, and the woman who Captain Harrington had humiliated in front of her peers over it.

And now here she was, inviting that same Captain Harrington's tac officer to a private and apparently secret meeting.

This was definitely Not Good.

But an admiral was still an admiral. "Yes, Ma'am," he said, circling the foot of the table and heading for the indicated chair. Captain Sandler, he noted, was heading for the likewise empty seat at Hemphill's right.

Hemphill waited until they were both seated. "My name is Admiral Sonja Hemphill, Lieutenant," Hemphill introduced herself. The corner of her mouth might have twitched. "I believe you've heard of me."

"Yes, Ma'am," Cardones confirmed, his parade-ground neutral expression firmly in place.

"You've already met Captain Sandler," Hemphill went on, gesturing to the man to Cardones's right. "This is Lieutenant Commander Jack Damana; on your left is Ensign Georgio Pampas."

Cardones exchanged silent nods with them. Damana was short and freckled, with brown eyes and the shade of carrot-colored hair that Cardones usually associated with cheerful, casual types. But if either of those characteristics was included in Damana's personality, he was hiding it well. Pampas seemed to have been extruded from much the same mold, except that he sported the olive skin and dark hair of a heritage stretching back to Old Earth Mediterranean stock.

"Across from you is Lieutenant Jessica Hauptman," Hemphill continued.

Cardones went through the nodding routine again. Hauptman was medium height and running a little to the plump side, with brown hair and eyes and a name that rang a bell as unpleasantly out of tune as Hemphill's. It hadn't been all that long ago that Klaus Hauptman, head of the huge Hauptman Cartel, had come charging personally out to Basilisk system for a raging confrontation with the then Commander Harrington over her war against smugglers operating out of the Basilisk Terminus. The details of that confrontation were still shrouded in secrecy, but normally reliable sources had it that Hauptman had had his head handed to him.

Still, there was no animosity in Hauptman's face that he could see. No real resemblance to Klaus, either, for that matter. If she was in fact related to him, it had to be something pretty distant.

"To her right," Hemphill concluded, "are Senior Chief Petty Officer Nathan Swofford and Petty Officer First Colleen Jackson."

Cardones wrenched his mind away from Hauptman's face and name and nodded to the others. Swofford had a heavyweight wrestler's build, with blond hair and a half smile that somehow never quite touched his gray eyes, while Jackson seemed to be entirely constructed of varying shades of black.

"Together," Hemphill said, settling back in her chair, "they constitute ONI Tech Team Four."

Cardones felt himself straighten up, his carefully constructed house of paranoia collapsing into embarrassed rubble. Whatever grudges or even vendettas Hemphill might carry against Captain Harrington, she was still an Admiral of the Red; and Admirals of the Red did *not* casually divert Naval Intelligence task groups for their own private purposes.

"I see," he said, the words sounding incredibly lame. "How can I be of assistance, Ma'am?"

Hemphill gestured to Sandler. "Over the past few months we've been hearing rumors of something new going on in Silesia," Sandler said, tapping the table's keypad. A hologram of the Silesian Confederacy appeared over the table, with the major systems marked. "Specifically, rumors that someone out there is using a new weapon or technique for taking down merchant ships. Up until a month ago the only hard data we had was the locations of the attacks."

Six flashing red dots appeared in the hologram, the intensity range indicating oldest to most recent. Off-hand, Cardones couldn't see anything significant in the pattern.

"It was only with this one—" a seventh dot appeared, brighter than the rest "—that we finally got something solid: another merchie in the system managed to get some sensor readings. They were too far away for anything really conclusive, but what they were able to get was highly suggestive."

"Of what?" Cardones asked.

Sandler pursed her lips. "We think someone out there's gotten hold of an advanced form of the grav lance."

"How advanced?" Cardones asked.

"Very," Sandler said bluntly. "Point one: it was able to take down the merchie's wedge."

Cardones felt himself sitting up a little straighter. The grav lance he and *Fearless* had been saddled with had been capable only of destroying an enemy's sidewalls, not the impeller wedge itself. Even granted that merchie impellers were weaker than those of a warship—

"And point two," Sandler added softly, "it took the wedge down from a million kilometers away."

Something with enough cold fingers for a dozen treecats began playing an arpeggio along Cardones's spine. The best grav lance the RMN possessed could hit an enemy from barely a tenth of that range, which was what made it such an unhelpful weapon in the first place. If this version was really able to take down impellers *and* could do it without needing to get into point-blank range first . . .

"I don't think you need the implications spelled out for you," Sandler went on. "We're still not entirely convinced that's what's going on out there; but if it is, we need to find out. And fast."

"Absolutely," Cardones agreed. "How can I help?"

"You're the only RMN tac officer who's ever used a grav lance in combat," Sandler said. "As such, Admiral Hemphill suggested you might be able to offer some useful insights as we go take a look at the most recent victim."

"Or what we suspect is the most recent victim," Hemphill added. "The *Lorelei*, seven and a half million tons, out of Gryphon."

"Yes, Ma'am," Cardones said, looking at Hemphill with an almost unwilling stirring of new respect. It must have taken a whole soup dish's worth of swallowed pride for her to have brought one of Captain Harrington's officers in on this. "I have to warn you, though, that I'm not very well versed in the grav lance's technical aspects," he cautioned.

"That part's already covered," Sandler said, gesturing to the end of the table. "Ensign Pampas, Chief Swofford, and PO First Jackson should have all the tech expertise we need. What we're looking for from *you* is the eye of experience."

"Yes, Ma'am," Cardones said, trying to suppress his quiet misgivings. Yes, he'd fired the grav lance in combat; but that hardly made him an expert on the damn thing. He just hoped Hemphill wasn't expecting more from him than he could deliver. "When will the orders be cut?"

"Already done," Hemphill said. "Captain Sandler has your copy; Captain Harrington's will be given to her after her conference with Admiral Trent. Your replacement will be ready to join *Fearless* at that same time."

Cardones felt his stomach tighten. "Replacement?"

"A temporary replacement only," Sandler assured him. "You're still officially assigned to *Fearless*."

"On the other hand, who knows?" Hemphill said.

"If you do well on this mission, ONI could decide they'd like you on staff full-time."

"I see," Cardones said. She meant it as a compliment, of course. Offhand, though, he could think of nothing he would like less than to be sitting in an Intelligence office somewhere trying to sift gold nuggets out of the effluvia of Peep propaganda 'faxes.

"Jack will fly you back to *Fearless* to pick up your kit," Sandler said. "We'll leave as soon as you get back. You can chew over the latest data and information once we're underway."

There must have been something in his face, because she smiled faintly. "No, we aren't taking *Basilisk* with us. We have our own ship, the *Shadow*. I think you'll like her."

"Captain Sandler will answer any other questions," Hemphill said, getting to her feet. "Needless to say, everything you've heard and seen here comes under the Official Secrets Act."

Her eyes locked like a pair of grasers on Cardones's face. "We're counting on you, Lieutenant," she said quietly. "Don't let us down."

Honor ran through to the end of the report and looked up at Admiral Trent, seated at the head of the bridge briefing room table. "I hope, Sir," she said carefully, "that this is some kind of serious misreading of either the data or the situation."

"So do I, Honor," Trent agreed heavily. "But even granting the extreme range the readings were taken at, and the low quality of the merchie sensors that took them, I don't see where there's much margin for error."

"And frankly, Captain, I don't see where there's *any* margin," the man seated across the table from Honor said, his voice a bit testy. "I know we all tend to think of the People's Republic as the only threat out there.

But they're not, and it's high time we started remembering to look in other directions."

Honor focused on him. Lieutenant Commander Stockton Wallace was probably a few years older than she was, with dark hair and eyes and a deep cleft in the center of his chin. He was also intense, verbally blunt, and, to her mind, a little quick to jump to conclusions.

But then, perhaps those were qualities Naval Intelligence appreciated in one of their officers.

"That's a little unfair, Commander," she said. "No one's forgotten the Andermani Empire, or their long-standing interest in swallowing up Silesia."

"Good," Wallace said. "Then I presume we also haven't forgotten that Manticore is all that stands in the way of that ambition?"

"No, we haven't," Honor said evenly. "But at the same time, starting a war of conquest by sneak-attacking Manticoran merchantmen seems a very non-Andy way of going about it."

She tapped the memo pad. "For that matter, we have no proof that this ship had anything to do with either of the attacks."

"Are you suggesting it just *happened* upon two dead merchantmen?" Wallace asked, his voice somehow managing to convey contempt without crossing the line into insubordination. Probably another talent ONI selected for. "*And* didn't bother to report it; *and* then turned and ran the minute he was spotted?"

Honor fought back a retort. Unfortunately, he had a point. In both instances the merchantmen who'd spotted the mysterious ship had hailed it, only to see it flee without making any response.

And when investigating ships had gone to the scenes, they'd found attacked and looted Manticoran merchantmen floating dead in space.

"Fine," she said instead. "Then let's talk about the identification itself. Even if this secondary emission spectrum *is* consistent with that of an Andy ship, there must be other possibilities."

Wallace pursed his lips. "With all due respect, Captain Harrington, you've had all of fifteen minutes to peruse the data," he reminded her. "My colleagues, on the other hand, have put quite a few hours into this analysis."

He jabbed a finger at the memo pad. "I assure you, this isn't just *consistent* with an Andermani emission spectrum. It *is* an Andermani emission spectrum."

And emission spectra can't be faked? With an effort, Honor swallowed the retort. Of course emission spectra could be faked. That was in essence what a warship's electronic warfare system did every time it made a superdreadnought look like a harmless little battleship.

But that kind of sleight of hand required a highly sophisticated selection of equipment. And especially when you considered the rest of the analysis . . .

"I'm simply concerned that perhaps we're being too clever," she said instead. "Or else perhaps not being clever enough."

"Meaning?" Wallace asked, an edge of challenge in his voice.

"It's the number of layers here that concern me," she explained. "We have the Silesian transponder on top—"

"Which is clearly a fake," Wallace cut in.

"Clearly," Honor agreed. Transponder signals, at least, were trivial to gimmick. Half the pirates and three-quarters of the privateers roaming Silesian space were probably running on faked transponder IDs. "But then underneath that we have a layer of emission spectra that *do* seem to fit with their Silesian merchie ID. It's only when you dig below *that* that you get to these Andy emissions."

"And your point is . . . ?"

"My point is who's to say that what we've got is two layers of camouflage and one real McCoy?" Honor said. "As opposed to, say, *three* layers of camouflage with something we still haven't spotted underneath everything else?"

Wallace took a careful breath. "I understand that you're not an expert in these technical matters, Captain," he said. "But my people *are*; and I can assure you that that is highly unlikely."

"Perhaps not an 'expert' by your standards, Commander," she said just a bit coolly. "I have, however, spent the odd hour or two playing with our own EW from a tac officer's perspective. And as a tac officer, I know that what I'm suggesting isn't exactly impossible, now is it?"

Wallace's lips puckered. "Nothing is *impossible*, Ma'am," he conceded grudgingly. "Especially not for *our* EW. But not everyone's capabilities are as good as ours, and we think it extremely unlikely in this instance."

"Regardless, it's a question that won't be resolved until we get a closer look at the ship itself," Trent put in. "And obviously, we need this nailed down as quickly as possible. Which is why, Honor, if you spot this emission spectrum, your new orders are to give complete priority to getting us that closer look."

He leveled a hard look at her. "*Complete* priority," he repeated.

Honor felt her breath catch in her throat. "Are you saying, Sir, that I'm to abandon my convoy in order to give chase?"

"If necessary, yes," Trent said. "I don't like it

any better than you do. But those are your orders."

He glanced at Wallace. "And to be perfectly honest, I agree with them," he added reluctantly. "If the Andies have decided to finally make their move on Silesia and are feeling us out by hitting our merchant-men, we need to know about it. Certainly before we allow relations between Manticore and Haven to deteriorate any further."

"That assumes we have some actual control over that deterioration," Honor murmured.

"True," Trent said. "But that's out of our hands. *This*—" he gestured to the memo pad "—is not."

"Yes, Sir," Honor said. She still wasn't completely convinced; but then, Trent hadn't invited her aboard for a debate on the subject. She was a Queen's officer, and once she'd been given her orders she was expected to carry them out. "I take it that the Andy connection is to be kept confidential?"

"Absolutely confidential," Trent confirmed with a nod. "As Commander Wallace pointed out, ONI had to do some serious digging in order to coax the Andy spectrum out from under the Silesian camouflage. We don't want word getting back to the Andies that we were able to do that."

"We can still identify the raider by his fake Silesian emission spectrum," Wallace added. "That's all the rest of the crew needs to know about for you to watch for him."

Unless he has a way of changing that, too. Still, as long as she knew about the underlying Andy spectrum, it should still work.

"Understood," Honor said. "I will need to bring my tac officer in on this, though. If we're going up against an Andy warship, he'll need to have some contingency plans prepared."

"No need," Wallace said, his lip twisting into something halfway between a smile and a grimace. "For the next few months, *I'm* your new tac officer."

Honor blinked. "What's happened to Rafe?"

"He's been temporarily detached for some other duty," Trent said, pulling out a data chip. "Something also connected with ONI, I gather, though they've been closed-mouth as usual about it."

"Really," Honor said, looking at Wallace. But if he knew anything, it wasn't showing in his face.

"I wouldn't worry about Commander Wallace," Trent went on, misinterpreting her look. "He's a perfectly adequate tac officer, as well as being thoroughly briefed on everything happening in Silesia at the moment." He held out the chip. "Here's your copy of the orders."

"Thank you," Honor said, resisting the impulse to point out that it would have been nice to have some advance warning. Apparently, this conversation—and the orders chip—was all the notice she was going to get. "Welcome aboard the *Fearless*, Commander. I trust you'll be ready to go by the time my convoy is assembled?"

"I'm ready to go now, Ma'am," Wallace said. "And allow me to say I'm looking forward to serving with you."

And to vindicating his belief that that was indeed an Andermani ship out there? Probably. "And I with you, Commander," she said softly. "If there's nothing more, Admiral . . . ?"

"That's all, Honor," Trent said, standing up and offering her his hand. "Good hunting to you."

Commodore Robert Dominick of the People's Navy gave a little grunt as he slid the data pad halfway across the polished conference table. "Satisfactory," he proclaimed. "Most satisfactory. Wouldn't you agree, Captain?"

"Yes, Sir," PN Captain Avery Vaccares said, reaching over and pulling the data pad the rest of the way across the table to himself.

"Yes, indeed," Dominick said, leaning back in his chair and folding his hands across his bulging belly. "Efficiently and professionally done. I think we can be extremely proud of our people, wouldn't you say?"

"Our people performed their duties quite efficiently, Sir," Vaccares said, choosing his words carefully. Yes, the men and women of the PNS *Vanguard* had indeed carried out their orders well.

But whether their actions had been *professional* . . . well, that was a different subject entirely. Certainly enemy commerce was a legitimate target in time of war; and certainly there had been enough provocation from the Star Kingdom of Manticore to try the patience of a saint.

But even if everyone for three hundred light-years in all directions could see the dark clouds gathering on the horizon, the bald-faced fact was that there was *not* a state of war between Haven and the Manties.

Which, in Vaccares's opinion, made what the *Vanguard* was doing nothing more or less than piracy.

Right down to the piratical tradition of dividing up of the loot.

"I presume your people will want first choice again?" Dominick asked, turning to the third man at the table.

The man they knew only as Charles waved a casual hand. "As a matter of fact, Commodore," he said in that soft, sincere voice that went so well with his genial smile, "I think that this time I'd like to donate our share to be distributed among the crew."

Dominick blinked. "The crew?"

"Certainly," Charles said. "As you so correctly

pointed out, they performed their duties well. It seems to me they should occasionally share in the rewards of their effort."

He turned the smile on Vaccares. "Wouldn't you agree, Captain?"

"The crew are servants of the People's Republic of Haven," Vaccares said, not returning the other's smile. "They do their duty, and they receive their pay accordingly. Personally, I feel that offering them a share of—" *the booty* "—the outcome of that duty is improper."

Dominick's face darkened; but Charles merely smiled some more. "Come now, Captain," he said soothingly. "This is really no different than the prize money traditionally due a crew for the capturing of an enemy ship."

Except that the Manties are not officially our enemies. "You asked for my opinion, and I gave it," Vaccares said, keeping his voice neutral. "But Commodore Dominick is in command here. Whatever he decides is what will be done."

"And I decide the crew deserves some reward," Dominick said gruffly, leaning over the table to snag the memo pad again and angling it so that he and Charles could both look at it. "Let's see . . ."

Vaccares leaned back in his chair, trying not to see his commander as one half of a pair of vultures discussing the best way to divide a particularly juicy sheep carcass.

And once again, as they had so often over the past few months, he found his eyes and thoughts drifting to Charles.

Charles. Medium height, medium build, light brown hair, dark brown eyes. Round expressive face, not handsome but not ugly either. As completely nondescript as it was possible for a human being to be.

Charles. He had no last name, or at least none he'd ever mentioned. He also had no age, no address, no family, and no planet of origin. His accent sounded distinctly Beowulfan, but that didn't help much. Vaccares had known too many people who could turn accents on and off like a set of light switches, and he wouldn't have bet a Dolist's savings account that Charles was letting his true voice show through.

Did the Octagon know anything more about the man? Vaccares fervently hoped so. Operating secretly in Silesian space this way, their necks were stretched out in six different directions. The last thing they needed was the chance that their new ally might suddenly cut the ground out from under them.

On the other hand, perhaps the Octagon didn't really care who Charles was or where he'd come from. Perhaps all it cared about was getting the PRH's hands firmly on the dazzling bit of technological magic he'd dangled under their noses: the magic weapon the *Vanguard* and her crew had been ordered out here to test.

And from all appearances, that magic weapon was performing exactly as advertised.

Which, for Vaccares, was precisely the crux of the problem.

Charles must have felt the unfriendly eyes on him. Maybe he felt the unfriendly thoughts, too, for all Vaccares knew. Whichever, he glanced up, gave the captain another smile, then returned his attention to the list of the goods *Vanguard*'s crew had looted from their latest Manty victim.

Vaccares rubbed gently at his chin, his eyes still on Charles. Yes, the weapon Charles called the Crippler worked, all right. Eight times in a row now it had completely knocked out its target's impeller drive, leaving it dead in space. And also as advertised, each time it had done so from a range of just over a million kilometers.

And the implications for those dark clouds on the horizon were profound. Classic military doctrine started from the most basic possible assumption: that a warship's impeller wedge was completely and totally impenetrable. Every ship design, every weapon, counter-weapon, and tactical approach—*everything* started from that point. And up to now it had been an assumption that had always been true.

Up to now.

Charles was a Solly, of course; that much Vaccares had long ago deduced. Only the Solarian League could possibly have the technological expertise to have created something like the Crippler. Only the Solarian League, too, would have the ability to keep something like this so dead a secret that no one had ever even heard a whisper of its existence.

So why was it now being offered to the People's Republic of Haven?

Vaccares knew all the standard answers, or what would be the standard answers if anyone else had been interested in discussing the issue. Haven's governmental public relations spin-masters had been successful in painting the Manties as the bad guys in all this. They'd used the "People" part of the PRN's name to turn the democratic instincts of the Solly man-in-the-street against the Manties; and they'd used the Manties' arrogance and control of the Wormhole Junction to alienate the Solly leadership, who weren't nearly so easily fooled by meaningless words.

But alienated or not, the official Solly stance was for strict neutrality, including a total arms and technology embargo against both Haven and Manticore. True, it leaked like every other embargo throughout the history of mankind, but the Solly leadership had proven themselves reasonably serious about clamping down on those they caught breaking the rules.

And the penalties for selling something with such an awesome potential for destroying the balance of power would be severe indeed.

So what exactly had Hereditary President Harris offered this man that could make those consequences worth risking? Untold wealth? Unbelievable power? A nice villa with a view and a different woman for every day of the month?

His eyes traced along Charles's slightly receding hairline. Given the effects of prolong, his age was as nondescript as everything else about the man. What were his desires? His ambitions? His appetites?

Vaccares didn't know. He just hoped like hell that someone farther up the chain of command did. *And* that they'd found some leash with which to hold the man firmly in check.

Because with this weapon, the defeat and subjugation of Manticore was absolutely guaranteed . . . unless, that is, Charles took Haven's money or power or women and then turned around and sold the Crippler to the Manties, too.

"All right, fine." Dominick straightened up and pushed the memo pad back toward Vaccares again. "Now. What's our next target, Captain?"

With an effort, Vaccares tucked his concerns carefully out of sight. Surely *someone* was keeping an eye on this man. "There are two possibilities on the list, Sir," he said. "If we have to choose one, I'd recommend the *Doppler's Dance*, which we could intercept on its way in to Telmach."

"*Doppler's Dance*," Dominick repeated, frowning. "That doesn't sound right."

"It isn't," Charles agreed, his forehead creasing at Vaccares. "The ship we want is called the *Harlequin*, with an intercept point at Tyler's Star."

"That's the one," Dominick nodded. "Sister ship to the *Jansci*. When is it due, again?"

Vaccares braced himself. "With all due respect, Commodore," he said carefully, "I believe that attacking the *Harlequin* would be unnecessarily pressing our luck. The more often we hit the Manties, the worse our odds become of being spotted and identified."

"Our odds are doing just fine, Captain," Charles soothed.

"Odds always look fine up to the point where they crumble on you," Vaccares pointed out. "In fact, to be blunt, Commodore, my recommendation would be to ignore the *Doppler's Dance*, too. I think we should head to the Walther System, get ourselves settled in, and wait for the *Jansci* to arrive."

"And, what, just let the *Harlequin* go?" Dominick asked, an edge of contempt creeping into his voice. "This is a strange time to be getting a case of the nerves, Captain."

"The *Jansci* is the real target, Sir," Vaccares continued doggedly. "The *Harlequin's* cargo won't be nearly as valuable as hers."

"We don't know that," Dominick disagreed tartly. "We *think* *Jansci* has the more valuable half; but all we really *know* is that together they make up the complete supply run."

"And what if they decide to reroute the *Jansci* because we've hit the *Harlequin*?" Vaccares pointed out. "If they shift *Jansci* to a different convoy, it won't come into Walther from the right direction. Either that, or they'll load it with so many escorts we won't be able to punch through even with the Crippler. Either way, the game will be finished."

"No." Charles was quietly certain. "There's no way for them to get word to *Jansci* in time to alter her course. And if they can't warn her, they can't shift any warships quickly enough, either."

He shrugged. "Besides, we've already hit a target in Walther. They'll believe their ships will be safe there."

"That's an assumption," Vaccares warned.

"But a valid one," Charles said in that same confident tone. "I know how military people think, Captain; and I'm certain that by now Manticoran Intelligence has a fairly good bead on our past activities. They'll surely have noted our meandering course across Silesian space, and they'll be expecting us to hit Brinkman or Silesia itself. Anywhere but Walther."

"Which is another point in favor of hitting the *Harlequin*," Dominick added. "An attack at Tyler's Star will help confirm that drift toward Silesia, putting Walther that much farther off their calculations."

"Only if they figure out it was us before the *Jansci* arrives," Vaccares said. But it was a losing argument, and he knew it. The commodore was so in love with this convoluted plan he and Charles had constructed that he would never believe the Manties wouldn't dance the proper steps to the tune Charles was piping for them.

But it was still his duty to try to inject some caution here. "Regardless, Sir, the fact remains that we'll be risking contact or possibly a direct confrontation for only questionable rewards."

"Wait a minute," Charles said, suddenly cautious. "Confrontation?"

"The Tyler's Star solar research station has been known to play host to Manty warships on occasion," Dominick told him. "Didn't I mention that?"

"No, you did not," Charles said darkly. "I trust you'll be positioning our attack well out of range of both the station and any guests it might have."

"Why?" Dominick demanded. "I thought you just said you were pleased with the crew's performance."

"I said they had performed their duties well," Charles corrected. "They're not ready to try the Crippler against a warship quite yet."

"And how much longer before this elusive bar is reached?" Dominick pressed, starting to sound angry. "First you said it would take five trials against merchies. Next it was seven. Now we've done eight, and you're still not satisfied."

"The ability of this crew to climb a learning curve is not under my control, Commodore," Charles said icily. "A warship's impellers are more complex than those of a merchantman, and that reduces the Crippler's effective range by anywhere from twenty to thirty percent."

Dominick drew himself up in his chair. "May I remind you that the primary goal of this mission is to confirm the effectiveness of this weapon you're so eager to sell us?"

"And may I remind *you* that President Harris put that decision in *my* hands?" Charles countered. "Besides, you *have* confirmed the Crippler's effectiveness. Eight times in a row, in fact."

He lifted a hand, palm toward the commodore. "You'll get your chance at a Manty warship," he said, all calm and quiet and soothing now. "But not until you're ready. I'm sure none of us wants to have the ship we're riding in blown out from under us."

Dominick took a deep breath. "No, of course not," he said, his voice still edged with impatience. "And I'll be the first to admit your plan has worked perfectly so far. But there were three prongs to this mission, and as yet I'm not sure we've achieved even one of them."

"I understand your frustration, Commodore," Charles said. "But when your goal is to take out two birds with one stone, the birds must come together at the right place and the right time. Patience is a necessary virtue."

He waved a hand. "And actually, Bird Number Two has almost certainly already fallen. The Manties will have penetrated our emission disguise by now and concluded an Andermani is running amok among their shipping. Once we've taken the *Jansci*, they'll be all primed to look the wrong direction for those responsible."

"I hope you're right," Dominick said with a sigh. "Looting Manty merchantmen can make for a satisfying afternoon's diversion, but it's hardly enough to return triumphantly to Haven with."

"Oh, you'll have your triumphant return, Commodore," Charles assured him, smiling tightly. "After all, it's not every day when a PRN officer brings home the weapon that will spell Manticore's death."

Dominick drew himself up again, this time with pride, and Vaccares mentally shook his head. Charles knew the buttons to push, all right. Knew them backwards and forwards, and could hit them with his eyes closed.

Who *was* this man, anyway?

"Captain, return to your bridge," Dominick said, his voice suddenly sonorous, as if he were speaking for posterity. "Set course for Tyler's Star."

Cardones had left the *Basilisk* with Admiral Hemphill's offhanded comment about him someday being snatched up by ONI still ringing in his ears, and with the private conviction that such an assignment was to be avoided like a Peep ship of the wall.

By the time Tech Team Four arrived in the Arendscheldt System, however, he wasn't nearly so sure about the latter.

The ship itself had been his first shock. From the

outside, the *Shadow* had looked just like any of the hundreds of other fast dispatch boats that darted through hyper-space carrying news and messages between the stars. Inside, though, it was another story entirely. Though designed for a crew of twelve, the ship was so crammed with sensors, esoteric surveillance gear, analysis workrooms, and fabrications shops that the seven of them were quite comfortably crowded. Half of the equipment was so new or so secret that he hadn't even heard of it, and better than half looked like it was fresh out of the box. The computer's tac systems alone, with the kind of sifting capability he would have given his right arm for back on the old *Fearless*, were enough to make his mouth water.

The team itself had been his second shock. The only Intelligence people he'd ever run into before had been the handful of officers who'd given lectures back on Saganami Island, and every one of them had come across as cold and drab. His first impression of this group, as they sat around the *Basilisk*'s briefing table, hadn't done anything to change that image.

But once aboard the *Shadow*—and, perhaps more importantly, out from under Hemphill's gaze—they had suddenly become human. Right from the start he'd been able to sense a close camaraderie between them, the kind of relationship that had existed among *Fearless*'s bridge crew once Captain Harrington had finally whipped them all into shape. On the surface, the relationship seemed to completely ignore rank, but after a few days of observation he realized that such considerations were indeed still there, forming an unseen foundation for everything else. As familiar and joking as Petty Officers Jackson and Swofford might get with Lieutenant Commander Damana, Cardones could sense an invisible line which neither of them would ever cross. And for his part, Damana scrupulously avoided invoking his own rank when kidding them back.

His third shock had been Captain Sandler.

His impression of her at the conference was that she was as cold and correct as her teammates, except that maybe she talked more than they did. But once again, those first impressions had been deceiving. Correct she undoubtedly was, and as the team's commander she made sure to keep herself aloof from the general verbal horseplay that went on among the others. But that didn't mean she was humorless, or that she hadn't connected solidly with the rest of her people.

And not only with her people, but also with this intruder who had been thrust into their close-knit company. Once they were underway, she personally gave Cardones a tour of the ship, reintroduced him to her team in their now more relaxed mode, and gave him full access to any of the analysis programs and equipment he might wish to use. She'd also sketched out for him the accomplishments of each member of her team, and in the process had subtly made sure to remind each of *them* of what Cardones and *Fearless* had pulled off at Basilisk Station. It was done so smoothly that only afterward did it occur to him that the history lesson had been carefully designed to slip him seamlessly into a place in the invisible shipboard hierarchy.

In retrospect, it was a lot like the way Captain Harrington had gone about turning a ship full of resentful, sullen misfits into an efficient, coordinated fighting force. And as the light-years disappeared behind them and he got to know her better, he realized there was a lot more about Captain Sandler that reminded him of Captain Harrington.

Her competence, for starters. Like Harrington, Sandler seemed to know everything about her ship. Not as well as the designated experts, perhaps, but well enough to keep up to speed on whatever the others were doing and to be able to offer informed suggestions. She was smart and quick-witted, too, able to pull together apparently unconnected bits of information in a way no one else had gotten around to seeing yet.

But most of all, he could see Captain Harrington's reflection in the way Sandler cared for her people. And as he'd seen once, that made all the difference when the excrement hit the fan.

Which, he realized as they eased alongside the darkened, silent hulk that had once been the Manticoran merchant ship *Lorelei*, might be happening very soon.

"All right," Sandler said as the boarding party finished the checks on their hardsuits. "Jack, you and Jessie keep a close eye on the sensors. If Rafe's analysis is right, they might have someone lying doggo out there waiting to take a crack at us."

Even through his nervousness, Cardones felt a trickle of pleasure at Sandler's mention of his name. It hadn't been his analysis alone—certainly Sandler and Damana had each had a hand in it—but it was typical of her to give her subordinates credit where it was deserved. And Cardones *was* the one who'd first noticed that the mysterious lad with the super grav lance seemed to be focusing on high-tech cargo shipments.

If that was true, and not just an illusion created by too small a statistical sample, a small ship loaded with top-of-the-line ONI gadgetry might be too good a target for them to pass up. Indeed, Damana had speculated that a ship like the *Shadow* might actually be the true prize the raiders were going for, and the destroyed merchies merely the bait.

But if Damana was worried about that possibility, it didn't show in his voice. "Don't worry, Skipper, we're on it," he called back from the command deck where he and Jessica Hauptman were standing watch. "We can have the wedge and sidewalls back up in nothing flat if we need to."

"Right." Sandler swept her gaze around the group. "All right, people. Let's go take a look."

She led the way through the hatch, handling her SUT thruster pack like it was something she'd been issued at birth. Pampas followed, with Swofford and Jackson moving up close behind him. Cardones, as the second senior officer of the party, brought up the rear.

It was an eerie passage. Every ship Cardones had ever seen before had been manned by *some*body, either its regular personnel or a refitting shipyard team or at least a skeleton crew. Some signs of activity, of a human presence, had always been present.

But the *Lorelei* had none of that. It was floating dead in space, alone and deserted, like a giant metal corpse.

Like a giant metal tomb.

He felt his flesh creeping beneath his suit. He'd seen dead bodies before, certainly, most recently those of his friends and shipmates aboard the *Fearless*. But there was something different about a military crew, somehow, with men and women who'd been trained for battle and had gone down fighting against an enemy of the Queen. The *Lorelei*'s crew, in contrast, had had neither the training or the weapons.

And if Hemphill and the ONI analysts were right, by the time their attackers arrived, they hadn't even had the protection of an impeller wedge. Or any way at all to escape.

"Like sitting ducks," someone murmured.

"Yes," Sandler said grimly.

Only then did Cardones realize that the first voice had been his.

✧   ✧   ✧

The carnage was as bad as he'd expected. To his mild surprise, though, his reaction turned out to be not nearly as bad as he'd feared.

For that, he knew, he had Sandler to thank. Instead of leaving him hanging, with nothing to do but stare at the floating bodies of the merchantman's crew and dwell on how they'd died, she had immediately ordered him to go with Pampas to examine the forward impeller nodes. At the same time, she'd sent Swofford and Jackson to the stern to look at the ones there.

Which, of course, left the grisly task of examining the dead solely to herself. Something else, Cardones thought as he and Pampas headed toward the bow, that Captain Harrington would have done.

The bow nodes looked just about the way impeller nodes always looked.

Pampas obviously saw the same thing. "No obvious damage," he reported as he drifted in front of the first node, fingering its surface like a phrenologist looking for bumps. "Guess we'll have to go deeper. Pop the tool kit, Rafe, and hand me a universal socket."

They stayed aboard the *Lorelei* for sixteen hours, approximately two hours past the point where Cardones's own brain began to fog over. Pride alone dictated that he hide his fatigue as he continued to assist Pampas, but apparently even ONI's supermen were subject to the same frailties as standard-issue mortals. As the last of those sixteen hours crawled past, the muffled curses at dropped tools or fumbled components grew steadily more frequent, until Sandler finally bowed to the inevitable and ordered everyone back to the *Shadow* for a hot meal and seven hours of sleep.

Seven hours and fifteen minutes later, they were back aboard the *Lorelei*.

And after twelve more hours aboard her, they had it all. Or at least as much they were going to get.

"There's not a lot I can tell you yet, Skipper," Pampas said tiredly as they gathered around the wardroom table with their steaming cups of coffee or tea or cocoa. "Not until we finish tapping into the rest of the diagnostic jacks and can build a complete system map. But the one thing that *is* clear is that all of them went down together."

"The forward and after groups both?" Damana asked.

"All of them," Pampas confirmed. "That alone tells us something new is going on here."

"Unless that's how a grav lance normally affects things," Jackson pointed out.

Sandler looked at Cardones. "Rafe?" she invited.

"It wasn't the way *our* grav lance behaved," Cardones said, shaking his head. "It didn't affect the Q-ship's impeller nodes at all, for one thing. And even in destroying their sidewall, it only took down the starboard side, the side nearest us."

"As far as you know," Hauptman put in pointedly. "Your sensors were pretty far gone by then, weren't they?"

"Yes, but they weren't so far gone that we couldn't get ranging readings as we pumped out our energy torpedoes," Cardones told her. "And the post-battle analysis of the destruction pattern clearly indicated that her port sidewall was still up when the torpedoes started ripping the guts out of her."

"Makes sense," Swofford murmured. "Just having that much metal between sidewall generators would make it hard for even a concentrated grav pulse to take out everything at once."

"Which makes this all the more ominous," Pampas said. "Something coming from the outside shouldn't be able to knock out every single node at the same time like it did."

"On the other hand, it's not like the nodes are running independently, either," Sandler pointed out. "In fact, aren't they pretty solidly interconnected, at least on a software and control level?"

"Right, but *only* on a software and control level," Pampas said. "You could bring down all the nodes at once by blowing the computer or frying the control lines, at least theoretically. But that's not what happened here. At least," he added, lifting his eyebrows questioningly at Swofford, "that's not what happened in the *forward* nodes."

"It's not what happened in the after ones, either," Swofford confirmed. "We took a good look at the control system before we started plugging into the diagnostics. None of the lines were fried."

"There is, of course, one other possibility," Cardones spoke up.

All eyes turned to him. "Yes?" Sandler prompted.

Silently, Cardones cursed the fatigue-driven fogginess that had made him open his mouth. It was such a ridiculous idea. . . . "It's a really slim possibility," he hedged. "I'm not sure it's even worth bringing up."

"Well, we won't know that until we hear it, will we?" Damana said reasonably. "Come on, we're too tired for Twenty Questions."

Cardones gave up. "I was just wondering if it was possible for the nodes to have been blown from the inside," he said hesitantly. "I mean, as . . . sabotage."

He had expected snorts of derision or at the very least a matching set of skyward-rolled eyeballs. But to his surprise—and relief—neither happened. "Interesting," Damana commented. "Seems to me there's one tiny problem with it, though."

"It would be tricky to pull off—" Cardones admitted.

"I wasn't referring to the technical difficulties," Damana cut him off gently. "I was thinking more about the fact that all the members of the crew have been accounted for out there."

Cardones grimaced. He'd felt vaguely like a fool even before bringing it up. Now, at least, he knew the specific parameters of that feeling. "Oh. Right."

"It was a good idea, though," Damana said encouragingly.

"And not one I'm ready to toss out with the bath water quite yet, actually," Sandler said, sounding thoughtful. "True, the number and gender of bodies match up with the official ship's manifest; but who's to say they didn't take on a passenger or extra hand somewhere along the way?"

"Wouldn't they have logged it if they had?" Jackson asked.

"They're supposed to," Hauptman said. "But if someone knew his way around a computer well enough to bring down the impeller, he'd certainly know how to edit a few log entries. *My* problem is why anyone would bother doing such a thing in the first place."

"Well, there's the cargo, for starters," Jackson said dryly. "Worth—what did we decide? Somewhere in the neighborhood of forty-three million?"

"Sure, but why cripple the ship?" Hauptman said. "If you're going to shut down the impeller, why not do it in such a way that you can bring it up again afterward? That way you can have the cargo *and* the ship."

"Unless it's a gigantic disinformation scheme," Sandler said. "We've already speculated that someone might have staged these attacks for the purpose of getting their hands on an ONI task ship."

"Which didn't happen," Damana pointed out.

"Yet," Pampas reminded him.

"If they haven't hit us by now, they're not coming," Damana insisted. "But if you're suggesting this is a variation of that scenario, Skipper, I can't see the point. What would they hope to gain?"

"Actually, the Captain may be on to something," Swofford said, rubbing meditatively at his lower lip. "Suppose we brought back a report saying that someone was able to do thus-and-so to a ship's impellers from a million klicks away. What do you suppose BuWeaps' response would be?"

"Ask for a bigger budget," Pampas murmured.

A slightly strained chuckle ran around the table. BuWeaps' appetite for money was legendary. "Right," Swofford said. "I meant *after* that."

"Well, obviously, they'd start a crash research project," Jackson said. "They'd first try to figure out what this theoretical weapon had done, then how to reproduce the effect, then how to devise a counter against it, and *then* how to build one for ourselves."

"All the while draining money and manpower from every other project in the pipeline," Damana said, nodding slowly. "It does make a certain amount of lopsided sense, doesn't it?"

"Especially when the whole thing drags on without anyone able to even figure out how the thing works," Sandler said. "A nice piece of distraction, especially with us in the process of gearing up for a war with the Peeps."

"I don't know," Pampas said, gazing down at the table. "Sounds too complicated for a Peep operation, and I can't see who else would bother. I'm still not convinced there really isn't something new out there."

"Neither am I," Sandler assured him. "But at this point it's worth brainstorming all possibilities."

"Well, in that case, you might as well throw this one into the hopper, too," Hauptman said. "It occurs to me that, along with creating a distraction for BuWeaps, this could also push the government into leaning even harder on the Sollies."

"Wait a minute," Jackson frowned. "Where'd the Sollies come into this?"

"No, she's right," Damana agreed. "I mean, where else could this superweapon have come from?"

"And pushing the Sollies any harder than we already have over the leaks in their embargo might goad them into getting their backs up," Hauptman said. "Maybe to the point of scrapping it altogether."

"Boy, *there's* a thought," Pampas muttered. "A Peep navy armed with Solly weapons."

"All the more reason to get this nailed down as quickly as possible," Sandler said. "Jack, did Arendscheldt Station send you a package while we were out?"

"Yes, Ma'am," Damana said. "I looked it over, and it looks like our next port of call will be Tyler's Star."

"Timing?"

"Seventeen days," Damana said. "A little tight, but we should be able to get there in time for the necessary preparations."

"Excuse me?" Cardones spoke up. "Is there something here I'm missing?"

"Sorry," Sandler apologized. "I forget sometimes that we've got uninitiated company aboard. We've now learned all we can—or at least we *will* have learned all we can once we get a full system map drawn up— from looking at the aftermath of an attack. What we'd really like next would be to actually witness the weapon in action so that we can get some real-time data on it."

"That would definitely be nice," Cardones agreed. "Are you telling me we have the raider's timetable?"

"In a sense, yes," Sandler said. "People tend to do

things in patterns, though they're sometimes not even aware of it. It turns out that the ONI unit in our Arendscheldt consulate has a little computer program that tracks patterns like this."

"With only seven data points?" Cardones asked, blinking with surprise. "That's one amazing program."

"We like it," Sandler said dryly. "At any rate, it says the best guess for the next target is Tyler's Star in seventeen days. So that's where we go."

"Mm," Cardones said, turning to Damana. This still sounded wrong, somehow, but he was hardly in a position to argue the point. "And the preparations you mentioned?"

Damana smiled. "You'll see," he said. "And as a tactical man, I think you're going to like it."

"The last merchie just came out of hyper-space," Lieutenant Joyce Metzinger reported from *Fearless's* com station. "Reconfiguring her wedge now."

"Group's forming up nicely," Lieutenant Commander Andreas Venizelos added, peering at his monitors. "Looks like we've got a clear run straight in to Zoraster."

"Good," Honor said, looking over the bank of monitors deployed around her command chair. The six ships were indeed shambling into their positions in the designated formation: five merchantmen, plus the heavy cruiser HMS *Fearless*.

Which was currently pretending very hard to be a sixth merchantman. Honor had ordered their impeller wedge set to low power, imitating that of a civilian ship, and they were running with the ID transponder of a Manticoran merchantman. To anyone out there with prying eyes, they should look like just another small herd of nervous sheep huddling together for mutual protection against the wolves prowling the starways.

The question now was whether or not there were any prying eyes out there. "Commander Wallace?" she called, swiveling toward the tac station.

"Nothing, Ma'am," Wallace reported, an edge of frustration lurking under the even tones of his voice. This was the third stop the convoy had made, and they had yet to see even an ordinary pirate, let alone their alleged Andermani raider.

Honor could understood Wallace's frustration, and could even sympathize with it. But if the fish weren't biting, the fish weren't biting, and there wasn't anything she could do about it. She swiveled back toward the helm display—

"We've got a wedge!" Wallace snapped suddenly. "Coming up from standby; bearing one-one-eight by oh-one-five."

"Confirmed," Venizelos said. "And he's definitely hauling—" he broke off, glancing at Wallace "—he's pulling some serious acceleration," he said instead. "I make it four hundred ten gees."

Four hundred gees, with the slowest member of their convoy able to pull barely two hundred. "I presume he's on an intercept course?" she asked.

"Yes, Ma'am," Lieutenant Commander Stephen DuMorne called from the astrogator's station. "Vector's firming up . . . okay. At present course and speed, he'll hit the edge of our missile envelope in seventeen minutes."

Honor studied the plot DuMorne had sent over to her astrogation screen. The bogy was coming in hard, all right. But given the relative positions and vectors, he still had time to break off without engaging if he got spooked.

They would just have to make sure that didn't happen. "Joyce, signal the other ships on whisker," she ordered. "Plan Alpha. Then sound battle stations."

"Yes, Ma'am," Metzinger said, and got busy at her board.

And now came the really crucial question. "Mr. Wallace?" she asked.

The other was hunched stiffly over his board, and Honor found herself holding her breath. If they really had found their Andy raider, first time out of the box . . .

But then Wallace straightened up, and even before he spoke she could tell from his body language that they'd come up empty. "According to the Silesian emission spectrum," he said, just slightly emphasizing the word *Silesian*, "it looks like we've got something on the order of a small destroyer."

"Convoy's breaking apart," Venizelos reported. "Alpha looks good."

Honor nodded. Plan Alpha had been carefully tailored to give any approaching pirates the one thing that invariably spurred them to greater effort: signs of panic among their victims. The faster merchantmen were starting to pull away from the group, pushing their impellers and inertial compensators to the limit as if trying to beat the pirate to his planned intercept point. Running for it, and to hell with the slower and more vulnerable members of the convoy.

It was, unfortunately, an all-too-common response, despite the fact that it was ultimately self-destructive. Not only did splitting up ruin any chance for a convoy to use their wedges for mutual protection, but it also strung the ships out into a space-going shish kabob, presenting the raider with a series of bite-sized morsels from which he could choose whichever looked the tastiest.

And as the convoy reacted exactly as the pirate expected, the pirate now unknowingly returned the favor. His vector shifted slightly to try to outrun the lead merchies, and he pulled out another fifteen gees of acceleration he'd been holding in reserve. He smelled fresh blood, all right, and he was charging full-bore in for the kill.

Unfortunately for him, the whole thing was a fraud. Some of the merchies were indeed pulling ahead in response to Honor's order, but it was a carefully plotted and controlled maneuver, one that would let them drop back into their original formation with only a few minutes' notice.

"Update," Venizelos called. "Bogy will now hit the edge of our envelope in twelve minutes. Point of no escape in fourteen."

"Chief Killian, ease us through the pack toward him," Honor ordered the helmsman. "Mr. Wallace, give me a targeting solution, but keep the active sensors off-line. All crews, stand by ECM and point defense, and be ready to bring the wedge to full strength."

A watchful silence descended on *Fearless*'s bridge. Honor listened to the quiet updates and watched as the red area on her tactical display shrank steadily toward nothingness. It was already nearly gone; and when it disappeared, so would any chance the pirate would have to evade contact. She checked her readiness status boards, feeling the usual slight pre-action quiver in her stomach and thankful she'd taken the precaution of putting Nimitz into his life-support pod in her quarters before they'd dropped out of hyper. With a pirate lurking this close to their exit point, she wouldn't have had time to run him down to her quarters by the time they'd spotted him.

Of course, James MacGuiness, her loyal steward, was perfectly capable of handling that job himself, and she could certainly have entrusted the 'cat to his care. But it was better all around that she'd been able to do it herself—

"Missile away!" Venizelos barked abruptly.

"Where?" Honor demanded, searching her displays. There it was, scorching away from the pirate.

"Well away forward," Venizelos said. "It's going to pass a hundred thousand kilometers in front of *Flagstad's* bow."

Honor felt her eyebrows lifting as she confirmed the missile's vector for herself. Most pirates didn't bother with anything as civilized as warning shots. "Are you getting anything from his ID transponder, Joyce?" she asked.

"Nothing useful," Metzinger said. "It reads out as the *Locksley*, with a Zoraster registry, but there's no ship of that name in our files." She paused for a moment, listening to her earbud. "He's calling on us to drop our wedges and prepare to be boarded," she added. "He claims to be with the Logan Freedom Fighters, and pledges we won't be harmed if we cooperate."

Venizelos snorted. "Cute. And, of course, your average merchie wouldn't know the Logan group doesn't operate in the Zoraster system."

"Actually, they may have just started," Wallace spoke up. "One of Logan's top lieutenants has been talking with the Zoraster Freemen about an alliance. They may have cut a deal."

"You're kidding," Venizelos said, frowning at him. "Where did you hear *that*?"

Wallace gave him a wry smile. "Try reading the ONI dispatches sometime," he said. "It's all in there."

Venizelos's mouth twitched. "I guess I'll have to start skimming them a little slower," he conceded. "I don't know, though. Boarding merchies sounds more like a pirate maneuver than something freedom fighters would do."

"Especially when their fight is supposed to be with

the Silesian Navy, not Manticoran merchantmen," Honor agreed. "Joyce, has he given any explanation for his demand?"

"Yes, Ma'am," Metzinger said, her voice suddenly grim. "He says they're looking for a shipment of shredder pulser darts. Apparently there's a special order on its way to the Ellyna Valley government."

"Yuck," Venizelos muttered under his breath.

"Agreed," Honor said with a disgusted feeling of her own. Pulser darts were lethal enough without adding in the shredding capability that could take out whole clusters of people with a single shot. All civilized nations, including the Star Kingdom, had banned them long ago. So, for that matter, had the Silesian Confederacy, at least on paper.

Unfortunately, there were still people out there who had no qualms about using them, which was why there were still people out there manufacturing the damned things.

"Tell them we don't have anything like that aboard any of our ships," she instructed Metzinger.

"Yes, Ma'am." Metzinger turned back to her board.

"I guess you can't blame them for not wanting to end up on the receiving end of shredders," Venizelos commented.

"Next question being whether they plan to destroy them if they find them, or simply load 'em in their own guns," DuMorne pointed out.

"They'll destroy them," Wallace told him. "The Logan group has consistently denounced the use of street-sweeper weapons, and there's never been a report of their own people using them. Any deal they made with the Freemen would have required that same restraint."

"So what exactly is our official stance toward these people?" Venizelos asked. "The usual hands-off thing, unless and until they threaten our shipping, at which point we can slap them down as hard as we want?"

"Basically," Honor said, turning back to Metzinger. "Joyce?"

"He apologizes, but says they have to check for themselves, Ma'am," the com officer reported. "He again promises we won't be harmed unless we do something foolish."

"He's certainly a polite sort of fellow," Venizelos commented. "So how hard *are* we going to slap him, Skipper?"

Honor studied her displays. The *Locksley* was well within the no-escape area now, and apparently still unaware that he was facing anything other than six helpless merchantmen. At this point, *Fearless* could basically do whatever she wanted to him.

And yet . . .

"Mr. Wallace, do you happen to know how well-supplied Logan's group is?" she asked.

"I don't know the numbers, Ma'am," Wallace said slowly. "A little better than the average Silesian rebel, probably, but not that much better."

"Can they afford to throw away missiles just for the fun of it?" she asked, though she was pretty sure she knew the answer.

"Not a chance," Wallace said firmly. "Not even the relatively piddling one he tossed across our vector."

Honor nodded, her mind made up. The *Locksley* had spent a valuable missile trying to get the convoy to stop without any further fighting. That meant he was either exactly who he said he was, with the more or less peaceful intentions he claimed to have, or else a pirate with the kind of chutzpah even a politician might envy.

"All right," she said. "Joyce, get a camera ready on me. Andy, when I cue you, bring up the wedge and sidewalls and paint him with the active sensors."

She settled herself in her chair and made sure her uniform tunic was straight. This should prove interesting. "He's hailing again, Ma'am," Metzinger said.

Honor nodded. "Put him through."

The screen before her cleared, and the face of a young man appeared, his cheeks tired and sunken, his eyes blazing with the fire of zealots and True Believers everywhere. "—one last time, Manticoran ships," he was saying. "If you don't drop your wedges—"

He broke off abruptly, his bright eyes goggling as he belatedly recognized her uniform. "This is Captain Harrington of Her Majesty's Ship *Fearless*," Honor said calmly into the stunned silence coming from the com. "I'm sorry; I didn't catch that?"

And with her final word she flicked a finger at Venizelos.

All around her, the bridge displays altered as *Fearless* suddenly surged to full combat readiness. The young man on the com display jerked like he'd been stung, his eyes darting to his own off-camera monitors, and Honor could hear the faint sounds of gasped consternation coming from the command deck around him.

"I've made my half of the introductions," she prompted. "Your turn."

With what appeared to be a supreme effort of will, the man pulled his gaze back to the com screen. "My name is Iliescu," he said, his cheeks looking more sunken than ever. "I—all right, Captain, you've got us. What now?"

"You've threatened my convoy, Mr. Iliescu," Honor reminded him coolly. "Verbally, as well as by putting a missile into space against us."

She watched his face as he opened his mouth, probably to protest that that had been a warning shot. But he subsided with the words unsaid. She knew that, and he knew that she knew it.

"All of which means that I would be within my legal rights to blow you to scrap," she continued. "Or do you see it differently?"

Iliescu took a deep breath. "I see that the use of shredder darts is an attack on all civilized human beings," he said. "I see that they're illegal, but that they're still being used by petty tyrants desperate to hold onto their power and their privileges. What would *you* do, Captain, if they were being used against *your* people?"

"We're not talking about me," Honor reminded him. "Do you have any evidence that there are Manticoran ships carrying these things?"

His lip twitched. "We don't know who's bringing them," he admitted. "All we know that they're supposed to be coming in soon, from a supplier on Creswell."

Honor nodded. Creswell had been the convoy's last port of call. So that was why Iliescu had been lying in wait in this particular spot. "So what are you planning to do? Stop every convoy coming from that direction until you find the shredders?"

Iliescu drew himself up. "If necessary," he said with stubborn dignity.

"All by yourself?"

"We have three other ships on loan from the Logan Freedom Fighters," he said. "We're running this in shifts."

"Who's your contact with Logan?"

The question seemed to take Iliescu off guard. "What?"

"I want the name of your contact," Honor repeated. "The one who negotiated the alliance with your Zoraster Freemen."

Iliescu's eyes were bulging again. "You're very well informed, Captain," he said. "I don't know if I should . . ."

"There's no deal possible unless you convince me, Mr. Iliescu," Honor warned quietly. "As far as I can tell from here, you could still just be another pirate with a gift for glib."

Iliescu swallowed hard. "His name is Bokusu. Simon Bokusu."

Honor glanced at Wallace, caught the other's fractional nod. "All right," she said, looking back at Iliescu. "Under the circumstances, I'm going to give you this one free pass. But from now on you leave Manticoran ships alone, or there *will* be trouble. Is that understood?"

"Understood," the other said. "What about the shredders?"

"None of the ships in my convoy are carrying them," Honor told him. "You have my word on that."

Iliescu hesitated, then nodded. "All right. Good-bye, Captain."

His image vanished as he broke contact. "Secure from battle stations," Honor ordered. "Signal the convoy to return to formation."

"Well, that was interesting," Venizelos commented. "Also pretty disgusting. What kind of a sick animal uses shredders anymore?"

"You heard the man," DuMorne said. "Petty tyrants desperate to hold onto power and privilege."

"And we have to look the other way," Metzinger murmured.

"Just one of the many fun things about duty in Silesia," Venizelos said. "Skipper, do you want to leave the wedge at full power?"

"We might as well, since the masquerade's blown anyway," Honor said. "And as long as the active sensors are on line again, let's give the area between us and the planet a good, hard look."

"Yes, Ma'am," Venizelos said. Honor turned back to

her tactical plot, watching the ships of her convoy shuffling back toward their original flight formation. The maneuvers were nowhere near military-precise, but not bad for merchantmen. Maybe there ought to be a course on this sort of thing at the Merchant Fleet Academy.

There was a beep from Venizelos's board. "Skipper, we've got another wedge coming up," he announced, frowning at his displays. "Off to port, about three million klicks out."

"Course is running skew across the ecliptic," DuMorne added. "Looks like she was just coasting through the outer system."

"We have an ID?" Honor asked.

"She's reading as an Andermani warship," Wallace said, his voice suddenly taut.

"Transponder identifies her as the IANS *Neue Bayern*," Metzinger confirmed.

"*Neue Bayern*," Venizelos repeated, punching keys on his console. "Battlecruiser, *Mendelssohn* class, massing just under nine hundred thousand tons. No sign of anyone else in her vicinity."

"Any idea what she's doing out here?" Honor asked, swiveling to look at Wallace. The other was working his board, his eyes intense but uncertain.

With good reason, she realized as she ran down the same logic track he was probably following. A lone Andermani ship, and one that had apparently been lying doggo as a pirate might, could very possibly be their raider.

Except that it wasn't fitting the rest of the ONI profile. A battlecruiser was too big, for one thing, and it wasn't running either the Silesian ID or the camouflaging surface emission spectrum.

On the other hand, considering the poor quality of the data on which it was based, the profile itself might not be all that accurate. Besides which, who was to say that the leopard might not occasionally trade in his spots for stripes?

"Well, if she's on escort duty, she seems to have misplaced her convoy, Ma'am," Venizelos observed. "And as for her vector . . . Stephen, what do you make of it?"

"We don't know what she was doing before we came in, of course," DuMorne pointed out. "But her current vector matches nicely with a straight-line course from Tyler's Star to Schiller. It almost looks like she's spent the past few days drifting her way across the system.

"Like someone hunting pirates?" Venizelos suggested.

Or perhaps something a little more personal? Honor caught Wallace's eye as he glanced up and lifted her eyebrows in silent question. He cocked an eyebrow of his own and gave a small shrug.

So at least they were agreed about their basic uncertainty. The *Neue Bayern* might well be out hunting a rogue Andy raider. On the other hand, she might be here to give that same raider tactical or logistical support.

"I hope she wasn't trying to sneak up on Iliescu's roadblock," Venizelos mused. "We pretty well ruined *that* one if she was."

"She'll get over it," Honor said, coming to a decision. Whatever this particular Andy was doing out here, she probably knew about the raider. Given that, it wouldn't hurt to let her know the Royal Navy was also in on the game. "Joyce, open a channel," she instructed. "Put it up when you get it."

"Yes, Ma'am." Metzinger keyed her board, and Honor silently began counting out the seconds. At the *Neue Bayern's* distance there was a twenty-second delay just for the signal's round trip, plus whatever time her captain took to decide whether or not he felt like talking to any Manticorans today.

The count was up to ninety-four seconds when the com screen came up, revealing a heavy-jowled man with close-cropped hair and full lips that seemed to be settled in a perpetual frown. "This is Captain Lanfeng Grubner of the IANS *Neue Bayern*," he said, his voice gruff and sounding like he wasn't at all happy about being disturbed. But maybe that was just his heavy German accent. "What do you want, *Fearless*?"

"This is Captain Harrington of the *Fearless*," Honor said, determined not to be intimidated by either Grubner's attitude or the fact that his ship outmassed and outgunned hers by a factor of three. "I wonder if I might impose on you for a brief conversation on a topic of mutual interest."

She waited as the twenty seconds ticked past. "And what topic might that be?" Grubner asked.

"I'd rather not discuss it on an open signal," Honor said. "If you could back off on some of your acceleration, I could bring a pinnace to within whisker laser range."

"Impossible," Grubner said flatly. "I'm on an important assignment for my Emperor. I have no time to exchange pleasantries with foreign naval officers."

"Not even if the conversation was related to your assignment?" Honor suggested.

Grubner smiled thinly, a neat trick with lips as thick as his were. "But we shall never know whether it was or not, shall we? Good day to you, Captain—"

Abruptly he broke off, his eyebrows drawing suddenly together. "Harrington," he said, his voice suddenly thoughtful. "Captain *Honor* Harrington?"

"Yes, Sir," Honor said.

The twenty-second delay seemed a lot longer this

time. "Well, well," Grubner said. "So *you* are the heroine of Basilisk Station."

"I wouldn't put it quite that way, Sir," Honor said, feeling her cheeks warming. She'd more or less resigned herself to the borderline awe she still got occasionally from her own people. But the same thing coming from a foreigner was a new and freshly embarrassing situation. "But yes, it *was* my ship and my people who pulled that off."

"Indeed," Grubner said, nodding slowly. "Well. This puts a different light on things. I would be pleased if you would join me aboard the *Neue Bayern* for the conversation you requested."

He smiled suddenly. "And, of course, I would like to show you proper Andermani hospitality, as well. Shall we say dinner this evening? Or whatever the next meal is your ship's clock is set for, of course."

Honor blinked, the sudden change in Grubner's attitude throwing her off-balance like a well-executed aikido move. "I'm very grateful for your offer, Captain," she managed. "But I don't wish to draw you off your schedule any longer than necessary."

He waved a hand negligently. "My schedule is not *that* rigid, Captain. And Imperial Naval orders always allow for unexpected events and opportunities."

Opportunities . . . "In that case, Captain, I would be honored to accept your invitation." Honor glanced at the ship's clock. "And dinner would be fine."

"Excellent, Captain," Grubner said. As near as Honor could tell, he sounded genuinely pleased. "Shall I send a pinnace for you, or would you prefer to bring your own? Mine is most likely faster," he added with a clear touch of pride, "and almost certainly more comfortable."

"Thank you, Captain," Honor said. "I appreciate the offer, but I'll come in my own. That way you'll be able to get under way again as soon as our meeting is finished."

"As you wish, Captain," Grubner said. "I will expect to see you at your convenience. *Neue Bayern* out."

The display blanked. Honor took a careful breath; and only as she glanced around did she notice that every eye on the bridge was pointed at her.

"What?" she asked, trying to sound casual. "Haven't you ever seen someone invited to dinner before?"

Venizelos found his voice first. "It must have been the German accent," he said, his voice studiously bland. "Though I've got to say, Skipper, that inviting you aboard wasn't what I expected him to do . . . until he caught your name."

"You seem to have picked up a new fan, all right, Ma'am," Metzinger agreed. "How many million does that make now?"

Honor shook her head. "I swear, when this is all over I'm going to change my name to Smith," she threatened. "I should have done it months ago."

"Oh, I don't know, Skipper," DuMorne offered. "Andermani food's really pretty good, they say. And some of their wines are excellent."

"I'll keep that in mind," Honor said dryly. "Joyce, call the boat bay and have my pinnace readied."

"Yes, Ma'am."

"You're not going alone, are you, Ma'am?" Wallace asked.

There was something in his tone that tickled the hairs unpleasantly on the back of Honor's neck. For the briefest second she wondered if he knew something about the Andermani she didn't. Something, perhaps, about hidden treachery beneath the surface courtesy?

But following a split second behind the reflexive xenophobic paranoia came the truth. It wasn't that

Wallace knew something she didn't. It was that there were things he *wanted* to know.

She swiveled her chair to look at him, and there was no mistaking the eagerness in his eyes. A Naval Intelligence officer, poised to get a first-hand look at an Andermani warship. A simple cajoling of his captain, he was probably thinking, and he would be on his way to an intelligence coup that might put his career on the express track.

And in fact, she could very probably accommodate him if she chose. Captain Grubner hadn't placed any stipulations on his invitation; if she showed up with a whole entourage tagging behind her, she doubted he would refuse them entry to his ship.

But at the same time, she knew that doing so would be a betrayal of his trust and the unspoken yet clear intent of his offer. *Especially* if that entourage included an ONI officer.

And given the steadily worsening situation with Haven, it didn't seem like a good idea for a Queen's officer to go out of her way to annoy an Andermani captain. Especially one who had already taken the initiative in extending his hospitality.

"I don't think I'll be in any danger over there," she told Wallace, deliberately misreading the true intent of his question. "Besides, all of you will be busy right here."

Wallace frowned. "Doing what, Ma'am?"

"Checking out our convoy," Honor told him. "I want you and Commander Venizelos to assemble some inspection teams to go across to each of the ships. Get Scotty Tremaine and Horace Harkness to help, Andy—they'll know the right people to pick for the teams."

"What kind of inspection?" Venizelos asked. "What are we looking for, Skipper?"

"Shredder darts, of course," Honor said grimly. "I

gave Iliescu my word that we weren't carrying them. Before we hit orbit, I want to know if I lied to him."

The *Shadow* had reached the hyper limit at the edge of the Tyler's Star system and had started its long trip inward by the time the three techs finally finished their analysis.

"Boiled down to the basics, what seems to have happened is that all the nodes went into simultaneous overload," Pampas said, gesturing to the exploded-view holo hovering over the wardroom table. "There were a whole series of blown junction points in each one, tracking right along the control lines."

"But the lines themselves weren't simply fried?" Sandler asked.

"No," Pampas said. "As I said, it looks more like an overload at these critical points."

"But an overload from where?" Damana asked. "There shouldn't be any way to get that much voltage in there. At least, not from the inside."

"Actually, we have come up with a couple of ideas," Pampas said. "They're both pretty shaky, but so far they're all we've got." He gestured across the table to Swofford. "Nathan?"

"The possible culprit is here," Swofford said, manipulating the controls. The exploded view vanished, replaced by a larger-scale technical schematic of a merchantman's power and control system. Another touch, and a pair of lines were highlighted at a point where they briefly paralleled each other. "We've got a control line running right up against one of the main power lines for about ten centimeters. If we somehow got a bleed-through of enough current, it could conceivably pop the junction points we found."

"Without burning the insulation?" Hauptman asked. "Or *was* it burned?"

"There weren't any scorch marks that we could find," Swofford admitted. "That's what makes it shaky. The other possibility is even shakier: something called Jonquil tunneling, where RF electric fields twist in such a way that you get quantum tunneling of electrons between the power and control lines."

"That would eliminate the intact-insulation problem," Pampas added. "Problem is, we can't come up with any way for the fields to twist that way without it showing up elsewhere in the power system."

"What about Rafe's scenario?" Damana asked. "The saboteur-in-our-midst thing?"

"Possible," Pampas said. "But even trickier to pull off than we first thought. In order to take down all the forward nodes simultaneously, our saboteur would have had to open up the system somewhere downstream of the control box but upstream of where the control lines branch off to the different nodes. There aren't a lot of places you can do that, and all of them are either in sight of the command crew or out in the open where anyone might happen by. That means he'd have to either distract an entire watch crew or else come up with a logical reason to be poking around access panels."

"And he'd have to do it for both the fore and aft nodes," Jackson put in. "The lines go off in different directions."

"Right," Pampas said. "Once into the wiring, he'd have to splice in a power boost with just enough juice to kill the junction points but not enough to affect anything else."

"And, of course, he would have had to sync both boosts to get the fore and aft nodes to go down together?" Sandler suggested.

"Right," Pampas said. "Then, after the boosters had done their job, he'd have to go in and take them out again."

"Though he would have had other cleanup to do at that point, anyway," Hauptman reminded them. "Erasing his presence from the logs, for starters."

"And of course, the rest of the crew would probably have been dead by then," Damana said.

"You said these were our choices if it was done from the inside," Sandler said. "What about from the outside?"

Pampas shrugged uncomfortably. "Then we're talking Admiral Hemphill's magic grav lance," he said. "Presumably if you boost a lance's power high enough, you could overload the impeller wedge in such a way that it would back-feed and blow out the junction points. But to pack that kind of power into a ship is beyond any theory I've ever heard of."

"Especially when you're going to do it from a million klicks out," Swofford added.

"Right," Pampas agreed. "Either of those two pieces represents an enormous technological leap. Put them together . . ." He shook his head.

For a moment there was silence.

"All right," Sandler said at last. "What I'm hearing is that our options run from the ridiculously unlikely to the completely impossible, and that we're at a stalemate until and unless we can see this thing work for ourselves. That about sum it up?"

"I'd say so, yes, Ma'am," Pampas said.

"So let's make that happen." Sandler touched her board, and the wiring diagram floating over the table was replaced by a schematic of the Tyler's Star system. "The problem with catching raiders in the act is that they've always got so much space to work with," she said. "Usually, of course, they like to sit right at the hyper limit and catch their prey as they leave hyperspace; but our raider seems to prefer attacking them somewhere in mid-system."

"Which he'd never get away with anywhere except Silesia," Jackson muttered.

"No argument," Sandler agreed. "Everywhere else the in-system sensor nets would be right on top of him if he tried this too close to inhabited areas. So let's see if we can use that confidence against him."

A slightly curved green line appeared, coming in from the hyper limit and running inward to end at Hadrian, the fourth planet out from the sun. "Here's the vector our bait will most likely be coming in from," she said. "You can see by the configuration of the planets that unless our raider is waiting right at the hyper limit, he won't have any decent chance to attack before they're in range of either in-system forces or someone's sensor cluster."

"What's that blue marker?" Cardones asked, pointing at a flashing light by one of the outer planets.

"An experimental ring-mining scheme," Sandler said. "A joint Silesian/Andermani venture, and as such under the protection of the IAN. The Andies usually don't have more than a destroyer and a few LACs on station at any given time, but that's enough to keep most raiders clear of the outer system."

"Including our boy?" Hauptman asked.

"We hope so," Sandler said. "Because we certainly can't cover the inner *and* outer systems at the same time."

"Even the inner system's a lot of territory for one ship," Cardones pointed out. "Or are we expecting help?"

"No, we're on our own," Sandler said. "But it's not quite as bad as it looks."

She touched keys, and the schematic shifted to a close-up view of the inner system. "Here's the incoming vector again," she said. "And *here's* the outgoing."

Another green line appeared, running off at about

a hundred forty degrees from the first. But instead of moving cleanly out toward the hyper limit, it split into three different paths a short distance out from the planet itself. "As you see, at this point our convoy suddenly loses its coherency," Sandler continued. "One of the merchantmen is slated to swing inward to a solar research station, two more are to head outward to a rendezvous with the fifth planet, Quarre, with the other four heading outsystem toward their next scheduled stop at Brinkman."

"I thought the whole purpose of a convoy was for the ships to stick together," Cardones said. "What are they splitting apart that way for?"

"Mainly because they haven't got much choice," Sandler said. "Three of the four ships in the latter group are carrying perishables, and they can't afford the extra time to divert either to the solar station or Quarre."

"So which group does the escort stay with?" Damana asked.

"Assuming there *is* an escort," Hauptman added.

"There is," Sandler assured her. "The heavy cruiser HMS *Iberiana*. The assumption is that no one's going to be interested in supplies being brought to a research station, so the plan is for the *Iberiana* to split the difference with the others. She'll run a course midway between them until the twosome reach Quarre orbit, then shift over, catch up with the main convoy, and take them out of the system."

"Pretty well coordinated plan," Cardones commented, frowning to himself. In point of fact, it was an amazingly well coordinated plan. Most convoys he'd ever known had been of the catch-as-catch-can variety, with merchies dribbling haphazardly into a system and the Navy then throwing them whatever escort they could scare up.

"Sometimes it works," Sandler said with a shrug. "Only when the merchantmen can stick with a real schedule, of course."

"So that's the two departing ships," Pampas said. "What happens with the others?"

"The two Quarre-bound ships—*Dorado* and *Nightingale*—will stay there for a few days, picking up cargo from the various asteroid mining operations and doing some maintenance," Sandler said. "At that point another convoy is scheduled to come through bound for Walther, and they'll link up with it. The *Harlequin*— that's the ship headed to the research station—will meanwhile join with a Silesian convoy going directly to Telmach."

"You seem to know a lot about their schedule," Cardones said.

Sandler smiled slightly. "Of course," she said. "We *are* ONI, you know."

"I meant all these specifics about the presumed attack," Cardones amplified. "From the way you were talking before, it sounded like all we knew was that there was a reasonable chance the raider would show up here looking for something to hit."

Damana shifted slightly in his seat, but Sandler's expression didn't even twitch. "That's all the predictor program *did* tell us," she agreed. "Only after we knew that could we pull up the shipping schedule and decide that this particular convoy was the likely target."

"Ah," Cardones said. He was still young, he knew, and still unsophisticated in the ways of the universe.

But he wasn't so young that he didn't know a flat-out lie when he heard it.

"At any rate, the point here is that the *Harlequin* is going to be the one off all alone," Sandler continued. "So that's the one I'm betting on."

"I presume we're not going to just follow it?" Swofford asked. "That would be just a bit obvious."

"Yes, it would," Sandler agreed. "And no, we're not."

The schematic shifted again, this time showing the merchantman's entire course from the convoy split to the research station tucked into its close solar orbit. "There's really only one stretch—granted, a big stretch—where the *Harlequin* will be out of sensor range of both the station and the *Iberiana*. We can cover about half the gap by putting the *Shadow* here."

A green blip appeared about three-quarters of the way from the split to the station "She'll be under full stealth, of course," she went on. "We'll then plug the rest of the gap right here."

Cardones frowned at the holo. There was something else already there, something that indicated a solid body and not a ship or base or anything else manmade. And the slender line marking its orbit . . . "What's that thing running the tight parabolic?" he asked.

"That, Lieutenant Cardones," Sandler said, a note of satisfaction in her voice, "is the comet officially designated Baltron-January 2479. Less officially, it's the Sun Skater Holiday Resort."

Cardones lifted his eyebrows. "It's the *what*?"

"You heard right," she assured him. "While the rest of the team takes the *Shadow* and goes into deep stealth—" she gave him a tight smile "—you and I are going to pay a visit to one of the most unusual resorts in the known galaxy."

Captain Grubner and another officer were waiting with the side party and a small Marine honor guard as Honor caught the bar and swung across from the free-fall of the tube into *Neue Bayern*'s gravity. She landed gracefully and felt Nimitz adjust his own balance on her shoulder with the ease of decades of practice.

"Welcome to *Neue Bayern*, Captain Harrington," Grubner said gravely.

"Thank you, Captain," Honor said, throwing him her best parade-ground salute. "Permission to come aboard, Sir?"

"Permission granted," Grubner said, answering her salute with one of equal snap.

"Thank you, Sir." Honor stepped across the line and walked to the group. "It's a great honor to be here, Captain Grubner. Once again, I thank you for your willingness to see me."

"It is my pleasure," Grubner said, gesturing to the man at his side. "My executive officer, Commander Huang Trondheim."

"Captain Harrington," Trondheim said, offering Honor his hand. He was a youngish man, younger than she would have expected to be XO of a battlecruiser. Either he was highly competent at his job, or—the cynical whisper brushed across her mind—he had good family or political connections.

"Commander Trondheim," she said, taking his hand and shaking it. "Pleased to meet you."

"The honor is mine, Captain Harrington."

Honor felt her forehead trying to frown. There was something in Trondheim's voice, she sensed, some underlying interest that wasn't making it to his face.

"Dinner will be ready shortly," Grubner said, gesturing to the exit. "In the meantime, perhaps we can retire to my day cabin to discuss this matter of mutual interest you mentioned."

They made small talk along the way, discussing the ins and outs of starship command in general and starship command in the Silesian Confederacy in particular. Occasionally, Grubner or Trondheim would point out some aspect of the ship as they passed, always something unclassified that Honor already knew from her classes on Andermani shipbuilding technology.

The third time it happened, she was tempted to add in a tidbit of knowledge that she knew but which the others hadn't mentioned. But she suppressed the urge. She wasn't here to show off, either her own knowledge or ONI's.

Grubner's day cabin was smaller than the captain's quarters would have been aboard a comparable Manticoran ship, but its efficient layout made it actually feel slightly larger. "Please; be seated," Grubner invited, gesturing to a semicircle of comfortable-looking chairs grouped around a low table on which a carafe and three glasses were waiting. "May I offer you some wine, Captain?"

"Thank you," Honor said, choosing one of the chairs and sitting down. The upholstery looked less sturdy than that in her own quarters aboard *Fearless*, so she settled Nimitz—and his claws—in her lap.

"I would like to first apologize for my earlier brusqueness," Grubner said as he and Trondheim settled themselves into chairs facing her, the executive officer taking charge of the carafe. "As I said, we're on an important mission for the Emperor, a mission which I confess is not going well, and I wasn't much in the mood for chatting with a Manticoran convoy escort."

"I understand, Sir," Honor said as Trondheim handed her a glass of the rich red wine.

"What changed my mind was your name," Grubner went on. "We in the Empire have examined the events of Basilisk Station with great interest."

He gestured to Trondheim as he accepted his own glass. "Commander Trondheim, in fact, has made quite a study of the strategy and tactics involved, both yours and those of the People's Republic. He has, I believe, published two papers on the subject?"

"Yes, Sir," Trondheim said, smiling almost shyly at Honor. "I'm currently working on a third."

"I'm impressed," Honor said, understanding now the reason for Trondheim's interest in her. "And also honored that you found our actions worth so much of your time and effort. I would very much like to read them, if they're not classified."

"I'm honored in turn, Captain," Trondheim said. "I'll give you copies before you leave." He glanced at his captain. "And I should perhaps advise you that I'd like to get at least one more paper out of the subject."

"So be forewarned that any questions from the commander during dinner will carry ulterior motives," Grubner said with a smile.

The smile faded. "But now to business. The floor, Captain Harrington, is yours."

Honor took a sip from her glass, studying Grubner's face as she did so. It was an excellent wine, one of her favorite Gryphon vintages, and its presence here in Grubner's day cabin was a clear and unapologetic statement that the two Andermani clearly knew more about her than she knew about them.

Such straightforwardness, she decided, deserved an equally straightforward response. "We have reason to believe, Sir," she said, "that an Andermani warship has been attacking Manticoran merchantmen in Silesia."

Accusing the IAN of complicity in piracy should have sparked outrage or icy denial. The complete lack of either reaction, from either man, spoke volumes. "Indeed," Grubner said calmly. "And what has brought you to this conclusion?"

"We have records of emission readings from two separate incidents that clearly indicate Andermani ship design," Honor said. "From the acceleration the ship pulled as it ran in on its victims, we deduce it must have been a warship."

Grubner pursed his lips. "But you have no actual visual confirmation of the attacker's identity?"

"No," Honor conceded. "But our people believe there can be no mistake."

"I see," Grubner said. "And what reason do you think the Empire might have to attack Manticoran shipping?"

"There are two theories," Honor told him. "One is that this is a rogue ship, running on some unauthorized and probably personal vendetta against us."

"And do these same theorists presume an entire ship's company can go insane together?" Trondheim asked pointedly.

"It wouldn't take more than a few of the top officers to create such a situation," Honor pointed out in turn. "Like those of Her Majesty's Navy, I expect the Empire's crews would obey orders, even if those orders didn't seem to make sense."

"You mentioned two theories," Grubner said. "What is the other one?"

Honor braced herself. "That this is in fact an official Andermani military operation," she said. "Top secret, but officially sanctioned."

"Certainly a much simpler theory," Trondheim said evenly. "All we need now is for a single man—the Emperor—to have lost his mind."

"It doesn't have to have anything to do with the Emperor," Honor hastened to point out, feeling a sheen of sweat beginning to collect beneath her collar. Being straightforward was one thing, but a dash or two of diplomacy might have been in order. "It could be a newly appointed Prime Minister or sector admiral who's decided to see how the Star Kingdom would react to such a threat."

"No such changes have occurred at the highest levels of our government," Trondheim countered. "And no sector admiral would dare presume such a unilateral change in policy on his or her own."

"Of course not," Honor said. "I merely mentioned it—"

"You mentioned it in order to gauge our reaction," Grubner said calmly. "But tell me, Captain. So far you've spoken of the theories of others. What do *you* think?"

"I think someone has found a way to fake Andermani ship emissions," she told him. "I think that same someone is trying very hard to play us off against each other."

Grubner's face seemed to harden, just slightly. "Really," he said, his voice carefully neutral.

"Yes," Honor said. *Straightforward*, she reminded herself. "Furthermore, I think that the fact that neither of you has reacted with surprise or outrage to my accusation means you already know all about this mystery ship."

Grubner lifted his eyebrows at Trondheim. "I told you she was quick," the executive officer said.

"Indeed," Grubner agreed, looking back at Honor. "Very well, Captain. You've been gracious enough to put your cards on the table. Let me do the same with ours. One of our light cruisers, the IANS *Alant*, has gone missing. The *Neue Bayern* has come to Silesia to look for her."

"Gone missing how?" Honor asked, frowning.

"Vanished while on patrol several months ago," Grubner said. "We assumed she had simply been destroyed, either accidentally or as the result of an attack."

He took another sip of his wine. "But then we began to hear reports of a raider which seemed on the surface to be Silesian, but which showed an Andermani emission spectrum underneath. Apparently, the *Alant* had been taken intact."

Honor sat up a little straighter. "Where did you hear these reports?" she asked.

Grubner smiled suddenly. "From Manticoran Intelligence, of course," he said. "Our information sources in the Star Kingdom are quite extensive."

Honor's throat went suddenly tight. "Then you knew all along what I was doing here?"

"We knew what your people were saying," Grubner corrected. "But as some of your people have reacted with caution to this situation, so have some of ours. This story of a rogue Andermani could have been a disinformation campaign by Manticore, designed to goad *us* into a confrontation."

He shrugged. "When you hailed me, I thought perhaps speaking with you face to face might help clear up some of those uncertainties."

Honor glanced at Trondheim, but his expression wasn't giving anything away either. "And has it?"

"To some degree, yes," Grubner said. "Of course, I'm like you: I can't believe Manticore would be so foolish as to provoke trouble between our nations, particularly at a time when war is brewing between you and the People's Republic. But regardless of what Manticore may or may not be doing, I am now convinced that you yourself are not a collaborator in any such secret conspiracy, or at least not an informed one. I am further convinced that you wish to bring this matter to a satisfactory conclusion, no matter where the chips may fall."

"The chips?" Honor asked carefully.

"Yes," Grubner said. "Because it *could* still be that this is a secret plan of your government's. A revelation like that would be highly embarrassing to your government. Are you willing to take that risk?"

Honor looked him squarely in the face. "Yes," she said.

"Good." Grubner's smile turned brittle. "Because despite Commander Trondheim's for-the-record indignation a moment ago, it could also be that the *Alant* has indeed gone rogue, in which case the embarrassment would be on *our* side. But either way, I believe it is in both of our interests that she be tracked down and dealt with as quickly as possible."

Honor felt her heartbeat speeding up. Was he actually offering to join in a cooperative venture here? "I agree, Sir," she said cautiously. "Are you suggesting . . . ?"

She hesitated, suddenly wondering if she should even ask the question. Though the Star Kingdom and Empire were officially at peace, there was a certain degree of coolness between their governments. A cooperative military venture, even one this localized, should properly require diplomats and ministers and a collection of Emperor's and Queen's officers far more senior than either she or Grubner. In fact, given all that, the question she'd been about to ask could even be taken as an implied insult of the Empire's chain of command—

"That we work together?" Grubner suggested into the hiatus. "Yes, that's exactly what I am suggesting."

Honor tried to keep her reaction out of her face. From Grubner's dryly amused expression, she obviously hadn't succeeded. "You seem shocked," he said.

"Yes, Sir, a little," Honor admitted. "Not that I'm unwilling," she hastened to add. "I'm just . . . surprised . . . that you would trust me that far."

"With anyone else, I'm not sure I would," Grubner admitted in turn. "I certainly have my fair share of distrust toward Manticore. *But.*"

He leveled a finger at her. "That distrust is based

on my suspicion of the Star Kingdom's motives regarding Silesia. The Confederation has a potential to create huge wealth for whichever of us wins out in the region. I'm sure you'll agree that love of money can quickly taint the purest motives."

"Indeed," Honor said. "At the same time, I'm not sure I would agree with your tacit assumption that I'm above such motives."

"Perhaps no human being is, entirely," Trondheim said. "But with you, we at least have evidence that such motivations are low on your list."

Honor frowned. "What evidence?"

"The fact that at Basilisk Station you refused to back down from your duty even in the face of pressure from Klaus Hauptman himself," Grubner said. "That speaks to me of an officer who is motivated by duty and what she perceives to be best for her nation and her service."

He regarded her thoughtfully. "I believe I can justify trusting such an officer. Certainly for a task of this sort."

"Thank you, Captain," Honor said, inclining her head to him as she ruminated briefly on the odd twists the universe could take. At the time she'd stood up to Hauptman she would have sworn nothing good could possibly come of it. "How do you propose we proceed?"

Grubner smiled as he leaned back in his chair. "No, no, Captain," he admonished gently. "This meeting was your idea; and somehow I doubt you came here without a plan already in mind. Please; enlighten us."

"Yes, Sir," Honor said, trying to organize her thoughts. She had indeed had some ideas swirling vaguely through her mind, but her main purpose in coming to the *Neue Bayern* had been to see if they could exchange information about the rogue ship. She hadn't in her wildest dreams expected Grubner to offer what boiled down to a temporary alliance between the Empire and the Star Kingdom, even such a private one. "Up to now, this raider seems to have been concentrating its attention on Manticoran shipping. It would seem reasonable, therefore, that if we're to catch him, I'm the one who needs to provide the bait."

"Reasonable," Grubner agreed. "And that trick you used of making yourself appear to be a civilian ship should certainly help lure him in."

"Still, Silesia is a large place," Trondheim pointed out, "with a considerable number of Manticoran convoys traveling its starlanes. How do you propose we attract his attention?"

"The best way would be to find a convoy that looks particularly appealing to him," Honor said. "I have a couple of ideas on how to do that."

She looked at Grubner. "But Commander Trondheim has a point. This may take some time; and in the meantime you won't be covering as much ground as you would if you searched on your own."

Grubner waved a hand. "We spent three weeks floating through Zoraster space with nothing to show for it before you arrived," he pointed out. "I doubt it will be any less efficient for us to shadow an actual convoy on its way."

"Though I trust you don't intend a literal shadowing," Trondheim cautioned. "I doubt we can crank back our impellers and emissions far enough to pass as a Manticoran merchantman."

"Certainly not long enough to entice an attacker into a no-escape situation," Grubner agreed, lifting an eyebrow at Honor. "Have you thoughts on that subject, Captain Harrington?"

"I agree that simply following us won't work," Honor said. "I do have another idea; but it'll require a certain amount of fancy maneuvering on your part."

Grubner smiled broadly. "A word of advice, Captain Harrington," he said. "Never issue a challenge like that to an IAN officer unless you are serious."

Setting his wineglass back on the table, he leaned forward expectantly. "Let's hear your plan."

Venizelos and Wallace were waiting for her when she swung out of the tube into *Fearless*'s boat bay. "Welcome back, Captain," Venizelos said, his casual voice unable to completely hide his relief that she was back safe and sound. "How was your dinner?"

"Excellent," she told him, studying Wallace out of the corner of her eye. From the slight tightness of his lips, she decided, he was still miffed at having been left behind. "Though I get the feeling they go out of their way to impress visiting non-Andermani just on general principles."

"And your meeting, Ma'am?" Wallace asked, with just a hint of that same tightness in his tone.

"Productive," Honor said. "Let's go to my quarters. We need to talk."

No one spoke again until they were in her cabin and seated around her desk. "All right," she said, reaching to her lap to stroke Nimitz. "First of all, we need to make some introductions here. Some *complete* introductions."

"Captain," Wallace warned, his tone reminding her that Admiral Trent had made it abundantly clear that his identity was to be kept a vacuum-black secret from everyone else in her crew, including Venizelos.

It wasn't something Honor needed reminding of. Unfortunately, given the current situation—

"Are you referring to Commander Wallace's affiliation with Naval Intelligence?" Venizelos asked calmly. "And no, she didn't tell me," he added as Wallace's eyes flashed. "She didn't need to."

"Terrific," Wallace growled. "How many of you know?"

Venizelos shrugged. "I haven't discussed it with anyone else, but probably only myself and maybe one or two others. Naturally, it won't go any further."

"Naturally," Wallace echoed ironically, in the tone of a man reluctantly accepting the inevitable. "If the introductions are now *complete* enough, Captain . . . ?"

Honor described her conversation with Grubner and Trondheim. "Interesting," Venizelos commented when she had finished. "You think they're serious?"

"They certainly seemed so," Honor said. "Besides which, I can't think of a good reason why they would lie to me that way."

"Unless this raider is in fact an official probe by the Emperor," Wallace said sourly. "In that case, having their denial on record would help if they had to pull the plug on the whole thing at some point."

"Except that I doubt a simple battlecruiser captain is high enough in the chain of command to be privy to any such high-level intrigues," Honor pointed out.

"But if he's simply been fed the official story—" Wallace broke off, nodding. "Oh. Right. If all he has is the official story, there's no reason for him to be setting up fall-back excuses."

"And certainly not with some Manticoran commander he happens to run across," Honor said. "Which brings me back to my opinion that we can trust him to do what he's promised."

"At least as long as it looks like sticking with us will gain him something," Venizelos said.

"Which gives us that much more incentive to smoke this raider out as quickly as possible," Honor said. "Which means finding the right kind of bait."

She turned to Wallace. "Over to you, Commander."

Wallace seemed taken aback. "Over to me how?" he

asked cautiously. "Are you saying you want *me* to find this bait?"

"You're the ONI man on the scene," Venizelos reminded him. "What do fake Andy ships eat for lunch?"

"I have no idea," Wallace said. "We only have two sightings, after all."

"Both of them alongside wrecked merchies," Honor reminded him. "Why don't we start with what the merchies were carrying."

Wallace's lips compressed briefly. "I don't know."

Honor and Venizelos exchanged glances. "I thought you were part of the team," Venizelos said.

"I was part of the team analyzing the attacker's ID and emission spectrum," Wallace said. "A different team was assigned to look over the merchantmen themselves."

"And, what, you don't talk to each other?"

Wallace's lip twitched. "Our report was instantly classified," he said. "That means no one below a field officer sees it without that field officer's authorization. If their report was classified too . . ." He shrugged. "At any rate, I haven't heard anything from that end of the investigation."

"That's just great," Venizelos muttered, shaking his head in disgust.

"That's SOP," Honor reminded him, sitting firmly on her own annoyance. "The system's there for a reason, so let's figure out how to work with it. Where's the nearest field office, Mr. Wallace? Posnan?"

"No, that one's been closed down," Wallace said. "The nearest actual station's now at Silesia."

Honor looked at Venizelos. "Any chance we can sneak over there while we're at Tyler's Star?"

Venizelos shook his head. "Not and stay with our schedule," he said. "Our next convoy should already be assembling when we get there with this one. We'll only have a couple of days; and after that we're off to Walther and Telmach, with no way to get back to Silesia."

Honor nodded; she'd pretty much come to the same conclusion. "Where's the closest base after Telmach?" she asked Wallace.

"Actually . . ." Wallace hesitated. "At the moment, Telmach should do just fine."

"I didn't know we had a base there," Venizelos said, frowning.

"We don't," Wallace said. "What we do have is the *Provisioner* about to set up shop."

Honor exchanged lifted eyebrows with Venizelos. The *Provisioner* was a depot ship, a sort of floating goody basket for Royal Navy ships working a long way from home. "I thought *Provisioner* was at the Gregor Terminus."

"It was," Wallace said. "She's being brought to Silesia as a sort of experiment. The hope is that if our escort ships can stay in the Confederacy longer without having to return to Manticore for supplies and replacement parts, we can guard our convoys more efficiently."

"Sounds reasonable," Venizelos said. "And you're saying there's an ONI field office aboard?"

"Not an office per se," Wallace said, "but there's an officer of command rank who should be receiving these reports on a timely basis."

" 'Should' being the operative word?"

"He *will* be receiving the reports," Wallace corrected himself tartly. "If you can wait until we reach there, we can hopefully get the merchantman data and start figuring out what sort of ship our raider likes to go after."

"Good enough," Honor said, keying for the bridge.

DuMorne's face appeared on her com screen. "Yes, Ma'am?"

"Is the *Neue Bayern* still within tight-beam transmission?"

DuMorne peered at something off-camera. "Yes, Ma'am, just barely."

"Good," Honor said. "Have Joyce get a lock while I record a message. And pull up our flight schedule for attachment."

"Yes, Ma'am."

Honor cut the circuit. "And after I do that," she told Venizelos and Wallace, "you two can bring me up to speed on the progress of our little impromptu cargo inspection."

"We're in position, Commodore," the *Vanguard's* helmsman reported. "Holding orbit true."

"Reduce impellers to standby," Dominick ordered. "Rig for full stealth."

"Yes, Sir."

The bridge crew started down the by-now familiar checklist; and from his unobtrusive seat beside the tac officer's station, Charles permitted himself a small smile.

It was a self-satisfied smile, though he was careful not to let any of that part show through. Dominick was hooked, all right; hooked like a prize bassine on a strand of thousand-kilo test line. And if the commodore was hooked, the People's Republic was hooked, too.

All he had to do now was reel them in. Reel them in, and hope that Dominick didn't accidentally bite on the bone before the deal was done.

The smile faded. No, Dominick wouldn't bite. Dominick was completely under his control, dazzled by his successes and by the booty pouring in from the Manticoran merchantmen he and his new toy had crushed beneath their heel. Dominick would follow

Charles straight into hell if Charles wanted him to. Even better, he would charge in fully convinced that the course setting had been his own idea.

Not that Charles had any intention of dragging him or the *Vanguard* anywhere near that sort of fire, of course. On the contrary, he had every intention of keeping this ship as safe as possible. And not only because his own precious skin was aboard. If they tumbled to the hook too quickly, that skin wouldn't be worth very much.

And therein lay the rub. Because if Commodore Dominick was safely under control, Captain Vaccares was another matter entirely. He was primed for that trip to the edge of hell, eager to give the Crippler the kind of baptism of fire that Charles couldn't afford for it to have.

Something would have to be done about that. Something that wouldn't rock the boat Charles had so carefully maneuvered along this potentially treacherous channel for the past few months.

"Charles?"

Charles turned his attention and his smile to Dominick. "Yes, Commodore?"

"If they're on schedule, we'll have another four days before the *Harlequin* arrives," Dominick said. "While we're waiting, I want to put the crew through some extra simulations."

"Excellent idea," Charles agreed. "How can I help?"

"I want you to supervise the Crippler crew," the commodore said. "We're going to practice going up against a Manty warship, and you're the only one who can tell us if the simulation is accurate enough."

"I'll do what I can," Charles promised smoothly, even as he felt his stomach muscles bunching up. So Dominick was smelling blood in the water now, too. Damn that Vaccares, anyway.

Still, it could be worse. If the attack on the *Harlequin* fell out as planned, this particular Manty escort should be too far away to be a problem. And if for some reason it was closer or faster than anticipated, he should still be able to get the *Vanguard* out before the Manty could move in on them.

And supervising the Crippler drills would be a perfect opportunity to lay the necessary groundwork for that kind of strategic withdrawal. "When do we begin?" he asked.

"Immediately," Dominick said, smiling wolfishly. "If you'll head down to the Crippler ops station, I'll sound battle stations."

"Certainly," Charles said, getting to his feet. Besides, he'd known going in that there was a fair chance this house of cards would eventually come tumbling down. That was why his own private yacht was snugged away in *Vanguard's* Number Four boat bay, and why he'd introduced that little bug into the battlecruiser's transponder and sensor systems so that the yacht wouldn't even be noticed if and when he had to leave.

And it was also why he'd made sure the up-front half of the price he'd negotiated with Hereditary President Harris for the Crippler would be enough to make him a respectable profit. If he never saw the half-on-approval money, he would survive.

He just hoped that if and when he had to vanish the *Vanguard* would be in a system where he had some contacts. His little sublight runabout wasn't going to take him anywhere else, and he would hate to still be stuck in some Silesian backwater trying to get home when the Havenites came looking for him.

He glanced at the main viewing screen as he crossed the bridge, noting the delicate sweep of a distant comet's tail slashing across the starscape behind it. Back

on Old Earth, he knew, comets had been considered
bad omens.

Groundless superstition, of course. He hoped.

Directly ahead, visible in all its glory on the cabin
viewscreen, the delicate sweep of Baltron-January
2479's tail arched its way across the starscape. Comets, Cardones remembered, had once been considered
bad omens.

Groundless superstition, of course. He hoped.

"Your attention, please," the pilot's voice came
over the lounge speakers, and the two dozen well-
dressed passengers scattered around paused in their
drinking or conversation to listen. "I'll put it on the
main display in a minute, but if you want to look
out the right side of the cabin at the comet's head,
you should be able to see the main building of the
Sun Skater Resort."

There was no mad rush for the viewports; people
with the kind of money these folks had, Cardones
reflected, made a point of not looking hurried.
Instead, they made a sort of concerted but leisurely
drift toward the starboard side, those with glasses still
sipping from them, most pretending it was no big deal
even as they jockeyed genteelly for the best viewing
positions.

Cardones glanced to his left, wondering if Captain
Sandler was as amused by it as he was. But if she was,
it didn't show in the bland, self-indulgent, wealthy-
beyond-all-belief expression she was wearing. It was
an expression designed to match those of the rest of
the passengers, just as the rest of her posture and
behavior let her mix seamlessly with them.

And, not surprisingly, she was doing it far better than
Cardones was. He looked back at the crowd by the
viewports and wished for the umpteenth time that he'd

been able to talk Sandler into picking one of the others for this role instead of him.

But she'd had all the logic on her side, not to mention the command authority to back it up. Even he had had to admit that the probability of the raider attacking the *Harlequin* within sight of anyone, even the dilettantes lounging around the Sun Skater, was really quite low. The *Shadow* was silently covering the more likely attack area, and Sandler had insisted the ship be fully crewed with pilot, copilot, and all three techs. Cardones and Sandler had thus been the only two people the spy ship could spare; and so it was Cardones and Sandler who were going to spend a couple of nights in Tyler's Star's premier resort.

In one of the four honeymoon cabins.

Cardones squirmed in his seat. Sandler had made it quietly clear that none of the standard honeymoon activities would be taking place between them, and that she'd booked the cabin solely for its distance and therefore privacy from the main resort complex. But that hadn't stopped Cardones from feeling excessively uncomfortable with the whole arrangement. Nor had it stopped the others, most notably Damana and Pampas, from ribbing him about it.

But all that was forgotten as the camera zoomed in on the resort and he got his first real look at the place.

Sun Skater had been the brainchild of some Solly developer who had noticed Baltron-January 2479 drifting in toward Tyler's Star and seen possibilities no one else had. The entire complex had been thrown up in a matter of months, built onto—and partially sunk into—the comet's five-kilometer-diameter head.

It must have seemed like a fool's fever dream back when the comet was nothing but a huge lump of ice and rock floating out beyond Hadrian's orbit. But now, with the comet in close enough for the solar wind to work its magic, the investment had paid off handsomely. Carefully positioned just past the comet head's mid-point, the resort was squarely in the flow of the ethe-real tail being gently boiled off the ice.

It was a vantage point virtually no one in the gal-axy had ever had before, and that alone would have guaranteed it at least a trickle of the rich and jaded. Adding in the highly ephemeral nature of the place—for the resort would most likely be abandoned once the comet had circled the sun and its magnificent tail faded away—and that trickle had become a steady stream.

"There's our place," Sandler murmured from his side, pointing to the left of the main building complex. "That little red-topped building off to the left. See it?"

Cardones patted her hand in what he hoped was a husbandly sort of way. "Yes, dear," he said.

Still, he had to admit that there was a certain kick in being able to call an attractive female superior officer *dear*. Especially when he'd actually been ordered to do so.

Honeymoon Suite Three was located a hundred meters from the main resort complex, accessible through a half-underground tunnel. Like the tunnel, the suite had been partially sunk into the rocky ice of the comet for stability; and like the rest of the com-plex, it had the comet's tail sweeping over it, drifting past its windows. It was a strange and curiously mag-netic sight, Cardones decided as he stopped their luggage cart just inside the main pressure door and peered out the kitchenette window. Rather like a horizontal snowfall, but without the howling windstorm that would be needed to create such a phenomenon on any normal planet. Here, instead, all was silence and calm.

He walked past the kitchenette and the bedroom door and stepped into the living room. There he paused again, his attention caught by the view out the back windows. Beyond the "rear" of the complex, the drifting ice crystals flowed together behind the comet head, coalescing into a tail that stretched out for millions of kilometers toward the brilliant starscape beyond.

"Nice view," Sandler commented.

Cardones jumped; he hadn't heard her come up beside him. "Sure is," he agreed, an odd lump in his throat. "I can see why people are paying these rates to come out here."

"Yes," Sandler said. "But Her Majesty isn't paying for us to gawk at the scenery. Let's get to work."

The spell vanished. "Right," Cardones said, turning away from the view and heading back to the luggage cart. "I just hope they were able to sneak in the sensor pod while we were catching the shuttle from Hadrian."

"We'll know as soon as we try firing up the remotes," Sandler said. "I think we'll set up here by the window. Get the receiver and display panel and bring them in."

Cardones picked up two of the suitcases and returned to the living room. She was in the process of rearranging the furniture, pulling the coffee table and a pair of end tables together in front of the couch that faced out toward the drifting tail. Opening one of his suitcases, Cardones pulled out a multi-channel short-range receiver array and carried it to the coffee table, trailing wires behind him.

It took them nearly two hours to set everything up, connect all the wires properly, and run the various self-checks. But after that, it took only a few minutes to confirm that the *Shadow* had indeed managed to place the sensor pod nearby.

"I'm surprised the tail isn't interfering with the

readings," Cardones commented, peering at the displays.

"Actually, there really isn't all that much substance to it," Sandler reminded him as she made a small adjustment to one of the settings. "It's only thin gas and ice crystals blown off by light pressure and solar wind. Mostly all it does is provide a little visual camouflage for the pod, which is what we wanted."

"Still, some of those crystals are ionized, and a lot of the rest are scattering photons and electrons all over the place," Cardones pointed out. "I'd have thought that would at least skew some of the more sensitive detectors."

Sandler shrugged. "They're very good instruments."

"Nothing but the best for ONI?"

"Something like that." Sandler stretched her arms back over her shoulders. "If the *Harlequin*'s on schedule, she should be hitting the edge of our sensor range anywhere from six hours to two days from now. Let's order some dinner from the kitchenette and then both grab a few hours' sleep."

They had their dinner and five hours of sleep, with Cardones on the large and comfortable bed while Sandler took the far less comfortable couch. Cardones had felt more than a little guilty about that, but Sandler had insisted. He had countered by insisting—with all due respect to a superior officer, of course—that he take the first watch after that.

He was two hours into that watch when the sensor pod made its first contact.

It was definitely a merchantman, looking alone and vulnerable as she lumbered along, and Cardones keyed a query pulse from the sensor pod to check the ID transponder. It was the *Harlequin*, all right, dead on the timetable Sandler had given him. For a civilian ship to hold so tightly to schedule was almost unheard of. Either Sandler was an incredibly lucky guesser, or else the *Harlequin*'s skipper was the most anal retentive in the merchant fleet. With a mental shake of his head, he began a systematic quartering of the sky for other impeller signatures. There shouldn't be any, he knew: the rest of the convoy would be well out of his detection range by now, and *Shadow* was supposed to be skulking along invisibly on full stealth well behind *Harlequin*'s current position, her own impellers shut down to standby.

And then, almost before he'd begun his search, another signature blazed into existence. A powerful signature, too strong to be that of a merchie or system patrol craft. Almost certainly a warship.

And it was burning along at four hundred gravities on an intercept course with the *Harlequin*.

"Captain?" he called toward the bedroom where Sandler had relocated when she began her watch. He keyed the computer for analysis, belatedly realizing he should have done that before waking her up. If this was nothing but an extra Manticoran escort laid on at the last minute, he was going to look pretty silly.

Too late. "What have we got?" Sandler said, fastening her tunic as she stepped into the living room.

"The *Harlequin* and a bogey," Cardones reported. "It's running a Silesian ID—"

He broke off as the analyzer beeped its results. "But the emission spectrum makes it a Peep warship," he finished. "From the impeller strength, probably a battlecruiser."

"Got to be our raider," Sandler said grimly, dropping onto the couch beside him and snagging one of the keyboards. "And a Peep, yet. Imagine my surprise."

"Look's like *Harlequin*'s come to the same conclusion," Cardones agreed as the merchie's vector and emission numbers suddenly changed. "She's making a run for it."

"Watch carefully, Rafe," Sandler said quietly. "Come on, Peep. Do your stuff . . ."

Abruptly, the bogey's impeller emissions began to fluctuate, bouncing wildly up and down and up again. Cardones opened his mouth to say something—

And without any other warning, the *Harlequin's* impellers suddenly died.

Cardones exhaled his intended warning in a huff of stunned air instead. "They did it," he murmured. "They really did it."

"They sure did," Sandler agreed, her voice somewhere midway between awed and horrified. "Damn and a half. They actually knocked out her wedge."

With an effort, Cardones shifted his eyes to one of the other displays. "And from nearly a million kilometers away."

Sandler muttered something under her breath. "I've been hoping we were wrong, Rafe," she said quietly. "Hoping we were misinterpreting the data, or that this was some elaborate disinformation scheme. But this—" She shook her head.

"Unless there's a saboteur aboard," Cardones suggested hesitantly. They still had that single thread to grasp at.

But Sandler shook her head. "No," she said firmly. "Not on that ship."

Cardones frowned sideways at her. There'd been something in her tone . . .

"Is there something else I should know about this?" he asked carefully.

Sandler's lips compressed into a tight line. "That's not just a regular merchantman out there, Rafe. She's a Royal Navy supply ship."

"Ah," Cardones said as the whole thing suddenly came together. No wonder Sandler had known where to wait for the *Harlequin*, and when to start watching for her. Regular merchantmen might not be able to hold to a schedule worth treecat-chewed celery, but RMN ships most certainly could. "Who are they supplying?"

"The research station, for one." She smiled tightly at his expression. "Oh, yes, it *is* a research station, and it *is* doing some studies of Tyler's Star. But we also have a presence aboard for some . . . other work."

The smile vanished. "But mostly, they were on their way to Telmach to resupply the *Provisioner*."

Cardones blinked. *Provisioner* was a depot ship, designed to be home away from home for far-flung RMN forces. What was she doing in Silesia?

And then the full import of it hit him. "They've got high-tech military equipment aboard," he breathed. "Sensor modules, ECM—even missiles?"

"No, no missiles," Sandler said. "And she shouldn't have much in the way of ECM, either. This one's mostly carrying non-classified stuff."

" 'This one'?"

"There's another ship on its way," Sandler said, the words coming out with the reluctance of pulled teeth. "The *Jansci*. She's due here in four days to join the *Dorado* and *Nightingale* at Quarre. They'll meet a new escort there and head to Telmach by way of Walther." Her lips compressed again. "*That's* the ship loaded with sensitive equipment."

Cardones gazed at the displays. No wonder she'd been so reluctant to talk about this back aboard the *Shadow*. "And yet they knew right where to hit it," he said. "*And* they knew which ship of the convoy they wanted."

"Not necessarily," Sandler said. But the words were

automatic, without any weight of conviction behind them. "It could have just been the luck of the draw."

The Peep warship had hit the midpoint of its vector and was starting its deceleration toward a zero-zero rendezvous with its helpless prey.

"Not a chance," Cardones declared. "They're getting information. They know exactly what they're doing."

He looked sharply at her as the last piece suddenly fell into place. "Just the way you do. This little hunch didn't fall out of some computer prediction program, did it? They knew what the *Harlequin* was carrying; and you *knew* that they knew it."

"Rafe—"

"There's a spy in the works somewhere," he cut her off. "ONI is feeding him all this information, letting him give it to the Peeps, all so we could get here ahead of time and be waiting for him."

"Get off the subject, Lieutenant," Sandler said, her voice soft but with a layer of warning laminated to it. "This is classified *way* over your head."

Cardones bit down hard against the retort trying to get out. "What about *Harlequin*'s crew?" he asked instead. "Or are they part of the bait, too?"

"They're already out," Sandler assured him. "They would have had a pinnace waiting, just in case."

She lifted her eyebrows. "But even if they hadn't, we would have done it this way," she added coldly. "The only thing that matters is getting a handle on this weapon of theirs and figuring out how to counter it. To do that we need to see it work; and to do *that* we had no choice but to let them go into harm's way."

The corner of her lip twitched. "And really, is that so different from what you do in the regular Navy? You go into battle fully prepared to sacrifice some of your own. Certainly you know that a number of your screening destroyers and cruisers will die in order to take some of the heat off your ships of the wall."

Cardones looked away from her, wanting to argue the point but no longer certain he could. They *did* go into battle knowing some were going to die, after all. Was that really any different from what Sandler and ONI were doing here? He looked back at the displays, searching the universe for answers.

There weren't any. But because he happened to be looking at the displays, he saw something neither he nor Sandler had yet noticed.

The raider had spouted a dozen assault boats, as both of them had known it would. But only eight of the boats were converging on the *Harlequin's* paralyzed hulk.

The other four were headed straight toward the Sun Skater Resort.

"You had better be right about this, Captain," Dominick warned the image on his com screen. "We know *Harlequin* got a distress signal off, and we have a very limited number of minutes before the system forces respond."

"I am," Vaccares said confidently. As if, Dominick thought sourly, the thought of a third fewer boats available to collect *Harlequin's* booty didn't even bother him. "It was definitely a transponder query pulse; and it definitely came from the direction of that comet."

Dominick grimaced. But if Vaccares was right, there was indeed no choice. One of the mission's standing orders was that no one was to get a good look at the Crippler in action—or, at least, not to get that look and survive to tell the story—until Charles decided they were ready to take on all comers, Manty warships included.

And speaking of the devil— "I agree with Captain Vaccares," Charles spoke up. "A hidden query pulse may be accompanied by an equally hidden sensor array. If it is, you need to get rid of it before it can transfer data to anyone."

Dominick felt his lip twist. Personally, he didn't give a rat's backside anymore whether or not the Manties got to see their new toy in action. A healthy dose of panic would be good for the overconfident little royalists, in fact. All he could see was the four fewer boats' worth of top-grade Manty technology going into *Vanguard*'s holds.

But the standing orders didn't care. "Fine," he growled. "Have them take a look. You sure you don't want to go along to supervise personally?"

"No, thank you, Commodore," Vaccares said, his voice grim. "If there's a Manty skulking by that comet, I want to be right here when he shows himself."

"No doubt about it," Sandler said tightly. "They're on their way. Must have spotted the pod."

"What do we do?" Cardones demanded, peering over the top of the displays at the window. Suddenly their spacious luxury suite was feeling downright claustrophobic.

As was the resort; and, for that matter, the whole damn comet. There were precious few places here to hide, and nowhere at all to run.

"First job is to get rid of the pod," Sandler said, crossing the room to an attaché case she'd earlier set unopened along the wall. "Maybe we can convince them that's all there is."

"Somehow, I doubt they'll be that gullible," Cardones said, watching in fascination as she settled the case on her lap and flipped it open. Inside was what looked like a miniature helm control board, complete with an attitude control stick and a set of compact display screens set into the lid.

"We'll see." Sandler flipped a pair of switches and the control board came to life, status lights starting to change from red to amber to green as the device ran its self-check. "Ever seen one of these before?"

"No," Cardones said. "I gather it's a remote control?"

"Best on the market," Sandler confirmed, settling her right hand into a grip on the stick and watching the last set of status lights with a patience Cardones could only envy. "Not that it's actually *on* the market, of course."

"Of course," Cardones said. "An ONI special, I presume?"

Sandler nodded. "We keep a couple aboard *Shadow* at all times," she said. "They're especially handy in that there's no hard-wiring needed. All you have to do is wrap the receiver pack around the control cables running between a ship's helm and auxiliary control and you're set."

"Really," Cardones said, looking at the case with new respect. "Even if someone else is trying to fly the ship at the time?"

"They're not quite *that* handy," Sandler said. "The induction signal's not nearly strong enough to override an actual control signal. At least," she added thoughtfully, "not yet. Maybe if you boosted the power enough you could even do that."

"All you'd have to do then would be find a way to smuggle a receiver pack and a spy aboard a Peep ship of the wall," Cardones said, trying to get into the spirit of the thing.

"You come up with the gadget and the technique and you'll retire rich," Sandler agreed. "Okay, here we go," she added as the last light turned green. "Cross your fingers."

She keyed the thrusters, and the relative-V numbers began to rise. Cardones shifted his gaze to the window, straining for a glimpse of the pod. It should be visible, he knew; the tail material wasn't all *that* dense.

There it was: a dark bubble in the tail, falling rapidly away from them. Sandler leaned the stick sideways, and the bubble moved left toward the edge of the tail—

And then, suddenly, the smooth stream of glowing gas was ripped apart as she kicked in the impellers. The pod darted away like a bat out of hell, turning straight into the sun and clawing for distance.

Two of the approaching boats responded immediately, breaking away from the others and charging off to the chase. "What are you going to do if they get close enough to grab it?" Cardones asked.

"They won't," Sandler said, concentrating on her controls. "I'll make sure to destroy it first."

"Okay," Cardones said slowly. "But won't that kind of ruin the illusion that there's a crew aboard?"

"They're not going to get hold of the pod intact," Sandler said tartly. "Other than that, I'm open to alternative suggestions. Here, make yourself useful."

She let go of the drive control long enough to dig a forceblade from her pocket and drop it into his lap. "Pull all the data chips from the recorders and put them in with the collection by the player over there."

"Right," Cardones said, standing up and slipping the forceblade into his own pocket.

"And then," Sandler added, "start cutting everything up."

Cardones froze in midstep. "You mean the recorders?"

"I mean everything." She glanced a thin smile up at him. "Yes, I know. Millions of dollars worth of equipment down the tubes." She nodded at the displays. "But two of those boats are still on the way, and I'm not expecting them to be satisfied with just looking in the windows. We're going to have company soon; and we'd better not have anything here the average honeymooning couple doesn't."

"Yes, Ma'am," Cardones said, looking around the room. "Only, once we've shredded it all, how do we get rid of the pieces?"

"You'll see," Sandler said, her attention back on her controls again. "Get to work."

Manticoran law required a forceblade to emit a horrible, tooth-twisting whine whenever its invisible blade was activated. Sandler's version, ONI issue no doubt, gave out only a soft buzz instead. Cardones had retrieved all the data chips and hidden them as instructed—they had come prelabeled, he noted, with music and vid titles—and he was in the process of slicing up the receiver when Sandler abruptly straightened. "Well, that's it," she announced grimly. "The pod is officially history. How's it coming?"

"Not very quickly," he admitted, glancing back toward the windows. The approaching assault boats were still too distant to be seen, of course, but even that illusory safety wouldn't last much longer. "I hope you're not planning to dump everything into the disposal."

"That's the first place a suspicious mind would think to look," Sandler said, crossing to the orange-rimmed emergency suit locker door and pulling it open. "Here."

Cardones looked up in time to catch the vac suit she'd tossed to him. "Throwing it all outside isn't going to be much better," he warned as he closed down the forceblade and started climbing into the suit. "Besides, won't we set off decompression alarms if we start cutting open windows?"

"Not if we're careful," Sandler said, already halfway into her own suit. "Suit up, and I'll show you a trick."

The vac suit was designed to accommodate a wide range of body sizes and types, and was therefore bulkier and looser than the skinsuits Cardones was used to. Still, emergency equipment was fairly standardized, and he had it on and sealed in ninety seconds flat. "Ready," he called as the status bar went to green.

"Right," Sandler said, her voice coming over his helmet speaker from her own helmet. She had pried the cover off the air-pressure sensor on the wall and was fiddling at it with a screwdriver. "Come over here."

Cardones stepped to her side. "See this little lever?" she asked, pointing with the screwdriver. "Hold it down. And *don't* let it up."

"Right." Gingerly, Cardones took the screwdriver and wedged the blade against the lever. "What does it do?"

"It tells the sensor that we're all breathing just fine in here," she said, stepping to the couch and retrieving the forceblade from where Cardones had left it. "It also keeps the ventilator system shut down, which means it won't try to add more air once we evacuate the suite."

"Handy lever," Cardones commented. "How come you know about these things? I thought you were a command officer, not a tech."

"You don't get to command a tech team without first having been a tech," Sandler said, crossing the room to the far corner, which sported a large potted plant on a low wrought-iron stand. Moving the plant and stand aside, she knelt down and set the business end of the forceblade against the wall. "Here goes."

She activated it; and suddenly Cardones felt a stirring of air around him. He shifted his attention to the window, wondering what would happen if someone aboard the approaching boats noticed the telltale plume of leaking air.

But of course they wouldn't, he realized suddenly.

Not with all the ice crystals and other gases already flowing past the suite. The perfect cover. "I think it's working," he said.

"Thank you for that update," Sandler said dryly. Shifting position, she eased the tip of the forceblade into the narrow gap between the wall and the thick carpet pressed up against it. A little cutting, a little probing with her gloved fingertips, and she was able to pry up a corner. "Okay," she muttered, getting to her feet and pulling on the loosened carpet until she'd exposed a square meter of flooring. "Now comes the tricky part."

"What's tricky about it?" Cardones asked, understanding the plan now. Instead of throwing the incriminating evidence out the window for everyone to see, she was instead going to bury it beneath their suite.

"The need to cut a hole in the floor without shorting out the grav plates down there," she said tartly. "Or don't you think they'd notice if they wandered into this corner and bounced off the ceiling?"

Cardones swallowed. "Oh. Right."

He watched in silence as Sandler carefully cut a rough circle in the floor, beveled so that it could be seated solidly in place once it was put back. Lifting it out, she set it aside and peered down into the opening. From his vantage point across the room, all Cardones could see was that there were pipes and cables laid out against a metal grid. "How's it look?" he asked.

"Tight, but doable," she said, kneeling down and starting to dig into the opening with the forceblade. "*And* there's nothing but open comet head underneath the support grid. Should work just fine."

A fresh cloud of white was beginning to boil out now as her slashing movements and the rapidly decreasing air pressure combined to sublimate the ice beneath the suite into vapor. "Provided we have enough time," Cardones warned.

"We should," Sandler said, stretching out on the floor as she dug deeper. "Keep an eye toward the main complex—that's where the boats will probably land. And no talking from now on. I've cranked down the gain on these radios, but we don't want them accidentally stumbling over our frequency when they get closer."

Nodding inside his helmet, Cardones shifted his attention to the view out the side window.

The minutes crawled past. The breeze in the room faded away as the last of the air vanished out into the passing mists. Faint white clouds continued to drift up out of Sandler's pit as she dug, until finally she straightened, gave him a thumbs-up, and crossed to the table and their equipment.

And as she did so, across the frozen landscape, the two assault boats touched down beside the main complex.

Cardones opened his mouth to speak, remembered in time, and waved his free arm instead. Sandler looked up, and he pointed out the window. She took a moment to glance that direction, nodded to him, and got back to work.

For the next few minutes Cardones alternated his attention between her and the window, the frustration of his situation welling up in his throat like excess stomach acid. At least aboard *Fearless* he had work to do, duties that could theoretically make a difference. Here, there was nothing for him to do but stand around and watch Sandler work.

That, and maybe think.

Okay, he thought, trying to clear his mind. The boats carried no markings that he could see—big surprise there—but they looked to be fairly standard Peep issue.

A maximum of thirty troops, fifteen if they were paranoid enough to put them in full armor, and they would probably go through the whole of the main complex before they tackled the outlying buildings.

That still didn't give them a tremendous amount of time, but Sandler was a lot faster at this kind of demolition work than he had been. She carried each piece of expensive hardware in turn to the hole she'd dug, slicing it up and dropping the pieces down the pit as if she'd done this sort of thing a hundred times before.

Maybe she had. The kind of budget ONI was rumored to have probably wouldn't even have winced at having the odd million dollars' worth of equipment turned into metallic cole slaw.

Finally, it was done. The last piece of the last console disappeared down the rabbit hole, and Sandler laid aside the forceblade and began setting the section of flooring back into place. She got it down and rolled the carpet back over it, tamping down the edges with her fingertips until it looked more or less the way it had before. An emergency patch from one of her suit pockets took care of the hole in the wall; and then she was at his side, taking the screwdriver from him at last and fiddling again with the sensor. He felt air begin to flow around him, and tensed for the scream of the low-pressure warning.

But again Sandler had done her job right, and there was no fuss or bother as the suite began to repressurize. Catching his eye, she nodded back toward the patched hole in the wall. He nodded understanding and crossed to the potted plant that had been sitting in that corner. Sitting around in vacuum that way couldn't have done it any good, but at least it shouldn't show any obvious signs of damage until after the raiders were long gone.

He got the stand back into place with the pot neatly hiding the patch, and stepped back to examine his handiwork. Like the carpet, the wall wouldn't hold up to a determined search, but people looking for a full data retrieval setup probably wouldn't be interested in tearing the room apart.

His suit indicator was showing adequate pressure now. Taking his first relaxed breath since those boats had started their direction, he reached up and twisted the helmet seal. It came loose with a gentle pop, and he glanced around the room as he pulled it off—

And froze.

Sandler had eliminated all the electronics, all right. *But she'd forgotten the empty suitcases.*

Sandler had popped her own helmet and was starting to unseal her suit. "Captain!" he bit out. "The suitcases!"

She looked around at the damning evidence, her throat going visibly tight as she realized—too late— how suspicious those empty cases would look to even the most casual searcher. And she knew better than Cardones that neither the wall nor the floor would stand up to any real examination.

And then, even as the first rumblings of panic started to surge up Cardones's throat, he had the answer. Maybe. "I've got an idea," he said, stripping off the rest of his suit and tossing it and the helmet to Sandler. "Here—put these away."

They had barely three minutes to work before the suite's pressure door abruptly slid open to reveal a nervous-looking woman and two hulking, combat-suited men.

But three minutes was enough.

"Please excuse the interruption, Mr. and Mrs. Kaplan," the woman said, her voice quavering only slightly as the two troopers bulled their way into the suite, their momentum carrying her in ahead of them. She was wearing the burgundy-trimmed gray suit of the hotel management and seemed to be sweating profusely. "These . . . gentlemen . . . would like permission to search your suite."

"What?" Cardones demanded, letting his genuine tension add a matching quaver to his own voice. "What do you mean? What do you want?"

The performance was mostly wasted; one of the troopers had already disappeared into the bedroom, and the other had turned his head to study the kitchenette area. "I'm sorry," the woman said. "They arrived a few minutes ago and—"

"What's all that?" the second trooper demanded, his voice coming out hollow and slightly distorted from his suit speaker.

"What's what?" Cardones asked quickly.

"Those." The trooper strode past the manager straight toward Cardones. Cardones hurriedly backed up at his approach; and then the trooper planted himself in the middle of the room and swept a gloved finger over the half dozen cases scattered around. "That's a hell of a lot of suitcases," he amplified, his voice darkening with suspicion. "Way too many for two people on a four-day trip."

Cardones worked his mouth and throat. "Uh . . . well . . ."

"Open them," the trooper said flatly. "All of them."

Cardones threw a helpless look at Sandler, whose eyes were wide with guilty panic. She really *was* a good actress, he decided. "It's just that—"

"*Open them!*"

Cardones jumped. "Yes, Sir," he mumbled. Kneeling down, he popped the catches of the nearest suitcase and lifted the lid.

The manager inhaled sharply. "Are those—?"

"We were going to put them back," Sandler insisted, her voice coming out in a rush, all scared and miserable. "Really we were."

"We just wanted to see . . ." Cardones let his voice trail off.

"How they looked in your luggage?" the manager suggested coldly.

Shamefaced, Cardones dropped his eyes to the open suitcase. To the open suitcase; and the towels, wine glasses, and plates he'd packed inside, all of them proudly bearing the Sun Skater emblem. "They were just . . ." he mumbled. "I mean, it's so expensive here . . ."

Again, his voice trailed off. The trooper made a little snort of contempt and turned as his partner emerged from the bedroom. "Come on," he said. "Nothing here but a couple of small-timers."

They lumbered toward the door. The manager gave Cardones a look that promised this wasn't over, then turned and hurried to catch up with them.

The pressure door slid shut behind them, and Sandler exhaled in carefully controlled relief. "Congratulations, Commander, and brilliantly done," she said. "I didn't think we were going to pull that one off."

"Neither did I," Cardones said honestly. "But I guess when you go around robbing merchies, petty thieves are sort of kindred spirits."

"Or else they just found the whole thing amusing," Sandler said, retrieving an armful of linens from the suitcase and heading back toward the bedroom. "Still, definitely worth a commendation for quick thinking."

Cardones smiled tightly as he lifted out a set of wine glasses. "Which of course no one will ever see?"

"Probably not," she conceded from the bedroom. "Sorry."

"That's okay," Cardones said. "It's the thought that counts."

Half an hour later, the assault boats lifted away from the comet and disappeared back into space. An hour after that, Sandler and Cardones were closeted with the manager, who no longer had any capacity left for new surprises, but simply and numbly accepted the money Sandler gave her to pay for the damage to their suite.

Six hours after that, they were back aboard the *Shadow*.

"Well, there's good news, and there's bad news," Ensign Pampas grunted as he slid into a chair across from Sandler, Hauptman, Damana, and Cardones and spread a handful of data chips onto the wardroom table in front of him. "First bit of good news: this weapon of theirs really does exist."

"That's part of the *good* news?" Hauptman asked.

"It means we're not going to look stupid as the Intelligence service that fell for someone's disinformation game," Pampas said dryly. "The *bad* news is that I can't see any way of stopping this thing."

"Explain," Sandler said.

Pampas ran his fingers tiredly through his hair. He and the other two techs had been sifting through the Sun Skater data for the past twenty hours, and the skin of his face was sagging noticeably. Swofford and Jackson, in fact, had already been ordered to bed, and Pampas himself was only going to be up long enough to give his preliminary report. "Near as I can explain it, it's like a kind of heterodyning effect between the two impeller wedges," he said. "A rapid frequency shift that creates an instability surge in the victim's wedge."

"From a million klicks out?" Damana asked. "That's one hell of a stretch."

"This isn't like a grav lance," Pampas said, shaking his head. "That *does* actually push the wedge out far enough to knock out a sidewall. What this thing does is more subtle. It runs the attacker's wedge frequency up and down, alternating between a pair of wildly different frequencies, setting up a sort of rolling resonance. Even at a million klicks out, there's enough of an effect to throw an instability into the victim's own wedge, which manifests itself as a transient feedback through the stress bands back into the nodes. The current goes roaring through a handful of critical junction points—" He lifted a hand and dropped it back onto the table. "And as we saw, poof."

A hard-edged silence settled momentarily onto the table. "Poof," Sandler repeated. "Is it focused, or does it affect the entire spherical region around it?"

"With only the one target in this particular attack, it's hard to tell," Pampas said. "But I'd guess it's focused. There may be a spherical effect at a much closer range, but the million-klick shot has got to be aimed."

"Well, that's something, anyway," Damana said. "If we can keep to missile-duel range, we should be able to stay out of its way."

"Unless they set the things up in stealthed probes," Hauptman said darkly. "Or even in a mine field."

"That's the other thing," Pampas said, his lips puckering slightly. "If we're right about how this thing operates, it won't work against a warship."

Damana and Sandler exchanged startled glances. "You mean one of *our* warships?" Sandler asked.

"I mean *any* warship," Pampas said.

Damana was staring at Pampas as if waiting for the punchline. "You've lost me. Why not?"

"Because warships generate two *different* sets of stress bands, remember?" Pampas said patiently.

"Thank you for that lesson in the obvious," Damana

said tartly. A bit *too* tartly, in Cardones's opinion; but then, Damana was tired, too. Certainly everyone here knew perfectly well that every warship generated two separate stress bands. The outer one was what kept an opponent's sensors from getting an accurate read on the inner one, because—in theory, at least—someone with an accurate read on the strength of a wedge could slip an energy weapon or sensor probe straight through. Preventing that from happening was one reason warships' impeller nodes were so powerful for their size. "So why can't it just take them down one at a time?"

"Because there's no specific frequency for a resonance to latch onto," Pampas explained. "The two wedges act like weakly coupled springs, with their frequencies in effect flowing back and forth into each other. Same reason it's impossible to scan through someone else's wedge. *We*—I mean the guys inside—know how the wedges flow into each other, because we've got the nodes and the equipment running them. But there's no way to figure it out from the outside."

"If you're right, that would explain why we haven't seen this thing used in combat before," Hauptman commented.

"Maybe," Sandler said. "But that doesn't make it any less of a threat to merchantmen and other civilian craft. You sure there's no way to block it, Georgio?"

Pampas held out his hands, palms upward. "Give us a break, Skipper," he protested. "We're not even sure we've got the exact method figured out right yet. All I said was that if we *are* right, the effect can't be blocked. It's like gravity in general, working through the fabric of the space-time continuum. I don't know any way to build a barrier to space itself."

"Well, then, how about trying to stop the effect?" Cardones asked hesitantly.

"How?" Pampas asked, his tone one of strained patience. "I just got finished saying we *can't* stop it."

"No, I mean stop what it's doing to the impellers," Cardones said. "If it's an induced current that's frying the junction points, can't we put in some extra fuses or something to bleed it off?"

"But then the—" Pampas broke off, a sudden gleam coming into his red-rimmed eyes. "The wedge would come down anyway," he continued in a newly thoughtful voice. "But then all it would take would be putting in a new batch of fuses instead of trying to cut out and wire in a complete set of junction points."

"Couldn't you even use self-resetting breakers instead?" Damana suggested. "That way you wouldn't need to replace anything at all."

"And your wedge would be ready to go back up as soon as the breakers cooled," Pampas agreed, nodding slowly. "Probably somewhere in the thirty-second to five-minute range."

"Either way, it would beat the hell out of lying there helpless," Hauptman said.

"Yes," Pampas said. "Yes, this has definite possibilities. Let me pull up the circuit layouts—"

"Negative," Sandler interrupted. "All you're pulling up right now is a blanket. Neck-level ought to do it."

"I'm all right," Pampas assured her. "I want to get going on this."

"You can get going after you've slept a few hours," Sandler said, her tone making it clear it was an order. "Go on, get out of here."

"Yes, Ma'am." Wearily, but clearly trying not to show it, Pampas got up from the table and trudged from the room.

"Best news we've had in months," Hauptman commented.

"Definitely," Damana agreed. "So what's our next move, Skipper? Back to Manticore to report?"

"Not quite yet," Sandler said slowly, fingering the data chips Pampas had left behind. "After all, right now all we've got is a theory as to what's happening. And a possible theory of how to counter it."

She lifted an eyebrow. "Wouldn't it be nice to be able to drop a complete package on Admiral Hemphill's desk instead?"

"Okay," Damana said cautiously. "So how do we go about doing that?"

Sandler was gazing thoughtfully out into space. "We start by setting course for Quarre."

"Quarre?" Damana asked, looking surprised.

"Yes," Sandler said, her eyes coming back to focus. "We're going to commandeer one of the Manticoran freighters waiting there for the next convoy and let Georgio play with circuit breakers on the way to Walther. If I'm right—if the *Jansci* is their next target—we may get a chance to see if we've really found the answer."

Damana glanced pointedly at Cardones, as if to remind his captain that the *Jansci* and her high-tech cargo were classified information from mere regular Navy types. "Except that they've never hit a whole convoy before," he pointed out. "Individual ships only. Certainly never one with a military escort."

"And now we know why," Sandler agreed. "But remember that they've been building this whole thing up for several months. They'll know we've been watching for a pattern; if the *Jansci* is their main target, they'll make sure *that's* the attack where they break that pattern. It's a perfect way to throw us off-balance."

"I don't know, Skipper," Hauptman said doubtfully. "Sounds too complicated for a Peep operation."

"I agree," Sandler said. "But I don't think the Peeps

are working on their own on this one. I think they've linked up with someone else who's plotted out the actual strategy."

"Who?" Cardones asked.

Sandler shrugged. "Sollies would be my first guess. Or maybe the Andies. Someone who has the technical expertise to come up with this gravitic heterodyne in the first place."

"And then foist it off on the Peeps?" Hauptman asked doubtfully. "Knowing full well it's only a matter of time before we figure out how to stop it?"

"Maybe they figure it's a chance to stock up on Manticoran merchandise until that happens," Sandler said. "Or maybe whoever owns the hardware is running a con game of his own on the Peeps."

"That's a kick of an idea," Damana said. "They'd sure be ripe for it, too, especially after Basilisk."

"Just be thankful he didn't dangle it in front of *us*," Hauptman said dryly. "I bet BuWeaps would be just as interested in this thing as the Peeps are."

"Don't laugh," Sandler warned. "The way these top-secret operations get compartmentalized, someone in Hemphill's office could very well have the sales brochure sitting on his desk right now."

An image flashed through Cardones's mind: Captain Harrington's expression as she was told she and *Fearless* would be given yet another new weapon to test out. The mental picture was accompanied by an equally brief surge of pity for whoever wound up delivering that message to her.

"Regardless, the sooner we nail this one shut, the better," Sandler went on. "Jack, get us on our way to Quarre. Jessica, pull up the stats on the *Dorado* and *Nightingale* and their crews. As soon as any of the techs wakes up, you'll put your heads together and figure out which one would be better for this test."

She looked at Cardones as she gathered up the data chips Pampas had left behind. "And while you do that, Rafe and I are going to go over this analysis with a fine-edge beam splitter. If there's anything Georgio's missed, I want to find it."

"*Fearless* to all convoy ships," Honor called over the ship-to-ship. "We're ready to leave orbit. Bring your wedges up and move into your positions."

She motioned to Metzinger, and the com officer closed the circuit. "How are they doing, Andy?" she asked.

"Looks good," Venizelos said, peering at his displays. "*Dorado* in particular seems really eager to take point."

"McLeod's ex-Navy," Honor told him, picking out the big merchantman on her own displays. "Warn him not to get too far ahead of the pack."

"Right," Venizelos said with a grin. Ex-Navy types, they both knew, sometimes forgot that the ship they were now commanding had about as much fighting power as a new-born treekitten. "You heard the Skipper, Joyce. Put a leash on him."

"*Dorado* acknowledging," Captain McLeod growled, cutting off the com with the heel of his hand. "You heard the *Fearless*, Lieutenant. Pull us back a few gees."

Hauptman, at the helm, glanced around at Sandler. "Go ahead," the real master of the *Dorado* confirmed for her, and it seemed to Cardones that McLeod's thin, dyspeptic face went a little thinner. It was bad enough, he reflected, to have had your ship commandeered by a bunch of hotshot ONI types barely twelve hours before departure.

But to have it commandeered by lunatics who had calmly announced their intention of ripping up and rearranging its guts in flight was even worse. The average merchie captain would probably have gone into hysterics at the very thought, or else fled to his cabin and the nearest available bottle. McLeod, former first officer of one of Her Majesty's destroyers, was made of tougher stuff.

Maybe he'd go find that bottle when he learned exactly what it was they were planning to rip up.

Sandler waited until the convoy was in hyper-space before turning Pampas, Swofford, and Jackson loose on the nodes. McLeod, to Cardones's mild surprise and quiet admiration, not only didn't come unglued, but even insisted on squeezing his way into the impeller room, dangerous high voltages and all, to watch them work.

Working on a ship's impeller nodes in flight was roughly equivalent to rebuilding a ground car engine while running a steeplechase. Sandler readily admitted she couldn't remember another case of anyone doing such a thing, but also pointed out that that alone didn't mean anything. Besides, as she reminded Captain McLeod roughly twice a day, surgeons routinely worked on living, pumping hearts without any trouble.

On the other hand, none of their techs were exactly open-torso surgeons. Still, as the days progressed and the new circuit breakers gradually began to appear at the critical junction points, McLeod's permanent expression of impending doom started to ease a little. He began to let the techs work without hovering over their shoulders, spending more time in the wardroom with his crew and any of the ONI team who happened to be off duty, sometimes regaling them with stories of his days in the Navy.

And since Cardones had little to do with either the refit or the day-to-day operation of the ship, he tended to be one of the more regular participants at McLeod's oral history lessons. It was all highly entertaining, and he suspected that at least some of it was actually true.

But mostly, he thought about the *Fearless*.

Sandler hadn't told him that his own ship would be running escort for their convoy. Maybe she hadn't known it herself. But it added just one more layer of frustration and dread to the voyage. Frustration, because so many of Cardones's friends were within easy com range and yet he couldn't even tell them he was here. He was on a secret mission, and Sandler had forbidden any contact, and that was that.

And dread, because if Sandler's analysis was right, the convoy was soon going to come under attack. Cardones was *Fearless*'s tac officer, and her bridge was where he was supposed to be during combat. Certainly not here aboard a merchantman, being about as useless as it was possible for a Queen's officer to be.

And he *was* useless. In the quiet dark of the night, that was what rankled the most. The rationale for bringing him into this in the first place had been Hemphill's assumption that this mysterious weapon was a variant of her beloved grav lance. Now that they knew it wasn't, there was no reason at all for him to be here. Sandler ought to call it quits, swear him to secrecy, and just send him across to the *Fearless*.

But that was out of the question. Sandler had her orders, and like Captain Harrington, she knew how to follow them. Cardones would stay put until they were all told otherwise.

The refit itself seemed to drag on at the pace of a lethargic banana slug, but Cardones recognized that as the skewed perspective of someone who wasn't actually doing any of the work. They were, in fact, still twelve hours out from the hyper limit when Pampas pronounced the job complete.

And at that point, there wasn't anything for *any* of them to do except wait.

"*Nightingale*'s out, Skipper," Venizelos announced, peering at his displays. "Reconfiguring her sails . . . looks clean."

Honor nodded, her own attention on her long-range sensor displays. As always, right at the hyper limit was the most likely place for a pirate to be lurking.

But there were no impeller signatures showing nearby. "Full active sensors," she ordered.

"Already running," Wallace said. "Nothing showing."

"Very good," Honor said. "Stephen, compute us a course for Walther Prime, and let's get moving."

"Commodore?" Lieutenant Koln, *Vanguard*'s tac officer, called from across the bridge. "They're here, Sir."

"Where?" Dominick demanded, swiveling toward his own tac displays.

"One-three-eight by four-two-three," Koln said. "About three light-minutes away."

Dominick had the images now. "Course?"

"Straight in, Sir," Koln said with a note of satisfaction. "Looks like the escort is riding the convoy's port flank."

"Good." Dominick looked at Charles. "Any last-minute suggestions you'd care to make?"

"None," Charles said. "They're playing exactly as you anticipated."

Dominick felt his chest swell with professional pride. Yes; as *he* had anticipated. This was *his* plan, and his alone, and he was looking forward to showing Charles a thing or two about Republican military tactics. "Yes, indeed," he said. "Mr. Koln, alert Captain Vaccares. Activate Plan Alpha."

❖   ❖   ❖

"Captain, we've got a disturbance," Wallace said suddenly, leaning over his displays. "Off to port, about three and a half million klicks. Looks like—"

He broke off. "Looks like someone's getting hit," Venizelos put in. "Silesian merchantman *Cornucopia*, by the transponder."

Honor swiveled toward her tac displays. From the target's impeller strength and acceleration, CIC was tentatively identifying it as a merchantman in the two-million-ton range. She was running full out, driving hard toward the relative safety of the inner system.

But she wasn't going to make it. Her attacker was already in energy range and coming up fast, blasting away with lasers and grasers both. "Damage?" she asked.

"No sign of debris," Venizelos said. "They may be firing warning shots, trying to get her to heave to."

But connecting or not, the sheer number of weapons being fired simultaneously indicated the attacker was at least the size of a light cruiser. Way too big for the average pirate ship—

"Captain." Wallace's voice was suddenly tight. "CIC's pulling a Silesian emission spectrum from the raider . . . with something *not* Silesian beneath it."

"What do you mean, 'not Silesian'?" Venizelos asked, frowning at him.

But Wallace's gaze was locked on Honor's face. And from the tension around his eyes, she knew there was only one thing his veiled words could mean.

They'd found their Andermani raider.

She took a deep breath. "Stephen, plot me an intercept course for that raider," she ordered, still looking at Wallace. "Full acceleration."

"Full acceleration?" Venizelos swiveled to face her. "What about our own convoy?"

"They'll just have to do the best they can," Honor told him, forcing her voice to remain calm. "Joyce, inform the other ships we'll be leaving them temporarily. Instruct them to follow our vector so as to stay as close to us as possible."

Metzinger glanced uncertainly at Venizelos. "Skipper, if someone else is lying doggo—"

"You have your orders, Lieutenant," Honor said, more harshly than she'd intended. It was one thing to sit in a calm briefing room aboard the *Basilisk* and acknowledge orders in a nice safe theoretical way. It was something else entirely to actually run out on ships full of men and women who were trusting her for their safety.

But she had no choice. "And then," she added quietly, "order battle stations."

On the *Dorado*'s nav display, the distant impeller signature suddenly shifted vector. "There he goes," Cardones announced.

"Who, the raider?" Sandler asked, leaving her quiet consultation with Pampas and McLeod at the back of the bridge and stepping to his side.

"Yes, Ma'am," Cardones told her. "Looks like he's pulling for the hyper limit."

Sandler hissed softly between her teeth as she leaned over his shoulder for a better look. "I don't like this, Rafe," she murmured. "There's something wrong here."

"What, you don't believe there could be two unconnected raiders working the same system?" Cardones asked.

"No," Sandler said flatly. "And neither do you. This is some kind of setup, and we both know it. What *I* don't understand is why *Fearless* was so damn quick to abandon us."

"Maybe Captain Harrington knows something we don't," Cardones suggested.

"Maybe," Sandler conceded. "I just hate sitting out here feeling helpless." She rubbed her chin. "And you're *sure* that raider isn't our Peep?"

Cardones shook his head. "He's pulling way too many gees to be a battlecruiser," he said. "Besides, his emission spectrum is definitely Silesian."

"As far as you can tell from these sensors, anyway," she said with an edge of contempt. "I wish we could pull *Shadow* out from under the wedge long enough to take some decent readings."

"I suppose we could," Cardones said doubtfully. Sandler had refused to leave the *Shadow* behind in an unsecured Silesian port, but the dispatch boat was too big to shoehorn into the *Dorado*'s cargo hold without everyone in sensor range knowing something funny was going on. The solution had been to moor her onto the merchie's hull near the upper bow, where the stress bands would hide her from prying eyes but where she could be slipped in and out quickly if necessary. "But if someone's watching," he added, "that could give away the whole show."

"I know," Sandler agreed reluctantly as she straightened up. "Well, whatever's going on, we don't have much choice but to keep going. Just keep your eyes open."

"Yes, Ma'am," Cardones said, frowning as something caught his eye. Had something happened to the *Fearless*'s impellers just then?

Yes—there it was again. A brief flicker, as if the nodes were having trouble keeping the wedge up.

Like something was interfering with them.

A hard knot settled into his stomach. They had only Pampas's professional opinion, after all, that this Peep heterodyning trick wouldn't work against a military wedge. That fleeing raider wasn't far out of the million-klick range; and if he was equipped with the same weapon and was testing its range . . .

He squeezed his hands briefly into fists, fighting against the almost overwhelming urge to pounce on the com and warn *Fearless* what they might be up against. But even if he did, there was nothing they could do to counter such an attack except turn and run for it.

And that was something Captain Harrington would never do.

He took a deep breath, forcing himself to let it out slowly. *You go into battle*, Sandler had reminded him, *fully prepared to sacrifice some of your own*. It was one of the truisms of warfare; and no one had ever promised him that the ones who died wouldn't be his friends and colleagues. It was the life he'd chosen, and he would just have to learn to accept the darker aspects of it.

Fearless's impellers seemed to be running properly now. Taking another deep breath, Cardones fought the demons from his mind and settled down to watch.

The minutes trickled into an hour; and finally, the time was right. The Manty warship had continued her chase, her course taking her farther and farther away from the alleged attacker's alleged victim.

More to the point, that course had taken her away from her own convoy. Even if she turned around right now, it would be over two hours before she could burn off her current velocity and get back.

Which meant it was time to strike.

"Prepare to bring wedge to full power," he ordered. "Lieutenant, has CIC sorted out yet which ship is the *Jansci*?"

"They've run all the transponders in range, Sir," Koln reported. "So far they haven't tagged her, but there are a couple that are still being blocked by impeller shadows."

Dominick nodded. Or *Jansci* might be running under a false ID. If the Manties suspected there was a leak in their Merchant Coordination office on Silesia, they might have taken such a precaution with this particular ship.

No matter. They were too far out from the inner system to draw attention from Walther Prime's laughable excuse for a government. Once they eliminated the escort, they could cut open each of the merchies at their leisure until they found the one they wanted.

And speaking of the escort— "Did CIC happen to identify the Manty warship?"

"Yes, Sir." Koln smiled slyly. "They make it the *Star Knight*-class heavy cruiser *Fearless*. Captain Honor Harrington commanding."

"Harrington?" Dominick echoed. "*Harrington?* The Butcher of Basilisk?"

"Yes, Sir," Koln said.

Dominick settled back in his chair and sent Charles a smile. "The Butcher of Basilisk herself," he repeated. "Well, well. This is going to be an extra pleasure."

"Indeed," Charles said.

A nice, neutral answer; from which Dominick deduced Charles had no idea who Harrington was. No matter. This operation had been intended to kill two birds with one stone: to prove the capabilities of a devastating weapon against the Manties, while at the same time driving a wedge of suspicion between the Star Kingdom and Andermani Empire.

Now, it appeared, there was going to be a third bird in the path of this particular stone: Captain Honor Harrington herself.

"Bring up the wedge," he ordered, admiring the way his voice rang around the bridge. The convoy, following its escort as best it could, was in perfect striking position now, situated more or less between *Vanguard* and *Fearless*. Dominick could head toward *Fearless*, picking off the merchantmen with the Crippler as he passed. Then, when *Fearless* turned back to defend them—as she undoubtedly would—he would have her pinned between himself and Captain Vaccares's appropriated Andy cruiser.

"We have the *Jansci* now, Sir," Koln announced. "Bearing two-four—"

"I see her," Dominick interrupted, a stirring of anticipation in his stomach. First the *Jansci*, then the rest of the merchantmen, then Harrington. Life was indeed good. "That's your target, Mr. Koln. Order the Crippler prepared for action."

For the first fraction of a second, Cardones thought his eyes were playing tricks on him, or else that something had gone wrong the *Dorado*'s sensors.

And then, the horrible truth rolled in on him. "Captain!" he snapped at Sandler. "That's not a merchie. It's the Peep battlecruiser!"

Sandler was at his side at an instant. "Damn," she bit out. "You sure?"

"She just brought her wedge up to military strength," Cardones told her tightly. "Better trick even than lying doggo—we knew something was there, and so we didn't look at it more closely."

"We *would* have looked if we'd had the sensors to do it with," Sandler ground out. "And you saw how that first ship drew *Fearless* off before she could get within range to see through the masquerade herself. Clever. Looks like someone's still pulling the Peeps' strings."

"So what do we do?" Damana asked from the helm console beside Cardones.

"What else?" Sandler said. "We let him come for us."

Her hand, resting on the edge of Cardones's sensor board, tightened against the smooth metal. "And find out if this defense really works."

The *Vanguard* was on the move now, and the first Manty merchantman was within range. "Fire Crippler," Dominick ordered.

The bridge lights dimmed as the weapon did its magic with the *Vanguard*'s impellers; and with a suddenness that still never failed to amaze him, the *Jansci*'s wedge collapsed.

"Target disabled," Koln confirmed.

"Very good, Mr. Koln," Dominick said. First the *Jansci*, then the rest of the merchantmen. "Lock onto second target. Fire when ready."

"Skipper!" Venizelos snapped. "We've got—what the *hell*?"

"What?" Honor asked, her eyes darting to the display holding the image of their fleeing raider. There was no indication it was firing or changing course or anything else that should have startled her exec that way.

"The *Cornucopia*," Venizelos bit out savagely. "She just fired up a military-class wedge."

"New identification from CIC," Wallace put in. "They now make it a Peep battlecruiser."

Honor felt her throat muscles tighten. Exactly the same trick they'd used themselves on Iliescu back in Zoraster system. Only this time it was *Fearless* who'd been caught like an amateur.

"She's moving on the convoy," Venizelos continued. "The merchies are starting to scatter. A lot of good that's going to do them. Looks like the Peep's going to— Skipper!"

"I saw," Honor said, staring at the displays in disbelief. Suddenly, without warning, the *Jansci*'s impellers had gone down. "Was she hit?"

"I didn't see any missiles," Venizelos said. "She *is* within energy range; but I didn't see any—"

He broke off, inhaling sharply. The *Poor Richard*'s wedge had collapsed, too.

"Commander?" Honor demanded, swiveling toward Wallace.

But Wallace looked as bewildered as everyone else on the bridge. "No idea, Ma'am," he said grimly. "I've never heard of anything like this happening before."

"Well, it's happening now," Honor said, watching her displays. Behind them, the *Sable Chestnut*'s wedge was the third to go.

And this time she spotted something else: an odd fluctuation in the battlecruiser's own wedge just before the merchie's had collapsed. Some new Peep version of a grav lance, maybe? Something powerful enough to take down an entire wedge, not just sidewalls?

Or had the fluctuation been for the same purpose as the flicker she'd ordered on *Fearless*'s own impellers an hour earlier? There were two known players on the Peep side now; could there be a third lurking in the shadows?

Abruptly, she came to a decision. "Turn ship and decelerate," she ordered. "We're going back."

Wallace's head twisted around. "Captain?"

"We're going back, Mr. Wallace," she repeated. "The convoy needs us."

"But the raider—"

"The raider will keep," she cut him off, warning him with her eyes.

His mouth worked, but he turned back to his board without comment, shoulders hunched in silent protest. Thinking of their orders from Admiral Trent, no doubt.

Or else thinking about the fact that the enemy was a battlecruiser that outgunned *Fearless* by probably three to one.

"Peep's altered course toward the *Dorado*," Venizelos announced. "From the data, CIC speculates that whatever they're doing to the merchie's impellers operates at a range of about a million klicks."

Or in other words, ten times the range of a grav lance. Or at least, of a *Manticoran* grav lance.

Which meant that Honor's gut reaction a minute ago had been correct. If this was indeed a new Peep weapon, they needed to find out as much as they could about it. Admiral Trent might not be happy that she'd let the Andermani raider escape, but under the circumstances—

"Aspect change in the raider, Skipper," Venizelos announced. "She's also flipped and decelerating."

"Run the numbers, Stephen," Honor ordered. "Assume the battlecruiser waits for us. What's our intercept time?"

"For a zero-zero intercept, two hours thirteen minutes," DuMorne said. "We'll be in missile range twelve minutes before that."

"And the raider?"

"She'll be in missile range of us four minutes after that," DuMorne said.

"Good," Honor said, forcing her voice to remain calm. So the enemy wasn't going to be content with just looting the convoy, or even with suckering *Fearless* into going up against a ship three times her size. Instead, they were going to guarantee victory by making *Fearless* fight both ships at the same time.

"Good?" Wallace echoed. "What's good about it?"

"They'll have us surrounded," Honor said evenly, remembering an old, old quote. "*This* time they won't get away."

She turned back to her displays, ignoring Wallace's look of disbelief. In the distance, the battlecruiser's wedge fluctuated again—

—and with a distant thundercrack and a jolt that could be felt straight through the deck plates, *Dorado*'s wedge collapsed.

"Hot diggedy damn," Captain McLeod's strained voice said into the sudden silence. "Is that what was supposed to happen?"

"Part of it," Sandler assured him, crossing to the engineering status board. "Georgio?"

"Don't know yet," Pampas said, his fingers playing almost tentatively with the keys. "The breakers are still popped, but they might just be too hot to reset."

Cardones looked back at his displays. The Peep was still moving among the scattering convoy, methodically popping merchie wedges as it went.

But something new had now been added to the picture. On the distant marker indicating the *Fearless*, the green number indicating acceleration away had been replaced by a red one.

Which meant *Fearless* had given up on the chase. She was decelerating hard, killing her forward velocity and preparing to come to the convoy's rescue.

Where she would face a Peep battlecruiser.

"Captain Sandler?" he called. "You'd better come see this."

"What is it?" Sandler asked, making no move to leave Pampas's side.

"*Fearless* is decelerating," Cardones told her. "I think she's going to come back."

"Understood," Sandler said, and turned back to Pampas's board.

Cardones blinked. "Captain?"

Reluctantly, he thought, she turned back. "What?"

"Aren't we going to do something?" he asked. "I mean, she's *coming back*."

"What exactly would you like me to do, Commander?" Sandler countered. "Warn the Peep off? Or shall we just charge to the attack ourselves? Don't worry, Captain Harrington can handle him."

"But—"

"I said don't worry," Sandler said, cutting his protest off with a stern look. "Kilo for kilo, *Fearless* has far better weapons than any Peep warship. You know that."

"Besides, this particular Peep has almost certainly had a lot of its armament gutted to make room for their wedge-killer," Damana added. "*Fearless* should be all right."

"Got it!" Pampas crowed suddenly. "There they go, Skipper. Breakers have closed, and the nodes are back up to standby."

He grinned up at Sandler. "We did it, Ma'am."

"We did indeed," she agreed, some of the lines smoothing out of her face as she clapped Pampas on the shoulder. "Well done, Georgio."

"So what are we waiting for?" McLeod asked. "They're moving away from us right now. We could bring up the wedge and make a run for the inner system, and they'd have to decelerate before they could even think about coming after us."

"No," Sandler said, an odd note to her voice. "No, leave the wedge down."

"But we might at least be able to distract them," Cardones put in. A number on his display caught his eye as it changed— "Uh-oh."

"What?" Damana asked.

"The raider's also flipped over and started decelerating," Cardones told him.

"ETA?"

Cardones was running the numbers. "Looks like they'll reach here pretty much together," he said. "They're trying to box *Fearless* between them."

"They're going to succeed, too," Damana agreed, eying his captain. "This changes things, Skipper. Even if *Fearless* can handle a gutted battlecruiser, adding a light cruiser's tubes to the mix stacks the odds the other way."

"Again, what do you want me to do about it?" Sandler asked.

"As Captain McLeod suggests, we could run for it," Damana said. "If we can draw the Peep far enough out of position, it would give *Fearless* a chance to take out the raider first instead of having to face both of them together."

"Unless the Peep decides we're not worth bothering with," Sandler pointed out. "She might just let us go, in which case we'll have done it for nothing."

"So?" Cardones said. "I mean, what have we got to lose by trying?"

"What have we got to *lose*?" Sandler demanded. "We have *everything* to lose."

She looked back and forth between Cardones and Damana. "Don't you see? Either of you? We now have the counter to their wedge-killer; *but they don't know we have it.* If they leave here without finding that out, who knows how much time and money Haven will waste building these things and putting them aboard their ships?"

Cardones stared at her in disbelief. "You mean you'd let *Fearless* die for *that*?"

"People die all the time in war, Mr. Cardones," Sandler said tartly. "If it makes you feel any better, they won't have died for nothing."

"Yes, they will," Cardones shot back. "The Peeps aren't going to just recall all their ships to base and load these things aboard them. They'll keep on testing; and sooner or later, they're bound to run into a merchie with the breakers installed."

A sudden cold wave washed over him. "Or weren't you going to tell anyone outside ONI about this?" he breathed. "Were you just going to let merchies continue to get slaughtered?"

"I'm not going to debate it with you, Lieutenant," Sandler said icily. "You have your orders. The wedge stays down." Deliberately, she turned her back on him. "Georgio, let's see the self-diagnostics on those junction points."

Cardones turned back to his displays, his stomach churning with anger, an odd sense of loss digging an empty spot into his soul. He'd been wrong. Elayne Sandler was nothing at all like Honor Harrington. Captain Harrington would never, ever sacrifice people for nothing this way. When she put people at risk it was for duty or defense, not for some stupid psychological game played by dark-minded men and women in dark-minded rooms. That was what she had done at Basilisk . . . and it was what she was about to do right now.

And *Fearless*, and all aboard her, would die.

There was no doubt about that. None at all. Sandler and Damana might be right about the limited combat capabilities of the battlecruiser, and *Fearless* could certainly take the light cruiser now coming in from behind her.

But she couldn't take on both at the same time. Not and survive.

He had to do something. *Fearless* was his ship, and Honor Harrington his captain. He had to *do* something.

He stared at the display . . . and like a row of dominoes toppling in sequence, the answer came.

Maybe. It would mean disobeying Sandler's direct

order, of course, and that would mean the end of his career.

But what was a career for, anyway?

Seated at the helm beside him, Damana was staring straight forward, his own expression a mask. Taking a deep breath, Cardones reached over to his board—

And before Damana could stop him, he activated the wedge.

"What in the *world*?" Koln said, his forehead wrinkling in surprise.

"What?" Dominick demanded, swiveling his command chair to face him.

"One of the merchies, Sir," Koln said, glancing at Charles before returning his frown to the displays. "The *Dorado*. Her wedge has come up again."

"What?" Dominick growled, and shifted his own frown to Charles. "What's going on?"

"What do you mean, what's going on?" Charles countered, filling his voice and expression with casual unconcern even as his heart sank a few centimeters within him. "Your crew missed, that's what's going on."

"Impossible," Koln insisted. "The wedge was *down*."

"Because you caught a corner of it," Charles explained patiently. "You caused enough of a surge to confuse the software, but not enough to actually fry the junction points. I've mentioned this possibility to you before."

He held his breath as Dominick frowned slightly, clearly trying to remember. Charles had mentioned no such thing, of course, because he'd just now made it up. But he'd thrown so much technobabble at the commodore over the past few months that the other hopefully wouldn't remember this one way or the other.

Apparently, he didn't. "Fine," Dominick grunted. "So what do we do about it?"

"Obviously, you hit her again," Charles said. "Try to make it a clean shot this time."

Dominick grunted again and shifted his attention back to the helmsman. "What's she doing?"

"Heading away at full acceleration," the helmsman said. "Looks like she's making for the inner system."

"Mr. Koln?" Dominick invited.

"There are four other ships we haven't hit yet," Koln reminded him. "Given our current position and vector, it would make more sense to cripple them first, then go back for the *Dorado*."

Dominick stroked his chin. "Will that give us enough time to get back into position before *Fearless* arrives?"

"No problem," Koln assured him. "The *Dorado* is hardly going to outpace us."

"Good," Dominick rumbled. "I wouldn't want Captain Vaccares to have to face *Fearless* alone. We deserve some of the satisfaction of pounding Harrington to dust."

"Just be sure you don't kill everyone aboard," Charles warned. As if that was actually going to happen now. "Remember that part of the plan is to leave survivors who will testify they saw the People's Republic and a disguised Andermani warship working together."

"Don't worry, we'll leave a few," Dominick said, settling back comfortably into his chair. "Carry on, Mr. Koln."

"Yes, Sir." Koln returned to his skeet shooting.

Charles heaved a silent sigh of regret. So the Manties had figured it out already. Too bad—he'd hoped he could get his hands on some of *Jansci's* *really* high-tech cargo before the house of cards came tumbling down. Some genuine, useful hardware would have made his next run that much more believable and profitable.

Still, such was the way of the game. And he was hardly going to leave this one empty-handed.

No one was paying any particular attention to him as the *Vanguard* swung around to target the next merchie. Casually, Charles got up from his chair and began to circle around the bridge in the casual urgency of a man making for the head. Just beyond the head was the bridge's exit.

Standing in the hatchway, he looked back one final time. *Sic transit gloria mundi*, he thought, and ducked quietly through the opening.

Nobody saw him go.

"I will have your head, Mister," Sandler ground out in a voice with broken-glass edges, glaring at Cardones as if trying to set him on fire through willpower alone. "You hear me, Cardones? You are *dead*."

"That'll be up to a court-martial to decide," Cardones said, rather surprised at how calm he had suddenly become. The die had been cast, and there was nothing to do now but ride it through. "But for right now, may I have your permission to help the *Fearless*?"

Sandler's glare only got hotter. "We might as well, Skipper," Damana murmured from her side. "The disinformation thing is out the window now anyway."

"No, it's not," she countered, shifting her glare to him as if astonished that he would dare come to Cardones's support against her. "They'll simply assume they missed."

"Until they get aboard and examine the junction points," Damana said, holding her gaze without flinching.

"Which they wouldn't even have thought to do if *he* hadn't reactivated the wedge," Sandler snarled.

Damana just stood there silently . . . and slowly the fire died from Sandler's eyes. "They won't let us get away, you know," she said, turning back to Cardones. "They'll come after us and disable us; and then they'll go back and blow *Fearless* into dust anyway. *Then* they'll come back as Jack said and find out how we spiked their toy and ruined all their fun. We had a plan; and now you've wrecked it. And for nothing."

"I don't think so," Cardones said, trying to match her gaze the way Damana had. "That is, it wasn't for nothing. Because you're right, they don't realize yet what we've done. And that gives us a weapon we can use against them."

He looked at Damana. "But we don't have much time."

"What do you need?" Damana asked evenly.

"Some equipment from *Shadow*," Cardones told him. "And I need Ensign Pampas and Captain McLeod to stay behind with me for a few minutes."

Damana threw a sideways look at Sandler's stiff profile. "I take it that means the rest of us are abandoning ship?"

"I'll be damned if I'll leave my ship," McLeod spoke up indignantly.

"You'll do what you're told," Sandler said coldly. For a long moment her eyes searched Cardones's face. Then, reluctantly, she gave a sort of half nod. "Jack, collect the team and get aboard *Shadow*," she said. "Captain McLeod, order your people to go with them."

McLeod started to sputter, took a closer look at her face, and choked back the objection. "Yes, Ma'am," he gritted instead, and turned to the intercom.

"So what's the plan?" Sandler asked, her eyes still on Cardones.

Cardones gestured toward the displays. "From the way we saw them operate at Tyler's Star, I'm guessing they'll move in close and launch boarding boats after they take out our wedge again."

"Probably," Sandler said. "So?"

"So," Cardones told her grimly, "we're going to prepare a little reception for them."

"That's odd," Wallace murmured. "Captain, CIC just reported one of the merchies has brought her wedge back up."

"I thought you said they'd all been knocked out," Honor said, looking over at her displays. He was right: the *Dorado* was up and running again, lumbering toward the inner system.

"They were," Wallace agreed. "McLeod must have gotten his nodes working again."

"Any idea how?"

Wallace snorted under his breath. "I don't even know how the Peeps knocked them out."

"Mm," Honor said, frowning at the numbers. Yes, the *Dorado* was running; but where was she running *to*? Surely McLeod didn't think he could outrun a battlecruiser in that thing.

And then understanding struck her, and she smiled a bittersweet smile. Of course. McLeod couldn't get away; but what he *could* do was try to distract the Peep. Possibly even drag him far enough out of position that *Fearless* would be able to engage the two enemy ships one at a time.

The catch was that if he was able to become enough of an irritation that he actually did any good, that defiance might well cost him his life.

Which left Honor with only two options: to take advantage of his proffered sacrifice, or to instead try to distract the Peep herself into leaving the *Dorado* alone.

Fearless had finished her deceleration and was finally

starting to close the distance back toward the convoy she'd abandoned. The raider behind her, she noted, was accelerating in her wake, continuing to herd her toward the battlecruiser while at the same time being careful not to get close enough that she would be tempted to turn and engage. It was still over an hour back to the convoy, according to DuMorne's plot. Plenty of time for the battlecruiser to deal with the *Dorado*.

For a moment she studied the numbers. *Fearless*'s acceleration was hovering right at five hundred and four gees. That was far above the normal eighty percent power the RMN normally maintained, but it still left a safety margin of almost three percent against her inertial compensator. . .

"Chief Killian," she said quietly to the helmsman, "increase acceleration to maximum military power."

Venizelos turned to look at her, but remained silent. He'd probably run the numbers, and the logic, the same way she had.

"Aye, aye, Ma'am," Killian acknowledged, and the safety margin dropped to zero as *Fearless* went to a full five hundred and twenty gravities.

"And prepare a broadside, Commander Wallace," she continued. "We'll fire as soon as we're within range."

Because, after all, it was the wolf's job to distract the rampaging bear from the cub, not the other way around.

And with a little luck, the Peep would find out just how distracting HMS *Fearless* could be.

"We're in range of the *Dorado*, Commodore," Koln announced. "Crippler reports ready to fire."

"Tell them to make sure they actually hit the damn thing this time," Dominick said pointedly. "Fire when ready."

"Yes, Sir," Koln said, touching the signal key.

Vanguard's lights dimmed yet again, and on Dominick's tac display *Dorado*'s wedge vanished. "Good," he said, weighing his options. As long as he was here anyway, he could send a couple of boarding boats to go and loot the attempted runaway.

But if he did, that would leave *Jansci* floating around on its own behind him, with all that top-secret military equipment aboard. Would the Manties have orders to destroy the most sensitive cargo in case of imminent capture? The *Harlequin*'s crew hadn't bothered with any such sabotage before they'd run; but then, *Harlequin*'s cargo hadn't been as sensitive as what was supposed to be aboard the *Jansci*, either.

There was no point in taking chances. He opened his mouth to order the ship around—

"Sir!" Koln said suddenly. "We've got another ship on scope. Small one—dispatch boat class, about forty thousand tons."

"Where?" Dominick demanded, scanning his displays.

"Behind the *Dorado*," Koln said. "It must have been hidden by her wedge. Probably moored to the topside hull; they had their belly to us when their nodes went down that first time. Really hauling gees, too."

"Yes," Dominick murmured. The dispatch boat was indeed eating up space, and at a rate that was impressive even for that class of high-speed ship. That implied it was something special.

He smiled, a sudden wolfish grin. "Well, well," he said. "The Manties are being cute, Lieutenant."

"Sir?" Koln asked.

Dominick gestured at his displays. "There's no reason for the average merchie to carry a boat like that." He cocked an eyebrow. "Which implies she's *not* an average merchie."

For a second Koln just looked puzzled. Then his face cleared. "The *Jansci*," he said, nodding.

"Exactly," Dominick agreed. "Somewhere along the line, she and the *Dorado* must have exchanged ID transponders."

And they might not even have tumbled to the deception if the crew hadn't panicked and jumped ship. Typical Manties.

His smile vanished. Unless the hurry they were in *wasn't* simply panic . . .

"Full scan of the *Dorado*," he snapped. "Look for odd energy or electronic emissions."

"Nothing showing, Sir," Koln said, sounding puzzled. "Except that the nodes are acting like they're on standby. That's impossible, of course—that last Crippler blast caught them dead center, and we *saw* the wedge collapse."

Dominick gnawed at his lower lip. Koln was right—he'd watched the wedge die himself.

So then what the hell was happening over there? Some new technological deviltry the Manties had come up with? A feedback loop in the nodes, maybe; something that would blow up the impellers and fusion plant after the crew had had time to get away?

He couldn't even begin to guess the details. But the details didn't matter anyway. He'd been right the first time: those Manties were the keepers of a ship full of secrets, and they were going to scuttle that ship.

Or at least, they were going to try.

"Man the boarding boats—double-time," Dominick ordered. "Helm, get us in as close as you can—I want the crews aboard as quickly as possible."

He glared at his displays. Because he would be damned if he would let the damn Royalists take his prize—*his* prize—away from him.

❖   ❖   ❖

They were nearly finished when the bone-cracking sound of the collapsing wedge once again echoed through the *Dorado*. "There it goes," Pampas called from beneath the sensor monitor panel. "Hope the breakers can handle all this stress."

"We'll send a nasty letter to the manufacturer if they can't," Cardones said, looking over his own handiwork. Just wrap the receiver pack around the control cables, Sandler had said, and the remote control would be ready to rock. He just hoped he'd wrapped it properly. "How's it going in there?"

"Two minutes," Pampas said. "Maybe less."

The bridge door slid open, and Cardones turned as McLeod stepped in. "Forward sensor interlocks are disabled," he announced. "And I checked the lifeboat on my way back. Everything's ready."

"Good," Cardones said. "Georgio says two more minutes and we'll be off."

"I hope so," McLeod said sourly, stepping over to the helm and peering at the displays. "The Peep's still coming."

Cardones nodded, craning his neck to look at the impeller status display. "Looks like the breakers just closed again," he said. "Georgio?"

"Finished," Pampas said. "Let me make sure the wires are sealed and I'll be right with you."

"What's he doing down there?" McLeod asked, the worry in his voice tinged with suspicion.

Cardones took a deep breath. "He's just taken the compensators off line."

McLeod's mouth fell open a centimeter. "On a ship with a functional wedge? Are you *insane*? You fire up the impellers—"

His face suddenly changed. "That's why you had me wreck the interlocks," he breathed. "No compensators, no limit protection on the wedge—you fire it up now, and anyone aboard will be smeared across the bulk-heads like jelly."

"Yes, I know," Cardones said evenly, looking back at the display. The Peep battlecruiser was on the move now, sweeping in with sudden new urgency toward the *Dorado*. Preparing, no doubt, to launch its boarding boats . . .

"Done," Pampas grunted.

"Good." Carefully, Cardones picked up the attaché case that contained Sandler's remote control system. "Let's go."

"They've dropped another boat," Koln announced. "Standard lifeboat this time."

"Never mind the lifeboat," Dominick growled. The boarding boats were in space now, driving hard toward the drifting *Dorado*, and there was no indication that whatever the Royalists had done to the nodes was gaining any ground. They should have plenty of time to get aboard and shut the system down before it blew.

But now, with the safety of his precious cargo assured, he was taking another look at the people who had tried to deprive him of it.

They were still fleeing, out there in their souped-up dispatch boat. Running as if their lives depended on it.

Which was, Dominick decided, as forlorn a hope as he'd ever heard of. Certainly *Vanguard* couldn't catch a boat that fast; but then, he hardly had to catch them to make his displeasure known. "Lock a graser on that dispatch boat," he ordered, shifting his eyes to the lifeboat. The merchantman's lower-ranking crewmen, most likely, left to fend for themselves when their superiors ran out in the faster boat.

Well, they would have the last laugh. They would get to see their former oppressors die.

"Graser ready, Commodore."

"Key it to me," Dominick ordered. This one he would do himself. A shame he couldn't use a missile, he thought regretfully. A missile would be even more satisfying, because that way the Manties would have a few seconds to see their doom bearing down on them. With a graser, unfortunately, they would be dead before they even knew about it.

But missiles cost money, and personal vengeance might as well be economical.

On his board, the fire-control command key winked on. Savoring the moment, he reached out a hand to push it.

Ten thousand kilometers away, seated behind Pampas and McLeod in the lifeboat, Cardones gave the remote-control displays one final check. The heading was keyed, the course maneuver settings locked in. All was ready.

Mentally crossing his fingers, he pressed the button.

"Commodore!"

Koln's startled cry cut across the bridge, jerking Dominick's finger away from the firing key before he could push it and jerking his eyes toward the displays.

The *Dorado* was moving.

Not just a reflexive twitch or jerk, either. The merchantman was swinging around, scattering away the boarding boats swarming toward it, bringing itself nose-on to the *Vanguard*.

And with its wedge blazing away at full power, it leaped forward.

But not at the pathetic acceleration of a normal merchantman. Not a lumbering, insignificant two hundred gees. Instead, the *Dorado* was burning through space at an utterly impossible *two thousand gravities*, fully four times *Vanguard*'s own top rate.

The very shock of it froze Dominick in his chair for that first horrifying fraction of a second. It was *insane*—the crew would have had to cut the safety interlocks, disable the inertial compensator, *and* crank the nodes up to a level they couldn't possibly maintain for more than a minute or two before vaporizing under the stress.

Impeller nodes that shouldn't have been operating in the first place!

"Evasive!" he snapped. "Ninety-degree starboard yaw—full power. Port broadside: fire at will."

The helmsman was on it in an instant, swinging the *Vanguard* hard over and kicking her into motion. But it was too late. The *Dorado* was turning right along with it, locked on and still coming.

"Shoot it!" Dominick shouted again, a note of desperation in his voice. He swung his chair around to snarl at Charles—

The snarl died in his throat. The seat beside the tac station was empty.

Charles was gone.

He swung around again, eyes darting to every corner of the bridge, knowing even as he did so that it was a pitiful way to waste his last few seconds of life. Charles had left the bridge and probably the ship, leaving nothing behind but empty promises and the acid taste of betrayal.

Belatedly, the port lasers and grasers opened fire. But with *Fearless* looming in the distance, all of *Vanguard*'s fire control had been locked into the long-range sensors, and there was no time to recalibrate for short-range fire. One graser beam did manage to score a direct hit, going straight down the *Dorado*'s throat and burning clear through its centerline, and for a brief moment Dominick dared to hope.

But there was nothing on that path of destruction but crew quarters, control systems, and cargo holds. Nothing that could disable those straining impeller nodes or otherwise halt the terrible Juggernaut bearing down on them.

And then there was no more time for firing. No more time for anything . . . except to appreciate a last bitter flicker of irony.

As he had those last few seconds to see his doom bearing down on him.

The *Dorado* reached the Peep battlecruiser . . . and with just under five hundred kilometers still separating them, their two impeller wedges intersected.

The nodes went first, in both ships, the sudden influx of gravitational energy shattering them into explosions of shrapnel and superheated gas that ripped through the impeller rooms, crushing decks and bulkheads and killing everyone in their path. Shock waves and electromagnetic pulses swept ahead of the shrapnel, crushing and killing and demolishing electronics as they passed. *Vanguard* writhed in agony; the *Dorado*, far weaker and more vulnerable than a warship, was already twitching her last death throes.

And then, the expanding spheres of destruction reached the fusion mag bottles.

The *Dorado*'s fusion generator had already died, hammered into useless rubble along with everything else inside the merchantman's hull. But the *Vanguard*'s twin plants, like the beating hearts of the still struggling ship, had somehow managed to survive.

They died now; and for a brief, eye-wrenching second there was a new star in the Walther System's night sky.

And then the star faded, and there was nothing left but a quietly expanding sphere of plasma and debris.

❖　　❖　　❖

Aboard the recently renamed light cruiser *Forerunner*, Captain Vaccares stared at his displays in disbelief. One minute the *Vanguard* had stood alone among a group of disabled merchantmen, waiting like a lion for its prey to be driven to it.

And now, in the blink of an eye, it was gone.

And that same prey, the HMS *Fearless*, was hailing him.

"Andermani Light Cruiser *Alant*," a woman's voice came from the bridge speaker, "or whatever you're calling yourself now, this is Captain Harrington aboard Her Majesty's Ship *Fearless*. You are ordered to strike your wedge and surrender your ship."

"*Fearless* has turned around again, Captain," the helmsman announced. "She's started accelerating toward us."

"Turn ship," Vaccares ordered. Between the two of them, he and Commodore Dominick could easily have taken a Manticoran heavy cruiser. But with *Vanguard* gone, he would have had to be insane to think of facing *Fearless* alone. "Give me full acceleration toward the hyper limit."

The images on the displays canted around as the *Forerunner* swung a hundred eighty degrees over. Vaccares double-checked the numbers and nodded to himself. The hyper limit was only about an hour away, he was still outside *Fearless*'s missile envelope, and he was faster than she was.

They were going to make it home. Not covered with glory, as Commodore Dominick had planned, or loaded with treasure and the key to Manticore's conquest, as Charles had promised. No, they would be returning to Haven like a dog with its tail between its legs. But at least they *would* be returning.

And then, even as he came to that conclusion, the

forward display flashed a sudden warning. "Hyper footprint!" the tac officer called. "Directly ahead of us."

"Identify," Vaccares ordered. Another Manty? Had the convoy had a second escort lurking out at the edge of the system?

But it wasn't a Manty.

It was far worse.

"Unidentified raider, this is His Imperial Majesty's battlecruiser *Neue Bayern*," a harsh, German-accented voice announced coldly. "You have no means of escape. Surrender, or be destroyed."

Frantically, Vaccares looked at the tac display. But *Neue Bayern* was right. Between the battlecruiser in front of him and the *Fearless* behind him, there was no vector he could take that wouldn't force him into engagement with one or both of the larger ships for at least ten minutes.

He could fight, of course. He and his crew could die for the glory of Haven, or at least to save it from the consequences of getting caught with a seized Andermani ship.

But too many people had already died in this fiasco. Most of them were Manties, but they were dead just the same.

He could see no reason to voluntarily add to their number.

"Strike the wedge," he ordered the helmsman quietly. "And then signal the *Neue Bayern* and *Fearless*.

"Tell them we surrender."

Admiral of the Red Sonja Hemphill looked up from the report and steadied her gaze onto the face of the young man standing stiffly at parade rest in front of her desk. "And what, Lieutenant," she said frostily, "am I supposed to do with you?"

Lieutenant Cardones's cheek might have twitched,

but there was no other reaction Hemphill could see. "Ma'am?" he asked evenly.

"You disobeyed a direct order from a superior," Hemphill said, tapping a fingertip on the memo pad in front of her. "Captain Sandler's report makes it clear she told you not to raise the *Dorado*'s wedge. Yet you did so anyway. Are you aware that that's a court-martial offense?"

"Yes, Ma'am," Cardones said. "And I make no excuse."

Hemphill felt her face settle into a familiar set of lines. "Aside from the fact that it saved every man and woman aboard the *Fearless*?" she suggested.

This time there was definitely a twitch. "Yes, Ma'am," Cardones said. "And the crews of the merchantmen, too."

"And do you intend to make a habit of placing individual lives over the value of official Naval or governmental policy?" Hemphill continued. "More to the point for a line officer, do you intend to place the value of these lives over the lawful execution of your orders?"

The young man's face had settled into lines of its own. "No, Ma'am," he said.

"That's good, Lieutenant," Hemphill said, letting her voice chill a few degrees. "Because if you were—if I even *thought* you were—you would be out of the service so fast it would take you three weeks just to catch up with your butt. Do I make myself clear?"

"Yes, Ma'am."

"Good," Hemphill said softly. "Then allow me make myself even clearer. You acted out of loyalty to Captain Harrington and the *Fearless*. I appreciate that. But loyalty must always be balanced with the larger perspective. Here we had a chance—a small one, admittedly, but still a chance—to feed Haven a line of disinformation that could have tied up its time and resources for years to come."

She lifted her chin. "And no matter what you, Captain Harrington, or anyone else aboard *Fearless* ever do with your careers, you will *never* accomplish anything that could possibly pay that kind of dividend for the Star Kingdom. Understood?"

"Yes, Ma'am," Cardones said.

"Good." Hemphill nodded toward the door. "You're hereby detached from your temporary ONI duty. You will return to duty aboard *Fearless* when she returns to Manticore in approximately one month; until then, you're on R and R leave. The yeoman will give you a copy of your orders."

"Thank you, Ma'am," Cardones said.

"And remember that everything you heard, saw, or did while with Tech Team Four is classified," Hemphill added. "Dismissed."

Cardones saluted, and with a crisp about-face he strode from the office.

With a grimace, Hemphill lowered her eyes to the report again. Yes, the kid had disobeyed orders, and she had needed to come down hard on him to make sure he didn't get casual about such things.

But in all honesty, it was hard to fault him for his actions. Even Sandler's own report had conceded it would have taken a miracle for Manticore to have kept up the deception long enough for Haven to commit any serious resources to the Crippler project. Balanced against that was the fact that the team had solved the problem, ended that particular threat to Manticoran shipping, and given the Peeps a sore nose along with it.

And even in the grand scheme of things, saving Her Majesty's Navy a heavy cruiser and its crew was nothing to be sneered at.

Especially when that ship had been instrumental in delivering a captured Andermani light cruiser back to its rightful owners, eliminating a potential source of tension before it really got started.

The Andies placated, and the Peeps humiliated. Two birds taken out with a single stone; and Hemphill was certainly realistic enough to appreciate the economy of such things.

And maybe there was a third bird waiting to be winged by this particular stone. That trick Harrington had used, flickering her impellers to signal the *Neue Bayern* lurking out beyond the hyper limit, had some definite possibilities. Not as a standard interception tactic per se; the Andies had had to do some very precise maneuvering in order to circle through hyperspace and plant themselves squarely in the escaping raider's path that way. Most Manticoran astrogators weren't competent enough to pull off a trick like that, at least not on a regular basis.

But the maneuver itself was almost beside the point. The point was that Harrington had found a way to use gravitational waves to send a signal to the Andies.

And since gravity pulses effectively moved faster than light *and* were detectable from much farther away . . .

Especially if they could combine this idea with the new high-yield fusion bottles and superconductors being designed for the next-generation electronic warfare drones, and maybe throw in something from the compact LAC beta nodes already undergoing testing over at BuWeaps . . .

A third bird, indeed. Maybe.

Pulling Sandler's report from her memo pad, she slipped in Harrington's and began to carefully reread it.

❖   ❖   ❖

Bracing himself, feeling a little like the new kid in school, Cardones stepped onto *Fearless's* bridge.

It looked just the same as when he'd left. Looked, felt, and smelled; and for a moment he just stood inside the hatch, taking it all in. It seemed like forever since he'd left this place. Since he'd left these people.

"There you are," a familiar voice said. "Welcome back, Rafe."

He turned, the new-kid feeling fading away like a light morning mist. Captain Harrington was standing with Andy Venizelos by the com station, consulting together over a memo pad. "Thank you, Ma'am," Cardones said. "How was the tour?"

"Interesting," the captain said. Her voice was casual, but Cardones thought he saw a flicker of something in the exec's face. "Yours?"

"About the same," Cardones said, matching her tone. "Permission to resume my station?"

"Permission granted," she said, and smiled. "Enough lazing around, Mr. Cardones. Get back to work."

"Yes, Ma'am," Cardones said, smiling back. Taking another deep breath, he crossed to his station.

It was good to be home.

A SHIP NAMED *FRANCIS*

by John Ringo & Victor Mitchell

CHAPTER ONE

SIBERIA IS A CONCEPT

Sean Tyler tapped on the open door to the sickbay and entered at a grunt from within.

Tyler was just pushing twenty-three T-years and was on the beginning of his second hitch with the Manticoran Navy. He was dark complected and stood a bit under normal height for a Manticoran, both of which would help him blend with his new Grayson crewmates. On the other hand, he seemed nearly as broad as he was tall, a situation of being "big boned" rather than massive. He had been assigned to the superdreadnought *Victory* until his sudden, unexpected and late in the "day" departure for his new assignment.

A chief warrant officer in his thirties, short and dark as most Graysons were, with a lean, gray face, was sitting at a desk staring at a pad as if the message on it might leap out of the screen and bite.

"Sick Berth Attendant Third Class Sean Tyler reporting for duty!" Sean said, snapping to attention and throwing a parade ground salute. He was mildly surprised to find the warrant still on duty; it was nearly 2400 hours, ship time.

The warrant tossed the pad on his desk and made a gesture towards his forehead that might graciously have been considered a salute and waved at a chair.

"Welcome, my friend, welcome to the *Francis Mueller*," the officer replied. "Grab a seat. I'll be with you in a minute."

Sean sat down and looked around at what was his new home, for however long he was going to be stuck here. His first impression was that the sickbay was small, less than a quarter of the size of the main sickbay on the *Victory*-class superdreadnought that had been his first assignment. It was even smaller than the three secondary sickbays scattered throughout that massive ship. On the other hand, the complement of the heavy cruiser *Francis Mueller* was less than a tenth the complement on the SD.

Not only was the *Francis* smaller than the SD, it was far older; indeed the class was among the oldest designs in the Alliance fleet. Although it was already obsolete, the ship had been sent to Grayson early in the current war against the Peeps. At the time it was one of the most powerful ships in that planet's fleet. Now, though, between the large number of converted Peep SDs, captured at First and Second Yeltsin, and the new Grayson SDs and cruisers that were starting to flow out of the yards, it was again in the position of being an outmoded and under-armed relic.

Furthermore, it looked it. No matter how many times a ship was sent into the yards for overhaul, no matter how thoroughly that overhaul was done, the ship always showed its age. It was apparent in the little patches of mold that crept out from bulkhead corners, in the worn spots on corners, even in the design of bunks, tables and other fittings, which had changed subtly over the years of war.

So there was a reason Tyler had a sour expression when the warrant finally tossed the pad on his desk.

"You don't look happy, SBA," the warrant said, pulling open a bottom drawer on his desk and extracting a half-filled, flaccid bladder of unidentified liquid. He squirted a generous measure into a mug of tea on the desk then waved it at Tyler. "Medicinal belt?"

"No, Sir, thank you, Sir," Sean replied, wondering if the clear liquid was anything other than water. Then the smell hit him.

"Chief Warrant Officer Robert Kearns," the warrant continued, putting the bladder away. "I'm the physician's assistant on this tub. You may call me Doc."

"Yes, Sir," Sean said.

"Did you get stowed away? Got a locker, bunk, all that stuff?"

"Yes, Sir. The Bosun met us and assigned us quarters."

"Good, good," the warrant replied. "Where'd they ship you in from? You're Manticoran, right?"

"Yes, Sir," Tyler said.

"Wanted to come slum with the religious nuts?"

"No, Sir," the SBA replied. "I had applied for a transfer to the Grayson service nearly a year ago. It's considered a good move promotion-wise, working with other Alliance forces."

"Uh, huh," the warrant said. "So, you're telling me you *volunteered* for the *Francis Mueller*?"

"Well, I volunteered for Grayson service and there was a priority opening on the *Mueller*, Sir, so here I am." He looked around, then decided to take a chance. "I made a serious mistake, didn't I?"

"Yup," the medic replied, taking a pull off of his reinforced tea. "You ever have to trank anybody on your previous ship?"

"Once," Tyler replied. "Is that . . . a particular problem?"

"We get about one trank call a week," the warrant admitted. "Sometimes more on bad weeks. What we do then is put 'em in a jacket and tie 'em to their bunk. When they come around we try to decide if it was temporary or permanent. If they talk nice, we let 'em out. If they don't, we leave them in confinement until we can get a transship to a safe ground area."

"One a *week*?" Sean gasped. In his six months on the *Victory* there had been a total of four people who had succumbed to "situational stress disorder" or "the bug" as most people called it. "And you've still got a crew *at all*?"

"We've got guys on this ship, I swear, are addicted to trank. Kopp, he's a missile tech, he's been tranked about six times. Cooper in Engineering, it's about once a month, like clockwork. Heck, the reason you were a priority replacement is that the other two SBAs were both medical evacs. If the timing had been different you would have met your predecessor on the way over; we transshipped him to the *Victory*."

"Weird," Sean said. "Any particular reason?"

"Oh," the warrant said with a slight catch in his voice, "I think you'll come to a few conclusions over time."

"Now hear this! Now hear this! Morning prayers! All hands not on watch, uncover for morning prayers!"

Sean hadn't had a chance to meet any of his fellow compartment sharers last night; they were all on second watch and had racked out by the time he entered the compartment. Now, as the lights came up and the other three stood up and clasped their hands, he wondered what to do.

Being a Manticoran, he was not a member of the Church of Humanity Unchained, so he was under no obligation to join in the morning prayers. But getting up and getting ready for the day wasn't exactly a good idea, either. So he figured he'd just bow his head and sit through it. How long could it take?

"*Tester,*" a nasally voice said over the enunciator, "*spare us this day from your Tests.*

"*Please, Tester, don't let any of the airlocks blow out. Let the environmental system, old as it is, shudder though another day of labor. Please, Tester, let the water recyclers make it through a few more days, even though Engineering says they're just about shot. Tester, please see fit to keep Fusion Two from terminally overloading and blowing us all into Your arms; we love you but we want to see our families again some day.*

"*Please, Tester, if you could maybe see clear to keeping the compensator on-line? If we don't have the compensator, we can't make our acceleration back home, and we'll drift in space, a derelict, until the systems begin to fail and the power runs out and the air gets foul and we all start eating each other . . .*"

It continued in the same vein for a good fifteen minutes as the quavering voice slowly worked its way through every imaginable disaster scenario.

Spaceships were, inherently, disasters waiting to happen. It was one of the main reasons that "the bug" was a problem; any reasonably intelligent individual dealt with a certain amount of "apprehension," as it was politely termed, as soon as he was out of the atmosphere. Vacuum is very unforgiving stuff and even the most advanced technologies could not make space truly safe.

But most people were polite enough not to mention that in public. Much less broadcast it, in detail, over the enunciator.

He began to see why people tended to flip out on the *Francis Mueller*. And he wondered, as he was getting dressed in the crowded but mostly silent compartment, how much worse it could get.

"What do you mean we're *lost*?"

Warrant Officer Kearns had just brought Tyler to the bridge to meet the captain. The first words out of his new commander's mouth were not ones to settle Sean's . . . apprehension.

Captain Zemet was incredibly handsome, with high cheekbones, an aquiline nose and a chin that you could use to crack walnuts. He probably could have been a holovid star with one exception; he was short, even by Grayson standards. On Manticore the word "dwarf" might have been used. He was looking up at the not much taller lieutenant with an expression of absolute perplexity on his face.

"We're not *lost*, Sir," the lieutenant standing braced in front of the captain replied. "We just appear to be . . . off course."

"Do you know *why*?" the captain asked.

"Not yet, Sir," the lieutenant said. "We appear to have suffered a change in course due to a . . . gravitational anomaly."

"Gravitational anomaly?" the captain replied.

"Yes, Sir," the sweating lieutenant replied.

"We're lost." The speaker was a tall man by Grayson standards, with a pale complexion and a thin, ascetic face. He was dressed entirely in black. Either Death had decided to visit the *Francis Mueller*, a possibility that had some validity all things considered, or Sean was in the presence of the ship's chaplain.

"We're lost, wandering helpless in the depths of space!" the chaplain said. It was the same reedy voice from morning prayers.

"We're not *lost*, Chaplain Olds," the captain said. "We simply have to make a course correction. How *much* of a course correction?" he asked the astrogator.

"We're still computing that, Sir," the lieutenant replied. "But we're at least a hundred and twenty thousand kilometers off base course."

"Good Tester," the captain swore. "It occurs to me that we made a close pass by Blackbird Six. You *did* figure that into your equations, didn't you, Astro?"

"Err," the lieutenant hesitated. "Let me check my notes."

"You didn't, did you?" the captain said. "It suddenly occurs to me that if you didn't figure it into your calculations, you probably *also* didn't consider that it was *out* there, did you? It crosses my mind that you didn't mention that we were doing a close pass until Tactical picked up the moon on lidar at under sixty-three thousand kilometers. I remember thinking that was cutting it a bit close, all things considered."

"I'm . . . not sure, Sir," the lieutenant said.

"Sweet Tester!" the chaplain exclaimed. "In my wildest nightmares, I never considered that we could slam unthinking into a celestial body! The ship would be strewn across its surface! Unless we noticed in time and sent out a distress call, we would be lost for all time! No one would ever find the wreckage! We would die, lost and alone, our bodies and souls left to drift helplessly in the depths of space!"

"Tomorrow's gonna be a doozy," the warrant muttered under his breath.

"Sir." The speaker was a short—how else—broad, lieutenant commander, presumably the XO. Tyler hadn't seen him arrive, he had just appeared out of nowhere as if teleported in. "There are penalties in the rules for court-martial regarding failure to perform prescribed duties and placing a ship in unnecessary hazard. We could convene a summary court and have the Astrogator spaced."

"I don't think that will be necessary, XO," the captain said helplessly. "Chaplain, why don't you go tend to your flock? Or maybe say a few private prayers for our well-being in your cabin. Astro, go punch in the gravitational pull of Blackbird Six and see if that works." He turned to Tyler and the warrant and gave them both a brilliant smile. "I take it this is the new medic?"

"Captain Zemet, Sick Berth Attendant Tyler," the warrant said. "Late of the Manticoran Navy."

"Good to meet you, Taylor," the captain said, holding out his hand. "You've joined the best ship in the Grayson Navy and, I think, the best in the Alliance. I'm sure you'll fit in well. All you have to do is give me one hundred percent of your abilities."

"Yes, Sir," Sean replied, wondering if a little 120,000 kilometer course error, not to mention forgetting that you were doing a close pass of a celestial body, was one hundred percent of the astrogator's abilities. The scary part was that it seemed to be. "I'll try to do my best. And it's *Tyler*, Sir."

"Glad to hear it, Taylor," the captain said. "Give him the tour of the ship, Chief. I've got a few things on my plate at the moment."

"Yes, Sir," the warrant replied.

"Good meeting you, Taylor," the captain said. "Glad to have you aboard."

❖   ❖   ❖

It appeared that the chief chose to skip the instructional walk-around as he led Tyler back to the sickbay.

Doc flopped into his chair and opened up the bottom drawer, pouring a shot into his tea again.

"So, what's your impression so far?" he asked, taking a sip.

"You only lose one guy a week?" Sean said with a quivering laugh.

"You noticed," the warrant said, lifting the bladder. "Medicinal belt?"

"Not yet," Tyler said, deeply tempted. "Is it just me, or is everyone on this vessel insane?"

"Certainly the entire chain of command," the warrant replied, taking another sip. "You haven't even *met* the Chief Engineer, who at least is competent."

"And . . . the Chaplain?" Sean asked, carefully.

"Chaplains, by law, have the run of the ship and are an entity to themselves," Doc replied with a grimace. "In the case of Chaplain Olds, he has two problems: an overactive imagination, and insomnia. I can't do anything about the former but I've tried to prescribe sleeping pills. No luck, he considers them to be a Devil's Brew. So he lies awake all ship's night, imagining all the horrible things that can, and very occasionally do, go wrong on the ship. He's also . . . egged on by some of the ship's company that have more of a sense of humor than common sense. Ribart, down in Engineering, is forever coming up with new things that 'need your prayers, Chaplain.' I've considered just tranking Ribart to get him off the ship, but that seems over the top. Then there's the automatic deference to chaplains that is instilled in Grayson at the bone."

"I'll admit that after the morning prayer *I'm* a little . . . apprehensive. And I've never considered that an astrogator might just *forget* that there is a planet around. But I still think that what the Chaplain needs is a good lay; he seems really uptight."

The chief grimaced and Sean realized what he'd said.

"I hadn't meant to impugn your faith, Chief . . ." Tyler said formally.

"Oh, it's not that," the warrant replied wearily. "You weren't here for the infamous STD incident." Doc took a healthy slug of his tea and then poured a straight-up refill.

"STD?" Tyler said. "I'm not sure what that stands for."

"Sexually transmitted disease," the warrant said dryly. "I'm aware that they've been wiped out among the Manticorans, but they do occasionally crop up in Silesia. We had a little . . . incident on our last cruise that way. Let's just say the Chaplain was not one of those who did not contract it."

Tyler looked at him questioningly and the warrant shrugged.

"Long story. Stupid story. Maybe some other time."

The chief took another sip, obviously gathering his thoughts.

"It's like this—you know the Grayson Navy has expanded nearly fifty fold since we joined the Alliance?"

"I'm aware of that, Sir," Tyler said. "Is that part of it?"

"That's *most* of it," Doc replied. "Whenever you do that fast of an expansion, you get people who rise beyond their level of competence. When that is realized, if nobody gets killed by it, you have a few choices. You can demote the person, which requires a lot of paperwork and time by *competent* authorities, time which is in short supply. Or you can shuffle them off where they aren't going to be much of a bother. Are you getting my drift?"

"Oh." Sean started to open his mouth and then closed it.

"And, yes," the warrant said dryly, raising his cup, "I'm included in that bunch. Whatever my competence as a doc, I've . . . got a bit of a drinking problem. So here I am, exiled to Siberia."

"Well," Tyler said with a laugh, "at least the Exec has a sense of humor."

"What do you mean?"

"Well," Tyler said, grinning, "when he said they should court-martial the navigation officer and sp—" He stopped when he saw the warrant officer's face. "He *was* joking, right?"

"Nope," the medic said, pulling out the bladder and taking a squirt from the neck. "Welcome to Siberia, friend."

"I think I'll have that drink now," Tyler said weakly.

CHAPTER TWO

THE CONSOLATIONS OF FAITH

"Tester, spare us this day from your Tests.

"Please don't let us slam into any celestial bodies, our souls to drift helplessly through the deeps of space as our families wonder what disaster has overtaken us and left us, Tester, bereft and alone, among the stars . . .

"Tester, spare us this day from your Tests.

"It's been three days now, Tester, and Astrogation is still trying to figure out where we are. If you could maybe see the way clear, Tester, to giving them a hint how to find our way back to Grayson before the air

*runs out or the environmental systems fail or one of
the shuddering fusion reactors explodes, spreading our
constituent atoms among the stars . . .*

"*Tester, spare us this day from your Tests.*

"*Tester, I understand that one of the beta nodes is
looking pretty bad. If we lose it, Tester, please don't
blast out the whole bank. We still don't know exactly
where Grayson is, Tester, and we won't be able to send
out a distress call that will be picked up unless we can
send it in their direction. We don't want to die, Tester,
drifting through the empty blackness of the Heavens,
our bodies shriveled by vacuum, fighting like rabid
dogs, Tester, over the compartments that still have
air . . .*

CHAPTER THREE

REACTIONS AND ALARUMS

Tyler was just stooging through the bridge, on his
way to the missile tech's quarters where there were
reports of illicit gambling being conducted, when the
alarm went off.

The captain was on the bridge three seconds after
the alarm started, in a crouch, looking as if he didn't
know which way to run.

"Is that the reactor alarm?!" the captain yelled.

"You're the Captain," Tyler said quietly, putting his
hand over his eyes and mentally kissing his butt
goodbye. "You don't *know*?"

"Fusion Two is in alarm!" the engineering watch PO
said. "But there's no sign of the fault on my screens."

"Prepare to jettison!" the captain yelled as the alarm shut off. "Or not." He cursed luridly and hit the button for Fusion Two.

"Two! What in the Sweet Merciful Tester's name is going on?!"

"Uh, sorry about that," the talker replied. "Kowalski dropped his coffee mug on the alarm switch."

"Sir."

"AH!"

The XO had just appeared behind the CO again, causing the already somewhat overwrought captain to nearly jump out of his skin. One of these days, Tyler was going to see the XO actually walk. So far, he appeared to travel by telekinesis. "I recommend that we convene a summary court and space Spaceman Kowalski."

"I don't think that will be necessary, Exec," the captain panted. "Tempting . . . but no. We'll talk about a Captain's Mast tomorrow. For now, I'm going to go to my cabin and change my shorts. Make that a general order."

"Medic to the missile compartment," the enunciator called. "Bring your syringe."

Tyler left the bridge shaking his head.

"He didn't know if it was the reactor alarm or not," he said, giggling helplessly. "He's the *captain*, and he didn't *know*. Hah-hah. Hah-hah, hee. Uhn hah, Oh My God . . ."

"Tester, spare us this day from your Tests . . ."

CHAPTER FOUR

THE POTATO SACK INCIDENT

By the fourth day on the *Francis Mueller*, Tyler had taken to carrying a tranquilizer injector with him at all times. He wasn't sure if that was to use it on other crewmen, or himself.

But he had it, and a straitjacket, with him when he was called to the bridge on second Day Watch.

"Taylor, you need to sedate Petty Officer Kyle," the captain said, pointing to a PO in the tactical section. The petty officer was rocking in his chair, playing with himself.

"Hah, hah! Planet! Missed the planet! Hah, hah," Petty Officer Kyle was clearly enjoying himself.

"Yes, Sir," Tyler said, walking over and hitting the PO in the shoulder with the injector. The sedative worked quickly and in a few moments the petty officer slid bonelessly out of his chair and hit the deck with a thump.

"Sir," the XO said, appearing again behind the captain.

"AAAH! Sweet Merciful Tester, Greene, wear a bell on your boot or *something*."

"Yes, sir," the XO replied, seriously. "Sir, I think that PO Kyle needs to go before the Mast."

"I don't," the captain replied. "He was clearly driven around the bend by Lieutenant Wilson's announcement that the fault in his calculations was that he forgot to account for Blackbird's mass as well as all of her moons! It turns out that if we hadn't had that forty minute delay when we were trying to get the course adjusted on the way in, we would have hit the *planet*."

Tyler unfolded the straitjacket and started to load

the tactical PO in as he kept one ear on the conversation behind him.

"Well, at least we know where we are, Sir," Lieutenant Wilson said. "And I've got a course laid in for Grayson."

"Are you *sure*?" the captain asked. "And are you sure there's nothing *in the way*?"

"Yes, Sir," the communication officer said. "We sent a ping to them. They replied asking where we've been for the last few days."

"I think the best response was that we were lying doggo, under communications silence, in case anyone was trying to sneak into the system," the captain said, rubbing his chin. "The less mentioned about the last week, the better."

"*Masterful* response, sir," the XO said. "Com, fire that off right away."

"Aye, aye, Sir."

"We've got two weeks before we're due in the yards," the captain said. "We're supposed to be doing workups, but with the crew in the shape it is, I don't think that's a good idea. We're already as worked up as any crew I've ever seen."

"We can do them, Sir," the XO protested. "All the crew needs is a little firm discipline. If you'd just see your way clear to giving me a free hand . . ."

"We don't *have* any thumbscrews, Greene," the captain said, shaking his head. "No, what they need is some *down* time: a day off. Bosun!"

"Yes, Sir?" The senior enlisted person on the ship was heavyset, with thinning hair and a bulbous, red nose that indicated he probably was in Siberia for the same reason as Doc Kearns.

"Adjust Axial One to a forty-five degree, one gee, gravitational cone," the captain snapped. He keyed the enunciator and cleared his throat. "All off duty watch, report to Axial One, and BREAK OUT THE POTATO SACKS!"

Axial One was a large "tube" running down the spine of the ship. Normally, it was set to low gravity and used for movement of personnel and equipment. Under the low G personnel could move materials quickly and efficiently. Or, alternatively, crewmen who thought they were "salty" could move like a bat out of hell down the tube, bounding along under the .2 G field at speeds of up to forty kilometers per hour or moving huge loads like missiles or pallets of explosive bolts at only somewhat slower velocities.

Of course, the law of conservation of mass applied, so all those salty crewmen eventually had to decelerate or dodge other crewmen who were moving down the corridor at speeds far in excess of sense. And since the human eye and mind are not designed to calculate automatically what is "too fast" a closing speed, quite a few of those crewmen ended up impacting on some other sailor, or his large and occasionally deadly load, sometimes at closing speeds that would do for a small air-car wreck.

Axial One produced about fifteen percent of the total "incidental casualties" on the ship.

Of course, "speeds in excess of forty kilometers per hour" had never made it into *official* reports, even in the Manticoran service. It would take a real jerk, like Hard-Ass Harrington or somebody, to report what *actually* went on in Axial One, but for some strange reason newer ships didn't have anything like it. Of course, BuShips *said* that was because Axial One was a structural danger. On the other hand, the admirals at BuShips had served on the companion ships of the *Francis Mueller*. It was a statistical likelihood approaching certainty that some of them had been involved in an "incidental casualty" report. Which was a much better explanation for removing Axial One, in Sean's medical opinion, than "structural anomalies."

Sean considered all this gloomily as he looked "up" the corridor towards the bow of the ship and wondered if it was one of *those* idiots who had invented Potato-Sack Tobogganing.

The "floor" of the circular corridor was normally scratched and scuffed alloy. But one strip of it, a U-shaped section about twenty meters across the chord and the full length of the corridor, had been quickly polished and waxed. At the same time, the gravitational pull in the corridor had been set to a forty-five degree "cone." That is, instead of pulling straight "down" or towards the exterior of the ship, the artificial gravity was pulling "sideways" at a forty-five degree angle. Combined with the slickness of the waxed portion, the tendency was to cause a person to slip, and keep slipping. Towards the after end of the corridor the gravity had been adjusted in the other direction. It was an artificial hillside with a catchment at the base.

"Down" which a succession of screaming spacers were now sliding at, literally, break-neck speed.

The potato sacks on which they slid were of a strange, rough material that had been identified for Tyler as "burlap." They were not, apparently, used for carrying potatoes anymore but were kept for the sole purpose of this highly idiotic sport. They also stank to high heaven. The nature of the "sport" tended to cause flatulence and storing them between times was best described as "marinating"; they smelled worse than any latrine Sean had ever encountered. But this was supposedly "fun."

At the bow end of the corridor the captain could faintly be seen, holding onto a stanchion and shouting encouragement. He was apparently a big advocate of "crew quality time" and considered it team-building for everyone in the ship's company to risk their necks in a suicidal game of "find the nearest stanchion with my head."

Now Sean crouched in a small aid station set off the corridor (BuShips was *slow*, not *stupid*) and watched as sailor after sailor slid past on fecal-smelling bags—some yelling, others with expressions of quiet, fear-filled, desperation—and considered his orders from the warrant.

"When somebody gets hurt in your area, triage them. If they're just contused or have a surface cut or abrasion, slap a dressing on it and send them on. If they break a bone immobilize it, give 'em a shot to keep 'em quiet and hold them at the station; we'll set them all later. If they sustain a head-wound or spinal damage, send them down to me."

"You mean if *somebody gets hurt."*

"No, I mean when.*"*

He currently had four of the crew stretched out at the back of the aid station, two with broken legs, one with a broken wrist and one with multiple breaks and contusions. The reason for the damage became apparent as he watched the next contestant.

One of the crew, Kopp, one of the senior missile techs, was just starting down the artificial "slope." He was one of the "face frozen in determination" crowd and it was well earned. Kopp had a reputation for being a hard-luck case, so naturally he didn't make it all the way to the braking field. Instead, he tried to fit in and "surf."

Although the corridor was curved, the artificial gravity drew on it equally across the surface so it "felt" flat. What that meant was that using the weight of the buttocks it was possible, with care and skill, to slide back and forth on the waxed portion and "slalom" down the corridor. The operative words were "care" and "skill." Failure to use either sent the tobogganer into what pilots euphemistically refer to as an "out of control" situation.

Kopp only made it about a third of the way down before he lost it. He had just started to slalom when he went too far to the side and hit the unwaxed portion. This slowed his left buttock abruptly and following the laws of Newtonian physics his right buttock, and most of the rest of his body, continued in the direction they were going. This, first, induced flatulence, as his anus responded to the conflicting forces, then a scream as the first pain hit, and last a pinwheeling figure, bouncing down the corridor, his potato sack spinning off in one direction and his shrieking body, spinning faster, in another.

The yelling stopped, or at least changed tone to low groans, as he hit the coaming of one of the corridor exits. Tyler worked his way out of the first-aid station and laboriously climbed "up" the gravity well on the unwaxed portion, dragging two bags of supplies with him, until he reached the injured missile tech.

Kopp was holding on to the coaming with one hand while cradling the other arm and trying to tilt his head to keep blood from pouring into his eyes.

Tyler felt his cradled arm and shook his head at an in-drawn breath. "Broken, probably a green-stick fracture." He slapped a bandage on the bleeding head wound, attached a splint to the arm and put on a cervical collar for good measure.

"HE'S GOING TO BE OKAY!" he yelled up to the captain.

"NOT WHEN I GET AHOLD OF HIM!" the captain bellowed back. "WHAT KIND OF A SHOWING WAS THAT, KOPP?!"

❖   ❖   ❖

"This is the quality of sailor we get these days!" the captain grumped.

"Sir," the exec said, apporting in behind him. "There are Regulations governing making oneself unavailable for duty through negligence."

"I'm not going to Captain's Mast Kopp for wiping out," the captain replied, stepping down off his perch and leaning sideways against the gradient. "But what *this* crew needs is a lesson in how to ride potato sacks. Not enough veterans in this crew, not enough instructors. It's up to the *officers* to pick up the slack!"

"Uh, Captain," the bosun said uncomfortably as the commander held out his hand for one of the sacks.

"It's up to us to *set an example*, Boats," Zemet said, snatching the square of cloth out of his resisting hand. "PREPARE FOR A DEMONSTRATION OF HOW TO RIDE A POTATO SACK!" the captain yelled. "PREPARE TO WATCH . . . A PROFESSIONAL!"

"Well, Astro is pretty sure we're on course for Grayson, but we got so well lost first that it's a four day run." Doc dropped into his chair and pulled out his bladder of whiskey, holding it away from his mouth and taking a hard squirt out of the neck. "How's the Captain?" he coughed.

"He's breathing," Sean replied. "Just looks like a standard coma, no evidence of subdural cerebral hematoma."

"Can you just say 'brain bruise' for Tester's Sake?" the warrant grunted. "Four days under the Exec."

There didn't seem to be much else to be said.

"Bosun," the XO said, standing on the bridge looking at the navigational readouts, "we have a problem."

"Yes, Sir?" the Bosun said, faintly.

"That problem," the XO intoned, "is *slackness*."

"Yes, Sir."

"The Captain scheduled his little game in the interests of jollying people up, but the root problem was *slackness*. They've all been slacking. Well, we're not going to have any slackness when *I'm* in command."

"No, Sir."

"I've got a work-up schedule," the XO continued, turning to face the NCO. Deep in his eyes, a little fire seemed to burn. As far as the Bosun was concerned, it was burning his retirement papers. "And we're all going to follow it. To the letter." He turned back to contemplating the Astro display.

"Yes, Sir," the Bosun replied.

"We're not going to have any slackness," the XO repeated. "We'll show the fleet that slackness doesn't happen on the *Francis Mueller*. Whatever it takes."

"But, Sir," the bosun said, regretting the words even before they left his mouth, "we don't *have* any thumbscrews."

"That, Bosun," the XO replied in a low, mad whisper, "is why they give us machine shops!"

"Tester, spare us this day from your Tests. It's been nearly a day, Tester, with the Captain in a coma, and the Exec is preparing capital charges for a quarter of the crew. Based on simple statistics, Tester, no one is going to be alive when we reach Grayson. The ship will be a tomb, drifting helplessly in the grip of gravity wells and the solar wind . . ."

"Doc, I've got a problem," the bosun said, slipping into the sickbay after a cautious look around.

"Don't we all," the medic snapped, looking up from the captain's recumbent figure.

"I don't suppose the dwarf's come around yet?"

"No," Kearns replied.

The bosun looked up as Tyler slid through the door.

"I'm not going out there," Tyler said. "It's a zoo."

"The crew's ready to mutiny," the bosun went on. "They agree with the Chaplain; if we let the Exec get away with spacing a quarter of us every day, there won't be any of us left by the time we get to Grayson."

"That's an ugly word," Doc said. "Mutiny."

"Yeah, but it's better than 'explosive decompression,'" Sean pointed out.

"That's not a word, it's a phrase," Doc replied.

"They're both going to be phrases we'll all get accustomed to if we don't figure something out!" the bosun muttered.

"Well, Manticore doesn't generally use the death penalty," Tyler pointed out, rubbing his chin in thought. "And if they do, they generally wait until the ship gets to a major port where a court-martial can take place with due process. Why not try to . . . Never mind."

"Yeah, he'd never go for that," the bosun said. "If we even brought it up we'd be added to the list."

"Is he talking about just *spacing* them?" Kearns asked. "I mean, not even a bullet in the back of the head or anything?"

"No," the Bosun replied with a grimace. "He wants to either shoot them or give them a lethal shot and then . . . Hey!"

"Yeah," Kearns said with a narrowed glance. "Now all we have to do is convince him not to space the bodies."

"Decent burial," Tyler said after a moment. "I mean, you're all religious nuts, right? Surely it would only be proper to return them to the cool green hills of Grayson or something."

The warrant looked at the senior NCO and the SBA for a moment and then narrowed his eyes.

"Okay, what we're talking about here is conspiracy

to mutiny by circumventing direct orders of a superior." He looked them both in the eye. "And the penalty for that *is* death."

"I'll take my chance on a court-martial on Grayson," the bosun responded.

"Me too," Tyler said. "Hell, I'd prefer *Peep* justice to this friggin' nut-case."

CHAPTER FIVE

The Quick and the Dead

The XO stomped down the deserted corridors of the crew compartment, looking around in delight at the near pristine conditions. With none of the pesky crew cluttering things up, it was possible to have a truly efficiently run ship. Suddenly he slid to a stop.

"BOSUNNN!" he shouted, pointing at the floor. "What is that??!"

"Gum, sir," the bosun replied.

"Who is in charge of this area?" the XO asked, furiously.

"Cooper," the bosun replied. It was getting easier and easier to remember as the number of crew dropped precipitously.

"Well, space him!" the XO said. "Gum on the floor is just *slackness*."

"Yes, Sir," the bosun replied. "You'll remember that we're returning them to their families . . ."

"Very well," the XO said, continuing on his survey. "Send him to the medics."

❖   ❖   ❖

"No, no!" Cooper yelled, hopping up and down in the grip from two men-at-arms and winking for all he was worth. "Don't kill me, Doc!"

"Oh, shut up and take it like a man," Tyler replied tiredly. He rolled up Cooper's sleeve and injected the engineering tech with a sedative. "Take him to the forecastle."

"I bet he dropped that gum on the floor on purpose," one of the men-at-arms grumped. "I could do with a three day vacation at this point."

"If we lose many more engineering techs, we're never going to make it," Sean replied darkly.

Captain Zemet opened his eyes and stared blearily into the face of Admiral Judah Yanakov. A quick glance to the side showed the two medics, the engineering officer and the astrogator lined up against one wall of what was apparently a hospital room.

"Captain, would you kindly tell me what in the Tester's name was going on up there?" the admiral said furiously. "I would especially like to know how you came to be in a coma and left that Masadan of an XO in charge. The one hundred and twenty-three personnel that your former XO had sedated have all been returned to duty, by the way."

"Well, Sir," the captain said, not even glancing at the figures against the wall, "we were drilling on compensator adjustments in movement. The ship went right and I went left and that's all I remember."

"Warrant Officer Kearns?" Admiral Yanakov asked. "Corpsman Tyler? Is that an accurate report?"

"He's our Captain, Sir," Kearns replied. "What he says is what happened."

"Hmmmph." The admiral peered at the captain for a moment then shook his head. "That's not quite the same as saying 'It happened like he said.' I don't have anywhere *more* out of the way to put you, Zemet, except Blackbird Base and I already stashed your XO there. So I guess I'll have to leave you in command. The rest of you are dismissed."

"That's *it*?" Tyler asked, collapsing into the sickbay chair. The flight back from Grayson had been made in total silence.

"What's it?" Kearns asked, pulling out his bladder of whiskey and pouring some into his cup.

"No investigation?" the Manticoran asked. "We just go back out on patrol?"

"You remember you're in Siberia, right?" the warrant asked, taking a sip of his tea. "And you know that Siberia was nothing but a giant prison?"

"Sort of."

"We're all prisoners, trapped in a Siberia called the *Francis Mueller*. You. Me. The Captain. Hell, even Kopp and the Chaplain, both of whom have been thrown out of at least one *decent* ship so far. And prisoners don't rat out other prisoners to the warden."

"Oh."

"I notice *you* didn't say anything," Kearns pointed out.

"Well . . . hell," Tyler said. "I guess you're right. Why didn't he just say he fell in the shower?"

"He's too professional for that," the warrant officer said, tossing the bladder over to the corpsman. "Only amateurs fall in a shower. Welcome to Siberia."

LET'S GO TO PRAGUE

by John Ringo

CHAPTER 1

A PLAN IS HATCHED

"Let's go to Prague, Johnny!"

John Mullins looked across at his partner and seriously contemplated pegging him in the head with his beer mug. Instead he slid the container of thin, sour brew aside and let the next drop of condensation hit the tabletop.

He recalled the heady days when they first arrived at Seaforth Nine. The most prestigious base in the entire Havenite Republic had just been taken intact by a coup de main and since ONI was already going to be pouring over it, what better use could it be put to than stabling the elite Covert Insertion Teams. Heady days indeed; the unit *had* been barracked in a converted warehouse behind the Manticoran consulate on New Ghuanzou.

As it turned out, there *were* worse things than New Guano; the "most advanced base" the People's Republic of Haven had ever produced turned out to be a dump. Make that a dump and a half.

Much of the interior partitioning was of *wood*, for Christ's sake. Combined with the fact that the dessicators didn't and the chillers wouldn't, the place was a perpetual steam bath. It said much that teams had been trying to get moved up in the mission roster, just to get the relative luxury of beating around on Silesian tramp freighters and risking their lives behind Peep lines.

But that didn't mean he was willing to take leave in Prague.

"So, for our leave, you want to go beat around on tramps for two weeks, maybe a month, spend a couple of tension-filled months hoping we don't get picked up by StateSec and then have to hop tramps back? In what *possible* way does that differ from work?"

"I hear it's lovely in the spring," Charles said with a sardonic grin. He pushed his hair back and chuckled. "And we can drink as much of that fine Peep beer as we choose. Besides, you know how much you love your work."

When Charles Gonzalvez wasn't on a mission he was the spitting image of a mad scientist. Same wild hair, same crazed, glazed expression, same oddball sense of reality. He would be discussing Peep information system security in one breath and be off on how best to kill a sentry in the next.

Come to think of it, that was pretty much how he acted when he *was* on a mission.

Gonzalvez been through a half a dozen partners before he and Mullins met up. Nobody wanted someone who was that . . . frenetic when they were snooping and pooping around in the Peep's back yard. But, somehow, he and Mullins made a great pair. The hyper aristocrat from Manticore A and the quiet farmboy from Gryphon balanced each other. Or, perhaps, enhanced each other; there was no question that they were both the most experienced insertion team and the most successful. The former sort of assumed the latter; losses in CITs ran upwards of thirty percent per mission.

Insertion teams had a variety of uses, from direct reconnaissance, checking out Peep installations and equipment, to retrievals. Sometimes there were defectors to be pulled out or cells to be extracted or the occasional deep mole to be rescued. There was one Manty intelligence agent, Covilla, who had been supplying information for years from deep in Peep territory. That operative was one of the survivors, but not all were so capable. Or lucky.

The People's Republic of Haven had some pretty decent counterintelligence goons in their State Security. They were quite good at compromising cells and rolling up lines. So all too often some poor unsuspecting CIT would go strolling into what was supposed to be a safe house, only to find out that "safe" is a relative term.

Gonzalvez and Mullins had, so far, managed to avoid that fate. Whether it was Johnny's habit of never accepting anything at face value or Gonzo's ability to extract any information he needed at the drop of a cred piece, the two of them had survived every mission, despite some hairy encounters. And if nothing else worked, they had both proven on several occasions that, stolid or wacky, they were, in that delightful phrase, "good with their hands"; the very few times that it had come down to violence the situation ended up in their favor.

But he still wasn't going to Prague.

"How are we getting there?" Mullins asked, finishing the beer with a grimace. It really wouldn't have taken that much to improve the living conditions on Seaforth, but the fact that insertion teams were on the base was so secret it was hard to complain to the right people. *"Minister, we need to upgrade the living conditions on Seaforth."* *"Why?"* *"Uh . . ."*

"It's not like going to Basilisk or Manticore; we can't just jump on a freighter. Where are the travel documents coming from? The cover gear? Where, precisely, are we going to get the internal Peep documentation?"

"Ah, well," Charles said with a grin. "That's not a problem, old boy. Let's just say that Q has some files on his computer he doesn't want coming to life."

"Well, sure, doesn't everyone?" Mullins said. "But . . . wait . . . you cracked *Q's* computer?"

"Boredom doesn't befit me, old boy," his partner replied. "I *asked* him, politely, for an upgraded extraction pack. When he said no, what was I to do but take it as a challenge? All I was *really* looking for was inventory information. How was I to know he had a thing for wee beasties."

Mullins choked back a laugh and shook his head. "You're serious."

"Disgusting really," Charles said, taking a swill of beer. "So, are we going to sit in this bleeding steam bath for the next few months or what?"

"What's wrong with just going home?" Mullins asked. "You go to Manticore and hang out at the family estates and I'll . . ."

"Go home to the farm?" Gonzo asked with a grin. "Wander down to the local pub and not show off the uniform you don't have? Not impress the girls with the medals you can't wear?"

"Oh, shut up."

"I suppose we *could* go down to south coast and hang out on the beach," Charles continued. "Watch all the swabbies wandering around in uniform, telling their tales of how they *all* fought with the Salamander at Basilisk and Grayson. Flexing their nonexistent muscles and flashing their measly collection of ribbons."

"I get the picture . . ."

"While the girls ooh and ahhh . . ."

"All right . . ."

"Then we can go to the bar and watch the bartender filling up their mugs for free . . ."

"I really do understand . . ."

"While we're spending all our credits on overpriced sex in a canoe beer . . ."

"All right . . ."

"You know, very close to water . . ."

"All right . . ."

"When we *could* be in Prague . . ."

"I'll go . . ."

"Wearing StateSec uniforms, not having to pay for our really *good* beer . . ."

"I'LL GO . . ."

"Impressing the girls with our stories of how we were in on the kill of the Salamander . . ."

"I said I'LL GO! Okay, enough. I give. You're right!"

"I knew you'd see it my way old boy."

"Thanks."

"And it really is lovely in the spring."

CHAPTER 2

SUPPLY AND COMPROMISES

"Hallo, Q! Beautiful day isn't it?"

The position of covert operative supply officer had been known as "Q" since time immemorial. The reason was lost in the mists of time, but various reasons, most dependent on the nature of the current holder, had been suggested over the years. "Quality officer" was one. The current holder of the title suggested "Queer Bastard" to most who had to deal with him.

"You don't have a mission scheduled," Q said, waving at the door. The severely overweight supply officer was bent over what appeared to be a beer flask, picking at the base with a dental tool. Whatever was involved must have been very small because he had a video loupe slipped over his right eye. "And I don't have any interest in listening to your whining. Get out."

"Oh, is that any way to treat a friend?" Charles continued. "We're just here to pick up a few items for our leave."

"And what makes you think I'd let you have anything to take on leave?" Q asked, straightening up.

Johnny always imagined Q as some weirdly transformed amphibian. He had a wide mouth with fat lips and a foreshortened forehead that gave his face a faintly piscine look. Combined with the hundred kilos or so that he could stand to lose, the impression of an annoyed toad was hard to ignore.

"Oh, nothing old boy, just these," Charles said, handing the supply officer an envelope.

Q accepted it suspiciously and opened it with a

closed expression. After a moment he took off the loupe and went to his computer. A few taps later he was rubbing his jaw.

"These were obviously planted on my system," the supply officer said with a questioning tone.

"Don't think so," Mullins interjected. "Files are logged onto secure systems."

Q made a moue of distaste and tapped a couple more keys. Only then did his expression start to become more waxen.

"I took the liberty of locking down the evidence while I was in there, old boy," Charles said. "Just doing my job as a good citizen. Those pictures are illegal just about everywhere but New Las Vegas; and they're questionable even there. What that fellow is doing with the goat . . . tch, tch, tch . . ."

"Err . . ."

"And that picture of you and the sheep . . ."

"What picture???!" Q said then hit a series of other keys. His head tilted to the side and an unfathomable expression crossed his face. "Hmmm . . . . But that's *definitely* a fake!"

"Hard to prove, old boy," Charles said. "What with all the others . . . I mean, you're not even a *Marine*."

"Hey!" Johnny said.

"Sorry old boy."

"Bastard," the supply officer said, giving up.

"Definitely," Gonzalvez said, handing him another envelope.

Q opened this one with a great deal more trepidation and his eyes widened as he read the list. "What in the hell do you want with these?"

"Going on *leave*, old boy," Johnny interjected with a creditable mimicry of his partner. "Prague's beautiful in the spring, don'cha'know."

❖ ❖ ❖

With Q's more than willing support, getting to Prague was remarkably easy. With their bags marked as "Secure Material: Courier Only" they got a ride on a destroyer headed for Basilisk easily enough. Once there they changed identities to Silesian diplomats and, again, cleared customs without incident. A tramp freighter to Chosan, another change of clothes and in less than two weeks they were sitting in a bar in downtown Prague.

"You were right, Charles," Johnny said in Allemaigne. "The beer is definitely better."

One of the oddities that had led the then Private John Mullins from the Marines to the insertion teams was his ease with languages. What oddity of genetics had permitted a farm boy from Gryphon to smoothly learn nine languages, and he was working on Egyptian, was unsure. All that he knew was that he only had to hear one for a few days and before he even realized it, he was idiomatic.

Stranger things had happened in the universe. But not many.

"So are the girls old boy," Charles said, slipping a ten credit coin into the thong of the dancer in front of him. "So are the girls."

Prague had been settled by a society of Aryan racial homongenists from old Earth. The planet itself was a paradise with a temperature and weather regime remarkably similar to Earth's and the residents were among the "prettiest" to be found in the human settled worlds. Soon after landing the initial nutcases that had founded the colony were tossed out and a more realistic social structure based upon constitutional democracy was installed. The colony, which had been rather small to start and well off the main trade lanes, was nonetheless undergoing a real renaissance when the Peeps landed.

Since then it had been turned into just another Peep slave planet. Albeit with very pretty blond and red-headed hookers.

The People's Republic of Haven was, technically, the most egalitarian society in all the galaxy. Or at least that was what their Ministry of Information would have the rest of the galaxy believe. In reality, the social stratification, especially on subject planets such as Prague, was horrible. There were a few Peep senior officials who lived like Roman emperors, their StateSec and Navy officers who enforced the peace and lived like barons and knights, and the common people. The last group survived however they could and many of the females survived in the oldest profession in history. Any of the remarkably good-looking girls in the room could be had for less than an hour's pay of the State Security captains he and Gonzalvez were dressed as.

Charles watched the dancer step down off the stage and into the arms of a StateSec major and sighed. "Story of my life, really." Then he gasped at the sight of the next girl up.

Her hair was red and long enough that the braid was woven into her minimal clothing, a half bra and a thong that left very little to the imagination. Her breasts were high and almost unnaturally firm, but the clothing was brief enough to determine that there were *no* scars; indicating that the lift was natural. Her shape was an almost perfect hourglass topped by a heart-stoppingly beautiful face.

"A girl like that should be in videos," Charles said, nudging his partner. "Not dancing in a cheap strip-joint."

When there wasn't a response he looked over at Johnny, who was frozen to the chair, his mouth open.

"She's good looking, my friend, but not *that* good looking," Charles said.

"Ugah . . ." was the only response he got.

"Are you all right, Johnny?"

"Oh, God," Mullins finally gasped. "I'm dead."

"What's wrong?"

"Never mind," Mullins said, starting to stand up. "Maybe she hasn't . . ." but before he could leave his chair the girl had danced her way across the raised stage and now was dancing directly in front of him.

To top off her looks, she was an extraordinary dancer.

"I think I need a cold shower," Charles said as she entered a series of complicated sinuosities. "Several cold showers."

"Hi, Rachel," Johnny said in New French.

"Hi, Johnny," Rachel replied. "Long time." She bent over backwards until she was a curve balanced on her toes and fingertips then swayed back and forth. "Remember this one?"

"So you used to *date* her?" Charles asked when the dancer had left the stage.

"It's a long story," Johnny replied. "I was on a mission in Nouveau Paris–" He stopped as Rachel walked up. She had thrown a light blue robe on over her bra and panties but the sheer material didn't so much cover as reveal enticingly.

"It's . . . good to see you again. Although unexpected," Mullins said huskily.

"Yes, no letters, no contact at all," she said then slapped him as hard as she could. "*That* is for promising to marry me and then running away like a coward."

"Marry?" Charles said getting to his feet and moving over a stool as Johnny rubbed his cheek. "What a cad; undoubtedly a ploy to get you into his bed. I, on the other hand, am a gentleman, milady. Charles Gonzalvez, at your service."

"Pleased to meet you," she said in Allemaigne, sitting down between them. "How did you get stuck with this jerk?"

"Ill-luck of the draw," Charles replied, kissing her hand. "If it permits me to worship at your feet, however, my luck has changed."

"Hah!" she replied turning back to Johnny. "I see you made captain. Apparently StateSec is dragging the bottom of the barrel."

"I got redeployed," he said lamely. "It was . . . suggested that marrying . . . well a lady with a shady background would be a negative influence on my career. Actually, it was a lot more direct than that; my commander told me that if I contacted you again he'd send us both to Hades. I didn't want to get you in trouble."

"Nice off-the-cuff excuse, there," she said. "I forgive you for leaving; it was the promise of marrying that ticked me off. I thought you were serious there for a while."

"I was," Johnny said, looking her in the eye. They were, as he remembered, a deep purple, also natural. For some reason the phrase "the wine-dark seas" came to mind. After a moment he shook himself. "I was. I . . . also promised to get you out of the Republic."

She carefully looked around, then at Charles. "I take it you didn't hear that?"

"What? My partner speaking treason?" Charles said. "Not yet. Get a grip, Johnny."

"I will," Mullins said. "I . . . It's good to see you, Rachel."

She paused for a moment then stroked his cheek. "It's good to see you, too, Johnny."

Mullins shook his head and then smiled. "I don't suppose you're free tonight?"

Even her laughter was perfect, a delighted peal like bells in a carillon. "You don't give up, do you?"

"Not where you're concerned," Mullins said.

"Well, no, I'm not free tonight," she said maliciously. "I've got a hot date."

"Oh . . ." Mullins sighed. "Okay."

"But maybe later," she continued, stroking his cheek again. "Come back tomorrow night, okay?"

"Okay," Johnny said.

"I have to go," she said, standing up and arranging her robe. "Take care."

"I will," Mullins said watching her walk away. Then: "Shit."

"Bit of a spark there, still, old boy," Charles said, patting him on the back.

"I nearly shot myself when I got back from that mission," Mullins replied carefully, taking a deep pull off of his beer.

"Well, I have to admit she is spectacular, but is that really an appropriate response?"

"I don't know," Mullins said. He upended the liter glass then raised the empty and waved it back and forth. "It was my response."

"I say," Charles replied with a shake of his head. "I have to ask, though: Is she . . . available for hire?"

"Only to the highest bidder," Johnny said with a laugh, picking up the new glass that the bartender set down. "When I was dating her she was a mistress to the second assistant minister of information."

"Bloody good conduit," Charles said with raised eyebrows.

"I wouldn't know; I never tried to recruit her," Johnny said. "And then the mission went bust and we barely got out alive. If I'd had the ability to blackmail Q back then, I'd have gone back to Nouveau Paris to find her. But I didn't; I just tried to forget. For a while, the only thing that helped was drinking myself into a stupor. And I think that's what I'm going to do tonight." He put the freshly refilled glass of heavy brown ale to his lips and sucked until it was empty. "Bartender!"

"CORDELIA RANSOM SHE HAS NO BALLS!" Mullins sang as the two of them staggered down the deserted street. As with most Peep planets, Prague City tended to roll up the sidewalks after dark.

"Why . . . extac . . . exac . . . why are we going home-ward without female accom . . . without some women?"

"SAINT JUST'S ARE VERY SMALL!"

"Really, we *should* be accomp . . . sup . . . there ought to be women."

"ROB PIERRE . . . oh, never mind I can' think of a rh . . . rhyme for Pierre. We're returning to our domi . . . domic . . . rooms without women because wine giveth the desire and taketh away the ability."

"Okay, Shakespeare," Charles said. "If you're so smart, where's a bathroom?"

"Vo ist eine toiletten!" Johnny yelled to the empty streets.

"We're returning to our domic . . . to our rooms unaccompanied because of your girlfriend aren't we?"

"Ah, an alleyway," Johnny said. "I haff found our toiletten."

"Aren't we?" Charles asked again as they both stumbled into the darkness of the alley and leaned against the wall.

"Aaaah," Mullins said in relief. "You could have taken anyone home you wanted. I was . . . un . . . disin . . . I didn't want to."

"So it *was* because of your girlfriend," Charles said, clearing the tubes.

"If you shake it more than twice, you're playing with it," Mullins declared.

"*Halt!*"

"Christ, I'm just peeing on a wall," he complained as a body rounded the corner and plowed into him.

Mullins might have been three sheets to the wind but his survival instincts were highly trained. The body, it appeared to be a male in uniform, was spun in place and slammed into the wall as he wrapped the head into a snap-grip. In another moment the struggling figure would be lying on the ground with a broken neck.

"Don't," Gonzalvez said in Allemaigne. "He's being chased by StateSec."

"Good point." Johnny shifted his forearms and applied pressure, clamping on the nerve juncture. The "sleeper" hold was almost considered a myth; it required training, precision and strength to apply it properly. But John Mullins had all three in abundance; in less than two seconds the figure slumped.

"Grab his legs," Mullins muttered, dragging the body behind a dumpster and coming back out. He resumed his position as a flashlight-toting figure rounded the corner.

"Get that damned light out of my eyes!" Mullins shouted. "Who the hell *are* you?"

"Sorry, Sir," the StateSec private said diffidently, lowering the light. "But I'll need to see some ID. We're after a fugitive."

"Bloody local buffoons," Charles muttered in Nouveau Paris–accented French. He waggled his member and put it away, pulling out his ID tag. "Here," he continued in Allemaigne.

The private ducked his head and scanned the badge and the "captain's" retina, returning it and doing the same with Mullins'. "Thank you, Sirs. Did you see anyone pass this way?"

"Negative. Who are you looking for and what is the

local contact point?" Mullins asked as clearly as he could enunciate.

"We were told that Admiral Mládek is attempting to defect," the private gushed.

"What?" Gonzo gasped, right on cue. "The head of Fleet Communications?"

"Yes, Sir. We've closed down three Manty spy operations tonight and the captain says we're closing in on two more! General Garson is in charge; he was sent here by StateSec command in New Paris."

"Damn, I suppose this *is* important," Charles said. "You're doing a fine job, Private. If you have any questions for us, or need any help, we're in the New Prague Hotel, room 313."

"Yes, Sir," the private said, making a notation on his pad. "I have to go continue the search, Sirs."

"Carry on, Private," Johnny said. "You're in the best traditions of StateSec there."

"Thank you, Sir," the private said, trotting back out of the alley.

"Oh, bloody hell," Charles muttered. "I'm sober old boy, how 'bout you?"

CHAPTER 3

A HATCH IS PLANNED

No operative has just one bolt hole and whereas their digs *had* been in the New Prague Hotel, room 313, they had *also* rented a seedy flat on the bad side of town.

Prague City was bisected into north and south sections by the Aryan River. The north section was the business district with the better homes and flats on the

north edge. Also on the north side was the Peep
Building, pardon, the "People's Building," and the
StateSec headquarters.

On the *south* side was the industrial region and the
local police headquarters. Prague City, like all Peep
cities, had no crime problem. Just ask Cordelia Ransom. Everyone was happy and industrious, focused on
the important mission of destroying Manticore, the
aristocratic enemy of the People.

Strangely, South Prague City never made it into any
of Cordelia Ransom's tridee broadcasts. In South
Prague City, carrying a body into a building was only
notable in that it was being carried *in*.

Not that anyone in South Prague City was going to
notice *anything* at any time.

Johnny turned away from the window as the figure
in the chair stirred. "Headache?"

The admiral, which was what they had by his uniform, was a heavy-set man, probably in his sixties by
his looks. He didn't have the appearance of one of the
jumped up proles that made up much of the modern
Peep senior officer corps. From his look he was probably a holdover from the Legislaturalists.

The officer felt the bonds restraining him to the
chair, moved his lips under the tape on his mouth,
looked at the two men in prole clothing and nodded.

"Three things," Charles said, standing up with a cup
in one hand and a knife in the other. "Listening?"

The admiral nodded again, looking at the knife.

"First thing. We're not StateSec, we're Manty
Intelligence. Second thing, you were trying to defect
and nearly got nabbed by StateSec. Third thing,
we're not your pickup group but we're going to try
to get you out. However, if you mess about, we'll
kill you just as happily. Still want me to cut you
loose?"

The officer nodded then grimaced as Mullins first ripped off the tape then cut his bonds.

"I have no knowledge of what you are talking about," the admiral said, looking around the dingy room. "I am a citizen admiral of the Fleet; there will be absolutely effective repercussions if State Security thinks they can simply 'disappear' me."

"Uh, huh," Mullins said. "That wouldn't even fly with the Peeps and it doesn't get far with us."

"And, let me guess, old boy," Charles said cocking his head. "'Absolutely effective' would be your code word to determine if we're really ONI. Sorry, chap, we're not actually part of your pickup team so we can't give you the counter-code."

"Again, I have no idea what you are talking about," the admiral said firmly. "I am a loyal citizen officer of the People's Republic."

"Ah, okay," Johnny said. "In that case, there's a StateSec private we got you away from who is probably angling for sergeant." He grabbed the admiral by the arm and yanked the larger officer to his feet. "He'd probably get an instant promotion if he caught you."

The admiral looked from one to the other as Charles cut the bonds. "I am not attempting to defect," he said desperately. "I am a loyal officer!"

"General Garson is here," Mullins said. "'All the way from Nouveau Paris!' I'm sure he'll be happy to listen to your protests."

"If . . ." the admiral paused and gulped. "If you're Manty Intelligence, shouldn't you be trying to kidnap me? I could be carrying important information."

"Nope," Mullins explained. "You're not worth our lives if you're not willing to talk; Manticore doesn't use harsh information extraction methods. And, besides, we have another mission here. We only picked you up because it looked like an op had gone bad. If you're really a 'loyal officer of the People's Republic' we'll turn you loose, finish our mission and depart."

"We'd *prefer* to kill you," Charles said, putting away the knife and taking the admiral by the arm. "But it's against our basic rules of engagement. Pity. So, let's go meet that private, shall we?"

"Wait," the admiral said, holding up a hand. "Just . . . wait. Okay. Yes, I was attempting to defect."

"Good, now that we have your confession . . ." Charles said in a harsh Nouveau Paris accent.

"Oh, shut up, Charlie," Mullins said with a laugh at the frozen expression on the admiral's face. "He's joking. Not a good one. Major John Mullins, Admiral and this idiot is Major Charles Gonzalvez. Pleased to make your acquaintance."

"A pleasure to meet you," the admiral said with a sigh. "What went wrong?"

"I have no idea; we really *aren't* part of your pickup team. What happened?"

The admiral shrugged and looked out the window where dawn was just beginning to break. "I was supposed to go to a dry cleaners and drop off a pair of uniform pants. The code was that I wanted triple pressing, no starch."

"I know the laundry," Mullins said. "Lee's Cleaners on Fleur De Lis Avenue?"

"That one." The admiral nodded. "I was halfway down the block on my way to it when I was knocked off my feet by an explosion. When I got back up . . . boom . . . no more Chinese laundry."

"Somehow I doubt it was a gas leak," Charles said dryly.

"My doubt as well. I started to walk away and then saw State Security officers coming from every direction. I . . . I admit I panicked. I dropped the pants and ran."

"Best thing you could have done," Johnny said. "StateSec would have hung you on suspicion."

"I had been running and hiding for nearly two hours when I ran into you two. And that's all I remember. Now, how are you going to get me out of here?"

"What?" Mullins said. "Why should we do that?"

"But . . . but ONI set up my defection! You *have* to get me out!"

"Not really, old boy," Charles replied. "It's not *our* mission. Just because someone else blew it, doesn't mean we have to fix their abortion. I think you're on your own."

"You can't do this!" Mládek said. "Admiral Givens herself is involved in the planning for this!"

"Sure she is," Mullins said disparagingly. "She gets involved in every two-bit admiral that jumps ship."

"I'm not just a 'two-bit' admiral," Mládek snarled. "I was in charge of Fleet communications operation and design. Although StateSec is fine at finding thugs to beat people in the head, they don't have a clue when it comes to Fleet communications and they had to use *my* personnel to design and maintain their systems. I saw *all* their traffic. And I know things . . . let's just say that I know a few things that Admiral Givens really wants details on. I'm serious. If you leave me here you might as well defect yourself or Givens will gut you alive."

Mullins looked over at Gonzalvez who nodded slightly.

"Well . . . crap," Mullins said. "Getting *us* out was going to be interesting enough. Getting you out, too, will be ugly."

"You have means," the admiral said with a wave. "Make contact with your chain; activate an emergency escape plan. Whatever it is you do when a mission goes bad."

"Well, as to that," Mullins replied with a chagrined look.

The admiral listened intently, occasionally shaking his head.

"You've been drinking," he said when Mullins finished. "But even though it smells like a distillery in here, I can't believe you've been drinking enough to make up that story. And I doubt you're joking . . ."

"He's not," Gonzalvez said. "But before you decide to launch into a lecture, consider the fact that if we had *not* chosen to take our holiday on your sunny little planet, you would now be at the tender mercy of StateSec."

"That's a good point," the admiral said, subsiding. "But it still doesn't help us get off the planet."

"The laundry's gone," Mullins said. "There's a butcher shop and Aunt Meda's in addition. You know any others, Charlie?"

"Aunt Sadie's?" Gonzalvez said. "There's a flower shop on Holeckova, but this is the first I've heard of Aunt Meda's."

"Aunt Meda's House of Pain," Mullins replied. "It's a whorehouse with a sadomasochistic workout center called 'The House of Pain' as cover. And I know two safehouses. But if much of the network has been burned, who knows if any of them are clear?"

"How come you get the topless dancers and Aunt Meda's and I always get the flower shops and laundries?" Charles asked.

"God loves me and He hates you," Mullins replied. He jerked his head toward the admiral. "We need to get him out so we need to make contact. There's also Tommy Two-Time, but if I've got my druthers I won't bother with a double agent."

"You go," Gonzalvez said. "The Admiral and I will stay here and play gin rummy or something."

"I'll need a contact term for the flower shop," Mullins said. "Just my luck it'll be 'I need some pansies for the prom.'"

"Flowers or friends, Johnny?"

CHAPTER 4

SOMETIMES YOU GET THE BEAR

John walked past The House of Pain on the far side of the street, his head down, feet moving in the approved prole shuffle.

Aunt Meda's had been the last contact on his list and it was open. Contact, however, was problematic. The gym was on a generally unfrequented side street but today, for some unknown reason, there were several people wandering around.

In this corner, wearing an old shabby overcoat and fingerless gloves, nursing a bottle of cheap red wine, was a common street person. Such could be found in the more out-of-the way areas of Prague City but Aunt Meda's was on the better side of the tracks and street people should have been swept up by security. Ergo, it probably wasn't a street person at all.

Coming in the opposite direction from John was another prole. This one was a female and fairly good-looking. In fact, too good-looking. She didn't have the sallow skin from low-quality food that proles generally sported and her prole walk wasn't quite right. There was just a bit too much of the bounce to it.

Ergo, not a prole. Maybe a hooker or dancer dressing up as a prole, but unlikely.

Confirmation that the prole wasn't came when the

woman, probably a StateSec officer, brushed against him and subjected him to a fairly professional patting down.

He apparently passed since she continued on her way but as he turned the corner to head back to the safehouse his heart sank; there was a group of local police waiting around the corner, their air car grounded on the sidewalk.

"You!" One of the patrolmen, faceless in heavy body armor and helmet, waved him over as two more took up positions on either side.

"Name," the officer said. It wasn't a question, it was a demand.

"Gunther Orafson," Mullins replied in badly accented French. He proffered his ID tag then spread his legs, placed his right hand behind his head and held the left out, palm up; it was a position that proles learned early.

The officer put the tag in a slot, then waved the pad in front of Mullins' face and over his outstretched hand.

What the system *thought* it was doing was reading personal information of one Gunther Orafson, assistant boom operator at the Krupp Metal Works factory. It took a retina scan, surveyed fourteen points on his fingers and palm, compared his facial infrared topography to its database and took a DNA scan, all in under two seconds.

What it was actually looking at was some very advanced Manticoran technology.

Gunther Orafson had been stopped years before by someone very like John Mullins, except at the time the Mullins counterpart had been dressed like a local police officer.

Using a device that looked identical to the one this officer was using, he had taken all of Gunther Orafson's vital statistics and put them into a database. One checkpoint, fifteen minutes on a busy day, could garner dozens of identities, and the CIT teams had access to all of them.

Now the results of all that labor bore fruit. The police officer's pad looked at Mullins' eyes, and adjustable implants reflected an excellent facsimile of Gunther Orafson's retinas. The pad scanned his face and a thin membrane reflected Gunther Orafson's IR patterns.

The rest was the same. DNA patterns on fingerprint gloves and even a pheromone emitter for the more advanced detectors, everything screamed "Gunther Orafson."

Except his face. And the Peep system was so "advanced" they didn't even bother with a picture on the ID tag.

All of it was dissected and spit back to central headquarters. There it was compared with Gunther Orafson's data and accepted or denied.

The system apparently liked what it saw because it quickly clucked green and spit out the tag.

"What are you doing here?" the officer asked.

It was an abnormal question so Mullins let a bit more nervousness enter his voice. "I live in the seventeenth block of Kurferdam Street. I went to the market on Gellon because I had heard they had meat. But they were out. I am returning to my flat."

"I know where you live you idiot," the officer said, handing the tag back. "Get home. There will be a curfew tonight."

"Yes, Sir," Mullins said with a duck of his head. He continued on his way immediately; despite the fact the cop-thug had probably come from a prole background, proles didn't talk to cops and vice versa.

It had seemed like a routine stop but given the proximity to Meda's it was unlikely. A pity, really.

For all her personal . . . quirks, Meda had been a
lady.

And, worst of all, it only left Tommy Two-Time;
every other contact had been taken down by StateSec.

"Hiya, Tommy," Mullins said, trying not to breathe
as he walked in the door. Among the many reasons not
to deal with Tommy Two-Time, the regular fecal smell
from his overloaded bathroom had to be high on the
list. It had to be the worst smelling "herb" shop in the
universe.

Thomas Totim was an herbalist. Often that was a
high profile profession; in a society where "universal
medical care" meant waiting four hours for a drunken
doctor to look at your skull fracture, herbalists and
midwives were the most medicine that many proles saw
in their lives.

The shelves were sparsely populated with a variety
of inexpensive herbal remedies while along the left wall
a locked case held "harder" or more valuable materials. The far wall was lined with refrigerators, cases and
aquariums; many of the odder materials available to
the modern herbal doctor had to be used "fresh" from
any of thousands of species alien to humanity's home
planet.

But Tommy wasn't that kind of an herbalist. He had
all the herbs, and he could do a pretty good herbalist patter. But people came to Tommy when they
needed something harder than St. John's Wort; the
shelves were covered in dust and most of the aquariums were filled with the dying remnants of their original populations.

"Oh, shit," Tommy said looking out the door. "I can't
believe you just walked into my shop."

"Long time," Mullins replied fingering a dangling
root that was covered in mold. It might be the way

it was supposed to be, but with Tommy it was more likely to just be neglect. "What are you scamming this week? Spank? Rock?"

Under the early Legislaturalists many common soft drugs had been legalized. The technical reason was to reduce the rationale for street crime but the unspoken rallying cry was "A drugged prole is a happy prole." There was even a Basic Living Stipend entry for "pharmaceutical drug use."

However, even the Legislaturalists, and later the People's Government, weren't stupid enough to legalize Spank, which turned a male into a tunnel-borer rapist then drove him insane after about five uses, or Rock, which turned a person so inward that addicts commonly drifted off and never came back. There were others that inquisitive researchers had developed over the millennia, and Tommy could get them all.

"What, you join StateSec, 'Johnny'?" the drug dealer asked. "I don't think so. You and your buddy are the hottest thing on the planet."

"That what you're hearing, Tommy?" Mullins replied, looking around at the dust-covered sundries on the shelves and tapping on the glass of an aquarium. It was the only one that wasn't filled with gunk. Instead, five Gilgamesh River Devils looked back at him. Each of the semi-sentient, highly carnivorous "fish"—actually a dual-breathing amphibian—followed his hand with all six eyes, clearly hoping he would get close enough to remove a nibble with their three-centimeter teeth.

The river devils were piscine shaped, with sucker-tipped "arms" in place of pectoral fins that they used for locomotion in their terrestrial mode. They were all flashing through a dozen colors as chromatospores changed the hue of their skin through all the colors of the rainbow. Some scientists theorized that the color changes were a primitive form of communication. Having seen a group of river devils first distract and then surround a cow on a Gilgamesh riverbank, Johnny was pretty sure the scientists were right. Except for the "primitive" part. "Who's looking for me?"

"You, your buddy and some admiral. And everybody," the dealer continued nervously. He had the shoulder-length hair that was practically the badge of the professional herbalist but the circular bald patch on the top ruined the look. Now he rubbed the top of his head nervously and looked out the door again. "I do mean *everybody*. StateSec has flipped; the admiral's got some of their codes and secret information. And the Manties are pissed; their whole network in Prague City is just *gone* and according to them *you* did it."

"Oh?" Mullins said carelessly. The news was like a punch to the gut, but he wasn't going to let Two-Time know it. "Where'd you hear that?" He noticed the river devils were spreading out with one raising a surreptitious suction cup towards the top of the tank and decided it was time to back up.

"There was a snatch team in town to pull the admiral. Some of them got caught but the rest left word that you guys were out of sanction. I guess you'd better head for Silesia and get a job beating up old ladies for quarters."

"Maybe," Mullins said. "But right now the question is getting off-planet. I need some papers."

"Like I'm going to help you with that," the dealer said with an honest laugh, a needler suddenly appearing in his hand. "You're worth a lot but the admiral is worth more. Where is he?"

"Tommy, you're going to get busy with me?" Mullins said with honest surprise.

"You got swept coming in the door," Two-Time replied. "No body armor, no weapons. So you can either answer the question or I can fill you full of needles and then call StateSec. Or just forget you were ever here after I feed you to the devils; they handle terrestrial proteins just fine and they even digest the bones."

"Tommy, after all the years we've been friends," Mullins replied, shaking his head. "For it to end like this."

"I was never your friend," the dealer said. "The admiral. One . . ."

Mullins shook his head and twisted sideways, grabbing the drug dealer by the hair as the needle-gun fired.

Most of the needles missed entirely, common even at short range when an untrained firer jerks the trigger, but a few hit him in the abdominal region. And slid off his T-shirt.

Mullins wasn't wearing anything that showed up as body armor to Peep scanners; despite the officially egalitarian stance of the People's Republic, armor was permitted only to police and senior members of the government; some pigs were more equal than others.

But that didn't mean he went out naked as a bird either; his T-shirt was made of a high-tech high-density microfiber material, uncommon outside of Manticore and a few Sollie systems, that absorbed much of the blow from the light-weight needles and stubbornly resisted penetration.

The effect was like a punch to the stomach but John Mullins had been hit in the gut plenty of times and shrugged this blow off as well.

Tommy Two-Time was not so lucky.

Ignoring the needles, Mullins slammed the drug-dealer's throat into the hard wood top of the counter, cracking the counter and filling Tommy's throat with blood. Then, to make absolutely sure he wouldn't be telling any tales, the Manty agent twisted Tommy's head around until he was looking back down his spine.

"I've been wanting to do that since the first time I saw you sell a kid Rock," Mullins commented quietly, stepping around the counter and shoving the body out of the way. The late drug dealer had voided himself on exit from this mortal plane, but it was unnoticeable over the stench from the toilet.

Mullins picked up the needler and hammered the lock off of the small lockbox under the counter. All it contained were a few unmarked vials and some change in the form of small sheets of silver and gold. Since the standard monetary form in the People's Republic was a highly traceable electronic transaction related to the identity chip, the metal currency was standard on the black market. However, since virtually everyone used the black market for even everyday purchases, probably the only person who didn't use the sheets was Cordelia Ransom.

It still couldn't be his main stash, or his main cash, so Mullins did some hunting. Finally he found both the drug and money cache under a panel behind the noisome toilet. From the looks of things Tommy hadn't caught up with his supplier recently; there was more than enough cash to sustain them for months. Or get them off-planet if they could find a trustworthy forger.

The toilet, once unplugged, served to deal with the drugs, and the sheets of metal were easy enough to secrete around his body. As long as he didn't get stopped on the way back, everything should be fine. And if he did get stopped, the local cops would just assume he was a money mule and confiscate the cash.

Which would be unfortunate since they were apparently going to need the funds.

He started to leave and stopped, looking at the body stuffed under the counter. After a moment he smiled.

A few minutes later he left the store after having wiped all the surfaces he touched. On his way out he turned the sign to "closed" and locked the door.

CHAPTER FIVE

SOMETIMES YOU BARE THE GETS

"I'd say something light and quippy," Charles said. "But the only thing that comes to mind is: 'Crap.'"

"Congratulations, Admiral," Mullins said. "You just changed from an annoyance to a life-preserver."

"Yes, if you get back with me, all, or most at least, will be forgiven," the admiral said. "That, however, is a large 'if.'"

"I'm out of contacts," Gonzalvez said. "And I don't have a prober system with me, so I can't try to play with the local police system and fake us up materials from that." He blew through his lips and shook his head. "I'm stumped, Johnny me lad." He hung his head and whistled through his teeth. "Bloody hellfire."

"I've got one contact," Mullins replied grudgingly.

"Oh, my," Charles chuckled, looking up. "You're serious?"

Mullins stepped out of the shadows and nodded. "Hello, Rachel."

The dancer was dressed in prole clothing, a heavy gray cotton jacket and similar slacks against the early spring night air. The style on Haven leaned more towards flashy clothing and bright, tawdry make-up, but on the "occupied worlds" there was no BLS for the commoners, it was a day-in-day-out struggle for survival under the unbending yoke of the Ministry of Industry and only the cheapest materials were made available for the "unassimilated" populations. However, like the police agent near Aunt Meda's, there was no mistaking her for a common prole.

She tilted her head to the side and sighed. "I guess StateSec officers don't have to worry about curfew?"

"Something like that," he said. "Can I come in?"

She paused and looked at him for a long time then nodded. "Okay."

The fourth-floor flat was surprisingly neat and clean, for all it was small. It was mostly one room with a fold-up bed, a couch, a small table, tridee and tiny kitchen. There was a small bathroom to the side with a shower just visible. There appeared to be no heat and the room was like an icebox.

"Nice," he said. "But not as nice as Nouveau Paris."

"It's a dump," Rachel replied, taking off her coat and pulling down the makings of tea. "What can I do for you as if I don't know?"

"It's . . . not what you think," Mullins said, sitting at the small table. "There are some things you don't know about me."

"Well, you're wearing prole clothing, so apparently one of them is that you're an undercover agent." She put a pot in the warmer and set it on heat.

"Not for StateSec," he said carefully. "I'm a Mantie."

"Sure you are," she said with a chuckle. "And I'm Cordelia Ransom. Pull the other one, it's got bells on."

"I'm serious, Rachel. That's why I wanted to get you out of Peep space. I couldn't be with you here; I'm from the Alliance."

She turned around and looked at him soberly. "You're serious."

"As a heart attack. And I'm in trouble."

"And you brought it to me," she said angrily. "You're a God-damned Manty spy and you've brought your troubles to me?"

"Yes, I did," he replied. "You're the only person I can trust anymore, Rachel. If you want to turn me in, fine. I just ask for a few minute's head start. But I need your help. Please."

"Oh, man," she said, shaking her head. "Why me? That question was rhetorical, buddy." She took the pot of tea out of the heater and poured two cups. "Honey, right?"

"You remembered." He smiled, wrapping his hands around the mug for warmth.

"I have a very good memory," she snapped as she sat down. "I can remember things like that for over four hundred men."

"Oh."

"This is not going to be cheap," she continued. "You had better have money."

"I do, and some materials that might help." He paused for a moment and then shrugged. "But we've got a couple of other problems. We also have a citizen to get out, a defector."

"This general that everyone is so up in arms about?" she asked, taking a sip of her tea.

"Admiral. Yes."

She took another sip and set it down, gripping the bridge of her nose and squeezing. "Oh, Johnny."

"How bad is it?"

"In case you didn't notice, our club gets a lot of military," she said softly. "It was nearly empty tonight; there has been a general call-up by StateSec. They're all looking for your friend. I don't even know how you made it to the flat."

"I want you to come, too," he said in a rush.

"Not that again!"

"I'm serious. I nearly drank myself to death when I had to leave Nouveau Paris. *Please* come with me this time; it won't be safe for you here after we're gone."

"We'll talk about it later," she said, patting his hand. "Right now we have to get you and your friends somewhere that StateSec won't find you."

"I'm not sure anywhere is that safe," he replied.

"Where are we going?" John said as they sloshed through another puddle.

They had proceeded to the basement of Rachel's tenement where a metal plate had given access to a series of tunnels. Most of them had to do with maintenance for the billion and one things that go on out of sight and mind in a city. Besides sewers, there were forced air pipes, electrical lines, active foundation supports and a host of other items, most of which required occasional maintenance.

And very few of which were ever seen by "surface" dwellers, including police.

It was through this gloomy world, lit only by occasional glow-patches and a pale chem-light in Rachel's hand, that they had progressed. Once, in response to an almost unnoticeable mark on a wall, she had rapidly backtracked. When a group of dispirited Naval personnel had gone by them as they huddled in a side tunnel the reason had become clear.

He had followed her slavishly, and carefully not asked any questions, for nearly an hour. But if his reading of signs and general sense of direction wasn't completely off, they were very near the river. And the police headquarters.

"Not much farther," she whispered. "The one place that no one will bother looking is?"

"Where nobody would be dumb enough to go?" he answered.

"Exactly," she continued, pulling aside another metal plate and glancing around the room beyond. "Specifically, in the basement of the police administration building."

He looked at the room beyond. It appeared to be completely filled with junk. There were old-style monitors, chairs with one wheel gone and piles and piles of manuals. All of it was covered in dust.

"How did you find this place?" he asked.

"I have friends in low places," she replied. "Where are your friends and how do I keep them from killing me when I tap on the door."

"They're over in Southtown." He gave her directions to the flat and shook his head. "Just knock and tell them who you are; secret taps are for amateurs. You'll need this, though."

He pulled what looked like a dangling thread off the prole jacket and licked it. Then he held it up to his mouth and said: "All Clear, Kizke."

"What is that?" she asked, taking the somewhat sodden string.

"Just give it to Charles. He'll compare it to my DNA map. There's a way to fake it, but it's hard and beyond Peep tech. We think. That's what professionals use. Also, we need some back-ups. If anything happens while you are gone, now or later, I'll make a chalk mark on the side of the postal box on the fourteen hundred block of Na Perslyne. And I'll leave a message about where to contact me on the underside of the south bench by the duck pond on Wenceslas Square."

"Okay," she said. "I guess this is real spy stuff?"

"We use the word 'agent,'" he replied with a grin. "And, yeah, the term is 'tradecraft.' Can you remember what I said?"

"Mark on the postal box in the fourteen hundred block of Na Perslyne, south bench, duckpond

Wenceslas, Mister Super-spy. But when I come back, if I don't tap like this," and she gave him a demonstration, "kill whoever comes through the door. Sometimes StateSec will mimic an appearance."

"I think StateSec would find it difficult to mimic you," he said with a smile. "Thank you for this, Rachel."

"You're welcome, and you owe me."

"Well, this is a pleasant little love nest," Charles said, ducking through the door.

"I'd say it was nerve-wracking waiting for you to get back," Mullins replied. "But I always figure you're dead anyway."

"Terribly uplifting old boy," Gonzalvez replied. "Glad I feel the same way about you."

"Rachel, we do have to talk," Mullins continued. "I don't get you having this little bolt hole or knowing your way around underground so well. I deal with Peeps and proles all the time; they don't generally find their way around underground by preference."

"I have friends . . ."

"I heard that one," Mullins replied as Gonzalvez subtly shifted to block the exit. "Now tell me the rest."

"Okay," she sighed. "I do have friends. Some of them are in the resistance."

"Friends like we were . . . are . . . friends?" Mullins asked.

"Sort of," she replied, stone-faced. "After you left things got very sour for me on Nouveau Paris; I had to leave in a hurry. 'Friends' got me here and have . . . helped from time to time. I help them from time to time in return."

"Mule?" Charles asked.

"Generally," she replied. "But I'm not really a member of the resistance; just a working girl trying to make her way the best she can."

"No warrant for you?" Johnny asked.

"No, it never got that far."

"Can these . . . 'friends' get us passage out?"

"For a chance to make contact with Manty Intelligence? Of course they will."

"I'm not sure we can support them," Charles pointed out. "Most of them have been designated as terrorist organizations by the People's Republic; supporting them is a political decision at that point."

"Understood," Rachel replied. "But this is a chance for a hard contact and some positive PR, if only in your intelligence service." She sighed, looking around the room. "They're really *not* terrorists; they have a strict military/industrial target only policy. Sometimes civilians do get killed, but only those working on military equipment and manufacturing; they don't go bombing restaurants."

"Or strip-joints," Charles interjected. "Do you feed them information?"

"No, I don't," she replied. "I mean, sometimes a little, but I'm not a spy for them or anything. Sometimes I find out something they really have to know and I pass it on to a cell I trust. I'll have to bring them in on you guys; they're my only source of travel documents."

"Stop here," Rachel whispered. "You're not going to crack on me, are you?"

The man who would only answer to the name "The Great Lorenzo" raised himself to his not inconsiderable height and gathered the rags of his suit.

"Am I not the Great Lorenzo?" he asked in a mellifluous voice. "It is not a great role, but it is a speaking part. I shall do my trouper's best."

"Lord, this was a bad idea," she whispered. "Okay, they probably put out sensors, so you'd better get into role."

The man nodded and reached in his pocket, extracting a bottle of cheap whiskey.

"You shouldn't need that," she snapped. "You already smell like a distillery."

"But if I do not, my hands will shake," he noted logically.

"They're *supposed* to shake!"

"Only in the role within the role," he returned and upended the bottle, taking a single hard slug. "Now I am prepared," he added, tucking the bottle away as his face slowly softened into subtly different lines. He now had the overall visage of a drunken bum, but there was a cold light in his eyes and his demeanor, while stooped, had a hint of athleticism. "Ah, what a tangled web we weave, when first we practice to deceive!"

"Aloman?" she asked, stepping deeper into the gloom.

"Shakespeare," he sighed. "So few remember the Bard."

John slid the plate aside and nodded at Rachel. "Glad you're back."

"No names," she said. "This is a friend in the resistance. He can get you passages."

John looked the rebel visitor up and down. He appeared to be just another street bum; sallow face, palsied hands. The torn clothing was better than most, but not significantly. However, if anyone knew looks could be deceiving it was Mullins. "You?"

The bum slowly straightened until he was at his full height and looked at the admiral. "Yeah, that's Mládek," he said in a deep, gravely voice, ignoring Mullins. "First you grind us under the Legs then you grind us under the Peeps and now that the fire's too hot for you you turn tail and run." He spat on the ground in front of the Peep officer and smiled at the Manticorans. "Give him to me for an hour; I'll sweat out everything you want to know."

"Enough," Rachel said. "We don't have time for this."

"Yeah, I can get you documents," the rebel replied after a glance at the woman. "But there's a problem. I've got three; Rach said you wanted four."

"How long to get four?" Charles asked.

"Why should we?" Mládek snapped. "For God's sake, I'll buy you a piece of ass when we get to Manticore; leave the bint."

"You know," Mullins replied mildly, not turning around. "I just need to get you to Givens alive. There's nothing saying I have to leave you the use of your legs." He cocked his head to the side and looked at the visitor. "We need four."

"Ain't gonna happen any time soon," the visitor replied, scratching his chest. "And eventually they *will* find you; they've got Mládek's DNA for sure and probably yours by now. They'll use chem-sniffers eventually."

"Rachel, you are not staying on this planet," Mullins said. "They *are* going to be looking for you this time." He paused and shrugged, looking at the floor. "We already drew straws. Just in case. I lost."

"He did," Charles replied sourly. "He really, really did. I was there."

"Well, that makes a hell of a lot of sense!" Rachel flared. "I go back to Manty space and you stay here? What, exactly, am I going to do in Manticore? And how are you going to survive here?"

"I can get by," Mullins said. "As soon as it's clear the admiral is gone, things will cool down. I can make it. As for you, the one more or less constant in Manticore these days is a labor shortage; you won't have to worry about finding a job and it won't be as a dancer, either."

"I've got nothing against being a dancer," she said narrowly.

"No, but I do," he replied. "When you get to Manticore, find another job. Okay?"

"Okay, I'm not staying," she said after a moment's glare. "Take the pictures. We'll retouch them as necessary for clothing; I'll have to get that later. Two male sets and one female."

"I can do those as well," the rebel said. "I've got a lovely set of three, by the way. You're Solarian business representatives."

"Good," John replied. "The Peeps bend over backwards for those."

"Rachel will be the head of the group," the bum continued, handing out briefing papers. "She's the CEO of Oberlon, Inc. and a really nasty individual. Unfortunately, the CEO of Oberlon is about ninety and looks it, so we'll have to age you a bit."

"I'll live," Rachel said as he took the first picture.

"You'll be her son," the rebel continued, handing Gonzalvez his packet. "You're the heir apparent, but the old biddy won't die. So you're stuck in an eternal 'momma's boy' routine."

"Joy," Gonzalvez said, smiling as stupidly as possible at the camera.

"That will look great," the visitor said. "You're the executive assistant, Admiral. You don't talk much, just open doors and make coffee."

"That I can handle," Mládek said, glowering at the camera.

"And one to grow on," the rebel continued, taking Mullins' picture.

"What in the hell was that for," he asked, suspiciously.

"If I come up with another identity in the next day or so, do you want it or not?"

"Want," Mullins admitted.

"So there you are," the visitor said, putting away his gear. "One big happy family."

"And already planning the murder," Gonzalvez said flipping through his briefing papers. They were remarkably professional for what appeared to be a completely amateur organization.

"You'd better get up pretty early in the day, sonny," Rachel quavered. "How do you think I took over the company from your father?"

"One big happy family, indeed," Mládek laughed.

CHAPTER 6

Cliché: Another Word for Inevitable

Charles waited until the rebel was gone, then smiled.

"Good news, the Manty team didn't get captured. The people who were picked up were all locals; they don't know what happened to the Manties."

"How do you know that?" Rachel asked.

"Between the Admiral and me, we managed to hack into the police databanks," Charles said with an impish grin.

"What?" Rachel shouted. "Are you crazy?!"

"Shh, keep your voice down," the admiral replied, gesturing at a dataport. "We were clean. We were already inside their physical security and their electronic security was laughable."

"Why take the risk?" she asked. "What if they tracked you internally?"

"Not much chance of that," Charles said, buffing his nails on his tunic. "I, am a genius."

"Well, genius, we're going to need to change locations," she snapped. "You have five minutes to make it look as if you were never here."

"Women," Charles said with a shake of his head. "Never satisfied."

"Men," Rachel replied. "Never paranoid enough."

Mullins smiled through the window as Rachel grounded a beat up air car in front of him.

"Hi, lady, can I get a ride to the Metropolitan Museum?"

She looked at him for a moment then shook her head. "We don't *have* a Metropolitan Museum; it got destroyed in the Peep War and never rebuilt. What did you do to your face?" He was much heavier looking with fat cheeks and dark hair in place of his natural aquiline blond look.

Mullins slid into the seat and worked his jaw. "Charles blackmailed our supply guy into giving him the latest and greatest ID kit. And it seemed like a good idea to change identities again."

Rachel had been unwilling to let them stay in the basement another minute and, realistically, they had already been in one place too long. She had led them back out through the sewers and tunnels to a temporary hide and told them to meet her in twenty minutes. That had been more than enough time for Charles to produce a few new local identities for all of them except the admiral. He had a new ID as well, but unfortunately the retina scan wouldn't match up.

"I've got another hide you can move to," Rachel said, pulling the car up and into traffic. Prague was no longer a rich world but the traffic was still fairly heavy, stacked up at least six levels. The ground level was relegated to hover-trucks with the next three levels dedicated to general traffic and the top two to "platoon" groups: cars moving under computer control over long distances. East–west streets were on interleaving sections with north and south so that only the ground level had to stop at intersections. This also created "dead zones" between lanes that the more aggressive drivers used for passing. "But it requires going up on the surface and with all the patrol activity . . ."

"How bad is it, lassie?" Charles asked as a patrol van passed overhead fast enough to rock the shuddering car. The van had been in the dead zone and at the intersection it quickly cut downward into a parallel lane then back up to pass the slower traffic.

"Lots of roadblocks, lots of random stops," she said. "StateSec is even more intrusive on the conquered planets than they are on Haven. I think we got you hidden just in time. It took them about a day to get organized and now they're all over the place. Oh, by the way, there's an all points bulletin out for Tommy Two-Time. A person of your general build was seen going into his shop but all the surveillance equipment was disabled or destroyed. You . . . wouldn't happen to know anything about that?"

"Tommy, he sleeps with the fishes," Mullins said. "God, I always wanted to use that line!"

"You are so weird," she snorted. "I think this is just about the time to have a car chase. It's always about this time in the movies. What do you think, Mister Super-Spy?"

"I've always managed to avoid them," Johnny admitted. "I hate flying, actually."

"Well, good," Rachel said as she rounded a corner. "Hopefully our luck will hold out."

"Or, maybe not," John said as he looked at the line of cars.

"This was *not* here an hour ago," Rachel snarled at the roadblock.

"It's cool," Mullins replied softly. "My ID should pass just fine. Just play it like any normal roadblock."

"What about the admiral?" she asked.

"Retina scanners sometimes act up," Charles answered. "All the other data will match just fine. And the local police retina scan for the admiral is wrong."

"You didn't tell me you diddled the ID database," Rachel hissed.

"You didn't ask," Gonzalvez replied with another grin. "Anyway, the retina scan should come back garbled and everything else will pass. They'll let us through."

"Okay, but I don't like it."

"And don't try to run," John added. "This POS will never be able to out-fly the police vans. For that matter, we'll be zoomed in on from every direction and they'll be tracking us a half a dozen ways. Just play it cool."

"I am," she replied as the first van passed, scanning her registration. It swung around behind her and took a position above and behind. "I was," she continued.

"That's not good," John said. "They don't scan ID internally, so they had to have reacted to the registration. Who's this registered to?"

"Me," Rachel said, adjusting her rearview mirror and checking her lipstick.

"I think they're on to *you*, Rachel."

"I think they are too," she sighed, touching up her hair. "Damn it, Johnny, I did not need this crap."

"Okay, on my mark we kill everyone in sight," Charles said with a snort. "Or at least try."

"Hopefully it won't come to that," Rachel replied quietly. "And unless it does, don't do anything stupid."

Mullins looked around at the block. There were four cars in front of them, three like themselves hovering at about five meters and the first one grounded and being checked by the local constables. There were two police vans there, and the one behind them. As he watched, two of the constables at the block walked back to their own vans, one going to the rear.

"I think we're screwed," Mullins replied. There was an alleyway on his side, but the vans were going to have IR sensors so unless they could get underground and lose the cops on foot, they weren't getting away. "When I say 'now,' put the car in drive and jump out on my side; hopefully some of them at least will chase the car."

"I don't think *that's* an option either," Rachel said as one of the two vehicle cops extracted what looked like a rocket launcher and fired at her car.

"JESUS!" Mullins yelled, pulling open his door as the rocket slammed into the side of the vehicle.

But instead of an explosion, there was a simple "pop" and the car shuddered in mid-air.

"EMP round!" Rachel yelled. "Get back in the car!"

"It's dead!" Mullins said but the sudden shudder as it lifted upward belied him. Then he was thrown backwards in his seat. "Whoooaaa!"

Mullins had been in enough simulators to have a fair clue about how many Gs he was pulling and the little "rattletrap" car was accelerating far too quickly for its appearance.

"Friends in low places?" he grunted.

"My cousin's a mechanic," she hissed in reply, banking around the side of a building at the sight of blue lights in the distance. The car narrowly missed the side of the far tower, actually tapping on one of the empty flagpoles jutting out from it. "He installed an engine from an old Prague Defense Force mobile gun. It's designed to drive a mini-tank."

"How did it survive the EMP round?" Mullins asked. "We should have been sitting on the ground!"

"It's a *military* engine," she said, in a tone reserved

for a not very bright four-year-old. "Ever heard of *shielding*?"

He glanced behind them and winced as another police van joined the chase, slipping into the upper lane to prevent a break in that direction.

"They're going to be tracking us on the satellites," he mentioned. "Not that it looks to matter."

"I've got the transponder turned off," she commented. "But you're correct about them being able to track us visually. Not that it matters at the *moment*. But hang on."

The traffic ahead was slowed by an air car in the center middle lane that seemed incapable of making up its mind. The driver was either old or drunk because the car was weaving a pavane up and down, crossing through the dead zones and nearly entering the lanes above and below, as well as from side to side.

Rachel appeared not to notice, diving into the lower dead zone and accelerating towards the car fast enough to rattle the cars above and below in her wash. Just as it seemed she would hit the wandering vehicle it drifted upwards and she slid through the slot into the relatively open area ahead of it. As they blasted past, Johnny caught one brief flash of a white patch of hair and a pair of hands that clutched the steering-yoke at least six inches over the driver's head.

Unfortunately, Rachel's maneuver placed the car in the intersection, going the wrong way. Her sudden appearance in the cross-lanes caused cars to veer in all three dimensions and windshields in at least a half dozen cars turned blue as the auto-pilots went into spastic fault-mode.

Mullins looked back and shook his head in wonderment at the snarled mess behind them. Half the cars that had been around them were down or bouncing from side to side, the police vans had either grounded or slammed into the surrounding buildings trying to avoid various obstacles and the intersection was filled with cars on apparently random ballistic tracks.

"You just made yourself very unpopular in this town," he commented.

"Stuff happens," Rachel said, pulling all the way up into the control lanes and then down to avoid a slow section of traffic. "I was getting tired of Prague anyway."

"Oh," he said as she banked through the next intersection, slammed on the brakes and turned into a mostly abandoned multistory garage. "So this isn't the first car chase you've been in, is it?"

"No," she replied, raising the car up a story through an open hole and then spinning it to tuck neatly between a pair of rusted hover-trucks. There was nothing else on the level, but while the position gave a good view of the garage, it was nearly impossible to see the car where it sat. She quickly shut down the counter grav and then looked though the back window.

"And now we go?" he asked. "We're out of sight; we should . . . leave. Right?"

"Wrong," she said, looking at her watch. Outside the sound of sirens got louder and louder. There seemed to be quite a few of them.

"They'll have picked up the signature of the engine," he pointed out. "They'll be looking all over for it."

"You think?" she asked. She looked at her watch again and then nodded. "Time." In the distance there was a dull boom. A moment later the sirens began to fade. She leaned forward and fiddled with an almost unnoticeable knob under the dashboard then turned the car back on. It no longer throbbed or rattled.

"Your cousin?" Mullins asked dryly.

"He's a very good mechanic," she replied, pulling out from between the trucks and dropping back down through the hole. Turning right she pulled around a stairwell and parked beside a stripped air car. Johnny didn't recognize the model—presumably it was a preinvasion Prague design—but it was pretty and clearly made for speed.

"Give me a hand," she said, leaning down and pulling a lever.

Johnny shook his head as the body of the car lurched slightly then he joined her in lifting it up and away from the chassis.

"I've really got to meet this cousin of yours," he said. The sports car body, like the clunker body, was made of lightweight plastic and dropped onto the "rattle-trap" chassis perfectly. In under thirty seconds a slightly the worse for wear sports car rocketed out of the top of the garage and into the sky.

"My, that was refreshing," Mullins said. "Okay, Rachel, give. Your average stripper doesn't have a military grade, shielded turbine in her car. In fact, on Prague, she doesn't even *have* a car."

Rachel sighed and shook her head. "I do a few things more for the resistance than I told you. I'm not an agent for them, but I do mule work and also some of what you would call 'tradecraft'; your lecture about putting a mark on a box wasn't the first time I'd heard of that. And I really *do* have a cousin who does conversions on vehicles; I'm the person who gets them to the resistance. And he does other work, including some sabotage. He's surveilling us and had placed a bomb on a chemical plant. When he saw us blocked in he set it off. Then the police had more important things to do than chase down a hooker who maybe had met one of the suspects they are looking for. And, of course, I'm very good friends with one of the local resistance leaders."

"Very good friends?" he asked.

"Is that all you can ask about?" she asked in exasperation. "If you're going to worry about each of my friends you're going to spend all your time on that subject alone. I've got *a lot* of friends, okay?"

"Okay," Mullins said with a shrug. "As long as we can get you off planet before your friends can't keep you alive."

"I've reluctantly come to the same conclusion," she said.

"Who is *this* vehicle registered to?" Mullins asked as a police van swept through an intersection; its carcomp would have automatically scanned their registration as it passed.

"The local StateSec commander's daughter," Rachel said with a faint smile. "As long as we don't have to go through another block, we're fine."

She pulled into another multistory car-park and placed the car in an out-of-the-way corner.

"They were going to be tracing us as soon as they reviewed the data from the satellite," she continued, getting out of the car. "So we need to get down in the underground again."

CHAPTER 7

If It's Stupid and It Works, It's Not Stupid

Johnny looked at the walls of the fumed wood elevator and shook his head. "Where, exactly, are we going?"

The travel from the abandoned car had been short, which in general was not a good idea. They had exited the car-park in the basement, gone through a few

tunnels and then entered the elevator in another basement. This one had been packed with the usual sort
of industrial laundry machines found in hotels. But if
this was a hotel, it was much more upscale than anything Mullins had previously found on Prague.

"This was the VIP quarters for visiting Legislaturalists," Rachel said. "It's since been taken over
by StateSec for pretty much the same use."

"You mean, we're in a *StateSec* building?" Gonzalvez
snapped. "Are you insane, woman?"

"No," she said. "I have an apartment here."

Mullins tensed for a moment then decided to let
her live. "Why?"

"Why do you think, Johnny?" she replied as the
doors opened. "Let's just say I'm . . . maintained in it
by a local StateSec officer."

"And if he decides to just drop by?" the admiral
asked. "We're to hide in the closet, yes?"

"He won't be dropping by," Rachel replied. "He's
off-planet at the moment. And everyone knows why
he has the apartment, but not for whom, and he's the
deputy commander for Prague. So they're not going
to be questioning his mistress. Not if they want to stay
off of Hades. And if you have a better idea where to
hide you, I'm open to suggestions."

There wasn't time for any as the doors opened on
the corridor. Rachel stuck her head out then gestured
right. A short distance led them to a door that opened
at her passkey.

The apartment was large and airy, two story with
the main hall rising to the full height with a balcony overlooking it. There was a mural on one wall
depicting a pastoral scene along the Prague River
and furniture that looked to be mostly Old Earth
antiques. A brief tour, conducted by Charles on a
careful sweep for any detection equipment, revealed

similar luxury throughout including a Jacuzzi, a shower area large enough for a platoon of drunken Marines, a sunken bathtub, a collection of "adult novelties" that was practically a store in itself and a shower-massage.

"Why a shower massage?" he asked when he got back to the overstocked kitchen.

"I have to have something for myself," Rachel pointed out. She was making a sandwich which consisted of two pieces of bread, a pile of alfalfa spouts and a half a bottle of hot sauce marked with a skull and crossbones. As soon as it was done she stuffed the entire load in her mouth.

"M g'ung sh'er," she mumbled, then cleared enough space to talk. "Nobody should come to the door. If they do, we're screwed. If there's so much as a knock, alert everyone and head out the window."

"I'll slip some tell-tales out the door," Charles said. He gestured at her open mouth. "Unless you know something I don't, the Peeps don't normally sweep in high microwave range."

"No, that's okay," she said after a moment. "Just don't get caught."

"They're self mobile," Gonzalvez replied.

"Next dibs on the shower," Mullins said, taking a bite of the sandwich. "This is really wimpy hot sauce."

Rachel laughed and gestured around. "Raid as you wish. I'm not planning on coming back and it's less than my pig of a boyfriend deserves." With that she walked out of the kitchen and towards the stairs.

"As long as everything's there tomorrow, we're set," Charles said. "Of course, something will go wrong. But I intend to worry about that tomorrow."

"I don't suppose . . . ?" Mládek asked, lifting the bottle of wine.

"Go ahead," Mullins replied. "Just don't get so drunk you can't move."

"Well, say what you will about her boyfriend," Gonzalvez said from the depths of the refrigerator, "but he has excellent taste." He leaned out and flourished a jar. "Arellian caviar, Nagasaki shrimps in wine sauce and New Provence compote."

"A going away party," the admiral said with a sad smile. "I suppose it's appropriate."

"Just don't party too hard," Mullins replied.

"The condemned man ate a hearty meal," Charles said. "I'm surprised you're eating as well as you are, frankly."

"Why worry about it?" Mullins replied. "You guys go, I'll keep my head down and eventually we'll make contact again."

"Sure, easy," Gonzalvez replied.

"I'm not planning on being here in the morning," Mullins said, taking another bite of sandwich.

"Cutting out early?" Mládek asked. "Don't get yourself picked up and blow our cover."

"I won't," Johnny replied. "I'll probably take the window exit. Anyway, I thought you should know."

"Well, I would have known anyway," Charles replied. "I laced that as well as the door."

"Just as well," Johnny said, finishing off his sandwich. "I'm planning on having another beer and maybe a few of those fish-eggs on toast."

"It's *caviar*, you Gryphon barbarian," Gonzalvez said.

"Sure, sure," Johnny replied, picking up a canister of caviar and scooping some out with a finger. "This isn't too bad. Any potato chips around?"

John opened up the door to the closet in case there was anything that fit. He was willing to put on the sweaty prole outfit he had been running around in but if there was anything a tad cleaner it would be nice. He hadn't been able to ask Rachel after her shower because she had yelled that it was free and then disappeared into one of the bedrooms.

As it turned out Rachel's mysterious boyfriend had plenty of clothes. He appeared to be a bit on the hefty side compared to the Manty but there was one suit that looked to be Mullins' size.

Johnny contemplated it balefully for a moment then dropped his towel and tried on the shirt. It fit. So did the cummerbund and pants.

He looked in the mirror and sighed.

"Okay, I guess there have to be some studs around here somewhere."

When he came down from the shower he felt a bit better about his outfit; Rachel had changed into an electric blue Beowulf pantaloon set. The material was semitransparent, responding oddly to reflected light; when the light was shining directly at it the material was opaque, but in shadow or with glancing light patches it would go completely transparent. As she moved it revealed and covered seemingly at random, always covering far more than it revealed. Try as he might, Mullins couldn't determine if she was wearing a cat-suit underneath or absolutely nothing at all.

It was frankly hypnotic and went remarkably well with the archaic tuxedo that was the sole clothing Mullins could find that fit.

"Well, aren't you the pair?" Gonzalvez said with a laugh.

"I thought that might work for you," Rachel said, lifting a glass of champagne in his direction. "I picked it up for Bonz hoping he could get it around his fat middle. No such luck."

"Well, it fits," Mullins admitted, shooting the cuffs

and rolling his shoulders uncomfortably. "But I'd rather be wearing prole clothes; if we have to run this is going to stick out like a sore thumb."

"Well then, we'll just have to avoid making a run for it," Rachel replied, handing him a glass of champagne. "To a flawless escape," she said, raising the glass.

"To a flawless escape," Mullins replied tapping his glass to hers and taking a sip. "That ain't half bad."

"It's an excellent vintage," Mládek said reaching past for a glass. He was back in his own prole outfit and still drying his hair. He took a sip and sighed. "I'll miss New Rochelle grapes."

"You should try some of the Copper Ridge sparkling wines," Charles responded, working the wine around in his mouth. "This seems a tad raw."

"Raw? New Rochelle's one of the finest vintages known!" Mládek responded hotly.

"I think we can leave them to this," Rachel said. "I seem to remember that you actually can dance."

"Well, my mother never admitted that I had gotten any good at it," Mullins said, as he set down the glass. "But mom had two left feet."

"Darling, your only problem as a dancer is that you're too tall and refuse to follow where I lead," Rachel said, her hips thrusting from side to side.

"You took the words right out of my mouth," Mullins replied, completing a complicated twist that ended with his ankles locked behind hers and his hips following her in time. "When did you learn to suvala?"

The had been dancing for over two hours, the tunes segueing through a dozen styles. From the mirror-dance to the minuet, from the suvala to the Hyper-Puma Trot, the two of them had been trying to best each other. Rachel was far and away the more natural dancer, but

Mullins, if anything, knew more styles and was more precise in each.

"I know a girl from New Brazil," she replied, her lips inches from his cheek.

"You know this dance is illegal on Grayson?" he asked in a whisper, leaning in to her ear, his hips grinding against hers.

"Silly people," she husked back then disengaged. "Charles? Admiral? We're going to bed."

"Ah, really?" Charles asked. "So soon? The Admiral and I were just about to come to a conclusion in regards to the superiority of the Tancre strain of grape bacterium."

"I'm afraid not, old boy," Mládek replied. "Dautit is still the superior bacteria."

"But only for higher sugar content! My God man . . ."

"No, I mean *we're* going to bed; you guys can stay up as long as you'd like."

"Oh."

"Since you're sacrificing yourself for me tomorrow, it seemed the least I could do," she said, taking John's arm.

"Well, I'd get all huffy," Mullins replied. "But what the hell; take what you can while you can get it is my motto."

"See if you get anything with a motto like that," she said with a chuckle.

But she relented after suitable persuasion.

Mullins rolled over and patted the bed beside him then opened his eyes to a pallid dawn light.

Rachel was gone.

"Charley?" he called, rolling to his feet and grabbing his head. "Ooooo."

"I see you're bloody up," Gonzalvez said, staggering in the door. "I think your girlfriend slipped us a mickey. According to my sensor logs she slipped out the window about three A.M. local time. Of course, I was sleeping the sleep of the dead."

"Blast," Mullins snarled. "Probably that damned champagne."

"I *thought* it was a tad bitter," Charles said.

"All the gear is set up for *her*. I *still* can't get off-planet!"

"Oh, I don't know about that," Mládek said, entering the room with a large package in his hands. "This was on top of my clothes."

Mullins rubbed his head as the admiral opened up the package and laid out the contents.

"Two sets of male clothing, one set of female," Charles said, picking up the documents. "I need to run these through my scanner, but they look good. And *you're* the female, Johnny my lad." He tossed the appropriate ID over to the admiral with a chuckle.

"Ooooh!" Mládek said with a snort. "Uggh. You make a terribly ugly female, Major Mullins."

"Thanks very much," Johnny said snatching the document out of the admiral's hand. "You're right, I do," he continued, looking at the documents.

"I do not care to be set up, John," Charles said.

"Neither do I," Mullins replied. "But so far she's been helping us. I mean, if she wanted to hand us to StateSec, she could have last night."

"So we just go with the modified plan?" Gonzalvez asked. "That doesn't feel right, Johnny."

"If you have a better suggestion, lay it out there," Mullins snapped. "I just had a great night, barely remember it and have one hell of a headache."

"And you're about to be dressed up as a very ugly woman," the admiral interjected, somewhat cruelly Mullins thought.

"Thanks. I needed that," Mullins replied. "And we're

short on time. We need to get into character and get
out of here. Now."

"Okay," Gonzalvez said. "As long as I don't have to
be the ugly woman."

CHAPTER 8

Beauty and the Beast

The airtaxi trip was uneventful, but when the taxi
pulled up to the curb, the shuttle port was crawling
with security.

"Get the bags Manny," Mullins said querulously as
he lifted himself out of the cab with the aid of a cane.
"These Haven barbarians don't have skycaps!"

"Yes, Mother," Gonzalvez said, paying the driver then
lifting the massive set of luggage out of the boot. "We
have to hurry or we'll miss our lift."

"They had better hold it until we arrive or their
captain will live to regret it," Mullins said loudly as one
of the local Prague cops arrived with his hand outstretched.

"Papers," the security man said, looking away. The
woman was obviously Solarian and you'd think she
would have taken advantage of a face-lift. Or, hell, a
full biosculpt.

"Manny! Give this idiot our papers!"

"Mother!" Gonzalvez replied as Mládek silently
handed over the papers for the whole group.

"We're on the 1550 shuttle," the admiral said def-
erentially. "Mistress Warax is a Solarian trade delegate
and must not be delayed."

"She will be," the cop grunted, scanning the

paperwork and then remotely scanning the threesome. "There's a one hundred percent increase in security; it's bound to slow you down somewhat."

"Whatever for?" Gonzalvez said, marshaling the bags.

"We've got three or four Manty spies running around," the cop replied with a nod. He handed back the paperwork and gestured into the terminal. "Sooner or later they'll either make a break for the spaceport or we'll run them to ground."

"Well, that's not *our* problem!" Mullins snapped, leaning on his cane. "I warn you, if you delay my departure, Rob Pierre *himself* will hear about it! You understand me, sonny?"

"Yes, Mistress Warax," the cop said. "If you'll please proceed into the terminal. Will you need assistance? A float chair can be arranged."

"Yes, of *course* I need assistance, you moron!" Mullins replied. "Do you think I use this damned stick as an affectation?!"

The float chair was hastily summoned and Mullins rode into the port in semi-regal fashion. It was a well-known fact that without the covert support of members of the Solarian League, the Haven/Manticore war would have been long over, in Manticore's favor. So it was no surprise that their cover as Solarian trade representatives was a key to favor. It would not, however, keep them from being intensely scrutinized on the way to the shuttle.

Gonzalvez confirmed their reservation on the Solarian liner *Adrian Bayside* then led the group towards the long line for the final security scan. As he did, an overly abundant blonde, obviously a local and gorgeous in a trimly cut suit, cut in front of him.

"It looks like they're choosing every fifth person for a full-body search," Gonzalvez said. "That's . . . new."

"And unpleasant," Mullins replied softly.

"I don't think you have to worry," Mládek said sardonically as the StateSec guards who were "assisting" the usual security started to swarm around the blonde who had cut them off.

As she approached the security scanner, the head of the StateSec detail waved her out of line and pointed towards a side door; she had apparently been "randomly" selected as a potential threat.

"Pass," the guard said to Mládek as they approached the scanner. He was looking towards the side door angrily in the realization that he was going to miss the show. "Pass, pass, just get on through," he snarled.

The scanner field was a more advanced system than the simple hand scanners of the guards; among other things, if it was set high enough, it could conceivably detect not only the fact that Mullins was male, but that he and Gonzalvez were loaded with special ops "goodies." They were well concealed, but with some of the technology transfers from the Sollies, there was a possibility of detection.

So it was with a certain amount of trepidation that Mullins clambered off the float chair and muttered his way through the scanner. As he did, however, he had to repress a chuckle.

The scanner had two lights, one red and one green. The green was supposed to shine all the time as a telltale. However, the lights occasionally went out and given the Havenite approach to maintenance it was no surprise that this one was dark. However, what was also interesting was that the scanner was unplugged; the plug was sitting on the ground, a meter from the wall socket.

Mullins was morally certain he knew what had happened. The local guards had been told to crank the scanner through the roof. But after a few hours of constant false alarms, they had surreptitiously unplugged it so they could return to their regular routine.

Whatever had caused it, they clearly had nothing to fear. Mullins unobtrusively tapped Gonzalvez on the ankle then gestured at the plug as he walked through. The scanner, naturally, gave nary a beep, even at the metal in his cane.

He suppressed a grin as he took Gonzalvez' arm for "assistance" then started to join Mládek. At that moment, though, there was a shout from behind them.

"You three, halt!" The captain of the StateSec detail, returned from his "security check" of the dangerous blonde, gestured at the bored local guard.

"What in the hell is that scanner doing unplugged?" the StateSec captain snapped.

"Uh," the local guard said.

"Plug it back in," the captain snarled. "You three, back through the scanner!"

"The hell if I will," Mullins said, waving his cane. "Do you know who I am?"

"No, and I don't care," the StateSec officer said dangerously.

"Now Mother," Gonzalvez said soothingly. "We should do as the Captain says."

"I'll have you know that I know Rob Pierre!" Mullins said. "And he will *not* be happy that you have slowed us on our way back to Despartia!"

"Captain," one of the local guards said, trotting up and panting. "Is your communicator turned on?"

"What?" he asked, reaching down and activating the device. "No. I was . . . monitoring a procedure that required my undivided attention. And what is it to *you*?"

"Nothing, Sir," the private said, coming to attention. "But you might want to contact Colonel Sims. *All* of the communicators in your team were turned off; he thought you'd been taken out but there wasn't any incident report. The thing is, the Manty spies have been cornered in a warehouse in the company of a local woman. Team Five has them pinned down, but the Manties have some heavy firepower. Colonel Sims is calling in all of the StateSec units."

"Shit," the captain snarled. "You," he said, pointing at the scanner operator. "Get that plugged back in and get the rest of them through the line. You," he continued. "My team is in the interrogation room. They should be about done. Get them while I call the Colonel."

"Yes, Sir," the private said sardonically. "In the interrogation room, huh?"

"Never you mind that," the captain snapped, striding away.

The scanner operator waited until he was out of sight then waved to Mullins.

"You can go, Mistress. My apologies for the delay."

"Not your problem," he replied in a querulous voice. "But I've got the name of that captain. If he thinks Colonel Whatsisname is a problem, just you wait until *I* get done with him."

He got back on his float chair, which had been helpfully brought around the scanners, and proceeded towards the gate.

"We're early," Gonzalvez said.

"I know. I'd figured more time getting through security."

"So we just lie low?" Mládek said.

"Yeah," Mullins replied, guiding the float chair over to a corner near the gate. "I'm going to take a nap; I had a long night."

Gonzalvez snorted then looked up as the blonde came into the gate, still straightening her clothing. "I'd like a long night with that."

"She doesn't look too happy, does she?" Mullins muttered.

"Not particularly," Gonzalvez said. "Ah, there's our scanner tech."

"Go see if he's got any information on what's going down downtown," Mullins said.

Gonzalvez walked over to the tech, who was obviously headed for his break, and waved him down.

"Pardon me, good fellow," Gonzalvez called. "I was just wondering if you could tell me something."

"Depends on what it is," the tech replied with a smile to reduce the sarcasm.

"The other fellow mentioned some sort of a shootout downtown," Gonzalvez said. "I'm just curious about it."

"Well, there was a group of Manty spies we've been chasing all week," the tech said. "That's the reason for the alert here. Anyway, they have them cornered someplace. That's all I know. I'll keep my ears open on break and if I hear anything else I'll tell you. But why do you want to know?"

"Just curious," Gonzalvez replied. "Excitement, danger, foreign adventures," he said with a relish. "It's all so wonderfully alien to my usual life, you know."

"I can tell," the tech said with a snort. "That's your mother?"

"Yes," Gonzalvez said with a sigh. "The head of Oberlon when she was twenty-nine and now no one can pry her out of the seat, don'cha'know."

"Well, good luck," the tech said with a chuckle. "I'll keep you posted."

Gonzalvez went back to the group and sat down. Mullins was flipping through a pad that contained very reasonable, if wholly imaginary, business reports on a company called "Oberlon" while Mládek was just sitting staring out the windows at the shuttle port.

Gonzalvez glanced back over at Mullins and realized that he was riveted on the blonde.

"Mother, is there something wrong?" he asked, clearing his throat.

"Uh, no, dearie," Mullins said, returning to his pad.

"She doesn't appear to be your type, Mother," Gonzalvez clucked.

"Go away, dear," Mullins said.

"On the other hand, she is *mine*." Gonzalvez chuckled and walked over to the blonde.

"That was idiocy at the security scanner," he said, holding out his hand.

"Thank you," the girl said, looking up at him with a pinched expression. "But I've had about all the male attention I can handle for the day."

"I'm sorry," he said with a rueful smile. "I can understand. But I thought you'd like to know that the guy in charge of the security detail caught some hell for a completely different reason. He's likely to lose his captaincy."

"Thank you," the girl said curtly. "Now if you'll just leave me alone I can try to get back some of my bearing. Or at least center my aggression."

"Okee-dokee," Gonzalvez said, stepping away as the scanner tech came across the gate area with a smile on his face.

"Good news?" Gonzalvez asked, intercepting him well short of the girl.

"For us," the scanner tech said with a grim grin. "Not for the Manties. When they saw all the reinforcements coming, including your captain friend, they blew themselves up. So it's over."

"Yes, it is," Gonzalvez said shaking his head. "Those poor people. I know they are your enemies, but I can't help but feel for them."

"Well, yes," the tech said, adjusting his perceptions.

"A terrible tragedy. But at least now the security won't be so intense and you'll be sure to catch your shuttle."

"Yes, that will be for the good," Gonzalvez said, shaking the tech's hand. "Thank you very much for all your help."

"No problem. Have a good trip."

Gonzalvez sat down by Mullins and took a breath. "You heard?"

"I heard," Mullins replied. "We'll talk about it when we get back."

"Boarding for the *Adrian Bayside* will begin in just a moment." A slim female in Bayside Lines uniform appeared at the gate door. "I would like to have anyone with mobility problems, very small children or priority passes to come up first."

"Well, two out of three ain't bad," Mullins said, holding up a hand. "Give me a hand sonny," he quavered.

"Yes, Mother," Gonzalvez said with a sigh. "Coming, 'Robert'?"

"I suppose," Mládek said, standing up and smiling. "Let me give you a hand, there, Mistress."

"Such nice boys," Mullins said, shuffling towards the personnel tube. "You'd never know I met his father in a spaceport bar, would you?"

"Mother!"

CHAPTER 9

Hell Hath No Fury Like a Woman Admiral. Period.

After surviving extraction from Prague, sneaking through Peep space and convincing the Manty contingent on Excelsior that they weren't *really* double agents—look, here's a Peep Admiral Defector for proof!—Mullins thought it was likely that he would die right here and right now. Or, at least, he halfway wished his heart would just stop or a rock would drop on him or *something*.

"What in the ever living hells was going through what might, with leniency, be referred to as your mind?!" Admiral Givens was not known for raising her voice. And she did not now. The very fact that they practically had to strain to hear her tongue-lashing, which was just winding up after more than thirty minutes that had traced the course of their idiocy from generations before, through infancy and up to the present day, made it worse.

"Well, we did get the Admiral back," Gonzalvez pointed out.

"It's clear proof that your mother dropped you on your head as a child that you think that question was other than rhetorical, Major Gonzalvez," the admiral continued. "The only reason that Excelsior didn't sanction you was that you brought the Admiral back. And that was a good thing. His information, I'll admit, was useful confirmation."

"*Confirmation*, Ma'am?" Mullins asked. "He had a head full of StateSec secrets and codes!"

"All of which, and more, Honor Harrington brought back two weeks ago," Givens said.

"Harrington?" Gonzalvez blurted. "She's *dead*."

"So we all thought," the admiral replied. "But, in fact, she ended up on the ground on Hades. She staged the largest prison breakout in history and returned with not only a half a million prisoners, but reams of data on StateSec procedures and communications and some political prisoners that the Havenites had insisted had been dead for years."

"So," Mullins said. "We went through all of that for *confirmation*?"

"Exactly," Givens snappped. "You two are the most consummate foul-ups I have in my entire organization. I cannot let you out of my sight for more than thirty seconds without you involving yourself in some intensely moronic encounter. I don't *care* if you live through them; the chaos that you leave in your wake more than makes up for your survival. The whole point is to enter and exit *seamlessly*, causing not a ripple while you are there. Not killing double agents, blowing up buildings, getting in car chases and otherwise disporting yourselves like you're playing a *game*. Is *any* of this getting through to you two hydrocephalic *morons*."

"Yes, Ma'am!"

"I'm not in this business to build structures just for you to kick them down like a couple of children who find a pretty vase to break! This is not going to be a short war and we need all the intelligence we can gather; sending you two to a planet is like asking to have the entire system shut out for the rest of the war! Am I getting through to you?"

"Yes, Ma'am!" they chorused.

"I don't even know why I waste my breath," she muttered. She finally took a deep breath and leaned back in her chair, steepling her fingers. "What I *want* to do is *space* both of you, both for the good of NavInt and for my own sanity. But, as a *personal* favor to Agent Covilla I have agreed to give you a reprieve."

"Ma'am?" Gonzalvez said, stunned.

"Agent Covilla said that the two of you were of some assistance to her in her mission to extract the Admiral," Givens replied, touching a button on her desk. She waved as a woman walked through the door. She appeared to be about thirty, standard, plain and blunt featured, with male-short blond hair. She was wearing the uniform of a captain with ONI markings. "She *personally* convinced me that despite your amateurish blunderings on Prague, not to mention the reason you were there, that I should let you off with no more than a warning. Do I have to spell it out for you?"

"No more unauthorized adventures?" Gonzalvez asked, glancing sideways at the woman. He had never seen her before in his life.

"*That* should go without saying. No, if you ever get that screwed up on a mission again, authorized or *un*authorized, I will personally strap you to a missile and fire you out the tube. Do I make myself clear?"

"Clear, Ma'am," they both chorused.

"Captain Covilla?" Givens said. "Do you have anything?"

"No, Ma'am," the captain said. Her voice was gravelly; she'd either spent a lot of time shouting at some point or she'd had a bad experience with death pressure. "I'd like a moment of Captain Mullins' time."

"Very well," Givens said, pointing to the door. "Dismissed."

All three found themselves out in the corridor, looking around at the busy scurrying of NavInt.

"Confirmation," Gonzalvez muttered. "We put our butts on the line for *confirmation*!"

"Typical," Covilla growled. "Captain Mullins, if you could step down to my office, please?"

"Yes, Ma'am," Mullins said. "What about Captain Gonzalvez?"

"Well, he can get started on the paperwork."

"Paperwork?" Gonzalvez said suspiciously.

"Your unauthorized adventure was expensive," Covilla said. "We're going to have to sort out which part was duty and which part was not. And you're going to be paying back the non-duty portion. Come on, Captain."

He followed her to her office, noting that she had a decidedly un-ladylike gait that bespoke significant time in small-craft. He came to attention as she walked around her desk and sat in the room's sole chair.

"Do you have anything you want to add to the debrief?" she asked, flipping a pad across the desk. "You can stand at ease."

"I just have a question," Mullins said, spreading his feet apart and placing his hands behind his back in a position closer to parade rest.

"If it doesn't violate your need to know," Covilla responded with a thin smile.

"How was the rest of your trip back?" he asked. "I mean, after the scene at the shuttle-port, Rachel."

Covilla leaned back and steepled her fingers in a manner identical to Admiral Givens. "How long have you known?" she asked, swinging her chair back and forth. Her voice was now honey smooth.

"I wasn't *sure* until just now," Mullins said. "But the blonde at the shuttleport smoothed her hair back in a manner *identical* to the way you do. And her pushing into line was a bit too coincidental. As soon as I'd made *that* connection, backing up and finding all the places where you'd managed us was easy. So what *really* happened?"

"I was the backup for the defection," she said. "I had figured out that the Chinese laundry was compromised, doubled, but I couldn't abort the Admiral. So I blew up the laundry."

"When you said you had 'something to do' that first evening, you were serious," Mullins said with a chuckle.

"And I drove the Admiral to you," she continued. "I couldn't get him out and spoof StateSec at the same time."

"And the apartment?"

"Oh, that was really my boyfriend's," she replied, tiredly. "You use the weapons that God gives you, John. One of my weapons is my body."

"And it's one hell of a weapon," he said with a smile. "So where does this leave us?"

"I'm not sure," she replied. "I'm not in your chain of command, exactly, but we're close. If we continue it *could* be construed as fraternization."

"You know what?" John replied. "I really could give a rat's ass."

"Same here," she said with a smile, reaching up and peeling off the mask. She picked at a few pieces of plasflesh and rolled them on her finger. "I'm due about a year's leave. How about you?"

"I'm not sure I can get any ever again," Mullins replied with a shrug. "And I'm not going to be able to afford it."

"Don't worry about Patricia, I know where the bodies are buried," Rachel said. "As for the charge issue, I just told Gonzalvez that to get him out of our hair. Where should we go?"

"Anywhere but Prague," Mullins said with a shudder.

"I hear Gryphon is beautiful in the winter," she said with a grin.

FANATIC

by Eric Flint

1

Citizen Rear Admiral Genevieve Chin stared at the holopic on her desk. Without even realizing it, she was perched on the edge of her chair.

Citizen Commodore Ogilve, slouched in a nearby chair in her office, put her thoughts into words:

"He looks like a real piece of work, doesn't he?"

Glumly, Chin nodded. The holopic on her desk was that of a State Security officer whose face practically shrieked: *fanatic*. The fact that it was the image of a young man did not detract from the impression in the least. Coarse black hair loomed over a wide, shallow brow; the brow, in turn, loomed over eyes as dark as the hair. The eyes themselves were obsidian flakes against an ascetic-pale, hard-jawed, tight-lipped, square-chinned and gaunt-cheeked face. Genevieve had no difficulty at all imagining that face in the gloom of an Inquisition dungeon, tightening the rack still further on a sinner. Or shoving the first torch into the mound of faggots piled under a heretic bound to a stake.

Chin couldn't detect any traces of the leering cruelty that had not been hard to find on the face of the officer's predecessor. But she took no great comfort from the fact. Even assuming she was right, that cold-blooded part of her which had enabled a disgraced admiral to survive for ten years through Haven's Pierre–Saint-Just–Ransom regime would have preferred an outright sadist to a sheer fanatic as the effective new head of State Security in La Martine Sector. One could at least hope that a sadist would be careless or lazy, too often distracted by his vices to pay full attention to his official assignment. Whereas this man . . .

"Is he really as young as he looks, Yuri?" she asked quietly.

The third person in the room, who was leaning against the closed door to her office, nodded his head. He was a somewhat plump middle-aged man of average height, with a round and friendly looking face, wearing a StateSec uniform.

"Yup. Just turned twenty-four years old. Three years out of the academy. Unfortunately, he seems to have done splendidly on his first major field assignment and caught Saint-Just's eye. And now, of course . . ."

Citizen Commodore Ogilve sighed. "Since all the casualties State Security suffered in Nouveau Paris when McQueen launched her coup attempt—what in *Hell* what was she thinking?—Saint-Just is throwing every young hotshot he's got left into the breaches." He wiped his face with a thin hand. "If we'd had any warning . . ."

"And what good would that have done?" demanded Chin. "Sure, we could have seized this sector, and so what? As long as Nouveau Paris stayed under Saint-Just's control, he'd have the whip hand." Chin leaned back in her chair wearily. "God damn Esther McQueen and her ambitions, anyway."

She glanced at her desk display. It was dark, at the moment, but she had no difficulty imagining what it would have shown if she'd slipped it to tactical mode. Two State Security superdreadnoughts keeping orbit close to her own task force circling the planet of La Martine.

Admiral Chin's task force was much bigger in terms of ships, true—fourteen battleships on station, along with an equivalent number of cruisers and half a dozen destroyers. And so what? Chin was fairly confident that under ideal conditions she could have defeated those two monsters—though not without suffering enormous casualties. She had the advantage of handpicked officers and well-trained Navy crews, whereas the officers and crews of the StateSec superdreadnoughts had no real battle experience. They'd been selected for their political reliability, not their fighting skills.

But it was all a moot point. The StateSec warships had their impellers and sidewalls up and she didn't. They'd gotten word of Esther McQueen's failed coup attempt in Nouveau Paris before she had, and had immediately gone to battle stations . . . and stayed there. By the time she'd realized what was happening, it had been too late. Any battle now would be a sheer massacre of her own forces.

It had almost been a massacre anyway, she suspected. McQueen's coup attempt had immediately placed the entire Navy officer corps under suspicion; especially any officers who, like Chin herself, dated back to the old Legislaturalist regime.

But when her own People's Commissioner had been found murdered three days before the news

arrived . . . As accidental as it may have been, the timing
had been unfortunate—putting it mildly!

Ironically, Genevieve suspected, she owed her life
to the Manticorans. If the Star Kingdom's Eighth Fleet
hadn't begun their terrifying onslaught on the People's
Republic of Haven, State Security probably *would* have
decided just to destroy her chunk of the Navy.
But . . . Oscar Saint-Just was between a rock and a hard
place, and he'd probably decided he simply couldn't
afford to lose any part of the Navy that he didn't
absolutely have to lose.

That, at least, had been the gist of the message sent
ahead to the two StateSec superdreadnoughts by Saint-
Just's handpicked hatchetman.

She studied the holopic again. *No further action to
be taken against Navy units or personnel until my
arrival. Military situation critical.*

And so things had remained for a very tense three
weeks, since the news of McQueen's coup attempt had
arrived at the distant sector capital of La Martine. The
entire Republican Navy in the sector had been under
arrest in all but name. *All* of it, for the past week—
the superdreadnought captains had demanded the recall
of every ship on patrol. Genevieve Chin and her people
had been under the equivalent of a prison lockdown,
with two ferocious State Security SDs standing guard
over them while everyone waited for the young new
warden to show up.

"Do you know anything about him, Yuri?"

Yuri Radamacher, the People's Commissioner for
Citizen Commodore Jean-Pierre Ogilve, pushed himself away from the door. "Personally, no. But I did find
this record chip in Jamka's quarters. It's a personal
communiqué from Saint-Just."

Ogilve stiffened in his chair. "You took that? For
God's sake, Yuri—"

Radamacher waved him down. "Relax, will you? Now that Jamka's dead, I *am* the highest-ranked StateSec officer in this task force—in the whole sector, as a matter of fact, even if the captains in command of those two SDs aren't paying any attention to my exalted rank. The fact that I searched Jamka's quarters after his body was found won't strike anyone as suspicious. In fact, suspicion would have been aroused if I hadn't."

He pulled a chip from his pocket. "As for this . . ." Shrugging: "I'll have to destroy it, of course. No way to just put it back without leaving too many traces. But I doubt its absence will be noticed, even if Saint-Just thinks to enquire." Radamacher made a face. "Not only was Jamka a slob, but after anyone studies more than ten percent of the chips scattered all over his quarters they'll realize . . ."

He shrugged again. "We all knew he was a vicious pervert. Let Saint-Just's fair-haired boy"—motioning to the holopic with the chip—"wallow in that muck for a bit, and I don't think he'll be worrying about a missing private message from Saint-Just."

Yuri slid the chip into the holoviewer. After a moment, the image of the officer was replaced by another. The same officer, as it happened. But this was not a formal pose. What began playing was a recording of an interview between the officer and Saint-Just himself, which had apparently been made in Saint-Just's office recently.

"I'll give the kid this much," murmured Radamacher. "He's StateSec through-and-through, but he doesn't seem cut from the same cloth as Jamka. Watch."

Fascinated, Admiral Chin leaned forward. The sound quality in the holoprojection was as good as the images themselves—not surprising, given that Saint-Just would have had the very best equipment in his own office.

❖   ❖   ❖

The first thing that struck Admiral Chin was that the head of Haven's State Security seemed a smaller man than she remembered. Genevieve hadn't seen Saint-Just in person for many years, and then only at a distance at a large official gathering. On that occasion, Saint-Just had been positioned behind a podium on an elevated dais, at quite some distance from Genevieve. He'd looked like a big man to her, then. Now, seeing him in a holoprojection sitting behind the desk in his own office, he simply seemed a small, unprepossessing bureaucrat. If Chin hadn't known that Oscar Saint-Just was perhaps the most cold-bloodedly murderous human being in existence, she would have taken him for a middle-aged clerk.

That accounted for some of it. But Genevieve knew that, for the most part, the reason Saint-Just seemed much smaller to her was purely psychological. The last time she'd seen Saint-Just she'd hated and feared him, and had been wondering whether she'd still be alive by the end of the week. She still hated Saint-Just—and still wondered how much longer she'd be alive—but the passage of years and the slow rebuilding of her own self-confidence as she'd forged La Martine Sector into an asset for the Republic had drained away most of the sheer terror.

The door to Saint-Just's office opened and the same young StateSec officer whose face she'd been staring at earlier was ushered into the office by a secretary. The secretary then closed the door, not entering the room himself.

The young officer glanced at the two guards standing against the far wall behind Saint-Just. The Director of State Security was seated at a desk near the middle of the room, studying a dossier open before him.

Chin was impressed by the officer's glance at the

guards. Calmly assessing, it seemed—just long enough to assure himself that the guards were not particularly concerned about him. Their stance was alert, of course. Saint-Just wouldn't have tolerated anything else from his personal bodyguards. But there was nothing visible in that alertness beyond training and habit; none of the subtle signs which would have indicated that a man about to be arrested or secretly murdered had just been ushered into Saint-Just's presence.

Chin knew she couldn't have maintained that much poise herself, in that situation, even with her advantage of many more years of life and experience. The StateSec officer was either blessed by a completely secure conscience, or he was a phenomenally good actor.

The officer marched briskly across the wide expanse of carpet and came to attention in front of the Director's desk. Genevieve noted that he was careful, however, not to get *too* close. The officer was not a particularly big man himself, and as long as he stayed out of arm's reach of Saint-Just, the bodyguards wouldn't get nervous. He would already have been thoroughly checked for weapons. It was quite obvious that neither of the two guards—much less both together—would have any difficult subduing him if he suddenly went amok and tried to attack the Director. The guards were not precisely giants, but they were very big men. Admiral Chin had no doubt both of them were experts in close-quarter combat, armed or unarmed.

Which the officer standing at attention before the desk didn't seem to be, from what Genevieve could tell. He had a trim and well-built figure, yes; she could detect the signs of a man who exercised regularly. But Genevieve was an accomplished martial artist herself—had been, at least, in her younger days—and she couldn't detect any of the subtle indications of such training in the officer's stance.

Then, noticing something else, she cawed laughter. "They've removed his belt and shoes!"

Radamacher smiled sourly. "After Pierre was killed, I doubt if Saint-Just is going to overlook *any* possible danger." He paused the recording and studied it. Then, chuckled. "Is there anything sillier-looking than a man trying to stand at attention in his socks? It's a good thing for him the Committee of Public Safety did away with the old Legislaturalist custom of clicking your heels when coming to attention, or that youngster would look like a pure idiot."

But the humor was as sour as the smile. Idiotic or not, Saint-Just's new version of the Committee of Public Safety had Haven and its Navy by the throat. And young men like the officer standing at attention before him were the fingers of that death-grip.

Yuri started up the recording again. For half a minute or so, the three people in the room watched Saint-Just simply ignore the young man standing before him. The Director of State Security—now also Haven's head of state—was perusing the dossier spread out on the desk before him. The personal records of the officer himself, obviously.

Chin took the time to study that young officer. And, again, was impressed. Most young subordinates in that position would not have been able to disguise their anxiety. She knew perfectly well that Saint-Just was dragging out the process simply to reinforce that he was the boss and that his subordinate was completely at his mercy. A word from Saint-Just could destroy a career—or worse.

But from this youngster . . . nothing. Just an impassive face and stance, as if he possessed all the patience in the universe and not a trace of its fears.

Something indefinable in the expression on Saint-Just's face, when he finally raised his eyes from the dossier and studied the officer, let Genevieve know that Saint-Just's petty little attempt at intimidation had fallen flat—and Saint-Just knew it. For the first time, words entered the recording, and Chin leaned forward more closely.

"You're a self-possessed young man, Citizen Lieutenant Cachat," Saint-Just murmured. *"I approve of that—as long as you don't let it get out of hand."*

Cachat simply gave Saint-Just a brisk little nod of the head.

Saint-Just pushed the dossier aside a few inches. "I've now studied this report on the Manpower affair which you brought back from Terra. I've studied it three times over, in fact. And I will tell you that I've never seen such a cocked-up mess in my life."

Saint-Just's right hand reached out and fingered the pages of the report. "One of the pages in this dossier consists of your own record. Terra was your first major assignment, true. But you graduated almost at the top of your class in the academy—third, to be precise— so let's hope you can match the promise."

"Oh, hell," muttered Ogilve.

"'Oh, hell' is right." Radamacher grimaced. "The top five positions in any graduating class at the StateSec academy require a pure-perfect rating of political rectitude from every single one of your instructors. I graduated third from the bottom, myself."

He jabbed a finger at the recording, which he'd paused again. "And take a look at the kid's face. First time he's had any expression at all. This'll be news to him, you know. He'd had no idea where he stood at the academy, since it's the academy's policy not to let any of the cadets know how they're doing in the eyes of their superiors. I only found out my own standing years later, and then only because I was called on the carpet for 'slackness' and it was thrown in my face. A charge which, you can bet the bank, nobody's ever thrown at *this* young eager-beaver. Look at him! His eyes are practically gleaming."

Chin wasn't sure. There was something a bit odd to her in Cachat's expression. A gleam in his eyes, perhaps. But there was something . . . cold about it. As if Cachat was taking pleasure in knowledge for reasons other than the obvious.

She shook the thought away. It was ridiculous, really, to think you could make that much out of a hologram recording, even one of the finest quality.

"Start it up again," she commanded.

Saint-Just was still speaking. "So now you tell me the truth, young Victor Cachat."

Cachat glanced down at the dossier. "I haven't seen Citizen Major Gironde's report, Citizen Chairman. But, at a guess, I'd say he was concerned with minimizing the damage to Durkheim's reputation."

Saint-Just's snort was a mild thing, quite in keeping with his mild-mannered appearance.

"No kidding. If I took this report at face value, I'd have to think that Raphael Durkheim engineered a brilliant intelligence coup on Terra—in which, sadly, he lost his own life due to an excess of physical courage."

Again, that little snort. More like a sniff, really. "As it happens, however, I was personally quite familiar with Durkheim. And I can assure you that the man was neither brilliant nor possessed of an ounce of courage more than the minimum needed for his job." *His voice grew a bit harsh.* "So now you tell me what really happened."

"*What really happened was that Durkheim tried to put together a scheme that was too clever by half, it all came apart at the seams, and the rest of us—Major Gironde and me, mostly—had to keep it from blowing up in our faces.*" He stood a bit more rigidly. "*In which, if you'll permit me to say so, I think we did a pretty good job.*"

"*'Permit me to say so,'*" mimicked Saint-Just. But there was no great sarcasm in his tone of voice. "*Youngster, I'll permit any of my officers to speak the truth, provided they do so in the service of the state.*" He moved the dossier a few inches farther away from him. "*Which I'd have to say, in this case, you probably are. I assume you and Gironde saw to it that Durkheim went under the knife himself?*"

"*Yes, Citizen Chairman, we did. Somebody in charge had to take the fall—and be dead in the doing—or we couldn't have buried the questions.*"

Saint-Just stared at him. "*And who—I want a name—did the actual cutting?*"

Cachat didn't hesitate. "*I did, Citizen Chairman. I shot Durkheim myself, with one of the guns we recovered from the Manpower assassination team. Then put the body in with the rest of the casualties.*"

Again, Radamacher paused the recording. "Can you believe the nerve of this kid? He just admitted—didn't pause a second—to murdering his own superior officer. Right in front of the Director! And—look at him! Standing there as relaxed as can be, without a care in the world!"

Genevieve didn't quite agree with Yuri's assessment. The image of Cachat didn't looked exactly "relaxed" to her. Just . . . firm and certain in the knowledge of his own Truth and Righteousness. She couldn't keep her shoulders from shuddering a little. Just so might a zealous inquisitor face the Inquisition himself, serene in the certainty of his own assured salvation. The fanatic's mindset: *Kill them all and let God sort them out—I've got no worries where I stand with the Lord.*

Radamacher resumed the playback.

The room was silent for perhaps twenty seconds, with Saint-Just continuing to stare at the young officer standing at attention before him—and the guards with their hands on the butt of their sidearms.

Then, abruptly, Saint-Just issued a dry chuckle. "Remind me to congratulate the head of the academy for his perspicacity. Very good, Citizen Captain Cachat."

The relaxation in the room was almost palpable. The guards' hands slid away from the gunbutts, Saint-Just eased back in his chair—and even Cachat allowed his rigid stance to lessen a bit.

Saint-Just's fingers did a little drum-dance on the cover of the dossier. Then, firmly, he pushed the entire dossier to the side of the desk.

"We'll put the whole thing aside, then. It all turned out well, obviously. Amazingly well, in fact, for an operation you had to put together on the fly. As for Durkheim, I'm not going to lose any sleep over an officer who gets himself killed from an excess of ambition and stupidity. Certainly not when we're in a political crisis like this one. And now, Citizen Captain Cachat—yes, that's a promotion—I've got a new assignment for you."

To Chin's surprise, the recording ended abruptly. She cocked an eyebrow at Radamacher, who shrugged. "That's all there was. If you want my guess, I suspect the rest of it was none too complimentary to Jamka and Saint-Just saw no reason to let the bastard see the nuts and bolts of whatever he discussed with Cachat thereafter."

He popped the chip out of the holoviewer and put it back in his pocket. "Cachat's official new title may not have registered on you properly. *Special Investigator for the Director* is not a title used too often in State Security. And it's not one any StateSec officer wants to hear coming his way, let me tell you. This recording must have been made before Nouveau Paris got the news that Jamka had been murdered. I don't think Saint-Just was any too pleased with Jamka, and this was his way of letting Jamka know his ass was on the line."

"And about time!" snarled Ogilve. "I don't mind so much having a People's Commissioner looking over my shoulder—no offense, Yuri—" For a moment, he and Radamacher exchanged grins. "—but having a swine like Jamka around is something else entirely."

He gave Admiral Chin a look of sympathy. As the top-ranked naval officer in La Martine Sector, Genevieve had been saddled with Jamka as her People's Commissioner.

She shrugged. "To be honest, I didn't mind it all that much. The pig was usually more interested in his own—ah, hobbies—than he was in doing his job. And since he kept his vices away from me personally, I could pretty much just ignore him and go about my business."

She went back to studying the holoviewer gloomily. The original image of StateSec Citizen Captain Cachat was back. "This guy, on the other hand . . ." She sighed and slumped back in her chair. "Give me a lazy, distracted and incompetent commissioner any day of the week. Even a vicious brute." With an apologetic glance at Radamacher: "Or one like you, that the Navy can work with."

Her eyes moved back to Cachat's image. "But

there's nothing worse I can think of than a young, competent, energetic, duty-driven . . . ah, what's the word?"

Radamacher provided it. "Fanatic."

2

Two days later, Victor Cachat arrived at La Martine. Eight hours after his arrival, Chin and Ogilve and Radamacher were ushered into his presence. The Special Investigator for the Director had set up his headquarters in one of the compartments normally set aside for a staff officer on a superdreadnought.

A part of Citizen Commodore Jean-Pierre Ogilve's mind noticed the austerity of the cabin. There was a regulation bed, a regulation desk and chair, and a regulation footlocker. Other than that, the compartment was bare except for a couch and two armchairs—both of which were utilitarian and had obviously been hauled out of storage from wherever the previous occupant had put them in favor of his or her own personalized furniture. *Official Staff Officer Compartment Accouterments, Grade Cheap, Type Mediocre, Quality Uncomfortable, As Per Regulations.*

The bulkheads showed faint traces where the previous occupant had apparently hung some personal pictures. Those were now gone also, replaced by nothing more than the official seal of State Security hanging over the bed and, positioned right behind the desk, two portraits. One was a holopic of Rob Pierre, draped in black with a bronze inscription below it reading *Never Forget*. The other was a holopic of Saint-Just. The two stern-faced images loomed over the shoulders of the young StateSec officer seated at the desk—not that he needed them in the least to project an image of severity and right-thinking.

Ogilve didn't spend much time contemplating the surroundings, however. Nor did he give more than a glance at the other occupants of the now-crowded compartment, who were seated on the couch and armchairs or standing against a far bulkhead. All of them were State Security officers assigned to the StateSec superdreadnoughts, most of whom he barely knew. People who—like the former boss of StateSec in the sector, Jamka—preferred the relative luxury and comfort of staff positions on the huge SDs to the more austere lifestyles of StateSec officers assigned to the smaller ships of the naval task force stationed in La Martine.

The young man sitting behind the desk was quite enough to keep his attention concentrated, thank you, especially after he spoke his first words.

There was this much to be said for Cachat—as least he didn't waste everybody's time playing petty little dominance games pretending to be busy with something else. There was no open dossier before him when they were ushered into the compartment. There were no antique paper dossiers in evidence anywhere, as a matter of fact. The desk was bare other than the computer perched on the corner, whose display was blank at the moment.

As Chin and Ogilve and Radamacher came forward, Special Investigator Cachat's eyes swiveled to Radamacher.

"You're Citizen People's Commissioner Yuri Radamacher, yes? Attached to Citizen Commodore Ogilve."

The voice was hard and clipped. Otherwise it might have been a pleasant young man's tenor.

Yuri nodded. "Yes, Citizen Special Investigator."

"You're under arrest. Report yourself to one of the State Security guards outside and you will be ushered to new quarters aboard this superdreadnought. I will attend to you later."

Radamacher stiffened. So did Admiral Chin and Ogilve himself.

"May I know the reason?" asked Yuri, through tight lips.

"It should be obvious. Suspicion of murder. You were second-in-command to People's Commissioner Robert Jamka. As such, you stood to gain personally by his death, since under normal circumstances you would have—might have, I should say—been promoted to his place."

Ogilve was having a hard time thinking straight. The accusation was so preposterous—

Yuri said as much. "That's preposterous!"

The Special Investigator's shoulders twitched slightly. A shrug, perhaps. Ogilve got the feeling that everything this man did would be under tight control.

"No, it is not preposterous, People's Commissioner Radamacher. It is unlikely, yes. But I am not concerned at the moment with probabilities." Again, that minimal shrug. "Don't take it personally. I am having anyone arrested immediately who might have any personal motive for murdering Citizen Commissioner Jamka."

The hard dark eyes moved to Admiral Chin; then, to Ogilve himself. "That way I can quarantine the possibly personal aspect of the crime in order to concentrate my attention on what is important—the possible political implications of it."

Yuri started to say something else but Cachat cut him off without even looking at him. "There will be no discussion of my action, Citizen Commissioner. The only thing I want from you at the moment is your proposal for who should replace you. I will, for the moment, assume Citizen Commissioner Jamka's responsibilities for overseeing Citizen Admiral Chin, until a permanent replacement is sent from Nouveau Paris. But I will need someone to replace you as Commodore Ogilve's Citizen Commissioner."

Silence. The dark eyes flicked back to Yuri.

"*Now,* Citizen Commissioner Radamacher. Name your replacement."

Yuri hesitated. Then: "I'd recommend State Security Captain Sharon Justice, Special Investigator. She's—"

"A moment, please." The loose fists opened and Cachat worked quickly at the console. Within seconds, an information screen came up. Ogilve couldn't be certain, from the angle he was looking at it, but he thought it consisted of personnel records.

Cachat studied the screen for a moment. "She's attached to PNS *Veracity,* one of the battleships in Squadron Beta. A good service record here, according to this. Excellent, in fact."

"Yes, Special Investigator. Sharon—Citizen Captain Justice—is easily my most capable subordinate and she's—"

The hard, clipped voice cut him off again. "She's also under arrest. I will notify her as soon as this meeting is over and order her to report herself to this ship at once."

Yuri ogled him. Jean-Pierre was pretty sure his own eyes were just as round with disbelief.

Genevieve's eyes, on the other hand, were very narrow. Some of that was her pronounced epicanthic fold, but Ogilve knew her well enough to know that most of it was anger.

"For what possible reason?" she demanded.

Cachat's eyes moved to her. There was still no expression on his face beyond a sort of detached severity.

"It should be obvious, Citizen Admiral. People's Commissioner Radamacher may be involved in a plot against the state. The murder of his immediate superior Robert Jamka suggests that as a possibility. If so, under the circumstances, he would naturally name a trusted member of his cabal to replace him."

"That's insane!"

"Treason against the state is a form of insanity, yes. Such is my private opinion, at least, although it certainly wouldn't serve as a defense before a People's Court."

Genevieve, normally a model of self-composure, was almost hissing. "I meant the *accusation* was insane!"

"Is it?" Cachat shrugged. The gesture, this time, was not so minimal. And whether Cachat intended it or not, the easy heaving of the shoulders emphasized just how square and muscular those shoulders were. Much more so than Ogilve would have guessed from the holopic he'd seen a few days earlier. Ogilve was quite sure the man was a fanatic about physical exercise, too. Cachat's frame was naturally that of a rather slimly built man, and the muscle he had added was not massive so much as wiry. But the force of his personality was driving home to the commodore just how ruthlessly this young man would tackle any project—including his own physical transformation.

Cachat continued. "I can tell you that I spent most of my time on my voyage here studying the records on La Martine, Citizen Admiral Chin. And one thing that is blindingly obvious is that the proper distance between State Security and the Navy has badly eroded in this sector. As is further evident by your own anger at my actions. Why should a Navy admiral care what dispositions State Security makes of its personnel?"

Chin said nothing for a moment. Then, her eyes

became sheer slits and Ogilve held his breath. He almost shouted at her. *For God's sake, Genevieve—shut up! This maniac would arrest a cat for yawning!*

Too late. Genevieve Chin didn't often lose her temper. Nor was it volcanic when she did. But the low, snarling words which came out now contained all of the biting sarcasm of which she was capable.

"You arrogant jackass. Leave it to a desk man to think that in combat you can keep all the rules and regulations in tidy order. Let me explain to you, snotnose, that when you put people together in hard circumstances—for *years* we've been out here on our own, damn you, and done one hell of a good job—"

The State Security officers enjoying the privilege of being seated in the Special Investigator's presence began spluttering outrage. Two of the StateSec officers standing against the wall stepped forward, as if to seize Chin. The admiral herself, despite her age, slid easily into a martial artist's semi-crouch.

It's all going to blow! Ogilve thought frantically, trying to find some way to—

Wham!

He jumped. So did everyone in the room. The palm of Cachat's hand, slamming the desk, had sounded like a small explosion. Jean-Pierre Ogilve studied the Special Investigator's hand. It was not particularly large. But, like the shoulders, it was sinewy and square and looked . . . very, very hard.

For the first time, also, there was an actual expression on Cachat's face. A tight-eyed, tight-jawed, glare of cold fury. But, oddly enough, it was not aimed at Admiral Chin but at the two StateSec officers stepping forward.

"Were you given any instructions?" Cachat demanded harshly.

The two officers froze in mid-step.

"*Were you?*"

Hastily, they shook their heads. Then, just as hastily, stepped back and resumed their position against the wall. Standing at rigid attention, now.

Cachat's hard eyes moved to the StateSec officers seated on the couch and two armchairs.

"And *you*. In case you have difficulty with simple geometry, it should be obvious that the proper relations between StateSec and Navy could not have collapsed in this sector without the participation of *both* parties involved."

One of the two StateSec officers granted an armchair in what Ogilve was coming to think of as *The Fanatic's Presence* began to protest. Jean-Pierre knew her name—Citizen Captain Jillian Gallanti, the senior of the two captains in command of the superdreadnoughts *Hector Van Dragen* and *Joseph Tilden*— but nothing else about her.

Cachat gave her as short a shrift as he was giving everyone else.

"Silence. Whether or not you can handle geometry, your grasp of simple arithmetic leaves much to be desired. Since when do two SDs need to keep their impellers up to handle a task force of battleships and cruisers? Leaving aside the useless wear and tear on the people's equipment"—the words somehow came out in capital letters, People's Equipment—"you've also kept the People's Navy paralyzed for weeks. *Weeks,* Citizen Captain Gallanti—thereby giving the Manticoran elitists free rein to wreak havoc on the commerce in this sector. All this, mind you, in the midst of the Republic's most desperate hour, when the blueblood Earl of White Haven and his Cossacks are ravening at our door."

Cachat's eyes narrowed a bit. "Whether your actions

are the product of incompetence, cowardice—or something darker—remains to be determined."

Gallanti shrunk down in her chair like a mouse under a cat's regard. All the StateSec officers in the compartment now looked like furtive mice. Their eyes moving, if nothing else; desperately trying to avoid the cat's notice.

Cachat studied them for a moment, like a cat selecting its lunch. "I can assure all of you that Citizen Chairman Saint-Just is no more pleased with the state of StateSec-Navy relations in this sector than I am. And I can also assure you that the man who created our organization understands better than anyone that it is ultimately *State Security* which is responsible for maintaining those proper relations."

After a moment, he looked back at Yuri Radamacher. "Name another replacement."

Yuri's lips twisted slightly. "Since Citizen Captain Justice didn't suit you, I'd recommend Citizen Captain James Keppler."

Cachat's fingers worked at the keyboard again. When the appropriate screen came up, he spent perhaps two minutes studying the information. Then:

"I will warn you only once, Citizen Commissioner Radamacher. Trifle with me again and I will have you shipped back immediately to Nouveau Paris and let you face the investigation in the Institute instead."

Mention of the Institute brought a chill to the compartment. Before the Harris assassination, the Institute had been the headquarters of the Mental Hygiene Police, and its reputation had become only more sinister since the change in management.

Cachat allowed the chill to settle in before continuing.

He pointed a finger at the screen. "Citizen Captain Keppler is an obvious incompetent. It's a mystery to me why he wasn't relieved of his duties months ago."

Like the admiral, Yuri seemed to have decided that he was damned anyway. "That's because he was one of Jamka's toadies," he snarled.

"I'll have Keppler assigned to escort my first set of dispatches to Nouveau Paris. Presumably the man can handle a briefcase shackled to his wrist. Which means I still want your recommendation for a replacement, Citizen Commissioner Radamacher. Your opinions on any other subject are not required at this time."

"What's the use? Whoever I recommend—"

"A *name,* Citizen Commissioner."

Yuri's shoulders slumped. "Fine. If you won't trust Captain Justice, the next best would be Citizen Commander Howard Wilkins."

A couple of minutes passed while the Special Investigator brought up another screen and studied it.

"Give me your assessment," he commanded.

By now, it was clear to Ogilve that Cachat had hammered Yuri into . . . not submission, exactly, so much as simple resignation. "Take my word for it or don't. Howard's a hard-working and conscientious officer. Quite a capable one, too, if you overlook his occasional fussiness and his tendency to get obsessed with charts and records."

The last was said with another little twist of the lips. Not sarcastic, this time—or, at least, with the sarcasm aimed elsewhere.

Cachat didn't miss it. "If that jibe is aimed at me, Citizen Commissioner, I am indifferent. Charts and records are not infallible, but they are nevertheless useful. Very well. I can see nothing in Citizen Captain Wilkins' record to disqualify him. Your recommendation is accepted. Now report yourself under arrest."

After Yuri was gone, Cachat turned to Genevieve.

"I'll overlook your personal outburst, Citizen Admiral Chin. Frankly, I am indifferent to the opinion anyone has of me other than the people of the Republic"—again, it came out in capital letters: The People Of The Republic—"and their authorized leaders."

Cachat gestured to the screen. "I spent a portion of my time on the voyage here studying your own records, and those of La Martine since you assumed command of naval forces here six years ago. It's an impressive record. You've succeeded in suppressing all piracy in the sector and even managed to keep Manticoran commerce raiding severely under check. In addition, the civilian authorities in the sector have nothing but praise for the way you've coordinated with them smoothly. Over the past six years, La Martine Sector has become one of the most important economic strongholds for the Republic—and the civilian authorities unanimously credit you for a large part of that accomplishment."

The Special Investigator glanced at Jean-Pierre. "Citizen Commodore Ogilve also seems to have excelled in his duties. I gather he's the one you normally assign to leading the actual patrols."

The sudden switch to praise startled Ogilve. It was all the more disconcerting because the words were spoken in exactly the same cold tone of voice. Not even that, Jean-Pierre realized. It wasn't cold so much as emotionless. Cachat just seemed to be one of those incredibly rare people who really *were* indifferent to anything beyond their duties.

From the expression on her face, he thought Genevieve was just as confused as he was.

"Well. I'm glad to hear it, of course, but . . ." Her face settled stonily. "I assume this is a preface to questioning my loyalty."

"Do you react emotionally to *everything*, Citizen

Admiral? I find that peculiar in an officer as senior as yourself." Cachat planted his hands on the desk, the fingers spread. Somehow, the young man managed to project the calm assurance of age over an admiral with three or four times his lifespan. "The fact that you were an admiral under the Legislaturalist regime naturally brought you under suspicion. How could it be otherwise? However, careful investigation concluded that you had been made one of the scapegoats for the Legislaturalist disaster at Hancock, whereupon your name was cleared and you were assigned to a responsible new post. Since then, no suspicion has been cast upon you."

Seemingly possessed of a lemming instinct, Genevieve wouldn't let it go. "So what? After McQueen's madness—not to mention Jamka found murdered—"

"*Enough.*" Cachat's fingers lifted from the desk, though the heels of his palms remained firmly planted. The gesture was the equivalent of a less emotionally controlled man throwing out his arms in frustration.

"Enough," he repeated. "You simply can't be that stupid, Citizen Admiral. McQueen's treachery makes it all the more imperative that the People's Republic finds naval officers it can trust. Do I need to remind you that Citizen Chairman Saint-Just saw fit to call Citizen Admiral Theismann to the capital in order to assume overall command of the Navy?"

The mention of Thomas Theismann settled Ogilve's nerves a bit. Jean-Pierre had never met the man, but like all long-serving officers in the Navy he knew of Theismann's reputation. Apolitical, supremely competent as a military leader—and with none of Esther McQueen's personal ambitiousness. Theismann's new position as head of the Navy emphasized a simple fact of life: no matter how suspicious and ruthless State

Security might be, they *had* to rely on the Navy in the
end. No one else had a chance of fending off the
advancing forces of the Star Kingdom. The armed
forces directly under StateSec control were enough to
maintain the regime in power against internal opposition. But White Haven and his Eighth Fleet would
go through them like a knife through butter—and
Oscar Saint-Just knew that just as well as anyone.

Genevieve seemed to be settling down now. To
Ogilve's relief, she even issued an apology to Cachat.

"Sorry for getting personal, Citizen Special Investigator." The apology was half-mumbled, but Cachat
seemed willing enough to accept it and let the whole
matter pass.

"Good," he stated. "As for the matter of Jamka's
murder, my personal belief is that the affair will prove
in the end to be nothing more than a sordid private
matter. But my responsibilities require me to priori-
tize any possible political implications. It was for that
reason that I had Citizen Commissioner Radamacher
and Citizen Captain Justice placed under arrest. Just
as it will be for that reason that I am going to carry
through a systematic reshuffling of all StateSec assignments here in La Martine Sector."

The StateSec officers in the room stiffened a bit,
hearing that last sentence. Cachat seemed not to notice,
although Jean-Pierre spotted what might have been a
slight tightening of the Special Investigator's lips.

"Indeed so," Cachat added forcefully. "Running
parallel to an overly close relationship between
StateSec and the Navy here, there's also been altogether too much of a separation of responsibilities
within State Security itself. Very unhealthy. It reminds
me of the caste preoccupations of the Legislaturalists.
Some are always assigned comfortable positions here
on the capital ships in orbit at La Martine"—his eyes

glanced about the compartment, as if scrutinizing the little luxuries which he had ordered removed—"while others are always assigned to long and difficult patrols on smaller ships."

His eyes stopped ranging the bulkheads and settled on the StateSec officers. "That practice now comes to an end."

Jean-Pierre Ogilve had occasionally wondered what Moses had sounded like, returning from the mountain with his stone tablets. Now he knew. Ogilve had to stifle a smile. The expressions on the faces of the superdreadnoughts' officers were priceless. Just so, he was certain, had the idol-worshippers prancing around the Golden Calf welcomed the prophet down from the mountain.

"Comes—to—an—end." Cachat repeated the words, seeming to savor each and every one of them.

3

Ironically, the cabin which Yuri Radamacher was taken to by the guards after he left Cachat's presence was larger and less austere than his own aboard the commodore's flagship. That was always one of the advantages to serving aboard an SD, where living space was far more ample. This didn't quite qualify as a "stateroom"—at a guess, some nameless StateSec lieutenant had been ousted to make room for him—but it was still a more spacious cabin than the one Yuri had occupied aboard Ogilve's PNS *Chartres*.

Still and all, it was only a ship cabin. After the guards left—locking the door behind them, needless to say—it didn't take Yuri more than five minutes to examine it completely. And most of that time was pure dithering; the psychological self-protection of a man trying to keep the little shrieks of terror in the back of his mind from overwhelming him.

Soon enough, however, he could dither no more. So, not having any idea what the future held in store for him, Yuri sagged into the compartment's one small armchair and tried to examine his prospects as objectively as possible.

The prospects were . . . not good. They rarely were, for a StateSec officer placed under arrest by StateSec itself. Even the fig leaf of a trial before a People's Court would be dispensed with. State Security kept its dirty linen secret. Summary investigation. Summary trial. Often enough, summary execution.

On the plus side, while he and Admiral Chin and Commodore Ogilve had become a very close team over the past few years—exactly the sort of thing State Security did *not* like to see happening between naval officers and the StateSec political commissioners assigned to oversee them—they had always been careful to maintain the formalities in public.

Also on the plus side, while they had received vague feelers from Admiral Esther McQueen, they had been careful to keep their distance. In truth, they never *had* belonged to McQueen's conspiracy.

On the other hand . . .

On the minus side, there wasn't much doubt which way the admiral and Jean-Pierre and Yuri would have swung, in the event that McQueen had succeeded in her scheme. None of them particularly trusted McQueen. But when the alternative was Oscar Saint-Just, the old saw "better the devil you know than the devil you don't" just didn't hold any water. *Anybody* would be better than Saint-Just.

He tried to rally the plus side again. It was also true, after all, that they had never responded to McQueen's feelers with anything that could by any reasonable stretch of the term be characterized as "plotting."

Or so, at least, Yuri tried to tell himself. The problem was that he'd been an officer in StateSec for years. So he knew full well that Saint-Just's definition of "reasonable characterization" was . . . elastic at best. The fact was that there *had* been some informal communications between McQueen and Admiral Chin over the past year or so, which Ogilve and Radamacher had been privy to. And if the messages sent back and forth had been vague in the extreme, the simple fact of their existence alone would be enough to damn them if State Security found out.

If they found out. Yuri tried to find some comfort in the very good possibility that they wouldn't. The communications had always been verbal, of course, transmitted by one of McQueen's couriers. And always the same one—a woman named Jessica Hackett, who had been one of the officers on McQueen's staff. True, StateSec was superb at forcing information out of its prisoners. But there was at least a fifty/fifty chance that Hackett had been one of the many officers on McQueen's staff who had died when Saint-Just destroyed McQueen's command post with a hidden nuclear device. Not even a State Security interrogator could squeeze information out of radioactive debris.

Still, that was small comfort. Yuri knew perfectly well that StateSec would be on a rampage after McQueen's coup attempt. Heads were going to fall, right and left, and lots of them. The only reason Saint-Just had been relatively restrained thus far was simply because the critical state of the war with the Star Kingdom made it necessary for him to keep the disruption of the Navy to a minimum. But, as with everything else, Oscar Saint-Just's definition of "relatively restrained" was what you'd expect to find in a psychopath's dictionary.

Yuri sighed, wondering for the millionth time how the revolution had gone so completely sour. As a long-time oppositionist to the Legislaturalist regime—which had landed him for three years in an Internal Security prison, from which he'd only been freed by Rob Pierre's overthrow of the government—he'd greeted the new regime with enthusiasm.

Enough enthusiasm, even, to have volunteered for State Security. He chuckled drily, remembering the difficulty with which an inveterate dissident in his forties had struggled through the newly established StateSec academy, surrounded by other cadets most of whom were fiery young zealots like Victor Cachat.

Victor Cachat. What a piece of work. Radamacher tried to imagine how any man that young could be *that* self-assured, *that* confident in his own righteousness. So much so that in less than a day Cachat had succeeded in intimidating the naval officers of an entire task force and the officers of two StateSec superdreadnoughts.

Had Yuri himself ever been like that? He didn't think so, even in his rebellious youth. But he really couldn't remember anymore. The long years which had followed Pierre's coup d'état, as he slowly came to understand the horror and brutality lurking under the new regime's promise, had leached most of his idealism away. For a long time now, Yuri had simply been trying to survive—that, and, as much as possible, bury himself in the challenges posed by his assignment in La Martine Sector. Other, more ambitious StateSec officers might have been frustrated by being posted for so long in what was a political backwater, from the standpoint of career advancement. But Yuri had found La Martine a refuge, especially as he came to realize that the two naval officers he worked most closely with were kindred spirits. And, slowly, La Martine began to attract and keep other StateSec officers of his temperament.

They *had* done a good job in La Martine, damnation. And Yuri had found satisfaction in the doing. It had been one way—perhaps the only way—he could salvage what was left of his youthful spirit. Whether the Committee of Public Safety appreciated it or not, he and Chin and Ogilve had turned La Martine into a source of strength for the Republic. Despite its remote location, for the past several years La Martine had been one of the half-dozen most economically productive sectors for the People's Republic of Haven.

He wiped his face. *And so what?* Radamacher knew full well that Saint-Just and his ilk considered competence a feather, measured against the stone of political reliability.

Victor Cachat. It would be his decision, now. The powers of a StateSec Special Investigator, in a distant provincial sector like La Martine, were well-nigh limitless in practice. The only person who could have served as a check against Cachat would have been Robert Jamka, the senior People's Commissioner in the sector.

But Jamka was dead, and Radamacher was fairly certain that Saint-Just would be in no hurry to name a replacement for him. La Martine was not high on Saint-Just's priority list, being so far away from the war front. So long as Saint-Just was satisfied that Cachat was conducting the investigation with sufficient zeal and rigor, he'd let the young maniac have his way.

There was something ludicrous anyway about the idea of Robert Jamka serving as a "check" to anyone. Jamka had been a sadist and a sexual pervert. As well ask Beelzebub to rein in Belial.

And so the day wore on, as Yuri Radamacher sank

deeper and deeper into despondency. By the time he finally dragged himself to his bed and fell asleep, the only thing he was wondering any longer was whether Cachat would offer him the honorable alternative of suicide to execution.

He wouldn't, of course. That had been the tradition of the Legislaturalist regime's Internal Security. Part of the "elitist privilege" which StateSec and its minions were determined to root out. None more so than men like Victor Cachat. Cachat's diction couldn't be faulted, but Yuri had had no difficulty detecting the traces of a Dolist accent in his speech. A man from Havenite society's lowest layers, now risen to power, filled with slum bitterness and rancor.

4

He was roused by Cachat himself, some hours later. The Special Investigator came into the cabin in the middle of the night, accompanied by a guard, and shook Radamacher out of his sleep.

"Get up," he commanded. "Take a quick shower, if need be. We have things to discuss."

The tone of voice was cold, the words curt; so much Yuri took for granted. But he was well nigh astonished by Cachat's offer to allow him time to shower. And he found himself wondering, as he did so, why Cachat was accompanied by a Marine guard instead of one from State Security.

For that matter, where had Cachat even *found* a Marine on a StateSec SD? Except for the rare instances when suppressing a widespread rebellion was required, State Security normally provided its own contingent of ground troops for duty aboard its ships. Saint-Just didn't trust the Marines any more than he did the Navy, and he wasn't about to allow large bodies of men armed and trained in the use of hand weapons aboard his precious StateSec superdreadnoughts.

He found out as soon as he stepped out of the shower stall, his hair still damp, and quickly got dressed.

Cachat was now sitting in Yuri's armchair. A pile of record chips was spread out on the small table next to him. Not official chips, but the kind used for personal records.

"Were you aware of Jamka's perversions?" demanded Cachat. His hand gestured toward the chips. "I spent two of the most unpleasant hours of my life examining these."

Yuri hesitated. Cachat's tone of voice was always cold, but now it was positively icy. As if the man was trying to restrain a boiling fury by layering it with an official glacier. Instinctively, Yuri understood he was standing on the edge of a crevasse. One false step . . .

"Of course," he said abruptly. "Everybody was."

"Why was it not reported to headquarters on Nouveau Paris?"

Can he be that *much of a babe in the woods?*

Something of his puzzlement must have shown. For only the second time since he'd met Cachat, the young man's face was filled with anger.

"Don't bother using the excuse of Tresca, damnation. I'm well aware that sadists and perverts have been tolerated—whether I approve of it or not, and I don't— on prison detail. But this is a task force of the People's Republic! Officially, on armed duty in time of war. The behavior of a deviant like Jamka posed an obvious security risk! Especially one who was also a sheer madman!"

Glaring, Cachat picked up one of the chips and brandished it like a prosecutor holding up the murder weapon before a jury. "This one records the torture and murder of a *naval* rating!"

Yuri felt the blood drain from his face. He'd heard rumors of what went on in Jamka's private quarters down on the planet, true. But, from the habit of years, he'd ignored the rumors and written off the more extravagant ones to the inflation inevitable to any hearsay. Truth be told, like Admiral Chin, a large part of Radamacher had been thankful for Jamka's secret perversions. It kept the bastard preoccupied and out of Yuri's hair. As long as Jamka kept his private habits away from the task force, Radamacher had minded his own business. It was dangerous—very dangerous—to pry into the private life of a StateSec officer as highly ranked as Robert Jamka. Who had been, after all, Radamacher's own superior.

"Good God."

"There is no God," snapped Cachat. "Don't let me hear you use such language again. And answer my question—why didn't you report it?"

Yuri groped for words. There was something about the youngster's sheer fanaticism that just disarmed his own cynicism. He realized, if he'd had any doubts before, that Cachat was a True Believer. One of those frightening people who, if they did not take personal advantage of their own power, did not hesitate for an instant to punish anyone who failed to live up to their own political standards.

"I didn't—" He took a breath of air. "I was not aware of any such murder. What went on dirtside—I mean, I kept an eye on him—so did Chin—when he was aboard the admiral's flagship—or anywhere in the fleet—which wasn't too often, he was lax about his duties, spent most of his time either on the SDs or on the planet—"

I'm babbling like an idiot.

"That's a lie," stated Cachat flatly. "The disappearance of Third Class Missile Tech Caroline Quedilla was reported to you five months ago. I found it in your records. You did a desultory investigation and reported her 'absent without leave, presumed to have deserted.'"

The name jogged Radamacher's memory. "Yes, I remember the case. But she disappeared while on shore leave—it happens, now and then—and . . ."

He forgot Cachat's warning. "Oh, God," he whispered. "After I did the first set of checks, Jamka told me to drop the investigation. He said he had more important things for me to do than waste time on a routine naval desertion case."

Cachat's dark eyes stared at him. Then: "Indeed. Well, for punishment I'm going to require you to watch this entire chip. Make sure you're near the toilet. You'll puke at least once."

He rose abruptly to his feet. "But that's for later. Right now, we need to finish your investigation. The situation here is such an unholy mess that I can't afford to have an officer of your experience twiddling his thumbs. I'm desperately in need of personnel I can rely on." He jerked a thumb at the sergeant; scowling: "I even had to summon Marines from one of the task force vessels, since I can't be sure which StateSec personnel on this ship were involved with Jamka."

The scowl was now focused on Yuri himself. "That's provided you can satisfy me of your political reliability, that is, and your own lack of involvement in Jamka's . . . I'm still calling it 'murder,' even if I personally think the man should have been shot in the head. As long as it was done officially."

Yuri hesitated. Then, guessing that Cachat would rush the matter, decided to take the chance to volunteer for chemical interrogation. And why not? Cachat could order it done anyway, whether Yuri agreed or not.

"You can give me any truth drug you want." He tried to sound as confident as possible. "Well, there's one I have an allergic reaction to—that's—"

Cachat interrupted him. "Not a chance. Among the people implicated in Jamka's behavior—there seems to have been a whole little cult of the swine—was one of the ship's doctors aboard this vessel. I have no idea how he might have adulterated the supply of drugs, precisely in order to protect himself if he came under suspicion. So we'll use the tried and true methods."

Cachat turned and opened the door. Without a glance backward, he led Yuri into the hallway. As Radamacher, following, came up to the big Marine sergeant, he suddenly realized that he recognized the man. He didn't know his first name, but he was Citizen Sergeant Pierce, one of the Marines attached to Sharon Justice's ship.

"Three squads of us from the *Veracity* just got called in by the Special Investigator," whispered Pierce. "Only been here four hours."

Radamacher left the room. Cachat was stalking down the corridor perhaps ten yards ahead of him. Just out of whispering range.

"What going on?" he asked softly.

"All hell's breaking loose, Sir. Been maybe the most interesting four hours of my life."

The citizen sergeant nodded toward Cachat. "That is one scary son-of-a-bitch, Sir. Would you believe—"

Seeing Cachat impatiently turning his head to see what was holding them up, the sergeant broke off.

Thereafter, they traveled in silence. Cachat set a fast pace, leading them through the convoluted corridors of the huge warship with only an occasional moment of hesitation. Yuri, remembering how he'd gotten lost himself the first time he came aboard the super-dreadnought, wondered how Cachat was managing the feat.

But he didn't wonder much. It was a long voyage from Nouveau Paris, and he was quite sure the Special Investigator had spent the entire time preparing for his duties. Part of which, he was sure, involved studying the layout of the vessel he would be working in.

Duty. The Needs of the State.

He spent more time wondering about something else. He finally remembered that the woman who had been murdered by Jamka had *also* been attached to Sharon Justice's ship.

That was . . . odd. Not the fact itself. The fact that Cachat, after throwing Sharon Justice—and Yuri himself—under arrest, would then turn around and use Marine personnel from the same ship for—

For what, exactly? What the hell is he doing?

As soon as they entered the large chamber which was their destination, Yuri understood. Some of it, at least.

The chamber was normally used as a gym for StateSec troopers. In a way, it still was. Insofar as administering a beating could be called "exercise."

He stared, horrified, when he saw the person shackled to a heavy chair in the center of the compartment. It was Citizen Captain Sharon Justice, nude from the waist up except for a brassiere. He could barely recognize her. Sharon's upper body was covered with bruises, and her face was a pulp. Blood was splattered all over her head and chest.

"Sorry, Sir," whispered the Marine. Sharon's groans covered the soft sound of the words. "We'll go as easy as we can. But . . . it's either this or get what the good doctor got."

Yuri's brain didn't seem to be functioning very well. Despite State Security's reputation, there were plenty of StateSec officers like himself who were no more familiar with casual brutality than anyone else. Radamacher had never found it necessary to enforce discipline with anything more severe than a sharp tone, now and then.

There was a huge pool of blood around the chair Sharon was strapped into. Yuri groped for the answer . . .

How can she bleed so much?

Finally, the Marine's whispered words registered. Dimly, Radamacher realized that there were a number of other bleeding bodies in the compartment. He hadn't noticed them at first, because they'd been hauled into two of the compartment's corners and there were perhaps twenty other people crowded into the other two corners of the compartment.

"Crowded" was the word, too. They seemed to be pressing themselves against the bulkheads, as if they were trying to get as far away as possible from the proceedings in the center. Or, more likely, as far away as possible from the Special Investigator. That they were all members of State Security, except for the Marine citizen major and three Marine citizen sergeants who had apparently administered the beatings, made the whole situation insanely half-comical to Radamacher. No wonder the Marine noncom had called it "maybe the most interesting four hours of my life." Talk about role reversal!

Then Yuri took a better look at the bodies in the other corner, and any sense of comedy vanished. The bloody and dazed people in the one corner had just been beaten. They were being attended to now by a couple of medics, but despite the bruises and the gauze he recognized all of them. Essentially, that little group constituted most of the top StateSec officers assigned to the naval task force. What Yuri Radamacher thought of as "his people."

The other group of bodies . . .

He didn't recognize any of them, except one woman he thought was one of the officers from the other superdreadnought. He was pretty sure they were all members of the SD personnel, who'd always kept their distance from "fleet" StateSec.

They were the source of most of the blood pooled around the chair, he realized. They'd all been shot in the head.

Jamka's accomplices, he was sure of it.

Dead, dead, dead. Six of them.

"Well?" demanded Cachat.

The citizen major overseeing the Marines was Khedi Lafitte, the commanding officer of the *Veracity*'s Marine detachment. He shook his head. "I think she's innocent, Sir." He gestured with his head toward the holopic recorder being held by a StateSec guard nearby. "You can study the record yourself, of course. But if she had anything to do with Jamka's killing—ah, murder—we sure couldn't get a trace of it."

Cachat studied the beaten officer in the chair, his jaws tight. "What about her political reliability?"

The citizen major looked a little uneasy. "Well . . . ah . . . we were concentrating on the Jamka business. . . ."

Cachat shook his head impatiently. "Never mind. I'll study the record myself. So will whoever Citizen Chairman Saint-Just assigns to examine my report, once it reaches Nouveau Paris." He turned his head to the StateSec guard holding the recorder. "You *did* get a good record, yes?"

The guard nodded his head hastily. He seemed just as nervous around the Special Investigator as everyone else.

Apparently satisfied, Cachat turned back to study Justice again. After a few seconds, he twitched his shoulders. The gesture seemed more one of irritation than an actual shrug.

"Get her out of the chair, then. Put her with the others and see to it she gets medical attention. Thank you, Citizen Major Lafitte. I'll question Citizen Commissioner Radamacher myself. By now I'm almost certain we've cauterized the rot, but it's best to be certain."

Two of the Marine citizen sergeants, moving more gently than you'd expect from two men who had just administered her beating, unshackled Sharon from the chair and helped her toward the medics in the corner. Once the chair was empty, Cachat turned to Yuri.

"Please take a seat, Citizen Commissioner Radamacher. If you're innocent, you have nothing to fear beyond a painful episode which will end soon enough." There was a pulser holstered on his belt. Cachat lifted the weapon and held it casually. "If you're guilty, your pain will end even sooner."

Yuri took some pride in the fact that he made it to the chair and seated himself without trembling. As one of the sergeants fastened the shackles to his wrists and ankles, he stared up at Cachat.

Again, he ignored the Special Investigator's dictum. "Jesus Christ," he hissed softly. "You shot them *yourself*?"

Again, that irritated little twitch of the shoulders. "We are in time of war, at a moment of supreme crisis for the Republic. The security risk posed by Jamka and his cabal required summary judgement and execution. Their perversions and corruption threatened to undermine the authority of the state here. It *did* undermine that authority, as a matter of fact, when Jamka's behavior got himself killed."

Yuri had to fight not to let his relief show. Whether he realized it or not, Cachat had just stated that the significance of Jamka's murder was personal, not political—and had done so on the official record.

Cachat spoke his next words a bit more loudly, as if to make sure that all the StateSec officers in the room heard him.

"Citizen Chairman Saint-Just will naturally review the whole matter, and if he disapproves of my actions he'll see to my own punishment. Whatever that might be." His tone was one of sheer indifference. "In the meantime, however"—his eyes left Yuri and swept slowly across the crowd of officers watching in the corners, glittering like two agates—"I believe I have established that Legislaturalist-style cronyism and backscratching between unfit and corrupt officers will no longer be tolerated in this sector. Indeed, it will be severely punished."

All three citizen sergeants were back. All of them donned gloves to protect their hands.

"Have at it, then," said Yuri firmly. For reasons he could not quite understand, he was suddenly filled with confidence. In fact, he felt better than he had in a long time.

The feeling didn't last, of course. But, as Cachat had stated, it was eventually over. Through one blurry eye—the other was closed completely—Yuri saw the pistol go back into the holster. And through ears that felt like cauliflowers, he dimly heard the Special Investigator pronounce him innocent of all suspicions. True, the words sounded as if they were spoken grudgingly. But, they were spoken. And properly recorded. Yuri heard Cachat enquire as to that also.

As Citizen Sergeant Pierce helped him over to the corner where the medics waited, Yuri managed to mumble a few words.

"Dink 'y noze id boken."

"Yessir, it is," muttered the citizen sergeant. "Sorry about that. We broke your nose right off. The Special Investigator's orders, Sir."

Cachat, you vicious bastard.

Later, after he was patched up, he felt better.

"You'll be okay, Sir," assured the medic who'd worked on him. "A broken nose looks gory as all hell at the time—blood all over the place—but it's really not all that serious. Few weeks, you'll be as good as new."

5

Radamacher spent the next several days in his cabin aboard the *Hector Van Dragen*, recovering from his injuries. Although he was no longer officially under arrest, and thus under no obligation to remain in the cabin, he decided that the old saw about discretion being the better part of valor applied in this case.

Besides, he got a full daily report from Sergeant Pierce anyway, concerning the events transpiring on the superdreadnought—indeed, throughout the entire task force. So he saw no reason to venture out into the corridors himself, since he had a perfectly valid medical excuse not to do so. Philosophically—especially with the aid of new bruises added to old saws—he thought that phenomena which went by such terms as "Reign of Terror" were best observed indirectly.

He got the term "Reign of Terror" from Pierce himself, the day after his interrogation.

"Just checking up, Sir," Pierce explained apologetically after Yuri invited him into the room, "making sure you were okay." The sergeant examined his face, wincing a bit at the bruises and the bandages. "Hope you don't take none of this personally. Orders, Sir. We Marines never had no beef against you, ourselves."

The sergeant's wince changed into a scowl. "Sure as hell never had no beef against Captain Justice. He shouldna had us do that, dammit. It idn't proper."

The injuries to Yuri's face caused his ensuing snort of sarcastic half-laughter to *hurt*. Especially his broken nose. He added that little item to his long list of grievances against Special Investigator Victor Cachat.

"Ide 'ay nod!" he wheezed. "Ma'ines an'd zuppose do bead dey own ovizuhs." He steeled himself for more pain. "'Ow iz Zha—Gabban 'Usdis—doin'?"

"She's fine, Sir," the sergeant assured him, almost eagerly. "We went as easy as—I mean, well—the Special Investigator left before we started on Captain Justice, Sir. So he wasn't there to watch. So—"

Pierce was floundering, obviously feeling trapped between human sympathy and duty—not to mention the possible Wrath of Cachat. Yuri let him off the hook. Given the difficulty of speaking, he also decided to ignore the citizen sergeant's unthinking use of the forbidden term "sir." He understood full well the word was an indication of Pierce's trust in him.

"Nedduh mine, Ziddezen Zajend. Z'okay. Iz 'uh noze boke doo?"

"Oh, no, Sir!" Yuri had to force down another laugh. The sergeant seemed deeply aggrieved at the suggestion. "Pretty a woman as she is, we wouldn't do nothing like that. Didn't knock out none of her teeth, neither. Just, you know, bruised her up good for the recorder."

Feeling two missing teeth of his own with a probing tongue—they also *hurt*—Yuri was pleased at the news. He'd always found Sharon Justice a very attractive woman. So much so, in fact, that on more than one occasion he'd had to remind himself forcefully of the prohibition against romantic liaisons between officers in the same chain of command. That hadn't been easy. He was a bachelor beginning to tire of it, Sharon was a divorcée about his own age, and their duties brought them into constant contact. Just to make things worse, he was pretty sure his own attraction to her was reciprocated.

The citizen sergeant began moving about the cabin, fussily tidying up here and there. As if trying, somehow, to make amends for the events of the previous day. There was something utterly ludicrous about the whole situation, and another little laugh wracked pain through Yuri's face.

"Nedduh mine, zajend," he repeated. Then, gesturing toward the door. "Wad's 'abbenin' oud deh?"

Pierce grinned. "It's a regular reign of terror, Sir. Look on the bright side. You're well and truly out of it, now. Whereas those sorry worthless bastards out there—"

He broke off, coughing a little. It was also against regulations for a Marine noncom to refer to the officers and crew of a State Security SD as "sorry worthless bastards."

Under the circumstances, Yuri decided to overlook the citizen sergeant's lapse. Indeed, with a lifted eyebrow, he invited Pierce to continue. Even went so far, in fact, as to invite the Marine to sit with a polite gesture of the hand.

❖   ❖   ❖

For the next half an hour, Pierce regaled Radamacher with Tales of the Terror. He'd had a ringside seat at the proceedings, since he and the other Marines from the *Veracity* had continued to serve as Cachat's impromptu escort and ready-made police force.

"Got some StateSec people with us too, of course, making the actual arrests. But those are all okay folks. From the fleet. The Special Investigator brought 'em over from half the ships in the task force."

Yuri was puzzled. "'Ow did 'e know widge ones do ged?"

The sergeant's face flushed a little. "Well. Actually. He asked us, Sir—we Marines, I mean, especially Major Lafitte—which ones we'd recommend. If you can believe it. Then he went into Captain Justice's cabin—she's just down the corridor a ways—and cross-checked the names with her."

Yuri stared at him.

"It was weird as hell," Pierce chortled. "He went over the list with the captain just as calm as could be. Didn't even seem to notice the bandages."

No, the bastard wouldn't, Yuri thought sourly. *Cachat would pass out beatings like he'd pass out any other assignment.*

But there wasn't really much anger in the thought. Radamacher was just fascinated by the peculiarities of the whole thing. Cachat's actions were like a grotesque Moebius strip concocted in the mind of a torturer. First, Cachat used the Marine contingent from Sharon's own ship to beat her into a pulp. Then, he turned around and consulted with those same Marines with regard to StateSec assignments—and cross-checked the recommendations with the same woman they'd just gotten through torturing!

Utterly insane. Not simply the actions of a fanatic,

but of one who was unhinged to boot. It wasn't *precisely* against regulations for an officer of StateSec to rely on Marines for their recommendations for StateSec staff assignments. But that was only because it never would have occurred to anyone that such a regulation was needed in the first place. It just wasn't *done,* that's all. As well pass regulations forbidding stars to revolve around planets!

As the days passed and the citizen sergeant continued his Tales of the Terror, however, Yuri soon realized that Cachat was not a man to concern himself with "what isn't done." Results were all that mattered to him, and—fanatic or not; unhinged or not—results he was certainly getting.

Seven officers and twenty-three crewmen of the *Hector Van Dragen* arrested, for starters, within the first week. Two officers and seven crewmen from the other SD, the *Joseph Tilden.* One of those officers and four of the crewmen subsequently executed, after Cachat finished examining the evidence found in their quarters.

Most of the officers and ratings had been arrested for routine corruption. Theft and embezzlement, mostly. Those Cachat slammed with the maximum penalties allowable under the official rules for shipboard discipline short of court-martial. But the others had been implicated in Jamka's activities. Clearly so in the case of the officer. The evidence had been fuzzier for the crew members. From what Radamacher could determine, the hapless ratings had been mainly guilty of being too closely identified as "Jamka's people."

No matter. They were all shot. By a firing squad this time, selected from StateSec members brought over from the fleet, not by Cachat himself.

Radamacher wondered how much of Cachat's

ruthlessness was dictated by typical StateSec empire-building. Guilty or not, the net effect of the purge was to completely shatter any residual Jamka network, and to intimidate anyone else from forming a different informal network. Or, at the very least, to keep it well under cover. By the end of his first week in La Martine Sector, Victor Cachat had established himself as The Boss, and nobody doubted it.

As cynical as he tried to be about the matter, however, Yuri didn't really think much if any of Cachat's behavior was motivated by personal ambitions. He noted, for instance, that although Cachat had ordered and personally overseen the beatings—okay, call them "interrogations"—of half a dozen of the top ranked StateSec officers attached directly to the task force, he had left it at that after pronouncing them all innocent. The Special Investigator had made no attempt to break up their own informal network, even though he was surely aware of its existence. As long as they were careful to mind their p's and q's—which all of them were doing scrupulously, now—he seemed willing to look the other way.

And thank God for that. Yuri still resented his bruises, and his broken nose and missing teeth. And he resented the bruises he saw on Sharon even more—which was every day, now, since they were both still on the SD and had cabins not too far apart. Still . . .

Any danger of being accused of being a McQueen conspirator was growing more distant as each day passed. Not just for Yuri himself, but for anyone in the task force. By hammering into a pulp the StateSec officers overseeing Admiral Chin's task force—and then declaring them all innocent of any crime—Cachat had effectively sealed the whole matter. Just as, by using task force Marines to do the blood work, he had effectively cleared them of any suspicion also; and, by implication, the naval officers in overall command of the task force. Neither Admiral Chin nor Commodore Ogilve had been subjected to anything worse than a rigorous but non-violent interrogation.

Granted, Saint-Just's regime didn't recognize the principle of double jeopardy, so any charges could theoretically be raised again at any time. But even Saint-Just's regime was subject to the inevitable dynamics of human affairs. Inertia worked in that field as surely as it did anywhere else. No one could question the rigor of Cachat's investigation—not with blood and bruises and dead bodies everywhere—and the matter was settled. Reopening it would be an uphill struggle, especially when the regime had a thousand critical problems to deal with in the wake of Rob Pierre's death.

Besides, whatever faint evidence there might once have been had surely vanished. By now, Yuri was quite certain that everyone in the task force who'd had any possible connection to McQueen had done the electronic equivalent of wiping off the fingerprints. Unwittingly—the young fanatic still had a lot to learn about intelligence work, Yuri reflected wryly—Cachat's week-long preoccupation with terrorizing the personnel of the two superdreadnoughts had bought time for the task force. Time to catch their breath, relax a bit, eliminate any traces of evidence, and get all their stories straight.

Radamacher was also aware that Cachat had made no move against either of the two captains commanding the SDs, even though Citizen Captain Gallanti in particular had made no secret of her hostility toward the young Special Investigator. Neither of the captains had been touched by Jamka's unsavory activities, and neither could be shown to be corrupt. So, punctiliously, Cachat had left them in their positions and did not even seem to be going out of his way to build any case against them—despite the fact that Radamacher was quite sure Cachat understood that the SD commanders would remain a possible threat to him.

When he mentioned that to Ned—he and Pierce had become quite friendly by the end of the week—the burly citizen sergeant grinned and shook his head.

"Don't underestimate him, Yuri. He might be leaving Gallanti and Vesey alone, but he's gutting their crews."

Radamacher cocked an eyebrow.

"Figuratively speaking, I mean," Pierce qualified. "You haven't heard yet, I take it, of what Cachat's calling the 'salubrious personnel retraining and transfer'?"

Yuri tried to wrap his brain around the clumsy phrase. Somehow, the florid words didn't seem to fit what he'd seen of Cachat's personality.

The sergeant's grin widened. "We lowly Marines just call it SPRAT. So does the Special Investigator. In fact, he says he got the idea from the nursery rhyme."

That jogged Yuri's memory. From childhood, he dredged up the ancient doggerel.

> *"Jack Sprat could eat no fat,*
> *His wife could eat no lean.*
> *And so betwixt the two of them,*
> *They licked the platter clean."*

"Yup, that's it," chortled Pierce. "Except the Special Investigator says it's time to do a role switch. So he's transferring about five hundred people from the SDs over to the fleet, and about twice that number from the fleet over here. Even some Marines, believe it or not. A company's worth on each ship. I'm one of them, in fact."

"*Marines?* On a StateSec superdreadnought? That's . . . not done."

Pierce shrugged. "That's what Captain Gallanti said to him when he told her. She wasn't any too polite about it, neither. I know; I was there. The SI always keeps two or three of us Marines around him wherever he goes." Half-apologetically: "Along with the same number of StateSec guards, of course. But they're okay types."

Radamacher stared at him. "*Okay types.*" He knew perfectly well that a Marine definition of that term would hardly match Saint-Just's.

His mind was almost reeling. Cachat was a lunatic! To be sure, an SI's authority in a remote sector could be stretched a long ways. But it didn't really include decisions over personnel—well . . . unless severe problems of discipline and/or loyalty were concerned . . . and Cachat had just littered an SD's gym with dead bodies to prove that it was . . .

Still. It just *wasn't done.*

He must have muttered the words aloud. The citizen sergeant shrugged and said: "Yeah, that's what Gallanti said. But, as you mighta figured, the SI's a regular walking encyclopedia of StateSec rules, regulations and precedents. So he immediately rattled off half a dozen instances where Marines *had* been stationed on StateSec capital ships. Two of the instances at the order of none other than Eloise Pritchard, Saint-Just's—ah, the Citizen Chairman's—fair-haired girl."

Yuri's face tightened. He knew Pritchard himself, as it happened. Not well, no. But he'd been close to the Aprilists in his days as a youthful oppositionist, and she'd been one of the leaders he'd respected and admired. But since the revolution, she'd turned into what he detested most. Another fanatic like Cachat, who'd drown the world in blood for the sake of abstract principles. Her harshness as a People's Commissioner was a legend in State Security.

However, it was indeed true that Pritchard was, as the sergeant said, Saint-Just's "fair-haired girl." So if Cachat was right—and he'd hardly fabricate something like that—he might get away with it.

"You can bet the bank Gallanti's going to scream all the way to Nouveau Paris," he predicted.

Pierce didn't seem notably concerned. "Yup. She told Cachat she'd insist on including her own dispatches with the next courier ship, and he told her that was her privilege. Didn't blink an eye when he said it. Just as lizard-cold as always."

The sergeant cocked his head a little, braced his hands on the edge of the seat, and leaned forward. "Look, Sir, I can understand where you'll be holding a grudge against the guy. What with a broken nose and all. But I gotta tell you that personally—and it's not just me, neither; all the Marines I know feel the same way about it—the SI's okay with me."

He grimaced ruefully. "Yeah, sure, I wouldn't invite him to a friendly poker game, and I think I'd have a heart attack if my sister told me she had a crush on the guy. But. Still."

For a moment, he groped for words. "What I mean is this, Sir. None of us Marines are gonna shed any tears over the shitheads he whacked. Neither are you, if you'll be honest about it. Scum, to call them by their right name. For the rest of it? He had a buncha decent people beaten up some, but—being honest about it—no worse than you mighta gotten in a barroom brawl. And then the slate was clean for them, and meanwhile he's been tearing right through all the crap that's piled up in these ships."

Yuri fingered his nose gingerly. "You must have been

in some worse barroom brawls than I ever was, Ned."

"You don't hang out in Marine bars, Citizen Commissioner," Pierce chuckled. "A broken nose? Couple of missing teeth? Hell, I 'member a time a guy got his— Well, never mind."

"Please. I grow faint at the description of mayhem. And remind me not to wander into any Marine bars in the future, would you? If you see me looking distracted, I mean."

The citizen sergeant snorted. "The only time I ever see you looking distracted is when Captain Justice is around."

Yuri flushed. "Is it that obvious?"

"Yeah, it's that obvious. For chrissake, Yuri, why don't you just ask the lady out on a date?" His eyes glanced around the room, then at the door, sizing up the surroundings. "I grant you, entertainment's a little hard to find on a StateSec superdreadnought. But I'm sure you could figure out something."

Yuri Radamacher had a little epiphany, then. The citizen sergeant veered away from the awkward personal moment into another tale of Cachat's Rampage. But Yuri barely heard a word of it.

His mind had wandered inward, remembering ideals he'd once believed in. How strange that a fanatic could, without intending to, create a situation where a Marine noncom would joke casually with a StateSec officer. A week ago, Radamacher had not even known the citizen sergeant's first name. Nor, a week ago, would that sergeant have dared tease a StateSec Commissioner about his love life.

The Law of Unintended Consequences, he mused. *Maybe that's the rock on which all tyrannies founder in the end. And maybe freedom's real motto should be something whimsical, instead of flowery phrases about*

Liberty and Equality. There's a line from a Robert Burns' poem that would do nicely.

> *"The best laid schemes o' mice an' men*
> *Gang aft agleigh."*

6

The next day, however, it was Radamacher's own half-assumed plans which suffered the mouse's fate.

The Special Investigator showed up at Yuri's door early in the morning. To his surprise, accompanied by Citizen Captain Justice.

As he invited them in, Yuri tried to keep his eyes off of the captain. Sharon's bruises were well on their way to healing now, and she looked . . .

Better than she ever had. Yuri realized that Citizen Sergeant Pierce's wisecrack the day before had broken through his last attempts at maintaining his personal reserve. To put it in the crude terms of a Marine, Yuri Radamacher had a serious case of the hots for Sharon Justice, and that was all there was to say about it.

The problem of what to *do* about it, of course, remained in all its stubborn intractability. So he told himself, firmly, as he forced his mind to concentrate on the unwelcome figure of the Special Investigator.

"Are your injuries sufficiently healed to resume your duties?" Cachat demanded. The tone of voice implied a sentence left unspoken. *Or do you still insist on malingering, mired in sloth and resentment?*

Yuri's jaws tightened. Law of Unintended Consequences or not, he just plain *detested* this young fanatic.

"Yes, Citizen Special Investigator. I am ready to resume my duties. I'll have my kit transferred—"

"Not your old duties. I have new ones for you."

The SI nodded at Sharon. "In light of her exonera-
tion and your own recommendation, I've appointed
Citizen Captain Justice—sorry, People's Commissioner
Justice, now; the promotion is only brevet, but that's
within my authority—to serve for the moment as
Citizen Admiral Chin's commissioner. Citizen Commander Howard Wilkins will be replacing you as the
commissioner for Citizen Commodore Ogilve."

Yuri frowned, puzzled. "But—"

"I shall require you to remain on board this
superdreadnought. The *Hector Van Dragen* will be
remaining in La Martine orbit while the *Joseph Tilden*
accompanies the task force in its upcoming mission."
Cachat scowled fiercely. "I cannot allow the needs of
the ongoing investigation to impede the State's other
business any longer. Three new incidents of Manticoran
commerce raiding have been reported—even a case of
simple piracy!—and this task force *must* be gotten back
into action. There being no valid reason for both SDs
to remain lounging about while Admiral Chin's task
force resumes its work, I am assigning the *Tilden* to
accompany them."

Radamacher scrambled to catch up. "But—Citizen
Special Investigator—ah, no offense, but you're not a
naval man—a superdreadnought really isn't suited for
anti-raiding work. Not to mention—ah—"

Cachat smiled slightly. "Not to mention that the SD
captains will raise a howl of protest? Indeed they will.
Indeed they have, I should say. I squelched them last
night."

Yuri was fascinated, despite himself, at the smile
which remained on Cachat's face. It was the first time
he'd ever seen the Special Investigator smile about anything.

It was a thin smile, naturally. But try as he might,
Yuri couldn't deny that it made the man's face look

even younger than usual. You might even call it an attractive face, in that moment.

"As for the other," Cachat continued, "while I'm no expert on naval matters, Citizen Admiral Chin *is*. And she assures me that she can find a suitable role for the *Tilden*. Given her own experience and track record— and the fact that my investigation has turned up no reason to question either her competence or her loyalty—I have ordered Citizen Captain Vesey to place the *Tilden* under Citizen Admiral Chin's command."

Yuri tried to imagine how loudly Vesey must have shrieked at *that* news. True, Vesey wasn't as mulish and intemperate as Citizen Captain Gallanti, the CO of the *Hector Van Dragen*. But, like all commanding officers of StateSec capital ships, Vesey hadn't been selected for his friendly attitude toward the regular Navy.

Cachat's smile was gone, now, his usual cold expression firmly back in place.

"Citizen Captain Gallanti will naturally include her and Vesey's protests at my decision in their dispatches to Nouveau Paris. I authorized sending a courier ship today, in fact, to ensure that Vesey's remarks could be included before he left orbit. But until and unless my decision is overruled from StateSec headquarters, the decision stands. And I will see to it that it is enforced, of course, by any means necessary. Fortunately, Citizen Captain Vesey did not press the issue."

Hey, no kidding. Who's going to "press the issue" with a man who's already demonstrated he'll personally shoot six people in the head in the space of a few hours if he thinks it's in the line of duty? It's one thing for a mouse to bell a cat, if he thinks he can get away with it. But he's not going to debate the cat about it ahead of time, that's for sure.

Yuri stared at Cachat, wondering if the SI's own thoughts were running on parallel lines. They . . .

Might be. Cachat might not be an experienced naval officer. But Radamacher was quite certain that the young man had studied naval affairs just as thoroughly and relentlessly as he did everything else. If so, he'd understand perfectly well that a single superdreadnought attached to a flotilla the size of Admiral Chin's would be outmatched in the event of—ah, "internal hostilities." Especially since—*Jesus, is he possibly this Machiavellian?*—Cachat had also seen to it that the internal security squads for both superdreadnoughts were now composed of Marines and StateSec troops who got along well with Marines.

While . . .

Jesus Christ. He is that Machiavellian. Now that I think about it, by transferring all the worst elements from the SDs over to the task force, he's split them up and scattered them over three dozen different ships. With no way to communicate with each other, and . . . surrounded by Navy and Marine ratings who'd hammer them into a pulp cheerfully—or shoot them dead—if Chin or Cachat gave the order.

Which leaves . . .

He couldn't help it. A little groan forced its way through Yuri's lips.

Cachat frowned. "What's this, Citizen Assistant Special Investigator Radamacher? Surely you're not objecting to a new assignment? You just got through assuring me your health had recovered sufficiently."

"Yes. But—"

His mind raced wildly. Cachat was a lunatic. *Lunatic, lunatic, lunatic!*

Yuri took a deep breath and tried to settle down. "Let me see if I understand you properly, Citizen Special Investigator. You're relieving me from my duties as a commissioner in order to serve as your assistant.

And since I assume you will be accompanying the task force in its mission—"

"That's essential." Cachat snapped the words. "I must oversee the operation of this entire combined StateSec and Naval force. In *action,* which is where it belongs. If nothing else, I intend to make sure that this important unit of the People's Republic is doing its duties properly and according to regulations. Which I can't possibly accomplish while everybody is lolling about in orbit twiddling their thumbs. There is no Manticoran threat to La Martine posed in the near future beyond commerce-raiding, so leaving a single SD on station in the capital should be more than sufficient to maintain order here."

He bestowed two piercing dark eyes upon Yuri. "The more so if the investigation on the *Hector Van Dragen* is concluded in my absence by a capable subordinate. You *do* have an excellent service record, Citizen StateSec Officer Radamacher. Now that any questions concerning your loyalty or possible involvement in the Jamka affair are resolved, I see no reason you can't accomplish the task quite successfully."

Cachat shrugged, as if moderately embarrassed to say the next words. "I dare say I've already rooted out the worst of the corruption and slackness aboard this ship. So all that really remains for you to do is oversee Citizen Captain Gallanti—"

She's going to love THAT! Yuri quailed a bit at the thought of Gallanti's temper.

"—and rigorously pursue whatever remaining traces of corruption and slackness you might uncover. To that end, I'll be leaving you the best of the new security units I've managed to put together. The best StateSec security teams—most of them from the task force, naturally, since the rot had festered too long here on the SDs—along with Citizen Major Lafitte and his Marines. I should think that would be sufficient."

That'll mean Ned Pierce will still be around. Thank God for that. I'll need his shoulder to cry on.

There didn't seem anything he could say. So, he simply nodded his head.

"Good." Cachat turned to leave, his hand on the door latch. Citizen Commissioner Justice began to follow, but not before giving Yuri a quick smile. Almost a shy smile, somehow, which was odd. Sharon Justice was normally a very self-assured woman.

The smile, even on lips still puffy from her beating, made Yuri's heart lift. Even more, the warmth in her brown eyes.

A sudden realization jolted him.

"Ah—Citizen Special Investigator?"

Cachat turned back around. "Yes?"

Radamacher cleared his throat. "I simply wanted to make sure my understanding of regulations is clear. As an assistant now attached to your office, I believe I am no longer in the task force's chain of command. Is that correct?"

"Of course," replied Cachat curtly. "How could it be otherwise? You report to me, and I report to State Security HQ in Nouveau Paris. How could we possibly be responsible to the same chain of command we're investigating?" Impatiently: "An officer of your experience simply can't be that ignorant of basic—"

He broke off. Then, glanced quickly at Sharon Justice. Then—

Yuri couldn't quite believe it, but . . . Cachat was actually *blushing*. For a moment, the young man looked like a schoolboy.

The moment didn't last long. Abruptly, as if summoned, the fanatic-face shield closed down. Cachat's next words were spoken in a very impatient tone of voice.

"If this involves a personal matter, Citizen Assistant Investigator Radamacher, it is no concern of mine so long as no regulations are broken."

He seemed to grope; the first time Yuri had ever seen the SI at a loss for words. Then, concluded in a half-mumble:

"I have pressing business. Citizen Commissioner Justice, the task force will be leaving orbit very shortly. I'll expect you to report for duty on time. Say, an hour from now."

He opened the door—flung it open, more like—slipped through, and was gone. Closing it firmly behind him.

Yuri stared at Sharon. Her smile now seemed as shy as a schoolgirl's herself. He suspected his own did likewise.

What to say? How to say it? After three years of scrupulously never crossing the line.

And in an hour?! A lousy HOUR?! Cachat, you bastard!

Sharon broke the impasse. The shy smile dissolved into a throaty chuckle, and all her normal self-assurance seemed to return.

"What a mess, eh, Yuri? We're both way too old—too dignified, too, especially you—to just hop into bed." She eyed the cabin's narrow bed skeptically. "Leaving aside the fact that neither of us have our youthful slender figures left. We'd probably fall off halfway through—and I don't know about you, but I'm still way too bruised to want another set just yet."

"I think you look gorgeous," Yuri stated firmly. Well. Croaked firmly.

Sharon grinned and took him by the hand. "An

hour's only an hour, so let's use it wisely. Let's talk, Yuri. Just talk. I think we both need it desperately."

They didn't *just* talk. Before the hour was up, there'd been a clinch or three tossed into the mix—and a very passionate goodbye kiss when it finally came time for Sharon to leave, bruised lips or not. But, mostly, they talked. Yuri never remembered much of the conversation afterward, although he always swore it was the most scintillating conversation he'd ever had in his life.

What was most important, though, was that after Sharon left and Yuri took stock of his situation, he realized that for the first time in years he felt just *great*. And, being by nature a cautious man but not a coward, was also sensible enough to ride that feeling out into the corridors and through the labyrinth of the SD's passages and into Citizen Captain Gallanti's office.

Even a newly enlarged and promoted mouse setting out to bell a cat has enough sense to do it with the wind in his sails.

7

Gallanti was not thrilled to see him.

"For God's sake!" she snarled, as soon as he was ushered into the stateroom she used for her command quarters when not on the bridge. "The maniac hasn't even left orbit yet and you're already here to give me grief?"

"There is no God," Radamacher informed her serenely. "Mention of the term is expressly forbidden in StateSec regulations."

That brought her up short. Her eyes rolled and Yuri could sense the woman's notorious temper rising. But he'd already gauged his tactics before entering the room, and knew what to do.

"Oh, relax, would you?" Radamacher gave her a wry

smile—he had a superb wry smile; people had told him so over the years hundreds of times—and eased his way into an armchair. "For God's sake, Citizen Captain Gallanti, just once can you assume we're adults instead of kids in a schoolyard? I didn't come here to play dominance games with you."

That threw her off her stride, as he'd suspected it would. Gallanti stared at him, her mouth half-open. The stocky blonde's heavy brow was frowning more in puzzlement now than anger.

Yuri pressed the advantage. "Look, as you said: The maniac hasn't even left orbit yet. So let's take advantage of all the time we've got to get everything straightened up before he comes back. If we work together, we can see to it that by the time he returns—that'll be at least six weeks, more likely eight—not even that fanatic can find anything wrong any more. He'll blow on his way and we'll have seen the last of him."

Gallanti was as notorious for her suspiciousness as her temper. Her eyes narrowed. "Why are you being so friendly, all of sudden?"

He spread his hands. "When have I ever *not* been friendly? It's not my fault you don't know me. I couldn't very well invite *myself* over to your staff dinners, could I?" He left unspoken the rest of it. *Although you could have, Exalted SD Captain—if you hadn't been such a complete snot toward every officer in the task force since you arrived on station.*

Gallanti's heavy jaws tightened. That was embarrassment, at first. But, like anyone with her temperament, Gallanti was not fond of self-doubt, much less self-criticism. So, within seconds, the embarrassment began transforming into anger.

Yuri cut it off before it built up any steam. "Let it go, will you? If you think *you* can't stand the maniac, try getting a beating at his hands." He fingered his still somewhat swollen jaw, opening his mouth to let her see the missing front teeth. He'd already begun regeneration treatment, but the gap was still obvious. And Yuri had rebandaged his nose before leaving his cabin, taking care to make the dressings as bulky as possible.

That did the trick. Gallanti managed a half-smile of tepid sympathy; then, flopped into the chair behind her desk.

"Isn't he something else? Where in creation did the Citizen Chairman dredge *him* up from? The Ninth Circle of Hell?"

"I believe that's the circle reserved for traitors," Radamacher said mildly, "which I'm afraid is the one fault you *can't* find in the man. Not without being laughed out of court, anyway. It's been a while since I read Dante, but if I recall correctly, intemperate zealots were assigned to a different level."

Gallanti glared at him. "Who's Dante?" Without waiting for an answer, she transferred the glare to her desktop display.

"As soon as I'm certain that bastard's into hyperspace, I'm sending off a purely blistering set of dispatches by courier ship. I can promise you that! Vesey is doing the same." Half-spitting: "We'll see what's what after they find out on Haven what the maniac's been up to!"

Radamacher cleared his throat delicately. "I would remind you of two things, Citizen Captain Gallanti. The first is that it will be at least six weeks before we can expect any answer, travel times being what they are between La Martine and the capital. I'd guess more like two months. StateSec is going to study all the dispatches carefully before they send back any reply."

She was still glaring at him. But, after a couple of seconds, even Gallanti seemed to realize that glaring at a man for simply stating well-known astrophysical facts was foolish. Grudgingly, she nodded. Then, summoning up her still-moldering anger and resentment, spat out: "And what's the second thing?"

Yuri shrugged. "I'm afraid I don't share your confidence that Nouveau Paris will be very sympathetic to our complaints."

That was a nice touch, he thought. In point of fact, Yuri Radamacher's name did not and would not appear on a single one of those "blistering dispatches." But, as he'd expected, a woman of Gallanti's mindset was always prepared to assume that everyone around her except lunatics would agree with her. So she took his casual mention of "our" complaints for good coin. That helped defuse her anger at his questioning of her judgement.

"Why not?" she demanded. "He had almost a dozen StateSec officers shot—"

"The figure is actually seven," Yuri countered mildly, "the rest were StateSec security ratings. Muscle, to put it crudely. And every single one of them was guilty— there's no doubt about this, Citizen Captain, don't think there is—of the most grotesque crimes and violations of StateSec regulations. You know as well as I do that Nouveau Paris will stamp 'fully approved' on each and every one of those summary executions."

Again, he cleared his throat delicately. "You'd do well not to forget that the Special Investigator is also—*has* also, I should say—sent dispatches of his own. I happen to know—never mind how—that those dispatches included a large sampling of the pornographic record chips found in the personal quarters of Jamka and his confederates. I don't know if you've seen any of those records, Citizen Captain, but I *have*—and I can assure you that the impact they will have on StateSec at the capital is *not*—not not not—going to be: 'why did Cachat blow their brains out?' The question is going to be of quite a different variety. 'Why was none of this reported prior to Cachat's arrival—*especially* by the commanding officers of the superdreadnoughts where the criminal activity was centered?'"

Finally, something seem to penetrate Gallanti's armor of self-righteousness. Her face paled a little. "I wasn't—damnation, it was none of my affair! I command an SD, I'm *not* assigned to the task force! Jamka was a people's commissioner—assigned to the task force—not someone under my command."

Try as she might, the words lacked force. Radamacher shrugged again.

"Citizen Captain Gallanti—do you mind if I call you Jillian, by the way, while we're speaking privately?"

Gallanti hesitated. Then, nodded her head brusquely. "Sure, go ahead. As long as it's private. Ah—Yuri, isn't it?"

Radamacher nodded. "Jillian, then. Look, let's face facts. We've all got our excuses, and you and I both know they aren't flimsy ones—not, at least, if you're willing to live in the real world instead of Cachat's fantasy one. But . . ."

He let the word fall into silence. Then:

"Face it, Jillian. Real world excuses always come up short against fantasy accusations whenever the fantasist can point to real crimes. So let's not kid ourselves. Cachat's rampage is going to go down very well in Nouveau Paris, don't think it won't." In a slightly cynical tone of voice: "Out of idle curiosity, I once did a textual analysis of several of our Citizen Chairman's occasional speeches to StateSec cadre assemblies. Back when he was still Director of State Security. Outside of common articles like 'a' and 'the,' do you know which word appears the most often?"

Gallanti swallowed.

"The word was *rigor*, Jillian. Or *rigorous*. So tell me

again, just how sympathetic our boss is going to be when he hears us whining that the fanatic Victor Cachat was too *rigorous* in his punishment of deviants using StateSec rank to cover their misdeeds."

Now, Gallanti looked like she was choking on something. Yuri segued smoothly into the opening of what he thought of as "the deal." Prefacing it by sitting up straight and sliding forward in his chair. Nothing histrionic, just . . . the subtle body language of a man suggesting a harmless—nay, salutary and beneficial— conspiracy. Say better: *private understanding*.

"We'll have a lot more luck with what I'm sure you raised in the way of your other complaints. It *is* outrageous, the way Cachat's been swapping personnel around. You can be damn sure Nouveau Paris is going to look cross-eyed at the way he's been using the Marines."

"They certainly will! 'Cross-eyed' is putting it mildly! They'll have a fit!"

Yuri waggled a hand. "Um . . . yes and no. Cachat's a sharp bastard, Jillian, don't make the mistake of underestimating him. Fanatics aren't necessarily stupid. Don't forget that he was always careful to assign an equal number of hand-picked StateSec guards to serve alongside the Marines."

Yuri saw no reason to mention that the Marines themselves, in effect, had done the handpicking. He pressed on:

"Yes, Cachat bent regulations into a pretzel. But he didn't outright break them—no, he didn't, I checked— and he'll still have the excuse that he faced extraordinarily difficult circumstances because Jamka had corrupted the normal disciplinary staff. Unfortunately, five out of the seven executed officers—and all four of the ratings—belonged to the SDs' police details. He'll claim he had no choice—and the claim isn't really

all that flimsy. Not from the distance of Nouveau Paris,
anyway."

Gallanti fell into gloomy silence, slumping in her
chair. Then, in a half-snarl: "The whole thing's *absurd*.
The one thing the stinkbug was *supposed* to do is the
one thing he didn't! We *still* have no idea who murdered Jamka. Somehow that 'little detail' has gotten lost
in the shuffle."

Yuri chuckled drily. "Ironic, isn't it? And after
Cachat's rampage, we'll never know. But so what? I
assume you saw the medical examiner's report, yes?"

Gallanti nodded. Yuri grimaced. "Pretty grisly business, wasn't it? No quick killing, there. Whoever did
Jamka was as sadistic about it as Jamka himself. From
looking at the holopics of his corpse, I'd almost be
tempted to say Jamka committed suicide. Except there's
no possible way he could have shoved—"

Yuri shuddered a little. "Ah, never mind, it's sick-
ening. But the point is—you know, I know, anyone with
half a brain knows—that Jamka was certainly murdered
by one of his own coterie. A falling out between
thieves, as it were. So when you get right down to it,
who really cares any more who killed Jamka? Cachat
shot the whole lot of them, and there's an end to it.
Good riddance. You really think *Oscar Saint-Just* is
going to toss in his bed worrying about it?"

Glumly, the SD captain shook her head. Even more
glumly, and in a very low voice, she said: "This is going
to wreck my career. I *know* it is, damn it. And—" Her
innate self-righteousness and resentfulness began to
surface again. "It's not my *fault*. I had nothing to do
with it! If that fucking Cachat hadn't—"

"*Jillian! Please.*" That cut her short. Yuri hurried
onward. "Please. There's no point to this. My own
career's on the rocks too, you know. Even when you're
found 'innocent,' having an official 'rigorous

interrogation' on your record is a big black mark. Worse than any on your record, when you get right down to it."

Gallanti almost—not quite—managed a smile of sympathy. Yuri decided the moment was right to strike "the deal."

This time, he slid all the way to the edge of his seat. "Look, the worst thing you can do is wallow in misery. There's still a chance to clean this up. Minimize the damage, at the very least. Cachat taking himself off on a romantic haring around after pirates and commerce raiders is the best thing we could have hoped for."

She cocked a questioning, vaguely hopeful eyebrow. Yuri gave her his very best sincere smile.

And an excellent one it was, too. Friendly, intimate without being vulgar, sympathetic; over the years, hundreds of people had told Yuri how much they appreciated his sincerity. Perhaps the strangest thing about it all—certainly in that moment—was that Yuri knew it for the simple truth. He *was* a sincere, sympathetic and friendly man. Using his own nature, since he was otherwise disarmed, as the only weapon at his disposal.

"I'm not a cop, Jillian. Cachat can plaster whatever labels he wants on me. I don't have the temperament for it. To cover my ass—everybody's ass—I'll find and bust up a few more pissant 'spots of corruption.' On a ship this big, there's got to be at least half a dozen illegal stills being operated by ratings."

"Ha. Try 'two dozen.' Not to mention the gambling operations."

"Exactly. So we'll fry a few ratings—slap 'em with the harshest penalties possible—while I go ahead with my real business."

"Which is?"

"I'm a *commissioner,* Jillian. And a damn good one.

Whatever other beefs any of my superiors have ever had about me, nobody's ever given me anything but top marks for my actual *work*. Check my records, if you don't believe me."

That, too, was the simple truth. Radamacher didn't try to explain any of it to Gallanti, for the task would have been hopeless. By the nature of her assignment, even leaving aside her own temperament, Gallanti was a StateSec *enforcer*. That was how her mind naturally worked, and she'd inevitably project that onto anyone else in StateSec.

The reality was more complex. Yuri, unlike Gallanti, had spent his entire career in "fleet StateSec"—one of those handful of StateSec officers on each ship assigned to work and fight alongside the officers and ratings of the People's Navy they were officially overseeing. Many if not all of such StateSec officers, as the years passed, came to identify closely with their comrades in battle. For someone with Yuri's temperament, the process had been inevitable—and quick.

Gallanti was too dull-witted to grasp that. Oscar Saint-Just, of course, was not. He'd always understood that he held a dangerous double-edged sword in his hand. The problem was that he *needed* it. Because bitter experience had proven, time and again, that the StateSec commissioners who got the best results in the crucible of war were not the whiphandlers but precisely the ones like Yuri Radamacher. The ones who did not "oversee" their naval comrades so much as they served them as priests had once served the armies of Catholic Spain. Inquisitors in name, but more often confessors in practice. The people just far enough outside the naval chain of command that ratings—officers, too— would come to them for advice, help, counsel. Intercession with the authorities, often enough, if they'd fallen afoul of regs which were intolerant on paper but could somehow magically be softened at a commissioner's private word. Despite the grim "StateSec" term in his title, the simple fact was that Yuri had spent far more time over the past ten years helping heartsick young ratings deal with "Dear John" or "Dear Jane" letters than he had trying to ferret out disloyalty.

Yuri had pondered the matter, over the years. And, with his natural bent for irony, taken a certain solace in it. Whatever else the Committee of Public Safety's ruthlessness had crushed underfoot, it had not been able to transform basic human emotional reactions. Yuri doubted now if any tyranny ever could.

"So what do you want, Yuri?" Gallanti's words were gruff, but the tone was not that of a woman issuing a rebuff. It sounded more like an appeal, in fact.

"Give me free rein aboard the ship," he replied at once. "In name I'll be the 'assistant investigator' scurrying all over rooting out rot and corruption. In the real world, I'll serve you as your commissioner. I'm *good* at morale-building, Jillian, try me and see if I'm not. By the time Cachat gets back, I'll have a handful of 'suppressed crimes' to wave under his nose. But, way more important, we'll have a functioning capital ship again—and a crew, including all the transfers, who'll swear up and down that the good ship *Hector* is a jolly good ship and Cap'n Gallanti a jolly good soul."

"And what good will *that* do?"

"Jillian, give Victor Cachat his due. I'd do that much for the devil himself. Yes, he's a simon-pure fanatic. But a fanatic, in his own twisted way, is also an honest man. *The kid's for real*, Jillian. When he says 'the needs of the State,' he means it. It's not a cover for personal ambitions. If we can satisfy him that the rot's been rooted out—even that we've got things turned around nicely—he'll be satisfied and go on his way. The fact is that La Martine Sector *has* been a stronghold for the Republic's economy for the past few years. The fact is that you *weren't* personally implicated in Jamka's crimes—and Cachat said so himself, in his official report to Nouveau Paris."

"How'd you know that?" grunted Gallanti. Skepticism mixed with anxiety—and now, more than a little in the way of hope.

He gave her his best worldly-wise smile, which was just as good as any of his other smiles. "Don't ask, Jillian. I told you: I'm a *commissioner*. It's my job to know these things. More precisely, to make the connections so that I *can* know."

And, again, that was the pure and simple truth. Even under arrest and self-restricted to his cabin, a man like Yuri Radamacher could no more help "making connections" than he could stop breathing.

He knew what Cachat had said about Gallanti in his report because the SI had asked Citizen Major Lafitte for his input and the Citizen Major had mentioned it to Citizen Sergeant Pierce, and Ned Pierce had told Yuri. None too cheerfully, as it happened, because like all Marines serving on the *Hector*, Ned Pierce and Citizen Major Lafitte detested the SD's CO. But Yuri saw no reason to tell Gallanti *that*.

It was just a fact of life; and now, finally, Yuri Radamacher accepted it entirely. People liked him and trusted him. He couldn't remember a time in his life when they hadn't—or a time when he'd ever repaid that trust except in good coin.

It was odd, perhaps, that he came to accept it at the very moment when—for the first time in his life— he was consciously plotting to betray someone. The woman sitting across the desk from him, whose confidence and trust he was doing everything possible to gain.

But . . . so be it. There was, indeed, such a thing as a "higher loyalty," no matter how cynical Yuri had gotten over the years. Something of the fanatic Cachat had rubbed off on him after all, it seemed. And if a middle-aged man like Radamacher shared none of the young Special Investigator's faith in political abstractions, he had no difficulty understanding personal loyalties. When push came to shove, he owed nothing to Citizen Captain Jillian Gallanti. In fact, he despised her for a bully and a hot-tempered despot. But he did owe a loyalty to the thousands of men and women alongside whom he'd served in Citizen Admiral Chin's task force, for years now—from Genevieve herself all the way down to the newest recruit. So, he'd use his natural skills to create a false front—and then use that front to save them from Saint-Just's murderous suspicions.

And if Citizen Captain Gallanti had to fall by the wayside in the process, stabbed in the back by her newfound "friend" . . .

Well, so be it. If a fanatic like Cachat had the courage of his convictions, it would be nothing but cowardice for Yuri to claim to be his moral superior—yet refuse to act with the same decisiveness.

As he waited for Gallanti to fall into the trap, Yuri probed more deeply into his conscience.

Well. Okay. Some of it's just 'cause I got the hots for Sharon and I will damn well keep my woman alive. Me too, if I can manage it.

Gallanti fell. "S'a deal," she said, extending her hand. Yuri rose, bestowed on her his very best trustworthy smile and his very best sincere handshake—both of them top-notch, of course. All the while, measuring her back for the stiletto.

8

Yuri did, in fact, have an excellent record as a people's commissioner. He had routinely been given top marks throughout his career for his proficiency—at least, once he got out of the abstract environment of the academy and into the real world of StateSec fleet operations. The one criticism which Radamacher's superiors had leveled against him periodically, however, had been "slackness."

By some, that was defined in political terms. Yuri Radamacher's actual loyalty wasn't called into question, of course. Had there been any question about *that* he would have been summarily dismissed (at best) from StateSec altogether. Still, there had been some of his superiors, over the years, who felt that he was insufficiently zealous.

Yuri could not argue the matter. He wasn't zealous at all, truth be told.

But the charge of "slackness" had another connotation. One which, several years earlier, had been put bluntly by the woman who had been his superior in the first year of his assignment in La Martine.

"Baloney, Yuri!" she'd snapped in the course of one of his personnel evaluation sessions. "It's all fine and dandy to be 'easy-going' and 'laid-back' and the most popular StateSec officer in this sector. Yeah, Citizen Mister Nice Guy. The truth is you're just plain *lazy*."

Yuri *had* argued the matter, on that occasion. And had even managed, by a virtuoso combination of razzle-dazzle reference to his record and half a dozen charmingly related anecdotes, to get his superior to semi-relent by the end of the evaluation. Still . . .

Deep down, he knew there was a fair amount of truth to the charge. Whether it was because of his own personality, or his disenchantment with the regime, he wasn't sure. Perhaps it was a combination of both. But, whatever the reason, it was just a fact that Yuri Radamacher never really did seem to operate, as the ancient and cryptic expression went, "firing on all cylinders." He did his job, and did it very well, yes—but he never really put in that extra effort to do it as well as he knew he could have done. It just somehow didn't seem worth the effort.

So he found himself amused occasionally, as the weeks went by, wondering what those long-gone superiors would think of his work habits *now*. Yuri Radamacher was still easy-going, and laid-back, and pleasant to deal with. But now he was working an average of eighteen hours a day.

He didn't wonder at the reason himself, though. With Yuri's love of classic literature, he could summon up the answer with any of a number of choice phrases. The one which best captured the situation, he thought, came from Dr. Johnson:

Depend upon it, Sir, when a man knows he is to be hanged in a fortnight, it concentrates his mind wonderfully.

Granted, Yuri Radamacher had more than a fortnight at his disposal. But how much more, remained to be seen. So, he threw himself into his project with an energy he hadn't displayed since he was a teenager newly enlisted in the opposition to the Legislaturalist regime.

A fortnight came and went, and another. And another. And still another.

And Yuri began to relax a little. He still had no idea what the future might bring. But whatever it was, he would at least face it from the best position he could have created. For most of those around him, not only himself.

More than that, it was given to no person to know. Not in this world at least; and, StateSec regulations aside, Yuri really didn't believe in an afterlife.

"Give me a break, Yuri," Citizen Lieutenant Commander Saunders complained. "Impeller Tech Bob Gottlieb is the best rating I've got. He can practically make those nodes sit up and beg."

Yuri looked at him mildly. "He's also the biggest bootlegger on the ship, and he's getting careless about it."

Saunders scowled. "Look, I'll talk to him. Get him to keep it under cover. Yuri, you know damn good and well there's *always* going to be an illegal still operating somewhere on a warship this size. Especially one that's been kept from having any shore leave for so long. At least we don't have to worry about Gottlieb selling dangerous hooch. He knows a lot about chemistry, too—don't ask me how or where he learned, I don't want to know. He's not a stupid kid who doesn't know the difference between ethanol and methanol."

"His stuff's pretty damn tasty, in fact," chimed in Ned Pierce, who was lounging in another armchair in Yuri's large office.

Yuri turned the mild-mannered gaze his way. The citizen sergeant was trying to project a degree of cherubic innocence which fit poorly with his dark-skinned, battered, altogether piratical-looking face. "That's what I hear, anyway," Pierce added.

Yuri snorted. "I need *something*, people," he pointed out. "Cachat'll be back any time now. I've got a fair number of screw-ups and goofballs on display in the brig, sure. But that's pretty much old stuff by now. About a third of them have almost served their time.

And I'm telling you: nothing will soothe the savage inquisitor like being able to show him a freshly nabbed, still-trembling sinner."

"Aw, c'mon, Yuri, the SI's not that bad."

From the tight expression on his face, Citizen Lieutenant Commander Saunders did not agree with the citizen sergeant's assessment of Cachat's degree of severity. Not in the least.

Yuri wasn't surprised. Saunders had been present in the gym when Cachat personally shot six fellow officers of the *Hector Van Dragen* in the head. So had Ned, of course. But Pierce was a Marine, and a combat veteran. Personal, in-your-face mayhem was no stranger to him. Had Saunders been in the regular Navy, he might have encountered the kind of battering which capital ships often took in fleet encounters, where it was not uncommon for bodies to be shredded. But StateSec capital ships were there to enforce discipline over the Navy, not to fight the Navy's battles. That was undoubtedly the first time Saunders had seen blood and brains splattered all over the trousers of his uniform.

Citizen Major Lafitte cleared his throat. He and his counterpart, a StateSec citizen major by the name of Diana Citizen—her real name, that; not something she'd made up to curry favor with the regime—were sitting side by side on a couch angled next to Yuri's armchair. The two of them, along with Ned Pierce and *his* counterpart, StateSec Citizen Sergeant Jaime Rolla, constituted the informal little group which Yuri relied on to handle disciplinary matters on the superdreadnought. The SD's executive officer knew about it and had been looking the other way for weeks. The man was incompetent at everything except knowing which way the political winds were blowing. He'd quickly sized up the new situation and—wisely—

decided that he'd be a nut crushed between Radamacher's skills and Captain Gallanti's temper if he tried
to assert the traditional prerogatives and authority of
a warship's XO.

Citizen Major Diana Citizen cleared her throat. "I've
got a sacrificial lamb, if you need one." Her thin, rather
pretty face grew a little pinched. "Except calling him
a 'lamb' is an insult to baa-baas. He's a pig and a thug
and I'd be delighted to see him slammed as hard as
you can. Assuming you can figure out a charge that
would stick. Unfortunately, he's slicker than your
average shipboard bully. Keeps his ass covered. Name's
Henri Alouette; he's a rating—"

"*That* fuckhead!" snarled Ned. "Me and him damn
near came to it, once, in the mess room. Woulda, too,
if the bastard hadn't backed off at the last minute. Too
bad, I woulda—"

"Citizen Sergeant Pierce." Yuri's tone was as pleasant
and relaxed as ever, but the unusual formality was
enough in itself to draw the citizen sergeant up short.
Normally, in this inner circle devoted to handling the
nitty-gritty business of a warship's "dirty laundry," infor-
mality was the rule. Over the weeks, rank differences
aside—even the traditional mutual hostility of StateSec
and regular military aside—the five people involved had
gotten onto very good personal terms. As usually happened with teams assembled by Yuri Radamacher and
overseen by him.

"I will remind you that I've stressed—any number
of times—the critical importance of keeping tensions
between the regular military stationed on this ship and
its StateSec complement to a bare minimum." He
smiled easily. "Which I dare say having a Marine citizen
sergeant pound a StateSec rating into a pulp—yes, Ned,
I'm sure you woulda and coulda—might cut against."

"Don't count on it," piped up StateSec Citizen

Sergeant Rolla. "Alouette's notorious all over the ship, Yuri. I'd give you three-to-one odds all the StateSec ratings in that mess room would have been cheering Ned on."

"You'd 'a won the bet," gruffed Ned. "Two of 'em offered to hold my coat. Another asked the fuckhead what blood type he was so he could make sure to tell the doctors in the ship's hospital."

Radamacher eyed Pierce for a moment. He'd been on such friendly personal terms with the big citizen sergeant for so long that Yuri tended to forget what a truly ferocious specimen of humanity the man was. Jesting aside, he didn't have much doubt at all that anyone who'd apparently angered Pierce that much *would* be needing transfusions after the brawl was over.

"Still." Yuri swiveled his chair around and began working at the keyboard of his computer. "We've gotten morale to such a good point on the *Hector* that I'd just as soon avoid any possible interservice problems." He glanced over his shoulder, still smiling. "I'm sure I can find a better way to nail Alouette than have Ned here try to frame him up on a brawling charge. Not even Special Investigator Cachat would believe for a minute that somebody deliberately picked a fight with *him.*"

He turned back, letting the easy laughter fill the room while he worked.

It didn't take long. Less than five minutes.

"I must be slipping," he muttered. "How'd I possibly miss *this*?"

"Working eighteen hours a day at everything else?" Major Lafitte chuckled. "What'd you find, Yuri?"

Radamacher jabbed a stiff finger at the screen. "How in the hell did Alouette pass his required annual spacesuit proficiency test when there's no record he's even been in a spacesuit once in the past three years? And how in the hell did he manage *that*—when he's rated as a gravitic sensor tech? Isn't external inspection and repair of the arrays sort of *part* of that specialization?"

He swiveled back around. "Well?"

The two Marines in the room had bland, blank *none-of-my-business* expressions on their faces. The sort of expressions which polite people assume when another family's skeletons are spilling out of an opened closet.

Radamacher approved. This was StateSec's dirty laundry. As was obvious from the scowls on the faces of the two StateSec officers and—even fiercer—on the face of StateSec Citizen Sergeant Rolla.

"That rotten SOB," Rolla hissed. "Give you three-to-one—no, make it five-to-one—that Alouette's been intimidating his mates and the section chief. Probably threatened the rating recording the test results, too."

Citizen Major Citizen looked uncomfortable. "Yeah, that's probably it. I hate to say it, seeing as how I sure didn't shed any tears over those bums that the SI blew away, but their absence did hurt us a lot in security. It left holes all through my department, which I still haven't been able to get filled up all the way. Especially since I had to start from scratch coming over from the fleet."

"Nobody's blaming you, Diana," Yuri assured her smoothly. "Isolated little tumors like this are bound to turn up, now and then, when a ship's security department was in the hands of human cancer cells for years. Which is about the most polite way I can think of to describe Jamka's cronies."

He rubbed the back of his neck. "To be perfectly honest about it—cold-blooded, too—this is damn near perfect. Cachat'll rub his hands with glee over a bust like this one. Beats a penny-ante bootlegging case hands down. Inquisitors, you know, thrive on real *sin*."

"Aw, c'mon, Yuri—" Ned started again. "The SI's not—"

The sudden burst of laughter from everyone else in the room caused a look of grievance to come over the citizen sergeant's face. "Well, he's *not* that bad," he insisted.

Radamacher didn't argue the point. At the moment, he was in such a good mood that he was even willing to grant that Special Investigator Victor Cachat probably didn't really match up to Torquemada. His understudy, maybe.

He looked to Citizen Major Citizen. "You'll handle this, Diana? Mind you, I want a good, solid, rock-hard case against Alouette. Nothing flimsy."

She nodded. "Won't be hard. Assuming we're right, everybody in the section will fall all over themselves spilling the beans—as long as they're sure that Alouette will get put away for a long time. Somewhere he can't retaliate against them."

"Have no fear on that score. Just going by a minimum reading of regulations, if Alouette has been threatening his mates with violence in order to cover up his skill deficiencies—much less a senior rating like a section chief—he's looking at five years, at least. That's five years served in a StateSec maximum security prison, too, not a ship's brig."

Yuri's face was grim. "That's if he's lucky. But I think Alouette's luck just ran out on him. Because his case will be coming up after the Special Investigator's return, and Cachat has the authority to mete out any punishment he deems proper. *Any* punishment, people. After I got my new assignment, for the first time in my life I studied carefully all the rules and regulations governing the position of Special Investigator. It's . . . pretty scary. And Cachat's already made crystal clear how he looks on StateSec personnel

abusing their positions for the sake of personal gain
or pleasure."

He studied the far wall of the stateroom. It was a
wide bulkhead, as you'd expect in a top staff officer's
suite in a superdreadnought. Almost as wide as the
bulkhead which Cachat had used as the backstop for
his firing squad.

Everyone else in the room seemed to share Yuri's
grim mood, judging from the sudden silence.

Not for long, though, in the case of the two noncoms. "Hey, Jaime," whispered Ned. "Any chance I
could volunteer—just the once—to serve on a StateSec
firing squad?"

"S'against regs," Rolla whispered back. "But I'll put
in a good word for you."

Yuri sighed. There were times—had been for
many years, now—when he felt like a sheep running
with the wolves. And wondering when someone was
finally going to notice that his moon-howl was distinctly off-key.

The half-rueful, half-amused thought lasted for
perhaps five seconds. Then the office hatch snapped
open with no notice at all, a commo rating burst
through the opening, and Yuri discovered that his long-
extended fortnight had come to an end.

Dr. Johnson's proverbial hangman had finally arrived.

9

The rating's face was pale as a sheet. "The task force
is back in the system. We just got a message from the
Citizen Admiral. They expect to be back in orbit inside
five hours."

Easy-going as Yuri was, the rating's lack of basic

military courtesy was just too extreme to let pass
unreprimanded. Yuri wondered what was wrong with
the woman. The task force's return was hardly unexpected, after all.

"What is your name, Citizen Rating?" he demanded
frostily.

The woman had apparently taken leave of her
senses. She didn't even have the excuse of being a
young recruit. From her age and the two hash marks
on her sleeve, she'd been in StateSec service for at least
six T-years. Even a wet-behind-the-ears newbie knew
enough to recognize a superior officer's *you-are-about-
to-be-fried-alive* tone of voice.

Utterly oblivious, it seemed. "You don't understand!
The SI sent a message too. Ordering Citizen Captain
Gallanti to disregard the message from the merchant
ship—"

Yuri felt his stomach drop out from under him. He
had a very bad feeling that the sensation was much like
that of a man feeling the trapdoor open under the
gallows.

"*What* message from a merchant ship?"

"—and stand down the impellers and sidewalls."

Citizen Lieutenant Commander Saunders bolted
upright in his chair, his head cocked as if straining all
his senses. He stretched out a hand and laid fingertips delicately against a bulkhead.

"She's right. The ship's getting under way. What the
hell—?"

Impellers couldn't be detected in operation inside a
ship. They were not reaction engines and produced no
discernible noise or vibration. But the impeller rooms
were close to Yuri's cabin and although Yuri himself still
couldn't sense anything, Saunders was apparently picking
up the subtle vibrations created by the various auxiliary
engines. That was Saunder's specialty—although even

he hadn't noticed until the rating brought it to his attention. Yuri didn't think to doubt him.

What was Gallanti doing? There was no logical reason for the *Hector Van Dragen* to be leaving orbit. And even if she were, why bring up the sidewalls unless . . .

Yuri forgot all his own by-the-regs proscriptions. "Jesus Christ," he whispered. Then, firmly, to the still-jittery rating:

"You're making no sense at all, woman! Settle down!"

That seemed to calm her, finally. She swallowed and then nodded abruptly. "Com Tech first-class Rita Enquien, Citizen Assistant Investigator. Sorry for the discourtesy. It's just—I'm not supposed to be here— the Citizen Captain finds out I left the bridge I'm dead meat—"

The sensation in Yuri's stomach was now definitely one of free fall. He wondered how long a man dropped before the rope ran out and the noose broke his neck.

"No problem, Citizen Tech Enquien," he said soothingly, in his best confessional tone of voice.

He realized, finally, what was happening. In general, if not the specifics. Something had completely panicked the rating and, in her confusion, she'd broken discipline and gone to the one person in the ship she'd come to trust in a pinch. Given that Yuri didn't know her, the woman's estimate was obviously based on what she'd heard from her shipmates.

Which meant . . .

The falling sensation vanished. Dr. Johnson's hangman be damned. Yuri had set out weeks ago to steal a capital warship right out from under its own captain, hadn't he? Just in case all hell broke loose.

All hell had broken loose, clearly enough. But the ship was there for the taking.

"Now, Enquien. Let's start from the beginning. What

merchant ship are you talking about? And what message did it send?"

The woman's mouth made an "O" of surprise. "Oh. How stupid of me." Then, in a rush:

"A merchant ship arrived in the system just half an hour before we got the message from the Citizen Admiral. It's from Haven. There's been—a revolution, I guess. Coup d'état, whatever you call it. Citizen Admiral Theismann's taken over, they say. And—"

She swallowed. Yuri suddenly knew what was coming next. Exultation flooded over him. Yet at the same time, oddly, a wave of fear also.

At least the Devil you know is the one you know.

"Citizen Chairman Saint-Just is dead. Nobody knows exactly how, I guess. Well, by whom exactly, I mean. They know *how*, that's for sure. The merchant ship sent us the recording, it was played all over Nouveau Paris' HD networks. I saw it myself. It was Oscar Saint-Just all right. The face wasn't touched. Just a great big pulser dart hole in the middle of his forehead."

The rating shook herself, as if chilled. "He's dead, Sir!" she cried.

And, in her voice also, Yuri Radamacher could sense the same conflicting emotions. His eyes scanned the room, seeing them on every face.

Exultation. The cold, gray, heartless man who had loomed over the Republic for years as the incarnation of murderous ruthlessness was finally gone. Dead, dead, dead.

Terror. And now what?

The paralysis lasted for perhaps five seconds. Then Yuri slapped his knees and rose abruptly.

"Oh, bullshit," he said, softly but firmly. "Now's the same as it always was. We do the best we can, that's all, with what we've got."

He looked at the rating. "I take it the Citizen Captain's gone berserk?"

Enquien jerked a nod. "Yes, Citi—uh, Sir. That's why I snuck out when she wasn't looking and came here." She hissed in a breath. "I'm scared, Sir. I think the Captain's really lost it."

Yuri sighed and shook his head. "I don't think she ever really had it, Enquien." Then, much like a priest might bestow absolution:

"Relax, you did the right thing. I'll take care of it."

The rating's taut face eased. Yuri turned to the other people in the room.

"Will you follow me?"

There was no hesitation. Five heads in unison—StateSec and Marine alike—jerked their own nods.

"Good. Citiz—the hell with it, the rating's got it right. Saint-Just is dead and his petty regulations went with him. Lieutenant Commander Saunders, I want you to return to your post and take control of the impeller rooms. Use whatever force you need to, in the event of resistance. Major Lafitte, you and Major Citizen go with him and see to it. Round up whatever Marines and reliable StateSec troopers you can. Whatever else, I want those impellers taken out of Gallanti's control. Understood?"

"Yes, Citizen Assistant Spec—uh, Sir." The stumbled phrase came in unison, and so did the rueful little laughs which followed.

The StateSec major grinned at her Marine counterpart. "This'll be worth it just so people won't keep making jokes about my last name." More seriously: "You're senior to me, Khedi. In years of service, anyway, and I don't know how else to figure this. Besides, you've got experience in boarding operations and I don't. So you take the lead and I'll follow."

Lafitte nodded. An instant later, the three officers

were out into the corridor and hurrying in the direction of the impeller rooms.

Yuri looked to the two sergeants. A quick glance at their hips confirmed the fact that neither was armed. There had been no reason for them to be, of course. In fact, it would have been against regulations. Aboard a StateSec ship, unless expressly ordered otherwise, only StateSec officers were permitted to carry sidearms. And they were required to carry them. From old habit, in fact, Yuri had a pulser on his own hip, even though the regulations were not entirely clear as to whether the provision applied to an Assistant Special Investigator.

He was hoping that single pulser would be enough. But given Gallanti's temper . . .

He'd planned for that eventuality also. "Come here," he commanded, stepping over to a locker along one wall. Quickly, his fingers punched the combination and the locker opened. Inside—

Ned Pierce whistled admiringly. "Hey, that's quite an arsenal. Uh, Sir. You allowed to have this?"

Yuri shrugged. "Who knows? You wouldn't believe how vague the regulations get when it comes to specifying what Special Investigators—their assistants too, I presume—can and can't do."

He stepped aside from the locker. "This really isn't my line of work. So I'll let the two of you choose whatever weapons you think most suitable."

Pierce reached eagerly for a light tribarrel—about the heaviest man-portable weapon made (short of a plasma rifle, at any rate)—with a thousand-round ammunition tank. The tank was coded for a mixed flechette, armor-piercing, explosive belt, and the Marine's eyes glowed with anticipation. But—

"For Pete's sake, Ned!" Rolla protested. "You'll slaughter everybody on the bridge with that thing. You

know how to fly a seven-million-ton SD? I sure as
hell don't."

"Oh." Pierce's face looked simultaneously embarrassed and frustrated. "Yeah, you're right. Damn. I love
those things."

"Just take a frickin' flechette gun, if you really *need*
to splatter people wholesale," growled the StateSec sergeant, plucking a hand pulser out of the locker himself. "At least that way you won't blow any essential
hardware apart, too! Or have you forgotten how to aim
at anything smaller than a moon?"

"Teach your grandmother how to suck eggs,"
retorted Pierce. Quickly, easily, the Marine sergeant
took out a flechette gun, examined and armed the
weapon.

Then, he and Rolla studied each other for a
moment. It was an awkward moment.

Yuri cleared his throat. "Ah, Sergeant Pierce, I
believe you're senior to Sergeant Rolla. In terms of service, certainly—and, as Diana said, I don't see any other
way to settle these things at the moment. Nevertheless—"

To his relief, Ned just shrugged. "Yeah, sure, Sir. Hey,
look, I ain't stupid." He nodded at Rolla. "Jaime can have
it. I really don't care."

"Good. What I *hope* we'll be dealing with is really
more a police matter than a military one. Not to put
too fine a point on it, but Sergeant Rolla has experience making arrests. Whereas, ah, you—"

Pierce's piratical grin was on full display. "I blow
people apart. Don't worry about it, Sir. Mama Pierce's
good little boy will follow orders."

Yuri's fears that they might face opposition on their
way to the bridge proved to be unfounded. All they
encountered, here and there, were a few small knots

of StateSec ratings huddled and whispering. Clearly enough, some scraps of the news had begun percolating through the ship. Just as clearly, the scraps were just that—murky, muddled, impossible to make any clear sense from. The huge size of the superdreadnought added to the confusion. Wild rumors in a smaller ship might have stayed concentrated long enough for people to boil down the truth from them. In an SD juggernaut, rumors echoed down endless passages, becoming completely distorted and incoherent the farther they went.

He was a bit puzzled, at first. He would have expected Gallanti to have at least stationed StateSec guards at the critical access routes to the bridge. But . . . nothing, until they finally reached the hatch leading into the bridge itself.

By then, Yuri had figured out the reason, and so it was armed with that knowledge that he marched forthrightly toward the two StateSec security ratings standing guard by the hatch. The two guards were not from a special unit, summoned by Gallanti for the purpose. They were from the unit which was routinely stationed there—and these two happened to have the bad luck to be on shift when the crap hit the fan. They looked as nervous as mice when cats are on a rampage.

Gallanti was just a stupid, self-centered, hot-headed bully, that's all. The explanation was no more complicated than that. A woman who'd gotten her way for so long simply because of her rank and her overbearing personality that she wasn't giving a second's thought to the fact that she might be facing a *tactical* situation.

He was almost surprised he couldn't hear her screaming even through the closed hatch.

The Boss is blowing her stack, and when the Boss

blows her stack everybody has to stand around and eat her shit. A law of nature, like gravity.

Idiot.

"Stand aside," he commanded, as soon as he came up to the guards. The words were spoken in a mild tone, but a very self-assured one.

The guards didn't think to question him. In fact, they were obviously relieved that he was there. Yuri jerked his thumb over his shoulder at Sergeant Rolla.

"You're now under the command of Citizen Sergeant Rolla. Is that understood?"

"Yes, Citizen Assistant Special Investigator." The replies came simultaneously. Then, seeing the figure of the commo rating following gingerly at the rear, their eyes widened.

Yuri opened the hatch and stepped through, followed by the two sergeants. Behind, he could hear one of the guards hissing to the commo rating.

"*Jesus*, Rita. You told us you were just gonna be gone for a minute. The Citizen Captain's ready to skin you alive. She finds out *we* let you pass—"

"Piss on Gallanti," Enquien hissed back. "I went and got the People's Commissioner. He's here now—and that bitch's ass is grass. *You watch.*"

The phrase she used made Yuri pause in midstep. Not "the Citizen Assistant Special Investigator." Just . . .

The Citizen Commissioner. No. Simply the People's Commissioner.

He found it all, then. All he needed for what had to be done. In that moment, for the first time in his life, he thought he understood that bizarre self-assuredness possessed by fanatics like Victor Cachat.

The People's Commissioner.

Indeed, it was so. For ten years he had carried that title, and made it his own. He had absolutely no idea what the future was going to bring, either for himself or anyone else, except for one thing alone. Whatever else happened, he was quite certain that the title "people's commissioner" was going to go down in history draped in the darkest of colors. As dark, he knew, as the term "inquisitors."

And rightly. Whatever the promise, the reality had turned it inside out. A post created to shield a republic from the possible depredations of its own military had been turned, not only against the military, but the republic itself. The old conundrum, reborn again. *Who will guard the guardians?*

Yet, he remembered reading of an inquisitor in the Basque country, in that ancient era when humanity had still lived on a single planet. Sent there by the Spanish Inquisition at the height of its power to investigate the truth behind a wave of accusations of witchcraft, the inquisitor had stopped the witch-burnings. Indeed, had insisted upon proper rules of evidence at all subsequent trials—and then released every supposed witch for lack of any such evidence.

Yuri had run across the anecdote in his voluminous reading. Years ago, that had been; but he'd taken a certain comfort from it ever since.

He even managed a chuckle, at that moment. Yuri Radamacher did not believe in an afterlife. Yet, if there was one, he was quite sure that at that very moment in Hell, some good-natured, round-faced, overweight, apprehensive little devil was being chewed out by Satan for "slackness."

It was time for the People's Commissioner to do his duty, then. The people of the republic needed protection against an officer run amok. Yuri advanced onto the bridge, with resolute steps.

❖   ❖   ❖

The bridge was . . . quite a scene.

Citizen Captain Gallanti was standing in the center of it, glaring red-faced at a display split into two screens. One screen showed the bridge of Admiral Chin's flagship. Yuri could see Genevieve herself standing there, along with Commodore Ogilve and Commissioner Wilkins. At their center, seeming to be in the forefront, stood Victor Cachat.

Cachat, as always, was an imposing figure. Even through a holodisplay, the young man's intensity seemed to burn. But Yuri's eyes were immediately drawn to the other screen. Sharon Justice was in that screen, which was showing the bridge of the other StateSec SD, the *Joseph Tilden.* So he assumed, anyway, given that the SD's captain Vesey was standing next to her.

He was relieved to see that Sharon seemed in fine health. Even in good spirits, for that matter. Her facial expression was one of solemnity, but Yuri knew her quite well after all these years and could detect the underlying . . .

Excitement? Maybe. It was hard to tell. But whatever else, she certainly didn't seem gloomy.

Captain Vesey, on the other hand, did look on the gloomy side. The words "nervous, worried, and more than a little depressed" might capture the expression on his face a bit better.

One thing was clear, just from the body language of the two people alone. Whatever was happening on the *Tilden,* it was obvious that Sharon was calling the shots and not the superdreadnought's nominal commander.

That was good enough, for the moment. Yuri looked away from the screens and quickly examined the bridge of the *Hector* itself. All of the ratings and as many of the officers as could possibly manage it had their heads buried as far down as they could get them into their work stations. As long-beaten underlings will do, when their mistress is having another temper tantrum, trying their very best to be inconspicuous.

That was not possible, of course, for some of the officers. The nature of their duties required them to be directly attentive to the citizen captain.

The *Hector Van Dragen*'s executive officer was standing not far from Gallanti, bestowing upon her his well-practiced look of fawning vacancy. The man's name was as comical in its own way as that of the long-suffering Diana Citizen. *Kit Carson*, no less. Fortunately for him, Yuri Radamacher was one of the few people in the task force who had the historical knowledge to understand how ridiculous the name was, given the man's nature.

Yuri dismissed him from consideration. Carson was a nonentity. Of the other top ship's officers on the bridge, most of his attention went to the tac officer, Edouard Ballon. Partly that was because of the nature of a tac officer's duties, since Ballon controlled the ship's armament. Mostly it was because Yuri knew that if there was going to be trouble from anyone other than Gallanti herself, it would come from Ballon.

The tac officer was not precisely a StateSec "fanatic." Certainly not one cut from the same cloth as Cachat. Ballon had no particularly strong ideological convictions. But he was the type of sour, nasty, mean-spirited person who tended to gravitate naturally to an organization like StateSec. Not a sadist, no. Just cut from the same cloth as the grim villagers who were always the first to raise the cry of "witchcraft!"—and always took satisfaction in the punishment of others. As if that validated their place in the world.

Neither Gallanti nor Ballon was watching him. Neither of them, in fact, had even noticed Yuri coming onto the bridge, they were so fixated on the screen.

Yuri took the opportunity to nod toward Ballon while giving both the sergeants standing behind him a meaningful look. Sergeant Rallo nodded back, relaxed; Ned Pierce just smiled thinly and hefted the flechette gun in his hands a centimeter or two higher.

It's time, then. Do it.

Yuri turned back to face Gallanti. And suddenly—did life *always* have to be ridiculously awkward?—realized that the first obstacle he faced was simply the pedestrian problem of getting the damn woman to *hear* him. She was making enough of a racket herself to drown a bugler.

"—at's pure horseshit, Cachat! I don't give a flying fuck what fancy titles you carry around! I'm the captain of this ship and what I say goes! And if you think when there's treason all about I'm going to disarm a StateSec capital ship, you're out of your fucking mind! The impellers and the sidewalls stay up—and I'll tell you what else, wet-behind-the-ears errand boy. Your sugar daddy Saint-Just isn't around any longer to cover your ass. You're on your own now, punk. You try shooting me in the head with that piddly pulser of yours, I'll show you just what kind of hell on earth a superdreadnought can unleash! Go ahead, try me!"

Yuri saw Captain Vesey wince. To the man's credit, he tried to intervene. "Jillian, *please.* Until we find out what's really happening on Haven—"

"Fuck off, you gutless bastard! What? Does that bitch Justice intimidate you? She doesn't intimidate me! Nobody does—and that includes you. That scow of yours may technically be a sister ship of mine, but command is what matters, don't think it doesn't. If the gloves come off here—and we're getting real close—I'll tear that thing down around your ears before I turn Chickenshit Chin's task force into so much dog food.

You'll see an SD turned into a funeral pyre faster than you can believe!"

Yuri had always heard about Gallanti's temper tantrums, but this was the first time he'd ever personally witnessed one. How in the world had this woman ever been given command of a capital ship? Even State Security should have had enough sense to realize she was unfit for such responsibility. If he wanted to be charitable about it, Yuri would have likened Gallanti to a spoiled five-year-old child throwing a fit.

Unfortunately, five-year-old children, no matter how spoiled, never had the terrifying power of a super-dreadnought under their control. Gallanti did. Which made the situation deadly instead of simply pathetic. Under the circumstances, she was as dangerous as a maddened bear.

Gallanti finally took a breath, and Yuri began to speak. But before he managed to get a word out, Victor Cachat's audio-amplified voice filled the bridge.

As always, it was a cold voice. "What took you so long, Assistant Special Investigator? I was beginning to wonder if you were slacking off again."

Yuri suddenly realized that he'd advanced far enough onto the bridge to enter the field of the comm pickup and become visible to those on the other two ships. Even though Gallanti herself hadn't noticed him until that very moment.

God, he was *tired* of that arrogant young voice.

"Have a certain regard for natural law if nothing else, would you, Cachat?" He took an admittedly petty pleasure in neglecting all honorifics. "I just got the news myself and got here as soon as I could."

The fact that Cachat didn't seem to take any umbrage at the lack of honorifics—didn't even seem to *notice,* damn the man—just irritated Yuri still further.

"And if you don't mind"—making clear by his tone that he didn't care if he did—"I prefer the title 'people's commissioner.' I don't really see where there's anything left to investigate, anyway."

Cachat stared at him. In the big display a capital ship could manage, the young fanatic seemed even larger than life.

Then, to Yuri's surprise, Cachat gave him a deep, slow nod. It had almost the sense of a ceremonial bow to it. And when his head lifted, for the first time since Yuri had met the man, Cachat's dark eyes seemed a warm brown instead of an iron black.

"Yes," said Cachat. "You have the right of it, Yuri Radamacher. Now do your duty, People's Commissioner."

Gallanti was gawping at Yuri. Then, burst into the start of another tirade.

"What the hell are you doing here? I didn't give you permission—"

Yuri had no desire at all to listen to more of that screech. When he needed it, he could manage quite a loud voice himself.

"You are under arrest, Captain Gallanti. I am relieving you of your duties. You are unfit to command."

That cut off her off in mid-screech. Again, she gawped.

Yuri, at the end, tried one last time. He put on his most sympathetic smile and added: "Jillian, please, there's no need for this. Just let it go and I'll give you my word I'll see to it—"

It was no use, and Yuri had a sick feeling that in his effort he'd simply condemned himself. Gallanti's hand was already grabbing the butt of her pulser—and, like a slack idiot, his own pulser still had the flap fastened.

"You fucking traitor!" Gallanti screamed. Her weapon was coming out of the holster and Yuri had no doubt at all she intended to fire. The woman had completely lost it. Out of the corner of one eye, as he scrabbled to get the flap of his holster open, Yuri saw the tac officer starting to rise from his chair. Ballon was reaching for his own sidearm.

Then—

Whackwhack. Whackwhack.

Small holes appeared in the foreheads of both Gallanti and Ballon, and the entire backs of their skulls exploded in a gory spray of splintered bone and finely divided brain tissue.

Rallo's doing, Yuri realized dimly. He'd double-tapped both of them. Yuri hadn't known the StateSec sergeant was that quick and expert a shot.

Brrraaaaaaaaaaaaaaaaaaaa!

Before Gallanti's body could even begin to slump, Sergeant Pierce's short, lethally accurate three-round burst flung her five meters against a bulkhead, the deadly flechettes literally shredding the body along the way. No one else was standing there, thank God. Thank Pierce, actually; even in the shock of the moment Yuri understood that the experienced veteran had made sure he had a clean line of fire. Although at least three of the bridge's officers and ratings were frantically scraping bits and pieces of Gallanti off of them—now one of the ratings started vomiting—nobody else had actually gotten hurt.

"Ned," Yuri heard Rolla complaining, "can't you do *anything* neatly? What do you use when you go fishing? Missiles?"

"Hey, Jaime, I'm a Marine. This is what we do. You wanna transfer? I'll put in a good word for you—so will at least ten other guys I know. Probably even be able to keep the same rank."

Rolla started to make one of his usual retorts about the mental deficiencies of Marines, but broke off before he got through the first four words. Then, after a moment's silence, said quietly: "Yeah, actually, I probably do. I've got a feeling State Security is about to get seriously downsized."

The StateSec sergeant had reholstered his pulser by now, there being clearly no other armed threat posed on the bridge. To Yuri's surprise, he pushed past him—not rudely, no; but firmly nonetheless—and came to stand at the center of the bridge staring at the figures in the display.

At Victor Cachat, to be precise.

"You tell me. Sir, or whatever else I'm supposed to call you. Who's running this show these days?"

Good question, thought Yuri.

"And what are we all supposed to do now?" Sergeant Rolla continued.

And that's an even better one.

10

Cachat didn't even hesitate, and Yuri damned him again. All the unfairness of the universe, in that moment, seemed concentrated in the fact that a twenty-four-year-old fanatic—*even now!*—never seemed to have any doubts about anything.

"I think the situation is clear enough, Sergeant—ah?"

"Rolla, Sir. Jaime Rolla."

"Sergeant Rolla. As for titles, I think we can all dispense with the curlicues." Cachat's razor-thin smile appeared. "I'll confess that I get tired myself of all those longwinded syllables. My standing rank in State Security is Captain, so I'll go with that. As for the rest—"

Cachat's eyes moved slowly across the people on the bridge of the *Hector;* then, briefly, at those he could see in his display on the sister SD; finally, at greater length, he looked at the naval officers standing next to him. Especially Admiral Chin.

Then he looked back at Rolla.

"Here's what I think. We have no real idea what's happened—or is happening—on Haven. The news brought by the merchant ship is simply too garbled. The only two things which seem clear at the moment are that Saint-Just is dead and Admiral Theismann holds effective power at the capital. But we still don't know what new government will emerge in its place— or upon what political principles that government will be based."

Genevieve's lips tightened. "I'll go with Theismann, myself."

Yuri could sense the StateSec officers on the bridge of the *Hector* stir a little. Not for the first time in his life, he found himself wishing that Admiral Chin would learn to be a *little* more diplomatic.

"Would you, Admiral?" Cachat demanded. "You know absolutely nothing about what sort of regime Admiral Theismann might—or might not—be putting into place. It might be an outright military dictatorship. Are you really so certain that's what you want?"

"It's better than Saint-Just!" she snarled.

Cachat shrugged. "Perhaps. And perhaps not. But Saint-Just is dead anyway, so he's irrelevant. Let's not all forget that our first responsibility—all of us—is to the republic and its people. *Not* to any organization within it."

"Fine for you to say! StateSec man!"

Yuri was practically grinding his teeth. *For Christ sake, Genevieve! We just barely averted disaster because one woman couldn't control her temper. Are you going to blow it now? In case you hadn't noticed—Admiral!—we've still got two fully armed StateSec SDs in this system. Yeah, sure, I might be able to control this one, seeing as how I've effectively created my own command staff. Except it's a jury-rigged hybrid staff, and if you start giving the StateSec people the idea that the Navy and Marines are going to start a counter-purge . . . Jesus, the whole thing could dissolve into a civil war!*

He broke off the angry, desperate thought. Cachat was addressing Chin again, still in that same calm, cold, controlled tone of voice.

"Yes, I am State Security. But tell me, Admiral, what is your grievance with *me*?" Cachat glanced at the screens. "Or Commissioner Radamacher. Or Commissioner Justice."

That—finally!—seem to rattle Chin. "Well . . . you had my people beaten up!"

Cachat's eyebrows rose. "*Your* people? Admiral Chin, I cannot recall a single instance where I had corporal punishment of any kind inflicted on any member of either the Navy or the Marines." He glanced at Ned Pierce, who was also in line of sight of the display. "Well, I suppose you could argue that I punished the Sergeant's knuckles by having him pound a number of *my* people into a pulp. Or have you forgotten—again—that Radamacher and Justice are part of StateSec, not the military."

If Yuri had had any doubts whether he loved Sharon Justice, she resolved them right then and there. She grinned at Pierce and said: "Sergeant, if you'll forgive me your poor knuckles, I'll forgive you my poor face. How's that?"

Pierce grinned back. "That's a deal, Captain. Uh, Commissioner."

Sharon's head swiveled a little, to bring Chin's image

into view. Yuri was getting a little dizzy with this three-way holographic discussion.

"Genevieve, cut it out," she said forcefully. "For six years now, you've rebuilt your career—and probably saved your life—by trusting StateSec people you thought you could trust. Why are you screwing around with it now? For years now, we've all managed to spare La Martine from the worst of what happened, by working together. I say we stick with it."

Genevieve's temper was fading, now, and her usual intelligence returning. Yuri could recognize the signs, and drew a deep breath.

"Okay, fine," Genevieve. "But that only applies to—you know, *you*. The fleet StateSec people."

Cachat's face was impassive, as usual. Vesey, the CO of the *Tilden*, on the other hand, was looking distinctly uneasy.

"I believe Commissioner Justice has had no complaints against Captain Vesey," Cachat stated curtly. "At least, all the reports I received from her throughout our mission were completely positive. Am I not correct, Commissioner Justice?"

From her moment's hesitation, Yuri suspected that Sharon's reports to Cachat had been somewhat edited. He doubted very much if she'd found working with the stolid SD captain all *that* positive an experience. But she piped up cheerfully: "Oh, sure. I've got no problem with Captain Vesey. Neither do *you*, Genevieve. You told me yourself you were happy with the captain's work—especially the way he participated when we nailed that Mantie battlecruiser in Daggan."

Yuri's eyes flicked to the image of Chin, and he had to fight down a laugh. Chin's hesitation lasted longer than a "moment." Yuri was quite sure that whatever praise Chin had heaped on Vesey, it had been grudging at best. However, Chin also did not argue the point.

"Yes, yes. Okay. I've got no bone to pick with the *Tilden*." Genevieve was starting to think like an admiral again. "And since I see that Yuri's got the *Hector* under control—thanks for taking down the impellers and sidewalls, Yuri, that makes me a lot less nervous—"

Radamacher was startled. He hadn't ordered . . .

Then Kit Carson caught his eye and he *really* had to fight down a laugh. The *Hector*'s XO had his most ingratiating expression on. Ever attuned to the changing of the political winds, Carson had apparently ordered the SD to stand down while Yuri had been preoccupied with forestalling another disastrous explosion. It was one of the few times in his life where Radamacher was willing to sing hosannas to the virtues of lickspittles.

"—I guess we can all consider the military situation something of a stalemate," Genevieve continued. Frowning: "As long as everybody agrees to *remain* in stand down. And remain here, in La Martine orbit. Assuming the merchant ship's report that there's a truce on in the Mantie war is right also, we shouldn't need to run anti-raiding patrols for a while. And—ha!—after what we did in Laramie and New Calcutta, I doubt if any pirates are going to be stirring around here for a while either."

Yuri picked it up and took it from there. "I agree with Genevieve. Let's face it, everybody. The crews of *all* the Republic's warships here in La Martine are so thoroughly mixed up by now—"

Thanks to the fanatic. Ha! The Law of Unintended Consequences works its will again!

"—that as long as we all stay calm—as Genevieve says, stay together in one orbit and remain standing down—then nobody can purge anybody. And besides," he added, shrugging, "does anybody really have that much of a grudge left, anyway? Not for anybody here in La Martine, I don't think. So I see no reason why we can't just keep on maintaining this sector of the Republic in a state of peace and calm. Just *wait*, damnation, until we find out for sure what's happening in the capital."

The relaxation everywhere was almost palpable, on all three screens. Yuri took another deep breath. That was it, he thought. For now, at least.

Cachat's voice interrupted his pleasant thoughts.

"You're overlooking one final matter, Commissioner Radamacher."

"What's that?"

"Me, of course. More precisely, what I represent. I was sent here by personal appointment of Oscar Saint-Just, then head of state of the Republic. And leaving formalities aside, I think it's accurate to say that for some time now I have effectively ruled this sector by dictatorial methods."

Yuri stared at him. Then, snorted. "Yes, I'd say that's accurate. Especially the dictatorial part."

Cachat seemed oblivious to the sarcasm. His image in the display was still larger than life. The grim young fanatic face, especially, seemed to loom over everything else. On the bridge of the *Hector*, at least; but Yuri was quite sure the effect was the same on the *Tilden*—and probably even more so on the battleship where Cachat was standing in person. The man was just so forceful and intimidating that he had that effect.

"What's your point, Cachat?"

To his surprise, Sharon interjected herself sharply.

"Yuri, stop being an ass. Captain Cachat has been courteous to you, so there's no excuse for you to be rude to him."

Yuri stared at her. "He—the bastard beat you up!"

"Oh, for pity's sake!" she snapped. "You're behaving like a schoolboy. Instead of using your brains. And aren't you the man whose favorite little saying—one of them, anyway—is 'give credit where credit is due'?"

The image of her head swiveled, as she turned to the screen showing Cachat. "Are you really willing to do it, Captain? Nobody's asking it from you."

"Of course, I am. It's my simple duty, under the circumstances." Cachat made that little half-irritated twitch of the shoulders which seemed to be his version of a shrug. "I realize most of you—all of you, I imagine—consider me a fanatic. I neither accept the term, nor do I reject it. I am indifferent to your opinions, frankly. I swore an oath when I joined State Security to devote my life to the service of the Republic. I meant that oath when I gave it, and I have never once wavered in that conviction. Whatever I've done, to the best of my ability at the time and my gauge of the situation, was done in the interests of the people to whom I swore that oath. The *people* to whom I swore that oath, may I remind you. There is no mention of Oscar Saint-Just or any other individual in the StateSec oath of loyalty."

The square shoulders twitched again. "Oscar Saint-Just is dead, but the Republic remains. Certainly its people remain. So my oath still binds me, and under the current circumstances my duty seems clear to me."

He now looked straight at Yuri and a thin smile came to his face. "You're very good at this, Commissioner Radamacher. I knew you would be, which is why I left you behind here. But, if you'll forgive me saying so, you are not ruthless enough. It's an attractive personal quality, but it's a handicap for a commissioner. You're still flinching from the keystone you need to cap your little edifice."

Yuri was frowning. "What are you talking about?"

"I should think it was obvious. Commissioner Justice certainly understands. If you're going to bury an old regime, Commissioner, you have to bury a *body*.

It's not enough to simply declare the body absent. Who knows when an absent body might return?"

"What—" Yuri shook his head. The fanatic was babbling gibberish.

Cachat's normal impatience returned. "Oh, for the sake of whatever is or isn't holy! If the mice won't bell the cat, I guess the cat will have to do it himself."

Cachat turned to face Sharon. "My preference would be to turn myself over to your custody, Commissioner Justice, but given that the situation in the *Tilden* is probably the most delicate at the moment, I think it would be best if I were kept incarcerated aboard the *Hector* under Commissioner Radamacher's custody. I think we should rule out Admiral Chin as the arresting officer. That might run the risk of stirring up Navy-StateSec animosity, which is the last thing La Martine sector needs at the moment."

Sharon chuckled. "Yuri might have you shot, you know."

"I doubt it. Commissioner Radamacher's not really the type. Besides, my reference to a 'body' was just poetic license. It should do well enough, I think, to have the most visible representative of the Saint-Just regime here in La Martine under lock and key." Again, that little shrug. "And if Commissioner Radamacher feels compelled to have me rigorously interrogated at some point, I won't hold it against him."

For a moment, the dark eyes seem to glint. "I've been beaten before. Rather badly, once. As it happens, because a comrade and I were overseen by the enemy conspiring against them, and so in order to protect both our covers he feigned an angry argument and hammered me into a pulp. I spent a few days in the hospital, true enough—the man had fists like hams, even bigger than the Sergeant's over there—but it worked like a charm."

Yuri shook his head, trying to clear it. "Let me get this straight . . ."

11

"Why," grumbled Yuri, staring at the ceiling of his stateroom, "do I feel like the poor sorry slob who got stuck with guarding Napoleon on St. Helena?"

Sharon lowered her book and lifted her head from the pillow next to him. "Who's Napoleon? And I never heard of a planet named St. Helena."

Yuri sighed. Whatever her other marvelous qualities—which he'd been enjoying immensely during the past month—Sharon did not share his passion for ancient history and literature.

Cachat did, oddly enough—some aspects of ancient culture, anyway—and that was something else Yuri had jotted down in his mental Black Book. The one with the title: *Reasons I Hate Victor Cachat.*

It was childish, he knew. But during the weeks since he'd arrested Cachat, Victor had found that his anger toward the man had simply deepened. The fact that the anger—Yuri was this honest with himself—stemmed more from Cachat's virtues than his vices only seemed to add fuel to the flames.

The fundamental problem was that Cachat *had* no vices—except being Victor Cachat. In captivity as in command, the young fanatic had faced everything resolutely, unflinchingly, with not a trace of any of the self-doubts or terrors which had plagued Yuri himself his entire life. Cachat never raised his voice in anger; never flinched in fear; never whined, nor groused, nor pleaded.

Yuri had fantasies, now and then, of Victor Cachat

on his knees begging for mercy. But even for Yuri the fantasies were washed-out and colorless—and faded within seconds. It was simply impossible to imagine Cachat begging for anything. As well imagine a tyrannosaur blubbering on its knees.

It just wasn't *fair*, damn it all. And the fact that Cachat, during the weeks of his captivity, had turned out to be an aficionado of the obscure ancient art form known as *films* had somehow been a worse offense than any. Savage Mesozoic carnivores are not *supposed* to have any higher sentiments.

And they're certainly not supposed to argue art with human beings! Which, needless to say, Cachat had done. And, needless to say, had taken the opportunity to chide Yuri for slackness.

That had happened in the first week.

"Nonsense," snapped Cachat. "Jean Renoir is the most overrated director I can think of. *The Rules of the Game*—supposedly a brilliant dissection of the mentality of the elite? What a laugh. When Renoir tries to depict the callousness of the upper crust, the best he can manage is a silly rabbit hunt."

Yuri glared at him. So did Major Citizen, who was the third of the little group on the *Hector* who had turned out to be film buffs and had started holding informal chats on the subject in Cachat's cell.

Well, it was technically a "cell," even if it was really a lieutenant's former cabin on the SD. Just as it was technically "locked" and there was technically always a "guard" standing outside the hatch.

"Technically" was the word for it, too. Yuri had no doubt at all that Cachat could have picked that simple ship's lock within ten seconds. Just as he had no doubt at all that nine out of ten of the guards stationed at the door would be far more likely to ask the former Special Investigator how he or she could be of service than to demand he return to his cell.

Sourly, Yuri remembered the arrest itself.

"Arrest." _Ha!_ It had been more like a ceremonial procession. Cachat emerging from the lock with a task force escort respectfully trotting behind him—and with both Major Lafitte and Major Citizen's Marines and StateSec security units lined up to receive him.

Theoretically, they'd been there to take him into custody. But as soon as Cachat had stepped across the line on the deck which marked the official legal boundaries of the superdreadnought, the Marines had snapped to attention and presented arms. Major Citizen's StateSec troops lined up on the opposite side had followed suit within a second.

Yuri had been startled, since he'd certainly given no order for that courtesy. But he hadn't tried to countermand it, either. Not after scanning the hard faces of the Marines and StateSec troopers themselves.

He'd never understand how Cachat had managed it, but somehow . . .

So, he imagined, had the Old Guard always reacted in the presence of Napoleon. Reality, logic, justice—be damned to all of it. In victory or defeat, the Emperor was still the Emperor.

"If you want to see a genuinely superb depiction of the brutality of power," Cachat continued, "watch Mizoguchi's _Sansho the Bailiff._"

Diana's glare faded. "Well . . . okay, Victor, I'll give you that. I'm a big fan of Mizoguchi myself, although I personally prefer _Ugetsu._ Still, I think you're being unfair to Renoir. What about—"

"A moment, please. Since we've ventured onto the subject—in a roundabout way—let me take the occasion to ask Commissioner Radamacher how much longer he's going to slack off before completing the purge."

"What are you talking about?" demanded Yuri. But his stomach was sinking as he said the words. In truth, he knew perfectly well what Cachat was talking about. He'd just been . . .

Procrastinating.

"You know!" snapped Cachat. "You're lazy, but you're not dumb. Not dumb at all. The fact that you've created a command staff throughout the fleet is fine and dandy. Fine also that, between the Marines and selected personnel from StateSec, you've put together a solid security team to enforce your authority. But this superdreadnought—and the *Tilden's* not much better; in some ways, worse—is still riddled with disaffected elements. Not to mention a small horde of pure hooligans. I'm warning you, Commissioner Radamacher, let this continue much longer and you'll start losing it."

Yuri swallowed. Cachat was speaking the truth, and he knew it. Both superdreadnoughts had enormous crews, whose personnel was entirely StateSec except for a relative handful of Marines. Some of those StateSec people—Major Citizen and Sergeant Rolla being outstanding examples—were people Yuri would stake his life on. *Was* staking his life on, as a matter of fact.

The rest . . . Most of them were simply people. People who'd enlisted originally to serve on a StateSec capital ship for much the same reasons that people from any society's lower classes volunteer for military service. A way out of the slums; decent and reliable pay; security; training; advancement. Nothing more sinister than that.

They'd all been willing enough to go along with the change of guard. Especially after it became clear that

Yuri had engineered what amounted to a truce so that none of them need fear any immediate repercussions as long as they kept the peace.

But there were still plenty of SD ratings—and plenty of officers—who were not at all happy with the new setup. They'd *liked* being in State Security, and would be delighted to see its iron-fisted regime return—since they had every reason to expect they could resume their happy days as the fingers of that fist.

"Damn it," he complained—hating the fact that even to himself his voice sounded whiny—"I didn't sign on to carry out a Night of the Long Knives."

Cachat frowned. "Who said anything about knives? And they wouldn't need to be long anyway. You can cut a man's throat with a seven-centimeter blade perfectly well. In fact—have you forgotten everything?— that was the blade-length of choice in the academy's assassination courses."

"Never mind," sighed Yuri. "It's an historical reference. There was once a tyrant named Adolf Hitler and after he came to power he turned on the most hardcore of the fanatics who'd lifted him to power. The True Believers who were now a threat to him. Had them all purged in a single night."

Cachat grunted. "I still don't understand the point. I'm certainly not proposing that you purge *Diana*. Or Major Lafitte or Admiral Chin or Commodore Ogilve or any of the excellent noncoms—Marine and StateSec both—who are the people who lifted *you* into power. I'm simply pointing out what ought to be obvious: there are lots of sheer thugs on these capital ships and you ought to have the lot of them thrown into prison. A real prison, too—dirtside, where they can't get loose— not this silly arrangement you've got me in."

Diana Citizen's face looked troubled. "Uh, Yuri, I hate to say it but I agree with the Special—ah, Captain

Cachat. I don't even care about political reliability, frankly. We're starting to have lots of problem with simple discipline. *Lots* of problems."

Yuri hesitated. Cachat's face seemed to soften, for a moment.

"You are a splendid shield, Yuri Radamacher," he said quietly. "But the republic needs a sword also, from time to time. So why don't you—this once—let a sword advise you?"

The young StateSec captain nodded his head toward the computer on his desk. The thing had no business still being there, of course. No one in their right mind would leave a computer in the hands of a prisoner like Cachat. Sure, sure, Yuri had slapped a codelock on it. Ha. He wondered if it had taken Cachat even two hours to break it.

But . . .

A computer was simply part of the dignity of a man like Cachat. To have removed it would have been like requiring Napoleon on St. Helena to sleep on the floor, or wear a sheet for clothing.

Cachat seemed to be reading his mind. "I haven't tried to use it, Yuri," he said softly. "But if you go into it yourself, you'll find my own records easily enough. The keyword is *Ginny* and the password is *Tongue.*"

For some reason, Cachat seemed to be blushing a little. "Never mind. It was a personal reference I'd . . . ah, be able to remember. That will get you into the list of personnel I spent quite a bit of time assembling while I was operating on this warship. That list will only contain *Hector Van Dragen* personnel, of course. But you can find the same for the *Tilden*— more extensive, actually, since I had more time on that ship—stored away on the computer I used while on the *Tilden* during our mission."

The peculiar blush seemed to darken. "The keyword

and password in that instance will be *sari* and, uh, *shakehertail*."

Diana burst out laughing. "Ginny—tongue—sari—*shakehertail*, no less. Victor, you dog! Who would have guessed you were a lady's man? I'd love to meet this girlfriend of yours, whoever she is."

The young man—for once, he didn't look like a fanatic—seemed on verge of choking. "She's not—ah, well. She's *not* my girlfriend. Actually, she's the wife—ah, never mind. Just a woman I knew once, whom I admired a lot." A bit defensively: "'Shake-her-tail' was a reference to her cover, and, uh, 'tongue' is because—well, never mind. There's no need to go into it."

For once, Yuri was inclined to let Cachat off the hook instead of needling him. Cachat the fanatic, he detested. Cachat the young man . . . was impossible to even dislike.

"Okay, Victor, we'll 'never mind,'" he said. "But what's on that list?"

The fanatic came back instantly. "Everyone I was planning to either arrest or, at the very least, break from StateSec service. Of course, I never thought I could do it all at once. Probably wouldn't even be able to do more than get started, since I had no idea how long Saint-Just would leave me on station here. But you can do the lot at a single stroke."

Radamacher eyed the computer. Then, sighing, got up and went over to it.

"Well. I suppose I should at least look at it."

The first name and entry on the list was: *Alouette, Henri. GravSen Tech 1/c.*

"Damn," muttered Yuri. "I forgot all about him, things have been so hectic."

The rest of Cachat's entry read:

Vicious thug. Incompetent and derelict at anything

*else. Suspect him of conducting a reign of terror in his
section, to the gross detriment of the section's performance. Arrest at the first opportunity. Most severe
punishment possible, preferably execution, if sufficient
evidence can be obtained. Certain it can once he is
arrested and his section mates no longer fear retalia-
tion.*

"Damn," Yuri muttered again. "I've been slacking
off."

The purge took place three nights later. On both
capital ships simultaneously.

Major Citizen led the purge on the *Tilden*, since that
ship was not as accustomed as the crew of the *Hector* to having Marines serving as a security unit. Captain
Vesey, by then more relieved to see discipline restored
than anything else, made no protest. Two of his bridge
officers did, including the XO, but that was to be
expected. They were led off the bridge in manacles,
after all. Both of them had been high up on Cachat's
list.

The purge on the *Hector* was, for the most part,
carried out by Major Lafitte's Marines. But it was
officially led by Jaime Rolla, whom Yuri had given a
brevet promotion to the rank of StateSec Lieutenant
the day before.

Again, he'd been slacking off. Yuri had found Rolla's
name on another of Cachat's lists in the computer. This
one under the keyword and password of *hotelbed* and
ginrummy.

The list had been entitled: *Prospects for Advancement*, and Rolla's name had been at the top of the list.
Cachat's entry read:

*Superb StateSec trooper. Intelligent, disciplined, self-
controlled. Commands confidence and inspires loyalty
from his subordinates. Absurd he still remains in the*

ranks. Another legacy of Jamka's madness. Promote to brevet Lieutenant immediately. Delay submission of name to OTS. May need him here.

Yuri had wondered at the last two sentences. He thought of asking Cachat why he hadn't wanted to send Rolla's name to Nouveau Paris as a candidate for StateSec's Officer Training School.

Then, realizing how much *he* would miss Rolla's steadying presence, he thought he understood. Although . . . why would Cachat care, really? *He* hadn't faced the problem of carrying through a revolution.

But he left the question unasked. He was irritated enough with Cachat as it was, the way each reading of the lists made him feel like a damn fool.

Just so, he was darkly certain, had Napoleon's jailor felt whenever the emperor beat him at checkers on St. Helena. Again.

Alouette was never arrested. Fleeing ahead of the arresting squad, finding himself cornered, the man tried to make his escape by climbing into his skinsuit, strapping on a sustained use thruster pack, and venturing onto the exterior of the *Hector*. Presumably—impossible to know—he'd hoped to make it across to the nearest commercial space station sharing orbit with the SD around La Martine.

It would have been an epic escape. Even a highly skilled and experienced EVA rating would have been hardpressed to cross that distance in a skinsuit without a hardsuit's navigation systems to go with the SUT pack.

Alouette was neither superb nor experienced. He never even made it off the warship. Apparently in a panic, he jammed the jets into full throttle and rammed himself into a nearby gravitic array. There he remained for minutes, crushed against the array by the flaring SUT thrusters; which he was unable to turn off, either because he couldn't remember how or—if the fates had mercy on him—because the initial impact had rendered him unconscious.

It was a moot point. By the time his body could be recovered after the SUT ran out of fuel, the impact and the thrusters themselves had shredded the skinsuit with magnificent irony upon the very array the grav tech had *not* serviced in all his time aboard the *Hector*. Decompression had done the rest. The body that was hauled back into the *Hector* had been nothing but a broken, soggy mess.

It bought him no mercy. Again, Yuri decided to follow Cachat's advice.

"When you drive in a sword, Commissioner, drive it to the hilt. Execute the corpse. Do it in front of a full assembly."

So it was. Ned Pierce got his wish, after all, emptying a full clip into the corpse of Alouette, propped up against a bulkhead.

The Marine sergeant did insist afterward—and loudly, too—that he got no satisfaction from the matter. But Yuri thought the cold grin on his face when he made the disclaimer belied the statement. And so, apparently, did the hundred or so of the *Hector's* ratings who had been assembled in the chamber to witness the event.

True, the dozen of them who had been in Alouette's own section had raised a cheer. But even they looked a bit pale-faced at the time. And Yuri had no doubt at all that none of them would be in the least bit tempted thereafter to emulate Alouette. Or do anything which might draw the wrath of the new regime down on their heads.

He took no pleasure in the fact, although he did appreciate the irony. He'd read the ancient quip, that if Satan ever seized Heaven he'd have no choice but to take on God's characteristics. Now, he was realizing that the converse was true: *If God ever took over the management of Hell, He'd make a damn good Devil himself.*

And so the weeks passed, in the distant provincial sector of La Martine. No word from Haven. Nothing but wild rumors brought occasionally by merchant ships. The only certain things were that the capital system was still under the Navy's control and that a number of provincial sectors had burst into rebellion against the new regime, led by StateSec units.

But La Martine Sector remained tranquil. Within a month, the civilian authorities were even so confident that they began demanding that Radamacher—now called, by everyone, *the Commissioner for La Martine*—resume the anti-piracy patrols. There had been no incidents, true. But the commercial sector saw no reason to risk slackness.

When Yuri hesitated, the civilian delegation insisted on speaking to Cachat.

"Why?" Yuri demanded. "He's under arrest. He has no authority here. He doesn't even have a title any longer, except captain."

No use. The faces of the civilian delegation were set, stubborn. Yuri sighed and had Cachat brought to his office.

Cachat listened to the delegation. Then—needless to say—spoke without hesitation.

"Of course you should resume the patrols. Why not, Commissioner Radamacher? You've got everything well in hand."

Yuri almost ground his teeth, seeing the look of satisfaction on the faces of the civilians. Just so—just so!—would the fishermen on St. Helena have appealed from his guard to the Emperor, over a dispute regarding the proper repair of fishing nets.

But, he ordered the resumption of the patrols.

He had no choice, really. Yuri was coming to realize, slowly, that Cachat had been right about his own arrest also. In some indefinable manner, Yuri's own legitimacy somehow depended on the fact that he was seen as the custodian of the man who had been the final representative of Saint-Just's regime in La Martine.

Had the man he held captive ever protested, or complained, things might have been different. Yuri often found himself wishing that the news reporters who appeared frequently on the *Hector* to take yet another shot of Cachat In Captivity would produce a suitable image. That of a scowling, hunched, sullen tyrant finally brought to bay.

But . . . no. The images published in the newsviewers were always the same. A young man, stiff and dignified, looking more like a prince in exile than an incarcerated fanatic.

When he said as much to Sharon, she just laughed and told him to stop pouting.

Then, finally, official word came. A courier ship from Haven, bearing an official message from the new government.

As soon as the dispatch boat made its alpha translation, Yuri recognized the distinctive hyper footprint of a courier vessel. Nothing else that small was hypercapable, after all, so it couldn't possibly be another merchantman . . . or a warship. Immediately, Yuri summoned all of the top commanders of the fleet to the bridge of the *Hector*. By the time the dispatch boat was within range to start transmitting messages, they were all present. Admiral Chin, Commodore Ogilve,

Commissioner Wilkins, Captain Vesey, Majors Citizen and Lafitte. Captain Wright, recently promoted to replace Gallanti as the CO of the *Hector.* And Sharon, of course.

As Yuri began reading the first of the messages, he sighed with relief. The message began by stating that a new provisional government had been set in place by Admiral Theismann. A *civilian* government. There would be no military dictatorship, after all. Short of a return of the old regime, that had been Yuri's worst nightmare.

The message continued with a list of names—the officials of the new provisional government. The first of those names almost caused his heart to stop.

Eloise Pritchard, Provisional President.

The King is dead, long live the Queen. Saint-Just's fair-haired girl. Ring-around-the-rosy and we're right back where we started.

We're dead meat.

But his eyes were already continuing down the list, and he realized the truth even before he heard Sharon's shocked half-whisper.

"Jesus Christ Almighty. She must have been in the opposition all along. Look at the rest of those names."

Others were crowding around now, trying to read over Yuri's shoulders.

"Yeah, you're right," agreed Yuri. "I know a lot of them, myself, from the old days. At least half this list is made up of Aprilists. The best of them, too, at least those who've survived the last ten years. Hey—look! They've even got Kevin Usher. I didn't think he was still alive. The last I heard he'd been shipped off to the Marines in disgrace. I thought by now they'd have vanished him away somewhere."

"Who's Usher?" asked Ogilve.

"One hell of a good Marine, I know that much,"

growled Lafitte. "I've never met him myself, but I've known two officers who served with him for a while on Terra." Lafitte chuckled. "Mind you, they said he drank like a fish and was hardly the model of a proper colonel. Even got into barroom brawls himself, now and then. But his troops swore by the man, and the officers I knew—good people, both of them—told me they'd be delighted to have him in a combat situation. Which"—the growl deepened—"is what matters."

"I *do* know him," Yuri said quietly. "Pretty well, once. It was a long time ago, but . . ."

His eyes rested with satisfaction on Usher's name. With even greater satisfaction, on Usher's title. *Director, Federal Investigation Agency.*

"What's the 'Federal Investigation Agency,' do you think?" asked Genevieve Chin.

"I'm not sure," Yuri answered, "but my guess is that Theisman—or Pritchard—decided to bust up StateSec and separate its police functions from its intelligence work. Thank God. And put Kevin Usher in charge of the cops. Ha!"

He practically did a little jig of glee. "Mind you, that's like putting a chicken in charge of the foxes. Kevin Usher—a *cop*, of all things! But he's a very very very tough rooster." He grinned at Major Lafitte. "Pity the poor foxes. I can't imagine who'd be crazy enough to pick a barroom brawl with him."

While he had been basking in the pleasure of seeing Kevin's name, Sharon had continued to read down the list. Suddenly, she burst into riotous laughter. Almost hysterical laughter, in fact.

"What's so funny?" asked Yuri.

Sharon, none too steady on her feet herself, took Yuri by the shoulders and more-or-less forced him into a seat on the bridge. "You need to be sitting down for

the rest of it," she cackled. "Especially when you get
to the names of the provisional sector governors."

Her finger jabbed at a line. "Take a look. Here's La
Martine."

Yuri read the name of the new provisional governor.

"Prince in exile, indeed!" Sharon howled.

Radamacher hissed a command.

"Get Cachat. Get him up here. *Now*."

When Cachat entered the bridge, Yuri strode up to
him and slammed the list onto a nearby console.

"Look at this!" he commanded accusingly. "Read it
yourself!"

Puzzled, Cachat's eyes went down the list. Quickly,
scanning, the first time through. Then, as he read it
slowly again, Yuri knew the truth. Knew it for a certainty.

The hard young fanatic was gone, by the end. There
stood before the commissioner only a man of twenty-
four, who looked years younger than that. A bit confused; very uncertain.

His dark eyes—brown eyes—were even wet with
tears.

"You swine," Yuri hissed. "You treacherous dog. You
lied to me. You lied to all of us. Best damn liar I've
ever met in my life. You played us all for fools!"

He pointed the finger of accusation at the list.

"Admit it!" he shouted. "It was all a goddam *act*!"

12

"Was it?" asked Cachat softly, as if wondering
himself. Then, he shook his head. "No, Yuri, I don't

think so. I told you once—it's not my fault if you never want to believe me—that I swore an oath to the *Republic*. I've kept that oath. Kept it here in La Martine."

His voice grew firmer, less uncertain. "I was specifically entrusted by the Republic to ferret out and punish traitors. Of which the two greatest, for years, were Rob Pierre and Oscar Saint-Just. Who stabbed our revolution in the back and seized it for their own ends."

No uncertainty, now: *"Damn them both to hell."*

"How long?" Yuri croaked.

Cachat understood what he meant. "I've been a member of the opposition since Terra. Since almost the beginning of my career. Kevin Usher was the commander of the Marine unit stationed at our embassy there and he— Well. Let's say he took me in hand, and showed me the way out. After I'd seen enough that I couldn't stomach any more."

Suddenly, Cachat's face lit up with a smile. A real, honest-to-God smile, too, not the razor Yuri had seen a few times before. "Though not before putting me in the hospital."

He gave Sharon a half-apologetic nod of the head. "If it'll make any amends, Commissioner Justice, I can assure you that Kevin Usher gave me a worse beating than you suffered at my order."

He looked back at Yuri, and shrugged. A real shrug. "Not, I admit, as bad as the one you got. But I'm sorry, Yuri, even before I got here I had you tagged as the key to the situation, and I needed to protect you as much as possible. So I used, on a broad scale, the same simple tactic Kevin once used on me. Had you— Sharon—many of you—beaten in order to establish your innocence."

"Why didn't you tell us?" asked Major Citizen,

half-whispering. "I mean—after Saint-Just died and it was all over? All these weeks..."

"*Was it?* 'Over,' I mean." Cachat's eyes were very dark. "I had no way of knowing what sort of regime was going to emerge. For all I knew, I was still going to have to continue as an oppositionist. But since I'd done everything I could to prepare La Martine for any eventuality—including the possibility of a restoration of the old regime—I needed to maintain my cover. It was my simple duty."

Every officer on the bridge was now staring at him. Precious few of the ratings seated at their stations were making any attempt to hide the fact that they were listening also.

Cachat frowned. "Why are you all looking so confused? You know how thoroughly I do my research. By the time I got to La Martine—it's a long trip—I was pretty sure I understood what was happening here. And what I needed to do. It didn't take more than a short time here to confirm it."

Of all the faces on the bridge, Major Lafitte's was the only one whose eyes weren't wide. As a matter of fact, they were narrow with suppressed anger.

"Why the hell did you order *us* to do your blood work?" he demanded. Glancing at Sharon. "Especially on our own commissioner. Best damn ship's commissioner any of us had ever served with."

"Don't be stupid, Major Lafitte!" snapped Cachat. The fanatic was back, it seemed. "The first thing I needed to do—"

He broke off sharply. Turned, and bestowed a hard gaze on one of the commo ratings. "Are the recorders on?"

Hastily—she didn't even think to look at the ship's captain—the rating pushed a button on her console. "Not any more, Sir."

Cachat nodded and turned back. "If you don't mind, Captain Wright, I'd prefer there to be no official record of this." He continued on, not waiting for the SD's CO to finish nodding his approval. "As I was saying, Major, don't be stupid. Jamka's insane rule—the results of it, I should say—had given me the opportunity to destroy the worst elements of Saint-Just's treason here in La Martine. Of course—"

He shrugged again; but, this time, it was the shoulder-twitch of old. "I had no way of knowing—never imagined it, in fact—that Admiral Theismann would shortly be overthrowing the traitor. But, no matter. My duty was clear. Sooner or later, Saint-Just's regime was bound to collapse. At the very least, start coming apart at the seams. No purely police state in history has ever survived for very long. So Kevin Usher told me, once, and I believe him. Saint-Just, without Rob Pierre, was bound to fall—and fairly quickly."

Usher's right, thought Yuri. *Beria without Stalin didn't last for . . . weeks? I can't remember, exactly. Less than a year, that's for sure. Terror alone is never enough.*

"It was therefore my clear duty to do what I could to prepare La Martine for the coming upheavals," Cachat continued. "Sanitize the sector, if you will. Jamka's murder provided me with the perfect opening, of course. But—to come back to the point, Major—doing so required me to enlist the aid of his killers immediately. Those were the only people I could count on for sure. Partly, of course, because their actions indicated their good character. But just as much because they'd see my presence as the surest way to cover their own tracks. Indeed, the quickest way to complete the mission they'd set out for themselves. I'm sure you'd planned—over time, of course—to execute everyone involved in

Rating Quedilla's murder. Jamka was just the beginning."

The room was frozen. There was no anger left in Major Lafitte's face. Only shock. And Sharon's face was that of ghost.

"Oh, Jesus," whispered Yuri. Half-pleading: "Sharon—"

"Desist, Radamacher!"

No one had ever heard Victor Cachat raise his voice. And this was a loud voice. Not cold in the least, but hot with anger.

"You slacker!" Cachat bellowed. Then, tightening his jaws and visibly clamping down on himself: "She only did what you *should* have done, Radamacher. You were second-in-command of State Security here in La Martine. It was *your* duty to have seen to the removal of a beast like Jamka, once his nature had become clear and the threat he posed to the people of the Republic was obvious. Not hers. *Yours.* Even if you had to go outside of channels to do it."

His nostrils fleered. "But, of course, you looked the other way. Slacked off. As always. *Commissioner.*"

The last word practically dripped sarcasm. But, as if that satisfied him, the angry contempt in his expression faded away within seconds.

"Oh, hell, Yuri," Cachat said wearily. "You are one of the nicest men I've ever met. But some day you'll have to learn that a shield without a sword is pitiful protection in a real fight."

Yuri was still staring at Sharon. She, staring back. Her face was still pale, but it was also composed.

"She was one of ours, Yuri," Sharon said quietly. "Caroline Quedilla was one of ours. When Jamka crossed that line—"

"A *shipmate*," Lafitte hissed. "And the best damn ship in the fleet, too." The major's shoulders seemed wider than ever, his big hands clasped behind his back. "Yeah, sure, Quedilla wasn't much of a rating and a screwball to boot. Always looking for thrills and a disciplinary pain-in-the-neck. Just the kind of nitwit that Jamka—he was a smooth, handsome bastard, if you'll remember; if you didn't know what lay beneath—could have suckered in while she was on shore leave. But she was still one of *ours*. God damn it! You don't *ever* let anyone cross that line." He took a slow, deep breath. "Not for something like this, anyway. If it'd been a matter of political loyalty or—or—"

The big hands seemed to tighten. "That's different. But this was just a monster at his games, thinking his position could protect him from anything. He learned otherwise."

The major swiveled his head to Cachat. "I had no idea you knew."

Cachat shrugged. "It wasn't hard to figure out, once I realized who the victim was. I'd already studied the personnel records, of course, on the voyage here. So I was aware of the *Veracity's* record—and the fact that its Marine unit in particular had an exemplary combat record. Three unit citations, no less. I'm quite familiar with Marines, Major. I spent months in their company on Terra after the Manpower incident, before Saint-Just recalled me to Haven for reassignment."

Cachat glanced at Sharon. "Captain Justice's record as a commissioner just sealed the matter. I don't know exactly how it all went down—nor do I care to know— but I imagine she was the one who gave you the nod. She'd have kept it away from the *Veracity's* captain, of course, to protect the ship as a whole in case it all came unglued. You would have organized the operation. Then—judging from the evidence I turned up over the next week or so, I'm quite certain Sergeant Pierce led the operation which executed Jamka."

He winced, slightly. "A bit flamboyant, that last part. But Pierce is a flamboyant sort of character. I certainly can't deny it was—ah—call it poetic justice. And the theatrical manner in which the killing was done—whether you or Pierce planned for it or not—did have the benefit of making it easy for everyone to assume that Jamka had fallen afoul of his cohorts." Cachat snorted. "It always amazes me how willing people are to jump to conclusions, as long as a handy conclusion is waved under their nose. The theory was ridiculous, of course. Jamka's cronies would have been the *last* people to kill him. His position and authority were what enabled them to operate with impunity. That's why I had them all shot at once, so they wouldn't have time to argue their case."

Yuri felt light-headed. "Evidence . . . ?"

Jesus, Sharon'll fry. Murder is murder, under any regime.

"Do you take me for an idiot?" demanded Cachat. "The evidence disappeared months ago. Vanished without a trace. I saw to that, I assure you. It was hardly difficult, since I was the Special Investigator assigned to handle the case."

Yuri was swept with relief. But only for a moment. His eyes began flitting around the large bridge. His stomach sinking as he realized how many sets of ears . . .

"And again!" Cachat snapped. "When are you going to learn?"

The fanatic—Yuri couldn't help but think of him that way; perhaps now more than ever—was giving him that cold, dark scrutiny. "Accept something as a fact, will you? I am far better at this than you will ever be, Yuri Radamacher. Better by nature, and then I was trained by the best there is. Oscar Saint-Just poured the iron, and—pity him!—Kevin Usher shaped the mold. So I know what I'm doing."

His eyes moved slowly over the bridge. As he came to each rating—none of them, any longer, even pretending to attend to their duty—most of them looked away. It was a hard gaze to face, after all. Oddly enough, though, Cachat's eyes seemed to lighten in color as they went. Black at the beginning; a rather warm brown at the end.

"There is no evidence," Cachat repeated, speaking to the entire bridge. "And there is no record of this discussion. I'm afraid all of you here are simply having a delusional experience. No doubt, wild and unsubstantiated rumors will begin appearing on this ship. No doubt, they will spread soon throughout the task force. Not much doubt, I'd say, they will eventually percolate throughout the Republic."

He turned back to the officers, smiling thinly. "And so? I see no harm to the Republic—none at all, as a matter of fact—if rumors exist that, even during the worst days of the Saint-Just tyranny, an especially vile leader of State Security was fragged by one of the ship's crews of the Republic."

For a moment, all was still. Then, as if they possessed a single pair of lungs, almost two dozen officers and ratings let out a collective breath.

Major Lafitte even managed a laugh of sorts. "Cachat, I don't think even Saint-Just—on his best day—or worst day, I'm not sure which—could have been that ruthless. *That's* why you used the *Veracity's* Marines as your fist, from the very beginning."

"I told you. I was trained by the best." Cachat's own little laugh was a harsh thing. "No one suspects a torturer, Major, of any crime except torture. The work itself obliterates whatever might lurk beneath. As Kevin once told me, 'blood's always the best cover, and all the better if it's on your own fists.' "

He turned to face Yuri. "Now do you understand, Commissioner?"

Yuri said nothing. But his face must have conveyed his sentiments. *You're still a damn fanatic, Cachat.*

Cachat sighed, and looked away. For an instant, he seemed very young and vulnerable.

"I had nothing else, Yuri," he said softly. "No other weapon; no other shield. So I used my own character to serve me for both."

There seemed to be some moisture back in his eyes. "So, was it an act? I honestly don't know. I'm not sure I want to know."

"Doesn't matter to me," said Major Lafitte firmly. "As long as you're on my side."

Sharon seemed to choke. "I'll drink to that!" she exclaimed. Then, turning to Captain Wright: "What say, Sir? It's your ship. But I think a toast might be in order."

Wright wasn't exactly a "jolly good soul." Precious few commanding officers of a StateSec capital ship ever were. But compared to Gallanti, he was a veritable life-of-the-party.

"It's straining regulations, but—I'm inclined to agree that—"

He got no further before an alarm sounded. Commander Tarack, Ballon's replacement as *Hector*'s tac officer, started in his chair—his attention, like everyone else's, had been riveted on Cachat—and turned quickly to his console. Fresh datacodes blinked on his display, and he listened hard to his ear bug.

Then he paled.

Noticeably.

"Sir," he said, unable to completely disguise his nervousness, "I'm getting a very big hyper footprint.

Uh, *very* big, Sir. And . . . uh, I think—not sure yet—
that we've got some ships of the wall here. Uh. Lots
of them. At least half a dozen, I think."

Whatever his other shortcomings, Wright was an
experienced ship commander. "What distance?" he
asked, his voice level and even. "And can you make
out their identity?"

"Twelve light-minutes, Sir. Bearing oh-one-niner,
right on the ecliptic. I won't be able to determine their
identity, or even the actual class types, until the light-
speed platforms report, Sir."

Twelve minutes later, Commander Tarack was able
to determine the identity of the incoming task force.
"They're Havenite, Sir."

The people on the bridge relaxed. Somewhat. It still
remained unclear whether the task force was from the
newly established regime or . . . who knew? There were
apparently StateSec-led rebellions in several provincial
sectors—one of which, at least, was not all that far from
La Martine sector.

But, ten minutes after that, that uncertainty vanished
also. The first message from the incoming flotilla had
bridged the lightspeed distance.

"They're from Haven itself, Sir," reported the comm
rating. "It's a task force sent out by President Pritchard,
to—ah, it says *'help reestablish proper authority in
Ja'al, Tetra and La Martine sectors, and suppress any
disturbances, if needed.'* That's a quote, Sir. Admiral
Austell's in command."

"*Midge* Austell?" asked Commodore Ogilve sharply.

The rating shook her head. "Doesn't say, Sir. Just:
'Rear Admiral Austell, task force commander.'"

"It's *got* to be Midge," said Admiral Chin. There was
more than a trace of excitement in her voice. "I don't

know any other Austell on the Captain's List. Didn't know she'd made admiral, though. Fast track, if she did."

"She could have, Genevieve," said Ogilve. His own voice sounded elated. "She never got smeared by Hancock the way we did, you know. She was too junior, at the time, just my tac officer in the *Napoleon*. So she didn't spend our time on the beach. God knows she's good enough. In my opinion, anyway."

"Here's another message, Sir," called out the rating. "Says that FIA Director Usher is accompanying the task force. *'To reestablish proper police authorities in provincial sectors.'* That's a direct quote, Sir."

Cachat collapsed into an empty seat. "Thank God," he whispered. He put his face in his hands. "I am so very tired."

A last spark of anger almost led Yuri to demand: *From what? You haven't done anything for weeks except rest.*

But he didn't ask the question. Wouldn't have, even if he hadn't seen Sharon's eyes on him. Hard eyes; questioning eyes—still pleading eyes, too. Yuri and Sharon would have a lot to talk through, in the days to come.

But Yuri Radamacher did not ask, because the commissioner knew the answer. Victor Cachat had not slacked off. Cachat had done his duty, and done it to the full.

And now, even a fanatic was weary of such duty.

Cachat still seemed weary, five hours later, when the first pinnace from the arriving task force docked at the *Hector*. He was there with the rest of them in the boat bay gallery, but his normally square shoulders seemed slumped; his face drained and paler than ever.

The sight of the first person coming through the lock

seemed to pick up his spirits, true. That sight certainly picked up Yuri's. He'd forgotten how large and excessively muscular Kevin Usher was, but the cheerful, rakish face was exactly as he remembered. Kevin Usher in a good mood could brighten up any gathering—and the man was obviously in a very good mood.

"Victor!" he bellowed, stepping forward and sweeping the smaller man into a bear hug. "Damn, it's good to see you again!"

He plunked the young man down and examined him. "You look like shit," he pronounced. "You're not exercising enough."

In point of fact, Yuri knew that Cachat exercised at least two hours a day. But Cachat didn't argue the point.

"I'm pretty worn out, Kevin," he said softly.

Usher's sharp eyes studied him for a few seconds. "Well, it's up to you. Your posting as provisional sector governor is rescinded, as of this moment. That was just an emergency stop-gap. You're not really the right type for it—as you and I both know good and well, heh—and we've got someone else in mind anyway. But I do need to appoint an FIA director for La Martine. I was going to offer the post to you, but . . . if you don't want it, you can return with me to Nouveau Paris. It's not like I don't have a thousand hot spots to squelch, and I do believe you've become one of my top firemen."

"I want to go home, Kevin." Cachat's voice seemed very thin. "Wherever home is. It's not here. Nobody here—"

He broke off, shook his head, and continued more firmly. "I'd rather return with you to Nouveau Paris and take on a different assignment. I'm tired of this one."

Usher studied him for a few seconds more, with that

shrewd gaze. "Been rough, huh? I figured it might have been, from what I could tell at a distance. Okay, then. Name your replacement."

Cachat didn't hesitate. Just turned his head and pointed a finger at Yuri. "Him. He's—"

For the first time, Usher caught sight of Radamacher.

"Yuri!" he bellowed. "Long time!"

The next thing Yuri knew he was being swept up into the same bear hug.

He'd also forgotten how *strong* Usher was. He couldn't breathe. But Yuri finally forgave Cachat for Sharon's beating. He didn't want to think what kind of punishment those huge hands had visited on the fanatic.

Usher plopped Yuri back on his feet. Then, one hand still on Yuri's shoulder, shook his head firmly.

"Not a chance. We've got another assignment for this one, if he wants it. We're putting our own people in as governors for most of the sectors, but La Martine's been so rock steady that we decided we'd just leave Yuri here in place running the show."

Everyone in the La Martine delegation looked surprised. "How'd you know—?" Chin asked.

Usher laughed. "For Pete's sake, Admiral, rumor flies both ways. Must have been thirty merchant ships pass through Haven, all with the same story. *Commissioner Radamacher's holding the fort in La Martine, steady as she goes and business is even good.* That's why we've left you on your own so long. Sorry 'bout that, but we had way too many other problems on our hands to worry about a problem that didn't exist. Besides—"

The other big hand clapped down on Cachat's shoulder. "I knew my number one boy Victor was out here, lending a hand. That was worth an hour's extra sleep for me every night, right there."

To Victor: "Name somebody else."

Victor pointed at Sharon. "Her, then. Captain Sharon Justice."

Sharon was standing frozen. Radamacher likewise. In fact, everyone in the La Martine delegation had a strained look on their face.

Usher frowned. "What's the matter?"

Cachat glanced around. Then, flushed a bit. "Oh. Well. Bad memories, I imagine. I once asked people here to name their replacements and—well. It all turned out a bit, ah, unpleasant."

Usher grinned. "Ran you all through the wringer, did he? Ha!" The hand rose, fell, clapping Cachat's shoulder. "A real piece of work, isn't he? Like I said, my number-one boy."

He focused the grin on Sharon. "Not to worry, I'm just passing out lollipops. La Martine Sector is the provincial apple of Haven's eye right now, don't think it isn't."

Now, to Yuri: "And you, what do you say? You'll have to give up the 'commissioner' part of it, Yuri. The name, anyway. Can you live with 'governor'?"

Mutely, Yuri nodded. Usher immediately shifted the grin elsewhere. He seemed determined to complete his business immediately. Yuri had also forgotten how much energy Kevin Usher possessed.

"Okay, then. Admiral Chin, you're relieved of command and ordered to report back to the capital for a new assignment. It's ridiculous to keep an admiral of your talent and experience running a provincial task force. Tom—Admiral Theismann—no, he's the new Secretary of War—tells me he's got a Vice-Admiralty and a fleet waiting for you. Commodore Ogilve, you're promoted to Rear Admiral and will be taking over from Admiral Chin here. Don't get too comfy, though. I don't think you'll be here long. We can find somebody else to squelch pirates. We've got some rebellions to suppress—and who knows how long the truce with the Manties will last?"

Even somebody like Usher wasn't completely oblivious to such things as "formalities" and "proper chain of command." His grin seemed to widen, though, as if he took great pleasure in tweaking them.

"Of course, you'll be getting the official word from Admiral Austell, not me. That's Midge Austell—she says she knows you, Commodore. She should be coming over on the next pinnace, which—ah. I see it's arrived."

Sure enough, the green light of a good seal flashed on the bay end of the boarding tube once more, and a woman swung herself from the tube's zero-gee into the bay. Piled through from the tube, rather, practically shoving Admiral Austell aside as she did so.

The woman was not wearing a uniform; was small; dark-skinned; gorgeous; and her face was tight with disapproval.

"Stupid red tape," Yuri heard her mutter. "Make me wait for the next pinnace!"

Then, loudly: "Where's Victor?"

She didn't wait for an answer, though, because her eyes spotted the man she was looking for.

"*Victor!*"

"*Ginny!*"

An instant later, they were embracing like long-lost siblings. Or . . . something. A close relationship, whatever it was.

"My wife," Usher announced proudly. "Virginia, but we all call her Ginny. She and Victor are good friends."

Yuri remembered various keywords and passwords. *Ginny. Tongue. Hotelbed. Shakehertail.* (True, *ginrummy* didn't seem to fit the pattern.)

Major Citizen happened to be standing right behind him. Diana leaned close and whispered into his ear: "You really don't want to know, Yuri. I mean, you really really really really don't want to know."

He nodded firmly.

Cachat and Usher's wife finally broke their embrace. Ginny held him out at arm's length and examined him.

"You look like shit," she pronounced. "What's the matter?"

Cachat seemed on the verge of tears. There was no trace left of the fanatic. Just a very young man, bruised by life.

"I'm tired, Ginny, that's all. It's been . . . real hard on me here. I don't have any friends, and—God, I've missed you a lot—and . . . I just want to leave."

Yuri Radamacher had survived for ten years under the suspicious scrutiny of the Committee of Public Safety. It had been quite an odyssey, but it was over. He'd weathered all storms; escaped all reefs; even finally managed to make it safely to shore.

The experience, of course, had shaped his belief that there was precious little in the universe in the way of justice. But what happened next, confirmed his belief for all time.

Not even Oscar Saint-Just could have advanced such a completely, utterly, insanely *unfair* accusation.

"So that's it!" Ginny Usher's voice was shrill with fury, her hot eyes sweeping over the La Martine delegation.

"Victor Cachat is the sweetest kid in the world! And you—" She was practically spitting like a cat. "You dirty rotten bastards! You were *mean* to him."

THE SERVICE OF THE SWORD

by David Weber

"Miss Owens is here, High Admiral."

High Admiral Wesley Matthews looked up at his yeoman's announcement, then rose behind his desk as the slender, shapely, brunette midshipwoman in the sky-blue tunic and dark-blue trousers of the Grayson Space Navy stepped past the yeoman into his office. She was tall for a Grayson—over a hundred and sixty-seven centimeters—and she carried herself with an innate grace.

She also, he noticed, had excellent control of her expression. If he hadn't been looking for it carefully, he would never have noticed the flash of irritation in her gray-blue eyes at the way Chief Lewiston had announced her. There was another flicker of emotion as he stood up, and he wondered if she was irritated about that, as well. If she was, he conceded, she might have a point. The uniformed commander in chief of the GSN was not really in the habit of standing to greet a lowly midshipwoman when she reported to his office.

Then again, he'd never greeted any Grayson midshipwoman in his office under any circumstances before today.

"Midshipwoman Abigail Hearns, reporting as ordered, Sir!" she said crisply, bracing sharply to attention with her visored cap clasped under her left elbow.

"Stand easy, Miss—er, Ms. Hearns," he said, and suppressed an urge to grimace as he started to make exactly the same mistake the yeoman had.

There might have been an ever so slight trace of amusement underneath her eyes' irritation this time as she obeyed his order. It was impossible to be certain, but Matthews wouldn't have been at all surprised. Abigail Hearns looked absurdly young to Grayson eyes, for she was a member of the very first Grayson generation to have received the prolong therapies. For that matter, at just over twenty-two T-years, she really was a mere babe in arms to someone the high admiral's age. But despite her youth, she possessed an air of maturity and assurance he was more accustomed to seeing in people twice her age. Which made sense, he supposed, given who and what she was.

He pointed at one of the chairs facing his desk.

"Sit," he said, and she obeyed with economic grace, setting her cap precisely in her lap and sitting with her feet close together and a spine so straight it never touched the chair back at all.

Matthews resumed his own seat and considered her thoughtfully across his desk. Intellectually, he was delighted to see her in the Navy's uniform; emotionally, he had his doubts about the entire business.

"I'm sorry to have taken you away from your leave,"

he said after a moment. "I know you haven't seen much of your parents over the last three years, and I know you're only home for a few days before reporting back. But there are a few points I feel we ought to discuss before you board ship for your midshipman's cruise."

She said nothing, only gazing at him with alert respect, and he tipped his chair back slightly.

"I realize that you're in a somewhat awkward position as Grayson's very first midshipwoman," he told her. "I'm sure you realized going in that you would be, just as you realized you were going to be under a microscope the entire time you were at Saganami Island. I'm pleased to say that your performance there was all anyone could have asked of you. Fourteenth in your class overall, and sixth in the tactical curriculum." He nodded approvingly. "I expected you to do well, Ms. Hearns. I'm gratified that you exceeded those expectations."

"Thank you, Sir," she said in a soft contralto when he paused.

"It's no more than the truth," he assured her. "On the other hand, that intense scrutiny isn't going to stop now just because your classroom studies are behind you." He regarded her levelly. "However much you may want to be just one more midshipwoman or one more junior officer, Ms. Hearns, it's not going to be that way. You do realize that, don't you?"

"I suppose, to a certain extent, that's inevitable, Sir," she replied. "But I assure you that I neither expect nor desire preferential treatment."

"I'm perfectly—one might almost say painfully—well aware of that," he said. "Unfortunately, I expect some people are going to insist on trying to show you preferential treatment, whatever you want. You *are* a steadholder's daughter, after all, and I'm afraid patronage and steadholder privilege are still very much a part of Grayson life. Some people are going to find your birth impossible to forget. And, frankly, other people aren't even going to try. Some of them, in fact, will be too busy trying to curry favor with your father to ever so much as consider whether or not he—or you— want them to."

Those gray-blue eyes flashed once more, but he continued in that same calm voice.

"Personally, I intend to do everything possible to disabuse them of the notion that you might. You've certainly demonstrated to my satisfaction that you genuinely don't want any special treatment, and I respect that."

And, he added silently, *even if you hadn't demonstrated it, your father made it crystal clear to me when he requested the appointment to Saganami Island for you. I don't think he had a clue why you wanted to go, but however bewildered he may have been, he made his support for your decision abundantly clear.*

"It's going to happen, anyway, of course." He shrugged. "It's an imperfect universe, and people will insist on being people, warts and all, no matter what we do. However, it wasn't the possibility of preferential treatment that I was getting at.

"You're going to be the very first Grayson-born female officer in history. For a thousand years, no Grayson woman has ever served in the military. I happen to agree that it's time that we put that particular tradition behind us, but there's an enormous amount riding on how well you perform. And, to be honest, your birth only makes that even more the case. As a steadholder's daughter, you will be held, rightly or wrongly, to a higher standard than those of humbler birth might be, and our . . . uncertainty over the entire notion of women in uniform will only underline that expectation for those who hold it. At the same time some of our people will continue to doubt that any Grayson-born woman can perform up to standard, however well you actually do. That's not fair, either. And given the fact that we've had female Manticoran officers serving as 'loaners' with us for the better part of fifteen years, now, it's downright silly, too. We've had ample evidence of how well women can perform as both officers and enlisted personnel, regardless of their birth. I suppose it's just our ingrained stubbornness that keeps us from making the conceptual leap from Manticoran women to Grayson women.

"Whatever the cause, though, you're going to find yourself serving with people whose expectations are so high not even a superwoman could meet them. And, conversely, with people who would love to see you fail miserably in order to validate their own prejudices and bigotry. And," he admitted with a wry grin, "all of us are probably going to be a bit awkward about adjusting to the reality you represent."

Despite herself, Abigail's lips twitched, as if to return his smile. But then his grin faded, and he shook his head.

"I'm sure you were already aware of all of that. What you probably never contemplated at the time you first entered the Academy was the extent to which interstellar events would conspire to make things even worse. As it is, all of us have to consider exactly that—thus your orders to report to me for this little chat. And, just for the record, what I'm about to say to you stays in this office, Ms. Hearns. Is that understood?"

"Of course, Sir!"

"Good." He rocked his chair back and forth a couple of times and pursed his lips as he considered his next words carefully.

"I doubt very much," he began after a moment, "that someone with your family background could possibly have spent the last three and a half years on Manticore without realizing just how . . . strained our relationship with the Star Kingdom has become since the cease-fire went into effect. I'm not going to put you on the spot by asking you to comment on the causes of that strain. Given the situation, however, I find myself forced to explain certain concerns to you, and doing that is going to require *me* to comment on certain events—and individuals—with an unusually brutal degree of frankness."

One of Abigail's eyebrows arched ever so slightly. Aside from that, it might have been a statue in the chair in front of his desk.

"The High Ridge Government's actions since Duke Cromarty's assassination have created an enormous degree of anger and ill will here at Yeltsin's Star," he said flatly. "Prime Minister High Ridge's unilateral acceptance of the cease-fire when we were on the brink of outright military victory angered many members of the Manticoran Alliance, but probably we were the angriest of all, with Erewhon coming in second. That would have been bad enough, but since then, his concentration on the Star Kingdom's domestic political concerns rather than on turning the cease-fire into a permanent peace treaty has made it still worse for all of Manticore's allies. And, of course, in our own case, the fashion in which he and his political associates have insulted and vilified Lady Harrington has only pumped hydrogen into the fire.

"At the moment, I can't think of a single segment of Grayson public opinion which isn't . . . irritated with Manticore for one reason or another. Lady Harrington's partisans are furious for obvious reasons, but High Ridge has managed to make her political enemies every bit as angry with him for reasons of their own. *They* feel that his conduct of what passes for 'diplomacy' validates every reason they've ever put forward for disassociating ourselves from the Star Kingdom, and, frankly, there are times I actually find myself tempted to agree with them. From the perspective of my own office, however, the military policy his government has elected to pursue, particularly in conjunction with his diplomatic policy, puts every other concern into the shade.

"Sir Edward Janacek is . . . not the ideal choice for First Lord of the Manticoran Admiralty," the high admiral said. "I realize that my saying this puts you in something of an uncomfortable position, given the fact that you're currently in the Royal Manticoran Navy's chain of command, but not to mince words, Janacek is arrogant, bigoted, vengeful, and stupid."

He watched her face carefully, but her expression never flickered.

"From High Ridge's viewpoint, Janacek is also the perfect choice for his current position, as his willingness to downsize the RMN so drastically at this point in time demonstrates. Others of his policies are creating their own problems for us and for our relationship with the Star Kingdom, but I'm not going to burden you with all of my concerns. The specific points you need to be aware of are first, that he's committed to reducing the Royal Navy's strength at a time when he ought to be increasing it. Second, that he doesn't like or trust us or our navy any more than we like or trust him. Third, that he thinks all Graysons are neobarbarian, unthinking religious fanatics. And, fourth, that he has a bitter personal enmity for Steadholder Harrington.

"To be perfectly honest, I strongly considered specifically requesting that you be permitted to make your midshipman's cruise aboard a Grayson ship, rather than a unit of the Royal Navy. In fact, I did very quietly arrange for several of your Grayson classmates to do just that. You, on the other hand, are too visible, both in your own right and as someone who is seen, rightly or wrongly, as Lady Harrington's protégée. I couldn't have arranged it 'quietly' in your case, however hard I tried. And making an official request would have offered far too much ammunition to everyone who's already angry at the Star Kingdom.

"Unfortunately, this was something of a no-win situation. If I requested 'preferential treatment' for you by having you make your middy cruise aboard a Grayson ship, I risked aggravating everyone— Manticoran, as well as Grayson—by emphasizing the strain between our two navies. But if I didn't get you reassigned to a Grayson ship, I left you in a very awkward position, one with the potential to turn out even worse than requesting your reassignment might have.

"With the reductions in the Royal Navy's ship strength, the competition for the remaining commands has become particularly fierce. At the same time, a great many Manticoran officers have been reduced to half-pay status because of their differences with the Janacek Admiralty—or, for that matter, have voluntarily gone onto the inactive list rather than serve under him. Coupled with Janacek's preference for putting officers who support his policies into the command slots available, the removal of the officers who don't support them from active-duty means that an increasing percentage of the Star Kingdom's current starship captains aren't what you might call huge fans of the GSN.

"All of which means that by not requesting your assignment to a Grayson ship's midshipman's berth I accepted the risk that you might be assigned to a ship whose captain shared Janacek and High Ridge's attitudes. I hoped that it wouldn't work out that way. Unfortunately, it looks like my hopes have been disappointed."

Somehow, without actually moving a muscle, Abigail seemed to stiffen in her chair.

"Officially, the assignments for midshipmen haven't been released yet, but we still have a few contacts within the Royal Navy. Because of that, I know that you've been assigned to the heavy cruiser *Gauntlet*. She's one of the newest *Edward Saganami*-class ships, and her CO is Captain (junior-grade) Michael Oversteegen."

He paused once more, and she frowned.

"I don't believe I'm familiar with the name, High Admiral," she said.

"We don't know as much about him as I wish we did," Matthews admitted. "What we do know is that he's young for his rank, that he's fourth in the line of succession to the Barony of Greater Windcombe, that he was promoted from commander out of the zone after Janacek selected Admiral Draskovic as Fifth Space Lord, that he's a junior-grade captain in what ought to be a captain of the list's command . . . and that his mother is Baron High Ridge's second cousin."

Abigail's nostrils flared, and Matthews grimaced.

"It's entirely possible I'm doing him a disservice, Ms. Hearns. But I'm inclined to doubt it given that pedigree and the preferential treatment he appears to be receiving from the current Admiralty. And if he is Janacek's man, then it's entirely possible that you're going to find yourself even more directly in the crossfire than you otherwise might have."

He sighed and shook his head.

"To be honest, I wish now that I'd gone ahead and insisted that you be assigned to one of our own vessels. No doubt that would have been awkward enough for you, since a crew full of Graysons would never have been able to forget that you're a steadholder's daughter. But at least it would have avoided something like this. And at least I could have been confident that you would have had superiors looking out for you rather than have to worry about superiors who may actually want you to fail. And, for that matter, it might have let you slip into the full rigors of shipboard life in an environment closer to one you'd be comfortable in.

"But what I wish I'd done is beside the point now. Requesting a change at this late date could only make things worse. Which means, Ms. Hearns, that I'm very much afraid that your middy cruise is going to be even more stressful than the norm. I don't like putting you in that position, and I wouldn't if I could see any way to avoid it. Since I can't, all I can do is remind you that you will be the first Grayson-born woman ever sworn into the service of the Sword, and that you wouldn't be, regardless of birth, if you hadn't proven that you deserved to be."

HMS *Hephaestus* wasn't as busy these days.

Everyone knew that, Abigail reflected. The Janacek build-down had slowed the Royal Manticoran Navy's pace everywhere, even here, aboard the RMN's premier orbital shipyard. But if that was the case, it certainly wasn't apparent as she made her way down the space dock gallery to HMS *Gauntlet*'s berth.

At least she'd never suffered from any of the anxiety or discomfort some of her Manticoran classmates at Saganami Island had seemed to experience in artificial environments. A child of Grayson grew up surrounded by environmental hazards which, in their own way, were far more dangerous than those that might have been experienced aboard an orbital habitat. Indeed, Abigail's problems at Saganami had been almost exactly the opposite. She'd been acutely uncomfortable, at first, when she found herself outside on windy days. Those were the sorts of conditions which kicked up atmospheric dust, and Grayson's high concentrations of heavy metals made dusty days dangerous.

Still, there was an enormous degree of difference between conditions here on *Hephaestus* and those which had obtained in Owens House. The swirling mass of bodies crowded far more densely together than would ever have been permitted back home. On the other hand, she conceded, the fact that the family's sections of Owens House had been spacious and uncrowded didn't necessarily mean the servants' quarters had been the same way.

She dodged a counter-grav come-along towing a long train of floating freight canisters. It required some fast footwork; the come-along's driver had strayed out of the inboard-bound tow lane, and she almost didn't see him coming in time. The tether for her counter-grav locker tried to wrap itself around her right ankle as she twisted out of the way, but he didn't slow down or even look back. She supposed it was possible that he'd never noticed her at all, but she couldn't quite keep herself from wondering if he'd seen her perfectly . . . and recognized her Grayson uniform.

Stop that, she scolded herself. *Paranoia is the last thing you need right now!*

She got herself untangled from her baggage, resettled her high-peaked, visored cap on her head, and proceeded along the gallery.

I wonder if I should have reported him? If he really didn't see me, he needs to be jerked up short before he kills someone. And if he did see me, maybe he needs to be jerked up even shorter. But whatever he needs, I don't need to look like I'm whining about how terribly people are treating me.

Her internal debate continued as she made her way through the crowd, but it brought her no closer to an answer before she suddenly found herself at the station end of *Gauntlet*'s boarding tube.

She felt her pace try to slow ever so slightly as the armed Marine sentry noted her approach, but she overrode the temptation sternly. Her heart seemed to flutter in her chest, with a surge of excitement she'd told herself firmly that she wasn't going to feel. After all, it wasn't as if this were the first time she'd reported for duty aboard a starship. There'd been all of those near-space training cruises from the Academy, not to mention the endless hours spent doing things like suit drill, both in simulators and under actual field conditions aboard *Hephaestus* or one of the training ships. This would be no different, she'd told herself.

Unfortunately, she'd lied. Worse, she admitted to herself, she'd known at the time that she was doing it. This was nothing at all like the near-space cruises, and it wouldn't have been even without High Admiral Matthews' personal little briefing.

She drew a deep breath and walked up to the sentry.

The Marine private saluted her, and she returned the formal courtesy with all the crispness her Saganami instructors had drilled into her.

"Midshipwoman Hearns to join the ship's company," she announced, and extended the record chip with her official orders.

"Thank you, Ma'am," the Marine replied, as he accepted the chip and slotted it into his memo board. The board's screen flickered alight, and he studied it for perhaps fifteen seconds, then punched the eject button. He extracted the chip and handed it back to her.

"You've been expected, Ma'am," he informed her.

"The Executive Officer left instructions that you're to come aboard and report to her."

"I see." Abigail kept her tone as expressionless as her face, but something about it must have given away her flicker of trepidation. The sentry's posture never changed, but she thought she saw the faintest hint of a twinkle in his eye.

"If you'll report to the boat bay officer, he'll have someone take care of your locker and get you directed to Commander Watson, Ma'am."

"Thank you, Private . . . Roth," Abigail said, reading his nameplate and making less effort to keep her gratitude out of her voice this time.

"You're welcome, Ma'am." The sentry came briefly back to attention, and Abigail nodded to him and launched herself into the tube's zero-gee.

After the hustle and bustle of *Hephaestus'* crowded galleries, *Gauntlet's* boat bay seemed almost quiet. Not quite, of course. There was always something going on in every boat bay aboard every warship in space, and *Gauntlet's* was no exception. Abigail could see at least two work parties engaged on routine maintenance tasks, and a Marine sergeant's voice sounded with less than dulcet patience as she put a squad through the formal evolutions of an honor guard. Still, there was something soothing about the sudden drop in energy levels and the press of bodies as Abigail landed neatly just outside the painted deck line which indicated where *Gauntlet* officially began and *Hephaestus* officially ended. She'd always wondered why the RMN bothered with that line. The Grayson Navy didn't. In the GSN, the shipboard end of a boarding tube belonged to the ship, and the outboard end of the tube belonged to the space station, which had always struck her as a far more sensible arrangement. But the Star Kingdom's navy had its own traditions, and this was one of them.

A junior-grade lieutenant with the identifying brassard of the boat bay officer of the deck looked at her, and Abigail saluted sharply.

"Permission to come aboard to join the ship's company, Sir!"

The lieutenant returned her salute, then held out a hand, and Abigail surrendered her orders again. The lieutenant spent a few more seconds glancing through them than Private Roth had. Then he popped the chip back out of his board and returned it.

"Permission granted, Ms. Hearns," he told her, and Abigail felt an odd little flutter deep inside as she officially became a part of *Gauntlet*'s crew.

"Thank you, Sir," she said as she slipped the chip back into its folio and put both of them back into her tunic pocket. "The tube sentry informed me that I'm supposed to report to the Executive Officer, Sir," she continued respectfully.

"Yes, you are," the BBOD agreed. He keyed his com and spoke into it. "Chief Posner, our final snotty—" he smiled slightly at Abigail as he used the traditional slang for a midshipman "—has just come aboard. I understand that you've been awaiting her with bated breath?" He listened to something only he could hear over his unobtrusive ear bug and chuckled. "Well, I *thought* that was what you said. At any rate, she's here. I think you'd better come collect her." He listened again, then nodded. "Good," he said, and returned his full attention to Abigail.

"Chief Posner is Lieutenant Commander Abbott's senior noncom, Ms. Hearns," he informed her. "And since Commander Abbott is assistant tac officer, which makes him our OCTO, that means the chief is more or less in charge of our snotties. He'll see to it that you get where you need to be."

"Thank you, Sir," she repeated, and her spirits rose.

She'd been even more braced against disaster than she'd realized in the wake of High Admiral Matthews' warnings, but so far things seemed to be going well.

"Wait over there by Lift Three," the lieutenant told her, and flipped a casual wave at the indicated lift shaft. "Chief Posner will be here to collect you shortly."

"Yes, Sir," Abigail said obediently and towed her locker across to the lifts.

"Welcome aboard, Ms. Hearns."

Commander Linda Watson was a short, solidly built woman with dark hair but startlingly light-colored blue eyes. Abigail guessed that the commander had to be in her late forties or early fifties, although it was sometimes hard for Abigail to estimate the ages of prolong recipients. Graysons hadn't had much practice at that yet.

Watson had a brisk, no-nonsense manner which went well with her solid, well-muscled physique, and her voice was surprisingly deep for a woman. But she also had a pronounced Sphinxian accent, and Abigail felt herself warming to the exec almost instinctively as its crispness flowed over her like an echo of Lady Harrington's accent.

"Thank you, Commander," she replied. She seemed to be thanking a lot of people today, she reflected.

"Don't let it go to your head," Watson advised her dryly. "We always welcome every snotty aboard. That's never stopped us from running them until they drop. And since there are only four of you aboard for this deployment, we'll have a lot more time to keep each of you running."

She paused, but Abigail didn't know her well enough to risk responding to her possible humor.

"All snotties are equal in the eyes of God, Ms. Hearns," Watson went on after a moment. "The reason

I invited you to drop by my office before you report to Snotty Row, however, is that not all snotties really are equal, however hard we try to make them that way. And, to be perfectly honest, you present some special problems. Of course," she smiled a bit wryly, "I suppose every middy presents some special problem in his or her own way."

She folded her arms and leaned a hip back against her desk, cocking her head to one side as she contemplated Abigail.

"To be perfectly honest, I was strongly tempted to just toss you into the deep end. That's always been my rule of thumb in the past, but I've never had a foreign princess as a midshipwoman before."

She paused again, this time obviously inviting a response, and Abigail cleared her throat.

"I'm not precisely a 'foreign princess,' Ma'am," she said.

"Oh, yes, you are, Ms. Hearns," Watson disagreed. "I checked the official position of both the Foreign Office and the Navy. Your father is a head of state in his own right, despite his subordination to the Protector's overriding authority. That makes him a king, or at least a prince, and that makes you a princess."

"I suppose, technically, it does," Abigail admitted. "But that's on Grayson, Ma'am. Not in the Star Kingdom."

"That's a refreshing attitude." Watson's tone added the unspoken rider *"if that's the way you really feel about it,"* but she continued briskly. "Unfortunately, not everyone is going to share it. So I thought I'd just take this opportunity to make certain that you didn't, in fact, expect any special treatment because of your birth. And to point out to you that you may find yourself laboring under some additional burdens if other members of the ship's company decide that getting on your good side could be a . . . career-enhancing maneuver."

The exec was carefully not, Abigail noticed, suggesting that those "other members" might be found among her fellow middies. Nor, she realized a moment later, had Watson suggested that some of *Gauntlet*'s more senior officers might share the same attitude, and she wondered if that was because the commander thought that some of them *would*.

"As long as you don't expect special treatment, and as long as we don't have anyone else trying to extend it to you anyway," Watson continued, "then I don't expect us to have any problems. Which would be a very good thing, Ms. Hearns. I realize you're actually in the Grayson Navy, not the Queen's Navy, but that makes your midshipwoman's cruise no less important to your career. I trust you fully understand that, as well?"

"Yes, Ma'am. I do."

"Good!" Watson smiled briefly, then unfolded her arms and straightened. "In that case, Chief Posner will see to it that you and your gear get safely stowed away in Snotty Row and you can report to Commander Abbott."

" . . . so we told the Chief that no one had told us Engineering was off-limits." Karl Aitschuler grinned and shrugged his shoulders. He sat at the table in the center of "Snotty Row's" commons area, looking, Abigail thought, remarkably like her younger brother had looked at age twelve after putting something over on one of his nannies.

"And he actually *believed* that?" Shobhana Korrami shook her head in disbelief.

Shobhana was the other midshipwoman assigned to *Gauntlet* for this deployment, and Abigail had been delighted to see her. Although she never would have admitted it to anyone, Abigail had been more than a little nervous about the RMN's normal shipboard accommodations, especially for "snotties." Each midshipman or midshipwoman had his or her own private, screened-off sleeping area, but they shared all of their other facilities.

The degree to which male and female students had been thrown together at the Academy had come as a distinct shock to a Grayson girl, especially one of noble birth. Intellectually, though, at least Abigail had known it was coming, which had helped some. Still, she very much doubted she would ever possess the easy acceptance of such proximity which seemed to be part of the cultural baggage of her Manticoran and Erewhonese classmates. And even at its most . . . coeducational, the Academy had offered at least a little more privacy than was going to be possible here. Having at least one other female middy along would have been an enormous relief under any circumstances, but the fact that it was Shobhana made it even more of one. Abigail and the slightly taller, blond-haired, green-eyed Korrami had become close friends during the many extra hours they'd spent together under the tutelage of Senior Chief Madison, the senior Saganami Island unarmed combat instructor.

"Of course he believed it," Karl said virtuously. "After all, who has a more honest and trustworthy face than me?"

"Oh, I don't know," Shobhana replied in thoughtful tones. "Oscar Saint-Just?" she suggested after a moment with artful innocence.

Abigail giggled, then colored as Shobhana looked up at her with a triumphant grin. Shobhana knew how much it embarrassed Abigail whenever she giggled. It wasn't something a steadholder's daughter was supposed to do. Besides, she thought it made her sound like a twelve-year-old herself.

"I'll have you know," the fourth person in the compartment said, "that Oscar Saint-Just looked much more honest and trustworthy than our Aitschuler ever did."

Abigail's temptation to giggle died abruptly. She couldn't quite put her finger on what it was about Arpad Grigovakis' tone, but what should have been another jab of friendly harassment came out with an unpleasant, cutting edge in his well modulated, upperclass Manticoran accent.

Father Church had always taught that God offered good things to offset the bad in any person's life, if she only remained open to recognizing them when they came along. Abigail was willing to take that on faith, but she'd come to suspect that the reverse was also true. And Grigovakis' presence aboard *Gauntlet* as a counterbalance for Shobhana's seemed further evidence that her suspicions were well founded.

Midshipman Grigovakis was tall, well built, so handsome she felt certain biosculpt had played a major part in his regularity of feature, and unreasonably wealthy even by Manticoran standards. He was also an excellent student, judging by his grades and where he'd stood in their final class standings. Which, unfortunately, did not make him a pleasant human being.

"I'm sure that if Saint-Just did look more honest than me," Karl said in a deliberately light tone, "it was purely the result of sophisticated imagery management by Public Information."

"Yeah, *sure* it was," Shobhana agreed, throwing her weight into the effort to keep the banter flowing.

"Do you think it was, Abigail?" Grigovakis asked, flashing improbably perfect teeth at Abigail in a smile which, as always, carried that overtone of patronization.

"I wouldn't know," she said as naturally as she could.

"I'm sure PubIn could have done it, if they'd wanted to. On the other hand, I imagine looking innocent and virtuous would have been almost as much of an advantage for a secret policeman on his way up as for a middy who got caught where he wasn't supposed to be. So maybe it was all natural protective coloration he'd acquired early."

"I hadn't thought of that," Grigovakis said with a chuckle, and gave her a nod that seemed to say *"My, how clever for a little neobarb girl like you!"*

"I thought you probably hadn't," she responded easily, and it was her tone's turn to say *"Because, of course, you weren't smart enough to."* A flicker of anger showed somewhere at the backs of his brown eyes, and she smiled sweetly at him.

"Yeah, well," Karl said in the voice of someone searching diligently for a change of subject, "innocent and virtuous or not, I'm not sure I'm looking forward to dinner tonight!" He shook his head.

"At least you won't have to face the Captain alone," Shobhana pointed out. "You'll have Abigail along. Just do what you always did at Duchess Harrington's dinners."

"Like what?" Karl asked suspiciously.

"Hide behind her," Shobhana said dryly.

"I did not!" Karl swelled with theatrical indignation. "She just happened to be sitting between me and Her Grace!"

"Three different times?" Shobhana asked skeptically.

"You were invited to Harrington House three times?" Grigovakis asked, looking at Aitschuler in obvious surprise leavened by something suspiciously like respect.

"Well, yes," Karl acknowledged with insufferable modesty.

"I'm impressed," Grigovakis admitted, then shrugged.

"Of course, I wasn't in any of her sections, so nobody in my Tactical classes got invited. I hear the food was always good, though."

"Oh, it was a lot better than just *good*," Karl assured him. "In fact, Mistress Thorne, her cook, makes a triple-fudge cake to die for!" He rolled his eyes in the epicurean bliss of memory.

"Yeah, but then she worked your ass off in the simulators," Shobhana told Grigovakis with considerably less relish. "She usually took the Op Force command herself and proceeded to systematically kick our uppity butts."

"I don't doubt it." Grigovakis shook his head with an expression of unusual sincerity. One of the very few points upon which Abigail found herself in agreement with him was his respect for "the Salamander."

"I tried to get into one of her classes when I found out she was going to be teaching at the Island," he added. "I was too late, though." He leaned back in his chair and considered his cabin mates. "So, all three of you had her for Intro to Tactics? I hadn't realized that."

"I almost didn't make it either," Shobhana said. "As a matter of fact, I didn't quite make the initial cut. I was number two on the waiting list, and I only got in because two of the people in front of me had family emergencies that made them miss a semester."

"And how many times did *you* get invited to dinner?" Grigovakis was working his way back to normal, unfortunately, and his tone clearly implied that he didn't expect to hear that Shobhana had ever received an invitation.

"Only twice," Shobhana admitted calmly. "Of course, everyone got invited at least once. To get invited more often than that, you had to earn it, and, frankly, Tactics wasn't my best subject." She smiled sweetly at Grigovakis' expression. Having even a single "earned" invitation to one of Duchess Harrington's dinners on her record was a mark of high distinction for any Tactics student at the Academy.

"But you had three invitations, did you?" he said, turning back to Aitschuler, who nodded. "And Abigail did, too?" That cutting edge of astonishment was back at the mere possibility that Abigail might have achieved such a distinction.

"Oh, no," Karl said, shaking his head sadly, then paused, waiting with perfect timing for the flicker of satisfaction to show in Grigovakis' eyes. "Abigail was invited *ten* times . . . that I know of," he said innocently.

"What *is* his problem?" Shobhana muttered later that ship's evening as she and Abigail shared the shower. It was the midshipwomen's turn to have it first today; tomorrow, it would be their turn to wait while the midshipmen had first dibs.

"Whose?" Abigail worked shampoo into her almost waist length hair. There had been more times than she could count that she'd been tempted to cut it as short as Shobhana wore her own. Indeed, once or twice she'd been tempted to cut it as short as Lady Harrington's hair had been on her first visit to Grayson. Just finding the time to care for and groom it properly had seemed an impossible task more often than not, and its length was scarcely convenient in zero-gee conditions, or under vac helmets, or during phys-ed class. She supposed her inability to actually bring herself to cut it was one of her few unbreakable concessions to the standards of her birth world, where no respectable young woman would ever dream of cutting her hair short.

Now she finished working in the lather and stuck her head under the shower and rinsed vigorously.

"You know perfectly well whose," Shobhana said just a bit crossly. "That asshole Grigovakis, of course! Every once in a while you'd almost swear there was a worth-while human being inside there somewhere. Then he reverts to normal."

"Well," Abigail said a bit damply from inside the cone of spray, "I always figured he just thought he was so much better than anyone else that we were being obtuse and rude not to acknowledge it spontaneously." She withdrew her head from under the shower, slicked her hair back into a thick rope, and began squeezing water out of it. "So since we aren't going to extend proper obeisance to him on our own, it's clearly his duty to extract it from us any way he can, instead."

Shobhana turned under the other showerhead to look at her in surprise, and Abigail bit her tongue. She knew the caustic bite she'd let into her voice had twanged her friend's mental radar.

"I wasn't exactly thinking about *all* of us," Shobhana said after a moment. "I was thinking about the way he seems to have a problem specifically with you. And unless my finely honed instincts are deceiving me, I think maybe *you* have a problem with *him*, too. No?"

"No, I don't—" Abigail began sharply, then stopped.

"You never were a very good liar," Shobhana observed with a slight smile. "Has to do with that strict religious upbringing, I bet. Now, tell Momma Shobhana all about it."

"It's just . . . well—" Abigail found herself suddenly very busy squeezing water out of her hair, then sighed. "He's one of those idiots who think that all Graysons are cave-dwelling barbarian religious fanatics," she said finally. "And he thinks our customs and notions of propriety are ridiculous."

"Oho," Shobhana said softly, regarding Abigail with knowing eyes through the shower's steam. "Came on to you, did he?"

"Well, yes," Abigail admitted. She knew she was

blushing, but she couldn't stop. It wasn't the way Shobhana was looking at her, even given the fact that neither of them had a stitch on at the moment. Women outnumbered men by three to one on Grayson, and for a thousand years, the only really acceptable female career on Abigail's home world had been that of wife and mother. Given the imbalance in births, competition for the available supply of men was often . . . intense. Moreover, Grayson's practice of polygamy meant that any Grayson woman could expect to find herself one of at least two wives, with all of the need for frankness and compromises that implied. All of which meant a Grayson girl grew up accustomed to a degree of explicit "girl talk" which was far more earthy and pragmatic than almost any Manticoran would have believed, given the SKM's view of the Grayson stereotype, just as they grew up accustomed to sharing living quarters and bathing facilities. But that was really part of the problem, wasn't it? She'd grown up accustomed to that sort of openness with other young women, not in a society which had prepared her for overt, direct expressions of masculine interest.

"I'm not surprised," Shobhana said after a moment, head cocked as she considered her friend. "Lord knows if I had your figure, I'd spend all of my time beating men off with a stick! Or, more probably, *not* beating them off," she admitted cheerfully. "And from what I've seen of friend Grigovakis, the fact that you're from Grayson probably added spice to it, didn't it?"

"I thought so, anyway," Abigail agreed with a grimace. "Couldn't wait to get the 'neobarb ice maiden' into bed where he could thaw her out. And probably brag to all of his friends about it, too! Either that, or he's one of the idiots who believes all Grayson women must be sex-starved, crazed nymphos, our frantic lust stayed only by our religious programming, just because our men are so outnumbered."

"You're probably right, given the crowd he hangs out with. Hell, for that matter, I wouldn't be surprised if he was dumb enough to believe both stereotypes at once!" Shobhana made a face. Then she waved a hand over the shower control and reached for a towel as the water stopped.

"Tell me," she went on, "did he take no for an answer?"

"Not very well," Abigail sighed. She closed her eyes and raised her face for one last rinse, then turned off her own shower and grabbed a towel. "Actually," she admitted through its folds as she dried her face, "I probably didn't say no as . . . gracefully as I could have. I'd only been on the Island for about two weeks at the time, and I was still in some pretty severe culture shock." She lowered the towel and grinned wryly at her friend. "The best of you Manties would curl the hair of any properly raised Grayson maiden, you know! As for someone like Grigovakis—!"

She rolled her eyes, and Shobhana chuckled. But the blonde's green eyes were serious.

"He didn't try to push it, did he?"

"On Saganami Island? With a Grayson? A Grayson everyone insisted on assuming was *Lady Harrington's* protégée?" Abigail laughed. "Nobody would be stupid enough to follow that closely in Pavel Young's footsteps, Shobhana!"

"No, I guess not, at that," Shobhana conceded. "But I'll bet he's never missed an opportunity to make your life miserable, has he?"

"Not if he could help it," Abigail admitted. "Fortunately, until we wound up assigned here, our paths didn't cross that often. Personally, I'd have preferred for it to stay that way indefinitely."

"Don't blame you," Shobhana said, picking up a fresh towel and starting to help Abigail dry her hair. "But at least you can look forward to the fact that the two of you will be in different navies after graduation!"

"Believe me, I thank the Intercessor for that regularly," Abigail assured her fervently.

An hour and a half later, Abigail Hearns, who was far more anxious than she strove to appear, found herself, along with Mr. Midshipman Aitschuler, seated at the foot of the large table in the captain's dining cabin of HMS *Gauntlet*. The only really good news, she reflected, was that Karl's class standing was eleven places behind hers. That made *him* the junior officer present, which meant that at least she wouldn't have to offer the loyalty toast. Although, at the moment, that seemed like a remarkably grudging favor on the Tester's part.

She looked surreptitiously around the dining cabin. One thing about growing up as a steadholder's daughter was that a girl learned at a very early age how to be aware of her surroundings at a social gathering without gawking with ill-bred and obvious curiosity, and that training served her well now.

Lieutenant Commander Abbott was the only person present—aside from Karl, of course—whom she felt she knew at all. Not that she knew him very well yet, of course. The sandy-haired Abbott seemed a pleasant enough sort, in a slightly distant fashion, but that might just be the separation he felt an officer candidate training officer had to maintain between himself and his charges. Aside from that, and from a general aura of competence, though, she had very little to go on in forming an opinion of him.

Which was only about a thousand percent more than she had for anyone else at the table.

Commander Tyson, *Gauntlet*'s chief engineering officer, sat to the right of the empty chair awaiting the captain's arrival. He was a solidly built, slightly stumpy man with muddy colored hair and a face that looked as if it had been designed to smile easily. Commander Blumenthal, the ship's senior tactical officer, faced Tyson across the table, and Surgeon Lieutenant Commander Anjelike Westman, the ship's surgeon, sat to Blumenthal's left. The sixth and final person at the table was Lieutenant Commander Valeria Atkins, *Gauntlet*'s red-haired astrogator. Atkins, seated across from Westman, was obviously a third-generation prolong recipient, and she was also an extremely tiny person. In fact, she was one of the few Manticorans Abigail had met who made her feel oversized.

Commander Tyson, as the senior officer present, had made the introductions all around, and the other three had acknowledged Abigail's and Karl's presence politely enough. But the two middies were too astronomically junior to any of them to feel truly comfortable. The dinners they'd shared at Lady Harrington's invitation helped some, but this was definitely a case of better to be seen than to be heard.

Abigail had just answered a question from Lieutenant Commander Atkins which had clearly been intended to help her feel more at ease, when the hatch opened and Captain Oversteegen entered the dining cabin. His juniors rose respectfully as he crossed to his chair at the head of the table, and Abigail found herself intensely grateful for the controlled expression any steadholder's child had to master at an early age.

It was the first time she'd set eyes on *Gauntlet*'s master after God, and her heart plummeted at the sight. Oversteegen was a tall, narrowly built, dark-haired man with limbs which seemed somehow just too long for the rest of his body. He moved with an economic precision, yet the length of his arms and legs made his movements seem oddly out of sync. His uniform, while immaculately neat, had obviously profited from the attentions of a high-priced tailor and displayed half a dozen small touches which were definitely non-regulation. But what caused Abigail's sudden sense of dismay was the fact that her new captain looked exactly like an athletic, fifty-years-younger version of Michael Janvier, Baron High Ridge, Prime Minister of Manticore. Even if High Admiral Matthews hadn't warned her about the captain's family connections, one look would have given them away.

"Be seated, Ladies and Gentlemen," he invited, as he drew his own chair back from the table and sat, and Abigail hid a fresh internal wince. Oversteegen's voice was a light baritone, and it was pleasantly enough modulated, but it also carried the lazy, drawling accent affected by certain strata of the Manticoran aristocracy. And *not*, she thought, the strata which were particularly fond of Graysons.

She obeyed the instruction to sit back down and felt intensely grateful when the captain's personal steward immediately bustled in, followed by two mess attendants, to begin serving dinner. The arrival of food and drink put a temporary hiatus into any table conversation and gave her an opportunity to take her emotions firmly in hand.

There was little enough conversation even after the servers withdrew. Abigail had already gathered from the ship's rumor hotline that aside from Commander Watson, none of Captain Oversteegen's officers had ever served with him before. That might have helped to account for the lack of table talk as his guests tucked into the really excellent dinner. On the other hand, it might just as well represent Oversteegen's own preferences. The captain had been aboard for over two months before *Gauntlet* departed *Hephaestus*, after all, so this could hardly be the first time he'd dined with any of his officers.

Whatever the reason, Abigail was just as happy for it, and she concentrated on being as politely silent as was humanly possible. At one point, she looked up to find Commander Tyson regarding her with a small half-smile, and she blushed, wondering if her efforts to remain seen and yet invisible were that obvious.

But in the end, the meal was finished, the dessert dishes were removed, and the wine was poured. Abigail glanced across the table at Karl, ready to administer a reminding knee kick, but he hardly needed his memory jogged. Obviously, he'd been looking forward to this moment with just as much trepidation as Abigail would have been in his place. But he knew his duty, and as all eyes turned towards him, he picked up his wine, stood, and raised his glass.

"Ladies and Gentlemen, the Queen!" he said clearly.

"The Queen!" came back from around the table in the traditional response, and Karl managed to resume his seat with an aplomb which did a very creditable job of masking the anxiety he must have felt.

His eyes met Abigail's across the table, and she gave him a small smile of congratulation. But then a throat cleared itself at the head of the table, and her head turned automatically towards Captain Oversteegen.

"I understand," that well modulated voice drawled, "that it would be appropriate for us t' offer an additional loyalty toast this evenin'." He smiled at Abigail. "Since it would never do t' insult or ignore the sensibilities of our Grayson allies, Ms. Hearns, would you be so kind as t' do the honors for us?"

Despite all she could do, Abigail felt herself color. The request itself was courteous enough, she supposed, but in that affected accent it took on the overtones of oh-so-civilized contempt for the benighted neobarb among them. Yet there was nothing she could do except obey, and she rose and picked up her own glass.

"Ladies and Gentlemen," she said, her Grayson accent sounding even slower and softer—and more parochial, she supposed—than ever after the captain's polished tones, "I give you Grayson, the Keys, the Sword, and the Tester!"

Only two voices got through the proper response without stumbling: Karl's and Oversteegen's own. Karl was no surprise; he'd heard the exact same phrase at each of the dinners he and Abigail had shared at Lady Harrington's Jason Bay mansion. Nor was it a surprise to her that the other officers around the table had been caught short by the unexpected toast. The fact that the captain got it straight *was* a bit of a surprise. Then again, it would hardly have suited his aura of superiority to have invited the toast and not been able to throw off the correct response with polished ease.

"Thank you, Ms. Hearns," he said in that same, intensely irritating drawl as she sank back into her chair. Then he looked around the other officers at the table. "I trust," he continued, "that the rest of my officers will recognize the need t' be suitably sensitive t' the courtesies due t' our many allies. And t' the desirability of respondin' t' them properly."

Abigail wasn't sure whether it was intended as a reprimand to his senior officers or as yet another way of underscoring the need to pander to the exaggerated sensibilities of those same primitive allies. She knew which one she thought it was, but innate self-honesty made her admit that her own prejudices might explain why she did.

Whichever his intention might have been, his comments produced another brief pause. He let it linger for a moment, then tipped back in his chair, his wine glass loosely clasped in one hand, and smiled at all of them.

"I regret," he told them, "that the press of events and responsibilities involved in preparin' *Gauntlet* for deployment has prevented me from gettin' t' know my officers as well as I might have wished. I intend t' repair some of that failure over the next few weeks. I could have wished for at least a few more days t' spend on exercises and shakin' down the ship's company, but unfortunately, the Admiralty, as usual, had other ideas."

He smiled, and all of them—even Abigail—smiled dutifully back. Then his smile faded.

"As Commander Atkins and the Exec are already aware, *Gauntlet* is headed for the Tiberian System. Are any of you—aside from the Astrogator—familiar with Tiberian?"

"One of the independent systems between Erewhon and the Peeps—I mean the Republic of Haven, I believe, Sir," Commander Blumenthal offered after a moment. Oversteegen arched an eyebrow at him, and the tac officer shrugged. "I don't know much more than that about it, I'm afraid."

"T' be completely honest, Mr. Blumenthal, I'm surprised you know even that much. There's not much there t' attract our attention, after all. And that was especially true durin' the shootin' war." This time his thin smile was downright astringent. "Most of the systems that did draw our attention out that way tended t' be places where the shootin' was goin' on, after all."

One or two people chuckled, and he shrugged.

"Actually, I didn't know anythin' at all about Tiberian until the Admiralty cut our orders. I've done a little research since, however, and I want all our officers t' familiarize themselves with the information available to us. The short version, though, is that we're headin' there t' look into the disappearance of several ships in the general vicinity. Includin'—" his voice hardened slightly "—that of an Erewhonese destroyer."

"A fleet unit, Sir?" Blumenthal's surprise was apparent, and Oversteegen nodded.

"That's correct," he said. "Now, I suppose it's reasonable t' assume, as the Admiralty has and as ONI's analysts agree, that the suspension of hostilities between the Alliance and the Havenites is logically goin' t' lead to a resurgence of the piracy which was so prevalent out Erewhon's way before the war. Certainly, no one in the area was prepared t' take responsibility for making the local lowlifes behave when everyone was busy worryin' about who the Peeps were about t' devour next. The Admiralty consensus, however, is that now that hostilities have ended, the Erewhonese and our other local allies between them have more than enough combat power t' deal with any pirate foolish enough t' set up business in their backyards."

He paused, and Commander Westman frowned.

"Excuse me, Sir," she said in a soft soprano, "but if the Admiralty believes that this is the responsibility of the Erewhonese, why exactly are they sending *us* out here?"

"I'm afraid Admiral Chakrabarti failed t' explain that t' me in any detail, Doctor," Oversteegen replied. "An unintentional oversight upon his part, I'm sure. However, my best guess, given the general tone of our instructions, is that Erewhon is just a bit upset over its perception that we no longer regard it as the center of the entire known universe."

Abigail hid a mental frown behind an attentive expression. The captain, it seemed, was less than overwhelmed with admiration for whoever had drafted his orders. At the same time, both his tone and his choice of words seemed to her to indicate a certain contempt for the Erewhonese, as well. Not surprisingly, she supposed, given his personal and political connections to the High Ridge Government.

"As nearly as I can tell," he continued, "our mission is intended primarily t' hold Erewhon's hand. Logically, there's nothin' much a single heavy cruiser can do that the entire Erewhonese Navy shouldn't be able t' do even better. However, there's been a persistent perception on the part of Erewhon and certain other members of the Alliance—" his eyes cut ever so briefly in Abigail's direction "—that they're no longer valued since the cease-fire. Our mission is t' demonstrate t' Erewhon that we do indeed place great value on our alliance with them by offerin' whatever assistance we can. Although, if I were the Erewhonese, I believe I would probably be somewhat more impressed by the deployment of a destroyer flotilla or at least a division of light cruisers than by that of a single heavy cruiser. We, after all, can be in only one place at one time. And as all of our experience in Silesia should indicate, what's really needed t' suppress piracy is a widespread presence, not individual units, however powerful."

Despite herself, and despite her instinctive dislike for the captain, Abigail found herself in total agreement with him in that regard, at least.

"If I may, Sir," Blumenthal said with a slight frown, "why, precisely, are we focusing on Tiberian?"

"Because in such a large haystack, we might as well start huntin' for the needle *someplace*," Oversteegen said in a poisonously dry tone. "More t' the point, Tiberian is located within the zone where most of these ships seem t' have disappeared. Hard t' be certain, of course, since all anyone really knows is that the ships in question never arrived at their intended destinations."

"That may be, Sir," the tac officer said. "At the same time, with the exception of a few psychopaths like Andre Warnecke, most pirates avoid setting up shop in inhabited systems. Too much chance that the locals will spot them and call in someone else's navy if they don't have the capacity to swat them themselves."

"That's certainly the case under normal circumstances," Oversteegen agreed. "And I'm not sayin' it isn't the case here, either. But there are three special considerations in this instance.

"First, there's the fact that Refuge, Tiberian's single inhabited planet, doesn't have much of a population. Accordin' t' the latest census data available, the entire settled area is concentrated on a single continent in an area somewhat smaller than Ms. Hearns' father's steadin' on Grayson." He nodded in Abigail's direction, and his eyes seemed to gleam with an edge of sardonic humor as she stiffened in her chair.

"The whole population amounts t' less than a hundred thousand," he continued, "and its deep space presence is strictly limited, t' say the least. Frankly, it's not much more likely that pirates would be spotted someplace like Tiberian than they would in a completely uninhabited system. Especially if they showed a modicum of caution.

"Second, one of the ships which seems t' have gone missin' out here was the *Windhover*, a Havenite-registry transport which was headed t' Refuge with another couple of thousand more settlers from the Republic."

"You mean Refuge was settled from the *PRH*, Sir?" Commander Tyson asked.

"Yes, it was," Oversteegen agreed. "It seems that some seventy or eighty T-years ago, there was a religious sect in the People's Republic. They called themselves the

Fellowship of the Elect, and they held to some pretty . . . fundamentalist doctrines."

This time he didn't even glance in Abigail's direction. Which, she reflected fulminatingly, only underscored the way in which he was oh-so-pointedly not saying "like the Church of Humanity Unchained."

"Apparently," the captain continued, "this Fellowship found itself at odds with the old Legislaturalist regime. Inevitably, I suppose, since they insisted on livin' in accordance with their interpretation of the scriptures. It's a bit surprisin' in some ways that InSec didn't squelch them, but I imagine even Public Information would've had trouble with that one, given that the Legislaturalists were always careful t' give lip service t' religious toleration. Oh, I'm sure InSec made itself highly unpleasant t' them, but tight-knit religious groups can be amazin'ly stubborn, sometimes."

Despite herself, Abigail shifted in her chair, but she also bit her lip and made herself show no other sign of the intense irritation that drawling accent sent through her.

"In the end," Oversteegen said, giving no indication that he'd just delivered a deliberate jab to one of his middies, "the Legislaturalists decided they'd be better off without the Fellowship, so they made a deal. In return for the nationalization of the Fellowship's members' assets, the People's Republic provided them with transportation t' Tiberian and the basic infrastructure t' set up a colony on Refuge." He shrugged. "There were no more than twenty or thirty thousand of them, and whatever their religious beliefs might have been, they'd done a better job than most of stayin' off the BLS, so the Legislaturalists actually showed a small net profit on gettin' rid of them. But not all of them accepted the offer, and a significant number remained behind . . . where," he added in a considerably grimmer tone, "StateSec proved less tolerant than InSec had.

"By the time Saint-Just was overthrown, there were only a few thousand of them left, and they were understandably bitter about the way they'd been treated. So when the Pritchart administration took office, they announced their intention t' join their coreligionists on Refuge. T' do her justice, Pritchart not only accepted their desire but provided state funds t' charter a ship to deliver them, and they departed for Tiberian just over one T-year ago.

"Unfortunately, they never arrived. Which would seem to suggest that although Tiberian is well over t' the side of the area in which most of the disappearances have occurred, it's apparently attracted the pirates' attention for *some* reason.

"Which brings us t' the third special consideration which applies t' Tiberian. When the Erewhonese launched their own investigation, they attempted to backtrack the courses of the ships they knew hadn't reached their final destinations in order t' determine how far each of those ships *had* gotten. The idea was t' more precisely plot the zone in which the vessels were actually disappearin'. One of the ships engaged in that effort was the destroyer *Star Warrior*, who was assigned, among other things, t' track the missing personnel transport with the Fellowship emigrés aboard. She started her investigation at Tiberian itself, where the Refugians confirmed that the *Windhover* had never arrived. After checkin' with the planetary authorities— which appears not t' have gone without a certain amount of friction—she departed for the Congo System, where another of the missin' merchies was headed.

"She never arrived. Now, *Star Warrior* was a modern ship, with first-line sensors and the same basic weapons fit as our own *Culverin* class. It would take a pretty unusual 'pirate' t' match up successfully against that. At the same time, I find it unlikely that an Erewhonese destroyer would be lost t' simple hazards of navigation."

"I would, too, Sir," Commander Blumenthal said after a moment. "At the same time, though, a rather ugly thought occurs to me about where a 'pretty unusual pirate' might have come from these days. Especially this close to Haven."

"The same thought has occurred t' Erewhon, and even t' ONI," Oversteegen said dryly. "Erewhon believes that some of the StateSec and PN warships that have been dropping out of sight as Theisman puts down the opposition t' Pritchart have obviously set up as independent pirates out this way. ONI is less convinced of that, since its analysts believe any such rogue units would get as far away from Theisman as they could. Besides, ONI feels that anyone who wants t' pursue a piratical career would naturally migrate t' Silesia rather than operate in an area as well policed as the one between Erewhon and Haven is rapidly becomin'."

"I'd have to say, Sir," Lieutenant Commander Atkins put in diffidently, "that if I were a pirate, I'd certainly prefer operations in Silesia, myself. Whatever else may be the case in this region, most of the system governments and governors are relatively honest. At least where something like conniving with pirates is concerned. And ONI has a point about how nasty things could turn for any pirate who pisses off someone like the Erewhonese Navy!"

"I didn't say ONI's analysis wasn't logical, Commander," Oversteegen drawled mildly. "And if *I* were a pirate, my thinkin' would be just about like your own. But it's probably worth bearin' in mind that not everyone in the universe is as logical as you and I. Or as smart, for that matter."

"God knows there are enough pirates already

operating in Silesia who don't have the brains to close the airlock's outboard hatch first," Commander Tyson agreed with a grimace. "And if these are some of StateSec's ex-bully boys, brainpower probably isn't exactly at a premium in their senior ranks!"

"That's certainly true enough," Commander Blumenthal put in. He leaned forward slightly, his expression intent, and Abigail was forced to concede that however arrogant and supercilious Oversteegen might be, he was at least managing to engage his senior officers' attention. "On the other hand," the tac officer continued, "apparently whoever these people are—assuming they're really here in the first place, of course—they've so far managed to keep the Erewhonese Navy from getting even a single confirmed sensor hit on them."

He looked a question at Oversteegen as he finished his last sentence, and the captain nodded.

"So far, we're lookin' for ghosts," he confirmed.

Abigail wished she were senior enough to contribute to the discussion herself without direct invitation. She wasn't, but a moment later Lieutenant Commander Westman made the point she herself had wanted to make.

"There's another thing about this entire situation that concerns me, Captain," *Gauntlet*'s surgeon put in quietly. Oversteegen crooked the fingers of his right hand, inviting her to continue, and Westman shrugged.

"I've deployed to Silesia three times," she said, "and most of the pirates out there hesitate to hit personnel transports. The kind of casualties that can cause is enough to get even Silesian System governors mobilized to go after them. But when they do hit a transport, they're very careful to minimize casualties and settle for collecting ransom from the passengers and then letting them continue on their way. Some of them even seem to enjoy playing the part of 'gentle-men buccaneers' when it happens. From what you're saying in this case, though, if there are pirates oper-ating out here, they just went ahead and slaughtered several thousand people aboard that transport headed for Tiberian, alone."

"That's my own view of what probably happened," Oversteegen agreed, and for once his voice was cold and grim, despite that maddening accent. "It's been over thirteen T-months since *Windhover* disappeared. If any of those people were still alive, they probably would have turned up somewhere by now. If nothing else, they'd be worth more t' any pirate as a poten-tial source of ransom from their relatives or the Refugian government than they would as any sort of forced labor force."

"So whoever these people are," Atkins mused aloud, "they're ruthless as hell."

"I think that's probably somethin' of an understate-ment," Oversteegen told her, and his drawling accent was back to normal.

"I can see that, Sir," Commander Tyson said. "But I'm still not entirely clear on exactly why we're headed for Tiberian." Oversteegen cocked his head at him, and the engineer shrugged. "We know that *Star Warrior* already checked Tiberian without finding anything," he pointed out respectfully. "Doesn't that indicate Tiberian has a clean bill of health? And if that's the case, then wouldn't our time be better spent looking someplace that *hasn't* been cleared?"

Abigail held her mental breath, waiting to see if Oversteegen would annihilate Tyson for his temerity, but the captain surprised her. He only gazed at the engineer mildly for a moment, then nodded.

"I see your point, Mr. Tyson," he acknowledged. "On the other hand, the Erewhonese are operatin' on exactly that theory. Their naval units are continuin' t' concentrate on the systems which haven't yet been checked out. Now that they've backtracked all of the shippin' movements as far as they can, they've moved their focus t' a case-by-case examination of the uninhabited systems out here where a batch of pirates might have set up a depot ship.

"It's goin' t' take them months to do more than scratch the surface, of course, and no doubt we could make ourselves useful helpin' out in that effort. But the way I see it, they've got enough destroyers and cruisers t' handle that job without us, and anything we can offer in that regard would be relatively insignificant in the long run.

"So it seems t' me that *Gauntlet* would be better employed pursuin' an independent, complementary investigation. The one Erewhonese warship that has been lost since Erewhon began investigatin' these shippin' losses is *Star Warrior*. And the last star system we know *Star Warrior* visited is Tiberian. Now, I'm aware that the Erewhonese have already revisited Tiberian and spoken to the Refugians again. But one thing ONI was able to provide me with was a recordin' of those interviews, and my distinct impression was that the Refugians were less than delighted t' cooperate."

"You think they were hiding something, Sir?" Blumenthal asked, frowning. He toyed with his dessert fork for a moment. "I suppose that if the pirates *did* contact them and offer to ransom the transport's passengers, one of the conditions might be that the Refugians keep their mouths shut about it afterwards."

"That's one possibility," Oversteegen acknowledged. "However, I wasn't thinkin' about anythin' quite that Byzantine, Guns."

"Then why would they hesitate to cooperate in anything that might catch the people responsible for the disappearance and probable murder of their colonists, Sir?" Atkins asked.

"This is a small, isolated, intensely clannish colony," the captain replied. "It has virtually no contact with outsiders—before the war, a single tramp freighter made Refuge orbit once a T-year; once the war started, no one visited them at all until after the cease-fire went into effect. And the system was settled by refugees who deliberately sought an isolated spot where they could set up their own society without any outside contamination. A *religious* society that specifically rejected contact with nonbelievers."

Once again, his eyes seemed to flick ever so briefly in Abigail's direction. This time, though, she couldn't be certain it wasn't her own imagination. Not that she was much inclined to bend over backward giving him the benefit of the doubt, because it was obvious to her what was going on behind his relaxed expression.

He might as well have me wearing a holo sign that says "Descendent of Religious Lunatics!" she thought resentfully.

"My point," he went on, apparently blissfully unaware of—or, at least, completely unconcerned by— his midshipwoman's blistering resentment, "is that the Refugians don't *like* outsiders. And that outsiders, like the Erewhonese, may not make sufficient allowance for that when they try t' talk to them. It certainly appears to me that the Erewhonese who interviewed the planetary authorities after *Star Warrior's* disappearance didn't, at any rate. It's obvious the locals got their backs up. It may even have started when *Star Warrior* dropped in on them in the first place.

"But if *Star Warrior* disappeared because she discovered somethin' that led her t' the pirates and the pirates destroyed her, then Tiberian is the only place she could have done it. The system was her first port of call, and so far as we can determine, she never made it t' her *second* port of call at all. So if there is an actual chain of events, not just some fluke coincidence, between *Star Warrior's* investigation and her disappearance, Tiberian is the only place we can hope t' find out whatever she did.

"If I'm right, and the Fellowship of the Elect just didn't want t' talk t' a secular bunch of outsiders who failed t' show proper respect for their own religious beliefs, then clearly the thing t' do is t' go try talkin' t' them again. It's entirely possible that no one on the planet realizes the significance of some apparently minor piece of information they gave *Star Warrior* which might have led her t' the pirates. If there was somethin' like that, then clearly, we have t' find out what it was. And the only way t' do that is t' get them t' open up t' us. And for that—" he turned his head, and this time there was no question at all who he was looking at, Abigail thought "—we need someone who speaks their language."

"Hard skew port! Come t' one-two-zero by zero-one-five and increase t' five-two-zero gravities! Tactical, deploy a Lima-Foxtrot decoy on our previous headin'!"

The thing Abigail hated most about Captain Michael Oversteegen, she decided as she manned her station in Auxiliary Control with Lieutenant Commander Abbott, and listened to the steady, rapid-fire orders from the command deck, was the fact that he actually seemed to be a competent person.

Her life would have been so much simpler if she'd been able to just write him off as one more under-brained, over-bred, aristocratic jackass who'd gotten his present command through the pure abuse of nepotism. It would have made his infuriating accent, his too-perfect uniforms, his maddening mannerisms, and permanent air of supercilious detachment from the lesser mortals around him so much easier to bear if he'd just completed the stereotype by being a total incompetent, as well.

Unfortunately, she'd been forced to concede that although it was obvious that nepotism did explain how a captain as junior as he was had snagged a plum command like *Gauntlet* in this era of reducing ship strengths, he was *not* incompetent. That had become painfully evident as he put his ship through a series of intensive drills in every conceivable evolution during the voyage to Tiberian. And given that Tiberian lay just over three hundred light-years from Manticore, with a transit time of almost forty-seven T-days, he'd had a lot of time for drills.

She was being foolish, she told herself sternly, her eyes obediently upon the tactical repeater plot while the current exercise unfolded, but she knew she would have felt a certain spiteful satisfaction if she could have assigned him to what Lady Harrington called the "Manticoran Invincibility School." But unlike those complacent idiots, Oversteegen obviously held to the older Manticoran tradition that no crew could possibly be too highly trained, whether in peacetime or time of war.

The fact that he had an obvious talent for cunning, one might even say devious, tactical maneuvers only made it perversely worse. Abigail had found a great deal to admire in the captain's tactical repertoire, and she knew Commander Blumenthal had found the same. Lieutenant Commander Abbott, on the other hand, clearly wasn't one of the captain's warmer admirers. He was far too good an officer to ever say so, especially in the hearing of a mere midshipwoman, but it seemed apparent to Abigail that her OCTO resented the accident of birth which had given Oversteegen command of *Gauntlet*. The fact that Abbott was at least five T-years older than the captain yet two full grades junior to him undoubtedly had more than a little to do with that. But whatever his feelings might be, no one could have faulted the assistant tactical officer's on-duty demeanor or his attention to detail.

There was an undeniable trace of stiffness and formality in his relationship with the captain, but that was true for quite a few members of *Gauntlet*'s ship's company. After the first week or so, no one aboard was prepared to question Captain Oversteegen's competence or ability, but that didn't mean his crew was prepared to clasp him warmly to its collective heart. The fact was that whatever other talents he might possess, he did not and probably never would have the sort of charisma someone like Lady Harrington seemed to radiate so effortlessly.

Probably, Abigail had concluded, that was at least partly because he had no particular interest in acquiring that sort of charisma. After all, the natural order of the universe had inevitably raised him to his present station. His undoubted competence was simply proof that the universe had been wise to do so. And since it was both natural and inevitable that he command, then it was equally natural and inevitable that others obey. Which meant there was no particular point in enticing them into doing what was their natural duty in the first place.

In short, Michael Oversteegen's personality was not one which naturally attracted the devotion of those under his command. Competence they would grant him, and obedience they would yield. But not devotion.

Arpad Grigovakis, on the other hand, seemed prepared to worship the deck he walked on. Abigail couldn't be positive why that was, but she had her suspicions. Grigovakis, after all, would never be described as a sweetheart of a guy himself. Although he was nowhere near so wellborn as the captain, he definitely belonged to the upper strata of Manticoran society, and he not so secretly aspired to precisely the same image of aristocratic power and privilege. In fact, Abigail thought, Grigovakis probably found Oversteegen a much more comfortable role model than someone like Lady Harrington, no matter how much he might recognize and respect the Steadholder's tactical brilliance.

In Captain Oversteegen's defense, Abigail had to admit that she'd never seen him lend the least encouragement to Grigovakis' apparent desire to emulate his own style. Of course, he hadn't *dis*couraged the midshipman, either, but that would have been expecting a bit much out of any captain.

"Bogey Two's taking the bait and going for the decoy, Sir!" That was Shobhana's voice, and she sounded calmer than Abigail suspected she was. Oversteegen had decided to make Commander Blumenthal a casualty fifteen minutes into the present exercise, and it was Shobhana's day to serve as Blumenthal's assistant, while Abigail played understudy to Abbott on Commander Watson's backup tactical crew. Which meant, Abigail thought just a bit jealously, that at the moment her classmate was in control of a 425,000-ton heavy cruiser's total armament, even if it was only for an exercise . . . and Abigail wasn't.

"Very good, Tactical," Oversteegen replied coolly. "But keep an eye on Number One."

"Aye, aye, Sir!" Shobhana replied crisply, and Abigail felt herself nodding in silent agreement with the captain's warning. The exercise was one of several simulations downloaded by BuTrain to *Gauntlet's* tactical computers before her departure from Manticore.

In theory at least, no one aboard the heavy cruiser had any advance knowledge of their content or the opposition forces' order of battle. Every so often, someone found a way around the security measures and hacked into the sims in an effort to make herself look better, but Abigail was confident that Oversteegen wasn't one of them. The mere suggestion that he might have required such an unfair advantage would be anathema to a personality like his.

Or mine, she admitted, *if not for exactly the same reasons*.

Sure enough, Bogey One was ignoring the decoy. CIC had identified Bogey Two as a heavy cruiser and Bogey One as a battlecruiser. That meant Bogey One should have better sensors, and in addition, she had a better angle on *Gauntlet*. She'd been better placed to spot the decoy's separation, but apparently the simulation's artificial intelligence had assumed that Bogey One wasn't positive of her own conclusions. She was allowing her consort to continue to engage the decoy just in case while she herself went after what she'd identified as the real enemy.

"All right, Tactical," Oversteegen said calmly. "Bogey One is comin' in after us. It's not goin' t' take Two long t' kill the decoy, even with its EW. So we need t' prune One down t' size a bit while we've got her all t' ourselves. Understood?"

That was much more of an explanation than Oversteegen usually bothered with. He was actually making a concession to the inexperience of his acting tactical officer, Abigail thought in some surprise.

"Understood, Sir," Shobhana replied.

"Very well, then. Give me a recommendation."

Shobhana didn't reply instantly, and Abigail felt herself lean forward in her own chair, urging her friend on.

"Recommend we change heading to starboard in six minutes, Sir," Shobhana said, almost as if she'd heard Abigail's encouragement.

"Reasons?" Oversteegen asked sharply.

"Sir, Bogey One will have closed into extreme energy range in approximately five-point-seven-five minutes, but she's still coming straight for us. I think she's convinced we're just going to go on running rather than turn and fight against such odds. I think she'll hold her course, trying to bring her own chasers into action, but according to CIC she's a *Warlord-C*, without bow wall technology. So if we time it properly, we might be able to put an entire energy broadside right down her throat even at extreme range."

There was a moment of taut silence. Then Oversteegen spoke again.

"Concur," he said simply. "Make it so, Tactical." He paused again, then added, "And call the shot."

"Aye, aye, Sir!" Shobhana replied exultantly, and Abigail's eyebrows arched in astonishment. That was the sort of order Lady Harrington might have given under similar circumstances, but she would never have expected to hear it out of Oversteegen.

She watched the crimson bead of Bogey One charging hard after *Gauntlet*, just as Shobhana had predicted. If Abigail had been in command of that battlecruiser, no doubt she would have been doing exactly the same thing. An *Edward Saganami*-class ship like *Gauntlet* was a powerful, modern unit, but scarcely a match for a *Warlord*-class battlecruiser in close action. The logical course for any ship as heavily overmatched as *Gauntlet* was in this instance was to run as fast and as hard as she could in the hopes that she might score a lucky missile hit on one of her pursuers' impeller nodes and somehow escape action.

The only problem was that *Gauntlet* had been surprised in a situation which gave the bogeys too much overtake advantage for even the newest generation of Manticoran inertial compensator to overcome. Which meant that escape was virtually impossible, whatever the heavy cruiser did. And Shobhana was right; if they couldn't outrun Bogey One, then their best choice was the bold choice.

Bogey One swept closer and closer, battering away at *Gauntlet* with her chase armament. Fortunately, the Peeps—no, she corrected herself, the *Havenites*—didn't have the equivalent of Ghost Rider. That meant they couldn't fire the same sort of effective off-bore missile broadsides a Manticoran or a Grayson ship might have. Bogey One was restricted effectively to the fire of her bow tubes and energy mounts, which meant her missile fire was far too light to penetrate *Gauntlet's* active and passive defenses, whereas *Gauntlet* was able to reply with a steady rain of fire from her broadside tubes. It wasn't as effective as it would have been if she'd had a proper broadside firing arc that let her use her main fire control. Even with Ghost Rider technology, she lacked the telemetry channels without a broadside arc to provide full-time control to more than eighteen birds at a time. She could share her available links on a rotating basis, but that could be risky in a high-EW environment, and it always led to at least some degradation in control. For that matter, not even a missile with Manticoran EW had much chance of survival at this range against the sort of defensive firepower an alert battlecruiser's forward point defense could pour out. But even though only a handful of them were getting through, they were enough to pepper the *Warlord* with what had to be an infuriating rain of superficial hits.

Of course, if Shobhana's maneuver failed and Bogey

One managed to get broadside-to-broadside with *Gauntlet* . . .

"Helm, come starboard nine-five degrees, roll one-five degrees to port, and pitch up four-zero degrees on my mark," Shobhana said.

"Starboard nine-five, roll one-five to port, and pitch up four-zero, aye, Ma'am!" the helmswoman responded crisply, and Abigail held her breath as another double handful of seconds trickled past. Then—

"*Execute!*" Shobhana snapped, and HMS *Gauntlet* snapped up and around to starboard even as she rolled to present her broadside to her huge, charging opponent.

It was the universe's turn to hold its breath, but the sim's AI decided that *Gauntlet*'s unanticipated maneuver had completely surprised Bogey One's hypothetical flesh-and-blood captain. The battlecruiser held her course, her chase armament continuing to hammer away at where she'd thought *Gauntlet* was going to be, even as the Manticoran cruiser swerved and rolled.

And then *Gauntlet*'s broadside grasers swung onto target and fired.

The range was still long, and the armor protecting a battlecruiser's forward hammerhead was thick. But there was no bow wall, the range wasn't long enough, and the armor was too thin to withstand the sledge-hammers of energy Shobhana Korrami sent crashing into it. It shattered, and the grasers ripped into the ship it had been supposed to protect. The range *was* too great for the grasers to completely disembowel a ship as big and tough as a *Warlord*, but they could do damage enough. The torrent of destruction smashed the battlecruiser's chase armament into wreckage, and the big ship's wedge fluctuated madly as her forward impeller ring was blown apart.

The savagely wounded ship swung sharply to port,

snatching her mangled bows away from her impudent opponent and bringing her own starboard broadside to bear. But Shobhana's helm orders had already sent *Gauntlet* streaking back onto her original course, and the Manticoran cruiser went bounding ahead under maximum military power at almost six hundred gravities. Wounding a kodiak max badly enough to run away from it was one thing; standing still to let it rip you apart *after* wounding it was quite another.

A tornado of missiles came crashing after *Gauntlet* from Bogey One's undamaged broadside, and Bogey Two—no longer in any doubt as to which was decoy and which was actual cruiser—charged after her, as well. Damage sidebars flickered as a handful of hits from the enemy's laser head missiles punched through *Gauntlet's* sidewalls, but her active defenses were too good and her passive defenses just good enough to fend off the tide of destruction while she pulled steadily away from the lamed battlecruiser.

Bogey Two continued the pursuit for another ten minutes, but she was no match for *Gauntlet* without the *Warlord's* support, and her skipper—or, at least, the sim's artificial intelligence—knew it. The enemy cruiser had no intention of finding herself all alone in energy range of a ship which had just crippled a *battle*cruiser, and she broke off before *Gauntlet* could lure her out from under the *Warlord's* missile umbrella.

"Well, that was certainly an interestin' . . . adventure," Captain Oversteegen remarked. "All hands, secure from simulation. Division officers, we'll convene in my briefin' room for the post-simulation critique at zero-nine-hundred." He paused for a moment, then surprised Abigail once again with something which would have sounded suspiciously like a chuckle from anyone else. "Commander Blumenthal, you may consider yourself excused from the debrief, in light of your many and serious wounds. I believe that Actin' Tactical Officer Korrami can take your place today."

Abigail didn't actually see Lieutenant Stevenson's hand coming. In fact, she couldn't have analyzed exactly what it was she did see. It might have been a slight shift in the Marine's weight, or perhaps it was the way his shoulder dipped ever so slightly, or it might even been nothing more than a flicker of his eyes. Whatever it was, her own right arm moved without any conscious thought on her part. Her forearm intercepted the left hand slicing towards her head and parried his arm wide to the outside, her own left hand shot out and upwards in a palm thrust to his chin, and her torso pivoted as she twisted in a circle to her left.

The lieutenant's head snapped back as her palm impacted on his jaw, but his right arm looped up and around, and his hand snaked back down on the inside of her left elbow. His fingers closed on her upper arm, his own arm straightened, binding hers, and he shifted his weight to the outside, even as his right ankle hooked into the back of her left calf.

Abigail's feet went out from under her, and the lieutenant's considerably greater weight yanked her sideways. She managed to break his grip on her arm, but not in time to keep herself from going down hard. She hit the mat on her left shoulder and rolled quickly, just managing to avoid Stevenson as he dropped, arms outspread, to pin her. He'd misjudged her speed, and he landed hard on his belly as she spun sideways, pivoting on her buttocks, and her scything legs slashed his arms from under him.

She rolled onto her side, snapping her torso backward, and her elbow slammed hard into the back of his head. The protective headgear they both wore shielded him from the full force of the blow, but it was still enough to knock him ever so briefly off stride, and Abigail used the opportunity to continue her roll. She twisted, supple as a serpent, and landed on his back. Both hands flashed, darting up and under his armpits from behind, and he grunted as they met on the back of his neck. She exerted pressure—not very much; the hold she'd secured was dangerous—but enough for him to recognize the full-Nelson.

His right palm slapped the mat in token of surrender, and she released her hold, rolled off of him, and sat up. He followed suit, and shook his head, then removed his mouth protector and grinned at her.

"Better," he said approvingly. "Definitely better that time. If I didn't know better, I'd have thought you were really trying to hurt me!"

"Thank you . . . I think, Sir," she said after removing her own mouth protector. Actually, she wasn't entirely certain how to take his last remark. Despite her natural athleticism, hand-to-hand combat had been the hardest course for her to master at Saganami Island. She'd enjoyed the training katas, and the way in which the training had sharpened her reflexes and coordination. But she'd had problems—serious ones—when it was time for her to apply her lessons.

The reason hadn't been difficult for her to figure out; it was *fixing* it that had been hard.

Grayson girls were reared in a culture in which actual physical confrontations were unthinkable. Unlike boys (who everyone knew were rambunctious, obstreperous, and generally ill behaved), well brought up girls simply didn't *do* things like that. Grayson girls and women were to be protected by those same obstreperous boys and men, not to demean themselves by engaging in anything so crude as fisticuffs!

It was a cultural imperative which had been societized into Graysons for the better part of a thousand T-years, and Abigail had been aware of it—in an intellectual sort of way—long before she reported to Saganami Island. She'd also thought that she'd prepared herself to overcome it. Unfortunately, she'd been wrong. Despite her determination to wear down her father's resistance to her decision to pursue a naval career, she was still a product of her home world. She didn't mind the sweat, the exercise, the bruises, or even the indignity of being dumped on her highly aristocratic posterior in front of dozens of watching eyes. But the thought of actually, deliberately *attacking* someone else with her bare hands, even in a training situation, had been something else entirely. And to her chagrin and humiliation, her hesitation had been even more pronounced against male sparring partners.

She'd *hated* it. Her scores had been abysmal, which had been bad enough, but she wanted to be a naval officer. It was all she'd ever wanted, from the night she'd stood on a balcony of Owens House, staring at a night sky, and watched pinpricks of nuclear fire flash among the stars while a single, foreign warship commanded by a *woman* fought desperately against another ship twice its size in defense of her planet. She'd known what she wanted, fought for it with unyielding determination, and finally won not simply her father's grudging permission but his active support.

And now that it was actually within her grasp, she couldn't overcome her social programming well enough to make herself "hit" someone even as a training exercise? It was ridiculous! Worse, it seemed to confirm every doubt every Grayson male had ever raised about the concept of women in the military. And, she'd been humiliatingly certain, it had done precisely the same thing for all of the Manticorans who believed Graysons were hopelessly, laughably benighted barbarians.

But worst of all, it had made her doubt *herself*. If she couldn't do *this*, then how could she ever hope to exercise tactical command in a real battle? How could she trust herself to be able to give the order to fire—to go all out, knowing her own people's lives depended upon her ability to not simply hurt but *kill* someone else's people—if she couldn't even make herself throw a sparring partner in the training salle?

She'd known she needed help, and a part of her had been desperately tempted to seek it from Lady Harrington. The Steadholder had made it quite clear to all of the Grayson middies that she was prepared to stand mentor and adviser to them all, and surely she, of all people, was uniquely qualified to advise anyone where the martial arts were concerned. But this was one problem Abigail had been unable to take to Lady Harrington. She'd never doubted for a moment that Lady Harrington would have understood and worked with her to solve it, but she couldn't bring herself to admit to "the Salamander" that she had it in the first place. It was impossible for her to tell the woman who had fought off the attempted assassination of the Protector's entire family with her bare hands and killed Steadholder Burdette in single combat on live, planet-wide HD, that she couldn't even make herself punch someone in the nose!

Fortunately, Senior Chief Madison had recognized the problem, even if he hadn't immediately grasped the reasons for it. Looking back, she supposed it was inevitable that someone who'd spent so many years teaching so many middies had seen almost every problem by now. But she suspected she'd been an unusually severe case, and he'd finally solved it by finding her a mentor closer to her own age.

Which was how she and Shobhana had come to become friends. Unlike Abigail, Shobhana had grown up with one older and three younger brothers. She'd also grown up on Manticore, and she'd had no compunctions at all about punching any one of them in the nose. She wasn't anywhere near as athletic as Abigail, and mastering the *techniques* of the Academy's preferred *coup de vitesse* had been much more difficult for her, but there'd never been anything wrong with Shobhana's *attitude* towards diving right in and bouncing someone around the salle!

The two of them had spent more additional hours than Abigail cared to recall working out under Senior Chief Madison's critical eye. Shobhana insisted it had been a fair exchange, that she'd gained at least as much in terms of proficiency and skill as she'd been able to give Abigail in terms of attitude, but Abigail disagreed. Her training scores had gone up dramatically, and she still treasured the memory of the first time she'd taken down a male classmate in just three moves in front of her entire class.

But even now, the ghost of her initial self-doubt lingered. She'd overcome her hesitance to tackle friendly opponents in a training environment, but would she be able to do the same thing in real-world conditions if she had to? And if she couldn't—if she hesitated when it was for real, when others depended upon her—what business did she have in the uniform of the Sword?

Fortunately, Lieutenant Stevenson was unaware of her self-doubt. He'd approached her as a sparring partner on the basis of her raw scores from Senior Chief Madison, and she'd accepted with every outward sign of enthusiasm. That accursed hesitancy had reared its ugly head once more, and he'd twitted her gently about it for the first couple of sparring sessions. But she was getting on top of it again, and this time she intended to stay there.

"I especially liked that variant on the Falling Hammer," he told her now, rubbing the back of his protective helmet. "Unfortunately, I don't think I'm limber enough to twist through it that way. Certainly not straight out of a sitting leg sweep like that!"

"It's not that hard, Sir," she assured him with a smile. "Senior Chief Madison showed me that one one afternoon when I started getting a little uppity. The trick is getting the right shoulder back and up simultaneously."

"Show me," Stevenson requested. "But this time, let's take it slow enough that we don't rattle my brain around inside my skull!"

"So how did Ms. Hearns' sparring session go this afternoon?" Lieutenant Commander Abbott asked.

"Looked like it went pretty well, actually, Sir," Senior Chief Posner replied with a slight chuckle. "Of course, *coup de vitesse* isn't really my cup of tea, y'know, Commander. But it looked to me like the Lieutenant thought he was going to take her down fast, only it didn't quite work out that way."

"I take it she's gotten over that shyness of hers, then?"

"I don't know if 'shyness' was ever really the right word for it, Sir. But whatever it was, yeah, she seems to be over it. In spades, actually! Seems like asking Lieutenant Stevenson to work with her was one of your better ideas."

"Her training file suggested that could be an ongoing problem area," Abbott said with a shrug. "It seemed like a good idea to get her back up on the horse with someone outside her Academy classes, and the Lieutenant is pretty sensitive and flexible . . . for a Marine."

"Well, Sir, I think he's gotten her out of whatever her shell was," the petty officer agreed with another chuckle. Then he grimaced slightly. "But now that we're more or less on top of that one, have you had any more thoughts about our Mr. Grigovakis?"

It was Abbott's turn to grimace. A good OCTO aboard any warship was half teacher, half taskmaster, half mentor, and half disciplinarian for the midshipmen committed to his care. Which came to quite a few halves. He doubted that any midshipman ever really appreciated the fact that an officer candidate training officer who did his job properly wound up running almost as hard and as fast as his snotties did. Which was one reason a *smart* OCTO depended heavily on his senior noncommissioned assistant when it came to managing his charges.

"I wish I knew," the lieutenant commander admitted after a moment.

"If I had my druthers," Posner said a bit sourly, "I'd arrange for *him* to spar with Ms. Hearns, Sir. I realize he's a pain in the ass to everyone, but he seems to have a special problem with Graysons. And nasty as he's been to her when he thinks no one's looking, she might just take the opportunity to trim him down to size. Painfully."

"Don't tempt me, Senior Chief!" Abbott chuckled. "It would be sort of fun, though, wouldn't it?" he went on wistfully after a moment. "I'll bet we could sell tickets."

"Sir, I don't believe you could get anyone to bet against you on that one."

"Probably not," Abbott conceded. "But we do have to figure out some way to show him the error of his ways."

"Could always call him in for a counseling session, Sir," Posner pointed out.

"I could. And I guess if it keeps up, I may have to. But I'd really rather find a way for him to figure it out for himself. I can always hammer him for it, but if he only acts like a human being because someone orders him to, it's not going to stick." Abbott shook his head.

"Sir, I agree that it's better to show a snotty the error of his ways than to just lecture him about it. But with all due respect, Mr. Grigovakis has the makings of a genuine pain in the ass as an ensign if someone doesn't straighten him out pretty quick."

"I know. I know." Abbott sighed. "But at least it looks like he's the only problem child we still have. And however . . . unpleasant a personality he may have, at least he's got the makings of a *competent* pain-in-the-ass ensign."

"If you say so, Sir," Posner said, with that edge of respectful doubt which was the privilege of the Navy's senior noncoms.

Abbott gazed at him out of the corner of one eye and wondered what the senior chief's opinion of *Gauntlet*'s commanding officer might be. It was a question the lieutenant commander could never ask, of course, much as he might like to. And to be fair, which Abbott sometimes found it difficult to be in Captain Oversteegen's case, the CO didn't seem to take malicious enjoyment in deliberately planting barbed comments under the skins of others the way Grigovakis did. And he never used his rank to snipe at someone junior who couldn't respond in kind, either, the way Grigovakis did with the ratings of *Gauntlet*'s crew when he thought no one was looking. Oversteegen could be equally infuriating, in Abbott's opinion, but he didn't appear to do it on *purpose*. In fact, if it just hadn't been for that incredibly irritating accent of his—and the way family patronage had obviously enhanced his career—even Abbott wouldn't have had any real problems with the captain.

Probably.

"Well, keep thinking about it," he told Posner after a moment. "If you can come up with something, let me know. In the meantime, we've got some non-snotty business to take care of."

He turned back to his desk terminal and punched up a document.

"Commander Blumenthal says the Captain wants a live-fire exercise for the broadside energy mounts this afternoon," he continued. Posner's eyes brightened, and the ATO smiled. "In fact, the commander says the Captain has signed off on expending a few decoy drones as live targets."

"Well, hot damn," Posner said. "Full-power shots, Sir?"

"Eventually," Abbott told him. "We want to get as much use out of them as we can before we expend them, though. So we'll go with the mount laser designators for the first couple of passes. We'll score hits regularly for evaluation on the lasers. But *then*," he continued with a grin, "we'll toss out the decoys on an evasion pattern and give each mount a single full-power shot under local control. Sort of a pass-fail exam, you might say."

He looked up from the outline of the exercise plan, and he and Posner smiled broadly at one another.

The graser mount compartment was crowded. It always was at action stations, even without the need to pack an extra body into the available space.

At least the designers had made some provision for the necessity, however, which meant that Abigail had a place to sit. It wasn't much of one, squeezed in between the mount captain's station and the tracking rating's. In fact, she just barely fitted into it, and she suspected that it had been designed specifically as a convenient niche for midshipwomen, since she doubted anyone much larger than that could have been crammed into the available space.

The good news was that Chief Vassari, Graser Thirty-Eight's mount captain, was a good sort. He didn't have that air of exaggerated patience some long-service noncoms seemed to assume naturally around any mere snotty. About the only positive thing Abigail could say about that particular attitude was that at least it beat the deliberate testing some enlisted and noncommissioned personnel indulged in. She was willing to admit that testing had its place—after all, she thought with a small, secret smile, she *was* a Grayson—but that didn't mean it was an enjoyable experience.

Chief Vassari fell into neither category. He was simply an all-around competent person who appeared to assume that someone could do her job until she proved differently. Which naturally made it even more important than usual to prove that she could.

Some of Abigail's classmates had always hated weapons drill, at least on the energy mounts. She understood intellectually that some people had an emotional objection to being sealed into a tiny, armored compartment while its atmosphere—and the atmosphere of its surrounding spaces—was evacuated. On an emotional level, though, she'd always thought that was a silly attitude. After all, a starship was nothing but a hollow space filled with air surrounded by an effective infinity of nothingness. If you were going to have trouble with spending time suited up in vacuum, then you should have made another career choice. On the other hand, she supposed it could be a simple case of claustrophobia. There really *wasn't* very much space in here, and it wasn't unusual for a weapons crew to spend hours at a time strapped into place, living on their suit umbilicals. All so that there would be a live, human presence on the mount if combat damage should suddenly cut it off from Tactical's central computers.

Of course, today's exercise assumed that every single energy mount in the starboard broadside had been thrown back into local control. Abigail couldn't imagine what sort of damage could have cut all of the broadside's weapons off from central control without destroying the ship outright, but that was hardly the point. The object was to train each individual crew for the unlikely day on which it might be the single lucky mount that *was* cut off.

Unfortunately, Graser Thirty-Eight was the last energy weapon in the starboard broadside, which meant that Abigail, Chief Vassari, and their people had been sitting here for what seemed like forever with nothing to do but watch other people miss the target.

"Stand by, Thirty-Six," Commander Blumenthal said over the com.

"Thirty-Six standing by," a cultured voice responded, and Abigail grimaced. Commander Blumenthal and Lieutenant Commander Abbott had decided to add an additional wrinkle to this afternoon's exercise and announced that each of *Gauntlet*'s four middies would be acting as the captain of the energy mount to which he or she was assigned. The announcement had not been greeted with universal joy by the crews of the weapons concerned. There was always fierce competition between crews during these exercises, both for bragging rights and because of the special privileges which were normally awarded to the winning mount. Having a mere snotty sitting in the command seat was not considered the best way to enhance one's chances of emerging victorious. Not that anyone would have guessed from Arpad Grigovakis' tone that he had any doubts at all about the outcome. Or that he'd been sitting there waiting almost as long as Abigail had, for that matter.

"Beginning run," Commander Blumenthal announced, and Abigail stared down into the minute plot provided between her and Chief Vassari's stations.

Although all control stations were manned, the grasers themselves weren't fully on line . . . yet. Instead, the crews would be "firing" the laser designators to which their weapons were normally slaved. Unlike the grasers themselves, the designators lacked the power to actually damage the sophisticated drones being used as targets, which would allow each target to be used several times. But the drones would sense and report the amount of energy each laser put on target—assuming it was lucky enough to score a hit at all—to establish the performance of each crew.

Unlike the master plot in CIC or the main fire control plot on the command deck, the tiny on-mount displays were not driven from the main sensor arrays. Instead, they relied upon their mounts' lidar, which had a much narrower field of view. Neither their software nor their imagers were as good as those available to CIC or Commander Blumenthal, either. But that was sort of the point, Abigail reminded herself, watching intently as the corkscrewing, rolling drone swept down *Gauntlet*'s starboard side.

The erratic base course was bad enough, but the drone's rotation on its axis made things even worse. She watched a sidebar readout as the drone flashed by at a range of fifty thousand kilometers, and her lips pursed in unwilling sympathy for Grigovakis. His crew seemed to be managing to track the bobbing, weaving drone surprisingly well, but its spinning motion turned its impeller wedge into a flashing shield. The drone wasn't rotating at a constant speed, either, she noted. At a mere fifty thousand klicks, there wasn't a whole lot of time to analyze its erratic rotation, and Graser Thirty-Six's energy-on-target numbers were abysmally low. Under three percent, in fact.

"Doesn't look so good, does it, Ma'am?" Chief Vassari muttered to her over their dedicated private com link.

"It's the rotation," she replied quietly. "The spin is blocking the laser. It's catching them between pulses."

"Yes, Ma'am," Vassari agreed, and Abigail frowned.

Like any shipboard energy weapon, *Gauntlet*'s grasers fired in burstlike pulses, and the laser designators were synchronized to simulate the grasers' normal pulse rate for the exercise. That pulse rate was high enough that a ship-sized opponent couldn't have rotated its wedge in and out of position rapidly enough to avoid significant damage. In the time it took an impeller wedge over a hundred kilometers across to rotate, each graser would have gotten off sufficient pulses to guarantee at least one or two hits, assuming that its targeting solution was accurate.

But the drone's wedge was less than *two* kilometers across, and at least ninety percent of Graser Thirty-Six's pulses were being shrugged aside by the spinning wedge. The same thing had happened to the other grasers which had engaged the drone, but Thirty-Six's energy-on-target totals were pretty pathetic even compared to the other mounts. Both Karl and Shobhana had done better, although neither of them was exactly in the running for the victor's trophy.

"Tell me, Chief," Abigail said thoughtfully, "do the on-mount computers keep track of *all* the firing runs?"

"They display all the EOT numbers, but they only log the totals for their own mounts to memory, Ma'am," Vassari replied. He turned his head, gazing at her narrowly through his helmet visor. "Why?"

"I wasn't thinking about performance numbers,

Chief," Abigail told him. "I meant, do the computers plot target motion each time the drone makes a run?"

"Well, yes, Ma'am. They do," Vassari said, then smiled slowly. "Are you thinking what I think you're thinking, Ma'am?" he asked.

"Probably," she admitted with an impish grin. "But is our software up to the analysis?"

"I think so," Vassari said, in the tone of a man who would have liked to scratch his chin thoughtfully.

"Well, we'd better get it set up quickly," Abigail said, gesturing with her helmet at the plot. "They'll be starting Thirty-Six's second run any minute now."

"Yes, Ma'am. How do you want me to handle it?"

"I'm hoping that the drone's running on a canned routine rather than generating random evasion maneuvers. If it is, then there's probably a repeat point where it resets. Look for that. And if we've got the capacity, let's run each individual pass for pattern analysis and see if we can't load an automatic recognition trigger into the firing sequence."

"If the Midshipwoman will allow me, Ma'am," Vassari said with a huge grin, "I like the way her mind works."

"Tell me that if we manage to pull it off, Chief," Abigail replied, and he nodded and began punching commands into his console.

Abigail sat back and watched as the drone flashed through the second of Graser Thirty-Six's firing passes. This time Grigovakis' crew did considerably better . . . which still left them with very low numbers. Not that they were alone, and Abigail wondered who was actually responsible for the drone's axial rotation. No one had warned any of the crews that it might be coming, and that didn't strike her as a typical Commander Blumenthal idea. It sounded exactly like something Captain Oversteegen might have decided to throw into the equation, however, and her smile grew nastier at the thought of possibly overcoming one of the captain's little ploys.

The drone returned to its starting point for Graser Thirty-Six's third and final solo designator run, and she turned to glance at Chief Vassari.

"How's it coming, Chief?" she asked quietly.

"Pretty good . . . maybe, Ma'am," he replied. "We've got good plots on about half the previous runs. Looks like we never got a tight enough lock with our on-mount sensors on the other half, so we don't have a complete data set. The computers agree that it's repeating a canned routine, but we'd really need at least half a dozen more passes to isolate the point at which the routine resets to zero. On the other hand, we've got hard analyses on at least twenty separate runs. If it repeats one of those, and if we've got good enough sensor lock to spot it, we should be in business."

"I guess that's just going to have to be good enough, Chief," she said, watching the numbers for Grigovakis' crew's final firing pass come up on her display. They were the best of the three, but even so they weren't anything to get excited about. The best energy-on-target they'd been able to come up with was under fifteen percent of max possible. That would have been more than sufficient to destroy a target as small as the drone, assuming the graser itself had been firing, but it was still a pretty anemic performance.

"We're up next," she pointed out, and Vassari nodded.

"Stand by, Thirty-Eight," Blumenthal's voice said, almost as if the tac officer had been able to hear her, and she keyed her com.

"Thirty-Eight, standing by," she acknowledged formally.

"Beginning run," Blumenthal told her, and Abigail

held her breath as the drone came slashing back down *Gauntlet*'s side yet again.

Graser Thirty-Eight's lidar reached out for the target. The drone was small and elusive, but they also knew exactly where to begin looking for it.

"Acquisition!" the tracking rating announced.

"Acknowledged," Abigail replied, and turned to look at Vassari. The chief was staring intently at his display, and when she glanced into her own, Abigail saw the red sighting circle projected across the drone's small bead of light. The targeting solution looked good, but although the energy mount was tracking smoothly, holding the drone centered in the cross-hairs, it wasn't firing.

Abigail felt the other five members of Graser Thirty-Eight's crew staring at her, but she kept her own eyes on the plot. It had seemed like a good idea when she and Vassari came up with it; now, she wasn't nearly as certain. The drone was almost a third of the way through its pass, and *still* the laser designator hadn't fired. If it didn't do something soon, they were going to come up with a score of zero, and none of the other mounts had managed to do quite *that* poorly. She hovered on the brink of ordering Vassari to open fire anyway, on the theory that at least something would have to get through, but she closed her lips firmly against the temptation. It either worked, or it didn't; she wasn't going to second-guess herself in mid-flight and risk losing any opportunity of success. Besides, even if she—

"Got it!" Chief Vassari barked suddenly, and the laser designator "opened fire" before the words were fully out of his mouth.

Abigail watched the plot's sidebar, and her face blossomed in a huge smile as the rest of her crew began to cheer and whistle. The computers had identified the repetition of one of the earlier fly-bys, and Vassari's fire plan had instructed them to synchronize the mount's pulse rate with the recognized spin rate of the target. It meant that they weren't pumping out the maximum possible amount of destructive energy, but what they *were* pumping out was precisely timed to catch the drone at the moment that it turned the open side of its wedge towards the ship. The energy-on-target total shot up like a homesick meteor, and Abigail wanted to cheer herself as the laser designator systematically hammered the drone.

"Sixty-two percent of max!" Vassari proclaimed exultantly as the drone completed its run. "*Damn*, but—!" He caught himself, and looked at Abigail with a sheepish expression. "Sorry about that, Ma'am," he said contritely.

"Chief," she said around a grin, "I'm from Grayson, not a convent. I've heard the word before."

"Well, in that case," he replied, "*damn*, but that was fun!"

"Damned straight it was," she agreed with a chuckle, and punched him lightly on the shoulder. "Now, if it just repeats the same maneuver sequence from where we got it indexed on this pass, we should really kick some butt on the next one."

"Not too shabby, Thirty-Eight," Commander Blumenthal observed over the com in a tone of studied understatement. "Of course, there are still two more runs to go. Stand by for second run, now."

"Thirty-Eight, standing by," Abigail responded, and the drone came slashing back at them again.

"I suppose we should all congratulate you," Arpad Grigovakis said.

The four snotties stood in the rear of the briefing room in which Commander Blumenthal and Captain

Oversteegen had just completed their dissection of the afternoon's exercises. Commander Watson hadn't attended, since she'd had the bridge watch, but all of the department heads had been present. By now, most of the other officers had already dispersed to other tasks, but Oversteegen, Blumenthal, and Abbott were still engaged in a quiet-voiced discussion, and the middies hadn't yet been dismissed by their OCTO. Which left them in the seen-but-not-heard-mode with which all middies were intimately familiar, and Grigovakis had kept his voice down accordingly.

Not that keeping its volume down had prevented it from sounding thoroughly sour.

"Darn right we should!" Karl Aitschuler grinned at Abigail and slapped her on the shoulder. There was nothing at all sour about his manner, and Shobhana was grinning even more broadly than Karl.

"I should think so," she agreed. "Seventy-nine percent of max possible overall? I'm not sure, but I think that probably ought to count as a record against a target like that!"

"No doubt it does," Grigovakis conceded, still in that sour-grapes tone. "On the other hand, what are the odds that that sort of targeting solution is going to come up in real life?" He snorted. "Seventy-nine percent or seven percent—either one of them would have destroyed a target that size if it had been for real."

"Sure, but I don't seem to remember Thirty-Six scoring *seven* percent overall, either," Karl said a bit more sharply.

"Well, at least we didn't take advantage of a freak opportunity that's never going to repeat against a real target, did we?" Grigovakis shot back.

"What, you don't think missiles are ever going to use canned routines?" Aitschuler snorted with an edge of contempt.

"Besides," Shobhana said, glaring at Grigovakis, "one of the things an alert tac officer is supposed to do is recognize *any* advantage or opportunity she can generate! Which is exactly what Abigail did."

"I never said that it wasn't," Grigovakis replied in a slightly more defensive tone. "All I said was that it's not a circumstance that's likely to repeat in real life, and that that leads me to question just how representative of our actual abilities the entire exercise was."

"What you really mean," Karl said coolly, "is that you're pissed off because Abigail and her crew kicked everybody else's butts—including yours."

"Well, yes." Grigovakis chuckled. It was obviously intended to be a rueful sound, but he didn't quite pull it off. "The truth is, I don't like coming in second best," he said with an air of candor. "And I like coming in seventeenth even less. So I guess maybe I didn't take it very well." He showed Abigail his teeth in what could have been called a smile by the charitable. "Sorry about that, Abigail. But don't think I'm not going to try to return the favor next time. And maybe next time *I'll* be in the Tail-End Charlie position."

"And what does that mean?" Shobhana asked tartly.

"Only that because Abigail's crew fired last, no one else had the opportunity to match her score by using the same technique," Grigovakis replied innocently.

"No one else had the opportunity because no one else came up with the same idea," Karl told him in disgusted tones.

"Well, of course they didn't. I didn't mean to imply otherwise. Although," he looked thoughtful, "to be perfectly honest, Abigail didn't, either."

"*What?*" Karl managed at the last moment to hold the volume down to something their seniors might not notice, but the strength of the glare he bent upon Grigovakis more than compensated.

"I only meant that she didn't run the actual *analysis* herself, Karl," Grigovakis said in the patient tones of the much put upon and misunderstood. "Chief Vassari did that."

Butter wouldn't have melted in his mouth, Abigail thought, but the unstated implication was clear enough. He was suggesting, without quite coming out and saying so, that the entire idea had been Vassari's and that Abigail had simply taken credit for it. Which, his tone and expression clearly emphasized, was no more than might be expected from a neobarb like her.

A wave of fury out of all keeping with the pettiness of the small-minded provocation rolled through her. Karl and Shobhana both made disgusted sounds, but Grigovakis only stood there, smiling at her with that smug sense of superiority. It didn't matter to him that neither Karl nor Shobhana agreed with him for an instant; he didn't need *their* agreement when he had his own. Besides, what else could have been expected from people with the lamentably poor judgment to side with someone like Abigail over someone like him?

She started to open her mouth, then clamped her jaw muscles firmly, instead, and asked the Intercessor for strength. The Church of Humanity Unchained was not exceptionally well known for turning the other cheek, but Father Church did teach that to assail a fool for being foolish was to assail the wind for being air. Neither could help what it was, and belaboring either of them was a waste of effort which might be more profitably devoted to meeting those aspects of the Test which mattered anyway.

And so, she didn't administer the salutary tongue lashing he so richly deserved. Instead, she smiled sweetly at him.

"You're quite right," she said. "I didn't run the analysis. Chief Vassari is much more familiar with the capabilities of the on-mount sensors and software than I am. Of course," she smiled more sweetly than ever, "sometimes it's not necessary to be personally familiar with the capabilities in order to identify a possibility, is it? You just have to be alert enough to recognize the opportunity when it comes along."

Karl and Shobhana chuckled, and Grigovakis' complexion darkened as the counter shot went home. He opened his mouth, but before he could say anything else, Lieutenant Commander Abbott cleared his throat behind him.

All four midshipmen turned to face him, and Grigovakis turned a shade darker, clearly wondering just how much Abbott had overheard, but the OCTO simply looked at all of them for a second or two.

"I'm sorry we kept the four of you standing around so long," he said finally, his tone mild. "I hadn't realized the TO and the Captain and I would be tied up quite so long. Mr. Aitschuler and Ms. Korrami, I'd like you to report to Commander Atkins. I understand that she's finished grading that astrogation problem she assigned you yesterday. Ms. Hearns, I'd like you to accompany me to my office. Chief Vassari will join us there. Commander Blumenthal has asked me to do a critical analysis of the technique the two of you used, and your input will undoubtedly be useful."

"Of course, Sir," Abigail replied.

"Good." Abbott smiled briefly, then glanced at Grigovakis and waved one hand towards the front of the briefing room, where Commander Blumenthal and Captain Oversteegen were still engaged in conversation. "While we're doing that, Mr. Grigovakis, I believe the Captain would like to speak to you for a moment."

"Uh, of course, Sir," Grigovakis said after the briefest of hesitations.

"When you're finished here, please come by my office," Abbott told him. "I imagine Ms. Hearns, Chief Vassari, and I will still be there, and I'd be interested to hear your input, as well."

"Yes, Sir," Grigovakis said expressionlessly.

"Good." Abbott smiled at him again, then nodded Abigail through the hatch.

Captain Oversteegen's conversation with the tactical officer lasted another fifteen minutes. Then Commander Blumenthal left, and Arpad Grigovakis found himself alone in the briefing room with *Gauntlet*'s CO.

Oversteegen appeared to be in no great hurry. He sat at the briefing room table, paging through several screens of notes on his private memo pad for five or six more minutes before he switched off the display and looked up.

"Ah, Mr. Grigovakis!" he said. "Forgive me, I'd forgotten I asked you t' stay." He smiled and gestured for Grigovakis to have a seat at the table.

The midshipman sank into the indicated chair with a wary expression. It was the first time, outside one of the formal dinners in the captain's dining cabin, that Oversteegen had invited him to sit in his presence.

"You wanted to speak to me, Sir?" he said after a moment.

"Yes, I did, actually," Oversteegen agreed and tipped back in his own chair. He gazed at Grigovakis long enough for the midshipman to fidget uneasily, then cocked his head to one side and arched an eyebrow.

"It's come t' my attention, Mr. Grigovakis, that you don't appear t' have exactly what one might call a sense of rapport with Ms. Hearns," he said. "Would you care t' comment on just why that is?"

"I—" Grigovakis paused and cleared his throat, then gave the captain a small, troubled smiled. "I really don't know why, Sir," he said earnestly. "It's certainly not anything she's ever done to me. We just don't click somehow. Of course, she's the only Grayson I really know well enough to consider myself at all familiar with. That may be part of it, though I know it shouldn't be. To be honest, I'm a bit embarrassed. I shouldn't needle her the way I do, and I know it. But sometimes it just gets away from me."

"I see." Oversteegen frowned thoughtfully. "I notice that you referred t' the fact that Ms. Hearns is a Grayson. Does that mean you're prejudiced against Graysons, Mr. Grigovakis?"

"Oh, no, Sir! It's just that sometimes I find them a bit . . . overly focused. I started to say 'parochial,' but that isn't really the right word. They just seem . . . different, somehow. Like they're marching to a different drum, I suppose."

"I suppose that's fair enough," Oversteegen mused. "Grayson *is* quite different from the Star Kingdom, after all. I would submit t' you, however, Mr. Grigovakis, that it behooves you t' overcome whatever personal . . . discomfort you may feel around Graysons in general, and particularly around Ms. Hearns."

"Yes, Sir. I understand, Sir." Grigovakis said earnestly, and Oversteegen regarded him silently for a moment or two. Then he smiled, and it was not an extraordinarily pleasant expression.

"Be sure that you do, Mr. Grigovakis," he said conversationally. "I realize some members of the Service— includin' some of its more senior ones—seem t' feel that somehow Graysons aren't quite up t' Manticoran standards. I suggest you disabuse yourself of that notion, if you should happen t' share it. Not only are

Graysons up t' our standards, but in many ways, particularly now, *we* aren't up t' theirs."

Grigovakis paled slightly. He opened his mouth, but Oversteegen wasn't finished yet.

"As a midshipman, you may have failed t' note that the Queen's Navy is currently in the process of buildin' down, Mr. Grigovakis. In my considered opinion, that is . . . not a wise policy. But however wise or unwise it may be, the Grayson Navy, on the other hand, is doin' exactly the opposite. And if you make the mistake of assumin' that simply because Grayson is for all intents and purposes a theocracy it must therefore be backward, ignorant, and inferior, you will be in for an extremely sad and rude awakenin'.

"In addition t' that, you are a member of my ship's company, and it is not my practice t' tolerate harassment of any member of my crew by another. Ms. Hearns has not complained t' me, or t' Commander Abbott. That does not mean we are unaware of the situation, however. Nor does it mean I am unaware that you have a tendency t' speak t' your enlisted personnel with a . . . vigor not yet justified by the level of your experience. I expect both of these practices on your part t' cease. Is that understood?"

"Yes, Sir!" Grigovakis said quickly, fighting a temptation to wipe sweat from his forehead.

"It had better be, Mr. Grigovakis," Oversteegen told him in that same, conversational tone. "And while I'm on the subject, perhaps it wouldn't hurt t' point out another reality t' you. I am familiar with your family. In fact, your Uncle Connall and I served together some years ago, and I consider him a friend. I am aware that your family is quite wealthy, even by Manticoran standards, and can trace its earliest Manticoran ancestors back t' shortly after the Plague Years.

"As such, you rightly enjoy a certain standin' and

prominence among the better families of the Star Kingdom. However, I think it would be wise of you t' reflect upon the fact that Ms. Hearns can trace *her* ancestry in unbroken succession through almost a thousand T-years of history t' the first Steadholder Owens. And that despite the fact that she bears no noble title—beyond, of course, that of 'Miss Owens,' which I've observed she never uses—her birth takes precedence over that of anyone below ducal rank in the Star Kingdom."

Grigovakis swallowed hard, and Oversteegen gave him another wintry smile.

"I'll leave you with one last thought about Ms. Hearns, Mr. Grigovakis," he said. "Your family, as I said, is noted for its wealth. That wealth, however, pales t' insignificance beside the Owens family fortune. We are accustomed t' thinkin' of Grayson as a poor planet, and t' some extent, that's no doubt justified, although I believe you might be surprised if you considered the actual figures and how they've changed over the past ten or fifteen T-years. Steadholder Owens, however, is one of only eighty steadholders . . . and Owens Steading was only the eleventh founded. It's been in existence for nine T-centuries, almost twice as long as the entire Star Kingdom. Steadholder Owens is wealthy, powerful, and unaccustomed t' acceptin' the discourteous treatment of members of his family. Especially its *female* members. I would be most surprised if Ms. Hearns would ever appeal t' him for assistance in such a minor matter, and I strongly suspect that she would be most upset if she ever discovered that her father had chosen t' take a hand in her affairs. Neither of which, I imagine, would dissuade him in the least. Aristocrats, you know, look after their own."

Grigovakis seemed to wilt in his seat, and

Oversteegen allowed his own chair to come fully upright once more.

"I commend t' your consideration the example of the treecat, Mr. Grigovakis," he said. "At first glance, treecats are simply fuzzy, adorable woodland creatures. But they, too, look after their own, and no hexapuma in his right mind ventures into their range. I trust the applicable implications will not be lost upon you."

He held the midshipman's eye a moment longer, then nodded towards the open hatch.

"Dismissed, Mr. Grigovakis," he said pleasantly.

The surge of vertigo-crossed nausea was something Abigail hadn't yet become accustomed to. Privately, she doubted that she ever would, but she had no intention of displaying her unsettling stab of discomfort before more experienced eyes, and especially not just now, with so many of those experienced eyes watching her. And not when Shobhana and Karl were about to have so much more of an . . . interesting time than she was.

Crossing the alpha wall from hyper-space back to normal-space for the first time was the equivalent of the old wet-navy tradition of "crossing the line" back on Old Earth. Just as crossing Old Earth's equator had turned the neophyte sailor into a true "shellback" mariner, it was the first alpha translation back into normal-space which transformed the neophyte spacer from a "dirt-grubber" into a "hyper-dog."

Despite their participation in half a dozen near-space and intra-system training cruises, neither Karl Aitschuler nor Shobhana Korrami had ever left the Manticore System prior to their deployment aboard *Gauntlet*. Which meant that they were about to suffer all of the traditional indignities inflicted upon those unfortunate souls who had never crossed the wall before. The ceremonies, which would include all sorts of initiation ordeals (many of which had been preserved and translated from Old Earth's oceans), were certain to take some time, and despite the uneasy flutter in her own midsection, Abigail rather wished that she could have been present to help officiate.

Fortunately, however, she was already a hyper-dog, and she'd been very careful to preserve the wall-crossing certificate she'd received from the captain of the transport which had originally delivered her from Grayson to Manticore to prove it. She'd been home six or seven times on leave during her assignment to the Academy, as well, which meant that compared to Karl and Shobhana, she was an old hand at hyper translations. That, at least, meant she wasn't likely to be smeared with grease, have her entire body shaved, be required to drink or eat assorted unpalatable substances, or otherwise be subjected to the rites of passage which the senior members of the lodge so cheerfully inflicted upon the newbies in their midst.

But it also meant that she and Grigovakis, who also had several commercial wall-crossings on his record, were available for regular duty assignment. So while Karl, Shobhana, and the handful of other dirt-grubbers among the enlisted members of the ship's company were undergoing the transformation into hyper-dogs, Abigail found herself working as Lieutenant Commander Atkins' assistant when *Gauntlet* emerged from hyper-space just outside the hyper limit of the Tiberian System. And also working very hard to project the same blasé attitude towards just another trip across the wall.

Of course, there were compensations to having the duty, she reflected. She might not get to help stuff Shobhana headfirst down a tube into a darkened, zero-gee compartment in her underwear to find and bring back "King Neptune's" floating, stolen "pearls" (usually lovingly saved over-ripe tomatoes or something similarly squishy) in her bare hands, but she did get to see the spectacular beauty of the main visual display as *Gauntlet*'s Warshawski sails radiated the blue glory of transit energy. She'd seen it before, of course. Passenger liners were very careful to make sure their paying customers got their money's worth and provided huge holo displays in their main salons expressly for moments like this. But there was a big difference between that and witnessing it as a member of a starship's command crew.

"Transit completed, Sir," Lieutenant Commander Atkins reported.

"Very good, Astro." Captain Oversteegen tipped his command chair back, watching the main maneuvering plot until it updated, showing *Gauntlet*'s position relative to the local primary and major system bodies. He gave Atkins a few moments to confirm the ship's position—a task Abigail was dutifully performing at her own backup station, as well—then let his chair come back upright.

"Do you have a course for Refuge, Astro?" he asked.

"Yes, Sir. Transit time will be approximately seven-point-six hours at four hundred and fifty gravities."

"Very well," Oversteegen replied. "Let's get a move on."

The captain waited while Atkins passed orders to the helmsman and *Gauntlet* brought up her impeller wedge and settled on her new heading. Then he stood.

"Commander Atkins, you have the con."

"Aye, Sir. I have the con," Atkins acknowledged, and Oversteegen turned to the exec.

"Commander Watson, would you and Ms. Hearns please join me in my briefing room?"

Abigail tried not to twitch in surprise, but she couldn't keep herself from looking up quickly, and he smiled ever so slightly at her. She felt herself color, but he only stood waiting patiently, and she cleared her throat quickly.

"Ma'am," she said to Atkins, "I request relief."

"You stand relieved, Ms. Hearns," the astrogator replied with equal formality. "Mr. Grigovakis," she looked past Abigail to where Grigovakis had been working with Commander Blumenthal's plotting party.

"Yes, Ma'am?"

"You have Astrogation," she told him.

"Aye, aye, Ma'am. I have Astrogation," he confirmed.

Abigail climbed out of her chair as Atkins moved to the chair at the center of the command deck and Grigovakis took over at Astrogation. She waited respectfully for the captain and exec to walk through the briefing room hatch first, then followed them in.

"Close the hatch, Ms. Hearns," Oversteegen said, and she hit the button. The hatch slid silently shut, and the captain waved her over to the conference table and pointed at a chair.

"Sit," he said, and she sat.

"I imagine you're at least a bit curious as t' why I asked you t' join the Exec and me," he said after a moment, and paused with one eyebrow arched.

"Well, yes, Sir. A bit," she admitted.

"My reasons are simple enough," he told her. "We're goin' t' have t' make contact with Refuge, and as I indicated when I first explained our reasons for comin' t' Tiberian in the first place, I feel it's important that we do so in a way which doesn't get their backs up. In addition, I feel it's equally important that we do so in a nonthreatenin' fashion. For that reason, I've decided that you will be in command of our shore party."

His tone was blandly conversational, but Abigail felt her soul stiffen in instant response.

After his remarks at that initial formal dinner, Oversteegen had seemed completely oblivious to the fact that Abigail was a Grayson. She'd been grateful for that, and even more grateful when she realized the captain must have . . . counseled Grigovakis about *his* behavior. The midshipman was never going to be a likable person, but at least he'd cut way back on the nasty little innuendos he so enjoyed directing at his fellows. For that matter, he'd eased up considerably on what Karl called his "little tin god" persona with the enlisted personnel with whom he came into contact, and she had no doubt that that, too, related directly to his private interview with the captain.

She'd been surprised at Oversteegen's intervention, and even more at the fact that he'd apparently chosen to intervene directly, rather than delegating the task to Commander Watson or Lieutenant Commander Abbott. But she'd also been undeniably appreciative. She'd never doubted her ability to handle Grigovakis if she had to, but it was a vast relief to have that source of friction removed—or at least considerably diminished—in Snotty Row.

But the gratitude she'd felt for the captain's intervention couldn't offset the stab of pure fury she felt at his present announcement. He might have come down on Grigovakis for creating unnecessary friction between members of his ship's company, but it clearly hadn't been because he disagreed with Grigovakis' view of Graysons. After all, who could be better to serve as spokeswoman to a batch of primitive, isolationist religious fanatics than another primitive religious fanatic?

"Captain," she said after the briefest of pauses in a carefully controlled voice, "I really don't know anything about the Refugians' religious beliefs. With all due respect, Sir, I'm not certain that I'm the best choice for a liaison with the planet."

"I believe you underestimate your capabilities, Ms. Hearns," Oversteegen replied calmly. "I assure you, I've considered this matter carefully, and on the merits, you *are* the best choice."

"Sir," she said, "I appreciate your confidence in my abilities." She managed to smile without even gritting her teeth. "And I will, of course, attempt to carry out any orders to the very best of my ability. But I'm only a midshipwoman. Isn't it possible that the local authorities will feel offended if someone as junior as I am is sent down as our liaison?"

"That possibility exists, of course," Oversteegen conceded, apparently totally unaware of her blistering resentment. "I believe, however, that it's unlikely. Indeed, I would imagine that a single middy and a squad or so of Marines would be seen as less threatenin'—and intrusive—than a more senior officer might be. And of the middies available t' me, I believe you're the best choice."

Abigail hovered on the brink of demanding to know just why he felt that way, but she bit her tongue and kept her mouth shut. After all, it was fairly evident why he did.

"In keepin' with my desire t' seem no more threatenin' or intrusive than absolutely necessary, Linda," he said, turning his attention to the exec, "I think it would be best not t' put *Gauntlet* into Refuge orbit. At least initially, I want our contact with these people t' be as low-key as possible. I'd like you t' spend some time with Ms. Hearns, briefin' her on exactly what sort of information we're lookin' for.

"Your object," he continued, looking back at Abigail, "will be t' explain why we're here and t' get a feel for the Fellowship of the Elect's attitude towards our presence. Any information you pick up directly will, of course, be welcome, but I don't expect you t' push hard. Your job is really more t' break the ice and put a friendly face on our visit. Think of yourself as our ambassador. If things proceed as I hope they will, you'll undoubtedly be involved in our further contact with Refuge, but we'll be sendin' down someone a bit more senior for the follow up contact and interviews."

"Yes, Sir," Abigail replied. There was, after all, nothing else she could say.

"Linda," he said to the exec, "in addition t' briefin' Ms. Hearns, I want you t' give some thought t' exactly how many Marines we should send down with her."

"Are you expecting some sort of trouble, Sir?" Commander Watson asked, and he shrugged.

"I'm not *expectin'* anythin'," he said. "At the same time, we're a long way from home, we've never had any previous contact of our own with Refuge, and I'll feel more comfortable sending someone along t' keep an eye on Ms. Hearns. I'm confident in her ability t' look after herself, of course." He smiled briefly at Abigail. "At the same time, it never hurts t' have some-one along t' watch your back, at least until you're certain you know the local ropes. Besides," he smiled more broadly, "it'll be good experience for her."

"Yes, Sir. Understood," Watson acknowledged with a slight smile of her own. *Just as if she were a nanny promising Daddy to keep me out of trouble back home,* Abigail thought resentfully.

"Once we've dropped her and her contact team," Oversteegen went on, "I'd like t' have some fairly obvious reason for takin' *Gauntlet* out of Refuge orbit. I don't want t' make too big a point out of how care-ful we're bein' not t' intrude upon them any more than we have to."

"Well, as you just pointed out, Sir, we're the first

Queen's ship to visit Tiberian," Watson said. "And everybody knows how compulsive the RMN is about updating our charts at every opportunity. It'd make perfectly good sense for us to do a standard survey run, wouldn't it?"

"Exactly the sort of thing I was thinkin' about," Oversteegen agreed.

"I'm sure we could draft a note from you to the planetary government explaining what we're doing, Sir," Watson said with a smile. "In fact, Ms. Hearns' official reason for visiting the planet could be to deliver the note in person as a gesture of courtesy."

"An excellent idea," Oversteegen said. "I'll explain that we're lookin' into *Star Warrior*'s disappearance in conjunction with our Erewhonese allies. That'll give Ms. Hearns an openin' t' pursue any avenues of inquiry which suggest themselves. And if we're prepared t' spend the time surveyin' just t' update our charts, it should make things seem routine enough t' help put them as much at ease as possible with our presence."

He leaned back in his chair and gazed at Abigail for a few seconds, then shrugged.

"You may believe I'm overly concerned with tiptoein' around the Refugians' sensibilities, Ms. Hearns. It's certainly possible that I am. However, as my mother has always been fond of sayin', you can catch more flies with honey than with vinegar. It will cost us very little t' avoid stepping on any exaggerated sensibilities these people may have. And t' be honest, given the fact that they've deliberately sought isolation in this system, I feel we have an added obligation not t' intrude any more deeply upon them than we must."

Abigail managed not to blink in surprise, but it was difficult. He seemed completely sincere. She would never have expected that out of him, and his apparent sensitivity to the Refugians' attitudes and concerns only seemed to underscore his *insensitivity* to her own reaction at being so casually shuffled off into a stereotyped niche in his brain.

"At any rate," he went on more briskly, "as soon as the Exec has briefed you and selected your landin' party, we can get you down there t' begin talkin' t' these people for us."

"Oh, shit. Are you serious? A *cruiser*?" Haicheng Ringstorff stared at George Lithgow, his sensor officer and second-in-command.

"That's what it looks like," Lithgow replied. "We can't be positive yet—all we really have is the hyper footprint and an impeller signature, but both of them are consistent with a single heavy cruiser or battlecruiser."

"A heavy cruiser is bad enough to be going on with, George," Ringstorff said sourly. "Let's not borrow trouble by thinking any bigger than we have to!"

"I'm only telling you what the sensor data says." Lithgow shrugged. "If whoever it is is headed for Refuge—and it looks like they are—our inner-system platforms should get a positive ID for us. In the meantime, what do we do about it?"

Ringstorff smiled thinly. Lithgow had said "we," but what he really meant was "you." Which was fair enough, he supposed, given that Ringstorff was the man officially in charge of the four-ring circus the entire Tiberian operation had turned into.

He leaned back in his chair and ran irritated fingers through his thick, dark hair. Ringstorff was tall for an Andermani, with broad shoulders and a powerful physique, and there were still traces of the Imperial Marine colonel he once had been. But that had been long ago, before certain minor financial irregularities in his regiment's accounts had come to the IG's attention. In light of his excellent record in combat and numerous decorations, he'd been allowed to resign without prosecution or even an official investigation, but his career in the Empire had been over. Which had worked out for the best, perhaps, because for the past twenty-five T-years, Haicheng Ringstorff had found much more profitable employment for his skills.

In many ways, his present mission promised to be the most profitable yet. Which it damned well ought to be, given the monumental pain in the ass it seemed determined to turn into!

"What's the schedule on Tyler and Lamar?" he asked Lithgow after a moment.

"Schedule? For these lunatics?" Lithgow snorted.

"You know what I mean," Ringstorff said irritably.

"Yeah, I guess I do," Lithgow admitted. He pulled a memo pad out of his pocket and punched keys, obviously refreshing his memory, then shrugged. "Tyler is due back sometime within the next seventy-two standard hours," he said. "If he and Lamar stayed in company with each other, we can expect both of them in that same window. If they split up, Lamar could be up to another full standard day behind him."

"Shit," Ringstorff muttered. "You know, the whole reason for picking this system was that nobody ever came here."

"That was the theory, anyway," Lithgow agreed.

"Yeah. Sure!" Ringstorff made a disgusted face and thought some more.

"The Four Yahoos might be a little easier to control if we could tell them why we're here and why we're supposed to lie so low," Lithgow pointed out rather diffidently after a moment.

"Not my decision," Ringstorff grunted. Not that Lithgow didn't have a point. But Manpower of Mesa was not in the habit of taking "captains" who were little more than common Silesian thugs into its confidence. For that matter, Ringstorff and Lithgow were the only two members of the hidden depot ship's Mesan crew who knew exactly why they were here. There were times the information restrictions made Ringstorff want to strangle people with his bare hands, but over all, he had to agree that they made better sense than usual in this case.

If everything went well with the main Manpower operation, the captains and crews of the four ex-Solarian heavy cruisers operating out of the carefully hidden base in Tiberian's outer asteroid belt would never know the real reason they'd been here. In that case, both they and the ships might well be useful to Manpower again, somewhere down the road. But if they *were* needed to support the current operation, then the odds were that once they'd performed their required function, Ringstorff would be instructed to use the remote-controlled nuclear scuttling charges carefully hidden aboard their ships to be sure there were no embarrassing witnesses.

Personally, Ringstorff would shed no tears if he got those orders. The universe would be a better place without Tyler, Lamar, or their two colleagues. Blowing up the ships *would* be wasteful, however, so preserving their crews' blissful ignorance—and thus obviating the need to eliminate them—was clearly the better option. But still . . .

"It was just a thought," Lithgow said. "Not a very good one, maybe, but a thought."

"I know." Ringstorff sighed. "It probably would have helped if the home office hadn't ordered me to let them play, for that matter."

"I think the geniuses who dreamed up this entire op probably figured there was no point even trying to keep the Four Yahoos from getting back up to their old tricks," Lithgow muttered. "And they were right. It'd make more sense to try to arm-wrestle entropy!"

"You're probably right," Ringstorff agreed. "I think HQ may have thought they could keep them on a leash initially, but after that transport blundered right into us—"

He threw both hands into the air with a grimace of disgust.

"It wasn't like we really had a choice with that one," Lithgow rejoined.

"I know. I know!" Ringstorff said irritably. "But you know as well as I do that that's what really started this entire mess."

Lithgow nodded. The original plan had been for the depot ship and all four of the converted cruisers to remain very quietly on station here in Tiberian until and unless they were required elsewhere. Unfortunately, there'd been some serious slippage in other parts of the schedule, and after four T-months of sitting here doing absolutely nothing, the cruisers' crews of Silesian outlaws had been so bored that Ringstorff had authorized a series of maneuvers and war games to let them play with and familiarize themselves with the capabilities of their vessels. It had made plenty of sense from a readiness viewpoint, after all, and the pirate captains and crews Manpower had recruited for the operation had been delighted by the sophistication of their ships. Most of their ilk had to make do with, at best, castoffs and obsolete units of the Confederacy Navy. The opportunity to trade in their old junkers and replace them with Solarian League technology that was no more than a few T-years out of date was one of the main reasons they'd signed on with Manpower in the first place.

But what Ringstorff hadn't known was that that goody-goody two-shoes Pritchart was going to send a damned transport full of colonists to *Tiberian*, of all places!

The inhabitants of Refuge had so little interest in contact with the rest of the galaxy that their total orbital infrastructure consisted of one primitive communications station that was probably the better part of a T-century out of date. Tiberian was one of the very few inhabited star systems in this entire region which had absolutely no surveillance platforms of any sort. For that matter, the Refugians had embraced their aggressively nonviolent, pastoral, agrarian lifestyle on their miserable little dirt ball of a planet with such enthusiasm that the system didn't even support a single asteroid resource extraction platform!

That was precisely what had attracted Manpower's attention to Tiberian in the first place. It was the closest star to the real objective, which meant it was ideally located to support the operation at need, and it might as well have been totally uninhabited in terms of the locals' ability to realize anyone was wandering around the outer reaches of their system. So it should have been totally safe to let the pirates play.

Except that the stupid damned transport had dropped out of hyper right on top of them. Not even a merchie's sensor suite could have missed them at that range, which had left Ringstorff no option but to order Tyler to capture it before it could translate back out with the word of their presence.

The elimination of the ship's entire crew and its passengers had been an unpleasant necessity, but one which Manpower's Silesian hirelings had protested. Not out of squeamishness, of course, but because dead passengers couldn't be ransomed by living relatives. They were being paid well for their services, but no self-respecting pirate was going to turn down the opportunity to enhance his profits, and they'd objected to losing this one.

Ringstorff hadn't liked it, but he'd passed on their complaints to the home office, at which point some REMF genius had come up with the notion of placating the pirates by allowing them to dispose of the transport itself through their own contacts in Silesia. At a little over two million tons it hadn't been all that large, but it was still worth the odd billion Solarian credit or two, and the pirates' credit accounts had done well out of it.

Which, unfortunately, had suggested to their stellar intellects that there was no reason why they shouldn't add a few more prizes to the list while they waited for whatever it was their employers had in mind. The same home office genius who had authorized the disposal of the transport in the first place had signed off on their new request, as well. Ringstorff wasn't certain whether that had been solely to keep the hired help happy or if there might not be a more devious motivation. It had occurred to him that the authorizer might have decided that if, indeed, it became necessary to eliminate "the Four Yahoos" and their crews after the main operation's conclusion, it could be convenient to have them identified as common, garden variety pirates. If it was handled correctly, it might even be possible to get the Erewhonese Navy, or the Manticoran Alliance, or even the Havenites to eliminate the "pirates" for Manpower.

It was the sort of complicated, theoretically neat and tidy plan that a certain variety of armchair strategist was fond of. Personally, Ringstorff had no intention of letting anyone else eliminate the Four Yahoos. If they had to go, he was doing it himself, before some half-way competent naval intelligence sort decided to wonder how a batch of "typical" Silesian pirates had gotten their hands on such powerful and modern vessels.

But in the meantime, he felt like a man juggling hand grenades. He was virtually certain that "his" captains had taken at least some prizes they hadn't mentioned to him at all. Certainly enough ships had disappeared in the area to begin attracting an unpleasant amount of attention . . . like the Erewhonese destroyer which had literally stumbled across the depot ship on its way out-system. Fortunately, the destroyer had already informed the Refugians that it was leaving Tiberian, and the Erewhonese appeared to believe that whatever had happened to it had happened somewhere else.

"You don't suppose that this cruiser is here because someone in Erewhonese intelligence has figured out their ship never got out, do you?" Lithgow asked, and Ringstorff grunted in amusement at the way his subordinate's thought processes had paralleled his own.

"The thought did occur to me," he admitted. "But if they had any serious evidence that we popped their ship here, they wouldn't have sent a single cruiser to check it out. They'd have responded in force, even if they didn't realize how much firepower we have, if only to give themselves some tactical flexibility if we tried to run for it."

"So you think they just happen to have turned up?"

"I didn't say that. Actually, I think they probably are here because of the Yahoos' operations. I'll bet you they've been jumping ships they've never bothered to mention to us. And if they have, the Erewhonese—or even the Havenites—could be turning up the heat trying to shake the 'pirates' out of the woodwork. In fact, it's more likely to be Haven than Erewhon, now that I think about it. Erewhon's already checked Tiberian out; Haven hasn't. It would make more sense for the Peeps to follow up their transport's loss here if they're just getting started on their own investigation than it would for the Erewhonese to backtrack through Tiberian for a third time."

"Good point," Lithgow conceded. "Still leaves us the problem of what we do about it, though."

"What I'd *like* to do would be to pull the hell out of here and take Maurersberger and Morakis with us. Unfortunately, we can't. Oh," he waved one hand, "we could sneak even farther out-system without whoever this is spotting us. I'm not worried about that. But if Tyler and Lamar come back before our visitor leaves, he's hardly going to fail to notice their hyper footprint, now is he? If that happens, it's the Erewhonese destroyer all over again, and in that case, I want all the firepower we've got right where I can put my hands on it in a hurry."

"You really think it would take all four of them to deal with one Peep cruiser?"

"Probably not, but I'm not about to take any chances I can avoid, either! And let's face it, however good 'our' ships are, their crew quality is a little suspect. Whereas if this really is a Peep, Theisman and his bunch have improved *their* crew quality significantly in the last couple of T-years. Better to have too much firepower than too little, in that case."

" . . . so, Ms. Hearns," Commander Watson said, leaning back in her chair and propping her elbows on its arms, "are there any questions?"

"I don't believe so, Ma'am," Abigail replied after a moment's thought. The exec gave a good brief, she thought. She still might not think very much of Captain Oversteegen's decision to send *her* down to Refuge, but she felt confident she understood what she was supposed to do once she got there.

Watson studied her for a moment, then frowned ever so slightly.

"Is something troubling you, Ms. Hearns?" she asked.

"Troubling me?" Abigail repeated, and shook her head. "No, Ma'am."

"I wasn't asking whether or not something about your instructions troubled you," Watson said. "But, frankly, Ms. Hearns, I believe that something rather more fundamental *is* troubling you. And I'd like to know precisely what it is before I send you off groundside out of my sight."

Abigail gazed at her, and behind her own calm expression she took herself sternly to task. *Tester, the last thing I need is to sit around sulking like a schoolgirl just because the Captain hurt my feelings!* she thought. *And just my luck the Exec should decide to call me on it!*

She considered denying Commander Watson's charge, but she wasn't about to compound her fault by adding lying to it. And so she drew a deep breath and made herself meet the exec's eyes levelly.

"I'm sorry, Ma'am," she said. "I don't mean to be overly sensitive, but I suppose that's what I'm being. It just . . . bothers me that the Captain never even seems to have considered assigning this to anyone else."

"I see," Watson said after a few thoughtful moments. "What you're saying is that you resent the fashion in which the Captain seems to have chosen you for this role because of your social and religious background. Is that a fair assessment, Ms. Hearns?"

There was no condemnation in the exec's cool voice, but neither was there any encouragement, and Abigail drew a deep breath. She started to defend herself by denying that she "resented" anything, but that would have been another lie. And so she nodded, instead.

"It sounds petty when you describe it that way, Ma'am," she said. "And maybe it is. I know there certainly have been times since I first reported to the Island that I've been overly sensitive. At the same time, and without seeking to justify myself, I do believe the Captain has made certain assumptions about me and about my beliefs based upon my planet of origin and religion. And I also believe he chose me for this particular assignment at least in part because he considers that the logical person to make contact with a planet full of religious reactionaries is . . . well, another religious reactionary."

"I see," Watson repeated in exactly the same tone. Then she allowed her chair to come back upright and leaned forward, planting her elbows on her desk and folding her forearms.

"I doubt that that was an easy thing for you to say, Ms. Hearns. And I respect the fact that you didn't attempt to waffle when I pressed the point. Nor, although I may have asked about it, have I seen any indication that you're allowing any . . . reservations you may feel about the Captain's attitudes towards you to affect the performance of your duties. Nonetheless, I would raise two points for your consideration.

"First, of the four midshipmen and midshipwomen aboard this vessel, the Captain selected you. Not simply to make contact with a 'planet full of religious reactionaries,' but to command an independent detachment of armed Marines making contact with a planet full of *anyone* for the very first time in the Star Kingdom's name. You may believe he made that choice because he has assigned you to a particular religious stereotype in his own mind. It is also remotely possible, I submit to you, that he may have made his decision based upon his confidence in your ability.

"Second, while I have been impressed by your

intelligence, your ability, and the degree of personal maturity you've demonstrated here aboard *Gauntlet*, you're still quite young, Ms. Hearns. I won't deliver the traditional timeworn homily on how your perspective will change as you grow older and your judgment matures. I will, however, suggest to you that while it's certainly possible that the Captain has allowed personal attitudes or even prejudices to shape his perception of you, it's equally possible that you've allowed personal attitudes—or even prejudices—to shape *your* perception of him."

Abigail felt her cheekbones heat, but she made herself sit very upright in her own chair, her head high, meeting the exec's gaze unflinchingly. Watson returned her regard for several seconds, then smiled with what might have been an edge of approval.

"I'd like you to consider both of those possibilities, Ms. Hearns," she said. "As I say, I've been impressed by your intelligence. I think you'll appreciate that I might just have a point."

She held the midshipwoman's eyes for a moment longer, then nodded her head towards the hatch.

"And now, Ms. Hearns," she said pleasantly, "I believe you have a landing party waiting for you in Boat Bay Two. Dismissed."

Abigail *did* consider the exec's points as *Gauntlet's* pinnace sliced downward through Refuge's atmosphere and steadied on its course towards the city of Zion, the planet's largest settlement. And as she considered them, she was forced, however grudgingly, to admit that they might have some validity.

She remained convinced that the captain had, indeed, pigeonholed her in his own mind as the product of a religion-blinkered, backward society. And that it was possible, even probable, that he had allowed that view of her to predispose him towards selecting her for her present mission. But however irritating she might find his accent, or his mannerisms—or even his tailoring—she had to admit that he'd never, in any fashion, engaged in the sort of snide, implied sniping Grigovakis and some of her other Saganami classmates had practiced. Neither had he, so far as she could tell, ever allowed any preconception about her on his part to affect the way he evaluated her performance. Nor was he the sort to risk the failure of a mission by assigning anyone to command it but the person he thought best qualified to carry it out.

Even if his prejudices might have inclined him towards selecting her in the first place, he wasn't the kind of officer to make his final decision without careful consideration. And Commander Watson had been right about another thing, as well—Abigail *hadn't* considered the fact that her assignment to make contact with the Refugians might just as well have reflected his faith in her capability as his prejudice against her own background.

She grimaced as she recognized the truth in the exec's analysis. Whatever Captain Oversteegen might or might not have been guilty of, Abigail had definitely been guilty of allowing her own prejudices and pre-conceptions to color her view of him. That was humili-ating. It was also a failure of her responsibility to Test, and that was even worse.

She gazed out the viewport as the pinnace dipped down below the cloudbase and the untidy sprawl of Zion came into sight. The fact that she'd failed to Test didn't necessarily mean she'd been *wrong*, but she resolved firmly that before she continued to accept her original conclusions, she would consider *all* the evi-dence.

That, however, would have to wait until she returned

aboard *Gauntlet*. For now, she had other things to consider, and whatever the captain's reasons for assigning her to her present task, it was her responsibility to discharge it successfully.

"Five minutes to touchdown, Ms. Hearns," the flight engineer told her, and she nodded.

"Thank you, Chief Palmer," she said, and glanced over her shoulder at Platoon Sergeant Gutierrez. Gutierrez was a San Martino. Quite a few San Martinos had enlisted in the Star Kingdom's military since the planet's annexation, but Gutierrez had joined the Royal Manticoran Marine Corps long before that. Like General Tomas Ramirez, Gutierrez had arrived in the Star Kingdom as a child when his parents managed to escape the Peep occupation of San Martin. In the Gutierrezes' case, they'd done so by stowing away aboard a Solarian League freighter which had dropped them on the planet Manticore with only the clothes on their backs. And like many refugees from tyranny, Sergeant Mateo Gutierrez and his (many) brothers and sisters were unabashed patriots, fiercely devoted to the star nation which had taken them in and given them freedom.

He was also the next best thing to two meters in height and must have weighed somewhere around two hundred kilos, all of it the solid bone and muscle only to be expected from someone born and bred to the heavy gravity of San Martin. Standing next to him in the boat bay, Abigail had felt as if she were five years old again, and his weathered, competent appearance had only emphasized the feeling.

But if he made her feel like a child, his was also a reassuring—one might almost say fearsome—presence. She felt reasonably confident that the pacifistic Fellowship of the Elect was unlikely to attempt to ambush and assassinate her landing party. But after considering all the possibilities, Commander Watson had decided to send not one, but two squads of Marines down with her, and Major Hill, the CO of *Gauntlet*'s Marine detachment, had picked the first and second squads of Sergeant Gutierrez's platoon. Abigail felt moderately ridiculous as the lowly midshipwoman escorted and guarded by no less than twenty-seven armed-to-the-teeth Marines, but she supposed she should take it as a compliment. Apparently, even if the exec had decided to whack her over the head for her sullen attitude, Commander Watson still wanted her back in one piece.

She chuckled quietly at the thought, then looked back out the viewport as the pinnace settled onto the "pad." It wasn't much of a pad. In fact, it was nothing more than a wide stretch of flat, more or less pounded-down dirt. Muddy water from a recent rain covered parts of it in a thin sheet that exploded upwards as the pinnace's vectored thrust hit it, and she shook her head.

Her aerial view had already made it painfully clear that the "city" of Zion wasn't much more than a not-so-large town of single and double-story wooden and stone buildings. From the air, it had appeared that the very oldest portions of the settlement had ceramacrete streets, but the rest of the streets were either paved in cobblestones or simple dirt, like the "landing pad." She'd seen cobblestones enough in the Old Town sections of Owens, but not dirt, and the sight—like that of the landing pad—emphasized just how primitive and poverty stricken Refuge really was.

She drew a deep breath, unbuckled, and climbed out of her seat while Sergeant Gutierrez got his Marines organized. One six-man fire team headed down the ramp and took up positions around the pinnace at Gutierrez's quiet command, and Abigail frowned slightly. They weren't exactly being unobtrusive about their watchfulness. She started to say something about it to Gutierrez, then changed her mind. Commander Watson wouldn't have sent the Marines along if she hadn't wanted them to be visible.

A trio of men stepped out of the neatly painted, thatched-roofed stone cottage which, judging from the aerials and satellite communication array sitting in front of it, was probably the settlement's com center as well as the "control room" for what there was of the landing field. She studied them carefully, if as unobtrusively as she could, as she followed Gutierrez himself down the landing ramp.

The greeting party had timed things pretty well, she thought, because they reached the foot of the ramp almost simultaneously with her.

"I am called Tobias," the oldest-looking of the bearded, brown and gray-robed threesome said. There was a certain watchful wariness in the set of his shoulders and the stiffness of his spine, but he smiled and inclined his head in greeting. "I greet you in all the names of God, and in accordance with His Word, I welcome you to Refuge and offer you His Peace in the spirit of godly Love."

"Thank you," Abigail replied gravely, even as somewhere inside she winced at how someone like Arpad Grigovakis would have responded to that greeting. "I am Midshipwoman Hearns, of Her Manticoran Majesty's Ship *Gauntlet*."

"Indeed?" Tobias cocked his head, then glanced at Sergeant Gutierrez and back at Abigail. "We are not precisely familiar with the Manticoran military here on Refuge, Mistress Hearns. But as a single small, lightly populated planet, we are—understandably, I think—cautious about unexpected contacts with outsiders.

Particularly with unexpected warships. As such, I took the precaution of consulting our library about the Star Kingdom of Manticore when your ship first contacted us. Our records are somewhat out of date, but I notice that your uniform doesn't match the imagery in the file."

He gazed at her expectantly, and she smiled back at him. *Sharp as a tack, this one. And it looks like the Captain was right about how wary these people might feel*, she admitted, and nodded in acknowledgment of Tobias' point.

"You're correct, Sir," she said, and waved one hand in a small gesture at her sky-blue tunic and dark-blue trousers. "I'm currently serving aboard *Gauntlet* while completing my midshipwoman's cruise, but I'm not Manticoran, myself. I'm from Grayson, in the Yeltsin's Star System. We're allied with the Star Kingdom, and I've been attending the Royal Navy's academy at Saganami Island."

"Ah, I see," Tobias murmured, and nodded in apparent satisfaction. "I've heard of Grayson," he continued, "although I can scarcely claim that I'm at all familiar with your home world, Mistress Hearns."

He gazed at her speculatively, and she wondered what, precisely, he'd heard about Grayson. Whatever it was, it seemed to reassure him, at least to some extent, and his shoulders relaxed ever so slightly.

"Your captain's message said that you're visiting us as part of an investigation into possible acts of piracy," he said, after a moment. "I'm afraid I'm not quite clear on exactly how he believes we can help you. We are a peaceful people, and as I'm sure is apparent to you, we keep much to ourselves."

"We understand that, Sir," Abigail assured him. "We—"

"Please," Tobias interrupted gently. "Call me Brother Tobias. I am no man's master or superior."

"Of course . . . Brother Tobias," Abigail said. "But, as I was saying, my Captain is simply following up the known movements of ships which we know were operating in this area and which subsequently disappeared. One of them was the Erewhonese destroyer *Star Warrior*, which called here some months ago. Another was the transport *Windhover*."

"Oh, yes, *Windhover*," Tobias murmured sadly, and he and his two companions signed themselves with a complicated gesture. Then he shook himself.

"I don't know that we have any information that can help you, Mistress Hearns. What we do know, however, we will willingly share with you and with your captain. As I said, we of the Fellowship of the Elect are a peaceful people who have renounced the ways of violence in all of its forms in accordance with His Word. Yet the blood of our murdered brothers and sisters cries out to us, as must the blood of any of God's children. Anything we can tell you which may aid in preventing additional, equally terrible crimes, we certainly will."

"I appreciate that deeply, Brother Tobias," Abigail told him sincerely.

"Then if you would accompany me, I will guide you to the Meeting House, where Brother Heinrich and some of our other Elders are waiting to speak with you."

"Thank you," Abigail said, then paused as Sergeant Gutierrez started to key his communicator.

"I think you can remain here, Sergeant," she said quietly, and it was Gutierrez's turn to pause, his hand on the com.

"With all due respect, Ma'am," he began in his deep, rumbling voice, and she shook her head.

"I don't believe I have anything to fear from Brother Tobias and his people, Sergeant," she said more crisply.

"Ma'am, that's not really the point," he replied. "Major Hill's orders were pretty specific."

"And so are mine, Sergeant," Abigail told him. "I can look after myself," she let her right hand make a small, unobtrusive gesture in the direction of the pulser holstered at her right hip, "and I don't think I'm in any danger. But these people are probably uncomfortable around armed personnel, and we're guests here. I see no reason to offend them unnecessarily."

"Ma'am," he began again in a dangerously patient voice, "I don't think you quite underst—"

"We're going to do this my way, Sergeant." Abigail's own voice was calm but firm. He glowered at her, but she held his eyes steadily with her own and refused to back down. "Keep an eye on the pinnace," she told him, "and I'll keep my com open so you can monitor."

He hesitated, clearly hovering on the brink of further objections, then inhaled deeply. It was obvious he didn't think much of her order, and she suspected he didn't think a great deal more of the judgment of the person who'd given it. For that matter, she was far from certain Commander Watson would approve of her decision when they got back to the ship and Gutierrez reported. But the captain had emphasized that they were not to step upon these people's sensibilities or beliefs.

"Aye, aye, Ma'am," he said finally.

"Thank you, Sergeant," she said, and turned back to Brother Tobias. "Whenever you're ready, Brother," she told him.

HMS *Gauntlet* moved steadily outward from the planet of Refuge. She wasn't in any particular hurry, but Captain Oversteegen had decided he might as well actually go ahead and update his charts on the Tiberian System. As Commander Watson had suggested, it provided a perfectly acceptable reason to move *Gauntlet* away from the planet. And if he was going to use it as a pretext, he might as well get some genuine use out of it. Besides, it would be a worthwhile exercise for Lieutenant Commander Atkins' department.

"How's it going, Valeria?" Commander Watson asked, and the astrogator looked up from a conversation with her senior yeoman.

"Pretty well, actually," she replied. "We're not turning up any serious discrepancies, but it's pretty obvious that whoever ran the original survey on the system wasn't exactly interested in dotting all the 'i's and crossing all the 't's."

"How so?" Watson asked.

"Like I said, it's nothing major. But there are some minor system bodies that never got cataloged at all. For instance, Refuge has a secondary moon—more of a captured hunk of loose rock, actually—that doesn't appear. We're finding some other little items like that. Small stuff, nothing significant or worth worrying about. But it's an interesting exercise, especially for my newbies."

"Good, but don't get too attached to it. I don't imagine we'll be hanging around very long after we recover Ms. Hearns and her party."

"Understood." Atkins looked around for a moment, then leaned closer to the executive officer. "Is it true she left her watchdogs at the pinnace?" she asked quietly, with a slight smile.

"Now, how did you hear that?" Watson responded.

"Chief Palmer made some observations for me on his way to the planet," Atkins said. "When he reported them to Chief Abrams, he . . . might have commented on it."

"I see." Watson snorted. "You know, the grapevine aboard this ship must be made out of fiber optic, given how quick it works!" She shook her head. "In answer to your question, however, yes. She left Gutierrez and his people at the landing field. I don't think the Sergeant was particularly happy about it, either."

"He doesn't think she's actually in any sort of danger, does he?" Atkins asked in a more serious tone.

"On a planet full of nonviolent religious types?" Watson snorted again, harder, then paused. "Well, Gutierrez *is* a Marine, so I suppose he could be a little less trusting than us Navy types. But my read right this minute is that he's just a bit on the disgusted side. I think he's put her down as one of those Little Ms. Sunshine types who think the universe is populated solely by kindly, helpful souls."

"Abigail?" Atkins shook her head. "She's a Grayson, Ma'am."

"I know that. You know that. Hell, *Gutierrez* knows that! But he's also down on a planet we don't know anything about, really, on a first-hand basis, and his pablum-brained midshipwoman has just gone traipsing off on her own with the locals. Not something exactly designed to give a Marine the most lively possible faith in her judgment."

"You think it was the wrong decision?" Atkins asked curiously.

"No, not really. I'm going to give her a little grief over it, when we get her back aboard, and suggest that I sent those Marines along for a reason. But I'm not going to smack her for it, because I think I know why she did it. Besides, she's the one down there, not me, and over all, I think I have considerable faith in her judgment."

"Well," Atkins said, after a glance at the bulkhead time/date display, "she's been dirtside for almost four hours now. Nothing seems to have gone wrong so far, and I suppose she should be heading back shortly."

"As a matter of fact, she's on her way back to the pinnace right now," Watson agreed, "and—"

"Hyper footprint!" The tactical rating whose report interrupted the exec sounded surprised, but his voice was crisp. "Looks like two ships in company, bearing zero-three-four by zero-one-niner!"

Watson wheeled towards him, eyebrows rising, then crossed quickly back to the command chair at the center of the bridge and hit the button that deployed the tactical repeater plot. She gazed down into it, watching until CIC updated it with the red caret that indicated an unidentified hyper footprint on *Gauntlet's* starboard bow at just over sixteen light-minutes.

"Well, well, well," she murmured, and pressed a com stud on the chair arm.

"Captain speakin'," Michael Oversteegen's voice acknowledged.

"Sir, it's the Exec," she told him. "We've got an unidentified hyper footprint at roughly two hundred and eighty-eight million kilometers. Looks like it might be a pair of them."

"Do we, indeed?" Oversteegen said in a thoughtful voice. "Now, what do you think someone might be doin' in a system like Tiberian?"

"Well, Sir, unless they're as noble, virtuous, and aboveboard as we are, then I suppose it's possible they might be nasty old pirates."

"The same thought had occurred t' me," Oversteegen said, and then his voice went crisper. "Send the crew t' Action Stations, Linda. I'm on my way."

Abigail leaned back in her comfortable chair in the pinnace's passenger compartment, watching the dark indigo of Refuge's stratosphere give way to the black of space, and considered what she'd learned from Brother Tobias and Brother Heinrich.

It wasn't much, she reflected. In fact, she doubted she'd learned a single thing that hadn't already been included in the captain's ONI analyses. Except that it was pretty evident that the captain had been right about the way *Star Warrior's* captain had rubbed the Refugians the wrong way during his own visit to Tiberian.

It wasn't anything Tobias or Heinrich had said, so much as the way they *hadn't* said it, she thought. She hated to admit it, but their attitude towards *Star Warrior* and her crew was precisely the same as the one certain Graysons must have had when Lady Harrington first visited Yeltsin's Star. The irreligious outsiders had come blundering into their star system, bringing with them all of their own, hopelessly secular concerns and all of their readiness to shed blood, and they'd hated it.

It seemed likely to Abigail that both *Star Warrior's* captain and the landing party from the Erewhonese cruiser which had followed up the destroyer's disappearance had taken exactly the wrong tack with the Fellowship of the Elect. She was sure they hadn't deliberately stepped on the Refugians' sensibilities, but they did seem to have radiated precisely the sort of eagerness to find and destroy their enemies which the Refugian religion would have found most distasteful.

And whatever might have been true in *Star Warrior's* case, the cruiser which had followed her to Tiberian had obviously been in vengeance-seeking mode. Clearly, the members of her crew who had spoken with Brother Heinrich and his fellow Elders had been both baffled by and at least a little contemptuous of the locals' rejection of their own eagerness to hunt down and destroy whoever had attacked their destroyer.

To be fair to the Fellowship's Elders, they'd recognized that however nonviolent their own religion might be, the suppression of the sort of piracy which had apparently murdered several thousand of their fellow believers was an abomination in the sight of God. That hadn't made them happy about their Erewhonese visitors' attitudes, however. Nor had it made them any less aware of their own religion's commands against violence, and their cooperation, however sincere, had been grudging.

It had taken Abigail a good hour to overcome that grudgingness, herself, and she'd come to the reluctant conclusion that Captain Oversteegen had chosen the right person for the job, after all. It irked her enormously. Which, she had been forced to admit, was petty of her . . . which only made it even more irksome, of course. Her own beliefs were in a great many ways very different from those of the Refugians. For one thing, while Father Church taught that violence should never be a first resort, his doctrine also enshrined the belief that it was the duty of the godly to use whatever tools were required when evil threatened. As Saint Austen had said, "He who does not oppose evil by all means in his power becomes its accomplice." The Church of Humanity believed that—helped, no doubt, she admitted, by the threat Masada had presented for so long— and she found the Refugians' hesitance to take up the sword themselves very difficult to understand. Or to sympathize with. Yet at least she understood its basis and depth, and that meant she was undoubtedly a far better choice as *Gauntlet*'s emissary than any of her hopelessly secular fellow middies would have been.

Now if only the trip had actually turned up some vital information that would have led them to the pirates! Unfortunately, as helpful as the Elders had been, in the end, they hadn't been able to tell her anything that seemed significant to her. She'd recorded the entire meeting, and the captain might be able to find something in the recording that she'd missed at the time, but she doubted it. Which meant—

"Excuse me, Ms. Hearns."

Abigail looked up, startled out of her thoughts by Chief Palmer's voice.

"Yes, Chief. What is it?"

"Ma'am, the Captain is on the com. He wants to speak to you."

"Oh, damn!" Haicheng Ringstorff muttered in tones of profound disgust. "Tell me you're lying, George!"

"I wish." If possible, Lithgow sounded even more disgusted than his superior. "But it's confirmed. It's Tyler and Lamar, all right. And our nosy friend couldn't have missed their footprints if he'd tried."

"Crap." Ringstorff shoved himself back in his chair and glared at his com display. Not that he was pissed off with Lithgow. Then he sighed and shook his head in resignation.

"Well, this is why we kept Maurersberger and Morakis on station. Has the Erewhonese challenged Tyler and Lamar yet?"

"No." Lithgow grimaced. "He's changed course to head directly towards them, but he hasn't said a word yet."

"That's going to change, I'm sure," Ringstorff said grimly. "Not that it matters very much. We can't let him go home and tell the rest of his navy about us."

"I know that's the plan," Lithgow said just a bit cautiously, "but is it really the best idea?" Ringstorff frowned at him, and Lithgow shrugged. "Like you, I figure even the Four Yahoos can take a single Erewhonese cruiser. But even after we do, aren't we still fucked? They obviously sent this fellow along to backtrack their destroyer, so if we pop him in Tiberian, they're bound to close in on the system—probably within another few weeks—which will make it impossible for us to go on operating here, anyway. At this point, we can still avoid action if we want to. So why not just pull out, if we're going to have to relocate our operational base whatever happens?"

"You're probably—no, you're certainly—right that we're going to have to find another place to park ourselves," Ringstorff conceded. "But the SOP for the situation was laid out in our initial orders. Now, mind you, I'm perfectly willing to tell whoever wrote those orders to go screw himself, under the right circumstances, but in this case, I think he had a point. If we zap this turkey, it absolutely denies the Erewhonese any information about us. All they'll know is that they lost a destroyer and a cruiser after investigating this system. They're bound to figure that they actually lost them *in* this system, but if there are no survivors and we nuke the cruiser's wreckage the way we did the tin-can's, they'll never be able to confirm that absolutely. And whatever they may suspect, they won't have any way to guesstimate what we used to take their ships out. If we let this one get away, they'll know we have at least two units, and they'll probably have a pretty good indication that the two they know about were in the heavy cruiser range themselves."

"I can see that. But they're going to figure we must have at least that much firepower, whatever it was aboard, to take their ships out in the first place," Lithgow pointed out.

"Probably." Ringstorff nodded. "On the other hand, they won't be able to be positive that we didn't somehow manage to ambush their cruiser with several smaller units. But, frankly, the main reason I'm willing to take this fellow on is that the Yahoos need the experience."

Lithgow's eyebrows rose, and Ringstorff shrugged.

"I've never been happy about the fact that the basic plan said we had to lie completely doggo—before the home office authorized our . . . peripheral operations, of course—but then be ready at the drop of a hat to produce four heavy cruisers prepared, if necessary, to take on light Erewhonese or Peep naval forces. You really think these jackasses are going to be prepared to stand up to regular naval units at anything remotely resembling even odds, Solly hardware or no?"

"Well . . ."

"Exactly. Maurersberger and Tyler nearly pissed themselves when they had to jump a single destroyer! Let's face it, they may be the best in the business when it comes to slaughtering passenger liners and unarmed merchies, but that's a whole different proposition from taking on regular men-of-war. So the way I see it, this busybody cruiser represents an opportunity, as well as a monumental pain in the ass. We ought to be able to take him out fairly easily, given the odds. If we can, well and good. It eliminates a possible information source for the other side, and simultaneously gives our 'gallant captains' some genuine combat experience and a victory which ought to be a morale enhancer if the balloon ever really goes up on the main op. And if we *can't* take a single Erewhonese heavy cruiser, then this is damned well a better time to find out than when the entire operation might depend on our ability to do the same thing."

"There *is* that," Lithgow agreed after a moment's consideration.

"Damned straight there is," Ringstorff said. Then he snorted in amusement. "And I suppose I should also point out that whatever happens to the Four Yahoos, *we* should be just fine. After all, we're only an unarmed depot ship. Not even Morakis could expect us to get into shooting range of an enemy warship to support her. So if anything unfortunate happens to the cruisers, we'll just very quietly sneak away under stealth. And tell whatever idiot back home in Mesa thought this one up that his precious Silesian pirates couldn't cut the mustard when it came down to it."

"The home office won't be especially pleased with you if that happens," Lithgow warned.

"They'd be even less pleased if we wound up committing these idiots to action during the main operation and they blew it *then*," Ringstorff replied. "And if they do manage to screw the pooch this time, I guarantee I'll make that point in my report!"

"What about that pinnace of theirs? According to the surveillance platforms, it's just left atmosphere headed after them, but it's never going to catch up before the shooting starts. So what do we do about it afterwards? For that matter, what about Refuge?"

"Um." Ringstorff frowned. "The pinnace is going to have to go," he said. "We have to assume that the cruiser's captain's already passed his intentions and at least some general info on to the pinnace crew. I don't know about the rest of Refuge, though."

He drummed lightly on the edge of his desk with both hands for several seconds.

"I'd prefer to just leave them alone," he said finally. "They don't have any surveillance net of their own, so the only information they could have would have to come from the cruiser's transmissions. I doubt a regular navy captain would want to get them into the line of fire if he could help it, though, so he may not have transmitted to them at all. Of course, the safest solution would be to go ahead and take them out, as well. It's hardly like there are enough people down there to

get the Sollies in an uproar over the Eridani Edict,
after all! But it would piss off Pritchart—she's already
irritated enough over what happened to her transport—
and remember that she was a frigging Aprilist before
the Pierre Coup. She wouldn't object to breaking
however many eggs it took to deal with a problem like
this, and it could get nasty if something we did convinced her government to begin actively cooperating
with the Erewhonese."

He pondered for a few more moments, then
shrugged.

"We'll have to play that one by ear," he decided. "If
we can nail the pinnace and its crew, that's the main
thing. If it looks like the other side did transmit to the
Refugians, we'll just have to take out Zion, as well. We
know their planetary com net sucks, so if we wipe out
their main groundside com node, we should wipe out
any information in it, as well. Hell, we can probably
get away with sending in a couple of assault shuttles
to take out just their com shack!" He chuckled suddenly. "Matter of fact, if we handled it that way, it
might even get us some brownie points for our
'humanitarian restraint'!" Then he sobered. "But if it
looks like the information's gotten beyond Zion, then
we'll do whatever we have to do."

" . . . so for right now, I want you t' head back t'
Refuge. We'll return t' collect you and your people after
we investigate this contact."

Abigail watched Captain Oversteegen's face on the
small com screen. He looked calm and confident,
despite the fact that CIC had confirmed that both of
the incoming impeller signatures belonged to something
at least the size of heavy cruisers. That was big for a
pirate vessel, yet far too small to be any sort of merchant ship. Of course, no pirate was going to be able

to match either the technology or the training of the RMN. But still . . .

"Understood, Sir," she told him, and waited out the light-speed communications delay until he nodded in satisfaction.

"Keep an eye out," he said. "Right now, it looks like we're lookin' at only a pair of ships. And it's still possible we're goin' t' find out that they're regular warships here for a legitimate purpose, too. But whatever they are, they're maintainin' their course along the outer edge of the limit. That's . . . unusual enough t' make me suspicious, but it also means they're not immediately tryin' t' evade us. So if it turns out they're pirates, they're mighty gutsy ones. Either that, or they've got something t' hide that's important enough for them t' risk taking on a heavy cruiser. And if they do, they're not goin' t' hesitate t' go after a pinnace, as well. Exercise your discretion . . . and try not t' get the Refugians involved. Oversteegen, clear."

The screen blanked. Abigail sat and gazed at it for a moment, then shook herself, stood, and stepped forward from the flight engineer's cramped cubbyhole of a compartment to the flight deck.

"You heard, PO?" she asked the pilot.

"Yes, Ma'am," Petty Officer First Class Hoskins replied. She gestured at her maneuvering plot, which was currently configured to display the entire system. The small display was too tiny to show much detail on such a large scale, but it was more than enough to show *Gauntlet*'s friendly green icon speeding rapidly away from the pinnace towards the two unknowns. "'Bout to get kind of lonely, Ma'am," she observed.

"I think I feel sorrier for whoever that is, assuming they're bad guys, than I do for the Captain," Abigail said, and realized she wasn't just preserving a confident front for Hoskins' benefit. "But in the meantime,

I suppose we should do what we were told. Let's turn it around, PO."

"Yes, Ma'am. Should I head for Zion, or just for planetary orbit?"

"I think we'll want to stay away from Zion, whatever happens," Abigail said slowly. "For right now, plan on sliding us back into orbit when we reach the planet. We can always change our minds later, if we have to."

"Aye, aye, Ma'am," Hoskins said, and Abigail nodded and turned to make her way back to the passenger compartment.

Sergeant Gutierrez looked up alertly, and she parked herself back in her own chair, across the aisle from the Marine.

"*Gauntlet* has picked up a couple of unknown hyper footprints," she told him. "She's moving to investigate them now."

"I see, Ma'am." Gutierrez considered her with neutral eyes. "And what about us, if I can ask?"

"The Captain wants us to head back towards Refuge. We can't match *Gauntlet*'s acceleration rate, and he doesn't want to delay to pick us up."

"I see," Gutierrez repeated.

"He doesn't want us to involve the Refugians if anything . . . unexpected happens," Abigail continued.

"Do we have some reason to expect that something *will* happen, Ma'am?"

"Not that I'm aware of, Sergeant," Abigail replied. "On the other hand, there *are* two of them. That we know of," she added, and Gutierrez looked at her for a moment.

"Do you really think there could be more of them hiding out there, somewhere, Ma'am?" The sergeant's tone was respectful enough, but that didn't keep him from sounding just a little incredulous.

"I think that, as far as we know, the Alliance has

the best sensor technology in space, Sergeant," Abigail told him, keeping her own voice serene. "I also think a star system represents a very large volume of very empty space, and we don't have a system-wide surveillance net in place. So while I don't necessarily think it's *likely* there are more of them around, I also don't think it's impossible. Which is why I'd like to be prepared for the possibility."

"Yes, Ma'am."

It was plain to Abigail that Gutierrez was humoring her, however respectfully he was doing it. Obviously, he was of the opinion that a midshipwoman who left her Marine bodyguards behind while she wandered off into the middle of an unknown settlement without a qualm and then worried about invisible bogeymen ambushing a Queen's ship had certain problems rationally ordering threat hierarchies. Not that he would ever dream of saying so, of course.

"What sort of preparations did you have in mind, Ma'am?" he asked after a brief pause.

"Well," Abigail said in a thoughtfully serious tone, moved by a sudden visitation from the imp of the perverse, "as I said, the Captain doesn't want us to involve the Refugians. So that seems to me to rule out a return to Zion. In fact, it would probably be a good idea for us to stay as far away from any of the Refugians' settlements as possible. After all, if there *are* other pirates in the system, they might decide to send one of their other ships after us, as well."

Gutierrez didn't say a word, but Abigail found it difficult not to giggle at his expression. Clearly, he was becoming even more convinced the midshipwoman with whom he'd been saddled was a dip. Now she thought pirates confronted by a Royal Manticoran Navy heavy cruiser would worry about chasing down a single *pinnace*? It must have been all he could do to not shake his head in disbelief, she reflected, but she kept her own expression completely serious.

"PO Hoskins is a very good pilot," she continued, "but there's no way a pinnace could avoid a regular warship in space. So if someone does come after us, I'm going to have her set us down somewhere on the planet—preferably clear on the other side of it from the closest Refugian settlement. Of course, if they track us in, they'll be able to find the pinnace without too much difficulty, whatever we might do to conceal it. So, in a worst-case scenario like that, we'll have to abandon the pinnace and seek to evade any pursuers groundside until *Gauntlet* can return to pick us up."

Gutierrez's eyes were almost bulging by now, and Abigail smiled at him with an expression of becoming earnestness.

"Bearing all of that in mind, Sergeant," she told him, "I think it would be a good idea for you to make a complete survey of the survival gear we have on board. Decide what would be useful to us and get it organized into man-portable packs in case we do have to abandon."

Gutierrez hovered on the brink of protest, but he was a Marine. He couldn't quite bring himself to explain to Abigail that she was a lunatic, so instead he swallowed all of the many arguments which must have presented themselves to him and simply nodded.

"Aye, aye, Ma'am. I'll . . . get right on it."

"You know, Captain," Commander Blumenthal said thoughtfully, "these guys seem to have really good EW."

"What d'you mean, Guns?" Captain Oversteegen asked, turning his command chair to gaze in Blumenthal's direction.

"It's really more of a feeling than anything else at this point," Blumenthal said slowly. "But I'm having a lot more trouble getting a lock on their emissions signatures than I ought to be." He gestured at his display. "The recon platforms are less than two million klicks out, and they still aren't getting as much as they ought to. If they were still under stealth, that would be one thing, but they aren't. Instead, they seem to be doing some sort of weird jingle-jangle on our drones' passives. I haven't seen anything quite like it before."

Oversteegen frowned thoughtfully. The possibility that the newcomers might have a legitimate reason for visiting Tiberian had become increasingly less likely. Without the RMN's FTL com capability, there'd been an inevitable light-speed transmission delay of just over thirty-two minutes built into any challenge/response com loop. But they'd passed that point some time ago, and the fact that the unknowns had completely ignored all of *Gauntlet*'s challenges and efforts to establish communications was certainly a bad sign. Unfortunately, neither the current RMN rules of engagement nor interstellar law gave him the right to preemptively attack someone simply because they refused to talk to him.

Normally, Oversteegen had no particular problem with that restriction. In this instance, however, he had quite a large problem with it. Although *Gauntlet* was only a heavy cruiser, without the magazine space or the launch tubes for the all-up multi-drive missiles which had given the Manticoran Alliance such a decisive advantage over the People's Navy during the final phases of the war, the missiles she did have were significantly longer ranged than those any other cruiser-sized vessel was likely to carry. But the unknowns were already inside his own theoretical envelope for a maximum-range engagement, and they were continuing to close. At the present rate of closure, in fact, he'd be inside *their* engagement range within less than another twelve minutes.

Which meant this was *not* a moment at which he wanted to discover that whoever they were had better hardware than they ought to have.

"We still don't have even a national ID, Sir," the tactical officer continued, "and I'm not happy about that."

"It's not just a class we haven't seen before?" Oversteegen's voice was more that of a man thinking aloud than that of someone actually asking a question, but Blumenthal replied anyway.

"Definitely not, Sir. I cross-checked what we do have against everything in the database. Whoever these people are, we don't know them. Not, at least, based on the emissions we've been able to pick up so far, even with the Ghost Rider platforms. That's what worries me. We ought to be able to make *some* stab at IDing them, and we can't."

Oversteegen nodded. The RMN's long-range, real-time reconnaissance drones gave it an enormous tactical advantage. At the moment, Blumenthal undoubtedly had a far better look at the unknowns than they could possibly have at *Gauntlet*. But that didn't help a lot if *Gauntlet* couldn't identify what she was seeing.

"Can you maneuver one of the platforms for a visual ID?" he asked after considering possibilities.

"I think so, Sir. But it'll take a while. And it'll have to be a down-the-throat look, and at that range, even Peeps could probably nail the platform, stealth or no stealth."

"Go for it anyway," Oversteegen decided.

❖   ❖   ❖

"You know," Ringstorff said, "I don't think I've had an operation get this fucked up in the last ten T-years. A Manty. A frigging *Manty*!"

He scowled down at his plot. The information it displayed was over nineteen minutes old, given the distance between the depot ship and the cruiser they'd identified as "Erewhonese" on the basis of the sensor emissions their stealthed inner-system platforms had picked up. But they'd forgotten that the Erewhonese weren't the only ones with Manticoran Alliance hardware, and the relayed challenge this HMS *Gauntlet* had transmitted to Tyler left no doubt about her nationality. His scowl deepened as he considered the implications, but Lithgow, on the other hand, only shrugged.

"No way you could have known until they challenged Tyler," he said. "Who would have expected to see a single Manty cruiser this far from home *now*?" He grimaced. "They've been pulling their horns in steadily ever since Saint-Just mousetrapped them into that cease-fire."

"Well, pulling in or not, they're here," Ringstorff grumbled.

"Doesn't really change anything, though, does it?" Lithgow asked, and Ringstorff looked at him. "What I mean is, they're obviously working with the Erewhonese, or they wouldn't be here. In that case, all of the arguments in favor of keeping them from passing on any scan data about us still apply, don't they?"

"Sure they do, but you heard Tyler's voice as well as I did. He's scared shitless by the very thought of crossing swords with a Manty!"

"So what?" Lithgow chuckled nastily. "He's already inside their missile range, so it's not like he has any choice about engaging them, anyway. And whatever the Peeps may think, I don't believe Manties are supermen. The Yahoos have state-of-the-art Solarian missiles and EW, and there are four of them. Two of whom the Manties don't even know are there yet!"

"I know." Ringstorff inhaled deeply and nodded, but despite that, he was far more anxious about the possible outcome than Lithgow was. Unlike Ringstorff, Lithgow was a Solarian himself, recruited by Ringstorff's superiors for the job. This was his first trip to what the League still referred to as the Haven Sector, and it had been obvious to Ringstorff for some time that Lithgow resented the enormous respect—one might almost say terror—which Manticoran technological superiority generated in the minds of the locals.

Part of that was the simple fact that Lithgow hadn't been here while the Manties' Eighth Fleet had been busy smashing every Peep fleet or task force in its way into rubble. But an even bigger part of it, Ringstorff was convinced, was the unshakable confidence in their own unassailable technological supremacy which seemed to be a part of the intellectual baggage of every Solly he'd ever worked with.

Still, he told himself, it was always possible Lithgow's view was at least as accurate as his own. He, after all, was an Andermani, and the Andermani—like their neighbors in the Silesian Confederacy, although to a lesser extent—were accustomed to the notion that the Royal Manticoran Navy was the region's premier fleet. No one in his right mind pissed off the Manties. That was a fundamental rule of survival for the various pirates and rogue regimes of Silesia.

Which was the real reason for his concern. Lithgow was certainly correct that Tyler and Lamar couldn't evade action at this point whatever they did, and he was also right that the Yahoos' capabilities were almost certain to come as a nasty surprise to the Manty. Not to mention the fact that the Manty seemed totally oblivious to the other two cruisers creeping up behind him. So by every objective standard, it ought to be the Manty who was in trouble.

Except that the Four Yahoos were all Silesians, which meant they were unlikely to see it that way.

"Who the hell *are* these people?" Commander Blumenthal demanded rhetorically as he glared at the visual image frozen on his display.

As he'd more than half-feared, the cruiser he was looking at had picked up the recon drone as it came sidling in for an optical pass. The target's forward missile defenses had promptly blown it out of space. In fact, they'd done it considerably more quickly than he'd anticipated, and he didn't like the acceleration numbers on the counter-missile they'd used. Nor did he care for the increasing evidence that their EW capabilities were much, much better than those of any "pirates" he'd ever heard of. For that matter, they were at least twenty or thirty percent better than anything *Gauntlet* had on file for first-line *Peep* systems!

"That, Guns," Captain Oversteegen murmured from where he stood at Blumenthal's shoulder, "is an excellent question."

The captain rubbed his lower lip while he furrowed his brow in thought. The visual imagery wasn't as good as he might have wished, and the angle was poor. But it was the first real look they'd gotten, and there was something about it. Something about the turn of the cruiser's forward hammerhead and the angle of the impeller ring . . .

"That's a Solarian design," he said suddenly, his aristocratic drawl momentarily in total abeyance.

"A *Solly*?" Blumenthal looked up over his shoulder in disbelief.

"I'm almost certain," Oversteegen said, and leaned closer to point at the visual image. "Look at that gravitic array," he said as more recognition features sprang out at him now that he knew what to look for. "And look at the impeller ring. See the offset on the beta nodes?" He shook his head. "And that might explain how good their EW is."

Blumenthal stared back down at the image, as if seeing it for the first time.

"You could be right, Sir," he said slowly. "But what in God's name would *Solly* heavy cruisers be doing *here*?"

"I don't have the least idea," Oversteegen admitted. "Except for one thing, Guns. If what they're here for was legitimate, they would have responded t' our challenges by now. And the fact that they're Solly-built, doesn't mean a thing about who's crewin' them, now does it?"

"But how would garden variety pirates this far from the League get their hands on Solly hardware? And if they could do that in the first place, then why waste their time on chicken-stealing level piracy in an area where all of the system economies are so marginal?"

"All very good questions, Guns," Oversteegen acknowledged. He straightened and clasped his hands behind him. "And it occurs t' me that they're also the sort of questions our friends out there aren't goin' t' want anyone to be askin' . . . much less answerin'. Which may explain why they're comin' in on us so steadily now. Of course, it still leaves the question of why they waited so long before they did, now doesn't it?"

He rocked slightly on the balls of his feet, eyes slightly unfocused as he thought hard. Then he nodded to himself.

"A nasty thought just occurred t' me, Guns. If these are Sollies—or, at least, Solly-built—and if the EW we've actually observed is this good, then what's their *stealth* technology like?"

"You think there are more of them around, Sir?"

"If there's two of them, I don't see any reason why there couldn't be more. After all, two of them are so unlikely, on the face of things, that I'm no longer prepared t' even hazard a guess as t' what they could be up to. But I think it's time we checked our back."

"Absolutely, Sir," Blumenthal agreed, and looked at his assistant.

"Deploy four more of the Sierra Romeo platforms, Mr. Aitschuler. I want a conic sweep of our after aspect immediately!"

"Shit!" Jerome Tyler, captain of the heavy cruiser *Fortune Hunter*, swore with feeling. No ship he'd ever commanded, or even served upon, before *Fortune Hunter* would have boasted the sensor sensitivity to have spotted the Manty's recon platform when it came in on her. Nor would they have been capable of spotting the additional platforms the bastard had just deployed astern of himself. Not even *Fortune Hunter*'s systems could manage to hold the drones once they cleared their mother ship's wedge and brought their own stealth systems fully online, but he knew where they had to be headed. Which meant they were probably going to find Juliette Morakis' *Cutthroat* and Dongcai Maurersberger's *Mörder* before they got properly into position.

This was all that asshole Ringstorff's fault! He was the one who'd figured it had to be the Erewhonese again. Now he'd committed them to taking on the Royal Manticoran Navy, and the one thing anyone who had ever operated in Silesia knew was that if you took on a single Manty warship, you'd better be damned sure you killed every member of its crew. Because if the Manties knew you'd hit one of their ships, and they had any clue that would let them identify you, they would stop coming after you only after you were dead . . . or Hell was a skating rink.

Tyler forced his thoughts out of their ever tightening circle and drew a deep breath.

Yes, it was all Ringstorff's fault. And, yes, they were up against a Manty. But that just meant their options were clearer.

And that they couldn't let there be any survivors at all.

"There *is* another one back there, Sir!"

Michael Oversteegen frowned ever so slightly as his repeater plot updated with the drones' report. The stealthed cruiser creeping up on *Gauntlet's* port quarter was much closer than any Peep could have gotten without being detected. On the other hand, she wasn't as close as another Manticoran ship might have managed, which suggested that the RMN's hardware remained superior to the other side's, even if those were Solly-built ships. Unfortunately, the margin of superiority looked like being much thinner than it should have been, and there were three of them.

That he knew about *so far*, that was.

He crossed his legs, considering the situation. The two ships he'd already known about were almost dead ahead of him now, but they'd been cautious, maneuvering along the outside arc of the hyper limit without ever crossing it while letting *Gauntlet* gradually close the range. The discovery of the third unknown unit might very well explain that caution; they'd shaped their course to draw Oversteegen into a position which would permit their consort to maneuver around astern of him.

But now that the third cruiser was almost into position, they'd changed their own vectors to head directly towards him. The current range was just over fourteen million kilometers, with a closing velocity of just over sixty thousand kilometers per second. Given that geometry, the effective powered missile range for a Peep missile would have been just over fifteen million klicks at 42,500 g, which would give them a minute and a half of drive time. *Gauntlet's* missiles could pull 46,000 g over the same time envelope, which gave her a current powered engagement range of over sixteen-point-three million klicks, but that theoretical advantage was rather cold comfort, given that both sides were already in their own range of the other. On the other hand, the other side's timing hadn't been perfect—not surprisingly, given the limitations of light-speed communications and the perennial difficulty of coordinating with someone whose stealth systems hid him from your sensors as completely as from the enemy's. Oversteegen knew the trailer coming up astern was there now, and that she'd need over eleven more minutes to get into missile range at all . . . assuming he let her do so.

"Things seem t' be gettin' a little complicated," he observed mildly into the silently roaring tension of his bridge. He drummed the fingers of his right hand lightly on his command chair's armrest and considered his options, which were becoming progressively less palatable.

"How do your targetin' solutions on Number One and Number Two look, Guns?" he asked.

"They're not as good as I'd like, Sir," Blumenthal replied honestly. "Against a Peep, my confidence would be high. Against whoever these people are, though—" He shrugged. "They haven't brought their ECM fully on line yet, so I can't be certain how it will affect our targeting solutions when they do. But given what they seem to be able to do to our passive sensors, I have to say I'd be cautious about their reliability."

"But they don't have it up yet," Oversteegen murmured.

"Not fully, no, Sir."

"Captain," Commander Watson said quietly from the com screen at Oversteegen's right knee which linked him to the exec and her backup command crew in Auxiliary Control, "it's my duty to remind you that the current Rules of Engagement require demonstration of hostile intent before one of Her Majesty's starships is authorized to open fire."

"Thank you, Ms. Exec." Oversteegen smiled thinly at her. "I'm aware of the ROE, but you're quite correct t' remind me of them, and the log will indicate you did so. However, under the existin' circumstances, and given these people's refusal t' respond t' any of our challenges, coupled with the obvious effort t' position their third ship t' ambush us from behind, I'm willin' t' consider that they've already demonstrated hostile intent."

A chill wind seemed to blow briefly around *Gauntlet's* command deck and the already palpable tension ratcheted higher.

"For what it's worth, Sir," Watson replied, "I concur in your evaluation."

"It would be nice if we were both wrong," Oversteegen observed. "Unfortunately, I don't think we are. Commander Atkins."

"Yes, Sir," the astrogator responded.

"Time t' hyper limit at constant accelerations and headin's?"

"Approximately twelve minutes, Sir."

"And how much can we shorten that?"

"Just a moment, please, Sir." Atkins punched new acceleration values and courses into her running plot, then looked back up. "If we go to max military power, Sir, we can hit the limit in ten-point-five minutes, assuming we change heading seventeen degrees to port for a least-time heading."

"Guns."

"Yes, Sir," Blumenthal responded.

"Number Three's current time t' maximum powered missile range at constant accelerations?"

"Assuming constant accelerations, and assigning Peep missile ranges, approximately ten minutes before Number Three enters her estimated engagement range, Sir," Blumenthal replied promptly. "However, I should point out that if these are Solarian-built units, they may be carrying Solly ordnance, as well, and we have no definitive figures on Solarian League missile performance."

"Noted," Oversteegen replied. "And if we go t' Astro's least-time course t' the limit?"

"Approximately nine-point-three minutes. The course change will let her cut the chord on us just a bit. But, again, Sir, that assumes Peep compensator efficiency at max military power, and a Solly-built ship may be able to pull a higher accel than that."

"Understood." It seemed to *Gauntlet*'s bridge crew that a small eternity passed, but it was actually less than five seconds before Captain Michael Oversteegen made his decision.

"Helm, when I give the word, put us on Astro's course for the limit."

"Aye, aye, Sir," the helmswoman said tautly.

"Guns, the instant we change headin', I want full broadsides *and* the chase tubes on Number One. I know you'll have t' share uplinks, but I want maximum weight of fire. Hit him hard, because I've got a feelin' any of these people who can are goin' t' follow us right across the wall."

"Aye, aye, Sir," Commander Blumenthal acknowledged in a crisp voice.

"Very well, Helm. *Execute!*"

❖   ❖   ❖

"What the f—?!"

Jerome Tyler stared at his plot in disbelief as no less than sixty missiles suddenly came roaring towards *Fortune Hunter*. No heavy cruiser packed a missile broadside that heavy! Had the bastards had missile pods on tow the entire time?

"Tactical! Bring up our EW! Point defense free! And open fire on that son-of-a-bitch!"

"There goes their EW, Sir," Blumenthal reported, and Oversteegen nodded. He also frowned, because the target's electronic warfare capability was enormously better than anything he'd ever seen out of any non-Manticoran unit. It came up faster, and it was far more effective.

The missiles' target faded into a fuzzy ball of jamming, and fiendishly effective decoys came to life on their tethering tractors. Blumenthal's systems didn't quite lose lock completely, but that lock became much looser and more tentative, and at least a quarter of *Gauntlet*'s missiles veered off to target the decoys as the combination of limited telemetry links and the decoys' efficiency came into play. The fact that *Gauntlet* was bows-on to her target even after course change let her engage with both broadsides and her bow chasers alike, but she had links for little more than a quarter of that many birds without sharing them, and it showed.

Yet however good their EW might be, it was evident that they couldn't match Ghost Rider's capabilities. Both Number One and Number Two returned *Gauntlet*'s fire almost instantly, but they fired only eight missiles between them. Clearly, those birds came solely from their chase tubes, which suggested that their broadside tubes couldn't match Manticore's off-bore capability.

But that was the only really good news, and Oversteegen watched as his own counter missiles and point defense engaged the incoming fire.

Just as the opposing cruisers' electronic warfare capability was far better than any Peep's would have been, so was their missiles' ECM. Point defense's firing solutions were much poorer than usual, and two of the incoming birds evaded no fewer than three counter missiles each. Blumenthal's last-ditch laser clusters managed to nail both of them before they reached laser head attack range, but Manticoran missile defenses shouldn't have let anything get that close from such a small salvo.

"Two hits on Number One!" one of Blumenthal's ratings announced just as the lasers stopped the second of the near-misses. Which, Oversteegen told himself sourly, wasn't anything to write home about coming out of a sixty-missile launch.

Still, it was better than the other side had done.

Fortune Hunter bucked, and alarms shrilled, as two X-ray lasers slammed into her bow. They came in from almost dead ahead, with no sidewall to interdict, and armor shattered under their ferocious power. Point Defense Four blew apart, and the same hit drove deep, severely damaging Gravitic One and breaching Magazine Two. The second hit came in at a broader angle, with no carry back into the hull, but it also came in directly on top of Missile Four. Seventeen men and women died under those two hits, and six more were wounded, and Tyler felt a deep, panicky stab of near-superstitious dread.

But then the Manty's change of course registered, and his eyes narrowed. He still didn't have any idea how the other cruiser had managed to target him with what had to be both broadsides simultaneously, but it was obvious that the enemy ship was running for the hyper limit. In the Manty's position, Tyler would have been attempting to avoid action from the very beginning against such numerical odds, but that wasn't the way Manties normally handled pirates. Now, though . . .

"The bastards are running," he muttered, and looked up from his plot. "They're running!" he repeated.

"Maybe so, but they're also hammering us a lot harder than we're hammering them!" his executive officer shot back.

"Hell, yes, they are," Tyler agreed with a snort. "And if we'd fired fifteen times as many missiles at them, we'd probably have hit *them* more often, too! Look at how close two of our birds *did* get before they stopped them!"

"Well, yeah . . ."

The exec had been with Tyler for almost four T-years, and he had a tendency to try to second-guess his CO. And he was also a fellow Silesian, with the same near phobic respect for the Royal Manticoran Navy. But his panic seemed to ease slightly as he considered the pirate captain's point.

"Damned right, 'well'!" Tyler shot back now, and looked past the other man at his helmsman. "Bring us hard to starboard! Put us as close to parallel with them as you can!"

"They're changing heading to open their broadsides, Sir," Blumenthal reported as *Gauntlet*'s third double broadside blasted from her tubes.

"Not surprisin'," Oversteegen replied in a calm, cool voice. "Only thing they can do, really. But they're not goin' t' be able t' put themselves on a headin' t' follow us across the wall. Stay with Number One, Guns."

❖   ❖   ❖

Jerome Tyler had already reached the same conclusion as Michael Oversteegen. Whatever he did, *Fortune Hunter* and Samson Lamar's *Predator* were going to slide in-system past *Gauntlet*. But they'd have time for at least eight or nine more broadsides first, and his lips skinned back from his teeth in an ugly smile. No Silesian raider had ever willingly engaged a Manticoran cruiser, but many of them had dreamed of the freak set of circumstances which might have let them do so successfully. The fact that the Manty *had* to be destroyed was the only thing which had inspired him to engage in the first place, but now that it had been forced upon him, he scented victory, and he wanted it. Badly.

"Pour it on, Tactical!" he snapped. "Communications, raise *Mörder*! Get her current position—now!"

Joel Blumenthal focused on his plot more intensely than he'd ever done anything before in his life. His eyes flicked across the display, noting shifting vectors, the enemy's fire patterns, and CIC's analysis of the other side's EW and decoys, and he grunted in partial satisfaction.

Number One and Number Two were firing full broadsides, now, and their turn had taken the vulnerable open front aspects of their wedges away from *Gauntlet*. Worse, the penetration aids and ECM of their attacking missiles were even harder to compensate for as the threat numbers multiplied. But his Ghost Rider recon platforms were real-timing close-range observations of the other ships' EW to him, which gave CIC's computers a much better look at them than the other side had at his own electronic defenses. And good as the pirates' EW might be, it wasn't as good as Blumenthal had originally believed.

Or possibly it was; it could be lack of skill on its operators' part.

Whatever the cause, the enemy's EW was slow. However effective their decoys might be, they were much slower to adapt their emissions than Manticoran decoys would have been. Perhaps even more importantly, their mother ships' onboard EW was slow to adapt to the active sensors aboard Blumenthal's remote recon platforms.

Those platforms' FTL grav-pulse transmitters fed his targeting computers with real-time data, and their radar and lidar was getting far better hits off of their targets than they should have done against jammers that capable. He wondered if the pirates even realized how close the platforms were. Or how quickly their targeting info could make its way back to *Gauntlet*. There was no way to tell, and it didn't really matter, he thought, as he updated his current missile salvo's attack profiles.

"Yes!"

Tyler pounded jubilantly on the arm of his command chair, and a hungry sound of triumph rippled around *Fortune Hunter*'s bridge as two of their laser heads broke through the Manty's defenses. The enemy cruiser's sidewall intercepted them, bending and blunting them, and it was unlikely they'd inflicted heavy damage, but it was a start, and more broadsides were already in space.

"I've got *Mörder*," Tyler's com officer announced. "I'm feeding her current position directly to Tactical."

Tyler waved one hand in acknowledgment. Then he looked down at his repeater plot as Maurersberger's cruiser appeared upon it, and his eyes flamed. *Mörder* was closing in on the Manty from almost directly astern, and Maurersberger was nearly in range already. The Manty's superior acceleration wasn't enough to overcome the velocity advantage *Mörder* had built up before the enemy ship altered course.

"Two hits forward of Frame Sixty," Commander Tyson reported from Damage Control Central. "We've lost Graser Fourteen, Laser Cluster Eight and Ten, and Lidar Two. No casualties from those hits. But we took another one aft of Frame One-Zero-Niner. It took out Missile Twenty and Graser Twenty-Four, and we took heavy casualties on the energy mount."

"Understood," Captain Oversteegen replied, but his eyes were fixed on his tactical plot as he watched Blumenthal's most recent broadsides roaring down upon Number One. Good as the enemy's missile ECM was, *Gauntlet's* was better, and Oversteegen's eyes glittered in anticipation as the target's counter missiles went wide and its point defense lasers fired late.

"*Shit!* Heavy damage to Laser Seven and Miss—" The voice from Damage Control chopped off in mid-word, and Jerome Tyler's hungry smile vanished as *Fortune Hunter* heaved madly. He clung to his command chair's arms on the bucking bridge, and his face was ashen as alarms screamed and the bridge lighting flickered. At least four missiles from the Manty's last salvo had gotten through this time, and he didn't need more reports from Damage Control to know *Fortune Hunter* had been badly hurt.

"Captain, our accel is dropping!" the helmsman reported, and Tyler grimaced as he stabbed a quick look at his own displays. Of course their acceleration was dropping—the goddamned Manty had just blown four nodes out of their after impeller ring!

"I've lost contact with Missile Niner, Eleven, and Thirteen," the tac officer reported. "Missile Defense

Seven and Niner don't respond either. And I've lost the port decoy!"

"Roll hard port!" Tyler barked. "Get our starboard broadside to bear on them!"

"Good hits on Number One!" Blumenthal announced jubilantly. "Their wedge strength is dropping, Sir!"

"Good work, Guns!" Oversteegen replied, even as he watched *Gauntlet*'s defensive fire annihilate an entire incoming broadside well short of laser head attack range. Number One was bleeding air and trailing debris, and her fire seemed to have dropped. And— yes, she *was* rolling ship to snatch her damaged flank away from *Gauntlet*! But it looked like she'd left it too late to evade Blumenthal's follow-up salvo.

"Time t' hyper limit?" he demanded.

"Four minutes, Sir," Atkins responded.

"Communications, record a transmission for Midshipwoman Hearns," Oversteegen commanded.

"Standing by, Sir," Lieutenant Commander Cheney acknowledged.

"Message beg—"

"*Incoming!* Missiles in acquisition, bearing one-seven-five! Impact in one-five-zero seconds!"

Oversteegen's eyes snapped back to his tactical repeater as the fresh threat came roaring in from astern. It couldn't be from Number Three—not on that bearing! Which meant there was a *fourth* enemy ship in the system, and they'd missed her completely!

"Stern wall!" he barked. "Get it up *now!*"

Tyler's eyes clung to the tactical display as the Manty missiles sliced through his badly battered defenses. He no longer had a port decoy, and his EW emitters had taken heavy damage from the hits which had lacerated *Fortune Hunter*'s port flank. His counter missile and point defense crews did the best they could, but it wasn't going to be good enough.

Gauntlet's missiles raced down upon their target and detonated at ranges as short as ten thousand kilometers. The powerful X-ray lasers ripped deep into *Fortune Hunter*, shattering bulkheads and opening compartments like knives. Energy mounts and their crews were smashed and mangled, missile tube mass-drivers arced madly as their capacitor rings shorted, and atmosphere gushed from the brutal wounds. The cruiser heaved bodily sideways, and then the last hit came slicing in, and Number One Impeller Room exploded with a cataclysmic fury that destroyed her entire forward hammerhead.

The ship tumbled madly as her wedge unbalanced, and then her inertial compensator failed.

Whether any of her crew were still alive when the savage torquing effect on her hull snapped her back scarcely mattered.

Michael Oversteegen was peripherally aware of Number One's spectacular destruction, but he had little attention to spare for it. Not with twenty-plus missiles racing straight for *Gauntlet*'s kilt.

Behind the mask of his features, he cursed himself for not having found whatever ship had just fired. He knew, intellectually, that Blumenthal had done extraordinarily well just to spot Number Three, given the effectiveness of these "pirates'" electronic warfare capabilities. But that was no comfort at all as he watched those missiles come.

Gauntlet's acceleration dropped abruptly to zero as her stern wall snapped up. She was one of the first *Edward Saganami-B*-class ships which had added that passive defense, and this was the very first time any of them had tested it in actual combat. It had worked well enough for the LACs who'd first employed it during Eighth Fleet's decisive offensive, but a heavy cruiser was scarcely a LAC.

More to the point, it took *time* for the wall to come up, and time was in very short supply.

Samson Lamar stared in horror at the broken, lifeless wreckage which an instant before had been a heavy cruiser. The sheer, blinding speed with which *Fortune Hunter* had been transformed into so much splintered rubble stunned him. And it also terrified him, because he knew who the next target of the Manty's wrath had to be.

He opened his mouth to order his helmsman to turn *Predator* up on her side relative to the Manty, sheltering behind the impenetrable roof of her wedge. But before he could get the order out, Dongcai Maurersberger's missiles exploded dead astern of the enemy ship.

HMS *Gauntlet* bucked in agony as the incoming laser heads detonated. Her after point defense had knocked out twelve of them, despite the surprise of their launch from stealth. Five more were sucked off by the cruiser's decoys. But the remaining six ran straight in on their target and detonated eighteen thousand kilometers astern of her.

If not for her stern wall, she would have died then and there. Even with it, the damage was terrible. The wall was still spinning up to full power when the lasers came slashing in. It could bend and attenuate them, but it couldn't *stop* them, and damage alarms shrieked.

"We've lost the after ring!" Tyson barked from Damage Control Central. "Grasers Thirty-Two, Thirty-Three, and Thirty-Four are gone! We've lost at least half the after laser clusters, and I'm getting no response from Environmental Four or Boat Bay Two!"

Oversteegen's jaw tightened. Raising the stern wall had cut *Gauntlet*'s acceleration to zero when it closed the after aspect of her wedge, but without the after impeller ring, it would be halved even after the wall came down. And with his after missile defenses so badly damaged, he dared not lower it at all until he'd wrenched his stern away from the previously unsuspected attacker.

"Can we get the wedge back?" he asked Tyson sharply.

"I can't say for certain, Sir," the engineer replied. He was hammering at his keyboard even as he spoke, eyes locked to the scrolling diagnostic reports.

"I don't like t' rush my officers," Oversteegen said, "but it would be most helpful if you could expedite that estimate."

"I'm on it, Sir," Tyson promised, and Oversteegen looked up from his com screen.

"Helm, reaction thrusters. Bring us ten degrees to starboard and pitch us up fifteen degrees."

"Ten degrees starboard, pitch up fifteen degrees, aye, Sir!"

"Tactical, we need t' find this gentleman astern of us," Oversteegen continued, swiveling his eyes to Blumenthal's section.

"We're on it, Sir," Blumenthal replied. "We've got a good fix on the missiles' launch locus, and these bastards' EW isn't good enough to hide from us when we know where to look for them!"

"Good. Astro," Oversteegen turned towards Lieutenant Commander Atkins, "recompute our course t' the wall t' reflect my last helm orders. Then generate a random course change as soon as we cross the wall.

With our after ring down, these people are goin' t' be able t' stay with us after all."

"Aye, aye, Sir."

"Guns," Oversteegen turned back to Blumenthal, "forget about Number Two for now. She's goin' t' slide past us whatever she does; it's Number Three and this Number Four we have t' worry about right now."

"Aye, aye, Sir. I'm recomputing now."

"And as for you, Commander Cheney," Oversteegen said, returning his attention to the communications officer with a thin smile, "I believe we were about t' record a transmission for Ms. Hearns."

" . . . so things are gettin' just a little tight up here, Ms. Hearns." Abigail stared at Captain Oversteegen's impossibly composed face on the pinnace's tiny com screen in something that wasn't disbelief simply because her shock was too deep for her to feel *anything* yet. She could hear combat chatter and the beeping of priority alarms behind him, but that irritating, aristocratic accent was as calm as ever.

"We've destroyed one hostile, but at least two are in position t' follow us into hyper," he continued. "If they're foolish enough t' come through separated, we should be able t' take them easily. If they stay concentrated, it's goin' t' be a little dicier, of course. Either way, we'll be back t' pick you and your people up as soon as possible.

"In the meantime, however, be advised that at least one enemy heavy cruiser is goin' t' be unable t' follow us. Since they chose t' engage us when they didn't have to, I'm assumin' that they feel they have somethin' here in Tiberian which they have t' conceal at all costs. If that's true, I anticipate that the cruiser which can't follow *us* will come lookin' for *you*. I can't advise you from here, Ms. Hearns. You're on your own until we can get back here. Evade any way you can, but avoid contact with the Refugians at all costs. It's our job t' protect people like them; not t' set them up t' draw fire.

"Good luck, Ms. Hearns. Oversteegen, clear."

The screen blanked, and Abigail inhaled deeply. As the oxygen filled her lungs, it seemed as if it were the first breath she'd taken in at least an hour.

She stood up in Chief Palmer's compartment, and her brain began to work after a fashion again.

The captain's transmission was over fifteen minutes old, because the pinnace had no ability to receive FTL transmissions. Which meant it was entirely possible that Captain Oversteegen and *Gauntlet*'s entire company were already dead.

No. She put that thought firmly aside. If it was true, then nothing she and her people could do to evade the enemy would succeed in the end. But if it wasn't true, and she allowed the possibility to paralyze her, then whatever slim chance of survival they had would disappear.

She squared her shoulders and stepped onto the flight deck.

"You heard, PO Hoskins?" she asked the pilot.

"Yes, Ma'am." The petty officer looked back over her shoulder at Abigail, her face taut. "Can't say I like the sound of it very much, though."

"I don't much care for it, myself," Abigail assured her. "But it looks like we're stuck with it."

"As you say, Ma'am." Hoskins paused a moment, then continued. "What are we going to do, Ma'am?"

"Well, one thing we're *not* going to do is try to evade a heavy cruiser in space, PO," Abigail said, and surprised herself with a smile which held a hint of true humor. "Any proper warship could run us down without too much trouble, and it's not as if we could hide from her sensors. Not to mention the fact that she's probably got at least a dozen or so small craft of her own she could deploy to come after us."

"That's true enough, Ma'am," Hoskins acknowledged, though her tone was dubious. "But if we can't evade them in space, how well can we hope to evade them dirtside?"

"Refuge's got some pretty rough terrain, PO," Abigail replied. "And we've got all of Sergeant Gutierrez's well-trained Marines aboard to help us hide in it. Of course, it would be best of all if we could convince them to not even look for us, wouldn't it?"

"Oh, yes, Ma'am," Hoskins said fervently.

"Well, in that case, let's just see what we can do about that."

"Are you sure about this, Ma'am?" Sergeant Gutierrez asked quietly, and Abigail smiled sourly. At least the towering noncom was asking the question as privately as the pinnace's cramped confines allowed. That, unfortunately, didn't change the fact that he appeared to be less than overwhelmed with her plan.

Such as it was, and what there was of it.

"If you're asking if I'm sure it will work, Sergeant," she said coolly, "the answer is 'no.' But if you're asking if I'm confident this is what will give us our best chance, than the answer is 'yes.' Why?"

"It's just— Well, Ma'am, no offense, but what you're talking about doing would be hard enough if we were all trained Marines."

"I'm aware that Navy personnel aren't trained in planetary evasion and concealment tactics the way Marines are, Sergeant. And if I had another choice, believe me, I'd take it. But you'll just have to take my word for it that there's no way this pinnace could possibly avoid detection, interception, and destruction if we try to stay in space. That's an area where we

Navy types have a certain degree of expertise of our own." She gave him a thin smile. "So, the way I see it, that only leaves us the planet. Understood?"

"Yes, Ma'am," Gutierrez said. He remained clearly unhappy, and she suspected he also remained somewhat short of total confidence in her leadership ability, but he couldn't avoid the force of her argument, either.

"Well," she told him with a more natural smile, "at least we already had our survival supplies ready to go, didn't we?"

"Yes, Ma'am, we did." Gutierrez surprised her with a chuckle which acknowledged that he knew she'd given him the initial assignment just to yank his chain. She grinned back wryly, but then their moment of shared humor faded, and she nodded to him.

"All right, Sergeant. Once we're down, I'm going to be relying very heavily on your expertise. Don't hesitate to offer any suggestion that occurs to you. I know *what* I want to do, but this isn't an area in which I'm trained to know *how* to do it."

"Don't worry, Ms. Hearns," he told her. "You know the Corps motto: Can do! We'll get through it when we have to."

"Thank you, Sergeant," she said, and she was genuinely grateful for his attempt to bolster her confidence, even though she was just as aware as he was of how slender their chances actually were against any determined orbital and aerial search for them. She smiled briefly at him, then returned to the flight deck.

"How are we coming, PO?" she asked.

"Almost there, Ma'am," Hoskins replied. Her co-pilot had the controls while Hoskins and Chief Palmer put their heads together over the autopilot programming panel. The petty officer looked up at the midshipwoman with an expression that was half-smile and half-grimace. "Too bad we didn't have any canned routines on file for this."

"I know. But Sir Horace didn't have one either when *he* set it up," Abigail pointed out. "And at least you and Chief Palmer get to work with our own software instead of the Peeps'."

"True, Ma'am," Hoskins agreed, and Abigail smiled encouragingly and returned to the passenger compartment.

"We should hit Refuge orbit in about twelve minutes," Commander Thrush said, and Samson Lamar nodded in acknowledgment of his astrogator's announcement just as if he didn't think this hunt for the Manty pinnace was ridiculous. And pointless.

He doubted very much that the cruiser had taken the time to squeal any sort of detailed download to the pinnace's crew. Certainly it must have had other things on its mind once it realized *Cutthroat* and *Mörder* were both behind it. Despite what the Manty had done to *Fortune Hunter*, the chances of its successfully defeating two more heavy cruisers had to be low, especially in light of the way *Mörder*'s fire had smashed its after impeller ring. And if the cruiser was destroyed, then there was certainly no rush in hunting down its orphaned pinnace! If, on the other hand, the cruiser succeeded in escaping destruction by some unlucky chance, then there was no point in destroying the pinnace, either.

But that pain in the ass Ringstorff had insisted, and Lamar had been unable to come up with any logical reason why he shouldn't just as well do what Ringstorff wanted. On the one hand, there'd been no way to decelerate in time for *Predator* to join *Cutthroat* and *Mörder*'s pursuit of the Manty, and, on the other, *Predator*'s base course had already been almost directly towards the planet.

So here she was, a fully armed heavy cruiser hunting for a single pinnace. It was rather like sending a sabertooth tiger to hunt down a particularly vicious mouse.

"Anything yet?" he asked his tac officer.

"Not yet. Of course, if they're lying doggo, they're going to be a pretty small target."

"I know. But Ringstorff says the remote platforms tracked them back to the planet, so they have to be around here somewhere."

"Maybe so, but if I were a pinnace that figured a heavy cruiser might be hunting for me, damned if I'd park myself in orbit where it could find me!"

"Yeah? Where would you hide?"

"The planet's got two moons," the tac officer pointed out. "Well, one and a fraction. Me, I'd probably look for a nice crater somewhere and hide in a ring wall's shadow. Either that, or find myself a nice deep valley down on the planet, somewhere. Damned sure I wouldn't hang around in space!"

"Makes sense to me," Lamar acknowledged after moment. "But we have to start somewhere, so let's get on with it. If they're not in orbit, Ringstorff is just going to make us look somewhere else until we find them, after all."

"What a pain in the ass," the tac officer muttered, unaware that he was paralleling Lamar's own opinion of Ringstorff. Lamar smiled at the thought, and returned to his own console.

Fifteen minutes passed. *Predator* slowed, killing the last of her motion relative to Refuge as she slid into a high orbit, and her active sensors began a systematic search for any other artificial object in orbit around the planet.

It didn't take them long to find one.

✧   ✧   ✧

"There she goes," PO Hoskins said softly, staring down at the palm-sized display of the portable com. The unit's transmit key was locked out to prevent any accidental transmission which might give away their position, but the signal from the orbiting pinnace came in just fine.

Not that it was much of a signal. Just a single, omni-directional burst transmission which would give away nothing about its intended recipients' location even if it was picked up. But it was enough to let them know what was happening.

High overhead, the pinnace which had returned to parking orbit under the preprogrammed control of its autopilot recognized the lash of radar when it felt it. And when it did, it activated the other programs Hoskins and Palmer had stored in its computers.

Its impellers kicked to life, and the small craft slammed instantly forward at its maximum accelera-tion, darting directly away from the planet in an obvious, panicky bid to escape.

It was futile, of course. It had scarcely begun to move when *Predator*'s fire control locked it up. The pirate cruiser didn't even bother to call upon the pin-nace to surrender. It simply tracked the wildly evad-ing little vessel with a single graser mount . . . then fired.

There was no wreckage.

"Well, that seems straightforward enough," Lamar said with an air of satisfaction.

"Yeah," his tac officer agreed. "Still seems pretty stupid of them, though."

"I think Al may have a point, Sam." It was Tim St. Claire, *Predator*'s improbably named executive officer, and Lamar frowned at him.

"Hey, don't blame *me*," St. Claire said mildly. "All

I'm saying is that Al's right—only a frigging idiot would have sat here in orbit waiting for us to kill him. Now, personally, I figure there's a damned good chance that anyone who's just seen his ship haul ass out of the system with the bad guys in hot pursuit *is* gonna act like a frigging idiot. Panic does that. But if he *didn't* panic, then this was way too easy. And if we don't go ahead and look for him some more on our own now, Ringstorff is just gonna send us back here and make us do it later. Besides, it'd give the crew something to do while we wait for Morakis and Maurersberger."

"All right," Sampson sighed. "Break out the assault shuttles and let's get to it, then."

"They didn't buy it, Ma'am," Palmer announced quietly, watching the display as the small tactical remote they'd deployed on a high peak several kilometers from their present position tracked the impeller signatures far above the surface of Refuge. The remote was too simpleminded to give them very detailed information, but it was obvious that the single pirate cruiser was deploying small craft.

"Not entirely, anyway," Hoskins put in, and Abigail nodded, even though she suspected that the pinnace pilot had only said it in an effort to make her feel better. But then another, deeper voice rumbled up in agreement.

"Chances are they're at least half-convinced they got us," Sergeant Gutierrez said. "At the very least, it's going to generate a little uncertainty on their part, and that's worthwhile all by itself. But whether they figure we're already dead or not, it looks like they're going to look down here until they're sure, one way or the other."

"We knew it was likely to happen," Abigail agreed,

looking about in the dusk of an early winter evening. Their carefully hidden position was tucked away in a narrow, rugged mountain valley on the opposite side of the planet from Zion. It was winter here, and winter on Refuge, she was discovering, was a cold and miserable proposition.

She shivered, despite the parka from the pinnace's emergency survival stores. It was warm enough, she supposed, but she was a Grayson, raised in a sealed, protected environment, not someone who was accustomed to spending nights outside in the cold.

At least it should be hard for them to find us, she thought. *Any planet's a big place to play hide-and-seek in.*

These rocky, inhospitable mountains offered plenty of hiding places, too, and Gutierrez and his Marines had rigged thermal blankets for overhead cover against the heat sensors which might have been used to pick them out against the winter chill. Unfortunately, they had only fifteen of the blankets, which wasn't enough to provide cover for all of them even when their smaller personnel doubled up. Worse, they hadn't been able to do away with power sources. Their weapons, the two long-range portable communicators they *had* to have if they were ever going to contact *Gauntlet* when she returned, and at least a dozen other items of essential survival gear all contained power packs which could be readily detected by an overhead flight, and the thermal blankets wouldn't do much to change that.

They'd done their best to put solid rock between those power sources and any sensors which might fly past, but there was only so much they *could* do.

"All right, Sergeant Gutierrez," she said, after a moment. "Who's got first watch?"

❖   ❖   ❖

"This has got to be the most *boring* fucking job yet," Serena Sandoval grumbled as she brought the heavy assault shuttle around for another sensor sweep.

"Yeah?" Dangpiam Kitpon, her co-pilot, grunted. "Well, 'boring' beats the shit out of what happened to the *Hunter*, doesn't it?"

Sandoval made an irritated sound, and Dangpiam laughed sourly.

"And while we're talking about things that 'boring' is better than," he continued, "I wonder just how 'interesting' things are being for Morakis and Maurersberger about now?"

"You've got an over-active mouth, Kitpon," Sandoval half-snarled, but she couldn't quite dismiss Dangpiam's question. It had been hours since *Cutthroat* and *Mörder* had translated into hyper in pursuit of the Manty cruiser. As badly damaged as the Manty had been, they *had* to have caught up with her quickly, so where the hell were they?

She concentrated on her flight controls, ignoring the moonless winter night beyond the cockpit canopy, and took herself firmly to task for letting Dangpiam get to her. Sure, it was a Manty, but there was only one of it, and it already had the shit shot out of it! It had just gotten lucky against *Fortune Hunter*, that was all, and—

A signal pinged quietly, and Sandoval's eyes dropped to her panel.

"Well, dip me in shit," Dangpiam murmured beside her.

"Wake up, Ma'am!"

The hand on Abigail's shoulder felt as if it were the size of a small shovel. It felt as strong as one, too, although it was obviously restraining itself, since it was only ripping one shoulder off at a time.

She sat up abruptly, eyes snapping open. The sleeping bag was like an entrapping cocoon, for all its warmth, and she squirmed, fighting her way out of it even as her brain spun up to speed.

"Yes? I'm awake, Sergeant!" she said sharply.

"We've got trouble, Ma'am," Gutierrez told her in a low voice, almost as if he were afraid of being overheard. "Overflight four or five minutes ago. Then whoever it was came back again, lower. They must have gotten a sniff of something."

"I see." Abigail sucked in a deep lungful of icy mountain air. "Should we move, or sit tight?" she asked the platoon sergeant, deferring to his expertise, and heard him scratching his chin in the darkness.

"Six of one, half a dozen of the other, at the moment, Ma'am," he replied after a moment. "We know they must have picked up *something*, or they wouldn't have come back. But there's no way to know *what* they picked up. For that matter, they could've come back around and missed us the second time, in which case they may decide that this is a clear area. In that case, it would be the safest spot we could find. And there's always the fact that people moving around are easier to spot than people bellied down in a good hide. I'd stay here, unless—"

Gutierrez never completed the sentence. The whine of air-breathing turbines seemed to come out of nowhere and everywhere simultaneously, filling the night with thunder. Abigail threw herself flat in instinctive reaction, but her eyes whipped around, seeking the threat source.

She caught a brief, nightmare image of a vast, black shape, looming out of the night like some huge, high-tech bird of prey. It wasn't a pinnace, she realized. It was an assault shuttle, the heavily armed, heavily armored kind that could carry an entire company of battle-armored infantry.

Then something flashed in the night.

"There!" Dangpiam shouted, pointing at the visual imagery as the low-light cameras swept the craggy mountain terrain. Sandoval darted a look at the display herself, but she couldn't afford to take her attention off the flight instruments this close to the ground. Not in terrain like this.

"I'll take your word for it," she said as she brought the big shuttle back around for a third pass. "Punch up the com. Tell *Predator* we've got them, and then tell Merriwell we're about to drop his people on top of the Manties. I'll stand by for support after that, and th—"

Lightning flashed somewhere beneath her and interrupted her in mid-word.

A Royal Manticoran Marine Corps rifle squad consisted of thirteen men or women divided into two fire teams and commanded by a sergeant. Each fire team consisted of a single plasma rifle, the standard heavy firepower of the Marines, covered by three pulser-armed riflemen and one grenadier, and was commanded by a corporal.

Platoon Sergeant Mateo Gutierrez had deployed his two squads to cover the narrow valley in which they'd found refuge, and his instructions had been explicit. No one was to fire without direct orders from Abigail or him, unless it was obvious that they'd been discovered. But if it *was* obvious, then he expected his people to use their own initiative.

Which was why four plasma rifles fired virtually simultaneously as Serena Sandoval, who'd forgotten that this time she was hunting Royal Manticoran Marines and not terrified, unarmed civilian spacers, swept back over them for the third time.

The assault shuttle was big, powerful, and well armored for an atmosphere-capable craft. But it wasn't well enough armored to survive simultaneous multiple plasma strikes at a range of less than three hundred meters. The incandescent energy ripped straight through its hull, and Abigail tried to burrow her way into the stony ground as Sandoval, Dangpiam, their flight engineer, and the seventy-five armed pirates who'd thought they were hunting mice, vanished in the brilliant blue flare of igniting hydrogen.

"God dammit!" Lamar slammed a fist on the arm of his command chair as the report came in. "God *dam*mit! What did those idiots think they were doing?!"

"I imagine they thought they were closing in on the Manties," St. Claire replied tartly. Lamar glared at him, and his exec glared back. "Don't let your emotions shut down your brain, Sam," St. Claire advised coldly. "It looks like Al was right—that pinnace *was* a decoy." He smiled sourly. "Ringstorff will be pleased we found them."

"Yeah? Well, now that Sandoval's gotten her silly ass blown out of the air, who have we got in position to go *get* them?" Lamar demanded scathingly.

"Nobody, right this minute," St. Claire admitted. "We've only got so many shuttles. But we can have another bird directly over them within twenty minutes, max. And this time, we'll come in smarter."

"Move, move, *move*!" Sergeant Gutierrez shouted, driving the Navy personnel before him while his Marines moved along the flanks. At least they all had decent low-light vision equipment, but that didn't make the terrain any less rugged, and Abigail had already discovered that running down a rocky gorge in the middle of a winter night was nothing at all like the track at Saganami Island.

She stumbled over a rock and would have fallen if that same shovel hadn't darted out and caught her. She was a slender young woman, but she knew she couldn't possibly weigh as little as Sergeant Gutierrez made it seem as he held her up one-handed until she got her feet back under her.

"They'll be back overhead as quick as they can," he told her, his breathing almost normal despite the pace he was setting. Of course, a corner of Abigail's mind reflected, Refuge's gravity wasn't that much more than half the gravity to which he'd been born. "The fire will screw up their thermal sensors, at least to some extent," he continued. "But they'll still be able to sweep for the power sources unless we can get back under cover in time."

Abigail nodded in understanding, but unlike Gutierrez, she had no breath to spare for conversation. She concentrated on putting one foot in front of the other. That was quite enough to keep her completely occupied, under the circumstances.

"Here! Turn left here!" It was Sergeant Henrietta Turner, the sergeant commanding the second squad Commander Watson had assigned to Abigail all those lifetimes ago. She looked up, and saw Turner literally pushing Chief Palmer down a narrow ravine. Gutierrez had scouted the vicinity carefully before he settled on their first hiding place, and he'd chosen it at least in part because there were others, almost as good, close at hand. Now Abigail saw Palmer disappear, and then it was her turn to follow him into the ravine.

It was so narrow that she couldn't believe Gutierrez would be able to squeeze his bulk into it, but the platoon sergeant fooled her again, following close on her heels as she ducked her head under a stone overhang. The northern wall of the ravine inclined steadily towards the southern wall as it rose, until the gap between them was no more than a meter or two wide. Over the years, debris had gathered, narrowing the gap still further and effectively turning the ravine into a cave, and the party of refugees pressed themselves back against the walls, panting gratefully as Gutierrez finally allowed them to stop.

The overhead cover was actually better than it had been in their original position, but the ravine was so much narrower that they were hard-pressed to fit all of them into the available space. Worse, there was only one entry and one exit.

"Check the remote, Chief," Abigail panted.

"Yes, Ma'am." Palmer slipped his shoulders free of his backpack's straps and delved into it. It only took him a moment to extract the com tied into the remote still watching over their old encampment.

"Damn," Gutierrez said softly as he peered over Abigail's shoulder at the small display and the image of the second shuttle grounded beside the roaring flames of the first. "I'd hoped they wouldn't be quite that fast off the mark." He checked his chrono. "I make it roughly twenty-three minutes."

Abigail only nodded silently, but her heart sank. She'd hoped it would take much longer than that for a follow-up flight to reach their original campsite. The speed with which the pirates had actually managed it dismayed her. This wasn't the sort of tactical problem they'd trained her for at the Academy, and somehow, when she'd devised her plan, she'd assumed they'd have more time to move from covered position to covered position.

She patted Palmer on the shoulder, then nodded to Gutierrez to follow her, and the two of them made their way back to the mouth of the ravine. Abigail crouched there, Gutierrez squatting behind her, and gazed back up the way they'd come. Their position was as close as they were going to get to a private conversation, she thought.

"They're fast," she said finally, and half-sensed Gutierrez's shrug behind her.

"People who fly are always faster than people who walk, Ma'am," he said philosophically. "On the other hand, people who walk can get into places people who fly can't."

"But if they can pin us down in a place like this," she said quietly, "they won't really have to get into here after us, will they?"

"No," Gutierrez agreed.

"And it won't take them long to work their way here," Abigail continued in that same quiet voice.

"Longer than you think, Ma'am," Gutierrez assured her. She looked up at him, and her low-light gear showed her his expression clearly. To her surprise, he seemed completely serious, not as if he were simply trying to cheer her up.

"What do you mean?" she asked.

"Ma'am, they can overfly us in just a few minutes, but we're under pretty good cover here. They're not going to see us from overhead, and that means they're going to have to send people in looking for us on foot. Now, we knew exactly where we were going, and it took us a good fifteen, sixteen minutes to get here at a hard run. It's going to take them a helluva lot longer to cover the same distance *not* knowing where they're going. Especially when they're going to be wondering if the same people who shot down their shuttle are waiting to shoot *them* up, too."

Abigail nodded slowly as she realized he was right. But even if it took the pirates four or five times as long to cover the same distance, they'd be to the ravine in no more than an hour and half or so.

"We need to buy some more time, Sergeant," she said.

"I'm certainly open to ideas, Ma'am," Gutierrez replied.

"How good are those thermal blankets at blocking sensors, really?"

"Well," Gutierrez said slowly, "they're pretty damned effective against straight thermal sensors. And they'll help some against other sensors. Not a lot. Why, Ma'am?"

"We don't have enough of them to cover all of us," Abigail said. "Even if we did, it will only be a matter of time until they work their way far enough down the valley to spot this ravine." She thumped the rock wall behind her. "And when they do—" She shrugged.

"Can't argue with you there, Ma'am," the sergeant said slowly, in the tone of a man who was pretty sure he wasn't going to like what he was about to hear.

"It occurs to me that if we just stay here, they'll get all of us once they reach this point," Abigail said steadily. "I'm sure you and your people will put up a good fight, but with us pinned down in here, all it would take would be one or two grenades or plasma bursts, wouldn't it?"

Gutierrez nodded, his expression grim, and she shrugged.

"In that case, our best bet is to decoy them away from the ravine," she said. "If we just stay here, we all die. But if some of us use the thermal blankets for cover while we move away from here, then deliberately show ourselves further down the valley, well away from the ravine, we can draw them after us, pull them past the others. There should even be a pretty good chance that they'll assume all of us are somewhere out there ahead of them and extend their perimeter past the ravine without ever realizing it's here."

Gutierrez was silent for several seconds, then he drew a deep breath.

"Ma'am, there may be something to what you're saying," he said very slowly. "But you do understand that whoever does the decoying isn't going to make it, don't you?"

"Sergeant, if we all stay here, we all *die* here," she said flatly. "It's always possible some of the decoy force might survive." She held up a hand before he could protest. "I know how heavy the odds against that are," she told him. "I'm not saying I think any of them will. I'm only saying that it's at least theoretically *possible* . . . whereas if we stay here, there's no possibility at all, unless *Gauntlet* somehow miraculously gets back in the nick of time. Or would you disagree with that assessment?"

"No, Ma'am," he said finally. "No, I wouldn't."

"Well, in that case, let's—" she looked up at the sergeant with a bittersweet smile he didn't quite understand "—be about it."

It wasn't quite that simple, of course. Especially not when Gutierrez found out who she intended to command the decoys.

"Ma'am, this is a job for *Marines*!" he said sharply.

"Sergeant," she shot back just as sharply, "it was *my* idea, *I'm* in command of this party, and I say that makes it *my* job."

"You're not trained for it!" he protested.

"No, I'm not," she agreed. "But let's be honest here, Sergeant. Just how important is training going to be, under the circumstances?"

"But—"

"And another thing," she said, deliberately dropping her voice so that only Gutierrez could hear her. "If—when—they finally catch up with the decoys," she said unflinchingly, "they're going to realize they've been fooled if all they find are Marines. That was a Navy pinnace. They may assume some of the crew stayed aboard to draw their fire and cover the rest, but do you think they're not going to be suspicious if they don't find *any* naval personnel dirtside?"

Gutierrez stared at her, his expression unreadable, as he realized what she meant. That despite anything else she might have said, she *knew* the decoys were going to die . . . and that she was deliberately planning to use her own corpse in an effort to protect the other personnel under her command.

"You could have a point," he acknowledged, manifestly against his will, "but you really aren't trained for this. You'll slow us down."

"I'm the youngest, fittest Navy person present," she said bluntly. "I may slow you down some, but I'll slow you down the least."

"But—"

"We don't have time to debate this, Sergeant. We need every minute we've got. I'll let you choose the rest of the party, but I'm coming. Is that clearly understood?"

Gutierrez stared at her for perhaps another three heartbeats. And then, slowly, obviously against his will, he nodded.

"It's taking too long," Ringstorff said.

"It's a big planet," Lithgow replied. The depot ship was far enough from Refuge that Lamar's light-speed message reporting the loss of his assault shuttle had yet to reach it.

"I'm not talking about that," Ringstorff said. "I'm talking about Morakis and Maurersberger. They should have been back here by now."

"It's only been fourteen hours," Lithgow protested.

"It could easily have taken them that long just to run the Manty down!"

"Not if this report from Lamar about her impeller damage was accurate, it couldn't," Ringstorff shot back.

"Unless she got it fixed before they caught her," Lithgow said. "Or maybe they got just enough of it back to stay ahead for a few extra hours." He shrugged. "Either way, they'll catch her, or after a few more hours, they'll turn around and come home to announce they've lost her."

"Maybe," Ringstorff said moodily. He moved morosely around the depot ship's bridge for a few minutes. He didn't care to admit, even to himself, how shocked he'd been by *Fortune Hunter*'s destruction. Despite all of his inbred respect for the Royal Manticoran Navy, he hadn't really believed that a single RMN cruiser stood the proverbial chance of a snowball in hell against no less than *four* Solarian-built cruisers, even with Silesian crews. But he'd viewed Lamar's report carefully, and he was privately certain that if *Mörder* hadn't hit her with that single totally unexpected broadside, *Gauntlet* could have taken all three of the ships she'd known about.

Which, he finally admitted to himself, was the real reason he was so antsy. If an undamaged *Gauntlet* could have taken three of the Four Yahoos, then it was distinctly possible that, even damaged, she could deal with two of them. And that assumed she'd really been damaged as severely as Lamar thought she had.

"Bring up the wedge," he said abruptly. Lithgow looked at him in something very like disbelief, but Ringstorff ignored it. "Take us out of here very slowly," he told his astrogator. "I want a minimum power wedge, and I want us under maximum stealth. Put us outside the outermost planetary orbital shell."

"Yes, Sir," the astrogator acknowledged, and

Ringstorff walked back across to his command chair and settled into it.

Let Lithgow feel as much disbelief as he liked, he thought. If that Manticoran cruiser *did* manage to come back, there was no way in hell Haicheng Ringstorff intended to confront it with an unarmed depot ship. The chances of anyone spotting them that far out from the primary were infinitesimal, and they could slip undetectably away into hyper anytime they chose.

"What about Lamar?" Lithgow asked in a painfully neutral voice, and Ringstorff looked up to find his second-in-command standing beside his command chair.

"Lamar can look after himself," Ringstorff replied. "He's got an undamaged ship, and he's way the hell inside the system hyper limit. He certainly ought to be able to spot a heavy cruiser's footprint in plenty of time to run before it comes in on him. Especially if his damned report about its impellers was right in the first place!"

"I'm picking something up," Sergeant Howard Cates announced.

"What?" Major George Franklin demanded nervously. Franklin wasn't really a "major," any more than Cates was a "sergeant," of course. But it had amused Ringstorff to organize his cutthroat crews' ground combat and boarding elements into something resembling a proper military table of organization.

"I'm not positive . . ." Cates said slowly. "I think it's a power pack. Over that way—"

He looked up from the display of his sensor pack and pointed . . . just as the supersonic whip crack of a pulser dart blew the back of his head into a finely divided spray of blood, bone, and brain tissue.

Franklin cursed in falsetto shock as the scalding tide of crimson, gray, and white flecks of bone exploded over him. Then the second dart arrived, and the major would never be surprised by anything again.

Mateo Gutierrez had his vision equipment in telescopic mode, and he smiled with savage satisfaction as Private Wilson and Staff Sergeant Harris took down their targets.

"Well, they know we're here now," he said, and Abigail nodded beside him in the dark. She'd seen the sudden, efficient executions as clearly as he had, and she marveled, in a corner of her mind, that it hadn't shocked her more. But perhaps that wasn't really so surprising after the last four or five hours. And even if it was, there wasn't time to worry about it now.

"They're starting to circle around to the west," she said instead, and it was Gutierrez's turn to nod. He'd managed, for reasons Abigail hadn't been prepared to argue against, to assign her as his sensor tech. They'd had less than a dozen of the sensor remotes, but they'd planted them strategically along their trail as they scrambled across the mountainside under the cover of their thermal blankets. Abigail was astounded at the degree of coverage that small number of sensors could provide, but very little of the information coming in to her was good.

There were well over two hundred pirate ground troops moving steadily in their direction. It was obvious to her that they weren't even remotely in the same league as Gutierrez and his people. They were slow, clumsy, and obvious in their movements, and what had just happened to the pair that had strayed into Sergeant Harris' kill zone was ample evidence of the difference in their comparative lethality. But there were still over two *hundred* of them, and they were closing in at last.

She leaned her forehead against the rock behind

which she and Gutierrez had taken cover and felt herself sag around her bones. The sergeant had been right about how untrained for this she was. Even with the advantage of her low-light gear, she'd fallen more than once trying to match the Marines' pace, and her right knee was a bloody mess, glued to her shredded trouser leg. But she was better off than Private Tillotson or Private Chantal, she thought grimly. Or Corporal Seago.

At least she was still alive. For now.

She'd never imagined she could feel so tired, so exhausted. A part of her was actually almost glad that it was nearly over.

Mateo Gutierrez interrupted his focused, intense study of their back trail long enough to glance down at the exhausted midshipwoman briefly, and the hard set of his mouth relaxed ever so slightly for just a moment. Approval mingled with bitter regret in his dark eyes, and then he returned his attention to the night-covered valley behind them.

He'd never thought the girl would be able to keep up the pace he'd set, he admitted. But she had. And for all her youth, she had nerves of steel. She'd been the first to reach Tillotson when the pulser dart came screaming out of the dark and killed him. She'd dragged him into cover, checked his pulse, and then—with a cool composure Gutierrez had never expected—she'd taken the private's pulse rifle and appropriated his ammo pouches. And then, when the three pirates who'd shot Tillotson emerged into the open to confirm their kill, she'd opened fire from a range of less than twenty meters. She'd ripped off one neat, economical burst that dropped all three of them in their tracks, and then crawled backward through the rocks to rejoin Gutierrez under heavy fire while the rest of Sergeant Harris' first squad put down covering fire in reply.

He'd ripped a strip off of her for exposing herself that way, but his heart hadn't been in it, and she'd known it. She'd listened to his short, savage description of the intelligence involved in that sort of stupid, boneheaded, holovision hero, *recruit* trick, and then, to his disbelief, she'd *smiled* at him.

It hadn't been a happy smile. In fact, it had been almost heartbreaking to see. It was the smile of someone who knew exactly why Gutierrez was reading her the riot act. Why he had to chew her out in order to maintain the threadbare pretense that they might somehow survive long enough for her to profit from the lesson.

She'd killed at least two more of the enemy since then, and her aim had been as rock steady for the last of them as for the first.

"I make that thirty-three confirmed," he said after a moment.

"Thirty-four," she corrected, never lifting her forehead from the rock.

"You sure?" he asked.

"I'm sure. Templeton got another one on the east flank while you were checking on Chantal."

"Oh." He paused in his rhythmic search and raised his pulse rifle. Her head came up at his movement, and she brought her own appropriated rifle into firing position.

"Two of them, on the right," Gutierrez said quietly from the corner of his mouth.

"Another one on the left side," she replied. "Up the slope—by that fallen tree."

"You take him; I'm on the right," he said.

"Call it," she said softly, her youthful contralto calm, almost detached.

"Now," he said, and the two of them fired as one. Gutierrez dropped his first target with a single shot;

the second, alerted by the fate of his companion, scrambled for cover, and it took three to nail him. Beside him, Abigail fired only once, then rocked back to cover their flanks while the sergeant dealt with his second target.

"Time to move," he told her.

"Right," she agreed, and started further up the valley. They'd picked their next two firing points before they settled into this one, and she knew exactly where to go. She kept low, ignoring the pain in her wounded knee as she crawled across the rocky ground, and she heard the sergeant's pulse rifle whine again behind her before she reached their destination. It wasn't quite as good a position as it had seemed from below, but the rough boulder offered at least some cover, as well as a rest for her weapon, and she rolled up into position, thanking the Marine instructors who had insisted on drilling even midshipwomen in the rudiments of marksmanship.

The pulse rifle's built-in telescopic, light-gathering sight made the valley midday bright, and she quickly found the trio of pirates who were engaging the sergeant. She took a moment to be certain of their exact locations, then swept the lower valley behind them from her higher vantage point, and her blood ran cold. There were at least thirty more of them, pressing up behind their point men, with still more behind them.

Gutierrez had the lead trio pinned down, but they had *him* pinned down, as well, and he couldn't get the angle he needed on them.

But Abigail could. She tucked the pulse rifle into her shoulder, gathered up the sight picture, and squeezed off the first shot.

The rifle surged against her shoulder, and the left shoulder and upper torso of her target blew apart. One of his companions darted a look in her direction and started to swing his own rifle towards her, but in the process, he rose just high enough to expose his own head and shoulders to Gutierrez.

The platoon sergeant took the shot, and then Abigail had her sights on the third pirate. Another steady squeeze, and she keyed the com they hadn't dared to use until they were certain the pirates were already closing in on them.

"Clear, Sergeant," she said. "But you'd better hurry. They brought along friends."

"Piss on this!" Lamar snarled as the latest reports came up from groundside. His ground troops had run the damned Manties to ground, but in the process they'd run into an old-fashioned buzz saw. He didn't believe the kill numbers they were sending up to him for a moment. Hell, according to *them*, they'd already killed at least forty of the bastards . . . and even at that, they'd lost forty-three of their own. Not that there was any damned way the Manties had sent forty people down to a dirt ball like Refuge in the first place!

"Piss on what?" St. Claire asked wearily.

"All of this—every damned bit of it! Those frigging idiots down there couldn't find their asses with both hands!"

"At least they're in contact with them," St. Claire pointed out.

"Sure they are! Such *close* contact that we can't get in there to use the shuttles for air support without killing our own troops! Dammit, they're playing the Manty bastards' game!"

"But if we call them back far enough to get air support in there, the Manties will break contact again," St. Claire argued. "They've done it three times already."

"Well, in that case, maybe it's time for a few 'friendly fire casualties,'" Lamar growled.

"Or time to give it up," St. Claire suggested very, very quietly, and Lamar looked at him sharply.

"I don't like how quiet Ringstorff's been being for the last several hours," his exec said. "And I don't like hanging around this damned planet chasing frigging ghosts through the mountains any more than you do. I say bring our people up, and if Ringstorff wants these Manties, he can go down there and get them himself!"

"God, I'd love to tell him that," Lamar admitted. "But he's still calling the shots. If he wants them dead, then that's what we have to give him."

"Well, in that case, let's go ahead and get it done, one way or the other," St. Claire urged. "Either pull them back far enough to get in there with cluster munitions and blow the Manties to hell, or else tell our ground people to get their thumbs out and *finish* the damned job!"

"We've lost Harris," Abigail told Gutierrez wearily, and the sergeant winced at the pain and guilt in her voice. The dead staff sergeant's thirteen-person squad was down to four Marines . . . and one midshipwoman.

"At least we did what you planned on," he said. "They're way the hell and gone this side of the others. No way they're going to backtrack and search for survivors that close to the original contact site."

"I know." She turned an exhausted face towards him, and he realized that it wasn't as dark as it had been. The eastern sky was beginning to pale, and he felt a vague sense of wonder that they'd survived the night.

Only they hadn't, of course. Not quite yet.

He looked back down their present hillside. All four of First Squad's survivors were on the same hill, and there was no place left for them to go. The ground broke down in front of them for just under a kilometer, but the hill on which they were dug in was squarely in the mouth of a box canyon. They were finally trapped with no avenue of retreat.

He could see movement, and he realized the idiots were going to come right up the slope at them instead of standing back and calling in air strikes. It wasn't going to make much difference in the end, of course . . . except that it would give them the opportunity to take an even bigger escort to hell with them.

Well, that and one other thing, he told himself sadly as he looked with something curiously like love at the exhausted young woman beside him and touched the butt of the pulser holstered at his hip. Mateo Gutierrez had cleaned up behind pirates before. And because he had, there was no way Abigail Hearns would be alive when the murderous scum at the foot of that hill finally overran them.

"It's been a good run, Abigail," he said softly. "Sorry we didn't get you out, after all."

"Not your fault, Mateo," she said, turning to smile up at him somehow. "I was the one who thought it up. That's why I had to be here."

"I know," he said, and rested one hand on her shoulder for a moment. Then he inhaled sharply. "I'll take the right," he said briskly. "Anything on the left is yours."

"About fucking time!" Samson Lamar swore, and gestured for the com officer to hand him the microphone. "Now, listen to me," he snarled at the ground troops' commander—the third one they'd had, so far, "I am sick and *tired* of this shit! You get in there, and you *kill* these bastards, or I will by God shoot every last one of you myself! Is that clear?!"

"Yes, Sir. I—"

"*Incoming!*"

Lamar spun to face *Predator*'s tactical section, and

his jaw dropped in disbelief as he saw the blood-red icons of incoming missiles. It was impossible! How could—?

Michael Oversteegen's eyes were bloodshot in a drawn and weary face, but they blazed with triumph as *Gauntlet*'s fire streaked towards the single surviving pirate cruiser. The idiots were sitting there with their wedge at *standby*, and it was obvious that they hadn't even bothered to man point defense stations!

He looked around his own bridge, counting the price his ship and crew had paid to reach this moment. Auxiliary Control was gone, and so was Environmental Two and Four, Damage Control Central, Boat Bay Two, and Communications One. Only two tubes and one graser remained operational in her forward chase armament, and none at all aft. Half her gravitics were gone, and her FTL com had been destroyed. Over thirty compartments were open to space, her surviving magazines were down to less than fifteen percent, and Fusion Two was in emergency shutdown.

Lieutenant Commander Abbott was dead, along with Commander Tyson and over twenty percent of *Gauntlet*'s total crew, and Linda Watson and Shobhana Korrami were both among the many critically wounded in Anjelike Westman's sickbay. Barely a quarter of *Gauntlet*'s after impeller ring—and only one of her after alpha nodes—were on line, and her forward impeller ring had taken so much damage that her maximum acceleration was barely two hundred gravities. Nine of her broadside missile tubes, six of her broadside graser mounts, and four of her sidewall generators had been reduced to wreckage, and there was no way in the galaxy he could take on yet another undamaged heavy cruiser and win.

But he and his people had already destroyed three

of them, he thought grimly. If they had to, galaxy or no galaxy, they would damned well take out a fourth. Either way, there was no way he was going to abandon Refuge to the animals who had already slaughtered so many, and he had people of his own down there.

And so he'd come back anyway. Made his excruciatingly gradual alpha translation almost twenty light-minutes out, well beyond detection range from the inner system, and accelerated inward steadily. Now *Gauntlet* came roaring out of the dark at over fifty percent of light-speed, and every one of her surviving tubes spat missiles at the totally unsuspecting *Predator*.

It was over in a single salvo.

"Holy shit!"

Gutierrez didn't know which of his surviving Marines it came from, but the exclamation summed up his own feelings admirably. The huge, blinding, sun-bright flashes as whole clusters of laser heads detonated almost directly overhead could mean only one thing. And then, almost instantly, there was a far larger, far brighter, far *closer* boil of fury, and he knew a starship's fusion bottle had just let go.

"Here they come!" somebody else yelled, and the platoon sergeant jerked his attention back down from the heavens as the pirates below started up the slope at a run. Pulse rifles, tribarrels, and grenade launchers poured in a heavy covering fire, trying to keep the defenders' heads down, but Gutierrez had positioned his people with care and built sangars of rock for cover.

"*Open fire!*" he shouted, and five pulse rifles poured darts back down the hill. The Marines were running low on ammo, but there was no point conserving it now, and they blazed away furiously. Their one surviving plasma rifle walked its fire across the slope, painting the pre-dawn dark with brief, terrible sunrises, and he could hear the shrieks of wounded and dying pirates even through the thunder of battle as the wave of attackers shredded under that savage pounding.

Still they came on, and he wondered what in God's name they thought they could accomplish now. They were done, damn it! Didn't they even realize what those explosions overhead had meant?!

Maybe they thought they could take some of their enemies alive, use them as hostages or bargaining chips. Or maybe it was simple desperation, the move of people too tired and too tightly focused on the job at hand to think about anything else. Or maybe it was simple stupidity. Not that it mattered either way.

Private Justinian died as a pirate-launched grenade detonated almost directly above her, and Private Williams went down as a head-sized lump of rock was blasted into the breastplate of his unpowered clamshell armor. But the armor held, and Williams dragged himself back up and opened fire once more.

The attack rolled on up the hill, melting under the defenders' fire but still coming, and Gutierrez saw Abigail drop her pulse rifle as her last magazine emptied. She drew her sidearm, holding the pulser in a firing range, two-handed grip, and he realized that even now she was choosing her targets, spending each round carefully, refusing to simply blaze away in blind, suppressive fire.

And then, suddenly, there were no more attackers. Perhaps thirty percent of the force which had come up the slope survived to retreat back down it, but they were the lucky ones. The ones who had just discovered what professionals like Gutierrez already knew. You did *not* charge into the teeth of modern infantry weapons, however outnumbered the defenders were.

Not without powered armor or a hell of a lot more support than those yahoos had had.

He raised his head cautiously and peered out and down. Motionless bodies and writhing wounded littered the frosty hillside between the roaring pockets of flame the plasma rifle had left in the underbrush in its wake, and Gutierrez blinked in disbelief.

They were still alive. Of course, that could still change, but—

"Now hear this," the voice rattled from every com on the planet, hard as battle steel and broadcast over every frequency, "this is Captain Michael Oversteegen, Royal Manticoran Navy. Any pirate who lays down his weapons and surrenders immediately will be taken into custody and guaranteed a fair trial. Any pirate who does *not* lay down his weapons and surrender immediately will not be given the opportunity t' do so. You will be shot where you stand unless you surrender at once. This is your first and last warning!"

Gutierrez held his breath, staring down the hill, wondering.

And then, by ones and twos, men and women began to step out of cover, lay down their weapons, clasp their hands behind their heads, and simply stand there as Tiberian rose above the eastern horizon at last.

"All right, Sergeant Gutierrez," a soft Grayson accent said beside him. "We've got some prisoners to take into custody, so let's be about it."

"Aye, aye, Ma'am!" Gutierrez gave her a parade-ground salute which somehow completely failed to look out of place, despite his filthy, bloodstained uniform. Or hers. She looked up at his towering centimeters for a moment, and then she returned it.

"All right, people!" Gutierrez turned to his survivors—all three of them—and if his voice was just a little husky, of course it was only due to fatigue.

"You heard the Midshipwoman—let's go take these bastards into custody!"

"Ah, Ms. Hearns!"

"You wanted to see me, Captain?"

"Indeed I did. Come in."

Abigail stepped through the hatch into the captain's day cabin, and it slid shut behind her.

The man sitting behind the desk in that cabin was exactly the same man she'd seen at that first formal dinner, down to the last non-regulation touch of the superbly tailored uniform. He still looked exactly like a younger version of Prime Minister High Ridge, and he still had all of the maddening mannerisms, all the invincible faith in the superiority of his own birth, and that incredibly irritating accent.

As if any of that mattered.

"We'll be dockin' at *Hephaestus* in about three hours," he said to her. "I realize that you'd prefer t' remain aboard until we hand the ship over t' dockyard hands. In fact, I requested permission t' retain you on board until that time. Unfortunately, I was overruled. I've just been informed that a personnel shuttle will be arrivin' in approximately forty minutes t' deliver you, Mr. Aitschuler, Ms. Korrami, and Mr. Grigovakis t' the Academy."

"Sir, we'd *all* prefer to remain aboard," she protested.

"I know," he said in a surprisingly gentle voice. "And I sincerely wish you could. But I believe there are people waitin' for you. Includin', if my sources haven't misled me, Steadholder Owens."

Her eyes widened, and he permitted himself a slight chuckle.

"It's traditional for immediate family members t' be present for the award of the Conspicuous Gallantry Medal, Ms. Hearns. Naturally, I feel confident that that

custom is the only reason your father has seen fit t'
become the first Grayson-born steadholder ever t' visit
Saganami Island. I believe I may also have heard that
the Queen intends t' be present, however. And I
understand there was some mention of Steadholder
Harrington's administerin' your oath as a Grayson
officer."

The young woman on the other side of his desk
blushed darkly, and his deep-set eyes twinkled. She
seemed at a loss for words, then shook herself.

"And will you be present, Sir?" she asked.

"I believe you may count on that, Ms. Hearns," he
told her gravely. "I'm informed that there will be more
than sufficient preliminary festivities and family greetin's
t' give me time t' hand *Gauntlet* over t' the yard dogs
and still make the award ceremony."

"I'm very glad to hear that, Sir," she said, and hard
though it would once had been for her to believe it,
she meant it.

"I wouldn't miss it for the world, Ms. Hearns," he
told her, and rose behind his desk. "Some of my com-
patriots have seen fit t' express contempt for Grayson.
They seem t' feel that such a primitive and backward
planet can't possibly have anythin' t' offer a star nation
so sophisticated and advanced as our own. I never happened t' agree with that position, and if I ever had, I
certainly wouldn't now. Especially not after havin' the
honor and considerable privilege of seein' firsthand just
what sort of young women Grayson will be calling t'
the service of the Sword. And havin' seen it, I intend
t' be there when the first of them receives the recognition she so richly deserves."

IT'S ALL ABOUT HONOR!

**David Weber's Bestselling
Honor Harrington series**